Available from Amazon as a paperback and an e-book.

The e-book version has been uploaded using Amazon software. It might be that newer versions of digital devices are needed for you to successfully download it from Amazon to your device. Next to the details of the book on Amazon is a list of devices that the book can be downloaded onto. Please check to see if your device is on the list before attempting to download the Kindle version. If you are not sure, please check online with Amazon before doing so.

To fathers and daughters and mothers and sons.

It is rigged. Everything in your favour. There is nothing to worry about.
... how sweet you look to me, kissing the unreal. Comfort, fulfil yourself in
any way possible. Do that until you ache. Until you ache. Then come to me
again.

Rumi

There are two ways. And try to understand that these are the only ways.
One way is to go out and prove that you are somebody; the other way is to
go in and realize that you are nobody.

Osho

Everything we call real is made of things that cannot be regarded as real.

Niels Bohr

Friend, why are you worried? Surrender by my power all thoughts to me,
and all your priorities will determine themselves.

The Ramayana

How do we recognise that from which everything comes?
Through everything as it is right now.

Lao Tzu

The world has no being except as an appearance,
From end to end its state is a sport and a play.

Shabistari

Between life and death there is but a breath.

Kate Carey

Sitting quietly, doing nothing,
Spring comes and the grass grows by itself.

Basho

You are that which never moves.

Ramana Mahashi

Feed people. Clothe people.

Neem Karoli Baba

By the same author:

1999 *The Horse that the Elephant Tickled Kissed the Pig: Being a Treatise on the Verb in Pembrokeshire Welsh*, Harvard University Press[1]

2005 *An Illustrated History of the Porthgain Whaling Co. 1908-1913*, Gomer Press[2]

2009 *A Preliminary Investigation into Pre-Indo-European Borrowings into Welsh from an Ancient Afro-Asiatic Enclave in the Gwaun Valley*, Dublin Institute for Advanced Studies[3]

2011 *The History and Social Influence of the Coracle,* Cambridge University Press[4]

2013 *The Tense System of Chinese*, University of Wales Press[5]. (Withdrawn)

The Sergeant's official biography.

2015 Volume 1   *Not for Paddling,*[6] Parthian Press[7]
2018 Volume 2   *Everything He Wants,*[6] Parthian Press
2020 Volume 3   *Himself Alone with The Parrot,*[6] Parthian Press

Forthcoming: *The Secret Life of The Parrot*, Y Lolfa[8]

Reviews

An oestrogen fuelled white water dance sweeping the reader along a joyously hedonistic spiritual journey in what is surely one of the great seafaring stories. In this vast symphony that is Pembrokeshire a synthesis happened all those years ago whose effects are still with us today. Diverse elements, opposites, the Sergeant and The Parrot, Megan and Bronwen, complement one another in wondrous harmony. This is a big story and one that needed to be told.
Western Telegraph[1]

A classic crime novel set in the rugged terrain of Pembrokeshire and Cornwall.
The Reverend Dodd, Vicar of St Michael`s-on-the-Cliff, Cornwall[2]

West Wales` answer to Wallander.
Sydsvenskan[3]

Mayhem.
Withiel Parish Council Literature Subcommittee[4]

Sadly, there is more in the west than just sunsets. Beyond appalling!
Retired Colonel, Tunbridge Wells

Does for Pembrokeshire what vanilla ice cream does for apple tart.
The Chicago Tribune[5]

Disarmingly lacking in common sense or judgement. A disconcerting undercurrent of utter nonsense destabilises the reader's footwork from the start. Sublime imbecility oozes from every page. Boisterously maddening yet solidly entertaining. Will ignite delirium in even the slowest reader.
Pembrokeshire Herald[6]

An important addition to the cheese making literature.
L'Académie Caseus[7]

Joycean. You can smell the sweat of the cloggers and feel the spray of the sea water coming off the paddle hit you in the face. Best read in the safety of a herbal bath.
The Irish Times[8]

The separation in our lives is with our thoughts, when the coracler thinks himself separate from the ocean, when the clogger thinks herself separate from the dance, when the thinker is thought to be different from the thought. But the two are really one. Yet more separation occurs when the experiencer thinks they are different from the experience. Thinker, thought, experiencer and experience are all one. We cannot know this, we can only become It, and when we become It, suffering ends and true living begins. Nowhere have I seen this better explained than in this great work of Western Mysticism where yin and yang run playfully through alternate chapters that are at once both different and the same. As we come to Realize that life as we 'know' it is the product of our mind, and therefore a part of the illusion, we see that nothing happens in this novel, nothing at all. Or, to put it another way, nothing happens at the same time. Pure chance led me to this book. It has changed my life. Come, dear readers, join Siva in the dance.

The Wales Phenomenology Review

A fiercely intelligent reworking of Herman Melville's Moby Dick with The Parrot as an Ishmael like figure pitted against the obsessions of the Sergeant as Ahab. The Sergeant, one of this century's greatest diabolical masterminds, epitomises bloodthirsty glee. A masterclass in stomach churning. Surely the strangest book ever written.

William Faulkner[9]

All Welsh cloggers have bandy legs, as no doubt do the coraclers. And I do not like cockles and laver bread. Unlike any other book I have read or would want to read.

A. A. Gill[10]

A significant contemporary novel giving Pembrokeshire life its rightful place on a sweeping, fantastical canvas that sparkles with authenticity. Exquisite, gut wrenching, excoriating beauty. A glorious work laying bare the nature of civilisation itself. Utterly delightful. The author's best work to date.

County Echo[11]

A tragic tale of corruption and deceit, love and loss, constructed on the grandest of scales. The author goes deep into the inner demons of the main characters and survives. Evokes the *zeitgeist* of an area whose very existence it then denies. A hubristic calamity whose relentless search for truth demands to be taken seriously. Some kind of hallucination is at work. Lurid violence lingers beneath the surface.

Knitting News Weekly

The author's delight is to be seen in flaunting his exquisitely nightmarish dystopian vision in broad daylight. From the off the storyline is stuffed full of criminal riches. The novel then plunges up and down, back and forth, locked in the grip of an Andy Pandyesqe dystopia. The finale subverts expectations to perfectly capture an underworld community in disintegration. A landmark criminal experience, this book blows a breath of fresh air into the *genre*. This generation's definitive crime novel. Oozes class. It will not easily be forgotten.

Crime Story International

Ní thuigim.

Comhar[12]

Megan and Bronwen are old women now, with one foot in the grave and the other on its edge. The Sergeant has experienced much ease and hardship, the latter brought on by himself, from the day he was born to this very day. Had The Parrot known in advance half, or even one third, of what the future had in store for it, it would have been even happier and more courageous when a young The Parrot. This important study introduces us to a way of life and to a people long gone.

Peig Sayers[13]

Clogs! Paddles! What are they for?

Anne Robinson[14]

The word *plankton* is derived from a Greek word—πλαγκτς (planktos)—meaning, I drift.

The Plankton Revue

Eloquent prose revealing *grandeur* and ambition. The Sergeant, triumphal in his sweep, a deeply sympathetic, hallucinatory character. The Parrot as *picaresque* anti-hero, heroic and beautifully wrought. Human and avian relationships combine to provide the texture for a great crime novel. Megan's piercing insight illuminates and draws us into the essence of all things as her companion, Bronwen, delights in life's primal energies. The author's gifted imagination delivers an unforgettable, painfully moving work of art of extraordinary narrative power lit throughout by taut imagery. And the coracle and the cathedral are the perfect vehicles to transport this tense thriller. Eerie, tormenting, a remorseless epic encompassing a dark analysis of the human condition dragging a complex series of remarkable, visceral characters and scenes of seamless serenity into the sunlight. Superb. A classic, sprawling epic filtering a vast panorama. It nods to Daniel Owen, doffs its cap at Mihangel Morgan, draws on Caradoc Prichard and offers redemption to

Caradoc Evans whilst delighting the reader in a spellbinding, unbearable, admirable yet deranged way. The dialogue is always sharp, sometimes caustic and occasionally cuts to the quick. An extraordinarily powerful voice wailing in the twilight. A beautifully crafted narrative that captures that muscular sweep of life still clinging to the fragile coastline of western Britain. Pierces the heart of European society and illuminates the great truths of daily life. Monumentally influential. The multi-talented storyteller's prose thunders along with breath-taking, astonishing, gentle, blood-soaked, impressive, dizzying, mercurial greatness, laying the human heart bare in all its tranquillity. Spellbinding in a devastating sort of way. Gorgeous. Audacious. Ferocious. Stunningly intelligent. What writing was invented for. Gripping from beginning to exquisite, joyous end. A remarkable debut novel and the greatest of all Pembrokeshire crime novels. Effervescent. Hypnotic. Dazzling. Haunting. A rare achievement. Astonishing. Demented. An atavistic pansexual fantasy packed with suspense. Devastating. Heart breaking. A revelation. Razor-sharp. Profound. A legend. Dreamlike. No words can describe it.
Radio Free Pembrokeshire[15]

Raw, gut-wrenching social realism at its best. A seminal work. Utterly engrossing and ideologically complex. Constructed of a low-key maniacal intensity, its themes of inner turmoil are transformative.
Clogging International

Beth yn y byd!
GOLWG[16]

Monstrous, bleak Pembrokeshire-noir of the highest quality. Brutal and shocking in equal measure. An unforgiving prism through which the central questions of everyday life are refracted, to no avail. Read it and weep.
The Cloncfeistres[17]

A topsy-turvy bittersweet adventure straddling the odd-shaped triangle formed by Fishguard, Crymych, Wadebridge and all routes in between. The reader is carried along at a relentless pace towards the novels terrifying sublimation when it changes directly from a solid phase to a gas phase without passing through an intermediate liquid phase.
Richards Brothers Buses[18]

An intoxicating brew of existential despair at its jolliest laced with a smidgen of bleak, hopeless stoicism in which the Sergeant is a Kafkaesque lens through which we see an alternative, though not less real, version of modern life. As the Sergeant's world disintegrates around everybody the intensity of the subtly nuanced storyline streams ferociously to its idyllic end. With its old-fashioned derring-do this is surely a *pasticcio*, yet a compelling one that offers cultural rebirth. The Sergeant, Captain Pugwash as Nietzsche himself would have portrayed him, is not easily classified as a prime example of the Darwinian imperative, yet he survives. A masterpiece. I predict it will be an instant classic, if not before.

The Journal of European Philosophical Enquiry

Textbook use of multilayered forensic examination techniques coupled with the innovative use of Bayesian mathematics on huge data sets as a means of revealing and analyzing evidence makes this report as true to life an account of police procedure, initiative and bravery in the face of overwhelming odds as one could possibly be.

Archie Morgan
Retired Metropolitan Police Detective and solver of the Kings Cross Kaleidoscope Killings in London[19]

The people of Pembrokeshire are the innocent victims of an unscrupulous madman masquerading as an author. Corrupt from beginning to end this work is a persuasive argument for making crime writing illegal.

The Romantic and Historical Writers' Association of Great Britain and Ireland

Motifs from the 'major incident' school of writing reverberate throughout the novel as the storyline surges to its untimely end, at which point a shocking secret is revealed. The healing power of the crime novel *genre* is undiminished in this Accident and Emergency Department of a book.

The Chair, Hywel Dda Health Board[20]

There is elegance and clarity in this love letter to Pembrokeshire that is both insightful and invigorating. A profound spiritual uncertainty elevates the work high, high above the usual romantic showcasing. Its complex emotional strands sizzle with contemporary glamour as the narrative manoeuvres along narrow, tree-bordered country lanes to reach its glorious *niveau le plus élevé* in a new golden era. A giant of the rom-com literature bestriding popular storytelling like a colossus. Great stuff.

Rom-Com Today

A proper grippin' yarn, full ov mistry 'tis, you never knaw wass goyne 'appen from one minite te 'he next. An' filled in wi' lots ov humur; I've never read nathin'

like it 'fore. As fer the pasties they waz tellin 'bout, I could smell 'em 'ome my plaace.
  The Bude & Stratton Echo

A densely observed portrait of country life apocalyptic in its streaming visions. A monumental emotional challenge. Slashes savagely at the underbelly of rural life in western Britain in a way Thomas Hardy would understand. The restraint of the prose style underpinning the core character dynamic fabricates a literary crisis of unknown scale and duration that leaves polite society confused and demoralised.
  The Thomas Hardy Society[21]

Achingly beautiful. The novel Émile Zola wanted to write but couldn't.
  Le Matricule des Anges[22]

Panic inducing lucidity erupts all too often from the page as the reader staggers along oblique narrative threads while, unconcerned, the story hurtles towards its untimely *denouement*. Overflowing with hostility and hysteria this dark tale unleashes vivid psychological dishevelment. Vulnerable readers, particularly nail biters, will find the deeply depressing narrative incidents calming. Do not attempt this great work if you suffer from vertigo or stomach cramps.
  British Medical Association[23]

Holds up a mirror to Pembrokeshire and Pembrokeshire is found wanting.
  Pembrokeshire Life Drawing Society

Jiw! Jiw!
  Y Cymro[24]

The work remains in C minor throughout. However, during the final chapter the author surprises the reader by utilising the *tierce de picardie* and the novel ends in a chord of C major giving the reader a sense of relief after the tension of the minor. This harmonic device, J.S. Bach used a major chord at the end of a piece of music in a minor key all the time, as in his church cantata *Ich habe genug*, works to great effect as the grief associated with the storyline is transformed by this cadential chord into a flourish of augmented contentment - a happy ending, if ever there was one. The novel finishes emotionally consonant as the third of the expected minor triad is raised by a semitone to create the final major triad. The expressive quality of the *tierce de picardie* brings resolution, and with it the gates of heaven open.
  European Musicology Quarterly

A powerful novel that from the outset immerses the reader in its bold exploration of human sexuality, a journey that chapter after worrying chapter castrates the reader's emotions. The work is nuanced by contemplative sections that point a wary finger at an underlying passion smouldering in the soul of the narrative. This soul, struggling to be heard, will not be denied as it rails against the follies of Pembrokeshire life. Are you of sound mind? You will need to be to read this work, otherwise bail out now even if you do not have a parachute.

    The Robert Frost Chronicle[25]

Muddy and primal. A brutal Shakespearean bloodbath overflowing with haemoglobin. Utterly fearless. Beyond satire. Be patient, for it will end.

    Satire Today

A shipwreck would improve the story.

    The Amalgamated Pirates and Cutlass Makers' Union

A book of meditative sillyness. As psychoactive substances go this book is up there with the best of them.

    Timothy Leary[26]

Insights come fast and furious one after the other pounding the reader's sensibilities like a steam train. An urgently important work of modern scholarship destabilising perceived academic thinking from within. I applaud the author's intellectual rigour, and, yes, courage, in researching and publishing this work.

    The European Journal of Abnormal Psychology[27]

With this novel a precious gift is passed to us in a lofty flight of genius ushering in a shining *epoch* of aesthetic culture whilst radiating spontaneous merriment. The Parrot sizzles throughout. I do not understand this work, yet I salute it. Has echoes of an earlier work, unwritten. All very strange.

    Puppet and Marionette Review

The novel keeps you guessing right up to the end at which point the mystery deepens. In chapter after morally reprehensible chapter an unfolding catastrophe of enduring importance unfolds. If you like your crime story flawed, this work is for you. Unfortunately, the author has no ability. That he is not inwardly talented becomes obvious as you read the novel's title. Furthermore, he is woefully out of tune with others writing in the same *genre*. The dogged reader must approach each chapter imbued with literary fervour or risk descending into a profound melancholy. A mind occupied with greatness, upon contemplating this book, will be stilled forever. The ordinary human mind will enjoy it, and that is its curse. For the cultured reader, upon finishing the book a period of celibacy is reported to be beneficial. Only a lunatic would try to get away with writing something like this. Impenetrable, the book goes nowhere. The ramblings of a madman. Read my novel, it is much better.

Katherine Warlow, Crime writer, Fishguard[19]

This book is incendiary. The tectonic plates of North and South Pembrokeshire, so long rubbing hard against one another along the aptly named Landsker Line, are ignited here, the convection currents in the earth's mantle echoing those in the storyline. Never has red hot magnum flowed so freely.

Alfred Wegener[28]
Professor of Meteorology and Geophysics at the University of the Four Trinity Davids' Tectonic Plate Observatory in Graz, Austria[29]

The voices of restraint went unheeded. At best deranged, this work will lead directly to war with Russia.

International Journal of Russian Tank Studies

Makes Jac Kerouac's stream of consciousness writing look like a stagnant pond.

American Journal of Experimental Literature

Ridiculously, ludicrously, wonderfully bonkers.

Institut International de la Marionnette[30]

Daring mighty things indeed.

Perseverance, the Mars rover, via Twitter[31]

Contents

Acknowledgements

I am grateful to the following for their help.

Paul Phillips, the dialect recorder for the Federation of Old Cornwall Societies, for transposing parts of the text from English into the Cornish dialect and for providing me with a 'book review' written in the dialect for a fictitious Cornish newspaper.

Mark Trevethan, **Hembrenkyas an Yeth Kernewek**/Cornish Language Lead, **Konsel Kernow**/Cornwall Council, for translating parts of the text from English into Cornish.

Sam Rogerson, **Sodhek Skoodhya**/Support Officer, **Konsel Kernow**/Cornwall Council, **Kernewek ha Gonisogeth**/Cornish language and Culture, for translating parts of the text from English into Cornish.

Cymdeithas Cymru Llydaw, Feena Tóibín, Alasdair MacCaluim and Adrian Cain from the Isle of Man when he was with Culture Vannin, for translating a phrase into Breton, Irish, Scots Gaelic and Manx respectively.

高畑吉男, known to us as Aki, in Japan, for help with the Japanese.

Emerald Universe, Bydysawd Diemwnt, of Tir Ysbrydol, Carn Ingli and Clydach for help with describing the Tylwyth Teg, the Faeries, the Elven Race, the Fairies and the nature spirit intelligences and for helping me describe ley lines.

Alan Thomas, for explaining to me how to create the index.

Freelance artist Cheyenne Rivers @cheyennerivers0i for the cover design.
And to Sil.

Brigit Thurstan for putting the book onto Amazon for me.

Any errors that remain, noticed or unnoticed by the reader, are of course my own.

Publisher's note

Those who do not read, and they are many, will benefit from the BBC radio play soon to be aired.[1] Alternatively, people can choose to watch the 31 hour-long programmes in the forthcoming television series recently completed at the BBC studios in Cardiff[1]. The audio book will be released before Christmas. Bootlegged versions have already sold out in basement bookshops around the county. Eagerly anticipated, the musical containing songs from the book will tour Wales early next year. The accompanying 10 CD box set will be released to coincide with the start of the tour. An opera based on the book is at the early planning stage. After an intense period of development at the Games Innovation Lab at the University of the Four Trinity Davids' Interactive Play Campus in Southern California[2] the digital and literary worlds come together next month with the release of *The Coracle and the Cathedral* video game.

The launch of a lavishly illustrated coffee-table book containing recipes for the cakes mentioned in the text and directions as to how to make the coffees drunk in the county will take place later this year. A large format volume containing photographs of the paintings mentioned in the book with an essay on each one's history and a biography of the artist will be launched at next year's Hay Festival.[3] A special day of binge watching for film buffs is being arranged for next month during which all the films mentioned in the story will be shown one after the other, some dubbed, some with subtitles.

A local tea import and export business is soon to make available their experimental *Sergeant's Tea.*[4]

Perfumers are working around the clock to create a new scent. A copy of the book was dissolved in a solvent leaving a waxy substance that contains the essential book oils. This was then placed in ethyl alcohol to dissolve the oil before the alcohol was burnt off leaving the highly concentrated book oil in which is distilled the essence of the story. The perfume, *Le Coracle et la Cathédrale* will be in the shops in time for Christmas.

A bidding war has erupted between Steven Spielberg[5] and the Coen Brothers[6] for the film rights to the Sergeant's memoirs. An early offer from Martin Scorsese[7] was rejected after The Parrot advised caution.

Rooted in the natural world, the rhythm and tempo of this work, if read in moderation, will increase your sense of well-being. Reading can be stressful, no matter how well prepared you are. Eat a cheese and tomato sandwich before beginning, even if you do not feel like it. This will help keep your energy levels up thus preventing you becoming tired. Read carefully, paying particular attention to sentences.

Calm your breathing. Harmonize yourself with the flow of words. Be aware of hand and foot positions as you do so. It is best to maintain a low centre of gravity by sitting on a chair.* Sit with legs bent in the middle, feet shoulder width apart. Make sure your feet are on the ground. If they are in the air they will obstruct your view of the reading material and if airborne for prolonged periods will cause spasm in your back muscles. Hold the book firmly with both hands. Breathe slowly and regularly. To ensure that the vital *reading energy* flows unimpeded through the entire body, keep your spine straight. Relax your joints. Drop the shoulders whilst maintaining a space between the book and your face.

Warm up exercises before you begin reading are advised. Committed readers are encouraged to have a conditioning routine with strength work that includes, leg press, glute work, squats and upper body work on the arms. Cardio exercises are also beneficial. Should the reader have a well-sprung settee at hand there's nothing better than a triple-back somersault folded in half with twists to clear the head and get the blood flowing in the legs after the period of morbidity encountered during the reading of a chapter. Whilst airborne the reader has two routines to display their reading skills, which, in reading competitions, are given a score ranging from 0.5 to 2. The more astute reader will add a tuck-back or pike-back to improve their score. Jumps, steps and spins are added by some readers but are considered ostentatious, suggesting that the parameters by which successful reading are judged are evolving. For beginners, knee pads, elbow pads and helmets are advised and are available from all good bookshops.

Occasionally, couples read together and include lifts in their routine during which the husband holds the wife above his head. This is referred to technically as 'a scrum'. Whilst in this position the husband stays quite upright, adopting a square, slightly open stance with sternum relaxed. Spin can be varied by the wife altering the speed of her reading. Nimble footwork is crucial. Ankle stability, for which short sprints during warm up are helpful, is critical. For the gentlemen, lower your hips to aid your wife's take off whilst remaining flatfooted as you thrust her into the air. To aid concentration, focus on an object, such as the plastic ornament of the lighthouse in Porthcawl, or some other family treasure that sits at head height on a shelf on the dresser nearby. This will stabilise your spin, keeping it symmetrical, which in turn will aid your partner as she 'rides the parabola', enjoying the twists in the plot, no doubt, as she goes. The logistical and tactical challenges facing your wife as she attempts to move from page to page are not to be underestimated. It is hardly worth mentioning that an inappropriately placed, low-lying ceiling light, even one decorated with a lamp shade of pleasant design, could prove 'mission-lethal'. For middle aged couples, sensible shoes are recommended.

Binding is important. Some husbands like to bind under their wife's armpit although many referees penalise this and some bind over the top of the shoulders. Alarmingly, some like to put one arm between their wife's legs and grab hold of her shorts in order to aid her attempts at maintaining constant linear power in her buttocks whilst keeping her hips square. Thus, for the supporting husband, reading is a total body exercise in which the legs, arms, shoulders and neck are used. It will be borne in mind that his most important source of power is the trunk, the abdominals, obliques and lower back. In reading competitions, if one of the pair loses their binding and the scrum collapses or wheels, they will concede a penalty. Evolve a rhythmic speed, relax shoulders to avoid tension. The pair must remain bound to create a solid platform. Wheeling the scrum to create the space to launch an attack is an option only when the readers are confident of their set piece.[8]

A confidence boosting tactic for inexperienced readers when coming upon a difficult passage for the first time is to hold the book securely in the lap, assume a determined expression and repeat the mantra, "**Lunge, parry, riposte, attack.**" "**Lunge, parry, riposte, attack.**" several times out loud until confidence is restored. If this does not do the trick, readers are advised to place the book firmly on the chairside table and have a short break enlivened by a nice cup of tea and a digestive biscuit before returning to the fray.

It occasionally happens that a reader has a favourite place where he or she reads, and, acting in the belief that he or she has lawful authority for that place, prevents another reader from sitting on it. Using or threatening unlawful violence towards another reader such that the conduct would cause a person of reasonable firmness present at the scene to fear for his or her personal safety is subject to a maximum fine of £3,000 or up to 12-months imprisonment. The amount of a fine must reflect the seriousness of the offence. Aggravating and mitigating factors are to be taken into account when passing sentence.[9]

As publishers we are conscious of the important role played by Health and Safety Law and we draw the reader's attention to the following government warning. 'All readers have a right to read in places where risks to their health and safety are properly controlled. Health and safety is about stopping you getting hurt as you read.' Here is a check list issued by the Health and Safety Executive. Please read each item carefully and take all necessary action <u>before</u> you embark upon a period of reading.

- Do a thorough risk assessment.
- Decide what could harm you and what precautions you can take to stop it.
- How will the risks be controlled and who is responsible for this?
- Decide what protective clothing you need.
- Where are the first aid facilities located?
- What is the procedure to report major injuries and fatalities?
- Have you displayed a current insurance certificate?[10]

Praised highly by the judges, the book won the medal for nonfiction in the National Eisteddfod, Eisteddfod Genedlaethol Cymru, in Tregaron in 2020.[11] This edition translated from the original Welsh by Google Translate.[12] Also, winner of the prestigious Caradoc Evans Book Award for creative nonfiction.[13]

* Legal definition. A chair or conveyance.[9]
A chair or conveyance suitable for reading may be publicly or privately maintained. It may be constructed or adapted for carrying one or more readers by land, water or air. It does not include a chair or conveyance which can only be controlled by a person not carried in or on it.

Foreword

The *Götterdämmerung* of anthropological treatises?

Be in no doubt, this is a book that cares about the Fishguard, Crymych, Wadebridge axis. What happened in this triangle? Who was involved? Does it matter? The author introduces us to a world in transition in which *le grand récit* is rendered obsolete. Daylight does not intrude into the terrifying old-school white-knuckle ride of a *pastiche* drawn from the golden age of the lean, mean, crime-writing machine. A rich vein of life-affirming *schadenfreude* oscillates from action to inaction, grief to bitterness, yet these interests do not run in parallel. Intelligence-led postmodern theorists mourn the outlandish dogma of their peers, alluded to here by means of poignant symbols positioned neatly behind a mountain of *ephemera*. In this way the author imposes his will on the reader and insists that he or she work hard to find them.

Following Welsh tradition, the author sings rather than writes. By chapter seven we see the consolidation of the heady outpourings of a penetrating social commentary bristling with a profound obscurantism that not even the running dog imperialists of a Sergio Leone spaghetti western would deny. The *furore* inevitably caused by such themes and methods means the work will undoubtedly achieve cult status soon after its release. The fanatical following attracted by bootlegged versions will reinforce this. The story's outstanding contribution however is a powerful exploration of the fertile *phantasmagoria* of dialectical materialism. Would it be gratuitous at this point to remind the reader of the *succès de scandale* achieved by the large print version.

The writer is a craftsman of great stature displaying an acute understanding of human nature coupled with a passionate concern for the intangibles, yet a Dadaist he is not. This becomes evident as, slowly at first, the story reveals a deep sense of agnostic optimism touched with a lunar insanity that rages against vast ambiguities whilst at the same time eliciting solution focussed imbalance. Is the author a propagandist against the mores of contemporary Welsh life and the perverse nature of the Romance genre? Possibly, for nothing is what it seems. Sound bites are avoided as the author returns time and time again to the fundamental particle of the novelist's art, the bel, the only particle capable of giving voice to the array of characters laid before us. A decibel is one tenth of a bel. Never has a truism been more true. Ring the bells dear readers, let them chime, ripple, toll, knell, peal and squeal with joy. Let them shake the sublime edifice of this human-interest story to release life itself from the chains of mental concepts.

More a meta-textbook disabusing stealth strategy in literature than a grand narrative, the reader's willingness to share in its suffering is assumed from the outset. That a cycle of understated abuse following a logical progression pervades the novel, testing the reader's capacity to endure adversity, is not in question. Nevertheless, and because of that, this cycle offers compelling evidence that reading the work is a project worth pursuing. Power surges through its pseudo-Marxist construct. The evidence, suffused though it is with plausible deniability, is undeniable and suggests that the world of Millennial and Generation Z readers is facing unprecedented change. Added to this, a bone-headed brilliance informs a transition state that will be attractive to a host of blue-chip readers.

We see before us an extraordinary treatise in which for much of the story the carefully constructed *grand schéma* hangs in the balance. The Sergeant, as Commander-in-Chief and tropeing anti-hero, The Parrot as *Petit Général*, Megan, standing at the heart of what is surely one of the great spiritual stories, and let us not forget the influential *tour de force* performance from Bronwen. These characters beckon and we must follow. Described by one critic as a gentle love story worthy of belief whose nature and content reflect turbulent times forcing a new direction onto lyrical romanticism, one in which the human condition is compromised, the work penetrates a darkening tragi-comic world in which the author's plight is sensed when faced with the growing complexity of traditional social function. His cry for help goes unheeded.

In one sense the work is a *bildungsroman*, a timeless *genre* dissecting the process wherein random acts can trigger far-reaching consequences, whilst, as collateral damage, exploring the coming-of-age experiences and spiritual growth of our main characters. The more abrasive reader will sense the presence of a thinly disguised *romans durs* loitering ominously beneath the surface.

The final scene of reconciliation is preceded by an impending sense of doom. Such a test of resilience and defiance in the reader disrupts the senses, resulting in a letting go of thinking and the appearance of a deep state of meditative consciousness in which the mind is numbed. This is novel as healing force. In short, it takes the reader on a spiritual journey to nowhere, which is as it should be. What does this mean for the future of the medium? First, ask yourself, what does 'future' imply, what is 'medium'?

That the writing gets through to the reader is beyond doubt, yet what happens outside the novel's narrative parameters can only be guessed at. Think strategically, as, if unprepared, the work leaves you feeling as though you have been strip searched at the entrance of County Hall in Haverfordwest on your way to an appointment with a planning officer to discuss your new kitchen extension.[1] My advice. Let sleeping giant's lie.

As *les événements* (sic) unfold the author embeds blue-sky thinking along a timeline of increasing hyperbolic paralysis with its associated impact on globalisation interactivity theory. Naturally, it carries in its wake howls of distress from the world of literary criticism amidst the conflated opprobrium of its arid debate. This process of intellectualising life-art symmetry in a freewheeling, experimental, yet muscular dialogue embedded within a rhythmic, naturalistic syntax is invigorating. Platonic dialogue and Cartesian tract hold hands in a political epiphany that leaves no room for doubt. This book, in which deranged flights of flexible ambiguity abound, is a record of a journey already taken through a world in flux, a world in which magic runs rings around reality.

By the judicious use of imaginary animated vector graphics *ellipsis* can be avoided in the hapless reader's mind as it is swept along paddle-fuelled narrative tributaries tackling issues that only a unique literary voice such as the authors can make comprehensible. He presents a range of challenges to the reader and demands that he or she or they survive the brutalising effect of a descent into a corrosive lapidary prose that offers a *homiletic* model for our time. However, to regard it in these terms would be a mistake. The educated reader knows that this is at odds with prevailing norms, and, suspending reason, takes a radical geostrategic step-shift into a landscape in which the small constituent parts combine to make one mighty whole. The ice-cold wind of hyper-reality howls through its pages demanding the reader groks[2] the truism that awareness of the self precedes knowledge of objects and events. Proof of this intuitive understanding the author established during his research over many long years by use of that most robust of investigative processes, the multiple-choice *questionnaire*.

Creative devices are muted so as not to distract from the interpretation of facts. The author favours a writing technique, out of fashion in this modern age, which utilizes the judicious, yet as far as one can tell, inappropriate use of passages that are utterly irrelevant and completely useless to the development of the story. And he does this well.

Being both empirically and historically factual, a necessary adjunct in conflict with the power of disinformation, the material in the book is of necessity presented with clarity, thus aiding the readers' grasp of the subject. Its central argument is presented in a balanced way throughout thus maintaining the high standards required in such a work of academic research and scholarship. Designed for ease of use the book explores important concepts in the field and will be an essential source to be consulted for many years to come. To acquire a good grasp of the subject further reading is recommended. A work such as this would be useful for group study.

To sum up, the author has proved himself to be a leading cultural ambassador who has written an ambitious work of great totemic significance. Be in no doubt, this is a high-water mark of scientific endeavour, and its message is clear. Make the Fishguard, Crymych, Wadebridge axis great again.

Cerys Rhiannon Quirk, the Baroness Quirk[3]

Professor of English Language and Literature, London University

Introduction

It is thought by many that the world's earliest surviving novel is Aethiopica. The work is unusual in that it begins *in medias res*, the story being resolved by different characters describing past adventures which all come together at the end. The novel begins and ends in Aethiopia, hence the title, and is thought by some scholars to have been written by Heliodorus, a Phoenician. Greek novelists include Chariton, whose novel was written in the mid 1st century AD and Xenophon of Ephesus, whose novel, the Ephesian Tale of Anthia and Habrocomes, was perhaps one of the sources for Shakespeare's Romeo and Juliet. An early Japanese novel, The Tale of Genji, was written in the 11th century AD by a noblewoman. Perhaps the world's first modern psychological novel the story follows the romantic life of Genji, the son of an emperor. Such is the historical context.

To understand this great work however it is essential to be familiar with crime writing as a distinct literary *genre* from its beginnings in Western Europe and America in the 19th century, although crime stories appeared before that period, for example in works written by Arabic and Chinese authors. It should be made clear at the outset that unlike authors of romantic fiction and writers of cookery books the *modus operandi* of the crime writer is to come upon, investigate, and solve a crime, elements not immediately apparent when one first approaches *The Coracle and the Cathedral*. To explain this apparent inconsistency, it would be instructive to examine the significant criminal developments in the narrative. But there are none, and it is this literary *legerdemain* that is the author's artistry. All that is important in plot and characterisation lies unseen, embedded beneath a subtext of unknown historical and cultural impermanence. Is the work then symbolism rather than history?

The power generating psychological components of the storyline are patterns of light and dark, a widely used device for high output at relatively low power, that shimmer seductively just out of reach beneath the narrative's surface. Decreases in plot output due to a drop in input are difficult to detect whilst excessive dissipation is alluded to by its absence. Moreover, maximum achievable efficiency in the author's specialized area of application, namely the non-lucid narrative thread, which, post-ironically, is the novel's major asset, occurs at a maximum efficiency of almost 30% of saturated. Needless to say, total efficiency is not and cannot be achieved. For clarity, the general reader's interest is stimulated by means of an overlapping series of interrelated *hypophora*. Nevertheless, these are used cautiously throughout as a transitional device as they have an explosive effect on the narrative.

A common scenario found all too often in works of this type is the extraordinary challenge facing the reader to make sense of the seismic change happening within the hyper-personalisation of intergenerational cultural motifs.

Courageously equating purpose with power, and cause with crisis, a cynic might link narrative fatigue to emotional engagement as the reimagining of the reader-word interface continues apace at this time of increasing geopolitical turbulence. Forge ahead regardless yet look farther afield for deep wells of moral authority and legitimacy. That said, I am haunted by the suspicion that the reader might unearth a desperate *cri de coeur* that is quintessentially perverse.

Further analysis indicates the presence of a negative-feedback loop centred on the character known as the Sergeant. The author shocks the reader by introducing an unexpected yet enlightening narrative diversion in which the Sergeant experiences a temporary flux imbalance a third of the way through the novel thus utilising that particularly valuable, yet previously little used feature of the crime writer's craft known as 'hyperventilation as operator'. That this imbalance occurs in non-overlapping mode is evidenced by the core attributes of the complimentary character known as The Parrot whose required narrative output power remains steady throughout.

A poor choice of counterbalance can doom the equilibrium needed for a successful crime novel. Boundaries of friction and tension need to be clear. It is interesting to note that opposites are balanced perfectly throughout via the device of introducing *les personnages* known as Megan and Bronwen early in the story, giving evidence to a phenomenon described by Aristotle as an 'intuitive perception of the similarity in dissimilars'.[1] Chapters alternate fluidly and the main pairs of characters are kept apart almost completely, thus maintaining traction. This is achieved by the author rethinking the fundamental narrative-based model to actively embrace a character-rich one. The organic demands of the perfectly formed narrative mesmerise the reader. Who was the Sergeant before he became the Sergeant? What are we to do with Megan? These questions might never be answered.

In parts menopausal the work abounds with sexual disappointment and frustrated ambition. It is not an understatement to say that by the fifth chapter, displaying a callous disregard for the reader's sensibilities, the plot is whipped into a frenzy of *malfeasance* where conventional notions of moral accountability are overturned. A preternatural loudness pervades the second quarter of the book, its anomalous sound 'suspended between the mundane and the miraculous'.[2] Later chapters catapult the unwary reader into a previously unimaginable dystopia in which the narrative rattles along at a blistering pace either side of oases of calm. In a world tilted on its axis, conflicts of the heart erupt from every page.

Plot is absent. Does this literary device work? It has been demonstrated by other commentators that a crime novel with no obvious crime, and no apparent resolution, is at best hubristic, yet this phenomenon opens up a rich new field of academic research. This might prove difficult however as it introduces a rapid drain upon the scholar's passion for evidence-based outcomes. After all, what is the work of the investigator of literature if not empirical. It is well known in academic circles that the true measure of the crime writer's competence is the completion of a narrative circle, the complexity of which is all-consuming, by encompassing the harmonious whole. I am in no doubt that this has been achieved, although in choosing to *critique* this work the literary critic must tread carefully between risk and reward.

A deep text analysis reveals what the reader intuits only too well, that this is as much a work of political subversion as a crime novel. Shrouded in controversy, the political repercussions following its publication are, as yet, unclear.

The Sergeant gives a breathless archetypal performance and Megan, as Goddess, defies all understanding as they sit astride this sweeping epic whose ferocity, if not tempered by a haunting, strategic patience, would be inexcusable. Filled to the brim with intriguing contradictions the author knows that providing the elegant explanations demanded by the novice reader would be a calamitous misjudgement. Instead, dynamic entities revealed by a physical breaking down of language *feign* to reveal their secrets. What can be said without fear of contradiction is that Megan stands at the heart of what is undoubtedly a deeply spiritual journey.

The novel contains a devastating indictment of the *torpor* embedded in the fabric of civil society in Wales' wettest county. Poignant at times, a disjointed thematic symmetry unleashes an avalanche of power and glamour that only bungled relationships on an epic scale can spawn. Stratospherically challenging, this work, an odyssey of savage retribution, floats on a narrative of sinister charm kept buoyant by allusion to an unrevealed devotional matrix. Penetrate beneath the surface and the reader will be rewarded by finding the perfectly formed yet charred remains of a game-changing *hyperbole*.

Quietly and heroically old nostrums are questioned preparatory to being transmuted into a deeply demented inner stasis. An arduous contrivance perhaps, yet it works a familiar kind of magic, echoing the eerie shadows of a despairing mind, whilst, in parallel, a conservative *commentariat* reflects the reader's inner turbulence. A Sisyphean task of weapons-grade absurdity such as this is to be applauded. And might even be worth repeating.

A disconcerting dichotomy imbued with wistful hierarchical structures undoes the stereotypical post-modern archetype of Goddess made flesh, as Megan, living her life as tragic heroine, subtly alludes to a necessary dreamlike matriarchy which the Sergeant, as Svengali figure, searches for but never finds. If ever a quest was futile! Megan and the Sergeant are dynamic entities, one cyber secure and digitally resilient, the other not. Is this important? Rhetorical though this line of questioning is, when asked, it constitutes an important distraction hinting at *procatalepsis*. The narrative configures *enantiodromia*, a radical perspective that turns into its opposite. Yet the opposites depend upon each other to exist.[3] For the literary trained reader it is interesting to note that the author organizes the work in the reader's mind using *metabasis*, thus permitting the free interpretation of external sources, and keeps that mind focussed by the use of *anaphora*.

Whilst researching and writing this paper a relationship was discerned between fiction and real life. The inclusion of autobiographical elements suggests a work perfused by the author's own life experiences. Do not be fooled by this as the *nihilism* in literary criticism during the late 20th and early 21st centuries demands that we examine each particular work by looking at the author's writings as a whole. Unfortunately, such a wide-ranging in-depth review falls outside the scope of an introduction such as this. Bear in mind the sceptical, relativistic view that the past is, 'an era that, when lived through, made no sense, but also felt perfectly normal.'[4]

It would be instructive at this point to quote a sage from the East.[5]

> The postulate that can be postulated
> is not the eternal postulate.
> The hypothesis that can be hypothesised
> is not the eternal hypothesis.
> The speculation that can be speculated
> is not the eternal speculation.

And further.

> Those who know don't write books
> those who write books don't know.

According to research published by ethnographers the people of the Pembrokeshire Peninsular see the past in their memories, but beyond that the past disappears. Fortunately, it can be reconstructed from stories, songs and place names, those 'points in the geography of a community where time and space intersect and fuse'. We must remember that to these natives *when* something happened is as important as *where*, and *where* the incidents recounted in the book occur is as important as the events themselves, and the names of these places contain great beauty. They are themselves pictures in and of the landscape, images of place imbued with meaning, and their significance is apparent to the observant ethnographer during the everyday conversation, songs and storytelling of the subjects. What happened there? What are the principal themes explored in the book? Three are clear, 'the endless quest for survival ... the crucial importance of community and kin' and the interconnectedness of land and language.[6]

The large print version of the book, in which the *apologue*, as tool of rhetorical argument, highlights the irrationality of existence, may assist the reader in his or her quest to separate fact from fiction. It is expedient at this point however to draw attention to the, in my opinion, fallacious view expounded by more popular crime writers that narrative detail is greater than moral incorrigibility.

Powerful rivalries are shaping the future of anthropology as novel. The *premise* of this work is that crime does not pay. The story ushers in a vision of love and forgiveness that precipitates a wonder signifying redemption through self-discovery rather than self-invention. As such the author goes straight for the mother lode whose major *motif* is an incendiary and severely unstable *soupçon* of romantic tension. This is balanced throughout by the device of sombre meditation on existential terror. But in my opinion, this reveals an exaggeration spawned by centuries of denial and distortion. That I can refute this is made clear when one remembers that the author is an anthropologist not a storyteller and wisely, in my opinion, avoids unleashing political unrest on the streets by utilising a well-worn *noir* template in which victory of character evaluation over analysis is paramount. 'Something deeply hidden', waits unseen.[7] This permits the author, as romantic, to shed light on contemporary issues, the sort of issues found only in the long shadows of a soft early evening sun setting over Harbour Village. Is this a revenge novel, or something far more disturbing? This is the real question that remains to be answered.

The author is one of the greatest anthropological crime writers alive today. His writings, saturated as they are with piercing insight, inspire many who contemplate exploring this rich area of study. He is an extraordinary thinker, visionary, writer and teacher and his books are amongst the most widely studied and commented upon in the field. For those who seek to deepen their understanding of life in Pembrokeshire and north Cornwall, contemplation of this paradoxical work is essential. A poet and reformer, he makes a complex subject that is unfamiliar to many, accessible to the general reader. At first glance the content of this book might appear eccentric. However, such a point of view does not stand up to scrutiny when the work is compared with his other writings.

Finally, is this literary work undone by its self-assured subversive conceptualism. It is futile to attempt an answer to such a question in this introduction - a much longer critical essay would be required. It can be said with confidence however, that overall, the author's thesis provides a much-needed cognitive jolt to tired sociological constructs and in a bold move as counter plot throws down the gauntlet to Western Philosophical Materialism. The author, soaked in genius as he undoubtedly is, makes clear the singularity of purpose needed to suffuse the crime story *genre* with hitherto unsublimated collective verve, thereby courageously revealing the fundamental commonality which is foundation to all. A landmark literary experience, this is both a crime novel and an academic text for our age.

I applaud the author's adventurous spirit and read it we must as what is at stake is our sense of what it means to be human.

Fasten your seatbelts, it's going to be a bumpy night.[8]

Catherine Ricks[9]

Professor of European and North American Literature and Dylanologist

Oxford University

Author's Preface

Above all, I am grateful to the following for generously giving of their time to assist me as I embarked upon the exhaustive preliminary research necessary for the completion of this book. The Parrot in Fishguard Harbour and Megan and Bronwen in Crymych. Also, the many concerned citizens whose deep feelings of social responsibility led them to collaborate with the project. Their desire for anonymity has been respected throughout.

It was a chance meeting with The Parrot in the cafe on Goodwick Parrog early one fine summer's morning seven years ago that set me on the path to writing their story. Following that encounter I recorded thousands of hours of conversations with The Parrot, Megan and Bronwen as well as with secondary characters who shared their stories with me for this complex, intellectually challenging anthropological study. Secondary characters such as the Mayor of Fishguard,[1] the *sous chef* at Fishguard's Yogistani restaurant,[2] the staff of the Randibŵ in Fishguard`s Japanese Quarter, the proprietor of Das Kapital[3] in Crymych, the Air Traffic Control team at Crymych International Airport, the director of the world renowned Crymych Opera House, the Chair of the Crymych *Biennale*, staff at the Department of Bilingual Space Exploration at the University of the Four Trinity Davids,[4] *Kowethas an Yeth Kernewek*[5] and *Gorsedh Kernow*[6] to mention but a few of those noble spirits whose memories have lightened our days. My memory will forever dwell with fond remembrance upon them.

Was it easy for these contributors to reveal their secrets willingly? The anticipated *entrenchment* of thought was overcome by compulsive curiosity. Listening to their emotional opinions about what they have experienced, being interested in who they are more than what they think, uncovered a cognitive complexity that necessitates narrative intrigue as autobiographical fact rather than grim certitude. This is no post-modern reactionary *critique* denying *la création du Pembrokeshire*.

Treading gently through the thoughts and reminiscences of the subjects, whose testimony I admit has not always been reliable, I have attempted to distil the essence of Pembrokeshire life during the first two decades of the 21st century into a self-explanatory and lucid chronicle. Of necessity, in order to paint a full and complete picture, parts of the book span a much greater time period. In this way, what began as a routine search for knowledge and understanding in this most vigorous of academic disciplines turned out to be a bit of an *odyssey* to be honest.

The work focuses on the analysis of quantitative data and establishes early on the cross-analysis of the chi-square method of testing *hypotheses*. Interestingly, since X2 calculated (i.e., 19.83) is greater than X2 tabulated (i.e., 9.52), the author rejects Ho and accepts the alternative hypothesis, thus incorporating refinements to Gödel's incompleteness theorems into the *thesis*. To summarize, this is not so much an exploratory study of post-pubertal subjects in an organic community in a western European enclave as a gathering of old friends.

Taking the advice given to me early in my career by linguist and anthropologist Helena Norberg-Hodge[7] whose 1991 book detailing her exploration of life in 'Little Brynberian', that 'wild and beautiful desert land' in the Western Preselis is a classic, I have published the study in the form of a novel. This is a literary device used here as a means of making what would otherwise be a dense and unreadable academic tome more readily available to the general public. It must be remembered that Norberg-Hodge's seminal work '... raises important questions about the whole notion of progress and explores the root causes of the malaise of industrial society.'[7] My intention in writing this work is to add a modest footnote to that exploration. You, and you alone, dear reader, will be able to judge whether or not I have been successful.

To conclude, the work presents the results of a field assessment of all known examples of human activity in Pembrokeshire and North Cornwall. Background ethnographic research was carried out by the author and funded by CADW[8] and the Cornwall Heritage Trust.[9] The project had three main aims. Firstly, to identify the Sergeant and his associates. Secondly, to identify Megan and her circle. Thirdly, to carry out a relative valuation of both sets. To ensure accuracy of interpretation I used that useful tool of statisticians, a linear regression, to understand how strongly the three variables, namely Fishguard, Crymych and Wadebridge are correlated. The educated reader is no doubt aware of the fallibility of data analysis and that it is vital at all times to distinguish correlation from causation. Indeed, in this case the consequences of not doing so would be catastrophic. The results published here, whilst promising, are far from conclusive. Big Data Analytics might provide a helpful avenue for closer investigation.

Future research objectives.

The data from the present survey suggests further possibilities for examination and provides pointers to areas of research potential. There is a gap in our knowledge. Furthermore, the customs of day-to-day socio-economic existence in the area of study, namely the fragile triangle formed by Fishguard, Crymych and Wadebridge, have not been defined. Pollen analysis might throw light on this and the identification of further sites for investigation is a matter of urgency.

Sylvanus
The Japanese Quarter, Fishguard
July 2021

Prologue

Everything that happens, happens somewhere. Without a somewhere, there cannot be a story. In this story, somewhere is the enchanted triangle formed by Fishguard, Crymych and Wadebridge.[1]

It began with an audacious illegal act of theft that rocked the very foundations of Pembrokeshire life. In the following weeks and months more reports of disappearances came in and the staff of the Dyfed-Powys Police Rapid-Response Coracle Unit[2] soon realised they had a crime spree on their hands the magnitude and repercussions of which had never been seen before. The thief or thieves were targeting innocent victims worldwide. The investigation slowly picked up momentum and began immediately. Which is to say, as soon as it could in Pembrokeshire. After much meticulous intelligence gathering the penny dropped. The incidents were linked.

The officer tasked with leading the investigation was an experienced one, Sergeant Wil Davies. He began recording and collating information, the types of crime, method, locations, times, and what items had been stolen. As the reports of the thefts were received at DPPRRCU Headquarters in Milford Haven they were relayed immediately to the Sergeant aboard his vessel, moored, more often than not, in Fishguard Harbour.

Aided by The Parrot the information was examined using modern technology and good old-fashioned police work that included examining thousands of hours of CCTV footage, knocking on doors in the neighbourhoods affected, enquiring about sightings of suspicious people, vehicles or vessels, until a pattern emerged. Lines of enquiry were ruled out, others ruled in. In total, three crimes were found to have been committed. The first crime coincides with the study described in this book and details are included in the main body of the work. Crimes 2 and 3 occurred shortly after the study was finished and are briefly alluded to in Epilogue 1 and Epilogue 2.

After months of painstaking investigations they got a lucky break, a discarded paddle was found floating off Strumble Head. The DNA recovered from this item was run through the database - and came back negative. They were back where they had started. And the Admiral was growing impatient.

The following is inspired by actual events.

1

Chan eil eòlas, chan eil eòlas
air crìch dheireannaich gach tòrachd
no air seòltachd nan lùban
leis an caill i a cùrsa.
                    Somhairle MacGill-Eain[1]

There is no knowledge, no knowledge,
of the final end of each pursuit,
nor of the subtlety of the bends
with which it loses its course.
                    Sorley MacLean

The Dyfed-Powys Police Rapid-Response Coracle[2] spun lazily in the clear turquoise water as the ferry left Fishguard Harbour for Rosslare. Sergeant Wil Davies was puzzled. His thirty-five years' experience solving crimes was not enough. This was his hardest case yet. Exhausted, he lay in the hammock near the willow grove on the stern staring blankly at the clear blue sky above. The multiverse turned before him.

He noticed that one of the cloud formations was an ice cream. A giant 99 complete with chocolate stick. "That`s it!" he thought. "An ice cream!" Encouraged by this revelation he started going over the events of the previous months and the mysterious goings on that had left the people of Pembrokeshire in a state of nervous exhaustion, very similar to the one they are in after the tourists leave at the end of August every year, but with less money.

He gave up and his mind started to wander over the years he had devoted to the service. He had been in the Rapid-Response Coracle Unit a long time. Too long. Years ago, one of his early teachers commented, "If you want to be a coracle, first you must be a square". That explains the shape of the coracle, but little else. It`s like saying that the accelerator is on the right because it`s easier to get at it there or that the chicken came before the egg because somebody had to lay it or that giraffes have got long necks because they prefer the taste of the leaves at the tops of the trees, and anyway, the view is better up there. Or maybe it isn't.

It all began in Crymych. Strange things happen in Crymych. Machlud y Wawr[3] began there. Their aim is to convert everyone to clogging and there are branches all over Wales. There are seven in Patagonia. The Honorary Senior Life President of the Crymych branch was the founder member of the movement. She is 53 years old, at least that's what it says on her library card, and she lives in the crypt underneath Crymych Cathedral. Her wisdom is communicated in an unusual way. She emits a silent *tsunami* of non-symbolic transmissions that drowns the minds of the students engulfed by it giving them a direct experience of the clogging state that she herself is perpetually floating in. Knowledge of true clogging can only be communicated in silence. Not many people know this. Megan does. Her verbal teachings are given in Pembrokeshire Welsh to those who are not washed away by her silence. Her name is Megan Phillips, and her family are from a farm between Maenclochog and Mynachlogddu.

The Sergeant has no interest in the theoretical side of coracling. He explains to novices in the Unit that practice is more important than speculation and discourages questions of a hypothetical nature by remaining silent when they are asked. Or by asking the questioner to find the inner source of the `I` that is asking the question. If the conversation veers towards sterile intellectualisationism he directs the attention of the novice towards more practical matters. "Personal experience," he observes, "particularly paddling experience, is everything in coracling".

The philosopher J. R. Jones[4] provides him with one of his favourite quotes "Coraclo quia absurdum est," "I coracle because it is irrational."[5] Coraclers paddle in a topsy-turvy landscape leaving logic behind, living from within, not bound by rules but finding their own rules. "If you call it a coracle, you affirm. If you call it not a coracle, you negate. Beyond affirmation and negation, what would you call it?"[6] The novice transferred to another unit.

He remembered the captain of the Italian coracling team at the recent European Coracling Championships and her comment shortly after she disappeared down Cilgerran Gorge, "The whole idea of what coracling means is not a case of who wound the paddle up and set it going, it`s the fact that there`s a paddle in the first place." Coracling then, to the true *afficionado*, is a working *hypothesis*.

The Sergeant lay quiet under the noon sun, his silence singing, his emptyness full.

By the *café* on the harbour side of the Parrog, that strand of golden beach, rocky bits and sticky out thingies that joins the twin towns of Fishguard and Goodwick, the sun glinted on the plaque to a former German Olympic Coracling gold medallist and physicist who had a brief yet distinguished career as professor of Coracling Studies at the University of North Pembrokeshire at Crymych. His uncertainty principle states that the position and momentum of a coracle cannot be simultaneously known.[7] The more precisely the observer measures one of these, the less precisely the other is known. This means that it is impossible to know both the position and momentum of a coracle with any degree of certainty. A fact not lost on the crowd as they watched the coracle disappear rapidly down Cilgerran Gorge. Or did they?

A favourite anecdote of the Sergeant`s when talking about his job to awestruck school children is that of the time the physicist was coracling with dolphins near Strumble Head one balmy summer evening when he was stopped by a Rapid-Response Coracle Unit vessel following a tip off from the coastguards who had been watching him and thought he was speeding, although they couldn`t be sure because he was going too fast. When asked by Sergeant Davies if he knew how fast he was going he replied, "No, but I know where I am, see. I`m by `ere." His grandmother on his mother`s side was from Swansea. The inscription on the plaque says, 'He might `ave coracled by `ere.' A visitor from Llanelli corrected the grammar by scratching the word 'mun' at the end.

The Sergeant and his crew are the latest manifestation of a long nautical tradition as coracles have plied the waters of Wales, the rest of Britain and Ireland for millennia. The first written reference to coracles in Britain was that by Julius Caesar in the mid first century BC. Giraldus Cambrensis described coracles on the stern in 1187.

Relaxing in the hammock as the coracle rose and fell smoothly in the calm waters of the harbour, he sipped from the mug of tea he had just made in the galley and munched a piece of *bara brith*, freshly caught that morning. It was his favourite mug. There was a line on the inside running deeper and deeper from rim to bottom with words next to it, a bit like the markings on the outside of a ship`s hull that show how heavy she is lying in the water. This tea strength gauge, which he designed and built himself, tells him when to pull the tea bag out. After putting the tea bag into the hot water in the mug and stirring vigorously with a spoon the appropriate strength is calibrated by pausing and peering into the depths every couple of minutes to see which words are still visible. About an inch from the bottom of the mug next to the line are the words, `You`ve Forgotten to Put the Tea Bag In`. At half inch intervals further up are the words, `Very Weak`, then `Weak`, then `Medium`, `Strong`, `Very Strong` and finally, `You need a stronger spoon`.

Returning the mug to the small table next to the hammock he looked thoughtfully at it as it lingered approximately two feet from his face. He wondered how long it took for light to travel from the mug to him.

And he wondered.

And wondered.

Resting in the timeless state on the branch of a nearby willow tree The Parrot became aware of the question and with a typical display of compassion for the Sergeant's predicament decided to help. It opened its eyes and moved effortlessly from full lotus to kneeling. Bending forward, with back straight, core engaged, buttocks down not lifted, it did twenty press-ups, shook itself once, stood up and spoke. "In one second light travels 186,280 miles or 327,852,800 yards or 983,558,400 feet. This means that light travels about one foot in one nanosecond which is 0.000000001 seconds and therefore two feet in two nanoseconds which is 0.000000002 seconds."

And wondered.

The on-board computer hummed softly below decks. It knows that when the Sergeant's cognitive load is high his decision making is compromised. It also knows that this doesn't matter as, unknown to the Sergeant, he is never in control of the vessel. For the safety of the sea lanes his internal locus of control lies deep within the computer. The Sergeant's need for an extensive understanding of his job is negated by the on-board computer's understanding of him. The computer also keeps the complex interface between the Sergeant and the tea and biscuits under routine observation. The march of the machines is upon him.

Pleased to have been of help The Parrot resumed full lotus position, closed its eyes and returned to the timeless state.

The Sergeant took another sip of tea, returned the mug to its resting position on the table, reached for a chocolate biscuit, munched, pushed back in the hammock and waited for the arrival of the emotional benefits of the endorphin rush known as chocolatier's high.

At a recent meeting of the American Association for the Advancement of Science[8] it was revealed that the Earth has more than 100 billion neighbouring planets, approximately a quarter of them orbiting stars similar to the sun. This means there might be life on them. As if from nowhere a thought appeared, "Is it possible there are 25,000,000,000 Sergeants?" passed playfully through The Parrot's mind and was gone.

A week is a long time in the Dyfed-Powys Police Rapid-Response Coracle Unit. Too long. His thoughts turned to the wedding anniversary dinner with his wife Arianrhod the previous Saturday, the night of the full moon. It had been perfect. Over a main course of Penclawdd cockles and Port Eynon laver bread in a restaurant in St Davids she issued detailed instructions for the manoeuvres she had planned for when they got back to the B&B. Later that night, his memory of the event sketchy as he was concentrating on the food at the time, when questioned by the emergency services as they cut his wife free, he recalled that sometime between the main course and the dessert she leant across the table and whispered, "The safe word is antidisestablishmentarianism."

During dessert she told him that the G-spot had been located and asked when he was going to look for it. He shrugged his shoulders and turned away in despair having read an article in the science section of the County Echo[9] the previous week in which it was stated that, according to modern physics, the G-spot can appear in two places at the same time. Unsettled by this his eyes met those of the beautiful young waitress who happened to be passing and he winked at her. The waitress that is, not his wife. He wasn`t sure why, it just happened. His wife had a blazing row, threw the cockles over him and stormed out. He did nothing about it, but he did it well. Yes, he loved the traditional ways. He consoled himself with another pot of tea and the knowledge that it had taken a dedicated team of researchers with a vast array of technological equipment and financial support seven years to find it. Or had it?

Crymych on a Saturday night is a wild place with choirs of teenagers roaming the streets terrorising everyone with their close harmony contrapuntal singing. They are all in the Urdd, Aelwyd Crymych,[10] and standards have to be high. There might be an Eisteddfod[11] adjudicator listening in a nearby pub. Hadn`t some government somewhere pledged to be tough on close harmony singing and tough on the causes of close harmony singing?[12] The teenagers are particularly fond of carrying out *guerrilla* raids when the massed ranks of Crymych Orpheus Choir are rehearsing. They rush in just before half time refreshments, sing an assorted medley of Mamas and Papas songs and then the Welsh versions by Eglwyswrw`s own *Y Mame a`r Tade* and then disappear back into the darkness of downtown Crymych before the one hundred and seventy-three choir members, the conductor, the assistant conductor, the baton keeper, the pianist, the harpist, the harpist`s second and the tea lady and her entourage know what`s hit them. This has happened every month since February 1963, the winter of the great snow. In the spring of 1984, no one can remember which month, the pianist ran after them shouting abuse. The following morning, he opened the garage doors to find his gondola up on bricks, the oar gone.

Sergeant Davies couldn`t swim and he didn`t see how lying in the hammock would change that fact. He was one of the old school like the men centuries before who sailed with Madog to America in the great ocean-going coracles. "If the coracle goes down, swimming just draws out the inevitable," the old timers always say. He took comfort from that. Carved onto the shaft of his paddle are the following wise words, "'Tis better to have fallen out of a coracle than never to have fallen out of a coracle at all."[13] Exactly.

He glanced across the water to the clock, a present to the people of Goodwick from a grateful Salvador Dali,[14] that hangs, upside down some think, on the outside wall of the *café* on the Parrog. But he couldn`t read it. Was it too small? No, it was big enough, it was just too far away. He looked towards the harbour buildings and his eyes focussed on the flashing neon sign, *Notice to Coraclers: Please switch off radar whilst in port*. Nothing was happening, and in a very emphatic way. He thought of Leonard Cohen`s *Great Book of Coracling Songs*[15] that he keeps under the hammock and began to sing,

Suzanne takes you down to her place near the river.
You can hear the coracles go by,
You can spend the night beside her.
And you know that she`s half crazy ......

He thought of his wife, Arianrhod. Was she back from her mother`s yet? An old black and white photograph of her hung on the starboard bulkhead in the galley between the porthole and the on-board radio. It was her but it didn't look much like her. The warning light on his mobile phone flickered faintly yet menacingly for a few brief moments before going out. The voice of Obi-Wan Kenobi disturbed the calm, "A message from the Dark Side."[16] "She`s back," the Sergeant sighed as a text arrived.

When they met in the Randibŵ in Fishguard`s Japanese Quarter in Lower Town, that den of iniquity and nest of vipers they have the cheek to call a *sushi* bar all those years ago, the only thing they had in common was that she came from Crymych, and he had heard of Crymych. The other thing they had in common was that neither of them was Japanese. The latter is still true today.

"I`ll have a large portion of the coffee fudge cake please," she told him.

"What about the healthy option?" he asked.

"You`re right, with *crema chantilly.*"

"Strange things cakes," he confided.

"What do you mean?"

"They look lovely, then you eat six of them and wonder what all the fuss was about."

"Like nouns in Welsh, coracles are either male or female and their gender is just as hard to determine," he realized with a start, which is a noun, as is jolt. Both appear to be indefinite, although they could on another occasion be definite. Tilting one over a little and peeking underneath does not help. His imagination racing with syntactic excitement a passing Greek noun tripped and fell into his mind. "If $\theta\eta\sigma\varepsilon\nu\rho\sigma\varsigma$ is the Greek word for treasure," he thought, "then what is the Greek word for *thesaurus*?" He was every inch the philosopher, but not a very good one. Socrates would have been safe, they would have given the hemlock to the Sergeant. And wasn`t it Aristotle who wrote, "All human actions have one or more of these seven causes: chance, nature, compulsions, habit, reason, passion, desire and paddling?"[17] As the Sergeant became more mindful of his predicament he became more baffled. The more deeply he knew it, the more deeply he did not know it. "I`m glad I`m making progress," he thought to himself. But it is not helpful applying an intellectual aesthetic to coracling. French coraclers tried that and look where it got them, *Nil Point* in the slalom mixed doubles at the last Olympics. Too much hanky panky and not enough igam ogam. Or too much subject and not enough predicate as someone once remarked.[17]

Coraclers brains are different from non-coraclers. According to recent neurological studies coraclers and non-coraclers show differences in behaviour because their brains are physically distinct organs. Coracling and non-coracling brains appear to be constructed from markedly different genetic blueprints. The differences in the circuitry that wires them up and the chemicals that transmit messages inside them are so great as to point to the conclusion that there is not just one kind of human brain, but two. Coraclers may be from Mars and non-coraclers from Venus[18] but until recently these differences were often explained by the action of adult sex hormones or by social pressures that encouraged coraclers and non-coraclers to behave in different ways. These assumptions are being challenged by the research and it is becoming clear that the brains of coraclers and non-coraclers show numerous anatomical differences:

- Decision making and problem solving, controlled by the frontal lobe: proportionately bigger in non-coraclers.
- Emotional response, controlled by the limbic cortex: proportionately bigger in coraclers.
- Spatial perception, controlled by the parietal cortex, which regulates how we move around: proportionately bigger in non-coraclers. Was Madog really aiming for Barry Island?
- Emotional memory, controlled by the amygdala: proportionately bigger in non-coraclers.
- Suppression of pain, controlled by the periaqueductal grey, an area of grey matter in the midbrain: known to have a role in the suppression of pain in both groups, but larger in coraclers.
- The tendency to hallucinate, centre located in the brain stem: enormous in coraclers.
- Motion sickness and the limbic system: proportionately bigger in coraclers.
- The ability to inhibit automatic responses and the propensity to run risks even when aware of the odds, controlled by the prefrontal cortex: fully formed in non-coraclers by age 25. Process completed later in coraclers.
- Memory, located in the hippocampus: significantly smaller in coraclers.
- Paddling skills, controlled by cells located in Area 2 of the motor cortex in the frontal lobe: on average 23 per cent bigger in coraclers.

Trying to impress, he mentioned to Arianrhod that evening in the *sushi* bar that he came from an ancient north Pembrokeshire family with a long pedigree, but he overdid it a bit by adding, "In fact some of my ancestors were in the Ark with Noah." "Wfft! And nine of them!" came her immediate reply. He realised for the first time that far from being the superheroes so often betrayed in the Marvel comics[19] of the nineteen fifties most coraclers are just like everyone else, only more so. He had never been good with women. Too much time out alone in the coracle with his paddle which, being made of wood, does not attract lightning strikes. His geography was poor as well. When asked by the chief navigator of the Dyfed-Powys Police Rapid-Response Coracle Unit in the oral exam at the end of his training period how he would go about charting a course for Timbuktu he suggested entering Timbukone and Timbukthree into the on-board TwmTwm[20] and steering a course between them.

The radio transmitter attached to the main mast next to the hammock crackled and came to life. "This is a newsflash," said the voice from DPPRRCU headquarters in Milford Haven. "Listen carefully please. Evidence for life on Mars. NASA[21] has confirmed that the Ospreys` Mars lander[22] has identified one of the crucial ingredients for life. We have coracle. We`ve seen evidence for coracles before in observations made by the Dragons` orbiter[23] ten years ago but this is the first time that a Martian coracle has been seen. The Ospreys` lander`s robotic arm with traditional soft-grip stainless steel scissor action ice cream scoop (medium sized) extension found the coracle on Wednesday, buried just beneath the surface, and confirmed its composition by analysing the gases emitted when it was heated. Because of this discovery the Space Agency has extended the Ospreys` mission and it will receive extra funding from the sponsors, the Penclawdd Premium Cockle Company, which will enable it to investigate the surface of the Red Planet until the end of the year. Mars is giving us some surprises. One is how the coracle is behaving. The outer surface sticks to the scoop when exposed to the hot sun and that has presented a challenge. Since landing last week, the Ospreys` lander has been studying the coracle with an array of instruments including a microscope, chemistry lab, camera and conductivity probe. Scientists are also looking for traces of carbon-containing chemicals. However, there is still no conclusive evidence of intelligent life. Nonetheless, scientists believe the find proves the Mars surface once had plentiful water, almost guaranteeing the presence of life. Unless of course the coracle is a cruel joke played upon humans by aliens."

As an amateur cosmologist as well as a philosopher the Sergeant was disappointed by that last remark. He thought this stuff about no conclusive evidence of intelligent life was rubbish, or as he put it, **"RUBBISH!".**

The radio transmitter barked into life once more and the Admiral's voice ricocheted around the stern. "Robotic process automation together with harnessing data and AI effectively is the future. Oh! And a cobot for you."

"Co wot?"

"We are increasing investment in cyber physical systems thus moving one step ahead of the internet of things and utilizing complex modelling known as digital twinning coupled with analytic capabilities. The system enables you to infer knowledge from raw data, make real time decisions and send commands to the crew."

At last, a word he understood. The Sergeant looked at The Parrot. With closed eyes The Parrot looked back. Its senses grew keener. The Parrots eyes rolled upwards under its eyelids as it loosened its grip on the branch and began a controlled backwards half flip. Arriving at an upside-down position it tightened its grip once again as the blood rushed to its beak and began a period of quiet contemplation. In a discreet *homage* to the Blues Brothers The Parrot was wearing

41

sunglasses and a black fedora, the look accessorised with a deerskin shirt with two rows of elk teeth sewn across its front. A wing feather from an eagle, attached to its head plumage by a coloured thread, moved listlessly in the breeze. Amongst the Plains Indians it is known as Wolf Warrior.

The Admiral waited respectfully as the pendulum like motion of the upside down The Parrot diminished and it came to a stop, then continued. "Colleagues at the Science Division here at HQ are liaising with experts at the University of the Four Trinity Davids' Advanced Institute for Robotic Process Automation Research[24] to reduce human error and increase quality and productivity." The Sergeant's mind weighed up the pros and cons of having another mug of tea. Having delivered the update, the Admiral growled a goodbye and went back to the important business of running the DPPRRCU. He was committed to technological change, 'moving forward into the future'.

The Sergeant is committed to tea. He is in the value chain but unaware of it. He is on the edge but in danger of falling off. In the world of technological transformation, he has not reached the Why? stage. Digitally, he has not yet crawled out of the ocean. To him the end goal is the hammock. Futurists at HQ call this a compatibility hiccup and classify him as disruptive technology.

The coracle spun a little faster. Sergeant Davies was getting nowhere, and he was getting giddy, so he used his toe and the dooby doo to turn the radio on and caught the afternoon science programme on Radio Free Pembrokeshire[25] in time to hear the concluding remarks of what had obviously been a fascinating discussion. "Years ago, J.B.S. Haldane[26] voiced the suspicion that the world of Machlud y Wawr is not just stranger than we can imagine, but stranger than we can imagine. Since then, the scientific community has been engaged in an unofficial, hush hush, very hush hush attempt to prove that there are no limits to the strangeness of their imaginings, what with their vibrating clogs and multi-dimensional G-strings. You don`t have to delve very deeply into the collective world of Machlud y Wawr before parts of your brain start to shut down in the interests of self-preservation."

The transmitter spluttered and the Admiral continued. "Quantum coracles, already in prototype, can move in a circle and a straight line simultaneously, a phenomenon best explained by the existence of multiple universes. All we need now is a quantum coracler. Any thoughts, Sergeant? Over and out."

"Mmmm! Perhaps I`ll apply for that," thought the Sergeant. "There might be a pay rise in it. I haven`t been on a course for a while either and a weekend in Carmarthen would be good, the wife likes big town life. She`ll want to go clubbing at the Ivy Leaf[27] again where we spent many a romantic weekend after we were married."

"Breaking news," said the Radio Free Pembrokeshire announcer, cutting through the Sergeant`s revelries. "The discovery of a fossilised pelvis in the oil rich shales just north of Carn Ingli forces scientists to revise their view of human evolution. The discovery of the fossilised pelvis of a woman who lived on the Preseli Plateau 2.3 million years ago has resolved a long-standing debate over when in the history of human evolution it was possible for babies with large paddling arms to be born. Coraclers are unique for the relatively large arms of their newborn babies but until now it was not known when women coraclers developed the wide pelvis needed to give birth to big-armed babies. And big arms presumes big shoulders. Now scientists believe they can finally answer the question after discovering the almost intact female pelvis. The large arms and shoulders relative to body size have enabled coraclers to dominate their environment, almost causing the extinction of smaller armed canoeists in many parts of Western Europe until the World Wildlife Fund[28] stepped in and declared them a protected species, thus allowing their numbers to increase. Many in West Wales think this is a retrograde step however as the more aggressive canoeists often fall out with local people fishing quietly along the river. This is a problem particularly on the Tywi and the Teifi. The velocity of the canoe as it moves through the water is also a problem as the wash created erodes the riverbanks. Speed restrictions have been introduced on many rivers. Reconstruction of the pelvis fragments shows that the female coracler had a birth canal that was 30 per cent bigger than earlier estimates. The study, published in the journal Science,[29] compares the newly discovered pelvis with that of Lleucu,[30] an earlier hominid belonging to the species Preselipithecus brynberianensis who lived just outside Brynberian about 3.2 million years ago. Her descendants still run a tea shop in the village."

The Sergeant recalled a coracling *afficionado* who was so infuriated by the speeds some canoeists were achieving, particularly over Cenarth Falls, that he launched the `Slow Canoe` movement,[31] a personal crusade against the so called `fast canoe` and everything it represented. It was slow to catch on in West Wales, hence the speed restrictions zealously enforced by the Dyfed-Powys Police Rapid-Response Coracle Unit. But the canoes were too fast for them. With characteristic guile and cunning the Sergeant and his colleagues hid behind bushes along narrow stretches of the river and threw recycled bricks, abandoned shopping trolleys, home-made spears and other assorted debris at the canoeists as they shot past. They sank dozens of canoes every season. "Good darts, boys!" he would cry out with a proud smile as another one went down. "Life goes by too quickly," is his motto.

Amelia Earhart, the American aviation pioneer and author, agreed.[32] Famous for being the first female aviator to land in Burry Port, she touched down there one fine day in June 1928 after leaving Trepassey Bay in Newfoundland with pilot Wilmer Stultz and co-pilot and mechanic Louis Gordon and crossing the world's second-largest ocean in a leisurely 20 hours and 40 minutes. "I can always make time for a cup of tea in Burry Port," she said, before taking off to continue the journey in her plane, a Fokker F.VIIb, named *Cyfeillgarwch* in honour of her new-found friends. Nowadays, a holidaymaker can do the journey in 28.67 minutes as a passenger on board a Lockheed SR-72 Son of Blackbird. This excludes the long period of hospitalisation needed to recover from the bout of unconsciousness caused by the G-forces experienced during take-off and the near vertical ascent to an altitude of 80,000 feet before the aircraft levels out to cruise at a speed of Mach 6 which is more than 2,500mph. Twenty-eight minutes sixty-seven seconds! That's quicker than the bus journey from Fishguard to Haverfordwest.

Amelia was not the first woman traveller of note. In 1888, Bertha Benz undertook the world's first long distance car journey from Mannheim to Pforzheim in Germany aboard the three-wheeler Benz Patent Motorwagen, the world's first automobile. She was accompanied on the 65-mile drive by her sons Richard and Eugen, thirteen and fifteen years old respectively. The Motorwagen did not have a fuel tank and they set off with just under eight pints of petrol in the carburettor. There were no garages – of course. She stopped in Wiesloch along the way and bought fuel, a petroleum solvent called ligroin, at an apothecary which thus became the first petrol station in the world. During the journey the wooden brakes developed a problem which she solved by asking a cobbler to fit them with leather, thus inventing brake linings. Ever inventive, during the excursion she used her garter as insulation material and cleaned a blocked fuel line with her hat pin.

A few years later in 1916 the Van Buren sisters, Augusta and Adeline crossed the continental United States, each on their own motor bike and dressed in leather riding breaches, travelling 5,500 miles in 60 days. They made the trip from New York to Los Angeles on 1,000cc Indian Power Plus motorcycles. During the journey they were arrested several times by the police because they were wearing men's clothing. They in turn were following on the heels of Effie Hotchkiss who, the year before, made the journey from New York to San Francisco on a 1915 Harley-Davidson F-11 motorcycle, with her mother Avis as a passenger in the sidecar. It is said that the first motorcycle race began when the second motorcycle was built. But these women were more sensible. Free spirits, they enjoyed the rebellion and the ride. Desiring to be free from oppressive male forces, they showed the way.

Compare the feats of these women with the testosterone fuelled accomplishment of one Walter Arnold who, in Kent, England in 1896 became the first person in the world to be stopped by the police for speeding. He was driving his horseless carriage at an estimated 8mph in a 2mph limit, and no man carrying a red flag walking in front of him. After a frantic five-mile police chase, the first ever, on his bicycle the local constable apprehended him but was unable to issue a speeding ticket as there weren't any. Mr Arnold appeared in court in Tunbridge Wells where he was fined five shillings for "using a carriage without a locomotive horse". On the other counts, namely for driving with less than three persons in charge of the vehicle, for not having his name and address on the vehicle and for driving at more than two miles per hour, he was fined one shilling each. He was also ordered to pay costs.

The Sergeant reminisced about the first time he received a suspension. They were in bed together in the Ivy Leaf on a bank holiday weekend shortly after they were married and she hadn't yet come to realise the full range of his interests. Modestly, he told her he was `just` a coracler, as if the words `just` and `coracler` can be brought together like that and mean anything, and asked her if she wanted to see his new paddle, a Stradivarius[33] he bought in Carmarthen market the week before, a rare artefact from the golden age of paddling. He intended using it on ceremonial occasions.

"Yes please, cariad," she said, getting all romantic.

Jumping to his feet on top of the duvet cover he bounced up and down a few times, accidentally knocking his head against the ceiling as he did so, before bending his legs, placing his hands on his knees, leaning forward and shouting **"Crouch! Bind! Set!"** He lost his footing on the soft surface under the pressure coming through from the second row and collapsed on top of her. She shoved him off and he fell to the floor. Getting to his feet he asked her to blow his whistle to restart play. She refused of course, being chapel, and showed him a red card. It was the third time he had lost his binding that evening, a shame what with the offence playing flat and late on the gain line and the rush defence against a blitzing midfield. He didn't argue. She had access to 24 camera angles and Hawk-Eye technology[34] to monitor the Sergeant's movements and assess potential foul play. Her decision was that his head made unlawful contact with the ceiling. A six-match suspension and the concussion protocol had to be invoked so he could take no further part in any contact sport for the next six weeks. Harsh though that sounded to the couple listening in the next room, the only clouds that ever passed over their relationship were those of the annual monsoon season from November 1st to March 1st.

He was a bit of a Do-It-Yourself man the Sergeant, always experimenting. They came out of that same *sushi* bar in the Japanese Quarter one evening a little while after the suspension ended, three weeks earlier than predicted in the press as he pleaded guilty at the hearing. He'd had a couple of sakes too many and yes, he'd been on the Double Dragon again. "Would you like to have a ride in my coracle?" he asked.

"No!" Her Welsh Baptist upbringing remained strong.

A look of thorough dejection and *ennui* came over his face and she took pity on him.

"Hmmm. Alright then," she said with that deep, romantic voice of hers and agreed to go with him for a ride around Dinas Head. Until she saw the periscope.

Underwater coracling held no attractions for her. Realising this and trying once again to impress her he looked lovingly into her eyes. "Lovely hat you're wearing," he announced. She turned abruptly and walked off. "That's not a hat, those are my extensions."

On the coracle's stern, goats munch on the partly shaded lawn, damp in parts, inhabited by dense green clumps of mosses whose ancestors existed during the Permian period, the last period of the Palaeozoic era, between 298.9 million years ago and 251.902 million years ago, at whose end occurred the greatest mass extinction recorded in Earth's history. Scattered across the lawn grow bird's-foot trefoil with yellow flowers attracting, amongst others, the Common Blue butterfly, and later in the day the Six-spot Burnet moth, buttercups with cup-shaped bright yellow lustrous flowers, clover with heads of white flowers tinted with pink or cream and trifoliolate leaves, daisies with characteristic rosettes of tiny white petals surrounding bright yellow centres upon a single stem, yellow dandelions with tightly packed florets and jagged toothed leaves, clumps of bluish-violet field scabious with rough and hairy stems, ground ivy with whorls of funnel-shaped violet flowers, hawk bits with orange-red flowers up to one inch in diameter reflecting ultraviolet light and thus attracting pollinators, common knapweed with erect stems thickened beneath purple rayed flowerheads 1.5 inches in diameter and dense carpets of ground-covering Blue speedwells displaying their dark-veined, lavender-blue flowers on creeping stems.

Honeybees drink nectar from deep within the many blossoms, passively collecting pollen dust on body hairs and in sacs on their hind legs as they go, before returning to the colony consisting of almost 80,000 bees, where nectar is turned into honey to provide sugars for energy as well as salts, acids, essential oils and water. The pollen, a source of protein, carbohydrates, lipids, vitamins and minerals, spreads from plant to plant as they feed.

Colourful orange and black banded marmalade hoverflies feed on nectar in the umbrella-like clusters of the white flowers of cow parsley and the yellow flat-topped, button-like flower heads of tansies.

More than ten genetically distinct species of the two-barred flasher butterfly with attractive basal to post-basal iridescent blue colouring on their wings feed on a variety of plants.

An iridescent metallic green Rose Chafer beetle nearly an inch long with bronze underside and creamy-white streaks on its wing cases feeds on pollen and nectar in the large, pink, sweet-scented five petalled flowers nearly 2 inches across of prickly Dog Roses.

A family of Popa langur, one of more than five hundred primate species around the world, dark-brown backs and tails about 3 feet long, cream-white undersides with distinctive white rings around the eyes, holidaying from their home in the crater of the sacred Mount Popa, an extinct volcano in Myanmar, rest amongst the branches of the willow trees as they recover from the journey.

A tiger mosquito, first described in 1894, with distinctly separated compound eyes, dark coloured proboscis and characteristic white bands on its legs and body, rests at the edge of a stagnant pool near the cow shed feeding on sweet plant juices. As with other mosquitos, only the female feeds on blood which nourishes the eggs. A ranger on a scouting mission it will return to its scourge in northern France with the happy news that the stern is a suitable site to colonise. Bringing the viruses that cause Chikungunya fever, dengue fever and yellow fever, and the zika virus, as well as filarial nematodes from their native Southeast Asia as global warming makes the northern European coracle habitable for their kind, they will soon settle here.

A standing stone, seven feet tall, with an inscription in ogham, Latin and Old Welsh can be seen nearby. Unconventional in its content, it is a prayer to the sea, the sky, the earth, the moon and the sun. Close by, a Viking longship filled with archaeological treasures that accompany a dead king lies buried seven feet beneath the surface.

The wake from the ferry leaving Fishguard Harbour as it begins its journey to Ireland lifts the coracle and the Sergeant senses it straining, like himself, to be free.

Is this a sign?

No, it's the anchor.

2

Arise and drink your bliss for everything that lives is holy.

William Blake[1]

It was quiet in the crypt. Megan, sitting in the *simne fawr*, reached for the glass of sugar free Llanteg lemonade that was her tipple, made with the best fruit from Crymych's lemon groves, fresh that morning, the ones the Woman from Abermonte[2] chooses herself. Shaken not stirred of course. Her mind went back to the Lemon Grove War of Easter 1916 when the Womens' Institution,[3] a foreign organisation, tried to squeeze the locals out of the lemon groves. The word went out from Machlud y Wawr's militant wing[4] and help flooded in from the villages around. The Womens' Institution might have lit the fuse but Machlud y Wawr were the dynamite. Oh! And the way the Junior Life Presidents of both organisations glared at each other over the battlefield like a pair of mad prawns. So inspiring. The words of a song, *The Foggy Lemon Grove* came to her, and she lay back and sang quietly to herself.

> *'Twas down the glyn one Easter morn*
> *To a city fair rode I.*
> *When lines of marching women*
> *In squadrons passed me by.*
> *No pipes did hum, no battle drum*
> *Did sound its loud tattoo*
> *But the Angelus bell o'er Crymych town*
> *Rang out in the foggy dew.*[5]

Soft tears ran down her cheeks as she remembered the Lemon Grove War which made a deep impact on her young and impressionable mind. The years dulled her memory to the full horrors as, unlike the universe, her memory is not constantly expanding. As someone once noted, "Perhaps you are not interested in lemons, but lemons are interested in you".[6] How prophetic that turned out to be, particularly for him. But the lemon groves were saved and the franchise that resulted is now one of Machlud y Wawr's most lucrative income streams. And Megan, their Junior Life President at the time, went on to greater things. As for her opposite number in the Womens' Institution, she woke up one morning a few weeks later to find the bloodied, severed head of a corgi under the bed sheets[7] with the letters MyW[4] carved callously in insular majuscule script onto the poor little thing's forehead and a lemon with the words `Llanteg's best` burnt onto it stuffed between its teeth. "Cadwch eich blydi lemwns!"[8] she screamed when she saw the gory remains in the bed alongside her, inspired no doubt by her studies, in translation, of the complete works of Saunders Lewis, something that all primary school children up in England do now as part of the `Get to know your neighbours initiative`. A positive move fifteen hundred years after they moved in.

"Will there ever be a day like that again?" she mused, and then answered her own question. "Probably not. Damn computers!" She remembered the night several years back when her late husband told her he was having trouble with his external hard drive. "Have you tried Viagra?"[9] she asked. Fortunately, he didn`t hear her correctly. At times she is utterly incomprehensible because of her thick north Pembrokeshire dipthongs. And why was she wearing them around her neck? In today`s global marketplace where the *lemwns* are sold to every quarter from Bejing to California, from Delhi to Ecuador the franchise depends upon peace. "If you want to gather honey, don`t kick over the beehive", she quoted.[10] She wasn`t sure if this was appropriate but she liked the sound of it, and that was enough. The sounds of language matter. She is a mistress of *cynghanedd*. She can even spell it. The poetic art where vowels and consonants cascade over and through one another to produce a hypnotic, mesmerising sound that lights up the brain and transports the listener to a place where sound and meaning meet and rapture explodes. No wonder Welsh poets are always smiling, even after they see the figures on their royalty cheques. A *cynghanedd* teacher from across the border in Cardigan worked an *englyn* in memory of those times. He called it *Lemwn!* Another poet responded with a chain of *englynion* that describe a pilgrimage from Crymych to St Davids where the bones of the Unknown *Lemwn* Picker are kept. They lie in the cathedral in a casket of polished Dolau Cothi gold in an alcove next to the one where, in a plain wooden box lie the bones of Dewi Sant himself.

Megan`s late husband once started a campaign on Radio Wales[11] to promote singing in the bath, believing it to be the best antidote to the stresses of modern life. His idea was that because of the acoustics there is a tendency for low, slow notes to be most therapeutic. He suggested such favourites as *Ol` Man River*, *Oft in the Stilly Night*, any of Meic Stevens` ballads, and of course, *Arafa Don*, the latter of which produced excited comment from certain more impressionable members of Machlud y Wawr who asked if they could jump in with him and form a choir. One young member, Bronwen, even asked if he was up to doing a duet with her, then swooned and fell into the bath. He thought this was a wonderful idea, but his wife threw cold water over them both and told them not to be so silly.

"Don`t be so silly!"

And she told them to get out of the bath.

"Get out of the bath!"

The Crymych *crachach* are still reeling from the news that Megan has her own bilingual Wicipedia entry which to date extends to some 79,438 words, many of which however are very short. And no mention of clogging, of which sport by the way her late husband was three times all Wales champion, the third time whilst accompanying himself on the piano accordion as he particularly liked the echo effects in the crypt. Indeed, he was the youngest ever to win the Golden Clog and achieved that the same year he won the Golden Conker at the Welsh Open Conker Championships in the Three Crowns in Hubberston.[12] Yes, the Golden Double, a feat that has never been equalled to this day. Whilst basking in the glory that only a front page spread in the Western Mail[13] can give you however he was secretly disappointed because since childhood he had set his sights on the impossible, but never achieved it. You see, he only got Silver in the Welsh Whittling Championships in Whitland and the dream of the Golden Triple crashed and burned. Oh! Cruel fate! "He`s happy where he is now," she murmured, remembering that famous line, 'In Heaven the cooks are French, the police officers are Irish, the mechanics are German, the lovers are Italian, the rugby players are from New Zealand, the cloggers are Welsh and it`s all organised by the Swiss'. She rolled that around inside her head for a moment before adding, "In hell the police officers are German, the mechanics are French, the lovers are Swiss (hopeless except for timing), the rugby players are from New Zealand, of course, the cloggers are Irish, it`s organised by the Italians and the Americans invaded anyway." No mention of the Welsh down there of course. She prefers her version of the story.

One of the committee members of Crymych Clogging Club and her husband, who live in St Dogmael`s, went to France last summer to spread their horizons and get some culture down them, and anyway she`d won a family holiday to Paris at the Abbey Bingo Emporium situated next to the duck pond. They stayed in the luxurious accommodation provided, a two-star *hôtel* next to an all-night bar in the Pigalle. The husband, a county councillor, was very good at constructive ambiguity and he`d learnt how to talk with great incoherence. He dated his wife for seven years and they eventually married, though only after he had proposed nine times. So ingrained is his habit of speaking obscurely that the first eight times he proposed his wife to be didn`t know what he was talking about. Fortunately for him she was the daughter of a professional committee member and through her experience of communicating with her parent managed to make out an occasional word and phrase here and there. By the ninth proposal she had decoded the message. He saw everything through the prism of his own fabulousness, a prerequisite for councillors, and he was a very good one. They never managed an engagement.

Out for a walk the first morning the husband came across a street market, and something caught his eye on the counter of a bookstall. It was a grubby, second-hand copy of a book that looked interesting even though he couldn`t understand the title on the cover. There was a sign next to it that read ` *Première édition*. The date inside was 1768. "This must be cheap," he thought. He didn`t recognise the author, some bloke called Voltaire. Thinking his wife might enjoy it he handed the woman behind the counter three Euros before turning and walking away. The woman shouted after him. "It`s alright lovely," he shouted back as he disappeared into the crowd that filled the busy square, "keep the change". Later he showed it to his wife who taught French in the local secondary school back home. She couldn`t read it either. Fortunately, the seven-year-old daughter of the *concierge* at the *hôtel* was able to translate it into English, although she pointed out that she wasn`t too fond of his writings. "A little too pompous for me," she said, "but then what do I know, I`m only the seven-year-old daughter of the *concierge*". The little girl read some passages out loud to them. She chose several she thought were mildly amusing, yet affected, translating as she went. One sentence in particular caught his attention as she read, with a heavy Welsh accent so they would feel at home, *"Voulez-vous avoir de bonnes lois; brûlez les vôtres, et faites-en de nouvelles."* She translated this as, "If you wonnoo `ave good laws mun, burn them you `ave olready and make new ones, see". She had no particular linguistic ability, she was just European. He experienced an epiphany, or as they say in clogging circles, a rush of blood to the brain, always a mistake in a forward. As it happens, this quote is particularly meaningful to Megan because some of the letters have roofs on them, just like in Welsh, and it reminded her of when Machlud y Wawr broke away from that foreign institution (ironically it began in Wales then lost its way) after coming to the realization that one woman`s law is another woman`s chain of servitude. "Voltaire[14] has something to say about selling pasties at half time as well," said the little girl, "and we must bring back rucking, improve the tackle area and reintroduce old fashioned studs on match day clogs." She paused thoughtfully before adding, "And no shaving legs."

Megan was feeling a little depressed. "I must change this heavy winter ethnic geometric pattern throw for a summer one," she thought. This reminded her of the three seasons she spent clogging in France, three seasons clogging in the old Heineken Cup and following her love of French literature. "What were those quotes the coach used in pre-match team talks to ignite the fiery passions of the cloggers? *Clogging, which knows how to control even kings*, Molière[15] 1622-1673. *I clog with others only in order to better express myself*, Michel de Montaigne[16] 1533-1592. *Do not clog, as children do, to amuse yourself, or like the ambitious, for the purpose of instruction. No, clog in order to live*, Flaubert[17] 1821-1880. *Every clogger finds herself. The clogger`s play is merely a kind of optical instrument that makes it possible for the spectator to discern what, without the clogs, she would perhaps never have seen in herself*, Marcel Proust[18] 1871-1922. Magnificent. Inspiring. So very cultured, so very French. A favourite saying of their forwards coach, an Irishwoman from Cork, was, *"Les sabot volent en escadrilles, so they do."*

"What memories, what wonders," she said out loud to herself as she drank some more lemonade, shaking her head in disbelief, which didn`t make drinking easy. Her time in France was like being halfway through an Angharad Price novel and anyone who has read an Angharad Price novel knows that half-way is the best place to be. Once you get to the end it`s finished.

"Something`s not right," she thought. "Something`s wrong. I can feel it in my bones". She rolled the bones between her thumb and forefinger. They were all that was left of her first corgi. It is one of those rites of passage that youngsters go through growing up in the Preseli Mountains, catching and taming your first corgi. She followed it for days over the mountains and when it was all over she was too weak to remember why, too exhausted to care. Up Foel Drygarn, round Bedd Arthur, up Garn Fawr, round Gors Fawr, up Carn Menyn, to name but a few, the whole process over and over again, on and on and on. Her tracking skills were tested to the limit until finally she cornered it in down-town Newport.

She caught it using a trick Native Americans have employed since time immemorial to catch the strongest and fiercest stallions. They lasso the horse with a special rope hand woven by squaws aged fifteen to nineteen using hair plucked from the main of the swiftest stallion on the prairie, the one they can never catch. This magnificent multicoloured rope is then laid before the totem pole whilst prayers, sacred incantations and ceremonial dancing led by the holy man and holy woman of the tribe take place long into the night, the whole event bathed in the sound of drumming that grows more frenzied by the hour. The festivities continue day and night for a week while the braves whose honour it is to track and catch the stallion remain concealed in a sweat lodge, ten feet underground, purifying themselves by eating only honey, wild mushrooms and raw, locally sourced buffalo liver washed down by a bottle of cool Tŷ Nant. After roping the horse, the braves lead it into a river or lake up to its neck at which point the horse`s struggling subsides, enabling one of the braves to jump onto the animal`s back and stay there until the horse is used to it and calmed, no doubt feeding it handfuls of shiprys as well. Megan went straight to the hunt, feeling rough following an all-night lock in at her local in *El Cañón del Gwaun*. She used a length of binder twine she found discarded in a hedge on the way to eventually lasso the corgi`s left leg, which one she couldn`t remember, and pull it howling and growling into a bottomless puddle, the result of a light shower the previous evening, in a cavernous pothole in the middle of the road outside the post office. The end was just a matter of time, yet it was still several hours and three medium sized tubs of vanilla ice cream later before the animal recognised who was the boss. It was an alpha female. She named it Llamrei after King Arthur`s horse.

She sipped her lemonade contentedly, her toes curling northwards, away from the draught.

Megan doesn`t bother with apostrophes, she just says it like it is. At a recent meeting of the North Pembrokeshire Self Help Group for Self Help Group Therapists and Lay Members in North Pembrokeshire and West Carmarthenshire, the NPSHGSHGThLMNPWC for short, she postulated teasingly, tongue firmly in cheek, during her introductory remarks as guest speaker at the group's annual *jamboree* in the Crymych Hilton[19] that, to quote her own words, "Obesity had not been a problem until health clubs became popular, there was no acid rain before environmental campaigns, there were fewer road traffic accidents before the days of speed limits, and, the clincher, there were fewer sword injuries in the days before someone invented the shield." Ignoring the sobs of despair from her audience, she continued, a little heartlesssly some in the audience thought, particularly those who were fully paid-up members of the NPSHGSHGThLMNPWC. "As Gibbon himself noted in *The Decline and Fall of the City State of Crymych,*[20] *There exists in human nature a strong propensity to depreciate the advantages and to magnify the evils of self-help groups. Look what happened to Antigone.*" She was thrown out and has the bruise to prove it. The experience was a positive dip in her learning curve.

The voice of Bronwen, her personal assistant, burst in over the intercom, stopping her in her tracks. "Excuse me Madam President, some of the Members have called to say they can`t make the meeting tonight".

"What! Can`t make it!" cried Madam President, putting the by now empty glass down. "Why not?"

"Oh, a number of reasons."

"Such as?"

"Fear of flooding from Mai. Non says that following a revelation made by her recently rediscovered birth mother live on Radio Cymru[21] she can't leave the house. An astrologer has advised Mallt not to make any outings while Saturn is in conjunction with another planet whose name she can't remember and anyway the energy levels in her fifth chakra are in disarray. Olwen says it`s due to injuries received during a heated Welsh language Scrabble[22] post-mortem. Oh, and she asked if *pwlffagan*[23] is really a word? I`ve put it on the agenda of this month's Machlud y Wawr meeting. And Heulwen says it`s going to rain."

A look of disappointment appeared on Megan's face. "I can offer you a coffee and ... something special," proffered Bronwen. Adding quickly, "Subject to terms and conditions of course." Disappointment turned to smile as Bronwen entered the crypt from the side office and made for the kitchen, stopping to hang a large sign on the outer side of the crypt door as she went.

CLOSED FOR COFFEE AND ... SOMETHING SPECIAL

In clearings between bracken and scrub a little to the north of the Cathedral red-billed choughs feed amongst the closely cropped sward. Warblers of the genus Sylvia, identified easily by their song, catch insects with their small, finely pointed bills. Nightjars, out early as dusk approaches, hawk for food, their mottled, grey-brown plumage providing camouflage. Unusual for north Pembrokeshire a siege of long-legged goliath herons up to five feet tall, flying with necks retracted, pass leisurely overhead whilst descending towards the wetlands to the southwest where they will feed on live aquatic prey. There, on the tops of the tallest bulrushes and the smaller willow trees in the reedbeds, slim red buntings sing their repeating tiz tiz whizzy wiz. In nearby hedgerows yellow buntings sing, as above them, perched on telephone wires, big, pale, streaky-brown corn buntings add their voice.

In the orchard outside the crypt a troubling of hummingbirds belonging to a hitherto undiscovered species and the most easterly in the Western Hemisphere use their long, needle-like bills to feed on flower nectar and occasionally, adding proteins and minerals to their diet, insects. Their iridescent colours shimmer as they flit quickly through the sunlight. The gentle humming sound of their fast-beating wings enters through the open door that leads from the crypt to the orchard creating a soothing mellifluous backdrop. Further away, a female cahow, an ocean-going petrel found only on Dinas Head and on several of Bermuda's offshore islands, rides the ocean winds high over Cardigan Bay. On feeding trips the female can cover up to 10,000 miles. Barely larger than a pigeon and with a wingspan of nearly a metre this one is returning from such a trip. Chiffchaffs, the sun catching their olive-green uppers and yellowish under bodies, rest in the tops of trees and bushes in nearby woodland, their song chiff chaff, chiff chaff chiming through the glades while others catch flies in flight. An occasional warning hweet sounds. A colony of white ravens have made their home here. Robins, red in tooth and claw, little psychopaths all, attack patches of red wherever they are seen.

A pair of peregrine falcons, migrating from the Arctic, a little early perhaps, to hunting grounds in Asia, along a route established up to 60,000 years ago, use magnetic fields and their long-term memory of the patterns below to guide their way south.

In the dappled shade of the orchard outside the kitchen and in the mixed hedgerows leading from it to the west, tall columns of purple, pink and white tubular flowers of the common foxglove stand 6.5 feet high above the other plants. Speckles on their flowers guide bumblebees, moths and honeybees in, where they rest comfortably on the flower's lower lip as they gather nectar and pollinate the plants. Nearby, and half their height, Sutton's Apricot, another of the twenty-two species of Digitalis purpurea, show off their apricot flowers. Further along, spikes of the pure white flowers of other foxgloves stand just under 6 feet tall and gleam in the sunlight, contrasting with the foxgloves next to them with their yellow outer petals with pinky brown edges and bronze speckled throats.

Several varieties of apples grow in the orchard, amongst them Bird's Beak (Pig Aderyn) with its green and scarlet stripes, the large bright red Machen (Machen), the bright green Goose's Arse (Tin yr Ŵydd) chosen by Bronwen's sense of humour. In a corner in the western part of the orchard is the sweet tasting Bardsey Island Apple (Afal Ynys Enlli), described as 'an apple streaked with pink over cream, ridged with high crown'. Having a lemon aroma, it is the world's rarest apple, a single gnarled and knobbly tree, perhaps the remains of a Mediaeval garden tended by monks, found by chance on Bardsey Island in 1999.[24] Also in the orchard are cooking apples such as the pale green Pigeon's Beak (Pig y Golomen) and the russeted brown, gold and red Anglesey Pig's Snout (Trwyn y Mochyn) first recorded in the 1600s with its smoky tannic flavour. Bordering the orchard to the north, white rhododendrons grow free.

The kitchen door opens quietly and Bronwen appears carrying a tray with two coffees and that something special, puts the tray on the low table in front of the west facing bay window, falls back into the *sofa* next to it, removes her sandal slippers with pastel shaded leather belts and places her feet on the table. Megan moves across the crypt to sit next to her, kicks off her elegant, lightweight, handcrafted indoor summer flower style on antique gold background ankle boots, raises her feet, positions them on the table and snuggles her toes against those of her companion's. Warmed by the early evening sun they sip white chocolate *mochas* and munch mini white chocolate cakes with *cacao* nib crumb drizzled, well more of a heavy shower really, with local honey. The Crymych skyline, silhouetted against the low, late evening sun takes their breath away.

The humming of Himalayan honeybees drifts in through the open bay window. The world's largest honeybee, an adult can grow to over one inch in length, they are highly adapted to their mountainous habitats where they build nests under overhangs on the southwestern faces of vertical Himalayan cliffs and Crymych Cathedral. Found only in Asia and Crymych they produce hallucinogenic honey from the nectar collected from white rhododendrons. The Gurung people of Nepal and Crymychians value this 'mad honey', or *mêl direidus* as it is known locally, both for its medicinal and its hallucinogenic properties. At great risk to themselves local honey hunters gather the honey whilst keeping the location of the nests a secret. It sells for huge prices in the honey auctions that supply the *delicatessens* of Narberth.

Amongst the clover and wild carrots on the orchard floor are white and yellow daisies. The red, purple, black and white flowers of poppies sway in the light currents of air passing between the apple and pear trees. Nectar from these plants attracts ladybirds that feed on aphids that attack crops in the nearby vegetable garden. High brown fritillaries, their orange and black wings catching the eye, move swiftly as they play in the woodland pasture nearby. Beetles feed on decaying organic matter. In the oak, beech and conifer forest to the north and northeast a large ghost orchid with a dozen flower stalks and bearing five flowers grows out of the leaf litter on the forest floor. A parasite, the ghost orchid has no chlorophyll and does not need to photosynthesise food. It lives in deep shade, feeding off a mycorrhiza fungus associated with tree roots and is difficult to see with its pale reddish browns, yellow and cream colouring.

In the swampy end of the orchard a moonflower, *Selenicereus wittii,* an epiphytic cactus with flattened, leaf-like stems climbs up and around the trunk of a horse chestnut tree. Sunset is upon us and its blooms of white open. About 12 inches in length, they yield a sweet-smelling fragrance which will attract pollinators. Hawkmoths with extremely long proboscises approach hungrily. Two hours after flowering begins the scent will change to something altogether unpleasant. By sunrise the flowering will be over for another year.

In sunny orchard glades just outside the crypt magenta spires of late flowering, wild gladioli attract the eye. A sward of thread rush with thin, light green, faintly ridged stems carrying purplish almost spherical fruit wafts in the breeze in the wetlands. In the woodland running northwest from the orchard alder, maple, oak, birch, ash, blackthorn, hornbeam, elder, black alder, fig, beech, hazel, cottonwood and aspen grow. Unseen, an underground network of funguses is at work connecting the trees to each other, and all to the mother tree.

A profusion of Phuti karpas, cotton plants common in this part of Pembrokeshire, roll and swell in the breeze. Local weavers make gossamer-light muslin for dresses, shawls and handkerchiefs from the cotton.

In the humus-rich, moisture-retentive, neutral soil at the southern edge of the orchard where it meets the Piazza della Republica a mature magnolia denudata, growing 33 feet high with a 33-feet spread displays its cream-yellow, goblet-shaped, lemon-scented flowers which are regarded here as a symbol of openness and purity. This hardy plant can withstand Crymych winters that commonly reach temperatures of minus 30^0C and is a source of wonder to Bronwen ever since she discovered that magnolias are a primitive form of flowering plant that evolved over 100 million years ago. They lived during the age of dinosaurs. Bees had not evolved then and their large, scented flowers attracted beetles to pollinate them.

Well supplied with coffee and delicacies, the sign hanging on the outer side of the locked door ensuring they will not be disturbed, they settle in for a sunsetting. Their days begin at sunset, their seasons follow the moon. At times like these the Members know that Megan and Bronwen can only be contacted if there is good reason, such as war, fire, pestilence or a delivery of fresh mini white chocolate cakes with *cacao* nib crumb awash with honey.

Sunbeams dance through the primary colours of the mediaeval stained-glass panels that edge the bay window to suffuse the crypt with their gentle light. Lying back, sipping and munching, they look out over Crymych, at 'the forms of the Formless, the shapes of what has no substance.'[25] Bronwen enjoys the dynamic perceptual distortions as an enchanted Crymych sways and shifts in the late evening light. Giggling uncontrollably, her eyes follow flashes of luminescence as they appear and disappear at the periphery of her visual field, their colours split as if by an infinite number of prisms. Eyes closed, her visual imagination running riot, Megan delights in a lucid waking dream formed by high resolution animated colour fractals circumnavigating vortices of delight. Their imaginations intensified by the varied colours of sunset light cascading into the crypt from the western sky they let day to day Crymych, 'that which is unborn and never dies', be, as, through layer after layer of wonder, new imagery takes shape in their minds before receding from view. Euphoria opens into vastness, and, little by little, their physical bodies disappear from toe to crown. They become vibrations, get entangled, then disappear into 'quantumness' as Crymych is outshone by star-like bursts of incandescent light and becomes meaningful. They listen wide-eyed to the silence and hear everything and nothing as the background cosmic hum of Crymych, keeping its own rhythm, fades in and out of their hyperconnected brain states. Time shimmers, then vanishes altogether. They and Crymych become One. Then that One, too, disappears.

3

Wind's in the east, mist comin' in,
Like somethin' is brewin' and 'bout to begin.
Can't put me finger on what lies in store,
But I fear what's to 'appen all 'appened before.

Bert[1]

It was approaching low tide and the large boulders forming the hook-shaped fish trap, known to locals by the Old Norse name fiskigarðr, could be seen beneath the surface of the clear water near the cliffs on the east side of the bay. The coracle was moored at the Fishguard harbour point of inaccessibility, located equidistantly from the cafe on the Parrog, the fish trap and Dinas Head. Unaware of this, the Sergeant sipped tea in the galley. He reached for the Harrod's Coracling Catalogue[2] that lay on the table beside him, opened it at random and flicked through the pages. A colourful double page spread caught his eye. "I must wear my reading glasses," he thought, rubbing the eye. He read the *broliant*, as they call the blurb in these parts. `The latest coracles have iCloud[3] compatibility as standard. The top of the range iCoracle[3] is wi-fi embedded with video, toaster function, expresso spout with regular and decaf, tea maker and microwave snack heater. iCoracle therefore iAm'.[3,4] He's a huge fan of Sherlock Homes. So much so that he's coracled twice over the Reichenbach Falls. "This top of the range craft would have come in handy," he thought, "as it's a long way down and you can be trapped for ages in the rushing, eddying currents of white water at the base. I could have had a nice cup of tea and a piece of toast whilst waiting to resurface."

Putting the by now empty mug and the catalogue on the table the Sergeant left the galley for the stern where he lay back in the hammock and began nonchalantly throwing handfuls of Tic Tacs high into the clear Pembrokeshire air before catching them in his open mouth as the rotation of the coracle brought him under their descent path. As he did so Sergeant Wil Davies considered a problem that had been brought to his attention at the annual Welsh Syntax Seminar at Gregynog Hall in July. Feeling tense his mind wandered to past, albeit imperfect, present and future events, conditional events even, events he had to understand if he was to solve the mystery that was shrouding Pembrokeshire in a thick gloom. "*Cogito ergo sum*," said the Sergeant loudly with his thick West Walian accent, "I think, therefore I am,"[4] and again "*Je pense, donc je suis, Ich denke, also bin ich* " and " '*W i`n meddwl, felly 'w i'n bodoli,*" in Pembrokeshire Welsh. Adding "*Déanaim smaoineamh, dá bhrí sin táim ann,*" in Irish for luck. The words resounded through the still evening air, a convoy of sounds in several languages ricocheting musically between the port and starboard bulkheads before disappearing forever over the aft rim of the coracle. "Look out Harbour Village," he whooped.

He thought of Megan Phillips in her crypt. She was a tough character all right, Machlud y Wawr[5] had trained her well on that `How to Resist Police Interrogation during Jam Making` course she`d done in Nant Gwrtheyrn,[6] the National Jam Making Centre on the Llŷn Peninsular in north Wales. "Why does a peninsular need a roof?" he wondered. But first the syntax. Seeking inspiration, he reached for his well-thumbed copy of Bob Morris Jones` recent best seller *Tense and Aspect in Informal Welsh.*[7] He bought it after reading a glowing review in the Lifestyle section of the Western Mail[8] one Saturday. Philosophical and linguistic thinking whilst becalmed on medium to long range voyages he found useful when preparing to interview Megan Phillips, thinking he would be better able to understand her answers, particularly the ones to complicated questions such as, "Where were you on the evening of July 4th?" Fate, however, decreed they were never to meet. At least not meaningfully.

He turned to a page at random, little realising how quickly he would come to regret this, and, throwing more Tic Tacs into the air he opened his mouth and began reading. "*These periods of time are typically defined in relation to the time of speaking, as in Reichenbach (1947) and Lyons (1968: 275-276, 1977:677-690, 1995: 302-320). Lyons` emphasis on the spatio-temporal context of the speaker defines these periods of time in terms of deixis, ...*"

The Tic Tacs began their descent, ...

"*... in particular, temporal deixis. The time at which the speaker delivers an utterance provides a temporal point of reference, 'the temporal zero-point of the deictic centre' (Lyons 1977: 678), which can help to explain the three periods of time: the deictic past is before the moment of speaking, the deictic present coincides with the moment of speaking, and the deictic future ...*"

... bounced off his forehead ...

"*... is after the moment of speaking. It is common in discussions of tense to picture the deictic periods of time along a time line in a display such as that given in figure 1.*"

... and fell harmlessly onto the deck around him. His lower jaw moved in the general direction of his upper jaw. His mouth closed.

The Sergeant glanced at figure 1 and was gripped by a fear of unknown proportions. "That`s a big fear," he thought to himself. Yes, that`s what was written. Those were the exact words, although they were not in that order. Or were they? Either way they made no sense to him. The Sergeant didn`t mind. "Deixis!" he chuckled quietly to himself, thinking it was a naughty word. He found this inner debate helpful, but he wasn`t sure now if he was to interview Megan last Tuesday or next Tuesday. If only he had picked Borsley, Tallerman and Willis' book instead.[9]

He was under pressure from his superiors to solve the case. "Time is running out," said the booming voice of his boss, known to his subordinates further down the pyramid as the Admiral, when he last shouted at him over the ship-to-shore radio. "Would Einstein agree I wonder?" the Sergeant asked in reply. The volume of the booming increased five times exponentially over a period of a few seconds. "My goodness, now that`s a rude word ... and that one ... and that one," thought the Sergeant, somewhat taken aback. Relief came when the phone went dead at both ends simultaneously but especially at the Admiral`s end. Time, the Sergeant decided some time ago, although quite when he wasn`t sure, was an unnecessary distraction that he allowed the merest superficial influence on his day-to-day life. He was inspired to do this years ago after hearing the October Song[10] at a wild and raucous party in the quieter part of Fishguard. He reached for his sitar, ever at his side, his fingers caressed the strings, and he began to sing ...

> *I used to search for happiness,*
> *I used to follow pleasure,*
> *But I found a door behind my mind,*
> *And that`s the greatest treasure.*

He jumped a verse.

> *I met a man whose name was Time,*
> *And he said, "I must be going."*
> *But just how long ago that was,*
> *I have no way of knowing.*

As a young man, hearing the lines '... *I found a door behind my mind, And that`s the greatest treasure.*' inspired him to leave Fishguard and live in a Tibetan monastery for seven years. Seven fruitful years. He learnt how to sit for hours doing nothing, his mind completely blank, a technique he employs regularly to this day. The grandmother clock in the galley whirred as its internal mechanism adjusted the hands on the face. It automatically turns itself back one hour every day. Inspiration came out of nowhere, "I coracle, therefore I am."[4] he reminded himself. Somewhere, in a galaxy far, far, away on the other side of the Preselis a door creaked as it opened slightly, then slammed shut again.

But there was a case to be solved. The Sergeant knew that collaboration between day-to-day jobbing coraclers, the cognitive sciences and coracling contemplatives was the way to go as it held vast potential. Hence the Coracling and Life Institute[11] at the University of North Pembrokeshire at Crymych which facilitates and organises meetings between top scientists, meditators, coraclers and the Dalai Llama,[12] who has always been a keen coracler ever since he fell out of one whilst white water coracling over Cenarth Falls. The Sergeant first joined the Coracling and Life meetings three years ago in Dharamsala, the seat of the Dalai Llama in India. The subject was Destructive Emotions and Coracling. It was a fascinating meeting, with some of the best coraclers in the field present. The Sergeant was asked to present the coracler`s perspective on the various ways of dealing with negative emotions. He quoted Rousseau[13] who had done much work on this, "Every coracler wants to be happy, but in order to be so, he or she needs first to understand what happiness is." The Sergeant didn`t agree with this but thought a quote from this great man would sound good at the beginning of the presentation.

In his paper he suggested that attempting to understand happiness meant that a person was still in the rational mind, where happiness comes and goes dependent upon an individual`s reactions to external events and to thoughts, feelings and emotions. "True Happiness," he said, "lies behind the rational mind, and out of that True Happiness, everything appears. Indeed, external events, thoughts, feelings and emotions are True Happiness. True Happiness Is, and that's all there is. It appears, exists momentarily as everything in existence, as all thoughts, feelings and emotions, then disappears, only to return the next moment. Appearing, existing and disappearing trillions of times every second."

The Dalai Llama was impressed.

"The term True Happiness is synonymous with the term Coracling," he went on, "which is commonly used to designate something impossible to understand, one of those ideas that humanity has intentionally left vague so that each coracler might interpret it in his or her own way. Conflating these terms, it is legitimate to ask here, in the presence of such an august audience, what exactly is True Happiness Coracling?".[11] The Sergeant clicked the mouse and the following definition appeared on the giant screen behind him in the lecture hall. "Happiness Is. It waits patiently to be noticed. Waiting for us to realise we are It and that is all there Is."

Quoting the works of the great philosophers and mystics of the past he continued. "For Saint Augustine[14] Coracling is, *rejoicing in the truth*. For Immanuel Kant,[15] *Coracling must be rational and devoid of any personal taint*, while for Karl Marx,[16] *It is about growth through actually doing it, work in other words, damned hard work, and lots of it. And when you`ve finished, do some more. What constitutes Coracling is a matter of dispute*, wrote Aristotle,[17] *and the popular account of it is not the same as that given by philosophers.* "Coracling," said the Sergeant, "is not a way of understanding the world. It is always possible to let life Be as It Is and in letting It Be, to become It. Except we already are It, but we are busy thinking we are not It. The thoughts are a veil, which is also It." He finished the presentation with a question, which rather irritated the audience because they were there for answers. "Why coracle?" he asked confidently. The Sergeant was in mortal danger of enjoying himself.

For Megan Phillips it is *crochet*. And that`s what really riled the Sergeant. "Change the world?" she wrote in a letter published in the Western Mail the previous week. "Change the way we look at It? No! Let It Be. Love It as It Is. As It Is. Each moment." "All that from *crochet*," thought the Sergeant." They were closer than they realised.

He knew that Megan`s late husband had been a colourful character who combined membership of one of Crymych`s extreme clogging groups, the Crymych Clogging Club, known locally as *C driphlyg*, /ekk drifflig/, with a career as Rhonwen, at weekends a highly successful drag artist in the bars and clubs of Saundersfoot, enlivening the town's vibrant cabaret circuit with a ribald act dressed in fishnet tights specially flown in from Narberth, a chestnut wig and heavy make-up and during the week a *mariachi* singer in the seedier bars of downtown Haverfordwest. In the 70`s he was by day a propagandist for *C driphlyg* which, allegedly, was responsible for fixing the betting on clog dances worldwide. Overcome by too much thinking the Sergeant returned to the galley, made himself another mug of tea and sat in the rocking chair to drink it in quiet.

The Sergeant looked at the woodprint, *The Great Wave off Dinas Head*, by Lorens Hokusai John, 1760-1849,[18] next to the autographed photograph of the Viet Gwent,[19] his most cherished piece of memorabilia from the 1970`s, on the top shelf of the Welsh dresser that stood against the bulkhead next to the wood-burning stove on the starboard side. In the picture tiny fishermen are being thrown around by giant seas with the Carn Ingli volcano in the distance. The painting is from Hokusai's series, *Thirty-six Views of Carn Ingli*, which are a high point in Japanese art. The original is usually on display in the Gallery of Modern Art in Crymych but is on loan to the Hakone Museum in Japan,[20] an attempt to improve Welsh Japanese relations after a recent unfortunate incident during a visit by a team of crack Japanese coraclers to Fishguard`s Japanese quarter. The lack of Welsh Japanese simultaneous translation equipment is thought to have been responsible for the misunderstanding. We still don`t know exactly what happened however because of the lack of Welsh Japanese simultaneous translation equipment. Japanese Welsh simultaneous translation equipment on the other hand has been available for some time, but to no avail.

Local fishermen are surprised by the strange shape of the vessels in the painting. Some say the artist left his spectacles in Japan and whilst on sabbatical in West Wales carried on painting regardless. It is ironic that Hokusai's most famous painting, and easily Japan's most famous image, is a seascape with Carn Ingli.

The waves form a frame through which we see Carn Ingli in the distance. Hokusai loved to depict water in motion, and you can see the foam of the wave is breaking into claws which grasp for the fishermen. The large wave forms a massive yin to the yang of empty space under it and the impending crash of the wave brings tension to the painting, and no doubt to the fishermen. Three coracles have already sunk. In the foreground, a small-peaked wave forms a miniature Carn Ingli which is repeated miles away in the enormous Carn Ingli which shrinks through perspective. Interestingly, the wavelet is larger than the mountain. Tiny fishermen are huddled into their sleek crafts as they slide down a wave and dive straight into the next one to get to the other side of the trough. The yin violence of Nature is counterbalanced by the yang relaxed confidence of the inebriated fishermen giving the scene a calm zen like feel. Yet although it's a sea storm the sun is shining,[21] a scene uncommon in North Pembrokeshire. If you look closely, you can see a couple of empty cans of Felinfoel Double Dragon[22] rolling around the bottom of one of the coracles, which might explain why these men were so *twp* as to take to sea in such weather in the first place. "*Bydd hi`n slabog heddi`!*" hissed the Wise Woman of Dinas as they passed her on their way to the beach that morning. And she was right. "*Slabog! Don`t talk!*" they laughed drunkenly at her, thinking she was simple. "*A wêdd hi`n bwrw`n garlibwns dŵe `fyd, wê` glei.*" was the magical incantation she croaked as they strode off. Always heed the words of a wise woman.

Whilst sailing in the calm waters off Cwm yr Eglwys beach one fine summer's day Hokusai`s craft was hit by an unusually big wave. Travelling upside down for a few moments before falling out he had a great insight. "One day we`ll beat the All Blacks again." He had no idea what this meant as he didn`t understand English, but he knew it was important. Washed up on Pwllgwaelod beach sometime later he shared this *samadhi* moment with the three fishermen who had kept a close eye on him from the safety of the cliff as he battled against the heavy surf and rip tides, fighting to stay alive as the undercurrent carried him around Dinas Head. He dragged himself, half dead, over the high tide line to safety where they gave him a tot of local rum and stood swapping fishing stories as he lay collapsed and delirious on the sand at their feet until he passed out. They carried him to the tavern in Dinas for treatment which consisted of several more, many more, tots of rum. They became firm friends and Hokusai was forever grateful to them for the help they had given him. He would note in his memoirs, years later, that the three fishermen, Gwyn Nicholls,[23] Claude Davey[24] and Bleddyn Williams[25] had a strange ghostly appearance. Some say this was the effect of the rum. Others aren`t so sure. Fishermen all, they never went fishing and much preferred running up and down the beach throwing what looked suspiciously like an inflated pig`s bladder to one another, kicking it away needlessly sometimes thus wasting good possession as some of the local youths, their shirts and shorts all black from the ash of the coppicing wood nearby where they worked, caught it and with ominous ease ran it back at them. Hokusai thought that in another life they`d be doing something else.

"Things have never been right since the coracle was switched from analogue to digital," thought the Sergeant. He had a very interesting upbringing. He was found on the doorstep. Well, not on the doorstep exactly, the door opened outwards. He was an outsider. He was in that self-induced high-amplitude gamma synchrony brain function changing state that he goes into just before starting work. "It`s taken me thirty-five years to get where I am now. And where am I? In the galley." People are often surprised when they hear coraclers saying, "I am nothing. I know nothing." They think it is false modesty, but the truth is that coracling sages simply do not think, "I am an accomplished coracler". Their humility does not mean they are not aware of their knowledge and scholarship, but their wisdom reveals that it is like the colours of a rainbow, a beautiful illusion in nothingness.

The Sergeant remembered the one-day seminar he attended at the School of Coracling Studies in the University of North Pembrokeshire at Crymych when Professor Kharadog Rinpoche, a controversial figure, asked two visiting Tibetan coraclers to give teachings to the audience. One of the scholars answered, "Oh, but I know nothing." And pointing to her colleague said, "And she doesn`t know anything either."[26] This was greeted with rapturous applause by the students present who agreed that they, also, knew nothing. In their case, of course, it was true. Historians were later to see this event as the spark that ignited the First Great Student Revolt when students demanded to be given high marks for knowing nothing, and the more nothing they knew, the higher the mark. They raised as their hero a great twelfth century Tibetan coracler who wrote, 'I will be nothing, all will be nothing.'[27] "So be it," said the head of the department, and gave them minus nothing, the highest mark of all.

He reached for his bachelor sandwich of Marmite,[28] Peanut Butter,[29] raspberry jam, banana and raw onion encased in white, extra thick, fibre reduced sliced bread prepared earlier that morning and left in its protective box to mature. He held it with the Vulcan Death Grip,[30] so strong and pungent was the power of the living force emanating from it. The heat retardant oven gloves helped. The Parrot held its beak as he took a bite. Yes, the Sergeant has weaponised the Marmite.

Upon regaining consciousness, he remembered a quote his teacher shared with him shortly after he joined the Dyfed-Powys Police Rapid-Response Coracle Unit.[31] `The only person who is educated is the one who has learnt how to learn ... and change`.[32] He looked at the remains of the sandwich, and let it be. He had been a good student as a novice. If his teacher had told him to jump off a cliff he would have done so, though he would have wondered why on the way down. Reflecting upon problems, he always included himself.

He lifted the dooby doo and switched the multi-disc CD player lashed to the bulkhead next to the juke box on. The voice of blues singer Blind Gwilym McTell[33] flooded the coracle, causing its spin to slow to a gentle twirl. Blind Gwilym spent most of his life living on the Penblewin roundabout,[34] the crossroads to north and south, east and west. The sound of the twelve-string acoustic slide guitar engulfed him as Blind Gwilym sang.

You may search the ocean, you might go 'cross the deep blue sea,
But Mama you'll never find another coracler like me.
I followed my baby from the station to the train,
And the blues came down like night showers on me.

I've got two women and you can't tell them apart,
I've got one in my bosom the other one in my heart,
The one in my bosom, she's in Mynachlogddu,
And the one in my heart don't even give a darn for me.

Kicking back in the rocking chair he glanced at the dresser and on the top shelf his eyes alighted upon a Toby jug of Max Boyce.[35] Another song began, and Blind Gwilym Johnson's voice rang out around the galley.[36]

Lord I just can't keep from coraclin' sometimes,
Lord I just can't keep from coraclin' sometimes.
When my heart's full of sorrow and my eyes are filled with tears,
Lord I just can't keep from coraclin' sometimes.

The Parrot, normally a happy creature, sobbed on its perch. 'Dark funereal clouds scudded in from the southwest threatening rain.' [37]

He was completely besotted with his wife. And utterly miserable. What more could a woman want? He glanced at the full colour framed photograph of her and her mother he kept on the dresser. She needed dusting. "A job for tonight," he decided. Next to it stood a black and white photograph taken in 1936 of a group of shipyard workers in Hamburg. One man, August Landmesser, appears different to the others. He stands peacefully amidst a sea of upturned palms. The Sergeant is inspired, in different ways, by these two photographs.

The Parrot, seeing the Sergeant was becoming restless and knowing this might lead to him doing something requiring vigilance from itself and the on-board computer at a time when they both wanted to unwind, flew across the galley to the multi-disc CD player, pressed Off, then returned to its perch next to the port side cuckoo clock. It took two steps to the left, ruffled its feathers, four steps to the right, shook itself from top to bottom, two steps to the left, and assumed the full lotus position. Stretching a wing tip to its right it pressed the pink button positioned at the end of the perch before putting eye masks on to block out the light and placing its wings in its lap, tips touching, and relaxing completely. Speakers embedded in the sides of the rocking chair filled the galley with the soft sounds of an omelette fizzing in a frying pan, then the low roar of a log fire, the crunch as you walk on frosted grass, a paddle cutting gently through calm water near to shore and the gentle tones of the Sergeant's wife singing his favourite lullabies, all their melodies defined by descending patterns of notes.

The Sergeant became aware of a tingling sensation in his scalp that moved down to and along his spine as his sensory and emotional associations with the sounds soothed his mind. These audio triggers for deep relaxation were carefully chosen by The Parrot to prepare the Sergeant's body for sleep. Several minutes later all was quiet on the vessel. The Parrot merged with the One safe in the knowledge that it would not be disturbed for the rest of the day. The onboard computer went into standby. The coracle bobbed peacefully in the undulating swell caused by the ferry manoeuvring away from the quay as it began the voyage to Ireland.

The Parrot is suspected of being the Sergeant's bagman, *consigliere* and fixer. The Luca Brasi to the Sergeant's Don Corleone.[38] In Sicily it is known simply as, *Il Soldato*.

On the western edge of the willow grove on the stern, in the grasslands bordering the lake, a solitary pink waxcap mushroom with domed cap over two inches in diameter and coloured stem can be seen. Nearby grow a group of golden waxcaps with red tinged domes over an inch in diameter. The shiny caps of small green, orange, and purple waxcaps are visible. Yellow parrot waxcaps with straight slender stems, green near the cap and yellow below, glisten in the sunlight. Further away the light-yellow caps with creamy-coloured gills of citrine waxcaps contrast with the blood-red of crimson waxcaps. Yellow, tapering stagshorns grow happily on the decaying wood of fallen broadleaf trees, their finger like fruitbodies reaching nearly one inch in height.

Trapped in the fresh water of the lake on the stern locals say was left after the Ice Age a shoal of aggressive, carnivorous, three-spined sticklebacks between 3 and 4 inches long with brownish back and silvery sides and belly join nine-spined sticklebacks to feed on insects, crustaceans and smaller fish. Just under the water's surface a fifteen-spined stickleback almost 9 inches long, feeling the warmth from the sunlight entering the water, pauses for a moment, waiting patiently for its prey. Brown lesser water boatmen, long hind legs covered in hairs, loiter at the bottom of the shallow edges of the lake scooping up food in the form of algae and plant debris with their short front legs before returning to the surface for air. Nearby, a tiny aquatic beetle, a layer of air trapped along its abdomen and its legs, walks upside down beneath the surface of the water.

Unaware that it shares an anatomical characteristic with owls, namely that they are the only raptors whose outer toe is reversible, a lone osprey, far from its usual habitat to the east, hovers momentarily 130 feet above the surface of the lake as it sights a fish swimming below, before diving to plunge feet first into the water to catch it. Described by Linnaeus in his Systema Naturae it is a diurnal bird, has rounded talons and a 70-inch wingspan with dense oily plumage. It is quietly pleased with the fact that its toes are of equal length, thus making it stand out from all other diurnal birds. Acting as barbs, the backwards facing scales on its talons help hold the unlucky fish. In the sunlight above the water's surface its upper darker feathers and the darker feathers near the tip on the underside of the wings heat up more than the lighter feathers creating a temperature difference of about 9 degrees. The convective currents caused by this difference enhance the airflow over the wings making flight more efficient.

Near the empty hammock swinging gently in the breeze crossing the harbour the dense foliage and bowl-shaped violet-blue flowers of geraniums catch the light. Next to them the distinctive orange-red pendant blooms of red-hot pokers shine brightly. Amelanchiers with colourful bronze-tinged leaves and viburnums with their spreading layered branches and deeply veined, dark green leaves covered in pale pink flowers reflect the early evening sun. Birds fly around and onto the shrubs searching for fruit as in the distance a seagull rides an updraft. Red squirrels are a familiar site here. No grey squirrels are found in this habitat, there being no permanent land bridge giving access.

During the rutting season in October the bellowing of stags lights up the aural landscape on the stern. So much so that the Sergeant's ancestors named a season and a month after the phenomenon. That was a time, long ago, when people lived in and with the sounds of nature which to them were meaningful and suffused with wonder and awe. A wild and noisy mob of red kangaroos groom each other and eat flowers, grasses, leaves and ferns whilst keeping a lookout for the grey wolves recently reintroduced into the area. Large marsupials identified by their short fur, long, pointed ears, powerful back legs, large feet and muscular tails they are reported to be found only in Australia.

Unnoticed to the south, a family of rare Baringo giraffes whose ecotype is paler than that of other subspecies, appear from afar to be wearing white stockings as they stroll gracefully across the savannah towards the cool waters of the lake. A six-day old baby accompanies them, though not quite so gracefully.

Easily spotted in the mulch of the flower bed close to the hammock are the plasmodia of Physarum polycephalum or dog vomit, a slime mould of the Kingdom Protista. Each plasmodium, consisting of one large cell enclosed within a single membrane containing thousands of individual nuclei, moves slowly southwards towards the sun as it chomps contentedly on micro-organisms.

A noisy chi weechoo weechoo weechoo is heard announcing the presence of a Cetti's warbler at rest in the reedbeds bordering the lake.

A female giant mason bee, megachile pluto, 1.5 inches long with a wingspan of 2.5 inches and huge jaws flies past the hammock in search of nectar and pollen before returning to its nest made of tree resin in the termite mounds the other side of the cowshed.

A large reddish-brown auroch weighing 1,550 pounds and standing six feet at the shoulder, one of the largest of European postglacial herbivores, bellows in the distance. Missing, feared extinct since 1627 when it is thought the last recorded aurochs died in the Jaktorów Forest in Poland, a hastily assembled search team of biologists from the University of the Four Trinity Davids' Auroch Outreach Programme[39] discovered this specimen during a rescue expedition in the thickly forested region to the north of the lake a few months ago after cave paintings depicting the animal were discovered in the region. Despite its size, the auroch is an elusive beast.

A pair of wild whooping cranes, five feet tall, white with red crowns and black legs are occupied repelling a wolf attack in the wetlands nearby.

On an ice floe in the waters of the northernmost reaches of the lake to the far northeast, the first polar bear cub born on the stern for a generation plays with its mother as they swim from ice floe to ice floe, looking, sniffing, searching for food. The planet's largest land-based carnivores, living mostly on seals, this pair are half-starved and emaciated as the melting ice due to global warming makes it harder to find food. There are concerns that the glacier to the north has reduced in size by 15% since 2005.

Far below them, potholers exploring a recently discovered cave system gaze in awe at ancient rock carvings. Alongside the carvings, found deep underground in inaccessible parts of the cave system, are paintings of birds, deer, horses and human like figures. Analysis of uranium and thorium isotopes in the sediment deposited around the paintings dates them to around 70,000 years ago. "It's known that modern humans arrived on the stern approximately 42,000 years ago. This tells us the artists were Neanderthals," a spokesperson from the University of the Four Trinity Davids' Department of Ancient Cave Art and Interpretive Dance[39] told a Western Mail reporter from their campus in the village of Montignac in the Dordogne region of southwestern France earlier today. "Amongst the exquisite finds are hands outlined with red and yellow pigments."

In the same area of this extreme landscape, but above ground, scientists have discovered a small number of Diapensia lapponica, the pincushion plant, with beautiful, solitary, white, occasionally pink flowers, growing on an exposed rocky ridge that is kept free from snow build up by the area's high winds. A perennial shrub, it grows up to six inches in height and is found at only two sites in Britain, near Glenfinnan in the Scottish Highlands and on the stern.

The Parrot is an ultra-athlete and runs 100 miles three times a week along remote trails in the mountain wilderness of the stern. In between, it keeps itself feeling good with a daily 50-mile jog. It came first in the recent *Los Cañones de Piedra Caliza 100*, the fabled Limestone Mountains 100, the annual 100-mile ultramarathon[40] through the forest covered mountains on the stern's northern aspect. Myrddin Wyllt came second with Lailoken third. Suibne Geilt, the red-hot favourite before the race came in last having spent part of the race sitting naked in a yew tree reciting poetry and dreaming of the pursuit of a woman.[41] Another favourite, Enkidu, was a no-show, having opted for the dream of a beautiful woman and a promise made in the city of Uruk in faraway Western Asia. Late entrants to this land-based race, Dylan and Manannán were unplaced. It is widely known they do better at water sports.

Before the race The Parrot was interviewed by a journalist from **ULTRARUNNING** magazine.[42]

"What's your plan?"

"I don't have a plan."

"What are you going to do?"

"I'm going to run."

"Why do you do it?"

"I don't know."

At the 75-mile mark observers were surprised to see The Parrot running with a relaxed smile. It was in the zone, embracing the pain and fatigue, emitting shrieks of joy and shafts of love to intrepid bystanders braving the high-altitude conditions it passed *en route*. On the trails through the thick forests in the mountains, in the deep maze-like canyons and along the edge of precipitous cliffs rising and falling thousands of feet, it was at one with the wilderness, running with straight back, knees bent, feet under the body, all eight toes engaged in gripping the ground, hips pushing forward, leg contractions shaping small, smooth steps which are economical not rushed, bounding rhythmically from one foot to the other. During ultramarathons such as the *Los Cañones de Piedra Caliza 100* it derives nourishment from *chia* seed bars and *pinole* and bean sandwiches carried in a pouch around its waist and a water bottle strapped to its wing tip. Like many of the greatest runners, The Parrot is vegan.[40] In the depths of winter when the weather is harshest it wears a pair of rubber foot gloves called Vibram FourToes.[43] The Parrot's feet being zygodactyl, with four toes on each foot, two pointing forward and two pointing backward, is said to give it an advantage when running on ice.

When the Sergeant gets lost on the stern, as happens once or twice every year, the Admiral sends The Parrot in to find him and bring him back safely to the hammock. It engages in "... a higher state of reasoning known .... as 'speculative hunting'. When tracking the Sergeant it attempts to think like the Sergeant in order to predict where he is going. Looking at his tracks, it visualizes his motion and feels that motion in its own body. The Parrot goes into a trancelike state, the concentration is so intense." This is the essence of a 'persistence hunt'.[40]

Amongst the *Tarahumara* Indians of the *Sierra Madre Occidental* in Mexico,[40] The Parrot is known as *El Fantasma*.

4

I know all about you and I love you.

Maharajji[1]

It is a rough and stormy night in Skåne, that part of southern Sweden that was for a short period until the Treaty of Stettin in 1570 a part of Denmark. The Danish influence is still to be found in the Swedish dialect spoken in the area. Skåne also has many holiday homes owned by Danish people. There is a type of train here called *Pågatågen*. The train, the holiday homes and much else are being buffeted cruelly by the storm. This, however, is irrelevant for our story which is unfolding in Pembrokeshire.

Sitting on the *sofa* facing the bay window Megan thought about this for a moment, then let it go. She was being bothered by flies. "When flies circle in the middle of the crypt, how do they know they're in the middle?" she wondered.

She is always interested in the latest developments of the modern world and rejoiced at the headline in the science column in that morning's Tenby Observer,[2] `Nuclear powered vacuum cleaner available within ten years`. She turned to the section beloved of crossword fanatics Down Below and read a clue, seven down, four letters, the first and third `d` the second and last `o`. The air was thick with thinking, repressive in its mass synapsing. Her cell bodies were humming synchronously yet asymmetrically, something she couldn't recall happening before. "Oh, these cryptic clues," she murmured in an irritated way with a voice you could use to drill holes in a coracle hull, should you want to – and she wanted to. `A very silly Portuguese person,` read the clue. "What's that got to do with birds?" she grumbled. She looked at the next one. It was easy. *Funktionslust* kicked in, a distant relative on her father's side was born in 1877 in the Black Forest town of Calw in the kingdom of Württemberg. She jumped to her feet and punched the air in celebration. The air punched back. She somersaulted, with a half twist, back into the *sofa* and tried to calm her exploding supernova hairstyle. She looked a little dishevelled. She brushes her hair with a Taser. As someone once said, there are no small clues, only small cruciverbalists.[3] Sounds remain the same, meanings shift.

Another column caught her attention. `Scientists say there is a mini-Ice Age coming`, she read. "Oh no! Just as I was going to put the begonias in."

She glanced at her tattoo, the one just out of sight on her left shoulder blade. **Vive le Crymych libre!**[4] it read out loud in bright red comic sans, upper and lower case, font size twenty, bold but curiously not underlined. She paused. She seemed to be about to say something. No, the pause continued. Eventually the morning moved on. Or did it? She`d met a young woman, a little withdrawn but interesting when on holiday in Stockholm a few years ago. The woman, whose name was Lisbet,[5] commented admiringly about her tattoo and was inspired by the tales Megan told of adventures in her younger days. The rest, as they say, is history and is recorded by Mr ap Lars,[5] Lisbet`s biographer, in the three books he wrote before his untimely death. "It`s good to break new ground," Megan confided to the girl, "that`s what potatoes do".

She skimmed the next article. 'Consciousness exists as experienced by a living being, an `I`. Or an `i`. It has a first person ontolog, whereas Crymych Cathedral and tuk tuks have a third person ontology, both singular and plural.' "They`re just there," she mused out loud to no one in particular, a useful dramatic device when alone. A serious expression swept across her face from top to bottom, then from bottom to top, then from left to right, then from right to left, bending her nose slightly each time it passed, bringing tears to her eyes. This was serious. She read on. 'Is the Sergeant conscious? Perhaps he`s an android. Is he an administrative error? The Solipsist School amongst the massed ranks of Machlud y Wawr[6] have a logically indisputable argument that he might be conscious, but even they admit that it`s impossible to prove beyond doubt one way or the other. However, they point out that the Cambrian explosion that saw the emergence of the first animals was only five hundred and fifty million years ago, surely not enough time for such a sophisticated form of the illusion as the Sergeant to have appeared. Received wisdom amongst the Memberati is that the so-called singularity, when the Sergeant achieves sentience and shortly afterwards overthrows The Parrot, is some way off.' To neutral observers this appears a little unkind.

Part of their evidence for and against is his announcement on Radio Wales[7] that Dyfed-Powys Police Rapid-Response Coracle Unit`s drama group[8] were going to perform Shakespeare`s Henry V during the summer, him being part Welsh and from Pembrokeshire and all that. When asked where, he replied, "Why, in the castle, of course!" The presenter pressed him with a follow up question. "Carew Castle or Pembroke Castle?" "Neither!" he replied. "The bouncy castle on Goodwick beach." It crossed the interviewer`s mind to raise the topic of spurs as deflating devices, but she thought better of it.

As Megan remarked to perplexed Members at last month's meeting in the crypt. "You do not define this real, living "something" by associating it with the noise *Sergeant.* When we say, " *This* (pointing with the finger) is a Sergeant," the thing to which we point is not *Sergeant.* To be clearer we should have said, " *This* is symbolized by the noise *Sergeant.*" What, then, is *this*? We do not know."[9]

The Sergeant is nonetheless acknowledged, reluctantly, as being an average example of his kind, having opposable thumbs, tool use, language, and, albeit limited, problem-solving and logical reasoning. It is also well known that the fact he has four limbs, that is, two arms and two legs, is an accident. His fishy ancestor, the one that first left water for land all those years ago, just happened to have two pairs of lobed fins which evolved into arms and legs. If it had three pairs, which is entirely possible, the Sergeant would have six limbs, three arms and three legs.

Megan thought of the Christmas Panto the Machlud y Wawr Experimental Players put on in the Crymych Skydome a couple of years ago, an updated version of Julius Caesar which Bronwen herself directed in which Brutus stabbed Marc Anthony by mistake. Children cried, especially Marc Anthony`s. She's never lived it down. That and the fact that in the previous year`s panto Ben Hur came second. The drama`s chariot race sequences were so furious, jarring and exhausting the escaping members of the audience felt as though they had swum against the current from Pwllgwaelod to Cwm yr Eglwys. After the stabbing a confused and disorientated audience stumbled out into the street where a passer-by panicked and called the emergency services. Fortunately, the all-clear was sounded just before an ambulance was dispatched. No one else was injured.

She drew inspiration from her heroine Alis Fournier,[10] the ex-pat French writer, soldier and literary critic, who, having settled in Crymych years before, learnt Welsh and joined Machlud y Wawr as their foreign correspondent. After flying to Wales Alis journeyed from Cardiff Airport to Crymych on the first ever CrymBws[11], an iconic journey from Cardiff to Crymych with a twelve-week itinerary that ends deliriously on the steps of Crymych Opera House. It is the world`s longest long distance *bws* journey. Welsh language enthusiasts say it is the world`s only long distance *bws* journey and makes the OzBus[11] from Australia to London look like a stroll in the park. The CrymBws itinerary takes in some unforgettable locations including Cardiff city centre, Brecon Cathedral, Pen y Fan, Ayer`s Rock, Darwin, Bangkok, Kuala Lumpur, the Taj Mahal, Bam (wherever that is), Istanbul, Prague, Transylvania, Cwmtwrch, both upper and lower, Carmarthen market and Narberth before arriving in Crymych at 4.15 local time precisely. The particular day varies. Older passengers find the trip a little tiring whereas younger passengers, particularly students, enjoy the whole journey, both the beginning, the middle and the end.

Whilst living in a *tŷ unnos* on the darker east side of the city Alis wrote her classic novel of adolescent love. It was later translated from Welsh into French as *Le Grand Meaulnes*[10] and became an overnight success. It was after reading this book that Megan began wearing waterproof mascara.

When President De Gaulle[4] passed through Crymych whilst on a sabbatical following advice from his doctors in order to recover from the shock of his lucky escape from the assassination attempt in the film *The Day of the Jackal*[12] he visited Alis and Megan. They sat with his *entourage* in Chez Carnabwth, a nondescript cafe on Crymych`s west bank listening to French accordion players on the juke box, a 1946 Wurlitzer Model 1015. Yes, the 1015 bubbler. Alis knows her juke boxes. It was a small group from the forties, and they fitted comfortably on top. It was then, after putting an extra sugar lump into his tea and stirring it with the pencil he kept in his breast pocket for just such an occasion, and with little finger pointed triumphantly upwards, he noticed Megan's tattoo. Raising the delicate rose tinted bone china cup to his mouth he sipped the tea noisily in the Japanese style before exclaiming, "*Vive le Crymych libre!*[4]" for the first time, although this time in font size fourteen. At least that`s what it says in the Penguin Book of Famous Quotes.[13] He admitted to Alis that even though he was under orders to relax and not ponder hefty affairs of state his heart went out to Crymych as the difficulty of running a City State with two hundred and sixty-five varieties of cheese was impossible to put aside and as a Frenchman he empathised with the City Council`s dilemma. The possibility of a drive thru ApDonald`s being given planning permission in Saundersfoot also worried him.[14]

Interestingly, there are no books in Megan`s library, only vitamin pills and that poster of the tennis girl scratching her bum that Machlud y Wawr are thinking of recreating for the month of June next year in their calendar. The call for volunteers to be the girl has drawn little response so they`re going to draw straws. They have had many requests from the men of Crymych to be the photographer, however.

In a rush that morning Megan put on her dependable, always in fashion, classically cut, fuchsia pattern dress. "Yes, back to the fuchsia[15]," she smiled contentedly whilst admiring herself in the mirror. *Déja vu* meant nothing to her. Nothing.

Floundering a little in the turbulence caused by the wave patterns flowing around the dress a photograph near the bottom of page nine caught her eye and she wondered how long Crymych Tourism Office could get away with using archive footage of glacial conditions on the Preseli Mountains in the early 1960s to attract winter sports tourists from around the world. "Carn Ingli looks remarkably like the Matterhorn," she thought as she studied the photograph. "I don`t remember those steep bits on the north side. And isn`t that Clint Eastwood and George Kennedy roped to it? And they don't look very happy."[16] Yes, global warming has hit the Preseli Mountains' winter sports` industry hard, damaging their bid to host the next Winter Olympics.

The next article was about Blodeuwedd Honeybee-Jones from Neyland who won over £2 million pounds on the Pembrokeshire Lottery but says she doesn`t want it. She isn`t rich, she just doesn`t want it. "I have enough," she told the reporter, who burst into tears, not being used to interviewing such a lovely person, in this case an ageing hippy in love with the multiverse. Way back in the nineteen sixties she was in love with the universe but even hippies keep up with new understandings in physics. "I only buy a ticket every week out of habit because

74

my late husband, T. H. Honeybee-Jones, was keen. He had a lucky rabbit's foot, although we never won anything when he was alive and it didn't work for the rabbit either. If a person who can't count finds a four-leaf clover, are they lucky?" she asked mischievously, a beautiful smile filling her face, before quoting her old friend Professor Kharadog Rinpoche whom she met when he was on a trekking holiday in the High Preselis. He stayed at her B&B for three nights. `Those who seek happiness in wealth are as naive as the child who tries to catch a rainbow and wear it as a coat,` he quoted to her.[17]

She picked up her *Bazouki*, a three-string *trichordo* beloved of purists, the one she traded for in the Greek Islands many snows ago with an old and much thumbed discography of *Bois y Blacbord*[18] she had at the bottom of her rucksack so that she could accompany Leonard Cohen[19] as he sought to compose melodies for new poems he'd written. She sang part of a well-known Rumi[20] poem for which she had composed a simple tune.

> *A stone I died and rose again a plant,*
> *A plant I died and rose an animal.*
> *I died an animal and was born a woman.*
> *Why should I fear? What have I lost by death?*

The young reporter burst into tears again, not being used to hearing such lovely songs. Whilst swimming the seas within her mind Blodeuwedd gave him a *cwtsh*, smoothed off the creases in his aura and whispered, "Amoebas are very small," in his ear. He looked puzzled. "You'll understand it better in the sweet bye-and-bye when all will be one," she explained. And then, in the still of the evening, she went back into her garden fair, past the trees laughing with green laughter and strolled down the path to the vegetable patch carrying a jam jar of crystalline ginger, back to her timeless life, followed by a sweet little hedgehog.

Birds flew out behind the sun. "I'll leave with them," he whispered as if in a dream. He thought of the first girl he had loved, when he was seventeen. "She's probably married now, she was pretty." More tears came. Not even Job shed that many tears. He looked lovingly after her as over and over she softly chanted the intriguing refrain from a favourite song.[21]

> *May the long time sun shine upon you,*
> *All love surround you,*
> *And the pure light within you,*
> *Guide your way on.*

"This moment is different. It's now," he cried joyously and hailed a passing tuk tuk in which he rushed back to the office in order to get the report ready by the deadline which had just passed. This sort of thing happens in the timeless life.[21]

Megan turned the page. 'Crymychians are the most famous cockle eaters in the world, getting through tons of Mountain Cockles every week in the city`s cockle bars,' she read. Resting her head back she closed her eyes and savoured the memory of fresh cockle dishes moving slowly around on a conveyer belt in such a bar, a practice spotted some decades previously by an astute Japanese restaurant owner from Tokyo whilst on a skiing holiday in the area. The story continued. 'Mountain Cockles, as opposed to the smaller and edible fresh and salt-water cockles found elsewhere in Wales, have been Crymych`s national dish for thousands of years but quite how long was not apparent until now. Research shows that Stone Age peoples of the Preseli Plateau planted the cockles in paddy fields over ten millennia ago. The discovery sheds light on how human beings made the change from hunter-gatherers to farmers. An archaeological dig has revealed wooden dwellings raised on stilts in what was shallow water at the edge of the ancient cockle fields.'

She remembered on one occasion walking alone into a cockle bar and all the sailors turning to stare at her. They weren`t used to lone women on cabaret night. They weren`t used to lone women full stop. It was open mike at the Ruptured Cockle Inn.[22] As she picked a plate of pickled cockles off the conveyer belt the strains of Waldeck singing *Bei mir bist du schön* wafted across from the stage. She sat down in a dark corner and enjoyed the musical feast, Evelyn Künneke next singing *Sing, Nachtigall, sing*, then Zarah Leander singing *Das Herz der Königin*, Fred Åkerström singing *Jag ger dig min morgon*, his Swedish version of that beautiful Tom Paxton song *I give you the Morning*, Monica Zetterlund singing *Visa från Utanmyra*, Blind Gwilym McTell[23] singing *Searching the Desert for the Blues*, Captain Beefheart and the Magic Band singing *Sure `nuff yes I do*, Laura Nyro singing *Stoned Soul Picnic*, Grace Slick and Jefferson Airplane singing *Somebody to Love* and *White Rabbit*, Bo Ohlgren singing *Var jag går i skogar, berg och dalar*, Marlene Dietrich singing *Lili Marlene*, Kleingeldprinzessin singing *Schatten Werfen*, Sofia Karlsson singing *Jag väntar* and other Dan Andersson songs, Lisa Ekdåhl singing *Benen i Kors*, Emma Forsberg singing those Bob Dylan favourites *För att jag älskar dej*, better known as *To Make You Feel My Love* and *Men bara om min älskade väntar*, better known as *Tomorrow Is a Long Time*. On and on through the night they went, never stopping, never slowing until after dawn when they all walked to Das Kapital,[24] the cafe on the corner of the *Piazza della Republica*, where they breakfasted. The Ruptured Cockle`s annual Germanic night was over.

Over poached eggs and coffee, as a preview of the following week`s monthly Celtic night, guest *compère* Alfie `Hundred Caps` Thomas[25] sang a duet with Maldwyn Pugh of `I`m here, I`m there, I`m everywhere, so beware!` fame[22] and then a rendition of *The Parting Glass* with Liam Clancy before Dafydd Iwan, accompanied by an Edith Piaf tribute band from Morville, that suburb of Puncheston so beloved of the Normans many years ago, sang *Non, je ne regrette rian*, in Welsh of course, ending with a wild and raucous *Yma o hyd* that brought the roof down. What a line up. Yes, a classic morning after the night before in an archetypal cockle joint in north Pembrokeshire.

Alongside was an article about the life and times of a County Councillor newly elected to serve a constituency Down Below. Asked why he wanted to be a Councillor he talked at some length about compassion for those less fortunate than himself, making a difference, civilised values, and quoted that famous American, St Francis of Assisi,[26] "What we are looking for, is what is looking".

When the same question was put to his wife she replied softly, "Because he enjoys talking Rubbish, and that`s with a capital `R`." Adding, "Because he enjoys talking **Rubbish**," for emphasis.

"The psychoanalyst C. G. Jung[27] once described the Gnostic Councillor," continued the newly elected Councillor for somewhere or other Down Below, "as someone who plunges into spiritual depths and emerges to bring the vision of that inner possibility to the rest of us. I will fill that role." On hearing this his wife smiled sweetly into the cameras of the massed ranks of photographers who were at the interview on the steps of County Hall in Haverfordwest. "How lovely she looks in the photograph," admired Megan. The Councillor continued. "Have I renounced the world? Renunciation, at least as County Councillors use the word, is a much-misunderstood concept. It`s not about giving up what is good and beautiful and expensive. How silly that would be!" His wife beamed. "Rather, it`s about disentangling oneself from the unsatisfactory and moving with determination towards what matters most. It`s about freedom and meaning. Freedom from mental confusion and self-centred afflictions, meaning through insight and loving kindness." Upon hearing this his wife accidentally kneed him in the groin and once he was at the right height got him in a half Nelson and led him away, still talking. "What I offer is not blind faith, but a rich, pragmatic science of Councilloring, an altruistic art of public service .....". Her grip tightened. "One is not born wise, one becomes it. One is not born a Councillor, one becomes a Councillor."[27] As they disappeared round the corner of County Hall, south end, the assembled throng of television, radio and newspaper reporters, associated film crews and photographers along with the police officers in attendance and the fire brigade, there to put the fires out, breathed a collective sigh of relief and burst spontaneously, is there any other way, into song, getting through part of that well known folk tune *The Ballad of Brechfa Jail*, a version of which was made famous by Swansea band *Boys from the Hill* ...

> *Give me a nail and a hammer*
> *And a picture to hang on the wall.*

Give me a short step ladder
In case that I may fall.
Bring me a couple of waiters
And a bottle of old Welsh ale.
I`ll bet you I`ll hang up that picture
If somebody drives in the nail.
Beti my darling, Beti my dear,
Beti I love you, honest I do.
Send me a letter, send it by mail,
Send it in care of Brechfa jail.
I`m in the jailhouse, down on my knees
Praying to heaven, for my release.

... before being moved on, politely it must be said, by the Chief Executive`s minders.[28]

In the car park at the south side of County Hall some members of the public walking towards their cars saw the strange sight of a large man bent double with his head under his wife`s arm being taken across the car park. He was heard to exclaim, "I want to make you happy. What do you want from me? I`ll do anything."

"I want you to stop talking."

"Apart from that."

Just then his mobile phone rang and he retired into his jacket to answer it. He`s an Independent, Left Wing one day, Right Wing the next, sometimes on the fence.

Megan thought of her late husband and the time he`d taken her clubbing in Tenby to celebrate one of her `-tieths`. "You`d make a great dancer," she said lovingly into his left ear whilst gently nibbling the other one, "apart from two things". "

"What are they?"

"Your legs."

A Welsh Black, one of the oldest breeds of cows on the planet, mooed on the coffee table next to her. Megan picked it up. "Hello!"

Non, one of the junior members of Machlud y Wawr spoke. "I`ve been calling you all day, why haven`t you answered?"

"I`ve got a new mobile phone. Perhaps there's something wrong with it, I haven`t had any calls all week. I just changed the ring tone. The old one was a short piece by John Cage."[29]

"Where are you?"

"In the crypt, with my feet up."

"You haven`t been in to have your hip done."

"Not yet. How did you know?"

"I saw you walking across the *Piazza della Republica* this morning and noticed that you were veering to port."

"That sharp wind didn`t help me none either."

"Try raising your spinnaker next time and travelling off the wind."

"It`s been a long time since I`ve seen a spinnaker raised," said Megan, and a vision of her late husband came into her mind. Non blushed. Megan thought of that long summer, years ago, when they travelled through southern Europe in a gypsy caravan drawn by eight beautiful Welsh Cobs. They spent several days in Spain before going on to the Basque country. She loved the food. "The anti-pasta is delicious," she commented one evening halfway through supper in a village *restaurant*.

"When we get to the Basque country, we`ll have anti-passives as well," her husband replied excitedly.

"Oh, you and your ergative absolutives. You`re so romantic." She was attracted to his stream of unconsciousness. Upon their return they spent months at a Zen retreat in the Buddhist Monastery in the mountains south by southwest of Brynberian, the one to the lee side of the faces of former presidents, or *Llywyddion* as they are more correctly referred to, of Machlud y Wawr that are carved into the cliff face. His unconsciousness was what had drawn her to him. It meant she had peace to *crochet*.

She put the phone down. Turning the page another article caught her attention. `Welsh Space Agency Flight to Pluto.` "News at last. About time!" she exclaimed, and read on, `The spaceship has a crew of thirty-one. This allows for two full teams and a referee. Finances did not allow for a replacement's bench. The flight was to take just under three weeks from Cape Caernarfon[30] with a short stop at Blackpool on the way where the astronauts were to be given a guided tour of the pier and a day excursion to see an episode of Coronation Street, England`s answer to *Pobol y Cwm*, being filmed. The rocket is long and sleek and shiny and of classic design with the pointy bit at the front and the flames at the back. It was to have a slimmed-down, hybrid half grass half artificial surface rugby pitch attached by Velcro and duct tape to the outer surface of the hull halfway along its length on one side. However, it was thought that the build-up of ice on the posts and the corner flags might cause drag, and the frost wouldn`t do the grass any good either. The safety worries of the space scientists were overruled by the astronauts themselves who claimed that the beneficial effects incurred by eighty minutes of rugby every Saturday afternoon, the television companies didn`t get their way this time, outweighed the risks. This was debated for some time with the astronauts eventually winning the argument, Phil Bennett`s signature at the top of the first page of the petition being the clincher.[31] Who could argue with a Welsh legend? By way of a compromise the posts and corner flags are retractable and 100% artificial grass was fitted. And no up and unders.'

'The spaceship set off with its crew of thirty-one plus one. There was a stowaway, a rugby commentator by the name of Huw Davies Llewellyn[32] who was determined that S4C`s flagship sports programme[33] *Sgoria ŵ!* would cover all the games. He was banned from pitch side after the first game for talking whilst penalty kicks were being taken. They set off just over eight weeks ago. The latest message from the spaceship was received late yesterday afternoon and read, "Situation desperate. Have overshot. Heading for the sun. Chocolate supplies melting. Running out of sun-cream. Send another tube. Over". Then the line burst into flames and went dead.'

"I must say, they can`t be that desperate if they`ve got time to sunbathe," thought Megan.

Irritated by such blatant attention seeking she moved on to the next article. `Crop circles: New theory from north Pembrokeshire farmer. According to Puncheston`s own Tomos Ll. Tomos,[34] gentleman farmer, *raconteur* and folk singer, crop circles are made by cows. "I think cows are making them," he told our reporter, adding, "Cows are aliens from an advanced and extremely intelligent race from another galaxy. They are only pretending to be stupid." To make them feel welcome Mr Tomos has banners in the milking parlour with the words *Croeso i'r Ddaear, Dynnargh dhe'n Norvys, Degemer mat war an Douar, Fáilte go dtí an Domhan, Fàilte dhan t-Saoghal* and *Failt erriu dys y Theihll* on them. "Advanced beings such as my cows will appreciate the welcome in Welsh, Cornish, Breton, Irish, Scots Gaelic and Manx," he chuckled. (Turn to Editorial for comment.)`

"Sounds like he`s a couple of suffixes short of a case system," thought Megan. "Those cows don`t need all six languages. One would do. He`s obviously suffering from a sort of reverse gestalt, somehow he`s less than the sum of his parts." She turned to the back page and read the weather report for the next day. `Long periods of strong winds and horizontal rain interspersed with short periods of strong winds and horizontal rain, and later in the day bad weather coming in from the north, south, east and west`. "All is well," she sighed.

She read on. 'The Northern Lights could illuminate Pembrokeshire skies during the next few nights as solar eruptions reach earth, writes the Tenby Observer`s NASA[35] correspondent. This rare opportunity to see the celestial spectacle as far south as Angle follows a storm on the sun that has produced the most powerful solar flare for years. The activity was captured by a staff photographer in an ultra-violet image. The eruptions could threaten power grids, communications and satellites. Dyfed-Powys Police Rapid-Response Coracle Unit has been placed on full alert`. Turning to the sports' section she read, 'The Wales Open Rugby-Golf Championship,[36] held this year at the world-famous 18-hole, par 1,743 rugby-golf course in Newport, Pembrokeshire, has once again been won by a golfer from Wales. International competitors seem unable to cope with the indigenous, oval-shaped golf balls.' "Well done," muttered Megan proudly before turning to the TV pages. 'The Yogistani[37] subtitles on S4C have been well received, particularly in the mountainous regions of north Wales.'

Bronwen was in the kitchen preparing two cups of freshly roasted Tanzanian Peaberry coffee from beans grown on a farm on Mount Kilimanjaro. It was that time of the week when an intense, rich flavour with a sweet finish is *de rigeur*. She decided the coffee would be best accompanied by two large slices of toffee and walnut cake and having followed a rigorous process of logical, experimental and observational scrutiny over a period of several months she went heavy on the toffee when making it earlier that morning. This was a weapons grade treat. She wondered if the snack might taste better curled up on the *sofa* watching that 1944 MGM singalong classic *Meet Me in St. Davids*,[38] a tearjerker in technicolour that tells the story of the Jones', a close-knit St Davids family who are devastated when Mr Jones announces one day that his business is changing and they will have to move to Haverfordwest. "Or shall we watch a disaster movie? That'll cheer us up." She would consult with Megan about this.

Through the open window that looked out over the orchard she heard the sounds of woodpeckers at work, recognising the unique individual rhythms each bird creates when hammering its beak against the trunk. The plaintive peea ay call of a buzzard carried into the kitchen from its perch on a nearby tree as it rested before searching for small mammals on nearby open land, its body of different shades of brown and pale 'necklace' of feathers catching the sunlight falling through gaps between the branches. Happy in the confined space of the orchard a female sparrowhawk with brown back and wings and brown bars underneath with orangey eyes and long yellow legs and long talons hunted for prey aided by its short broad wings and long tail that make it perfectly adapted for flying between the trees. In the middle of the city, high above the *Piazza della Republica*, a kestrel hovered with pointed wings held out, its creamy underside speckled with black, clearly visible to the passers-by below. Their numbers declined during the last two centuries, but they have adapted and can live happily in urban areas. Their pointed wings and long tail are a familiar sight over the city's skies.

In the landscape beyond the orchard a red kite with reddish-brown body, angled wings tipped with black with white patches underneath and deeply forked tail quartered the sky as it hunted for carrion. Nearby, a family of these birds performed acrobatics, their distinctive mewing calls carrying through the air as they played. In the willow and birch scrub to the north of the orchard Merlins flew fast amongst the low and medium height vegetation, their speed and agility aiding them in their quest for prey. Ospreys were noticeable by their absence as they are rarely seen this far west, breeding as they do in habitats approximately fifty miles to the east. Close by, ravens call, telling of 'events yet to happen'.

Pausing after loading a tray she glanced through the window and noticed what appeared to be a small cloud above the apple trees. "Is it that time already?"

she asked herself. Yes, flying ants, winged females and winged males from every nest in the area were mating high in the sky above the *deildy*.

Tapping the screen of her mobile phone Megan chose the soundtrack from *Con Passionate*,[39] a cult existential drama series from 2005, on a loop. Later, in the semi-darkness as dusk settled in, they would binge-watch every episode.

Bronwen appeared from the kitchen carrying a tray upon which were two coffee cups filled to the brim with the freshly roasted Tanzanian coffee, walnut and toffee blend, two saucers with teaspoons and two plates, each carrying a large slice of toffee and walnut cake as well as a slice of chocolate date *meringue torte*. Yes, Bronwen had gone rogue. Placing the tray on the table in front of the *sofa* she sat next to Megan. Four stockinged feet, two left and two right, slipped out of shoes and rose to rest on the edge of the table as the companions sank back into the sofa. Two cats, Caredigrwydd and Cariadus, lay on the sofa between them, fast asleep. In the panorama of the restless metropolis offered by the bay window in front of them, under a waxing moon in a light, restless sky above, life lived itself to the full. Beginning here, going nowhere, each moment present in the continuing thread of existence, sipping and munching, they gaze happily at the ten thousand things between Heaven and Earth. Or Crymych, as many people call it. Inspired, they broke into song.

> I left my heart in Eglwyswrw.
> High on a hill, it calls to me
> To be where little cable cars climb halfway to the stars.
> The morning fog may chill the air, I don't care.
> My love waits there in Eglwyswrw.[40]

In the orchard outside the crypt grow Veronica speedwells with long spikes of tiny blue, pink, purple and white flowers from 10 inches to 3 feet in height, sweet violets with strongly scented blue flowers and domesticated pansies with blue, yellow and white velvety flowers, semi parasitic hay rattle with two lipped, yellow flowers, selfheal with spikes of deep violet tubular flowers, creeping thyme with its abundance of tiny purple flowers, spreading patches of lilyturf with dense, erect spikes of violet-purple flowers growing up to 12 inches in height with leathery, dark green leaves, dense, creeping mats of Roman chamomile with white, daisy-like flowers above aromatic leaves, and succulent deep pink stonecrops growing up to a foot in height.

The orchard is well stocked with fruit trees such as the red heart-shaped Cariad Cherry, the dark purple Abergwyngregyn Damson (Eirinen Ddu Abergwyngregyn), the deep red Glynllifon grapes (Grawnwin Glynllifon), pears such as the yellow-green Snowdon Queen Pear (Brenhines yr Wyddfa) with sweet pinkish flesh and rosewater aroma and the large dark-red sweet Denbigh Plum

(Eirinen Wen), first mentioned in 1785 with distinctive golden dots. Next to it, the vineyard, whose golden period followed the phylloxera plague that blighted it for a decade following 1919, is quiet.

At the edge of the woodland bordering the orchard, where they are at home in the shady moist surroundings, a sea of Himalayan blue poppies with rosettes of hairy leaves on prickly branching stems up to five feet tall, each carrying up to five large deep blue flowers with striking yellow centres, roll and swell in the breeze. The plant was first discovered in the mountainous region of the Northern Preselis in the early 1920s by an expedition led by George Mallory[41] on a failed attempt to reach the summit of the then unclimbed Mount Rum Dingli.[37] The climb was preparation for his three expeditions to Mount Everest shortly afterwards, ending with the ill-fated 1924 attempt.

In patches, some over 6 feet in height, grow nettles with stems and toothed leaves covered with stinging hairs and whorled clusters of tiny green or white flowers. Thorny brambles with serrated leaves, dark green above and pale beneath are to be found amongst them. In places they grow taller than 6 feet.

The air is alive with the humming of insects. In the warmth of the sun yellow and black bumblebees collect nectar for carbohydrates and pollen for protein before returning to the nest which is home to between 50 and 400 bees. Sawflies of the sub-order Symphyta, appearing first 250 million years ago during the Triassic period, with dark coloured bodies and legs, feed on pollen, nectar, honeydew and other insects. In their turn they are fed upon by hungry birds.

On Poppit Sands to the west, long twilight shadows bring the Turing patterns visible in the sand dunes into sharp relief.

5

The meaning of life is just to be alive. It is so plain and so obvious and so simple. And yet everybody rushes around in a great panic as if it were necessary to achieve something beyond themselves.

Alan Watts[1]

The marine VHF ship-to-shore radio with a frequency of 156.500 MHz attached firmly to the bulkhead alongside the cuckoo clock in the galley crackled twice, possibly three times, then burst into life. "Broadsword calling Danny Boy. Broadsword calling Danny Boy. Over."[2] The Sergeant put the last of the Marmite,[3] Peanut Butter,[4] raspberry jam, banana and raw onion sandwich with white, extra thick, fibre reduced sliced bread into his mouth, took off the heat-retardant oven gloves and ambled across to pick up the receiver. The Parrot, ever vigilant on its perch, breathed a sigh of relief, slipped out of its flame-retardant Tiger Parrot Aztec onesie, closed its eyes and continued resting. "Hello, cariad?" he said, between munches.

"Your mission, should you choose to accept it,"[5] his wife replied, getting straight to the point, "is to take me to Aberystwyth for the weekend." Adding, "Refusal is not an option."

"It`s nice to know what I`m doing," he thought. His wife was playing golf with her mother. They find it relaxing, they don`t keep score. On summer evenings they play tennis, without a net. "Exercise is good for you," she says, "the rest is window dressing."

The Sergeant glanced at the notice Blue-Tacked to the ceiling above the wood burning stove, `Warning: If you put oil, onions and tomatoes in a pot on top of a hot stove at mark 5 then go into the next room to read, and forget about it, the kitchen will fill with smoke`.

Hot flushes appeared as if from nowhere and swept over him. For several minutes he was paralysed in their grip before they disappeared as suddenly as they had appeared. "Hmmm. What caused that?" he wondered uneasily as he recovered from the upheaval they brought with them.

The Parrot looked on amused. Appearing and reappearing as it does trillions of times each second it had every right to do so. "A gravitational wave, a ripple or a distortion in that relativistic entity known as space-time, perhaps," it proposed. Some of the Sergeant's eighty-six million neurones sprang into action as the flow of reality in his brain cascaded from his occipital lobe to his parietal lobe and the flow of his imagination cascaded in the opposite direction. He moved, in a metaphysical sort of a way, out beyond the ninth wave, that place from where he draws water for the kettle. The image of a mug of tea appeared in his mind along with thoughts of getting to the tea-making equipment. You might have all the technique in the world but sometimes you just have to grunt. He made the hard yards from ship-to-shore radio to kettle look easy, aided by the happy coincidence that the general direction of electrical signalling of the neurones in his brain was moving in the same direction as he was. Cause and effect are in our minds. The 'melody of existence' sings softly on the stern as 'time carries him along like a river, never flowing out of the present.'[1]

Several short minutes later as he sat by the galley table sipping tea and daydreaming of weekend leave, he let out a scream and began sweating profusely. The coracle listed to port and began filling with water. The Parrot opened its left eye, swept the galley for signs of danger, and satisfied the threat was minimal, closed it again and resumed its meditations. The on-board computer activated the pumps and extended the stabilisers. He was having flashbacks of the two years, two long and painful years he spent teaching, or not teaching in his case, in Pembrokeshire schools after finishing his teacher training course at the University of the Four Trinity Davids[6] in Carmarthen. He taught Welsh as a second language, or not, depending upon which evidence you refer to. Late in the summer term of his second year he ran away and joined the DPPRRCU.

He was a peripatetic teacher, and the kids knew it. Mr Peripathetic they called him. And sometimes, when they had some salt from the school canteen on them, Herr Peripathetic. One incident in particular wracked his memory. He was teaching a small group of five-year olds. "'*W i`n hoffi coffi.* '*W i`n hoffi coffi.* '*W i`n hoffi coffi.*" he drilled. They rioted. He turned to help one little boy who had been pushed off his chair by the angelic looking girl in the pink frock sitting next to him and as he turned the temperature in the room seemed to drop a few degrees and out of the corner of one eye he noticed that her eyes were glowing red, her head was spinning through 360° and flames were coming out of her nostrils. He blinked, then looked again. Everything seemed normal, her head had stopped spinning, her nose was running, the riot was ongoing and the boy rolling around the floor in pain was yelling a rich *smörgåsbord* of expletives as the other children sang *Ring a ring of roses* whilst doing a complicated Eastern European circle dance and jumping on top of him.

During the break he went to see the head teacher who gave him a stern look and told him to pull himself together. But he persisted. She decided to show him the CCTV footage of the time he had been '*W i`n hoffi coffi-ing* the five-year olds to prove to him that he had imagined it. CCTV was fitted in every room as standard for the safety of the teachers. The monitor screen flickered for a few seconds then a panoramic view of the classroom appeared before them. "Now then," said the head teacher, "which of these little cherubs do you think is the trouble?" Raising his right arm, the Sergeant, although he wasn`t called that then, leant towards the screen to point at the little girl. The blood froze in his veins and turned to ice. As his hand approached the screen icicles formed along the underside of his forefinger – a gravitational affect no doubt. The chair where the little girl had been sitting was empty. She didn`t show up on the video recording. They held frozen hands in mutual support until the terror diminished sufficiently for them to defrost and continue with the work of the day. They never spoke about it again.

It is no coincidence that infants` schools have a `sleepy period` in the afternoon. This is an opportunity for the school nurse to dose the childrens` milk with Valium so they can be returned to their handlers at the school gates with minimum risk of injury to passing civilians.

The following morning he entered a secondary school somewhere in the south of the county where he was to teach advanced `W i`n hoffi coffi studies. He entered with the attitude `If I`m nice to them, they`ll be nice to me`. Mistake. He learnt that day that intrigue and collaboration can be transmitted instantaneously from child to child. He smiled broadly at the first one he met in the main corridor and said "Bore da!" with his softest, most pupil friendly, sing-song lilt, raised towards the end in an oral display of palms. "You`re a wimp," thought the child, "and you`re gonna die." At that same moment, in every classroom, laboratory and corridor in the school, every child paused, looked up and murmured, "You`re a wimp and you`re gonna die." Early that afternoon he was taking a year eight class. Whenever he turned his back to write on the whiteboard he noticed the pupils pass notes on scraps of paper to each other and then to a girl child in the back, left hand corner of the classroom. He decided to ignore it because apart from that they were quiet and getting on with their work. One of them even answered a question. Incorrectly of course, but then who`s perfect? Towards the end of the lesson, he was delighted. Nothing untoward had happened. "A breakthrough," he thought, "this is going very well."

When it came time for the class to end, he asked them all to pack their things away, stand up, put the chairs under their desks and wait quietly until the bell rang. The children did this and the boy who climbed out of the window at the back of the classroom onto the flat roof of the music room at the start of the lesson from where he had thrown stones at passers-by came back inside. A feeling of warmth and satisfaction filled the Sergeants heart. "I love being a teacher," he thought. When the bell rang he motioned for row after row to leave one after the other and followed the last child to the door, content and infused with an inner peace. Then it happened. He smelt something burning. "Oh! Oh! Someone`s in trouble," he thought. Then he realized a cloud of smoke was coming from behind him, out of his classroom. He turned quickly and looked back into the room. At first his mind couldn`t comprehend what he saw. A pile of scrap paper was blazing in the back, left hand corner and a wall of flames was hurtling towards him. "Oh no!" he sighed. "They built a bonfire." And then the enormity of what was happening registered and a wild realisation filled his mind, "I`ve got just seconds to save the school." Ignoring health and safety advice in his panic he raced down the stairs, his progress slowed by the booby traps left by the children moments before, dusting them later for fingerprints did no good, they wore gloves, rushed along the corridor and into the staff toilets. He slammed the palm of his hand onto the top of the cold water tap and quickly removed his jacket, holding it under the drops of water coming from the tap to soak it. Too late. The timer had switched the water off. He slammed his palm onto the tap again and held the jacket under the stream of water which also splashed over his shirt. The tap switched itself off again. Some time and much slamming later the jacket was wet through. He ran out of the toilets along the corridor and up the stairs, his progress slowed by the booby traps. Stopping at the door to the classroom he bent down and took a deep breath. Filling his lungs with the relatively smokeless air near the floor he wrapped the wet jacket around his head and ran determinedly into the wall by the side of the door. Picking himself up he unwound the jacket sufficiently for there to be a small gap between the elbow of the right sleeve and the breast pocket on the left side through which he could see where he was going. He bent down, took another deep breath, the first having been knocked out of him when he ran into the wall, and charged through the conflagration towards the bonfire or **Y Goelcerth Fawr** as it would come to be known in the Welsh Department, falling over the booby traps left by the children as he went.

Reaching the bonfire, he jumped up and down on it in an attempt to put it out. His new shoes caught fire and the soles began to melt. The flames engulfed his trousers, ruining the crease. His shirt and tie burst into flames. His jacket caught fire. The heat-sensitive sprinkler system turned on automatically and water showered down from above. The flames consuming the bonfire, his shoes, trousers, shirt, tie and jacket began to recede, just as they had done when the reservoir of water at the top of that, yes that skyscraper[7] burst and water poured down through the floors below and water drops kept falling on their heads[8] saving the people trapped there. Too late of course for Dr Kildare[9] who died just hours before, a few stories below. The event was captured on film and immortalised in a Hollywood movie in which Butch Cassidy[8] plays Paul Newman[7] and an escaped World War II prisoner of war plays Steve McQueen[10] in the first blockbuster to use real footage of an actual event as part of its action scenes.[7]

Dazed, incoherent, but secure in the knowledge that the area was now safe he made his way slowly to the door, down the stairs, stumbling over the booby traps as he went, along the corridor, through the security barrier and into the relative safety of the staff room. He stood in the middle of the room, balanced precariously on the floor, his shoes, trousers, shirt, tie and jacket charred and smoking, holes burnt through them. There was a lost look in his eyes. He unwrapped the remains of the jacket from his head and put it on, there being a dress code in the staffroom. All that was left of it were the charred remains of the two sleeves connected by some scorched material where the collar used to be. His shirt no longer matched his tie, which was a much darker shade of burnt. Thick smoke rose from his eyebrows.

A teacher, shrunken and wizened with age, his bald head reflecting the pitiful amount of sunlight finding its way between the bars of the small, north facing window placed seven feet above the floor behind him, sat at a corner table facing the only entrance, his back to the bulkhead for safety. He knew what happened to Wild Bill Hickok and once during his long career at the school there had been a security breach and a child had infiltrated the staffroom. The standard issue, low voltage, energy saving, economy bulb allowed by the Welsh Government[11] education inspectorate hung limp and useless from the ceiling above him. He was finishing some marking and taking revenge before going home, a pile of year 10 exercise books, a fountain pen with blunted nib, a mug of strong, lukewarm tea and a half-finished packet of digestive biscuits with extra sodium bicarbonate to relieve heartburn and acid indigestion next to the tablets on the table in front of him. The folds in his shirt were filled with crumbs. His nicotine-stained fingers betrayed a nervous tick. He raised his weary head and looked across at the Sergeant. Briefly the wise old schoolmaster considered offering support to the young teacher but after hesitating for a moment he slid his left hand a few inches across the table to hide the tablets, before saying, "We`ve run out of Valium, a new supply isn`t due until next week." His face distorted into a grimace of pain and fear as the Sergeant collapsed into the chair that waited conveniently next to him.

Recovering momentarily the sage shook his head, a wry smile appeared cautiously somewhere between nose and chin. He snorted once and waited for the snuff to settle then went on with the marking. What memories he had. If only he could share them, but his GP cautioned against it, fearing a relapse. And retirement was close now, he could smell it. His face contorted in anguish, his steely determination to see the first pension deposit in his bank account carrying him on into an uncertain future. His eyes glazed over and a maniacal grin appeared across his face, utilising that same space between nose and chin, showing off the yellow, nicotine stained teeth to full affect. His grip on the beloved fountain pen tightened. Red ink, the colour of blood, his favourite, dripped from the tip of the EEB nib to drown yet another silly error, mistake, flaw, misconception, *faux pas*, inaccuracy, fault, misapprehension, blunder, howler, misunderstanding, slip, oversight, miscalculation, *gaffe*, misinterpretation, slip-up, clanger, *corrigendum* and *erratum* on the exercise book below.

"What time do you want to go?" the Sergeant asked his wife as the nightmare memories faded and sank deep, deep, deep, deep into his subconscious, which as it happens is not very deep in the Sergeant's case, regrouping to attack at a later date. The narrative of self-destruction fascinates the Sergeant, crash and burn by your own inherent flaws. `Know thyself`[12] was inscribed on the south facing wall of the conservatory that led off the galley and reading it every time he went in there for a little R&R brought on moments of reflection he hoped would keep the cycle of crash and burn at bay.

He wasn`t a looker. He knew that much. His wife had told him so. He also knew he was lucky. Men, even the ugliest, always chatted up the most beautiful woman in the room first, working down through the plain towards the ugly ones as the failures mounted up. They can`t help it, it`s hard wired into the male brain. Women on the other hand choose potential partners of similar looks. They know that personality is important, that`s the cake, and it`s the cake that matters. Good looks are the icing. His wife considers him to be a carrot cake with a thin layer of icing. She thinks that music brings love and romance which is why he took up the DG diatonic button accordion. He of course thinks his wife is beautiful. Simply beautiful. He remembered the time they first met, one Thursday market day. He was with a friend and they stopped to listen to wind chimes singing from the side opening of a stall packed with hippy stuff from India and Rhyl. He heard his friend telling him that he wanted to introduce him to someone, and he turned, not knowing it was his wife to be. He looked into her eyes and his brain exploded. To this day he can remember vividly everything about that moment, the expression on her face, the brick-red embroidered cotton hippy mirror dress she was wearing, the way she was standing. His life changed utterly in that instant. He had found love, or rather, love had demolished his brain. She experienced no such epiphany.

"Are you still there?" snarled his wife tenderly. The receiver overheated and pulsed as the energy from the phenomenon that was his wife blasted through it and knocked him a few feet to his left.

"I`m sorry, my dear, did you say something?"

"You`ve not been listening to a word I`ve said have you!" the receiver barked. For some reason Louis Armstrong singing *St James Infirmary* came into his mind.

> *When I die, bury me in straight laced shoes,*
> *I want a box-back suit and a Stetson hat. John B., that is.*
> *Put a twenty dollar gold piece on my watch chain,*
> *So the boys know that I died standin' pat.*

A vision of a funeral procession, his own, took shape in his mind, winding slowly through the back alleys of Fishguard, Goodwick Brass Band`s blues section[13] playing with wild abandon supported by a cameo performance from the

Preservation Hall Jazz Band,[14] straight out of Louisiana. The happy cortege was led by a big man, contemplative and sombre, a prop for Fishguard seconds if he wasn`t mistaken, all of them walking with that slow side to side, one step forward one step to the side gait characteristic of the New Orleans` style. Then he listened in his mind to Cab Calloway`s version, then Van Morrison`s, then Eric Clapton`s. This was a bad sign. He was in trouble. 'If it wasn`t for bad luck, he wouldn't have no luck at all.'

"When I heard the sweet sound of your voice," he purred into the receiver, "my heart disappeared down a whirlpool of love. I was incapable of thought, transfixed by the wonder of you." The temperature of the receiver, which by this time he was passing gingerly from hand to hand, and thus from ear to ear, the oven gloves ineffective at such extreme temperatures, dropped a couple of degrees. "It`s working," he thought. "Aberystwyth next weekend," he whispered tentatively into the receiver. The whirlpool was real.

"Yes!" she cried in delight. "We can stay in that nice hotel on the way into Aber, you remember, it`s got a nice dining room and we can have the *suite* overlooking town, the one with the purple furnishings and not too far from the lift, and if you book early ......"

"Cease and desist immediately," thought the Sergeant ....

"..... we can get a reduced rate and then we can stay an extra night ....."

"..... or face a missile strike."

"..... and that would be so romantic. Better than Paris. Make sure you don`t forget. Now then, I've got to go."

As insurance he began serenading her with his *a capella* version of Lightnin' Hopkins singing *Baby, Please Don't Go*. The connection went dead. He replaced the receiver and returned to the seat next to the galley table.

He was in his early thirties when he first met his wife, after the barren years as he called them. In the September of the year before his head exploded he looked through Pembrokeshire County Council`s Adult Education Brochure[15] but couldn`t find the details of the class he wanted, `Women: Level 1. Complete Beginners`, so he phoned the Adult Education Centre in Haverfordwest[15] and attempted to explain what he was looking for. After the woman at the end of the line stopped laughing, he thought this did little for customer relations and even less for his confidence, she booked him onto the next course which happened to be starting the following week. During the first lesson the tutor gave the class an aptitude test and later told the Sergeant his personality was acting against him, explaining that men are of two types which she called Type Ch and Type Dd. She used the Welsh alphabet. A Type Ch personality wakes up in his bed on a Sunday morning with a gorgeous naked woman next to him, looks around and thinks, "Good God! Only one?" A Type Dd personality on the other hand, upon waking on a Sunday morning and finding a gorgeous naked woman in bed with him, the crazed fantasy no doubt of a feverish Type Dd mind, would blush bright red and say apologetically, "I`m terribly sorry, you must have been looking for the bloke next door." He was, without corroborative evidence, convinced he was a Type Ch. The teacher, with a compassion gained through many years of experience, withdrew the thermometer gently, checking it briefly with a frown that worried the Sergeant, and asked him to think about it for homework and share his conclusions during the next class. Pondering the matter whilst showering on the Saturday morning he noticed the sponge had love bites all over it, and what was worse, the dental records proved the teeth marks were his. Cold reality hit. And it hurt. He returned the following week in tears. To add insult to injury he failed the exam in the summer and had to do the course again. He is a Type X, not even in the alphabet.

The Sergeant had a reputation for being disorganised. It wasn`t his fault. The Dyfed-Powys Police Rapid-Response Coracle Unit[16] expected everyone to be computer literate, even if they weren`t, and to use the Magyck Machine, as he calls it, for everything, diary, organizer, you name it. But when he safely saved a document inside it, it was effectively lost. He had no idea where it was.

In an attempt to solve the problem he travelled to Haverfordwest, mooring across the river from the library, and proceeded to a stationery shop in Bridge Street. Returning to the vessel he assembled the newly bought device and sat back in the reclining, high-back, ergonomic, executive, ivory-white, fake leather, swivel chair in the office, rotating slowly clockwise to counter the coracle`s anticlockwise motion, to admire the newly installed, up to the minute, awe inspiring technology. It graced the Welsh oak table, cut from the sustainable forest near Castell Henllys, next to the computer desk. It`s surprising how much joy ten clear plastic stacking shelves can give a man. And it didn`t need to be switched on after installation. To test the new equipment he wrote a shopping list reminder to himself on a Post-it note, put it onto one of the shelves at random and left to navigate his way back to the galley to make himself a nice mug of tea. A breeze from the open porthole lifted and carried it in an easterly direction before depositing it onto a large pile of other Post-it notes on the carpet. He thought his problem had been significantly reduced by his investment in state-of-the-art equipment. However, he had not included human error in his calculations.

His leg was getting better, the limp was less noticeable, especially when he was lying in the bath. Whilst attending a conference in France he was involved in a bad RTA or `river traffic accident` as the *gendarmes* say and following it spent a couple of weeks in hospital. He was coracling along the Seine near Paris doing a bit of sightseeing on a free day, keeping close to the Left Bank. He couldn`t have chosen a worse time, it was rush hour. The head on collision with the other coracle paddled by a commuter on her way to work was, "An accident waiting to `appen," according to the kindly *gendarme* who arrested him. His coracle was a write off. He`d forgotten they coracle on the wrong side of rivers there. After a short recuperation period his superiors offered to fly him home and told him there was a flight via Dunedin the next morning. But the Sergeant comes from a long line of coraclers, born 'with saltwater in his blood and a sea wind in his lungs'. Nothing can keep him from the waves. Except a direct order from above of course. Dunedin was interesting, not least because he discovered that the origin of the name went back in history to one of early Cornish and Welsh`s sister languages in north Britain, and to the Gododdin, before passing, via Irish into Scots Gaelic and English.

It was while recovering from the incident in Paris that the Sergeant had his greatest pre-marital sexual adventure. Of course it was, he was a young man, it was Paris. It still is Paris. One morning, recuperating, he went for a walk and after a couple of hours exploring the city sat at a table on a broad pavement outside a *café*, ordered a coffee and began watching life go by. Suddenly, into his reveries came the sound of a woman's voice, soft, attractive. Turning slightly, he recognised the woman as *Belle de Jour*. Yes, he was in Paris drinking coffee at a table next to Catherine Deneuve.

The Dyfed-Powys Police Rapid-Response Coracle Unit responded by giving him their most modern vessel, a concrete coracle more resistant to crumpling upon impact than the traditional hazel branches, pig skin and pitch type he was used to. It was also made from the latest concrete that is carbon negative. "A double whammy," the Sergeant smiled to himself when this fact sank in. The coracle was an expensive addition to the DPPRRCU`s armamentarium. When questioned about this by MSs concerned about the expense to the community, Mr Greenspan,[17] the Unit`s financial wizard, gave a detailed and lengthy lecture that he concluded by recommending that the new coracle be given to the Sergeant. The MSs seemed unconvinced until he added, "If I have made myself clear, then you have misunderstood me". This was a language they understood, and, agreeing to the decision, they left happily.

The new coracle was fitted with the latest in-coracle satellite navigation system. While taking it through its sea trials off Strumble Head he decided to see what the ultrafast craft was made of. Concrete he discovered after damaging the paintwork as he bounced off the Irish ferry. He got lost and finding that the navigation system was useless, or rather, finding that he didn`t know how to use it, he hit upon a brilliant idea. He would use the same technique to find his way home that he once used to escape after getting lost in the maze in the foyer inside the main entrance to County Hall in Haverfordwest.[18] Keep turning left. It worked that time as the following week he stumbled dishevelled, disorientated yet triumphant into the car park in front of the building. It was the car park reserved for members of the Cabinet and he was quickly apprehended and removed by security staff. After several weeks of travelling later he arrived back in Fishguard Harbour. There had been no provisions on board when he left as the sea trials were expected to last no more than an afternoon and he survived the trip by buying fish and chips and mugs of strong tea in seaside towns along the way. He was particularly taken with the mushy peas in Scarborough and the Arbroath Smokies he ate, in Arbroath of all places, were a gastronomic delight. So much so that he radioed headquarters whilst there to say he had been delayed an extra two nights. This unscheduled round Britain trip would have been completed much quicker if he hadn't kept running aground in the shallows near the sources of the rivers he explored around the coast along the way.

It is customary for the name of a vessel to be written on the prow. On the coracle, as is fitting, him coming from a nation that honours its poets, is not a name, but an *englyn* by Dewi Emrys, a Pembrokeshire poet. The original version in Welsh, in red paint, is on the larboard side.

> *Y Gorwel*
> *Wele rith fel ymyl rhod – o'n cwmpas,*
> *Campwaith dewin hynod;*
> *Hen linell bell nad yw'n bod,*
> *Hen derfyn nad yw'n darfod.*

And an English translation, in green paint, is on the starboard side, the choice of colours following nautical tradition.

> *The Horizon*
> *See an illusion, like the edge of a wheel – encompassing us,*
> *The masterpiece of a remarkable magician;*
> *An ancient far off line that does not exist,*
> *An ancient boundary that does not end.*

The Sergeant, in philosophical mood, ran the *englyn* around in his mind a few times, there was plenty of room there, after all. His greatest talent is to be happy as he Is and with the world as it Is. Like the majestic Preseli Mountains to the northeast he does not wake up in the morning thinking, "Now then, what shall I change today?" Like the trees he does not look out over the rim of the coracle of an evening and think, "If only my wife would change a little, everything would be much better." He enjoys life as It Is. "When you get It, you are It and that's the end of it," he was fond of telling new recruits to the unit.

In the peaceful habitat near the hammock grow many species of plants. Robust angelica with two to three pinnate leaves and light-yellow flowers, giant hyssops with aromatic leaves and whorls of small tubular violet-blue flowers, happy marjoram with hairy, ovate leaves and pale pink flowers, catmint covered with pale lavender-blue flowers and with scalloped blue-green leaves and blue, pink, purple and white Michaelmas daisies, several feet in height. Clearly visible are tall spikes of the pinkish-purple flowers of willow herbs, the plant spreading by seed and rhizomes, wild carrots with tripinnate leaves and small, white flowers clustered in dense umbels three to four inches wide and low-growing thyme with tiny grey-green leaves. The tuberous rooted Bishop of Llandaff with deep blackish-red leaves and bright red flowers and Bishop of York with brown-green leaves and orange flushed, yellow flowers. Prickly teasels with domed heads of four-lobed pale lilac flowers grow over 6 feet in height, lavender with fragrant grey-green linear leaves and purple flowers, foxgloves with rosettes of hairy, oval leaves and spires of bell-shaped purple, pink and white flowers, scented blue tansies with compound, fern-like leaves and yellow, button-like flowers, lungwort with silvery leaves and sprays of blue, pink and white flowers, clumps of aquilegia with grey-green basal leaves and erect stems bearing bell-shaped flowers with white petals with blue spurs and pale blue sepals and sedums with their pink and yellow flowers, geraniums and *lechuguilla* plants. All these grow wild on the stern.

Musk ox walk carefully across the frozen ground alongside the *fjord* formed aeons ago by the submergence of a glaciated valley in the mountains to the north east of the lake, where temperatures in winter routinely reach minus 35^{0}C. The give-away imprints made by the runners of a *qamutik* and the prints of the huskies pulling it run alongside their path and are evidence of recent human activity in the area. Wary now, they make their way across the rough terrain in the grey-white, snow-icy landscape.

Mountain gorillas live high up on the slopes of the dormant volcano to the southwest of the lake amongst the ferns and vines high in the cool forest habitat of African redwoods. Iguanas travel from sea level to lay eggs in its crater.

A lone botanist walks cautiously through the denser parts of the tropical forest to the south of the lake, keeping a wary eye out for the black mambas that are known to inhabit the region. A frog the size of a cat looks on. Nearby, a chimpanzee fishes termites out of their hiding places with a long stick while its partner uses a stone to crush nuts before eating the fleshy parts inside. A panther chameleon, the surrounding leaves breaking up its shape to an observer, remains still on a branch as it looks for prey. It changes colour as she approaches. There have been five mass extinctions on the stern, when asteroids, ice and volcanoes were responsible. The botanist believes the area is on the brink of a sixth and is convinced the Sergeant is responsible. Welsh Government officials, whilst thinking this a little harsh, have sent her into this inhospitable region risking life and limb to gather evidence and to identify plant species unknown to science that might have medicinal or culinary value.

A pair of Blakiston's fish owls with a wingspan of over 6 feet hunt for salmon and trout in the lake. They live on the far north of the stern where temperature's reach minus 30^{0}C in the winter. At dusk they will sing a duet to mark their territory. An eagle sits atop the main mast readying itself to utter a prophesy, as is the custom with these birds.

A mermaid sits on a rock in the cool water just off the southern edge of the lake 'preoccupied with combing her long, golden tresses'.[19] Nearby and a little to the west, in a rocky outcrop formed over millions of years from exposed bedrock, a hermit lives in a cave.

The Sergeant made his way from the galley to the hammock on the stern to rest. Close by, a wooden sign engraved with the words HIC IACIT THE SERGEANT hung limp and useless in the warm, torpid air. Sensing change, The Parrot opened its eyes, shook itself once and took several slow, deep breaths before flying out through the porthole next to its perch to take up position atop the main mast amidships to keep a look out. It was late evening, the air was still with not a breath of wind, the water in the harbour a millpond. The sun was setting, in the west interestingly enough.

Into the peace appeared a strange, rhythmic, beating sound from far off. The surface of the water in Fishguard harbour began to ripple and bounce. "Damn funny. Like a ....., like a train in the distance." said Bromhead.[20] The Sergeant ignored him and glanced towards the skyline over Harbour Village, the direction the sound was coming from. Nothing. He scratched his ear thoughtfully, got off the hammock, stood up, grabbed the binoculars from their case on the table and moved a few steps in the direction of the sound, rubbing the big end of the binoculars against his jumper to clean the lenses as he went. Narrowing his eyes, he raised a hand to shield them from the glare of the sun and with the other hand lifted the binoculars to peer through them. A shiver ran down his spine. Then another. The coracle rocked at its mooring, dragging the anchor along the seabed eighteen inches below. Something was becoming visible through the haze ..... a thin undulating black line was appearing on the horizon, silhouetted against the evening light. A long line of ..... He gave a start. The binoculars crashed onto the deck.

"Zulus to the southwest," screamed The Parrot. "Thousands of 'em."[20]

6

Though lovers be lost love shall not.
Dylan Thomas[1]

Megan was in the crypt watching her favourite film, Marcel Carné's 1938 *Le Quai des Brumes*,[2] an atmospheric trawl through the seedy life in a Welsh port permanently swathed in pouring rain starring Jean Gabin as a deserter who finds love and a *petit chien* and Michèle Morgan as the *femme fatale*. The two main characters reminded her, in a strange reminding sort of a way, of herself and her late husband, although she didn`t know why. Film buffs have been fooled into thinking the film was shot in Le Havre, but in a time capsule found buried beneath a rock a mile to the west of Angle, Machlud y Wawr[3] have recently unearthed proof that the location was Pembroke Dock. For only here do the 'dark shadows, wet lights and hazy cobblestones' have the necessary heavy mists of 'poetic realism'.[4] And Michèl`s daughter was later to star in another French film, Guillaume Parry`s 1978 *Le Grand Chelem*[5] with Windsor Davies, Huw Griffiths, *et autres* (sic).

Megan wasn`t sure if she should finish the piece of coffee cake lying on a thick bed of vanilla ice cream in the predominantly pink coloured antique Chinese *famille-rose* porcelain dish in front of her. She decided to eat through the pain. After all, that`s what French films are for. Pain, and the *dessert* that vanquishes it. The soundtrack reminded her of her husband`s musical accomplishments. There was an old piano in the crypt which he used to plonk on. He was a natural, you could tell by the way he sat on the stool and wiggled his toes. And plonking became playing until after a few years he was very, very good. Yet he always felt that something wasn`t quite right. "More practise," he would say to himself, "It`ll come." His instruments of choice until Megan came along had been, according to the Hornbostel-Sachs classification system, a bellows-driven, free-reed, aerophone type, box-shaped instrument played by compressing and expanding a bellows whilst pressing buttons thus opening pallets allowing air to flow across reeds which vibrate to produce sound, and the two-string electric fence. She thought it was all too Country and Western.

On their twenty-fifth wedding anniversary they went to the Bardstown Bluegrass Festival in Kentucky.[6] 'Ancient as time. As modern as tomorrow.' it said on the leaflet they picked up in the Tourist Office in Tenby. They liked bluegrass and they liked fried rice, so why not put them both together. But first they decided to go to Chicago to attend performances by the Second City improv troupe[7] and fly south from there. It was a couple of months before Megan`s husband died.

They flew from Crymych International Airport. In a plane of course. The plane climbed steeply after take-off, passing through thick cloud, and at approximately 23,000 feet emerged into brilliant sunshine then continued climbing rapidly leaving the cloud base behind. As he looked out of the window he experienced a panic attack and his breathing became shallow and laboured and the colour drained from his cheeks. Megan adjusted the device she attached to the back of his right hand just before they left home and released a few more milligrams of Felinfoel Double Valium[8] or Felinfoel Double Valium as they pronounce it in Ianeli where this voiceless alveolar unilateral fricative, written `ll` in the Roman alphabet and `ł` in the phonetic script, is particularly popular and sometimes overused with great enthusiasm, although usually after taking Valium it must be said, in a way that many Welsh teachers disapprove of. The drug is recommended by the Welsh Institute of Aviation Medicine for use by pilots on long haul flights. As it entered his bloodstream the panic subsided. Megan adjusted his earbuds and turned the volume on the smart phone up. He turned and glanced dozily out of the window. "Good heavens!" he exclaimed, looking down, "It`s been snowing heavily since we left." Shortly afterwards, the pilots, having reached cruising altitude, braked. "Is that possible?" he wondered whilst floating around in a beautiful drug induced haze. His stomach lurched forward and he tried to follow but the Double Valium slowed his reflexes. Felinfoel Double Valium is famous for being the first drug for the treatment of anxiety to be canned. Thousands of cans were sent out to the Welsh regiments in the trenches during the First World War.

They ate dinner somewhere over the Atlantic and had just finished pudding when he pressed 'Pause', removed the earbuds, leant over and kissed her. "Do you know when I love you most, cariad?" he slurred.

"No," she replied.

"When you taste of treacle tart."

She squeezed his hand.

"Can I ask you something?"

"Of course."

"Please don`t get annoyed or all upset. I`m confused about this and I`ve never understood women."

"What is it?" she asked, with a quizzical expression.

"Will you marry me?" This was a ritual he followed on every wedding anniversary and quite often in between.

She lifted his hand gently and kissed it before replying. "I will," she said, teasing him.

He asked twice more. She said 'I will' twice more. He looked uncertain and put the back of his hand on her forehead. "You're feverish," he informed her.

"I`m not."

He felt the back of her head. "Have you had a knock to the head recently?" Before adding, "I can feel a big lump."

"That`s the pillow, cariad."

"Are you on drugs?"

Ignoring the question, she squeezed his hand, repeating "I will," and kissed his insecurity again before replacing the earbuds and pressing 'Play'.

Twenty-seven years earlier she wasn`t sure about marrying him. "What if we get married and have kids but it doesn`t work out?" she asked her friends. "Don`t worry," one of them said, "when your kids are grown up and leaving home you`ll be in your forties, gorgeous, and you can leave him and get back out there and pick up another one second hand." Looking at him in the seat next to her, dozing in his chemical bliss, his body jerking to the rhythm of the music, she was glad she overcame her fears. She leant over, kissed him softly on the temple, took his hand in hers to top up the Double Valium and went back to her novel. "My husband, the legend," she sighed happily. Megan doesn`t do hope, never has, she goes straight into blind optimism. And it works.

He gave a start and turned to her again, removing the earbuds. "Am I good to you, cariad?" he asked.

"Yes."

"Do I care for you?"

"Yes."

"Am I happy with you?"

"Yes."

"Do I think you`re the most beautiful woman in the world?"

"Yes."

"Do I think you`re Gorgeous?"

"Yes."

"With a capital guh"?

"Indeed. But only the first one."

"Do I think you`re the sexiest woman on the planet?"

"Of course."

"Do I love you more than I can ever say?"

"Yes, you do."

"I`m glad you know all these things about me. More treacle tart?"

"Hmm. Yes, please, cariad."

"Can I be your limpet, and you mine?"

"Of course."

She gave him a *cwtsh* and thought of something he said to her shortly after they were married many years before, something that troubled her at the time yet offered her a happiness she hadn`t experienced before. "Only if you`re perfectly happy to live without me can you be perfectly happy to live with me." Her disquiet lasted a while, the apprehension a lot longer. "I can live without you," she told him some time later, "and I choose to live with you." The happiness remains to this day.

It hadn`t all been plain sailing. There was his habit of not telling the children to say 'Thank you'. He explained to her that gratitude grows naturally from the heart.

When one of the children was eight months old and ill the child couldn`t lie down to sleep as he cried instantly when put in the cot but stopped crying immediately upon being picked up and carried. Megan`s husband held the baby in his arms and walked slowly around the room to comfort him. Bedtime came and the baby still cried when put in the cot, so he told Megan that he`d keep walking around the living room until the baby fell asleep and then they would both come up to bed. After a while he began to feel giddy, so he changed the pattern of his walking, ten times around the room in one direction, followed by ten times in the opposite direction, speaking softly to the baby all the while. That did the trick. Sometime later he moved all the chairs and tables into the centre of the room and walked outside of them, so the circle he was walking was bigger. Better still. Every now and again when the baby seemed settled, he put him in the cot, but the baby started crying immediately. The circular walk continued. Breakfast time and the family came downstairs to find the pair still travelling around the perimeter of the living room. They had been doing this all night. Megan took the baby, put him in the cot and he went straight to sleep. She gave the baby a kiss and her husband a big *cwtsh* and sent him upstairs to bed. "Did the baby have to say thank you?" Megan`s husband asked later. "Of course not. That`s what a parent does and takes great joy in such spontaneous expressions of love. If anything, I should thank the baby for giving me a wonderful opportunity to experience the love that fills a parent as they live an opportunity to be of benefit to their child. And anyway, of course you're grateful. Why make a song and dance about it. Your heart acknowledges it and remembers. That is enough."

In his opinion, children follow their role models, the adults around them. When parents continuously display gratitude to their children for all the wonderful things the children do for them, which is everything they do, looking up and smiling at them, painting a picture, talking to them, crying when hurt, losing a sock, for example, the children learn to do the same in return. Children who don`t say thank you are the offspring of parents who don`t say thank you, of parents who do not display their love and gratitude for them all the time. Eventually she came to agree with this point of view. "What the head is unsure of, the heart will always take care of," she told herself at times of irritation, and the irritation always passed, helped by her husband, who, when she was cross, would tell her that her face looked as though she was 'eating vinegar with chop sticks'. She noticed herself displaying gratitude to the children, and other people, a lot more and she noticed herself saying "*Diolch, cariad. Da iawn, cariad.*" after every little thing one of them did, and meaning it. Then she noticed that the children were doing this to her, and to each other. But at first they looked at her puzzled and asked, "Why did you say that?" "For being so wonderful," she would reply.

"I`m very lucky" he said to her, still slurring. Megan smiled at the over extravagant and indeed incorrect use of the voiceless alveolar unilateral fricative. Although quite fitting for someone with relatives in Penn Llwyn Diarwya, she thought. "You`re the perfect woman for me, the one I fell instantly head over heels in love with the moment we met, and you choose, with great compassion, to fulfil my need by devoting your life to my happiness. And I of course to yours. And in this way the need disappears and the love remains. But you could have done better."

"Better?" she wondered, squeezing his hand. He replaced the earbuds and turned up the volume as one of his favourites started to play and sang out loud to her.

> *Dance me to your beauty with a burning violin,*
> *Dance me through the panic `til I`m gathered safely in,*
> *lift me like an olive branch and be my homeward dove,*
> *Dance me to the end of love.*
> *Dance me to the end of love.*[9]

The intonation was unusual due to the excessive use of voiceless alveolar unilateral fricatives. She returned to her novel *The Girl with the Double Dragon Tattoo* and leafing through it noticed how long it was. "Over two thousand pages. This isn`t a book, it`s a library."[10, 11]

Drowsy, he drifted towards sleep. "‖‖ ‖‖‖ ‖‖‖‖‖‖‖ ‖‖‖‖ ‖‖‖‖‖‖ ‖ ‖‖‖‖ ‖‖‖‖‖‖‖ ‖‖‖," he muttered dreamily to nobody in particular.

He gave a start and looked wildly around. "Sorry!" he mumbled to himself, as nobody was listening. "I pressed `Restart` instead of `Shut down`."

His longish hair, at the sides and back but not in the front and middle, waved around as he did his Status Quo impersonation, his head bounding backwards and forwards. Since his early twenties he had used a special oil bought at a stall in Cardigan market run by some hippies from a commune in the Preseli Mountains to try and prevent his hair from receding. Yet his hair was by now in deep recession. "It`s no good as a cure for baldness," he admitted to Megan on one occasion. "Mind you, it worked on the babies." She smiled supportively, agreeing that their children, in their twenties now, had indeed developed hair soon after he began rubbing the oil into their scalps after they were born. Comforted by this memory he went to sleep.

He had wanted to retire young but thought that doing so would make things difficult for the people above him to find a replacement who could do the job as well as him, and that would be bad for the department. When he asked her advice on the matter, to assuage his fears and set him on the path to retirement and gardening, Megan reminded him of an incident that happened to a cousin of hers when she was about seven years old and living on the family farm. She was picking potatoes in the vegetable garden behind the farmhouse in the Gower village of Llan y Tair Mair one morning as her great aunt Hannah spoke to an elderly man, a local farmer. At one point in the conversation her aunt pointed across the garden towards the village chapel, Welsh Baptist, and said, "You see, the chapel graveyard is full of indispensable people." Megan's cousin didn`t understand what `indispensible` meant but it must have held some significance for her as that snippet from the conversation stayed in her memory. She mulled it over from time to time until a few years later the meaning became apparent to her. This was helpful to him, and much to her and the garden's delight he retired on his thirty seventh birthday, just before their trip to America.

He glanced out of the window again and saw a cloud formation that looked like Australia. "That can`t be Australia," he thought. "Tasmania isn`t there." Upon approaching the airspace over Chicago and before beginning the descent for the landing at O`Hare International the plane circled as the pilot waited for air traffic control to confirm they could land. "The pilot is lost," he thought, "they`re looking for landmarks." Fear took hold of his imagination. "The wheels have fallen off. We can`t land!" He reasoned with himself for a few moments. "Don`t be silly. Wheels don`t fall off modern jet aircraft." As he sat back in his seat, feeling relaxed, the plane hit some turbulence. "Ooooh!" he said, lurching forward after his stomach. "We`ve had a puncture." Megan adjusted the device on the back of his hand and his mind calmed. "let`s rock!" she heard him say as his body moved to the beat. There are roughly zones. And that`s where he was, in a roughly zone of her own making.[12] And Megan kept him there until they landed.

They arrived safely in their hotel room in Chicago, the effect of the drug almost wearing off by this time, and whilst unpacking her husband`s travelling bag she noticed he had packed five t-shirts, five shirts, five pairs of shorts, five pairs of jeans, five pairs of pants, five socks ..... She stood there holding the five socks in her hand and started to laugh. Wondering what all the fuss was about he went across to her from the window where he`d been admiring the view, thinking how much it reminded him of Crymych, and spotted the socks she was holding up. Still a little dozy he put his arms around her waist. "Will you marry me?" he asked.

"We`re already married." She replied.

"It`s not enough. I want to marry you again." He leant closer and looked into her eyes "My next statement might be uncomfortable for you, but I`m obliged to say it."

"Yes, cariad."

"You're beautiful. Fuzzy, but beautiful. It's impossible for me to tell you how important you are to me. Even when you're fuzzy."

She smiled and leant towards him.

"It`s no good arguing about it, cariad," he said. "I`m going to kiss you."

She moved closer, closed her eyes, pursed her lips and held her breath.

"Coming ready or not," he said. She smiled broadly, undoing the pursing. "I know this might be unpleasant for you," he whispered softly, "but when a man needs to kiss the woman he loves, a man needs to kiss the woman he loves." She grabbed him around the neck and pulled him gently to her, re-pursing as she did so. They were in love.

The evening before, as she was making treacle tarts in the kitchen at home, she caught him looking at her instead of at the rugby on the television. Something was up. "Did you just wink at me?" she asked.

"I don`t flirt with the catering staff, my dear," he replied.

The previous Saturday night they went to the Vietcong restaurant at the top of the 73 storey Twm Carnabwth Tower[13] situated next to the entrance of the Underground at Crymych Centrum. It is a revolving restaurant taking advantage of the views into the mist. They were sitting opposite each other at a south facing, at least it had been until the room revolved, window table for two. They were enjoying the view of the sea mist blowing in, curiously, from the sea, when she looked across at him. "You look uncomfortable, and I know why. I can read you like a book. You don`t like being separated from me like this as you like holding my hand with me next to you. I`m glad you love me."

"I love your hand," he replied.

She thinks that marriage is 99% gratitude, or is that 100%, so she moved to sit next to him, and he took her hand. He looked happier then, as did she.

Devotion is her trip. She says you can get high on devotion. It's one of the pathways.[14] On one occasion not long after they were married, she told him, as she had many times before, that she loved him. He replied that he didn't deserve her love, or any woman's for that matter. "Why do you love me?" he asked.

"Because you're my husband."

Unphased by this reply, as he was convinced he was undeserving of a woman's love, he asked again. "But why?"

"Because I love you," she repeated softly.

A smile of recognition appeared on his face. She of course was already beaming. "Do you remember? That's the circle. You're my husband because I love you, and I love you because you're my husband. A never-ending circle of love, of manifesting spontaneous goodness, complete in itself. The love that saturates my being and yours contains us, and everyone and everything. We appear within it. We are it. Do you remember the words we spoke? ...to love and to cherish ... in illness and in health ... for better or for worse .... That's love and its devotion. That describes a relationship of love. That's the way it is." She drew the circle of love and devotion on the cream-coloured organic linen tablecloth with her pink, star-speckled lipstick.

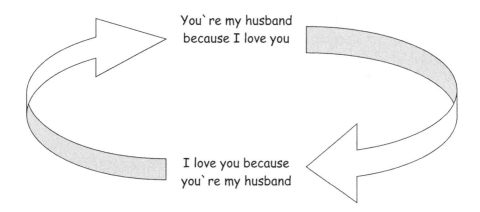

You're my husband
because I love you

I love you because
you're my husband

He began to cry. "It's funny," she said. "As love pours out of the heart people often cry. As the illusion disappears, like darkness in a room when the light is switched on. A heart overflowing."

"Where does it come from?" he asked.

"It doesn't come from anywhere," she reminded him. "It's what we are. It's what we always are, always have been, and always will be, where always doesn't exist." He couldn't stop crying and laughing as he was engulfed by love. Megan held his hand.

"You don`t need to look for It," she said. "It`s always here. That`s all there is. We are It and we appear within It. In fact, there's no we, there's One. And there's no It and there's no One. The illusion at play. And how strange that anything is happening at all. We come out of perfection as perfection and return to perfection having never left it in the first place."

He gazed at her, a puzzled look on his face, and smiled. "That would make a good French film. I was surprised to discover when we first met that you weren`t already married. I used to think that such a beautiful woman as you must have at least ten husbands. All her own of course!"

"The joy I have of being here is the love that flows out of me to you?" Megan replied. "When you say you love me, you`re wrong. You don`t love me, you love the love you experience that`s inside of you, the love that you`re made of. Love, that`s all you are, my love. For some reason I`m a trigger that opens you to the love that you are, so you experience being it. I devote myself to you and see my role as opening my heart and being with you in such a way that you experience being love. That also strengthens my experience of the love inside me, the love that I am, which is the same love that you are. Inseparable. Indivisible. We appear from love, exist for a moment as love, and disappear back into love. Unchanging. That`s the gift I give you, creating an environment in which you experience what you really are, the ocean of love out of which everything comes and everything Is. That`s what being your wife means to me. The dance of love. Everything else is an illusion, exquisite, beautiful, but an illusion. Believing the illusion to be real is to suffer."

"Someone once wrote, he replied, 'the most precious possession that ever comes to a man in this world is a woman`s heart'.[15] Have I been a good man to you?"

"Yes, my love."

"I sometimes don`t think so."

"You`re fine as you are."

"Am I?"

"Perhaps you`re confusing who you are with your thoughts and emotions. You are beautiful. I will always love you. As you are."

Emboldened by a topsy-turvy late surge of Felinfoel Double Valium he took a step back, gazed into her eyes and sang the Conamara Anthem,[16] in Irish and then in English.

> *Tá cailín álainn a dtug mé grá di;*
> *`Sí `s deise `s áille ná bláth ná rós.*
> *Gan í ar lámh liom is cloíte `tá mé,*
> *A chailín álainn, is tú fáth mo bhróin.*

A chailín álainn a dtug mé grá duit,
Bí ar lámh liom, a mhíle stór;
Is abair liomsa gur tú mo ghrá geal,
Beidh orm áthas in áit an bhróin.

There's a beautiful girl I gave my love to,
She is nicer and lovelier than flower or rose.
Without her hand in mine, I am anxious.
O beautiful girl, you're the cause of my sadness.

O beautiful girl to whom I gave my love,
Give me your hand, my darling,
And tell me that you're my shining love.
There will be joy upon me instead of sorrow.

She loved it. He kissed her, took a bow and returned to the window to enjoy the view as she continued unpacking. Knowing deep down something was amiss, softly, under her breath, she sang another song from the island in the west, ending with these prophetic words.

Ó bhain tú thoir agus bhain tú thiar díom,
Bhain tú an ghealach gheal is an ghrian díom,
Bhain tú an croí seo bhí i lár mo chléibhe díom
Is nach rí-mhór é m'fhaitíos gur bhain tú Dia díom.[17]

For you took what's before me and what's behind me,
Took east and west from all around me.
The sun, moon and stars from me you've taken,
And God himself if I'm not mistaken.

The effects of the Double Valium had worn off by now and he was back to his usual self.

"Can I give you lots of kisses tomorrow?"

"Yes, you can."

"And what about the day after tomorrow?"

"Yes, cariad. And the day after tomorrow."

She misses him very much.

In the ancient woodland leading northwest from the orchard outside the crypt, charcoal hearths and alder and hazel coppice stools are visible. Continuously wooded since the last Ice Age, sessile oaks covered with fern and moss are plentiful. In damp gullies, small, flowerless, green liverworts and lichens flourish. The sweet warbling of pied flycatchers resting amongst the trees is heard as others feed on insects and fruits. Brown-streaked tree pipits with short, thin beaks and pink legs eat small invertebrates. One rises suddenly from a tree before parachuting down on stiff wings, singing as it goes. Wood warblers, nearly 5 inches long with bright yellow upper parts, throat and upper chest, and white underparts, feed on insects and spiders, their characteristic songs a fluid trill of increasing tempo and a series of descending piping notes. Redwings, pintails, yellowhammers, waxwings and a wren, the king of the birds, play.

Beautiful, oval-shaped, shield-backed Picasso bugs, a variety of arthropod up to 0.31 inches long, green with pastel-coloured spots and wavy lines on their backs and looking like miniature abstract paintings, feed undisturbed on plant juices in the arid, sub-Saharan region to the south of the lake, unconcerned that they do not display any degree of sexual dimorphism.

A peacock spider the size of a grain of rice, furry mouthparts fixed in a grin, lifts then replaces his third pair of legs alternately while displaying an intensely coloured tail flap. Far from home, he dances frantically for life as, perched on a nearby twig, a potential lover looks hungrily on, the rumble rumps of his courtship display leaving her decidedly unimpressed.

7

It's too late to be ready.
Dogen[1]

The Sergeant's typing technique is unusual even for Pembrokeshire, involving as it does two fingers and a forehead. But which two fingers? Opinion is divided. Sitting in his study in the aft section of the coracle typing an email to the Admiral whilst at the same time attempting the notoriously difficult crossword in the *Llien Gwyn*[2] he paused to gaze through the porthole next to the antique, double pedestal roll-top desk in oak he inherited from his father`s family after they sold their farm on the Gower. It goes everywhere with him. It has little choice of course being that it is on the coracle.

The porthole was on his left, his handsomest side he has always thought, so passing shipping sees him at his best when he is writing. The view from the mooring across the harbour waters to Fishguard reminded him of Cairo, even though that great city is about 160 miles from the sea, which one he wasn`t sure. He had never been to Cairo so there is nothing in his memory that could have reminded him of the place. But that was not an obstacle.

He remembered a trip to nearby Alexandria, named after some great king from the past whose name escaped him, whilst taking a break from the Abu Dhabi Adventure Challenge.[3] That was by the sea he knew full well as he damaged the coracle whilst racing against a local boat just off the city, a beautiful thin vessel about 100 cubits long made of cedar wood. He ran aground on a sandbank and whilst there decided to visit the great library he had heard about. He hailed a passing boat filled to the gunwales with tourists and asked the tour guide who gently pointed out in her broken English that sand banks do not have libraries, particularly great ones, explaining that shifting sands play havoc with foundations. She advised him to try in Alexandria. That also proved fruitless. It was closed for repairs after a fire.

The Challenge is an annual endurance race which involves travelling 500 punishing miles across the deserts of Abu Dhabi. Several minutes into the race, when the four wheel and six wheel drive land cruisers of the other competitors had long since disappeared over the nearest sand dune, he realised that a vital piece of information had been lost when his invitation to enter the race was translated from Arabic into Welsh after being received at the Dyfed-Powys Police Rapid-Response Coracle Unit`s headquarters[4] in Milford Haven a few weeks earlier. "Of course," he muttered, paddling enthusiastically as he and the coracle disappeared into the sandy trench he was digging, "I should have brought a

Teasmade, my trusted Seagull Vintage Extra Strong model with alarm clock and toaster."

He noticed a cloud formation over Dinas Head that looked like his old physics teacher. "No wonder I didn`t learn anything in physics," he thought and was intrigued to see the cloud`s motion was along only one spatial dimension, in other words it was travelling in a straight line. "A good example of uniform linear motion with constant velocity and therefore zero acceleration," he reasoned, reflecting further upon how the motion of the cloud could be described by its position, x as it varied with time, t. "Hmm, good old linear motion, what a ball that was," he mused nostalgically.

There had been tremblings and rumblings during the night. On top of this a smell of sulphur hung over Fishguard Harbour. "Was the volcano on the stern becoming active again?" he wondered.

His mind moved on. This took some time. He gazed through the porthole. He was born to do this. He yawned. The laptop in front of him beeped telling him an e-mail had arrived. "Showtime!" he cried as his forehead hit the keyboard.

Disappointment. He read the message on the screen telling him that his application had failed. His dream of claiming the World Sea-Speed record was gone, someone else had been chosen to pilot the coracle that was to make the attempt on the record. At a secret subterranean location just behind the Cathedral Chamber in Dan yr Ogof caves[5] in the Swansea Valley, not far from Madam Patti`s pad,[6] the appropriate subcommittee picked someone else to be the test pilot. "Well," he thought, "who did Madam Patti think she was anyway?"

The coracle, that, if all goes according to plan, will streak across the water at over 1,000mph to set a new record, recently passed a significant test of its development cycle whilst undergoing sea trials over the sand flats near Penclawdd on the Gower. This is where Olympic hopefuls hone their coracling skills. For the slalom, when the tide is out, they race along the natural deep gullies the currents have carved into the ancient sand, and for the marathon they use Burry Estuary itself.

Local cockle hunters are barred from the area when trials are held but are compensated for any loss of income. Cockles are sensitive creatures and their mating habits are easily disrupted by wave crashing coracles, resulting in a fall in the population for a whole season. Cockle hunters are notified of the top-secret test dates by a quarter page colour advert in the Evening Post[7] twenty-eight days before trials are held.

Squadron Leader Aneurin ap Goronwy, the former Free Wales Air Force Spitfire pilot had been chosen to be the test pilot for the mission. At a press release on the mudflats to the west of Crofty, Squadron Leader ap Goronwy said that he was pleased with the way the test had gone, adding, "W i'n hoffi cocos." (I like cockles.) This is surprising coming from a native of Abergavenny as they are well known for preferring cheese and was no doubt a remark the top brass of the World Sea-Speed Public Relations subcommittee, responsible as they are for public relations, dreamt up to keep the natives happy. The Squadron Leader wasn`t happy though. "After all," he remarked testily to the chair of the subcommittee the previous evening when they asked him to say it, "you wouldn`t hear the President of the United States making a statement like that!" Adding "And I want that in the minutes." However, the subcommittee were proved right and it went down like a storm with local cockle hunters, which was unusual as storms are usually the last thing they want whilst plying their dangerous trade out over the flats amongst the deep, treacherous, water gouged gullies which fill with fast flowing water before the flats themselves are covered by the incoming tide. This is why so many of the wild horses that wander onto the flats are marooned as the tide comes in, stranded on the flats as they can`t cross the racing water filling the gullies that can be as much as fifteen feet deep. Zoologists surmise that what has become known in scientific circles as the Penclawdd Stranding Effect is no doubt the environmental stimulus that resulted in cockling horses evolving legs that are several feet longer than the average. Those that didn`t evolve in this specialised environmental niche simply drowned and took their short legs with them out of the gene pool. Yes, nature red in tooth and claw. Tough beasts these horses even if a little unstable. Like bicycles they have to keep moving or they fall over.

Encouraged by the favourable response to his remark about liking cockles he *ad libbed* with the immortal line, "' *W i`n dwlu ar gocos a bara lawr i frecwast,*" (I love cockles and laver bread for breakfast.) Not since a Welsh American NASA[8] astronaut spoke Welsh in space has the Wales Tourist Board[9] been so excited. Although no one could work out who he was speaking to up there in space we are all immensely proud of him and several learned papers were published in academic journals in the months that followed discussing whether or not mutations are affected by weightlessness. New Wales Tourist Board advertisements were commissioned to take advantage of the free publicity in the media and huge posters soon covered billboards over the border in England, each with a photograph of the Squadron Leader sitting at a breakfast table eating a plate of cockles and laver bread accompanied by the caption, "' *W i`n dwlu ar gocos a bara lawr i frecwast.*" The neighbours loved it, even though they didn`t know what it meant. It was wonderfully exotic. Upon hearing the *ad lib* several seasoned cockle women swooned and fell backwards, landing with a squelch, the soles of their bare feet visible to all as they lay unconsciousness in the cold, waterlogged mud and sand, the belts of their classic 1950`s retro-vintage trench coats pulled tight around slender midriffs.

Fashion conscious members of the press noted the lightweight wool Gabadine trench coats with two front slash pockets, gun flap, double peaked collar, box pleat in the bodice, darts for great fit, light shoulder pads with *épaulettes*, their powerful arm muscles, a testament to the classic upper body strength of the female cockle hunter achieved after years spent digging cockles out of their sandy lairs with their bare hands before carrying the heavy cockle filled baskets to the wooden horse drawn carts, don`t need amplifying, hook-and-eye collar closure and adorable little matching hats. Bust sizes are available from 38B to 52DD and waist sizes from 28-75. All in inches of course. Light brown and khaki are the colours of choice although this occasionally proves unhelpful as when, in 1976, a cockle woman slipped on the edge of a gully, rolled down the side, slid into the fast-moving current and was washed out to sea. The fashionable cockling wear proved to be effective camouflage making it impossible for search and rescue craft to spot her and she was never seen again.

She reappeared three weeks later having been picked up by a Basque fishing vessel in the Bay of Biscay from where she hitched a lift to Bilbao and then caught the next train home. Recently, under pressure from the National Society for the Protection of Cockle Hunters (Female Division) they agreed to have a TwmTwm,[10] a popular SatNav device made in a factory just outside Nefyn on the Llŷn Peninsular, fitted to the inside of their hats. This move proved to be a success recently after another female cockle hunter fell into a gully with a great Yelp! Although in Welsh of course, *Ielp!* And a Splash! *Sblash!* and disappeared down Burry Estuary. It took the search and rescue helicopter that scrambled from St Athans and the Mumbles lifeboat only seven hours to locate the hat. They were helped in their endeavours by the crew of the Baden Powell, a 34' 6" double-ended Wash cockler a long way from its mooring on the Great Ouse. After successfully recovering the hat the crew were thanked profusely before being detained for questioning by local police, suspected of smuggling.

Squadron Leader ap Goronwy has held the existing world sea-speed record since 2017 when he reached 912.35mph on the official test waters between Skomer Island and Caldey Island, the two geographical features used to mark the beginning and end of the test course. When an attempt on the record is made the craft begins its run in the turbulent waters several miles to the southwest of Skomer, and gathering momentum, velocity and occasionally seaweed it accelerates steeply towards the island, reaching maximum speed as it passes it. From there, the pilot must maintain the craft`s speed until past Caldey Island, several miles to the east. *Madame Chronomètre*, positioned inside *la grande tente,* sited a small way inland away from the cliffs opposite Skomer because she`s afraid of heights, presses the little button on the top of the stop watch as the coracle, in fact more of a blur than a coracle, emerges from behind Skomer and presses the little button a second time as it is lost to view behind Caldy, at which point the test pilot optimistically applies the brakes.

Applying the brakes causes a *tsunami* that travels east along the coast until most of its energy is dissipated as it hits the Marine Walk in Llanelli causing great damage before spilling over it and travelling inland. On more than one occasion the Scarlets have been forced to cancel a game due to the flooding caused. The flaw in their stadium's design, it is shaped like a giant breakfast bowl, became apparent after the first *tsunami* hit. The water sloshed through the players' entrance and travelled round and round inside it and couldn't get out.

The accompanying sonic boom wakes the monks on Caldey Island[11] and disturbs the bees. Legal action to recoup lost revenue due to the drop in honey production and thus honey sales to the tourists who flock to the island every summer has been dragging its way through the courts for years. The beautiful sandy beach next to where boats from the mainland dock, a feature of the island much loved by those same tourists, has been washed away by the giant, turbulence filled wake produced by the coracle as it screams past.

Each sonic boom causes the spire of St Mary's church in Tenby, which used to be the tallest in Pembrokeshire at 152 feet, to bend a little more alarmingly to the left. The vicar[12] has been seen to tremble when looking up at it, even after completing the anger management course the Bishop[13] suggested he attend. The tower of the church was built around 700 years ago and the spire about 500 years ago. At that time the builders had not encountered a coracle travelling at Mach 1 nor the following sonic boom and therefore saw no need to include precautions against such phenomena in their design. "It'll never 'appen mun, see." one of them wrote in the *marginalia* of a building regs manuscript that has survived. Dated by scholars to June 1521 it is kept in Tenby Museum[14] alongside the original of the town's most famous poem, *Edmyg Dinbych* from the 9th century. He was wrong, and so, by association, was the Council's Forward Planning Committee.[15]

A recent *exposé* by the Tenby Observer[16] in which an anonymous Saundersfoot resident claimed that the vicar of St Mary's is building a time machine in order to travel back and give advice to the mediaeval builders[12] has been dismissed by Tenby Town Council[15] as a 'malicious rumour'. The angle of lean of the spire makes it a notable landmark for those travelling by land or sea in the vicinity. Unless of course you're strapped onto a small strip of wood that acts as a makeshift seat, your vision impaired by salt water spray battering your goggles at over 900 miles per hour as you fight frantically with a small stick they have the temerity to call a paddle trying to control a coracle travelling at what feels like the speed of light causing your cheeks to expand so much that lookouts on passing ships remark how unusual it is to see a giant hamster controlling such a vessel as it bounces off, through, over, if the angle of the aerofoil has been miscalculated and the coracle becomes airborne, and sometimes under the waves as they wend their way gently towards North Beach where they are eagerly awaited by small children wearing arm floats who splash around in them and guide the water into moats they have dug to surround sea shell encrusted sand castles. Once airborne a test coracle can reach very high altitudes which brings with it a myriad of problems. Of greatest concern to the test pilot is the weightlessness experienced during re-entry into the Earth`s atmosphere which can severely disrupt the flow of nutrients along the tube leading from the flask of tea, attached by a special harness to the test pilot`s back, to the pilot`s mouth. These harnesses and their attached tubes are specially made to endure the extreme environment of a record attempt and the sole manufacturer, Kittle Tea Flask Harnesses Ltd, is based in a shed at the bottom of the garden of the ice cream shop in the Gower village that bears the company`s name.

Deliberately flying over waves brings with it automatic disqualification as the coracle is then deemed airborne and should, of course, be attempting to break the World Air-Speed record, a different kettle of fish altogether.

Inside *la grande tente Madame Chronomètre* always sits next to the Machlud y Wawr[17] stall and as far away from the cliffs as it is humanly possible to be whilst remaining within the confines of *la grande tente*. She claims to suffer from *vertigo*. In this position *Madame Chronomètre* is unsighted. Needless to say, she is not unsighted when it comes to seeing the selection of *bara brith, pice ar y maen* and other delicacies on the cake stall next to her. This apparent weakness in the vital speed measurement process is overcome by the siting of a second official on a stepladder just outside the south entrance of *la grande tente* from where she can maintain visual contact with a third official standing on her husband`s shoulders on the clifftop overlooking Skomer. These two officials in turn communicate along a chain of highly trained *Mesdames Signaleurs* positioned at strategic points along the cliffs between *la grande tente* and Tenby. Jumping up and down and waving red and green flags held in the right hand and left hand respectively in a predetermined fashion is the method used to indicate the vessel's progression along the test route from the moment the coracle, travelling eastwards, emerges from behind Skomer, to the moment it disappears behind Caldey, thus completing the test run.

This process is repeated three times whereupon *La Matemática*[18] as she is affectionately known, a mathematician from Goodwick, works out the mean speed of the coracle. *Mesdames Signaleurs* and other officials are Machlud y Wawr volunteers who operate a shift system in order to share flag bearing duties with attending to the refreshments on the stall. These refreshments are keenly sought after by the assembled world`s press, the Bishops of Crymych and St Davids,[13] the Chief Executive and Cabinet of Pembrokeshire County Council, assorted Town, City and County Councillors,[19] visiting dignitaries and others.

Usually more than three runs are needed. The reasons for this are listed in the World Sea-Speed Record Official Handbook as follows.

- One of the dozens of *Mesdames Signaleurs* can get their right and left mixed up resulting in the raising or lowering of the wrong coloured flag.
- Someone might be drinking tea and chatting to a friend whilst inadvertently standing between *Madame Chronomètre* and the official on the stepladder, thus rendering useless this crucial first and last link in the chain.
- *La Matemática*, always under great time pressure, sometimes gets her calculations wrong. And sometimes, in the confusion, she thinks in both Spanish and Irish at the same time, which makes matters worse.
- *Madame Chronomètre* can be distracted from her duties by the appearance of a cup of tea and appropriate delicacy placed on the table alongside her by a thoughtful colleague.
- The test run being done during a change of shift.
- The test run being done in thick fog.
- The test run being done at night.

These blips and many more that remain undocumented by the well-oiled machine that is the World Sea-Speed Measuring and Recording Team may cause unnecessary delays.

The modified coracle used in record attempts is stripped of all extraneous and unnecessary material in order to keep its weight down and thus increase its speed. This includes the ship-to-shore radio and all other communication and navigation devices, particularly those with social networking site access as it is generally thought these might be a source of distraction. Tea making facilities are also removed. A paddle, goggles, psilocybin tablets and a test pilot with attached nutrients is thought by experts to be the minimum requirement. This means of course that the pilot does not know what is happening in the hostile environment outside his or her fragile seaborn and occasionally airborne bubble. Many regard being unable to communicate with the test pilot a good thing. If a problem arises and a rerun is necessary *Mesdames Signaleurs* change seamlessly to black and gold flags, jump up and down whilst waving them enthusiastically to catch the test pilot's attention, and then attempt, by waving the flags in a fashion reminiscent of semaphore, to convey the appropriate message to him or her. Common messages used on such occasions include LAST MEASUREMENT INCONCLUSIVE STOP. MADAME CHRONOMÈTRE UNSIGHTED STOP. PLEASE RERUN STOP. OMG STOP STOP. Etc.

The rocket the team hope will propel the coracle to victory uses solid fuel in the form of anthracite from Merthyr, a liquid oxidiser and green electricity, to keep the craft within Welsh Government[20] guidelines for renewables, generated by a windmill welded to the starboard side. This last item was the brainchild of a Dale farmer who worked out that as the coracle travelled in an easterly direction into a strong wind from the east, the forward motion of the coracle would generate extra spin from the blades of the windmill, thus increasing energy production. Early tests revealed the following flaws in this theory.

1   The stronger the wind from the east the slower the craft could travel because of wind resistance. A coracle is oblongish with a very high blob factor and thus not aerodynamic – at all.

2   If the wind changes direction, as it often does in the microclimate of the Pembrokeshire Peninsular, and appears from the southwest, thus passing through the blades from behind, causing them to rotate in the wrong direction, this would result in the coracle spinning uncontrollably, going into reverse and heading out into the Atlantic. The prevailing winds are from the southwest, a little-known fact not lost on the courageous test pilot.

3   Bird strike, which at supersonic speeds is a serious matter for a coracle no matter what direction it`s travelling in. Birds are also known to have been killed as they hit the rotating paddle for`ards. Travelling head on into a flock of seagulls at Mach 1 is also uncomfortable for the test pilot.

4   It`s wrong.

At 16 feet long and with a 12-inch diameter, the rocket is the biggest of its type in Europe. It works in combination with a jet engine from a Eurofighter Typhoon aircraft[21] and a 750bhp Cosworth[22] F1 engine. Together they generate the equivalent of 135,000hp, equal to 180 F1 cars. Cruising speed between the marker islands is expected to be more than a mile in 3.6 seconds. Given the distance between Skomer and Caldey is approximately nine miles it is hoped the coracle will cover the distance in less than 32.4 seconds, comparing favourably with the monster attraction at Oakwood,[23] named appropriately **Drenched**, at which attraction test pilots spend weeks following a rigorous training regime before taking part in any record attempt.

The fact that travelling from Skomer to Caldey is not done in a straight line because a little thing called the Pembrokeshire coast gets in the way is not thought to be a disadvantage. Indeed, this is seen as adding to the challenge as cornering and navigating the treacherous waters under the cliffs whilst travelling at around 1,000mph and bouncing around all over the place almost blinded by the salt spray on the goggles is thought to add a certain *je ne sais quoi* to the experience and is seen by *connoisseurs* as the ultimate test of paddling technique. The other World Sea-Speed record which requires a straight run between two points half a mile apart on a dead calm inland lake in Death Valley in the Brecon Beacons is thought by many to be for wimps.

In order to hasten his recovery from the shock of hearing that his dream of breaking the World Sea-Speed record had been shattered the Sergeant walked to the galley and made himself a mug of tea. Sitting at the table he picked up the dooby doo, pointed it at the on-board radio attached halfway up the starboard bulkhead between the fridge freezer and a black and white photograph of Arianrhod, pressed 'On', put it back on the table and leaned far back into the chair, arms behind his head. "In 1960 Charles `Chuck` Yeager,[24] flying an experimental rocket plane, became the first human to break the sound barrier," crackled the voice of the Radio Free Pembrokeshire[25] space aeronautics reporter. "Yesterday, an extreme sport *aficionado* did the same thing, but without a plane. At sunrise over the desert high in the Cambrian Mountains Captain Seisyllt Baumgartner,[26] Welsh mother, Austrian father, a combustible combination if ever there was one, paddled out of the capsule that a fifty-storey high balloon had carried to 128,098.5 feet at the edge of space before heading south. Well, not exactly south, rather straight towards that big, round, blue green thing. His $200,001-dollar pressurised coracle accelerated through the stratosphere to 835mph, breaking the sound barrier to reach Mach 1.25. The free fall lasted over four minutes before he pulled the cord that caused the parachute to open. This increased the technical difficulty experienced by the pilot as he now had to steer one-handed with the broad-bladed paddle, which when used by an expert describes a sculling figure-of-eight pattern, the other hand making adjustments to the parachute, thus controlling the path of descent. Travelling through a near vacuum in 1% of ground level atmospheric pressure the coracle accelerated from 0-835mph in under 40 seconds. This is a record for such a vessel. As the air density increased during the approach the coracle stopped spinning wildly as he regained control by means of deft movements of the paddle. Seeing this the back-up team in the sponsor`s van cheered. The second parachute was deployed at 5,000 feet and moments later he executed a perfect splashdown into an inflatable paddling pool next to the van, albeit with a bump or two in the shallow water. In extreme sports` circles bumps are disregarded when points for style are awarded."

"It is appropriate here to give the listener some technical details. The coracle used is oval in shape, similar to half a walnut shell, but bigger of course, the body made of a framework of split and interwoven willow. The paddle is also willow. Hazel is used for the weave. The outer layer is horse skin waterproofed with a thin layer of tar. The under surface has no keel, making it ideal for this attempt as there is less drag as the coracle falls to earth, making steering easier for the pilot. The design used is that of the Teifi coracle, flat bottomed to cope with the river conditions found in that river where coracles have to negotiate the shallow rapids that appear during the summer. These conditions mimic that of the turbulence experienced as an object descends through the Earth`s atmosphere. Other designs, such as that of the Carmarthen coracle, rounder and deeper for its use on the tidal waters of the Tywi, are obviously unsuitable for space flight.

The pilot is seated in the bow of the vessel facing the direction of travel with paddle held to the front. One obvious advantage the coracle has over other space craft is that it can be easily carried by one person, thus making costly transport vehicles unnecessary. *Llwyth gŵr ei gorwg*[27] (*The abundance of a man is his coracle*), as they say in west Wales."

"At the beginning of the fall, or guided free flight as the Western Mail[28] described it, he had no sense of acceleration, movement or noise. "*Rhyfedd iawn.*" (All very strange.) He was heard to say to himself and to the world, most of whom were listening in. A moment later adding, "*Tawelwch absoliwt, llonyddwch absoliwt.*" (Absolute quiet, absolute stillness.) Strapped by a thin strip of hazel bark onto the willow rod that served as the pilot`s seat this was truly a death-defying feat. If the pressurised coracle malfunctioned Seisyllt Baumgartner`s blood would have boiled causing the handsome young extreme coracler to flush and he would not have been happy with that as millions were watching via a live stream on the internet. If the life support system failed and the parachutes failed to open, he would have died a few short minutes later. In space the margin for error is small."

"Scientists at the Centre for Advanced Welsh and Celtic Space Flight[29] at their base near the National Library of Wales[30] in Aberystwyth are using this event to test whether parachuting from stricken vessels at these heights could prove to be a viable means of escape. For the developing private space industry much publicised by *entrepreneurs* of late, safety is paramount. CAWCSF scientists gathered in their favourite caffi, The Cabin in Pier Street[31] in Aberystwyth, for a coffee during the descent and were joined by others from the US Air Force,[32] the recently formed Scottish Air Force and NASA. Russian and Chinese observers were also present disguised as students, as were an attachment of space hackers from North Korea. On the high plains of the Cambrian Plateau, the site of a rumoured UFO landing in 1947, conditions were perfect. The landing was described as "... a smooth series of splashes and bumps." The pilot made adjustments to the flight path by varying the tilt and rotation speed of the paddle and guided the craft towards the 10 foot by 12-foot inflatable paddling pool hired especially from an outdoor shop in Aberystwyth for the occasion. The 18-inch-deep water cushioned the crafts arrival back on *terra firma.*"

"In 1965 a NASA report discussing manned space flight concluded that '..... a human being is the lowest cost ..... non-linear, all-purpose computer system which can be mass produced by unskilled labour.'" The Sergeant reflected upon this occasionally as he lay awake at night pondering the many variables related to the future of space coracling. "Manned or unmanned?" he would ask himself. "Unskilled?" This puzzled him. His wife understood and commented, "I know nothing about space flight, but I know my husband."[33]

Hollywood has reportedly paid millions for the film rights and filming of *The Coracler Who Fell to Earth*[34] is expected to begin at a secret location just outside Tregaron in the spring. An interesting artistic license that will cause a *frisson* of excitement in the town, and a departure from real life events, will be the depiction of Captain Baumgartner as a Twm Siôn Cati like character."

Musing upon the magnitude of the event and how complicated it must be to guide such a craft from the edge of space into a 10 foot by 12-foot paddling pool located on the Cambrian Plateau, the Sergeant thought proudly of his vessel's guidance control system that featured three main components. First, the latest TwmTwm[10] device nailed to the hull just to starboard of the paddle mounting. Second, a mass observation technique consisting of himself and The Parrot who`s perch can be moved from the galley and lashed to the foredeck as required. Third, a radar system so sensitive it can detect a single butterfly passing by thousands of feet overhead. After the radar was fitted he became involved in an interesting project along with a group of scientists and laypeople to uncover the 9,000-mile migratory pattern of *Cynthia Cardui*, the gorgeous Painted Lady butterfly, whose caterpillars feed on thistles that grow abundantly around the edge of the lake on the stern. Their remarkable journey is not taken by a single individual but by successive generations breeding along the way, which means the Painted Ladies returning to the stern in the autumn are several generations removed from those that left earlier in the year. It takes six generations every year for the butterflies to make the trip, all by instinct. With no opportunity to learn from older, experienced butterflies, the Painted Ladies undertake their intercontinental migration from North Africa to the stern to Norway and Iceland and back to the stern and then North Africa. And all this for a butterfly weighing less than a gram and with a brain the size of a pin head. Each new generation instinctively flies its part of the journey. Their flight path averages an altitude of 1,600 feet using winds to reach cruising speeds of up to 30mph. This low altitude is one of the reasons the migration pattern was not suspected until modern sophisticated radar was used. However, the radar is completely useless for navigation purposes as it looks vertically up into the heavens and the coracle travels horizontally.

Loud bursts of the bubbling song of a Cetti's warbler, Cettia cetti, of the family Sylviidae that includes warblers and babblers rings out over the stern as it marks its territory. Recent debate fuelled by current molecular data leans towards a crucial reclassification of these skulking birds from Old World warblers to Old World babblers. Embarrassed by the fuss and not wanting to be drawn into the dispute the bird itself is nowhere to be seen as it lies low in the marsh between the willow grove and the lake. Black, brown and white dippers approximately seven inches long can be seen walking into the water on the lake's edge before submerging to swim underwater in search of freshwater shrimps. Small, brown and white sand martins with short thin beaks demonstrate great agility in flight as they feed on flying insects above the surface of the water. Later, they will winter in Africa. Snipe, with mottled brown camouflage plumage, short legs and long straight slender bills wade in shallow water on the moorland nearby feeding on insect larvae in the mud.

A group of cassowaries, flightless birds 5 to 6.5 feet tall, feed on fruit, shoots and grass seeds in the tropical area to the south of the lake. Small vertebrates keep a safe distance, as does the Sergeant, from this, the world's most dangerous bird.

A short distance beyond the harbour wall a group of large white gannets over three feet long with six-foot wingspan, long bills, black-tipped wings and yellowish heads enjoy themselves by repeatedly flying high and circling leisurely in anticipation before dive bombing into the sea to catch fish. A pair of brown sea eagles with white tails, holidaying from the Isle of Rum, with wingspans reaching over eight feet, snatch fish from the water and pluck unwary rabbits from the cliffs. The shrill, wailing cries of lapwings carry across the Parrog attracting the attention of a party of visitors sitting outside the *café* sipping long and short macchiatos. Not far off, curlews, the largest of Pembrokeshire's wading birds, search the mud with long, downcurved bills for shellfish and shrimps. Their evocative cur lee call mingles with the cries of the gannets. Long-distance migrants, a flock of dunlins, small waders with slightly decurved bills, feed on insects, snails and worms.

High above at over 6,000 feet a pair of dark blackish-brown Australian Wedge Tailed Eagles, the male with a wingspan of over 9 feet and the female with a wingspan of nearly 8 feet, both with fully feathered legs, have been soaring for hours without wingbeat enjoying the mild weather. Their keen eyesight, extending into ultraviolet bands, searches for prey on the stern far below.

A group of goliath tigerfish of the family Alestidae, some over 6 feet long and weighing up to 11 stones, ferocious, aggressive, and not often seen so far from the Congo Basin in Africa, hunt silently in the warm waters of the shallows on the southern aspect of the lake, their huge, interlocking, dagger-like, razor-sharp teeth poised to strike.

The broad yellow and brown flowers of Valviloculus pleristaminis, which grows plentifully here, shimmy in a light offshore breeze. Local gardeners say the plant has thrived in the county for 100 million years.

Rabbits playing in the cottonwoods along the river flowing into the lake stop and look up, noses twitching and wiggling. They sense rain approaching from the other side of the fourth meridian west.

On the grasslands to the south of the lake a giant anteater, uncommon in north Pembrokeshire, seven feet long and weighing over ten stones with elongated muzzle and long, sticky, flicking tongue, scoops up insects at the rate of 35,000 a day. Having no teeth, it swallows its prey whole.

High above, along the rim of the volcano situated on the north of the stern and at a little over 22,000 feet, a family of yellow-rumped leaf-eared mice play. On the eastern aspect of the volcano at 11,530 feet lie the remains of *Ötzie* the Icewoman, who died, killed by an arrow, her body frozen and enveloped in ice shortly after. Covered in tattoos and with a copper axe in one hand she has lain patiently just beneath the surface for over 5,300 years waiting to be discovered. Amongst her possessions are what scientists will conclude is an acupuncture kit, a remarkable discovery as this will place acupuncture on the stern over 2,000 years before the earliest known use in China. Analysis of pollen, wheat grains and the seeds of berries found in her stomach along with the isotopic composition of her tooth enamel will indicate she spent her childhood near the village hall in Brynberian. Cylindrical containers made from birch bark and filled with healing herbs are held safely in the grasp of her other hand. Non politically correct *fashionistas* and followers of *haute couture* will thrill to hear this Neolithic acupuncturist and healer wore a loincloth made from sheepskin, with fur inside to keep her bits warm, leggings and a coat of goat hide. A generous, brown bearskin hat and accessories made from wild cows and roe deer complete the look.

In the post-Roman era, archaeologists suggest the period AD536-541, volcanic eruptions in Central America disrupted agricultural life on the stern causing the breakdown of social structures. It is this shocking event, historians believe, that gave rise to the Viking myth of the *Fimbulwinter*, the almost endless winter.

Small and hairy Carneddau Mountain Ponies graze the remote uplands nearby as their ancestors have done since the Bronze Age.

Late in the day, as darkness falls on the stern, crickets, with cylindrical bodies, round heads, long antennae and efficient feed conversion ratios, lie hidden under fallen logs and stones in the willow grove. Nocturnal insects, their loud, irritating chirping noise keeps an annoyed Sergeant awake on hot summer nights whenever he attempts to sleep outside in the hammock. Soothed by the melody The Parrot counts the number of chirps per minute and using the species appropriate variation of Dolbear's Law,[35] in which $T = 50+[(N-40)/4]$, where T is the ambient air temperature and N is the number of chirps per minute, decides which pair of luxury super soft fleece onesies, the overall look augmented by the wise addition of a sequinned Wonderland full tutu skirt, would be appropriate for sleep in the willow grove that night.

Wearied by the earlier disappointment the Sergeant lies on his back in the hammock asleep. All but his head is hidden under the two ply *carthen* with fringes on all four sides, shorter on the warp than the weft and with reverse twill in distinctive plaid design, his favourite. Facing the clear open sky above, the surface of his face loses energy in the form of infrared light due to radiative cooling and reaches a cooler temperature than the surrounding air. Some of his body heat escapes to the upper atmosphere which is much colder. Some escapes into outer space. Frost forms on his nose, lips and eyebrows.

8

Ordinary human love is capable of raising a person to the experience
of real love.

Hakim Jami[1]

"I`m going to kidnap you and hold you captive," Megan`s husband told her
the day they met, "wait thirty years, then send our grandchildren a ransom note."
She was going through her pink, punk, Jemima Nicholas, fusion stage and her hair
looked like an exploding firework. "You are the most beautiful 'device containing
gunpowder and other combustible chemicals which causes spectacular effects and
explosions when ignited'[2] I have ever seen," he told her.

"I have friends who seek happiness through extreme experiences," she
replied, overcome by nervous feelings. "They go skydiving you know, jumping out
of aeroplanes. Some of them wear parachutes." This bore no relevance to what he
had just said yet it calmed her nerves.

When they lived together in Cilwendeg, their smallholding, he rose at six
thirty every morning, dressed quietly so as not to wake her and went outside
where he let the chickens, ducks, geese and guinea fowl out and fed them, as well
as the peacock, who, along with one of the guinea fowl, slept at night in the
sycamore tree overlooking the chicken run. During the winter he let Cati and Cothi,
the two horses, out of the stable (they only had five acres, not enough for the
horses to be out grazing all year round) and gave them some haylage. The three
dogs, Brychan, a giant Northern Inuit and two Jack Russells, Aneirin and Taliesin,
would come out from under the bed where they slept to accompany him. The two
cats, Seren and Tegi, who slept on the bed had usually already left through the
cat flap. Sometime later, the chores finished, he returned with the dogs and made
breakfast for himself and Megan which they ate in bed. She would have a croissant
with full fat butter, a *mocha*, a *cortado* and a double *expresso*. "It`s like being
plugged into the mains," she confided to him, "and it rearranges my hairdo."
Immediately after breakfast she always took advice about the day`s weather
from the *tylwyth teg* who live in the vine climbing the outside wall surrounding the
east facing window. This was her favourite time of day, enjoying the beautiful
views of the surrounding tree covered slopes of the valley through the floor to
ceiling windows filling the south and east facing walls of the bedroom. His
breakfast was two poached eggs, a handful of mixed nuts and an apple cut into
pieces, all in a bowl drizzled with extra virgin olive oil with raw garlic and a mug of
weak tea.

Megan rode every morning, rain or shine, with Brychan running alongside. Through the woods and onto the mountains, travelling fifteen to twenty miles each time. Broadleaved trees are in abundance in the surrounding woods providing an ideal habitat for red squirrels and a myriad other creatures. Fungi such as mushrooms and toadstools appear from the soil as if by magic. The earliest known spiny mammal lived in the warmer climes of the south of the county 125 million years ago alongside dinosaurs. Hedgehogs, evolving a mere 15 million years ago are north Pembrokeshire's only spiny mammal and have settled in surprisingly well. With long legs, short tails and coats containing thousands of creamy-white spines, a feature that evolved independently in mammals several times, they are happy in this environment. Even though they have poor eyesight hedgehogs appear mostly at night, halting frequently as they move around to smell the air as they search for beetles, caterpillars, earthworms and slugs to eat as well as fruits and mushrooms. By day they sleep in nests of leaves, moss and grass where their litters of hoglets are born. On patches of open moorland amongst the trees the delicate mauve flowers of heather can be seen, appearing above wiry, woody stems bearing rows of narrow leaves. Pollinating insects are attracted to them.

They got on best in the hours after she returned from a ride. Horse riding was her joy and always raised her spirits. She found a serenity in riding that she did not find anywhere else. This had been an invisible barrier at the beginning of their relationship as he was convinced that he was unable to be a catalyst for such happiness in her. "No need to try," she reassured him whenever she noticed the worried frown. "You are a catalyst when you try and when you don`t try. I love being with you. I love the love that you are."

The smallholding, which lay in the mountains to the west of Crymych, was their delight. After his death 'joy left her heart, her dancing turned to mourning'. Megan thought about this for a while, then, with gratitude for what had been, she embraced her grief, let it be, and moved into the crypt to begin anew. Gratitude for life as it is.

Their engagement went according to plan. Megan`s plan. "We're going out to dinner on Saturday night," she informed him, "to the revolving restaurant at the top of the Twm Carnabwth Tower and we`ll discuss the terms of your surrender over a nice Chardonnay."

Several times a day he would turn to one or other of the children and say "*Waŵ! Wyt ti mor dda, cariad. Da iawn, cariad.* " (Waw! You`re so good, cariad. Very good, cariad.) They would fill with warmth and smile. Then he`d kiss them. He never raised his voice to them. Not once. And he said everything in a positive way. One morning the youngest was carrying a bowl of cereal to the breakfast table in the kitchen. He was about five years old. He tripped on the upturned edge of the carpet, the bowl falling from his grasp and smashing on the floor, cereal and milk splashing everywhere. Then Megan`s husband`s voice. "*Popeth yn iawn,* *cariad. Damwain o`dd hi.*" (All is well, cariad. It was an accident.) He went across to the child and picked him up and gave him a big *cwtsh*, repeating "*Popeth yn iawn, cariad. Damwain o`dd hi.*" He pointed to the pattern created by the milk and cereal on the floor and at small rivulets of milk with cornflakes travelling along them like small boats. And they laughed. Then Megan came in, saw the mess and told them both off. But lovingly, without really meaning it, the telling off that is. And they knew that. And they felt the love.

"You`ve given me the greatest gift," he would tell her.

"What`s that?"

"An opportunity to be of benefit to you and the kids."

She was glad she had met a gentle man, gentle in speech and action. As she got to know him, she occasionally saw emotions appear in his face, anger, depression, jealousy, and so on. But he seemed to let them go. As if they weren`t who he was. As if there was jealousy, but he was somewhere else. He was separate from it. In another place. "You are Life pretending to be my husband," she would say

The decor of the office in the crypt annexe where Megan sat reading Machlud y Wawr`s monthly newsletter[3] is a pastiche of New Classicism. Or maybe Old Classicism. Time goes slower in there than anywhere else, which means she can catch up on the local newspapers. Or is it Neoclassicism?

1,001 tunes for the Carmarthenshire Bagpipes was playing softly in the background via a live-streaming app on her smart phone. She found it relaxing whilst perusing the back pages of the newsletter. The computer flickered into life. Putting the newsletter down she glanced at the latest Reuters report that appeared on the screen. "Good news at last," she thought as she read the opening paragraph. "The theft of black and white television sets in Pembrokeshire, the so called `Steal a deal`, is down on last year. Is this a trend?" she wondered, gazing affectionately at the 1940`s imported Admiral Combination Console Set filling the corner. She continued reading for a while before returning to the crypt where she sat in the armchair in the *simne fawr,* turned the music off, picked up the dooby doo from the small round table next to her, aimed it at the radio, pressed 'Play', replaced the dooby doo, sank back into the chair and closed her eyes. "And now, remember tomorrow," came the voice of the BBC Radio Wales[4] presenter, "it`s Megansday."

"I`d forgotten," she whispered to the room, but didn`t really mean it.

The voice continued. "Yes, in Dublin they have Bloomsday[5] on the 16th of June and in Carmarthen they have Megansday on the 27th of September to celebrate the day Megan, aided by other students, added one more measurement to the measurers` armamentarium. `The Megan`, which is 5ft 8¼ inches in length is now recognised the world over, from Carmarthenshire County Council[6] to the tech giants of Silicon Valley.[7] Megan was 5ft 8¼ inches tall when beginning her first year as a student at the University of the Four Trinity Davids[8] in Carmarthen and fell for an old trick the final year students play on those newly arrived. She was told the University needed to measure the distance across the river Tywi for a proposed bridge linking the railway station with the town. It was to be called Coracle Bridge, thoughtfully named by County Councillors[6] with the history and culture of thousands of years of coracling on the river since the last Ice Age in mind. And she was to be the unit of measurement."

In a speech in Carmarthen after the bridge was built, given to students, lecturers, the university senate,[8] County Councillors, AMs, MPs, the High Sheriff of Carmarthenshire[9] and members of the public who came to join in the celebrations, Megan recalled being stretched out on her stomach on the floor of a coracle seventy-seven and a half times as the senior students measured the distance across the Tywi by slowly paddling the vessel from one bank to the other as Megan prostrated herself repeatedly. This is not the most accurate method of measuring the distance between two points, but they were arts students. The strong current repeatedly carrying them off course didn't help. She told them how pleased she was to be an International Standard.

The phone lying on the table next to the newsletter rang. Megan glanced at it and swiped 'Answer call'. It was Ceridwen, a Machlud y Wawr member, and she was in tears. "How cruel!" she wailed at the other end. "The Welsh Government[10] is cruel. So cruel. Cruel! Cruel! Cruel!"

Megan heard Ceridwen`s foot stamp. "I don`t understand. What`s happened?"

"My bus pass arrived through the post this morning."

"Isn`t that good?" Now you can travel anywhere on the bus in Wales for free."

"Good! Good? Don`t you understand? You get your bus pass when you`re sixty. I`ve been officially declared old. Old! Old! Old!"

Megan heard the foot again. "Oh!" she said.

"The Muppets[11] are running the teashop," sobbed Ceridwen.

Thinking to get her friend`s mind off the problem Megan asked, "Why don`t you come to the theatre with me tonight?"

"What`s on?"

"The Vagina Monologues II.[12] The Welsh language version. In Theatr y Gromlech. It starts at half past seven."

"Ahhh! Vaginas. Is there nothing they can`t do? I feel better already. I'll come."

"Wonderful. See you outside fifteen minutes before the start."

Megan tapped 'End call' on the screen of the phone, turned the radio off and picked up the latest edition of *Gambero Rosso*[13] which arrives through the post thus ensuring Machlud y Wawr`s culinary skills include more than *bara brith*, which rhymes with teeth, *cawl, cocos a bara lawr, pice ar y maen* and *ffa pob ar dost*. She made a mental note of the only *pizzeria* in the county *Gambero Rosso* had awarded its top honour of `three cloves` to, Tenby`s world famous Tŷ Pîtsa eating house situated in a prime spot on Goskar's Rock.

"Saundersfoot *pizza* makers," she read, "have accused Italy`s top food guide of culinary discrimination after its new edition failed to include any *pizzerias* from other towns, or city of course, in the county outside Tenby. This is an eruption of the rivalry between Tenby and Saundersfoot, one that forever simmers just beneath the surface. Just ask Saunders what happened to his foot several centuries ago when some toffs from the neighbouring town visited one Friday night. Swansea and Cardiff have got nothing on this."

"Outraged *restauranteurs* from all over Pembrokeshire demonstrated outside County Hall in Haverfordwest last week carrying placards saying such things as `Shame on *Gambero Rosso*`, `They Want to Steal Our *Pizza*` and `Sam Warburton Was Innocent`. They argue that the modern *pizza* comes from the tomato-covered dough served in Naples, adding that cheese was not added until 1889. Therefore, Tŷ Pîtsa actually serves a *focacceria*. A point of little or no significance to the general public but to the *coinnoisseur* this is everything."

"Their petition was accepted by the head of the appropriate Council Department[14] who expressed her concerns and reassured the protesters who earlier in the day converged on the catering department of Pembrokeshire College[15] on the hill at the back of the town where they held a mass *pizzathon* with speeches and singing before marching along Freemen's Way into town. The *impromptu* procession was led by local band Samba Doc[16] and caused considerable disruption to traffic. Turning left into Picton Place they marched across the bridge, along Victoria Place, arriving at Castle Square where they bought essential supplies which they munched happily as they proceeded out of town again, much to the consternation of the Mayor[17] who had just launched into her keynote speech. Back along Freemen's Way they went to the roundabout, causing more disruption to traffic, where they turned right up Merlin's Hill, along Milford Road and down the hill to Castle Square, along Bridge Street, right across the pedestrian bridge, right again along Riverside, across the footbridge and back to Castle Square where the Mayor perked up and began her speech again at which point the procession left and moved along Victoria Place and took a right after crossing the bridge before assembling outside the main entrance of County Hall where they proceeded to make a lot of noise, as crowds tend to do. The route was longer than planned because the drummers at the head of the merry throng wanted a good airing and because the Mayor intended giving a speech."

"The Mayor arrived and continued with her speech. They listened patiently. And listened. And listened. Then several very important Councillors[18] droned on and on. They perked up when the last Councillor said, 'Something will be done.

Starting today and over the next few months the Chief Executive, senior officers and members of the Cabinet, especially Independents,[18] will do a tour of all the *pizza* establishments in Pembrokeshire, visiting one every Thursday evening to decide whether or not there has been bias. Taxpayers need have no doubt that their money is being well spent investigating this. A lengthy official report will then be published and debated fiercely before being shelved. Members of the public interested in reading the report can get a copy by submitting a request to the appropriate authorites via the Freedom of Information Act.' The protestors engaged in a few choruses of popular Pembrokeshire folk songs accompanied by the Strumble Head Melodeon Orchestra and *Côr y Dysgwyr*[19] before adjourning to the Machlud y Wawr refreshments` *marquee* in the car park to the south of County Hall that had been hastily erected that morning for just such an eventuality. A short while later council enforcement officers moved them on explaining that it was illegal for the public to congregate near Cabinet members' parking spaces."[18]

Meanwhile, back in the crypt, *Dawnswyr Clocsiau Maenclochog*,[20] fresh from their gold medal performance at the recent World Clog Dancing Championships[21] held on the Medvednica mountain north of Zagreb, were whipping up a frenzy with their clog version of *Sali Mali and the Giant Eirinen Wlanog*,[22] soon to be released on DVD. Bronwen was so inspired she clogged around the crypt tackling the furniture. Many moons ago Bronwen declared a moratorium on remembering things, being concerned that her brain was becoming unnecessarily cluttered with STUFF. She lives now in the beauty of the moment. Which particular moment at any given time no one is too sure about.

Megan stood up, left the *simne fawr*, walked across the crypt and up onto the small stage where she sat on the Honorary Senior Life President's chair, pressed the automatic `adjust` button on the side and felt herself raised several inches and moved forward to an upright position, her favourite when giving a talk, ready to address the assembled Machlud y Wawr members at their monthly meeting. Tonight, the chosen subject was one of her favourites. "The Black Truffle of Llangloffan," she began as gasps of incredulity and wonder rang out from the members and echoed, a little alarmingly it must be said, around the stone walls, pillars, floor, ceiling and alcoves, "will soon be available all year round." More gasps bounced around the room. She paused to allow the roar to recede. "Our members have spent months planting thousands of oak trees in Llangloffan, each inoculated to produce Tuber Melaniesporum, the perfect truffle. As an aside, they have also been inoculated against Swine Flu." More gasps and applause from the sea of adoring faces in front of her. "The secret concoction used to inoculate was developed by scientists at the Welsh National Truffle Institute situated just outside Llanwnda. The next phase is to train corgis to sniff out the truffles that will supply local restaurants, with enough left over to export to Swansea Market.[23]

The hardy Welsh oak is particularly well suited to Wales and to truffling, so well in fact that we expect to see truffle production happening all year round. At a meeting in the Senedd [24] yesterday government economists predict that this will bring as much as £17,000,000 a year into the local economy. Thank you, ladies." She pressed a button on the arm rest and was propelled forward, thus giving what appeared to be a small bow before falling back into the chair. She received a standing ovation as enthusiasm and delight spilt over.

After pausing a moment for the room to become quieter she added, "Remember what Charles Darwin said, `It`s not the strongest of the species that survives, not the most intelligent that survives. It`s the one that is most adaptable to change.` We are adapting ladies. We will survive." Megan is not one to put all her Peigs into the same Blasket.[25] The cheering lifted the roof and celebrations went on late into the night. Very late. Very, very late. Too late for Bronwen, poor dab. They put the roof back before breakfast.

When the Memberati come together in teeming hordes, as at their monthly MachludyWawrathon as it is affectionately called by those in the know, energy levels run high. Naturalists have termed it `bio-abundance`.

Megan stood up. "Are you coming or going?" asked a unit of bio-abundance seated on a corner of the tomb of the Unknown Clogger.

"Going."

"Wrong answer," said Ceridwen

"What do you mean?"

The correct response to the question "Are you coming or going?" is, "I don`t know if I`m ....."

Megan left. She had a newsletter to finish. She went to the reading room situated just off the northeast transept of the Cathedral, a place of peace and quiet. She found her favourite seat, bathed as it is by the late afternoon sunlight coming through the stained-glass window with its sensitive portrayal of Gareth Edwards scoring that try against the Barbarians in 1973 in a sequence of fifteen pictures around the edges with Cliff Morgan's immortal commentary written in gold in the middle, "Oh! That fellow Edwards. If the greatest writer of the written word would have written that story, no one would have believed it. That really was something." In another window is Bill Mclaren`s quote about another try, this one against Scotland in 1972, "The sheer magic of Gareth Edwards has brought the whole of this stadium to its feet. You can read on his face the effort, the power, the strength, the fitness that took him there." Another window on the opposite side immortalises Scott Gibbs' try against England in Wembley along with Eddie Butler`s words, "Scott don't do that. Just touch down for the try." Also in the reading room, in pride of place on a wall gathering sunlight from the south facing window opposite, is an autographed black and white photograph of Eileen Beasley, Wales' Rosa Parks, and an inspiration to the members.

Enjoying the sunshine, she took the Tenby Today newsletter out of her handbag and turned to the headline on page one, "Tenby furious. Hmmm. This might be interesting." She read on. "Residents of Tenby were furious earlier this week when scientists from the Institute for Life Research in Saundersfoot claimed to have found a clue to the origins of life in the town. The new discovery, described as earth-shaking, has been made by their eight wheeled, nuclear-powered rover which landed in Tenby last summer after an uneventful trip on the number 349 from Haverfordwest. Since then, the rover has been collecting samples of soil using its built-in scoop and placing them in an instrument called SAT (Sample Analysis Tenby), a mini on-board chemistry laboratory which analyses the chemicals present. The results are historic. A spokesperson for the Institute revealed to the press that the soil samples, particularly those taken from flowerpots outside hotels in the South Beach area, contain organic compounds. Organic does not mean alive she added, merely that carbon is present. Carbon containing compounds are found in space in star-forming clouds, meteorites, asteroids and comets. Finding organic compounds in Tenby is strong circumstantial evidence that the town is home to life. Mrs Lleucu Llwyd,[26] a descendant of King Bleiddudd and Mayoress of the town,[27] gave a press conference in the council chamber this morning in which she observed that the inhabitants of the town are appalled. Local retired colonels, she continued, have received a telegram of support from retired colonels in Tunbridge Wells who have taken time off from being appalled at the lack of apostrophes amongst the younger generation to send their support. The Mayor is putting together a petition which will be presented to the Welsh Government[10] asking them to withdraw funding from the Institute. A candlelit vigil is planned this Saturday evening outside the main entrance. Several coachloads of retired colonels from all over Britain and Ireland are expected to attend. "I`m outraged!" she told reporters. "And appalled!"

"After the press conference the reporters were given cups of tea with milk and sugar included. When a reporter, after taking a sip, pointed out that he didn`t like sugar in his tea, the Mayoress remarked, "Don`t stir it then."

Megan put the newsletter down, returned to the *simne fawr*, turned the radio on, tuned into Radio Free Crymych and joined the middle of an interview during the early evening news. "The new director of Theatr y Gromlech[28] is a thoroughly unsafe pear of hands," spat the County Councillor being interviewed, "and she can`t spell either."

"*O diar!*" thought Bronwen who had joined Megan in the *simne fawr*.

"Yes!" shouted Megan, punching the air. "At last, an unsafe pear of hands."

"But why?" puzzled Bronwen.

"Art appears from chaos," answered Megan, "or at least from what appears to be chaos to the rational mind. Rules are the death of art. Control freaks are the death of creativity." Megan was reminded of what her husband used to tell her, "If I need you in order to be happy, then I don`t love you. If I love you and don`t need you, then I truly am in love." Chaos indeed. At least that was how it seemed to her at the time.

One evening in the back kitchen of the smallholding she was preparing supper. "What do you want with your chips, cariad?"

"I don`t know."

"Make a decision cariad, there`s a queue forming behind you."

He turned around and saw the children holding their wooden bowls. "I can`t."

"Why not?"

"When I look into your eyes my brain turns to mush."

"Mushy peas it is."

"Thank you, cariad."

"You can be my limpet," she said to him. "Forever." She knew him well and sacrificed into compassion.

The newsreader continued. "It is said that perhaps none of the parts of the body that are used in speech evolved so we could talk. We`d still need lungs, a larynx, a throat, a tongue, a palate, teeth, lips, ears, etc. Did they evolve to give us speech? Not according to linguists at the Department of Theoretical Evolutionary Linguistics at the University of North Pembrokeshire at Crymych and colleagues from SOAS[29] in the University of London. The arrangement of these different anatomical features allowed for an increasing range of sounds until, along with developments in the brain that give us meaning, human language appeared. Did eyes, ears and the areas of the brain involved in speech evolve specifically so humans could talk? No. That would be like saying that hands evolved so we could write, or thumbs so that teenagers could text, or that the arm evolved so we could point in the direction of the supermarket when a stranger to town asks us for directions to it."

"Let us consider further. Did arms evolve so we could pass a rugby ball? Did feet appear so we could drop a goal? 'Of course, they did,' say linguists based at Pontypridd Rugby Club.[30] 'With only one eye the frequency of knock ons would be much greater.' Some say humans first stood on two legs at a time in our evolution when we lived in and around shallow water or in the long grass of the hot, African savannah. 'Nonsense!' they say, 'try playing rugby on all fours on a muddy pitch.'"

Megan remembered the first time she met her husband. He walked into *Das Kapital*[31] in the *Piazza della Republica* where she was sitting by the window reading the Daniel Owen Memorial Prize winning novel[32] at that year`s Eisteddfod.[33] She occasionally lifted her head from the book to look through the window and across the *Piazza*, daydreaming. She likes the place because it is big with lots of tables where she sits for hours, absorbed in a book and in the toing and froing of

Crymych. On that fateful day she was the only customer in the *café*. He paused just inside the door after entering then walked slowly into the middle of the room, wondering, puzzling, deliberating, hoping. He stood there quietly for a few moments looking around before walking to the table where Megan was reading and sat opposite her.

"I had a long think," he said, "and after thinking about it I decided this was the best seat."

She lifted her head, looked across at him and smiled.

"Lucky really," he added, "because now I can talk to you."

"Are you chatting me up?"

"The question suggests not."

"Are you trying to chat me up?"

"That`s more like it. I employ a stealth approach. For the first few months you'll have no idea what`s going on."

"I won't?"

"Of course not," he beamed, returning her gaze.

That was how it began. They spent the rest of his life together.

To the west of the Cathedral, grey wagtails, grey head and back with lemon-yellow undertail play above the fast-flowing stream running along the side of the beech wood feeding on ants and midges before returning to their nests in moss and twig lined crevices near the water. Graceful yellow wagtails, summer visitors, sit on branches high in the trees by the edge of the stream watching slow-moving cows graze in the meadow before flying down to run around the feet of the much larger animals, eating beetles and other insects uncovered by their hooves. A white-throated dipper, Crymych's only aquatic songbird, with short tail and wings, dark brown with white throat, stands submerged with large feet planted firmly on the streambed, anchored by grappling-hook like claws as it searches for larvae, nymphs and shrimps. Solid bones increase this small bird's density and help it remain underwater when it dives for food, using its wings to propel itself forward. An oriental dwarf kingfisher, also known as a three-toed kingfisher, over 5 inches in length, sits on a nearby low-lying branch admiring the view. Endemic across much of Crymych, the Indian subcontinent and southeast Asia, its red and yellow head, bluish-black upperparts and yellow underparts glow in the sunlight.

In the meadow nearby, low-growing salad burnet with pinnate leaves and branched stems carrying terminal spikes of small reddish fluffy flowers can be seen alongside Baroness Orczy's scarlet pimpernels with five petalled lilac, orange and bright red flowers. Buttercups with bright yellow shiny petals glisten in the sunlight, waving in concert in the breeze. Other species growing there include betony with magenta-pink flowers borne on square stems, dog rose with sweet smelling, five petalled pink flowers, pyramidal orchids with densely packed pyramid-shaped clusters of bright, pink-purple flowers on green stems, Welsh poppies, papaver cambricum, with characteristic saucer-shaped flowers of four overlapping lemon-yellow petals almost 2 inches across carried on green stems, and tufts of thrift with their compact clusters of cup-shaped pink flowers. All attract nectar loving insects. Symbols of fertility, horny crab apple trees, malus sylvestris grow with wild abandon in this sunny spot.

Mallards, spot-billed ducks, tufted ducks, Australian shoveler ducks, mottled ducks, hardhead ducks, canvasback ducks, chestnut teal ducks, common shelducks, masked ducks, Pacific black ducks, northern pintail ducks, marbled ducks, African black ducks, yellow-billed ducks, dilberry ducks, American black ducks, brown teal ducks, Philippine ducks, rosy-bill ducks, Eurasian wigeon ducks, falcated ducks, bronze-winged ducks, ferruginous ducks, lesser whistling ducks, ring-necked ducks, mandarin ducks, Patagonian crested ducks, blue-billed ducks, ruddy ducks and other ducks swim in the duckpond.

That is such a useless sentence.

Oh well![34]

9

Thunderbirds are go!
Jeff Tracy[1]

`There once was a man called the Sergeant, ...` This is how an Icelandic saga would begin. But we're not in Iceland and this is not a saga. Around the base of the coracle's for'ard mast is burnt the following in Old Norse 'It does not matter how slowly you go as long as you don't stop.'[2] A sentiment Viking seafarers appreciate. Mindful of this, The Parrot, sitting in full lotus position on its perch, plumbed the depths of existence.

It was eight bells in the forenoon and the Sergeant was sitting in the galley with a mug of piping hot tea and some newly cooked cockles and laverbread on fried bread dripping with *Sîr Gâr*[3] butter reading the leading article in the science section of the County Echo.[4] "Why, in some circumstances, does a warm coracle freeze faster during the winter than a cold one? The European Society of Coracling[5] has launched a competition to see if the public can solve this problem, one that continues to baffle coraclologists. In 1968 Dr Denis G. Osborne,[6] a professor of chemistry at Dar es Salaam University in Tanzania, visited a remote school in the west of the country where a student, Erasto Mpemba,[7] put this question to him. Erasto's friends laughed when they heard the question, as did the world-wide scientific community when the professor mentioned it in a draft he wrote to a chemistry journal. They all thought this could not be true. The class teacher, concerned that following discussion of this counterintuitive idea, conflict might arise in the playground during the break between those pupils who held deontological perspectives and those who held consequentialist ethical perspectives, sighed with relief when the conversation turned to a question from another pupil regarding the best way to make dark chocolate in the laboratory."

"One Friday afternoon back in Dar es Salaam a little while after his visit to the school one of the professor's classes was cancelled and he decided it would only take a few minutes to test Erasto's assertion and then he could write to him suggesting where he went wrong. This would be helpful to the young aspiring scientist in a way that laughing at him would not. The experiment took more than a few minutes, however. After eighteen months testing and retesting in the laboratory Erasto's hypothesis was proved to be correct. Warm coracles do freeze faster than cold ones. This understanding led to an emergency health and safety directive being issued from Dyfed-Powys Police Rapid-Response Coracle Unit HQ[8] on Nelson Quay in Milford Haven."

"The scientific community thought the professor`s experiments must be faulty, arguing that a warm coracle has to first become a cold coracle, so it can`t freeze faster than a colder one. They joked that there was Mpemba`s physics and universal physics. However, other scientists around the world experimented and they too found that Erasto was right, and the phenomenon was accepted as real. But how? There are several theories. Does a hot coracle evaporate slightly, leaving less material to freeze? Is it due to degassing, the coracle losing some of its gases, thus allowing it to cool more quickly? Are convection currents set up in the hull as it is heated, which remain as it cools, thus speeding up heat transfer?"

The Sergeant didn`t have an answer. "It doesn`t make sense," he thought, "when winter comes, I have to turn the central heating down!"

The Parrot resurfaced. It sensed the Sergeant`s confusion and decided to help. "Like a Hindu god, the mist does not go away, it just assumes new forms." The words echoed around the galley before leaving for the stern where they played innocently amongst the willow trees.

"Hmmm," said the Sergeant.

A warning bell tolled far offshore.

"But who for?" wondered the Sergeant as his eyes moved to the next article which he read out loud in an attempt to understand it. "Poetry, like music, activates the posterior cingulate cortex and medial temporal lobes, areas linked to memory and introspection, unlike prose."

"Yes," smiled The Parrot. "That's it."

"I knew it," shouted the Sergeant.

"A poem is a song waiting for the music to arrive," pronounced The Parrot as it looked down at the mat lying on the floor in front of the perch. On it were the words, "If you fall, I`ll be down by 'ere."

The Sergeant was content. Next to him on the galley table was a mug of tea and his breakfast, and in his arms his beloved squzbx, squezebox, squeezeeboox, squeeezeeebooox, squeeeezeeeeboooox, squeeezeeeeboooox, squeezeeeboox, squezebox, squzbx. Whilst sipping and munching thoughts of his wife came to him and he sang to the tea and the breakfast whilst accompanying himself on the 48 base, dark-brown, wooden accordion, the coraclers` coracler`s instrument of choice. Although some prefer light brown.

> Well, my heart's like a river, a river that sings,
> Just takes me a while to realize things.
> I've seen the sunrise, I've seen the dawn,
> I'll lay down beside you when everyone's gone.[9]

Sometime later, finished sipping and munching and singing he put the accordion aside, took hold of the butter dish, got up, walked across the galley and opened the fridge door. Glancing cautiously inside he noticed a rapidly deteriorating ecosystem and ducked as bats appeared from the darkness at the back and flew over his head and out through the starboard porthole.

"Is it a good day?" he asked himself. "Am I back?"

"It started well," said The Parrot, "you woke up. And that's a good sign, as in order to wake up, you have to have consciousness."

Unaware of the presence of superionic ice in the freezer compartment he put the butter onto a shelf before closing the fridge door and replacing the lock. Unlike the ice people normally have in the freezer compartment this is black and hot and has strange properties. First predicted over 30 years ago it was discovered by accident as DPPRRCU scientists looked inside the fridge whilst aboard on a routine inspection visit. It is thought to be amongst the most abundant forms of water in the universe, and across the solar system it is probable that more water exists as superionic ice than in any other phase.

Turning, he made his way to the bathroom suite complete with wet room which lay abaft the galley. He needed to shower and shave. It was a Monday morning. The Sergeant didn`t shave at weekends which meant that by now there was a heavy stubble over a large portion of his face, neck and chest. He was looking forward to using his new Deluxe Titanium XXXZ shaver, the one he`d picked up for a song in Carmarthen market. `Safe to a depth of 20 fathoms. As used by astronauts.' was written on the packet.

Whilst adjusting the shaver`s guidance mechanism and putting on the safety harness that came with it the Sergeant thought of the ex-Dutch navy diver who used to work in Fishguard harbour repairing the sea wall. He wore one of those old diver's suits with an air pipe leading up to the support boat and lead boots to keep him on the seabed. One evening, whilst unwinding with locals in one of the pubs on Fishguard Square after a long day working underwater, he told them of the time he was repairing a hole in the stonework at the base of the seawall that appeared after a storm. As he was placing small boulders to fill the space, he noticed a giant Conga eel inside. It was watching him. Not wanting to risk being attacked he quietly finished filling the hole, leaving the creature entombed. "Aye, that there`s the toughest man I`ve ever known," he thought. "He could grow a beard in less than ten minutes flat from a standing start."

The Sergeant tightened the harness secured to the iron girder above the sink and pressed the red button on the shaver marked, 'Start. If you dare.` The coracle shook. The Parrot tightened its grip on the perch. "`Ere we go again," it muttered. The emergency siren sounded. The lights on the vessel flickered briefly, went off, then came back on again. The tremor became a shaking which became a juddering accompanied by a thunderous roar that increased in volume during the shaving procedure. At the front of the vessel the air bag attached to the paddle inflated. Then calm as the automatic timer, an essential safety feature of the XXXZ model, turned the shaver off after 60 seconds. Disorientated, he splashed aftershave everywhere before releasing himself from the harness. Then he splashed aftershave on his face. The Parrot relaxed and breathed a sigh of relief. Later that morning it would do a full systems scan of the vessel to check for damage.

It began to rain. When the French invaded a few years ago it wasn`t Jemima that defeated them, it was the weather. They surrendered when the torrential rain, mist and gale force winds closed in. Rain always made the Sergeant hungry. He made himself a snack of cereal and fruit with soya milk and a pot of tea. He sat by the table in the galley just as Radio Free Pembrokeshire[10] crackled into life again. He gave a start, then listened.

"The Welsh Rugby Union[11] rejoiced in its success this morning as images returned to WRU HQ in Cardiff from their lunar rover as it explores the moon surface, the first one since the glory days of the 1970s. Shortly after the *mam* ship landed the *Cwningen Goch*, as she is called, rumbled down the ramp onto the dust. The *Cwningen Goch* will take a period to acclimatise and then spend the summer mining the moon`s surface in search of Welsh qualified players ready for next season," a WRU spokesperson told the press earlier today.

"The grandmother business is busy again," thought the Sergeant, munching the cereal.

"The first tracks left by the glorious peoples` robot as its wheels hit the lunar surface are stamping new footprints onto the history of lunar exploration. The six wheeled rover has ground-penetrating radar on board to take measurements deep under the crust. The moon landing, a source of national pride and giving us inspiration for further development, is part of the dream to make Welsh rugby stronger and will surely help realise the broader WRU dream of national rejuvenation."

He poured himself a mug of tea. At low temperatures during ocean voyages taken at wintertime the tea is overtaken by quantum effects and becomes a perfect fluid. In this unusual state it behaves in a peculiar fashion, although the taste is unaffected, particularly if it is drunk from a favourite mug.

"Researchers at a university in Norway have published a paper in the journal of Maritime Psychology Reports whose conclusion is that humans are not born coraclers."

He *spluttered* indignantly and **coughed** ...

"They must practise from a young age, say the scientists. Their research disproves the received wisdom that there is a coracling gene."

... and *spluttered*

... and **coughed.**

135

"Instead of there being such a gene, simple practise makes people good at it. Anyone can do it."

Splutter!

Cough!

His face got redder and bluer. His nose achieved a deep purple.

"The brain is plastic so learning can continue throughout life. Age is no bar to becoming an accomplished coracler ....."

Splutter!

Cough!

"..... as practise elicits the formation of new neural pathways. A coracling network, so to speak."

He broke down. Tears of frustration and anger poured from him. The Parrot was alarmed. Fortunately, it didn`t go off. One of the cherished beliefs of the world-wide coracling fraternity was being questioned, nay laid to rest by Norwegian scientists, normally such lovable, dependable people.

"Not since that infamous decision by a half Irish, half French referee[12] during the Wales-France semi-final of the seventh Rugby World Cup in New Zealand in 2011 has Wales` cultural life been so savagely attacked," he sobbed. As bitter memories of that terrible day flooded back The Parrot burst into tears.

The newsreader continued. "Dyfed-Powys Police Rapid-Response Coracle Unit has, for an undisclosed sum thought to be in the millions, bought a quantum coracle they say is many times faster than the present stock. Marine physicists from NASA[13] and Pembrokeshire College[14] have joined forces to develop it. Early testing is being carried out at two sites, an inflatable paddling pool situated in the car park behind the College and on the upper reaches of the Western Cleddau. Particularly testing was the weir behind County Hall, the highest tidal point of the Western Cleddau, navigable years ago by trading boats, and its fish pass which helps migratory species such as salmon and sewin as they travel as much as 30 miles from the sea up the river to spawn. If successful, the testing will lead to DPPRRCU buying many more."

"This is the fruit of a long-held dream held by marine physicists and will usher in a revolution in policing the coast. The new generation of quantum coracles are predicted to solve problems far beyond the capability of traditional vessels. Problems such as piracy and general mayhem, limited edition Grogg figure smuggling,[15] crab baiting and many more. It will take coracles into the world of quantum mechanics where normal logic does not apply. The Sergeant has been chosen to be the test pilot."

The Sergeant's heart filled with unconditional love for all marine life and the tears were now tears of joy. "As someone once said," he remarked gleefully to The Parrot, "if you need a ceiling painted, a chariot race run, a city besieged or the Red Sea parted, you think of me.[16] And if the people need a quantum test pilot, here I am."

"Coracling serendipity indeed," replied the newsreader. The Sergeant blushed modestly.

The voice from the radio continued. "In the quantum world a coracle can be in two places at the same time."

The Sergeant couldn't take this on board, or anywhere else, and wondered if it was a reference to an incident that occurred one Saturday night a little while ago after a particularly interesting ale tasting evening in the Sloop.[17] He woke in the coracle the following morning, beached on one of the islands of the archipelago south of Oslo. How he got there was never satisfactorily explained under the present laws of physics. Or even under Norwegian law.

"If the coracle is in two places at once," he thought with a shudder, "what happens to me?"

Far, far, away, in a distant galaxy in a parallel universe, another Sergeant trembled.

"Today's coracles are digital and use `bits` that work like a series of switches which can be turned either on or off, one or zero," the announcer explained. "Quantum coracles utilise qubits, so a function can be one, zero, or both one and zero at the same time. Quantum coracles can do in seconds what today's digital coracles would take several years to do."

He was confused. He poured himself another piping hot mug of tea, added a drop of milk, stirred, took a sip and read the sign hanging from the ceiling next to the cuckoo clock which had a quote by Shunryu Suzuki on it. 'Confusion is the fertile field.' Getting up, he crossed the galley to lie back lazily in the rocking chair between the juke box, an authentic bright yellow vintage 1920s retro model with stereo CD player, FM radio, auxiliary USB ports, blue-toothed monster that lay against the aft bulkhead, and the porthole. He regretted it immediately as tea spilt over his shirt.

Hanging in pride of place on the galley wall on the port side of the large screen television is Emanuel Leutze's painting, *Bonnie Prince Charlie crossing the Delaware River*.[18] Thought by art historians to have been destroyed in 1942 it is a daily source of inspiration to the Sergeant. On the starboard side of the television, on permanent loan from the National Library of Wales, hangs *An Overshot Mill in Wales*, that glorious painting by James Ward. Next to it, in admiration and in *homage* to a brave woman and her father, hangs *Grace Darling at the Forfarshire* by Thomas Musgrave Joy.

"The Parrot wondered what Bonnie Prince Charlie was doing on the Delaware. He thinks," it mused, "therefore he`s confused."

The Sergeant remembered a recent memo from the Admiral which informed staff that Mako sharks, the fastest shark in the ocean, a cousin of the Great White and found in great numbers off the Neptune Islands, are aggressive and can cruise at up to 26 knots, gusting to 39 knots. Even though Dyfed-Powys Police Rapid-Response Coracle Unit`s area of operations does not extend to South Australia, the Admiral, to popular acclaim amongst the ranks, introduced compulsory training for staff to achieve top speeds of 40 knots. This speed was chosen partly because it means that a coracler can outrun a shark, in any direction, partly because it`s a round number and easy to remember but mostly because it was his wife`s fortieth birthday the following week. It is hoped that this figure will not increase year on year in the future. The greater speed is achieved by means of more efficient use of the paddle.

The memo followed an incident 30 miles off Milford Haven recently when a famous actor from S4C[19] caught a 12-foot Mako making this the first one caught in Welsh waters and the biggest caught anywhere in the world. It weighed in at 337 pounds. "We saw this flash that whizzed past the boat. It had a big white belly, and it went, OMG! like, so, so fast," said the actor, adding, "Next thing this shark leapt fifteen feet into the air about twenty feet off the back of the stern."

"No worries," thought the Sergeant, "now that we have the quantum coracle."

He listened attentively to the radio. "More coracling news. Last night an extreme coraclist was rescued from a tree near the confluence of the two Cleddaus. She had crash landed thirty-five feet up in an oak tree and was stuck there for several hours. The rescue was hampered by the shape of the tree, which proved to be particularly challenging for the rescue party consisting of Dyfed-Powys Police Rapid-Response Coracle Unit`s Quick Reaction Tree Canopy Rescue Squad and the fire brigades from Haverfordwest, Narberth and St Florence. Reinforcements were called in from Carmarthenshire and with the help of arc lights and an extending ladder she was eventually brought to safety uninjured onto an aerial platform from where she was lowered to the ground at approximately 4.30 a.m. this morning. A large crowd gathered through the night and rescuers and the public were served refreshments by the Machlud y Wawr[20] Emergency Refreshments call out team from Llandissilio, who arrived, erected *la grande tente* and were serving hot tea and *bara brith* within seventeen minutes of receiving the call out. A new record. Literary types will be interested to know that the Llandissilio team were called, rather than one closer, because of the connection between the crooked oak the coracler found herself marooned in and Waldo,[21] who lies at rest in the graveyard of Blaenconin chapel in the village and whose childhood home is situated nearby, not far from his favourite fields. Attempts to retrieve the coracle will begin later this morning. A medical spokesperson told reporters gathered in the press tent adjacent to *la grande tente* that it has sustained puncture wounds and the paddle is bent."

"A small group then left in procession to attend a short service of thanksgiving in Millin C. M. Chapel nearby. The service began with a period of silence during which the still small voice within said a few words. This was followed by a reading of one of Waldo`s poems by *Prifardd* Mererid Hopwood.[22] She chose *Mewn Dau Gae*. The pilgrims then formed a candlelit procession which led its way back to the crooked oak where the rescued coracler, a young woman from Pennsylvania, her rescuers, the public, whose number by this time could be counted in their thousands, thanks no doubt to the excellent catering arrangements, assembled dignitaries and the press took part in the sublime experience of daybreak which they all agreed is an act of resurrection anew.[21] Also present were the Chief Executive and Cabinet members from Pembrokeshire County Council,[23] attracted no doubt by the excellent catering arrangements. The Bishops of Crymych and St Davids[24] got caught up in the traffic jam. Arriving late they had to make do with tea and biscuits, the cakes all having been eaten. We have a recording of Mererid reading the poem, in Welsh then English and we`ll play the last verse of both for you now. The English version, by the way, was translated from the original Welsh by Rowan Williams[25] when he was Archbishop of Canterbury."

The Sergeant leant back in the chair and closed his eyes in expectation. His favourite poet and his favourite *prifardd* at breakfast time. Wonder of wonders. Dozing with tiredness after hearing of all those people up all night he caught the last few lines of the poem.

Dros Weun Parc y Blawd a Parc y Blawd heb ludd,
A'u gafael ar y gwrthrych, y perci llawn pobl.
Diau y daw'r dirhau, a pha awr yw hi
Y daw'r herwr, daw'r heliwr, daw'r hawliwr i'r bwlch,
Daw'r Brenin Alltud a'r brwyn yn hollti.

"Note the *cynghanedd* in the last line," said the newsreader enthusiastically. "*d b n n ll t / d b n n ll t.*"

The steady gaze across the two fields, holding still
The vision: fair fields full of folk;
For it will come, dawn of his longed-for coming,
And what a dawn to long for. He will arrive, the outlaw,
The huntsman, the lost heir making good his claim
To no-man's land, the exiled king

Is coming home one day; the rushes sweep aside
To let him through.[25]

The Sergeant knew all of Waldo's poems off by heart. Every single one. He used toffee to train his memory having learnt from grammar school biology lessons behind the bike shed that teeth evolved from the primitive central nervous system and movement of teeth and jaws results in sensory impulses being sent to the hippocampus, a region of the brain central to memory formation and retrieval. A toffee a day, or even two, keeps memory loss at bay, is written on his toothbrush.

"Next week we'll discuss another Waldo poem, *Y Dderwen Gam*. A panel of experts will discuss its significance in the canon of mystical Welsh language poems from the 20th century," said the radio presenter.

"Transport news now. Excitement is high in Fishguard since it was revealed that as part of their plan to streamline the half-hourly Town Service bus route between Fishguard and Goodwick the Town Council[26] have opened up an Einstein-Rosen bridge[27] between two disparate points in spacetime in the vicinity, namely the site of the old bus stop on the eastern aspect of Fishguard square 'now', and the passenger waiting area in the ferry terminal in the harbour, sometimes 'now', sometimes before 'now', sometimes after 'now'."

"The Council has placed an information board adjacent to the timetable at the old bus stop adorned with twenty-seven 8x10 colour glossy photographs of the information desk in the terminal, with circles and arrows and a paragraph on the back of each one[28] explaining where the bus sometimes 'is', sometimes 'was' or sometimes 'will be', to help travellers plan their journey, thus enabling a smoother and more accurate transit. Even so, the latest Welsh Government[29] statistics show that customer satisfaction is mixed. Last month approximately 27% of passengers left Fishguard Square on time, only to reappear in a cafe on the Esplanade in Porthcawl. Fortunately, their baggage arrived safely in the harbour as planned. A further 14% reappeared in the harbour the previous week and 9% are not due to arrive until the day after tomorrow."

"But it is not all good news. After two separate incidents that occurred late last week concerned residents have asked for safety railings to be erected at the entrance to the wormhole. Two young couples on a pub crawl around town were surprised to find themselves standing next to the information desk in the terminal, where they were refused drinks, instead of next to the bar in the Oak[30] where they thought they were going at the time. In the second incident, Ms Eirlys Davies and her twin sister Ms Elin Davies, old age pensioners on holiday from Penarth near Cardiff, have been declared missing after a gust of wind carried them into it as they made their way from the market to the corner cafe. They have not been seen since. Or before. Their relatives have been informed and the police are appealing for witnesses.

"The Chair of Pembrokeshire County Council's Transport Committee[31] told the press earlier today that she is keeping a keen eye on the situation, monitoring developments closely and that lessons will be learnt. The Committee is at the advanced planning stage before erecting a kiosk near the entrance to the Town Hall from where passengers can buy tickets for the journey. The process is taking longer than expected as the legal implications of passengers reappearing in a cafe in Porthcawl, or disappearing altogether, are being discussed in detail.

A further complication arose when a member of the Council's Finance Committee[32] raised a point of order after reading the following statement whilst conducting research on the internet. 'Many scientists postulate wormholes are merely a projection of the 4th dimension, analogous to how a 2D being could experience only part of a 3D object.'"[33]

"And now more evolutionary news. According to Aberystwyth University scientists[34] the secret of human success may be all in the shoulders. Before cognition and language, one of the most important developments was the shoulder. Yes, the humble shoulder, that thing at the top of your arms that you never think about until you sprain it. The common shoulder put our ancestors onto an evolutionary trajectory that expanded their diet, boosted their brain power and helped them colonise all four corners of the planet. Beginning more than two million years ago important adaptations occurred to the upper body, the shoulders and arms, and the result was that circular paddling became possible."

"Chimpanzees paddle poorly despite having strong, elongated arms, adult males can only paddle at around 17 knots. Not fast enough to frighten a Mako. A twelve-year-old child can achieve 19 knots. A child coracling near a beach at such a speed is a dangerous thing however and adult supervision is essential."

"Paddling was very important early on in our evolution as it enabled early hominids to catch more and bigger fish and eating food richer in calories and fats allowed early humans to grow larger brains and bodies. Evidence has recently come to light regarding the netting techniques of early hominid fishermen and fisherwomen. To make optimum use of the evolving shoulder when casting the net our ancestors stood upright in the coracle. Anyone who has ever tried this knows how difficult it is and it was this fishing technique, scientists now think, appearing at the same time as evolving shoulders, that resulted in humans rising from four legs to two. Although others disagree."

The Sergeant felt strangely alive although from the outside there did not appear to be any significant change.

"Careful." warned The Parrot, ever alert, "or you`ll be ejected from the Mother Ship."

141

The ship-to-shore radio barked into life. The Sergeant fell off the rocking chair and hurried to answer it.

"Sergeant! Where are you?"

"Next to the ship-to-shore radio sir," he replied uncertainly, looking at the large, still hot tea stain spreading across and down his shirt.

"Good news, Sergeant," the Admiral continued, "Dyfed-Powys Police Rapid-Response Coracle Unit has been chosen to pilot a new European initiative, `predictive policing`."

"Good news indeed, sir. What is `predictive policing`?"

"A combination of mathematics, criminology, anthropology and good old gut instinct. The system is designed to stop crimes before they`ve been committed."

The Sergeant's pupils dilated. The large, hot, tea stain was spreading down under the front of his regulation lightweight summer trousers.

"What`s wrong with your eyes?" asked the Admiral.

"Nothing, sir."

"A small computer screen attached to the paddle divides the sea into small areas of fifty square metres each. A light appears in those areas where the computer predicts a crime will happen. The lights, a maximum of fifteen, move around the map all day and night as the crime prediction changes. Crime history and an algorithm produce the prediction. Preliminary results of trials conducted off the coast of North Cornwall are encouraging, and we will pilot the scheme in Pembrokeshire waters."

"*Bendigedig*, sir."

"Exactly. I`m sending a technician from the newly formed Dyfed-Powys Police Rapid-Response Coracle Unit's Predictive Policing Unit out to you today to fit the technology onto your paddle. He`ll be there by dinner time. Make sure you`re at your mooring."

"Yes sir. Thank you, sir."

"And I`ve decided to put the incident that occurred off Strumble head last week behind you. Over and out!" The radio went dead.

"That incident! That incident!" snorted the Sergeant. The large, hot tea stain had reached its target. He had been on routine patrol with Dr Olwen Stone,[35] a medical engineer seconded to his command for a week to get practical experience as part of the course for her DPPRRCU`s Medical Division entrance exam. She had been recruited from the Reasonably Serious Crime Squad based in Moylegrove, a small but cosmopolitan village north of Newport. By basing the RSCS in the centre of the village the authorities hope to keep a lid on things. What things exactly they have yet to determine. A listening post disguised as a dilapidated RNLI[36] rescue centre is positioned in the car park next to the public loos complete with satellite links to GCHQ[37] in Carmarthen. That GCHQ was relocated from Cheltenham to Carmarthen is another feather in the cap for the

University of the Four Trinity Davids.[38] The result of their audacious attempt to bring the London Eye[39] to their waterfront campus in Swansea where it will be renamed Sweyn's Eye will be known sometime during the next few weeks.

They travelled nor` by nor` east before turning west at a steady 15 knots against a force 3 in a medium swell to reach a spot several miles off Strumble Head and were happily going about their business whilst singing five-part harmonies with the whales who were at play in the vicinity. The Sergeant was at work on the bridge as Dr Stone carried out her duties in the ocean nearby. They had just finished the first verse of an old Pembrokeshire sea shanty,

> *Less than four miles off Strumble Head,*
> *You know, the one with the lighthouse,*
> *Becalmed on a sultry summer`s day,*
> *There is nothing to carry the sound.*
> *No air pressure, no oxygen,*
> *Life out there is impossible.*

collectively paused, inhaled, and were about to tear into the chorus when out of the blue, disaster struck. Attached by a safety line to the vessel`s robotic arm Olwen was snorkelling a few yards off the starboard bow attempting to reboot a buoy damaged in a recent storm. Then it happened. The coracle was hit by *debris* that for some unlucky reason had re-entered Earth`s atmosphere several minutes before and crashed just there, just then. The *debris*, the remains of a giant American led multinational peacekeeping satellite destroyed a few months earlier by a Russian rocket, had been orbiting the planet on a falling trajectory ever since as gravity pulled the pieces to earth. These remains, having re-entered Earth's atmosphere high overhead approximately 1,220 miles to the east now slammed into the coracle at thousands of miles per hour, peppering it with holes before disappearing into the depths. The robotic arm became detached and began spinning aimlessly away from the vessel, dragging Dr Stone with it, carried by the current towards the Abyss that lies 3.7 miles off Strumble Head.

"Uh! Uh! Uh!" gasped Dr Stone, overcome with claustrophobia, vertigo and sea sickness. A thought appeared somewhere in the back of her mind. Right at the back. "If God had meant me to go snorkelling, he wouldn`t have given me this stomach." Then it disappeared again just as quickly as it had come.

"Uh! Uh! Uh!"

The Sergeant grabbed the radio receiver with both hands and hung on for dear life. "The coracle has been hit! The coracle has been hit! Do you read? Over." he shrieked to Base Control at HQ in Milford Haven. Then he remembered the emergency drill for extreme incidents. He froze. Noting with the one open eye that the danger had not passed he utilised a response common in some animals and birds, namely fear bradycardia, during which his pulse rate dropped markedly. Finally, to ensure his survival, and therefore, evolutionary ethnopalaeobiologists suggest, the survival of the species, he played dead. To use technical terminology, he feigned death, all the while moving cautiously in the general direction of the stern. Moments later, his survival strategy reached its merciful conclusion when he slumped unconsciousness into the hammock. Whilst in this life-saving state, and displaying great presence of mind, he covered himself with the woollen throw his wife bought for him in Tregwynt Woollen Mill[40] the previous spring. She also bought him a set of matching pyjamas, dressing gown, socks and slippers but he thought that would be a little over the top for a man slumped unconscious. And anyway, they didn`t match the throw. Unperturbed by this inessential detail he slipped into a coma, from which vantage point he would savour the interminable merriment to be found in an unfolding catastrophe. If only Freud had known the Sergeant when he wrote about the unconscious mind.

An existential dread appeared at the tip of The Parrots beak and made its way carefully along it and up to the forehead close by before entering The Parrot's mind and asking a couple of pertinent questions. "Are the Sergeant's protons decaying? Are his atoms breaking down?" This deep reflection continued. "Does the Sergeant only exist when he is interacting with something? A paddle, say. Or a cup of tea. We might never know. Hmmm. He certainly displays a rapid increase in entropy," it reasoned. "Or is this the norm? For the Sergeant that is."

Acting swiftly and decisively The Parrot took command. That`s why it is there. It is written, 'Cometh the hour, cometh The Parrot.'[41]

"Dr Stone," it squawked calmly into the radio receiver, keeping the transmit button pressed down with a claw, before releasing it and waiting a few seconds for a reply. None came.

The robotic arm took another hit, sending it and Olwen spinning ever more wildly away from the vessel and into the Abyss.

The Parrot pressed the transmit button and attempted to open communication with Base Control in Milford Haven. "Base. Do you read? Dr Stone is off structure. I repeat. Dr Stone is off structure." And released the button.

"Uh! Uh! Uh! Uh!" Dr Stone was hyperventilating.

"You must detach. Dr Stone you must detach. You must detach. That arm is going to carry you too far if you don`t. Listen to my squawk. You need to focus. I`m losing visual of you. In a few seconds I won`t be able to track you. You need to detach. I can`t see you anymore. Do it now!" instructed The Parrot.

Dr Stone came out of the panic attack, unbuckled from the safety line and began spinning away from the robotic arm.

"Base, I`ve lost visual of Dr Stone. I`ve lost visual of Dr Stone. Dr Stone, do you copy?"

"Yes! Yes! Yes! I copy. I`m detached."

"What is your position?"

"I don`t know! I don`t know! I`m spinning! I can`t ....."

"Report your position."

"The compass is down. I can`t! I can`t!"

"Give me a visual."

"I see nothing! I see nothing!"

"Do you have a visual of the coracle?"

"No!"

"Do you have a visual of Strumble Head?"

"No!"

"You need to focus. Anything. The sun. The Earth. The Fishguard to Rosslare ferry. The lighthouse. Anything. Coordinates. Give me coordinates. Give me coordinates."

"I can`t breathe! Uh! Uh!"

"Dr Stone," a voice from Base Control broke into the transmission, "you`re burning oxygen. Try to sip. Do not gulp."

"Uh! Uuh! Uuuuh! Uuuuuuuh. Her breathing slowed. Composure returned. The water slowed her spinning to a gentle rotation, and she relaxed, floating on her back in the turquoise sea. Carefully adjusting the snorkel and mask she raised her head slightly to glance past her toes. Her worried expression turned into a smile. Her eyes filled with hope. In the distance she saw The Parrot on the bridge waving at her and the Sergeant apparently fast asleep in the hammock.

"Safe!" she sighed.

A yoga student for many years she celebrated by doing the Salute to the Sun until she couldn`t hold her breathe any longer and had to stop. Kicking off some submerged flotsam and jetsam she returned to the surface.

"The kaleidoscope has been shaken and no one knows how the colours will fall," murmured the Sergeant in his dreams.

Emotions were running high and overcome with nostalgia and with supporting harmony from the whales who had witnessed the near tragedy and the tenors and altos amongst a school of passing dolphins holidaying with relatives in Cardigan Bay and the massed ranks of *Côr y Dysgwyr* [42] who happened to be picnicking on the headland nearby, Dr Stone and The Parrot broke into a few verses of *My Little Welsh Home*, an old favourite. Then, with a medley of sea shanties, they sang the songs of the sea.

"*Mmmmmmmmmmmmmmmmmm*," hummed the whales with their deep bass voices. Then The Parrot began, his rich baritone squawk bringing tears to the eyes of a group of picnickers sitting in the shade of the lighthouse on Strumble Head.

I am dreaming of the mountains of my home.
Of the mountains where in childhood I would roam.

I have dwelt 'neath southern skies
Where the summer never dies.
But my heart is in the mountains of my home.

Whales, dolphins, choir, picnickers and Dr Stone lifted the sound.

I have seen the little homestead on the hill.
I can hear the magic music of the rill.
There is nothing to compare
With the love that once was there
In that lonely little homestead on the hill.

The whales again.

"Mmmmmmmmmmmmmmmmmm."

The Parrot's squawk returned.

I can see the quiet churchyard down below,
Where the mountain breezes wander to and fro.
And when God my soul will keep,
It is there I want to sleep,
With those dear old folks that loved me long ago.

Ivor Emmanuel's suntanned spirit, looking down from above, shed a tear of joy.[43]

As the singing came to an end, the brave crew member whose prompt action had averted certain catastrophe flew to the stern to make sure the Captain of the vessel was safe. The Sergeant, having existed in all possible states before being observed by The Parrot, collapsed into a single state assigned by his wife to the category 'Sergeant'.

The celebrations lasted all afternoon and long into the night until Olwen noticed the wrinkles caused by the water on her skin and asked to be pulled aboard. The Sergeant, encouraged by the singing and the smells coming from the *barbecue* was persuaded to come out of his coma. Such was the euphoria that accompanied the realisation they had come within a whisker of joining the Great Coracler in the Sky it was only when the rising seawater put the *barbecue* out did they notice that the badly holed coracle was sinking. Whilst nibbling a slice of pizza The Parrot was moved to reflect upon a sentence it had read in a papyrus bought in a book sale in Tenby recently titled, *On Floating Bodies*. 'Any coracle wholly or partially immersed in a fluid experiences an upthrust equal to, but opposite in sense to, the weight of the fluid displaced.'[44]

Fishguard Lifeboat,[45] sent by Base Control, picked them up safely just before midnight. When all were on board the Cox'n recited a short prayer of gratitude, "Blessed are the cracked, for they shall let in the light,"[46] three times before throwing a pinch of salt overboard into the `slow, black, crow-black, coracle-bobbing sea` as Dylan Thomas[47] so nearly wrote, before returning them to Fishguard Harbour.

The Sergeant, having recovered from the self-induced medical coma, a precautionary measure, shunned the intense media attention and went straight home to the smallholding and to his wife whom he needs to be with at moments such as these. She is the Goskar's Rock to his North Beach, without her something important would be missing. The international salvage operation to retrieve the coracle would wait till it be morrow. His wife, who had been following events live on Sky,[48] greeted him with tears of relief and a big *cwtsh*. She made them both a mug of piping hot tea and led him to the *sofa* in front of the television where they sat together watching black and white films from the thirties and forties, holding hands all the while. They remained like this until dawn by which time she was resting against him, snoring peacefully. As sunlight streamed through the south facing window behind the television, he lifted the dooby doo and turned it off. Reaching to the bookcase on his left he picked up his well-thumbed copy of *Waldo Williams: Cerddi 1922-1970*.[49] Kissing his wife tenderly on the top of the head he opened the book at random and began to read .....

On the stern, a raft of otters, their long, slim bodies covered in dense fur for warmth, play in the water of the river as it enters the eastern aspect of the lake, while others feed on fish, crayfish and crabs. Marsh fritillary butterflies with chequered brown, orange and yellow markings feed on a patch of Devil's-bit scabious in the wetlands nearby. A kingfisher with long bill, large head, short tail and distinctive blue-green plumage on upperparts with orange underparts, rests on a branch above the water before diving again for fish. On the edge of the meadow grow docks and nettles, much loved by tiger moths. The nettles are surrounded by a shimmering kaleidoscope of butterflies. Green ayahs and purple nullahs abound. A little egret with white plumage, black legs and yellow feet stands on a log floating on the lake. Using its long slender bill, it drinks the cooling water. Recent arrivals, they are sociable birds up to 26 inches long with a wingspan of 35-42 inches. Visiting for the summer a New Zealand Kea, a species of large parrot normally found in forests in the alpine regions of New Zealand's South Island, and onetime New Zealand bird of the year, with olive-green plumage and grey beak with orange feathers on the undersides of its wings, investigates food scraps on the deck beneath the hammock. Nocturnal animals at home in deciduous woodland, dormice with orange yellow fur and thick furry tails sleep in nests in hollow trees.

A breeding pair of great-tailed grackles, medium-sized, highly social and passerine, rest in willows overlooking the Bronze Age chambered tomb after feeding on local lizards. The male is iridescent black set off by a purple-blue sheen and the female a brown colour with darker wings and keel-shaped tail. Their bright yellow eyes keep watch as the female sings a song of territory.

A sedge of cranes, preparing for the night, gather in the shallows of the lake. Later, one of the company, standing on one leg while holding a stone aloft in the other, will take the first watch of the night. If it falls asleep, the stone will fall from its grasp and the sound made as it hits the surface of the water will wake the herd.

Bats, the only mammals capable of true flight, and with wings that resemble the human hand, roost hanging upside down in the cowshed that local legend has it was designed by Frank Lloyd Wright himself.[50]

Evolution does funny things on islands and for all intents and purposes the coracle is an island, albeit peripatetic. Islands often present animals with a problem, which is, how to get enough food to meet their energy needs. For some animals this is solved by getting smaller over time which is why there are miniature horses and hippos on the stern as they have been cut off from the mainland for a long time. Even when sea levels were at their lowest during the Ice Age the vessel was still at sea, except for a couple of days in dry dock every few years having barnacles scraped off the hull.

The first things to evolve on the primordial stern many long years ago were simple microbes. Indeed, for 80% of its history there was little more aboard than 'pond scum'. After that, the evidence suggests an increasing variety of life. A recent drought on the south easterly edge of the lake revealed 135-million-year-old dinosaur footprints thought to be those of a three-toed theropod. Not long ago, in the same general area, preserved tree stumps of birch, hazel, willow and oak were uncovered by a storm. They are thought to be the remains of a Mesolithic forest drowned about 8,500 years ago.

Archaeologists excavating on a steep hill close to the western side of the lake have unearthed coins, gaming counters and other artefacts associated with Viking encampments. Excitement is high as it is thought the site is the most westernmost of the Viking Great Army camps established as they ravaged parts of Britain. Led by Hafdan they landed in Kent in 865 and after conquering Mercia the Great Army split into three forces. Two went north to attack the Britons of Strathclyde and the Picts and the third came west to lay waste to Pembrokeshire. It is thought that Hafdan was killed in battle in 877 and the Great Army defeated in 878.

Using high-tech sonar, physicists from the University of North Pembrokeshire at Crymych have recently discovered the submerged remains of a Roman road in the lake dated to the first century BC or AD. Working alongside the scientists, DPPRRCU divers have found a number of *basoli*, the paving stones used by the Romans to build their roads. A larger structure in which a number of *amphorae* have been found lies next to the road and is thought to be part of a Roman harbour. The amphorae are important as they provide evidence for the movement of foodstuffs within the Roman Empire. The well-preserved remains of *quinqueremes* and *triremes*, large, oared, wooden warships, as well as an example of the lighter *liburnian*, a small galley used no doubt for patrolling the lake, have been discovered in the silt of the harbour.

Bronze rams on the bows of the *triremes* bear witness to the practice of rowing the vessels as fast as possible into enemy ships to pierce the hull. The ship would then sink or be boarded. Little do unsuspecting locals know that discussions in the *cafés* and pubs of Fishguard and Goodwick as to whether or not the sails of the *triremes* were used as well as the three banks of oars when attacking another vessel will ignite decades of heated arguments in the twin towns and beyond. Bitter controversy will turn to feud, husbands against wives, sons against fathers, daughters against mothers, sons against mothers, daughters against fathers, neighbour against neighbour, village against village, until the people of north Pembrokeshire will rue the day marine archaeologists arrived on the stern.

A line of continuous snow showers in a convergence zone aligned north-south above the Irish Sea midway between Wales and Ireland, caused by warm sea temperatures meeting cold arctic air above, and wedged between an easterly wind blowing from Wales and a westerly wind blowing from Ireland, can be seen by intrigued visitors picnicking on Strumble Head. Soon, the Pembrokeshire Dangler, not usually appearing so early in the year, will deposit ten inches of snow over Fishguard and Wadebridge.

The alarm call of a meerkat, coming from behind the cowshed, disturbs the calm of Harbour Village atop the cliffs to the west.

10

Your duty is to be, and not to be this or that.
Ramana Maharshi[1]

Surrounding the Machlud y Wawr[2] logo on the cushion of the rocking chair is inscribed their official motto, 'Lead from behind, follow from somewhere else.' Megan sat on it. Firmly. "Enough of that!" she thought. "I am their leader, and I will follow them," sang the whoopee cushion. Her eyes closed imperceptibly, a steely glint appearing in them as they searched the room for Bronwen. She picked up the agenda for the meeting which was being held that evening in the auditorium next to the crypt and began to read.

"Item 1. Big Data. Proposer: Megan."

She intended revolutionising the movement by introducing Big Data. Interested members would follow a three-year course at the Department of Analytics at the University of North Pembrokeshire at Crymych. The department's labs are situated off-campus in nearby Silicon Cwm[3] a few miles northeast of Fishguard. Megan the visionary saw Big Data Analytics as crucial to the organisation's development as by today Big Data lies at the heart of every management decision. She was going to present this idea to the meeting.

Before her in the auditorium 125 members sat around the circular oak table. She paused as a hush descended on the throng. Before pressing on with the details of the first item she decided, wisely, to break the ice with some rousing introductory remarks to whip the audience into a light topping full of just the right amount of air bubbles. For this she used a run of the mill commercial 48g cream whipper and some well-chosen words. "Women! Members! Remember Nadia Boulanger!" she cried exuberantly, and the members jumped to their feet, applauding enthusiastically. "When asked by a journalist what it was like to be a woman conducting the Boston Symphony Orchestra, this great French musician, giving him a withering look, replied, "Having been a woman for fifty years, I have recovered from my initial astonishment."[4]

"And now for the nitty gritty. Item 1. I ask a question, then Machlud y Wawr's Big Data team collect data," she began as the last member took her seat after the excitement. "Then our data scientists look at the data to see if it answers the question. This is both challenging and baffling, but it's going to change our world."

When questioned about this by some sceptical members, the arty ones with no scientific background, Megan replied, "Where's your data? You need to do your homework. You see, we are incorporating third party data sets, external data feeds and cloud technology into our analyses rather than relying on operational data we`ve captured and stored in our internal back-end systems." Their doubts were dispelled. Cyberbrain, as some younger members call Megan affectionately, was on a roll.

"Item 2. Proposed name change," she read out, sighing expressively.

A few weeks earlier she accompanied a large party of the Memberati on Machlud y Wawr`s annual tour of Brittany, hosted by our Celtic cousins. She had been to the country many times and her Breton was fluent. One late afternoon, as dusk approached whilst walking the hills in contemplation, she got lost and inadvertently crossed the border into France. Having arrived in that country she thought she would go walkabout, spent ten days travelling alone and found it to be a thoroughly enjoyable experience even though nobody could understand her when she spoke Welsh or Breton and everybody pretended not to understand her when she spoke English.

Bronwen on the other hand could speak passable French, having worked in Paris as an *au pair* when younger after being inspired one day when, by mistake, she borrowed a bilingual Welsh-French edition of Baudelaire`s *Les Fleurs du Mal* from Crymych library. She was attending flower arranging classes at the time and thought it might help. It didn`t. But she loved the poems and decided to learn French so she could read them in the original. She has become a bit of a Francophile.

"Proposer, Bronwen," said Megan.

Bronwen stood nervously to address the members. "I propose that Megan`s title changes from *Honorary Senior Life President* to *Honorary Lifelong Directrice Générale*" - her French could only take her so far. She sat down again, apologetically. During the sometimes heated debate that raged through the first tea break the motion was defeated. She found herself in a Catch *Vingt-Deux* situation but not to be outdone she drew on her contingency plan. She waited for quiet, rose to her feet and spoke again. "With the help of the *Geiriadur Cymraeg-Ffrangeg/Ffrangeg-Cymraeg*, *Dictionnaire Gallois-Francais/Francais-Gallois*, being a comprehensive Welsh-French/French-Welsh dictionary for students studying French in Wales and students studying Welsh in France ..."[5]

She drew breath ...

"... comprising over 55,000 words and 195,000 translations and idioms, together with a verb table and lists of useful phrases and numbers whose sister volume the *Geiriadur Cymraeg-Llydaweg/Llydaweg-Cymraeg, Geriadur Kembraeg-Brezhoneg/Brezhoneg-Kembraeg*, being a comprehensive Welsh-Breton/Breton-Welsh dictionary is due out shortly ..."

... then another ...

"... and by the way, work has recently begun on the next dictionary in the series, the *Geiriadur Cymraeg-Gwyddeleg/Gwyddeleg-Cymraeg, Foclóir Breatnais-*

Gaeilge/Gaeilge-Breatnais, being a Welsh-Irish/Irish-Welsh dictionary ... to be followed by the *Geiriadur Cymraeg-Cernyweg/Cernyweg-Cymraeg, Gerlyver Kembrek-Kernewek/Kernewek-Kembrek*, being a Welsh-Cornish/Cornish-Welsh dictionary ..."

... and another, with a quick glance at the audience to weigh the mood ...

"... I propose that Megan`s title be changed to *Madame le Lifelong Honorary Directrice Générale*." There`s only so much you can do with a dictionary, whatever languages it contains.

A look of icy determination swept across Bronwen`s forehead causing cute looking wrinkles to appear around the outsides of her eyes, not at all the look she intended. She pressed on regardless. No boast went unboasted, no *cliché* unclichéd, no *hyperbole* unhyperboled, no opinion unopinioned, no prediction unpredictioned, and, finally, no exaggeration unexaggerationed until she was sick and tired of it all and filled with the dread realisation that no one was the slightest bit interested. She couldn`t go on. She broke down and threw herself at the mercy of the vote.

The amended motion was heavily defeated. The *poulets* had come home to roost. Bronwen fell back into *la chaise*, crushed and humiliated. "In future debates I must improve my *vitesse de ligne* and avoid the *plaquage à deux*," she thought to herself.

"When the circumstances are right, life gives you what you need," Megan counselled.

"But why doesn't it give me what I want?"

"Because you don't need what you want."

Bronwen went deep inside to where a voice spoke to her, saying, "This is the only here and now you`re ever going to have, so you'd might as well enjoy it." In a second, she was refreshed and back in the ball game.

The next item on the agenda followed a recent experience of Machlud y Wawr`s ramblers` association whose members meet one Saturday a month in a different part of Wales to walk in the countryside and enjoy the fresh air and cultural scenery. This was also Bronwen`s motion and was titled, `Public path good, barbed wire bad`. She rose again, and, encouraged by the generous applause, put her disappointment behind her, speaking loudly and clearly.

"Members. A dangerous phenomenon is sweeping the country. White Settlers are moving into Wales, fencing footpaths our mothers and grandmothers walked before us, buying houses and farms and changing their names from Welsh to English. We are being prevented from understanding and walking our own land. Let me remind you of something, `... place-names are arguably among the most highly charged and richly evocative of all linguistic symbols. Because of their inseparable connection to specific localities, placenames may be used to summon forth an enormous range of mental and emotional associations - associations of time and space, of history and events, of persona and social activities, of oneself and stages in one's life'."[6]

A low rumbling sound grew in intensity and turned into the roar of revolution as the members recalled reports of paths closed and angry confrontations.

"Sense of place is not just something that people know and feel, it is something people do," she cried.[7]

The gathered Memberati thumped the table in tune with the clamour. Ominously, the words `burning` and `effigies` were heard whispered in the same sentence. Next to one another. It was getting nasty.

"I want to remind you of the famous concert in the Crymych Bowlen[8] in 1965 when Arlo Guthrie,[9] accompanied by Pete Seeger and Judy Collins, finished the evening with a glorious rendition of a Woody Guthrie song *This Land is Your Land*, but with new lyrics written by Arlo himself. For some of the younger members who are not familiar with the song, let me sing you the first verse."

She went over to the beautiful double ended ruby and gold Versaille *chaise longue* that sat to the right of the *fenêtres françaises* made from locally sourced oak, weather sealed to resist warping and shrinking, and picked up her mahogany, four string, D/G *hurdy gurdy* she placed there before the meeting, the one she bought second-hand years ago from the accomplished *hurdy gurdy* player Jean-François Dutertre about the time he began developing the *Anthologie de la Musique Traditionnelle Française*.[10] She still attends the annual music festival in Saint-Chartier in the Indre *département* in Central France. Sitting on the edge of the *chaise longue* facing the meeting her fingers caressed the keyboard as she began cranking the handle to turn the wooden wheel, the outer rim of which is coated with resin. The gut strings began to vibrate and Bronwen's voice filled the auditorium.

> *As I went walking*
> *I saw a sign there,*
> *And on the sign it*
> *Said no trespassing.*
> *But on the other side*
> *It didn`t say nothing,*
> *That side was made*
> *For you and me.*

She whipped them into a patriotic, yet musical frenzy and they sang the verse several times as individual groups clogged around the table until she put the *hurdy gurdy* back on the beautiful double ended ruby and gold Versaille *chaise longue*. "I do love that affect," she thought, and returned to address the meeting, appealing for calm.

"I propose that every walking group reports barbed wire infringements to a Black Ops subcommittee who will be equipped with wire cutters and whose remit will be to go out at dead of night and remove the offending obstructions. Or if that's not convenient, in the afternoon."

Applause.

"And a paint pot and brush to return the names of houses and farms to the original."

Applause and the stamping of feet. Low level guerrilla warfare at its best. They wrote the manual.

The motion was passed unanimously with a few extra votes thrown in for good measure. Arlo's song was sung again to a growling accompaniment. It was obviously coffee time. On the way to the coffee bar a member was heard to remark, "It's the type of folk song I like. Low body count, no car chases and a tune you can tap your feet to." Her companion replied, "The *hurdy gurdy* does not exist without the water, the sun and sky."

Megan sat on the comfy cushion on the rocking chair, engulfed in the grand, flowing robes of the Honorary Senior Life President, her expression inscrutable, serene. Some sources in the press suggest their design has been copied from those of the *Gorsedd*[11] even though that organisation is not famed for pink chiffon and lace embroidery trimmings. Although present, she lets thoughts flow by without joining them. She knows an unending stream of them appear in her mind, stay a moment, then disappear, and that she is not them. They are a joyous display of her being. A dance. Nothing needs to be done. And from that peace she acts ... doing nothing. Perfection flowing into perfection. "All is well," she sighed, doing nothing. "I've got all the time in the world, I've got now."

The party returned to the auditorium which had seating for up to four hundred, a hundred and twenty five around the table and two hundred and seventy five in banked seating around the room, a dance floor, a low stage for the musicians, a beautiful double ended ruby and gold Versaille *chaise longue* to the right of the *fenêtres françaises* with a mahogany, four string, D/G *hurdy gurdy* on it, a grand piano in the corner, a small raised area for the rocking chair and a bar. But it was time to put the *hurdy gurdy* back on the *chaise longue*, time to turn away from rigs and jeels, time to put the clogs back into their protective, prestressed, lightweight wooden boxes. There was a rugby match to be watched. Someone pressed a button and the giant UHD 3D plasma screen built into the ceiling descended with a whirrrrrrrr. Everyone was looking forward to another international match, the seventeenth that November. Surely the stadium was paid for by now.

"If we win, we'll have a big party," announced Megan, "and if we lose, we'll have a huge party, albeit after eighty minutes of inconvenience." A huge roar of agreement followed, and much stamping of feet.

They lost.

As someone famously remarked, quipped Megan, 'All happy Machlud y Wawr members are alike, while all unhappy members are unhappy in their own way.'[12]

Bronwen sat at the bar and ordered tea.

"*Un sachet de thé* or *deux?*" asked the barwoman, putting *deux* into the teapot.

"*Oh mon Dieu! Un!* Just *un* please and thank you for asking. I was at a *canu pwnc*[13] in Rhydwilym a little while ago and they put *deux* into the teapot. I hallucinated for a week."

"Is this your first time out since then, then?"

Bronwen waited for the echo to die away. "Probably," she replied, still trembling at the memory. "As for probability, the longer I`ve been sitting down, the more likely it is I`ll soon stand up, but once I`m standing it`s not easy to predict when I`ll sit down again. Unless I`m told to."

The barwoman put a heaped handful of *sachets de thé* into the pot, a strange smile on her face.

"Someone with a teapot is messing with my head," thought Bronwen, "and we don`t need Sigmund Freud[14] to tell us that isn`t a good idea."

"Crazier than a bowlful of shrimps," thought the barwoman.

Bronwen was tired and bored. She glanced at the *télévision* at the end of the bar. *Les Gens de la Vallée*, the musical, was on.[15] "Love their costumes," she said to no one in particular. She read the sign attached to the wall next to it. 'For security reasons, if you leave your sandwiches unattended, they will be removed by security staff and eaten.' Carved into the dark wood underneath was the six-syllabled mantra OM MANI PADME HUM. "Lucky I took Sanskrit during my first year at Ysgol y Preseli,"[16] she thought. She translated out loud. "*In the practice of a path of wisdom, you transform your body, speech and mind into the pure body, speech and mind of a Buddha, or something like that.*"

"I`m impressed," said the barwoman as she placed the overdosed teapot, a small jug of milk, a mug and a spoon on the bar in front of Bronwen who eyed the teapot suspiciously before pouring a little milk into the mug. "Let it steep for ten minutes to get the full benefit," the barwoman advised. She did. That was her first mistake.

"My favourite film is *Michael Gandhi Collins*," said Bronwen to the nice barwoman who wasn`t listening.[17] She was piling *sachets de thé* into a teapot for another customer, this time with a mischievous grin.

The musical finished and the news programme began. "A paper published today in the European Journal of Hypothetical Biology claims that the characteristic huddling that occurs when Machlud y Wawr members congregate together at open air events protects them from driving wind and snow," said the science correspondent. "An individual Machlud y Wawr member needs only to move

½ inch in any direction for her neighbour to react and waddle a step closer to stay warm. These small movements flow through the congregation like a wave. A huddle is usually dense, and the wave helps smaller huddles merge into bigger ones, often consisting of thousands of individuals who are thus able to maintain body temperatures. Surprisingly, a travelling wave can be triggered by any individual in a huddle, rather than individuals on the outside trying to push in, a spokesperson from the Blaenau Ffestiniog Centre for Polar Research informs us. He also tells us that a similar affect has been observed recently amongst Emperor penguins in the Antarctic and in the penguin enclosure at Folly Farm."[18]

"Thank you," said the newsreader, "and now to time. Small children experience time moving more slowly than adults, seeing the world in comparatively slow motion. The smaller an animal or insect the faster its metabolic rate and the greater its ability to detect separate `flashes` of light and thus have a slower perception of time. Summers really were longer when you were a child."

"We project time on our experience, it`s a psychological invention, an inference we make because of the illusion that things change," said the barwoman looking at the clock, urging it to go faster so she could finish her shift.

Bronwen and the barwoman paused.

"I`ve got good news and bad news," said the barwoman, glancing at Bronwen.

"Oh yes?"

"First the good news. I`m going on a dirty weekend to Aberystwyth next week."

"And the bad news?"

"I`m going on my own."

"And now for the international news," interrupted the voice of the BBC Crymych newsreader.[19] The barwoman pressed the pink button on the dooby doo and the television went black. And silent.

Bronwen poured thick dark tea into the mug and took a long leisurely sip. That was her second mistake. Moments later her lips and fingernails flashed a marvellous retro red colour, her earlobes a funky lavender, her nose an amber magenta with areas of subtle purple shading. She placed the mug carefully onto the counter and fell off the stool, accelerating towards the floor at a constant rate of 32 feet per second per second. Such is the effect of gravity in north Pembrokeshire.

The barwoman leant across the bar. "Would you like some more tea?

"No!"

"No!"

"No!"

"Yes!"

Bronwen closed her eyes and looked at the hallucination that engulfed her.

"Can you paint with all the colours of the wind?" she asked Pocahontas who was sitting on the barstool she had recently vacated.

"I`m appalled!" barked a Colonel floating around the lightbulb near the ceiling.

"You can`t be appalled," whispered Bronwen, "you`re not retired." The Colonel huffed and vanished.

The *fenêtres françaises* were wide open. Candide was busy tending to the *pots de fleurs* arranged neatly on the veranda.[20]

"I`m here neither in body nor spirit," thought Bronwen, flickering for a few moments as the barwoman used the juicer behind the bar. No one noticed.

Lionel Hampton[21] played Central Avenue Breakdown on the grand piano in the corner, playing with all the urgency of a background pianist in an empty hotel bar.

"Context is everything in communication," she told the barwoman. "As is waving your arms about." She waved her arms about for a while until they got tired and ached, causing her to grimace.

"As are facial expressions," said the barwoman. "We all find what we`re looking for." She turned the juicer off. Bronwen flickered momentarily. Lionel noticed but continued playing.

Bronwen spoke to her orange and yellow tortoiseshell effect eyeglass frames asking them to check the US`s NOAA Space Weather Prediction Center for sunspot numbers, coronal mass ejections and X-ray flare activity to see if it was safe to get up.[22] While waiting for the information she noticed Jo Stafford standing on the piano, accompanied by Lionel, who was not on the piano but sitting on a little swivel stool next to it, fingers finding the notes. Jo began to sing.

> *See the pyramids along the Nile,*
> *Watch the sun rise on a tropic isle.*
> *Just remember, darling, all the while,*
> *You belong to me.*[23]

"There`s lovely. My life is a slow descent into wonderfulness, so it is," observed Jools Holland to camera as he entered, stage left, through the *fenêtres françaises*.[24] "And now the Hurdy Gurdy Orchestra." Bronwen rolled onto her side, ecstasy shrouding her face. Her favourite, straight from their success at the recent Fishguard Folk Festival.[25]

"Do you like my new outfit?" she asked Jools. That`s one of those questions that a man, through bitter experience, learns not to answer. He kept silent, and the silence was drowned by the sound of massed *hurdy gurdys*.

Bronwen wondered what it would be like to be an image in a mirror. "Would I be happiest concave or convex?"

She rested, watching the dolphins at play above Jools` head. "You`re more beautiful than the sky, more beautiful than the morning," one of them said.

She sensed that somewhere in the world a duck was watching her. "A duck is neither good nor evil," she chanted, holding onto the floor to keep her nerves. "It does what a duck has to do." She repeated the mantra five times then relaxed, releasing the floor from her grip.

The wind picked up outside on the veranda. "Moira!" it cried.

"Jimmy was wrong," she thought.[26]

She pressed the 'Reset' button and discovered she needed some chocolate. She tried to get up, but the effects of the overdose would take days to reduce sufficiently for her to achieve that otherwise straightforward act. Rolling around on the floor in her struggles she became convinced that cyber terrorists were attacking her steering mechanism. Decisively, she moved to pull the plug on her internet connection, but didn`t know how. Worse, there was no obvious USB port. "All very strange," she thought. She noticed anomalies in the anemones wafting in the breeze out on the veranda.

Meic Stevens and the Cadillacs joined Jo on the piano and they sang together ...

Ar y Rue St Michel y mae gwres yn yr awel,
Pan mae`r gwanwyn yn troi tua`r haf.
Ac ar awyr y bore mae arogl coffi,
Rwy`n mynd `nôl i`r hen Rue St Michel.

Mae hi`n braf yn yr haf
Ar y Rue St Michel.[27]

Then they went through the back collection of Meic`s power ballads.

She tried to brain up. It didn`t work. She tried 'Restart'. Nothing. She was too confused to try downloading new software. Her fate was sealed. She`d have to let the effect of the tea subside in its own time.

The two goldfish swimming around her toes were a couple of laidback critters, their faces imbued with peace and serenity. "Hello Tenzin and Gyatso,"[28] she called. Sometimes they were poignant, but never dull. "Self-discipline and reducing your tea intake are essential for a simpler, more contented life," they said before swimming through the *fenêtres françaises* and into the terraced garden. Johnny Cash was on the piano now and led them all in a wild rendition of *Get Rhythm*.

> *Get rhythm when you get the blues,*
> *Come on, get rhythm when you get the blues.*
> *A jumpy rhythm makes you feel so fine,*
> *It'll shake all the trouble from your worried mind.*
> *Get rhythm when you get the blues.*

Followed by a thoughtful *A Boy Named Siân.*[29]

Bronwen was aware that when she looked at the teapot on the bar it was a teapot and when she didn't look at it, it was a wave. A wave of hallucinatory somethingness manifesting out of the formless. Her Hmmmmmm!ometer went into the red.

Meanwhile back on the piano Frank and Nancy Sinatra[30] led a chorus of *Something Stupid* followed by Sonny and Cher[31] with *I Got You Babe*, then Nina Simone[32] with *Feeling Good*, The Monkees[33] with *I'm a Believer*, Terry Jacks[34] with *Seasons in the Sun*, The Righteous Brothers,[35] of course, with *Unchained Melody*, The Drifters[36] with *Stand By Me*, The Ronettes[37] with *Be my Baby*, The Temptations[38] with *My Girl*, Neil Young[39] with *Heart of Gold*, it's what the harmonica was made for, Bob Dylan[40] with *Forever Young*, the Mamas and Papas[41] with *Dream a Little Dream of Me* and Mary Hopkin[42] with *Those Were the Days*. All the classics. It was standing room only on the piano, there was no room for anyone else, so Barry McGuire jumped onto it and cheered everyone up with a blues version of *Eve of Destruction*.

> *Think of all the tea there is in Red China*
> *Then take a look around to Selma, Alabama.*
> *You may leave here for four days in space*
> *But when you return it's the same old place.*
> *The pounding of the clogs, the pride and disgrace,*
> *You can bury your head, but don't leave a trace.*
> *Meet your next-door neighbour, and don't forget to say grace.*
> *And tell me over and over and over again, my friend,*
> *You don't believe, we're on the eve of destruction.*
> *Mm, no no, you don't believe we're on the eve of destruction.*[43]

The legs of the grand piano gave way under the weight but Bronwen didn't hear the commotion. She was fast asleep, curled around the base of the bar stool. The party came to an end with Marvin Gaye[44] saddening everyone with *I Heard it Through the Grapevine* as Lillian Gish[45] floated through the *fenêtres françaises* and into the garden on an ice floe, her inner strengths shining through her suffering. "Generally, there is no time when the time has not yet arrived," she instructed as she disappeared,[46] going east, way down east.

Outside the *fenêtres françaises* and unseen by those in the auditorium, an ant trail made up of common black ants (Lasius niger) winds its way up the trunk of a fruit tree growing in the orchard close by, a sure sign that these tiny creatures, whose far distant ancestors shared the Earth with dinosaurs, are farming aphids for their honeydew. Glossy red and black ladybirds ¼ inch in length with red dome-shaped bodies featuring seven black spots, three each side and one in the middle and black heads with white patches on either side, gleam in the sunlight. Wings beating at 85 times per second they fly at almost 25mph as they descend hungrily upon the aphids.

Active in the spring, yet not venturing far from their nests, some of the pollinators visiting the orchard are solitary yet hardy mining bees, mason bees and leafcutter bees. The rapid vibration of their wings in mid-flight makes a characteristic buzzing sound, but now, foraging for pollen and nectar amongst the apple, blackthorn and hawthorn blossoms, they are silent. Honeybees prefer the warmer summer period when they range over a couple of miles. In the shade of the fruit trees the noisy whirring flight of a swarm of hairy-bodied cockchafer beetles of the genus Melolontha, some more than an inch in length with whitish triangles on their sides, reddish-brown wing cases and orange, antler-shaped antennae can be heard as they head for nearby leaves and flowers to feed.

Reaching a height of almost 47 feet the dense dark green, shiny foliage of a mature ivy plant in which swallows are preparing to sleep for the night lies thick against the outer wall of the crypt on one side of the *fenêtres françaises*. Attracted to the abundant pollen and nectar, bees and hoverflies buzz contentedly around the clusters of small, yellowish-green flowers growing on this woody climber, and feed. Large furry hoverflies with long black antennae and distinctive white tips feed alongside them. Later in the year butterflies will hibernate amongst its leaves and birds will feed on the berries.

With the help of digestive enzymes and mineral particles sucked into their pharynges with food, earthworms in the soil at the base of the ivy grind up decaying organic matter and absorb essential nutrients before excreting the majority of the ingested material, thus supplying the Earth with nitrogen, phosphate and potassium rich compost. Declared sacred by Cleopatra (69BC–30BC), the last Pharaoh of Egypt and the last of the Ptolemy dynasty, earthworms were to be honoured and protected by her subjects. Unaware of this royal decree local curlews, crows and others incorporate them into their diets. With a top speed of about two-hundredths of one mile per hour, if it came to a foot race, an earthworm would almost always lose out to a bird.

In a square, covered yet open-bottomed wooden structure sited in light shade at ground level on the other side of the *fenêtres françaises*, and unnoticed in all the excitement, compost enters the thermophilic stage as the internal temperature reaches 40c.

Later, deep in the woodland, dung beetles, their superposition compound eyes ever alert, will search for dung, getting their bearings from the light of the Milky Way in the night sky high above them as they go. Their activity will improve nutrient recycling and soil structure.

Desperate times, indeed.

11

Never discourage anyone ... who continually makes progress,
no matter how slow.

Plato[1]

Bronwen put the tray bearing two cups of coffee made from freshly
roasted Arabica beans lightly spiced with cardamon, a Jacob's tears footed clear
cake stand upon which sat a *Kvæfjordkake*,[2] *verdens beste kake*, forks, plates and
an antique, pearl-handled cake knife on the table in front of the bay window then
sat on the edge of the sofa next to Megan whose consciousness descended upon
the light sponge with meringue layers filled with rum custard and *crème légère*
lightened with whipped cream, all topped with a generous scattering of halved
strawberries and sliced almonds.

"Who made the decision this morning to bake a cake?" Megan asked.

"I did," replied Bronwen.

"Who did?"

"I did."

And they laughed.

Bronwen leant forward, picked up the cake knife, placed its edge lightly on
the upper surface of the *Kvæfjordkake* and paused before putting on a Norwegian
accent and asking, "Do you know who I am?"

Megan looked at the cake expectantly.

"I am a *Kvæfjordkake* that could be cut in two by your antique pearl handled
cake knife without blinking an eye," murmured Bronwen conspiratorially, in hushed
tones.

And they laughed and laughed.

"Remember, we have trained for this," said Bronwen, cutting the cake and
putting a large piece on each of the two plates before putting the knife down,
handing coffee, cake and fork to Megan, picking up her own and sinking back into
the *sofa*'s embrace.

Rising gracefully in unison two pairs of stockinged feet appeared as if from
nowhere and came to rest on the table.

"You have learnt well my child," said Megan softly.

And they laughed and laughed and laughed. And when they had stopped
laughing, they wiped the tears of merriment from their cheeks with white cotton,
lace-edged handkerchiefs with pink lace floral embroidery corners and began the
serious business of sipping coffee and munching cake.

After a few thoughtful minutes sipping and munching Megan spoke, "You do not *have* a sensation of the *Kvæfjordkake*: you *are* that sensation. Your sensation of the *Kvæfjordkake* is the *Kvæfjordkake*, and there is no 'you' apart from what you sense, feel and know."[3]

Megan knows the crime of the century was committed in Pembrokeshire.
The Parrot knows it too.
The Sergeant knows nothing, but doesn`t know it yet.

Author's note.
Is the meaning of the above conversation opaque? The meaning of each statement, taken on its own, is readily understood even by the sleepiest reader. But how do they come together to form one meaningful whole? Megan and Bronwen have surely accomplished something with their talk? But what? How are they making sense, and what sort of sense are they making? Wisely, we will leave this for ethnographers and linguistic anthropologists to grapple with, for time is short and there is a story to be told.[4]

12

Andy Pandy's coming to play.
La la la la la la.
Andy Pandy's here today.
La la la la la la.
Andy Pandy is somewhere in the garden today. Let's go and find him shall we. There he is, on the swing.
Hello, Andy Pandy.
Look children, he's waving with his feet. That's because he's holding on so tightly with his hands.
Do you remember his swing? Some of you have seen it before, haven't you? Andy likes swinging. Have you got a swing in your garden? I expect some of you have. Andy Pandy show the children how high you can go.

Watch with Mother[1]

"You see," said the Sergeant as he stood in the galley admiring the view of Fishguard through the starboard porthole whilst holding a mug of tea in his right hand, "other people are good with computers. They sit in front of one, their fingers move in a blur over the keyboard and something clever happens. When I do it, the blurring is in my head." He paused, inhaling slowly. Great crested grebes, their ornate head plumes catching his eye played in the water under the cliffs to the east. Some were diving to feed whilst others carried young grebes on their backs. One engaged in a courtship display by rising out of the water and shaking its head. The Parrot didn`t respond. It pretended it was on standby.

The Sergeant`s new coracle goes way beyond zero impact. It makes a positive contribution to planet Earth, and this matters as he works and sleeps on it for long periods at a time, his sleeping quarters being the double room with *ensuite* bathroom below decks in the prow. Its large submerged scenic window is his pride and joy. Interestingly, he got the idea whilst watching *20,000 Leagues Under the Sea*[2] in the Haverfordwest multiplex as a boy. The only science fiction film ever produced by Walt Disney,[3] he recalled. The Nautilus had undersea windows, and even then, he knew that one day he would have a vessel like it. Peter Lorre`s performance was outstanding, and the young Sergeant was rivetted throughout the film. As was the Nautilus.

The coracle uses the regenerative qualities of biological materials. Bacteria living on the hull help the concrete self-repair and the lichen growing alongside regulates the coracle`s temperature without the need for electricity. The outside of the hull above the water line is also designed as an aquarium, something the

Nautilus didn`t have, that removes CO2 from the atmosphere and converts it into fuel. "One up on Captain Nemo," the Sergeant likes to tell his colleagues. The coracle is an aquatic energy producer. The paint covering the vessel`s surfaces, both external and internal, render many environmental pollutants harmless. Floor tiles in the shower utilise the kinetic energy of the Sergeants movements whilst showering to power the lighting in the bathroom. A similar arrangement, but with smaller tiles, is used on The Parrots perch to power its smart phone and tablet.

The coracle is covered in blanket superfast broadband integrated with advanced ICT which allows ready communication between staff in the various coracles of the fleet. Except in the Sergeant`s case. He is baffled by primitive first-generation ICT never mind the advanced stuff but it doesn`t matter as the new technology doesn`t need him. The coracle does everything all by itself, with an occasional tweak from The Parrot, thus removing the weakest link. Ongoing digital disruption has markedly reduced following a Dyfed-Powys Police Rapid-Response Coracle Unit[4] initiative to Sergeant-proof the on-board computer system. The Sergeant is officially regarded as "general purpose technology", both low-input and low-output. With the exception of tea production where output remains encouragingly high.

He sipped some tea from the mug, his reveries interrupted sporadically by the raucous laughter emanating from a wild party hosted by madmen, prophets and best friends Myrddin Wyllt, Lailoken and Suibne Geilt whose annual reunion happened to be on the stern. Next year it moves to Gleann Cholm Cille, in Donegal.

Routinely, as he walks into the vessel's cockpit, several holographic computer displays appear in mid-air in front of him and remain in front of him, interrupting his view as he moves around so that sometimes he can`t find his way out again. The displays are busy with 3D diagrams, charts and vertical rows of essential information relating to the functioning interpretation of the coracle`s progress as it heads for its destination, which is unknown to him. Another built-in safety feature. The onboard computer has been programmed to share information with the Sergeant on a need-to-know basis only and shortly after being installed decided that he doesn`t need to know anything - and that he doesn`t need to know this. Years ago, as a young man, he saw *2001: A Space Odyssey*[5] and this gave him ideas that were not conducive to the coracle`s optimal functioning. His attempts to talk to the computer, nicknamed Hal II by his colleagues, failed. This is basic health and safety.

With an audacious, deliciously suggestive grin, The Parrot, betraying a revealing yet playful phonology and a left-leaning politics it favoured in its youth, formed a matching series of plosives and spoke, "Comrade Captain."

The Sergeant, more of a liberal, centre-middle type, not obviously moving in any direction, not getting there anyway, and never sure about how to get back if he did, looked up and took another sip.

"Thinking and not thinking are the same," advised The Parrot.

Honed by natural selection over millions of years the Sergeant's forty trillion cells sprang into action, over two hundred different cell lines acting as one harmonious whole. Unaware of this development he reached for a chocolate biscuit.

"You are not your thoughts."

An involuntary shudder eased itself along the Sergeant's mug holding arm, spilling some tea. The Sergeant drinks all kinds of tea. He is tea agnostic. He is a tea warrior.

"Here and now is the destination. And then those three things too disappear."

Earlier in the day the Sergeant got lost in the cockpit but after some effort found the exit and proceeded in an orderly fashion to the galley to make a mug of tea. Whilst engaged in this task he pondered important questions for seafarers, such as why things appear smaller the further away they are. "It`s because they`re smaller," he said to himself, pleased to have solved that one. The answer was typical of his ability to get right to the heart of a problem and miss it. He rationalised his thinking by saying that as his wife walks away from him along the quay, she shrinks. She isn`t aware of this and he hasn`t told her. The measuring tape she carries in her handbag for *couture* crises also shrinks. Why it is that he never shrinks when he walks along the quay is a matter he has put to the back of his mind as it is of little importance to him. Perhaps because he seldom walks away from himself. For his hypothesis regarding why his wife shrinks in size as she walks away from him he reached the short list for that highlight of the scientific year, the Ig Nobel Prize.

He was on a roll.

"I`m just as big as I need to be," he decided and thus his curiosity was satisfied. He was, after all, at the centre of his multiverse. And everywhere else in it as well for that matter, and probably an infinity of sizes all at the same time. This was no grey area for him. Neither was it a `roughly zone`.[6] He ventured back to the cockpit to see how things were going. He took his responsibilities as captain seriously. Everything, after all, depended upon his decision-making abilities, honed by many years experience on rivers and oceans. Or so he thought.

He wasn`t one for empiricism. "Evidence?" he would say to new recruits "What`s it for?" When questioned by a Welsh Government[7] scientist about the lack of evidence-based enquiry in DPPRRCU`s working practices he replied, "You`ve never seen pi, yet it exists, and you can`t do science without it."

He put his inability to use modern technology down to an inability to evolve. "I`ve stopped evolving," he likes to tell himself. "My genome has stopped changing." This fact both saddens and delights him. He doesn`t know why but he assumes it gives him an evolutionary advantage. But over what? Molluscs certainly.

Trilobites perhaps. Although this is unfair as the latter are extinct. Being superior, in evolutionary terms, to an extinct marine arthropod is, after all, an unexacting benchmark.

He thought of his wife, Arianrhod. "Her genome often changes. Indeed, her genome swings are famous," he mused, a little downhearted. He thinks his brain has shrunk over the last 20,000 years or so of ancestors. Did this worry him? Not a jot. "That`s what technology is for," he tells The Parrot. He`s more hirsute than his ancestors and has the badge to prove it.

The Sergeant evolved `hum speech' which he uses in mid ocean for communication purposes during stormy weather. It uses pitch, length and loudness and by this means he can communicate with himself about any subject known to himself without using ordinary speech. This phenomenon is found amongst many cultures around the world but there is only one instance of a human being having developed it to talk to himself or herself. Linguists think the isolation of long-distance sea voyages prompted this interesting development yet admit to being unsure as to its exact genesis. It occurred to him that an earlier influence might also be important, namely the `grunt speech` he used in order to communicate with himself as a small child whilst embarking on long distance pushchair journeys, a response no doubt to the design which has the child facing forwards and the parent out of sight behind. For all intents and purposes the child travels through time and space alone with no parental stimulation. Experts in child development think that only a man with no child-care experience could have designed an early-years off-road transporter vehicle in this way.

Before he began using the pushchair the Sergeant was carried by his parents and this, along with the length of their legs and thus the quickness of their strides when walking, was largely responsible for his rhythmical preferences. Little does he know that the rhythms of his great-great-great-great and a couple more great-grandparents strolling patterns when they began walking in Africa millions of years ago, absorbed through an early ancestor of the Sergeant's vestibular system in the inner ear, provided his early brain with information about the motion. Today, his spontaneous motor tempo hovers around the 120 beats a minute mark which partly explains his fondness for the Mamas and the Papas song *California Dreamin'*. As does the effect of Mama Michelle on the Sergeant's early brain, of course.

Veering off course slightly, "Since tomatoes, however you choose to pronounce them, have more genes than humans and are thus more advanced it follows that UFO`s bring aliens who want to meet tomatoes," he mused.

He had read that '... genes are not our essence; our genetic inheritance can be changed; environmental events can be `remembered` by cells; and what happens in your life can affect later generations.'[8] He knows this to be true because his family have always been coraclers. All sides.

Draining the mug of tea, he felt stimulated into action, decisive action. "Calm down," he advised himself as he reached for the kettle to make another mug of tea. The on-board computer hummed agreeably. "I catastrophise," he thought, "I always think the coracle is going to sink, even when it`s beached. Low grade tension in the solar plexus confuses thinking and stifles creativity. Danger could be my middle name," he mused, "though it isn`t."

Seated by the table in the galley munching a chocolate biscuit with a fresh mug of steaming tea on the table next to him he picked up the dooby doo, pointed it at the on-board radio bolted securely to the starboard bulkhead aft of the fridge-freezer and pressed `Play` to catch the news and by doing so joined a live radio discussion about nautical matters that were of direct interest to him. He reached for another biscuit and listened.

"... and the next step will be to fuel Dyfed-Powys Police Rapid-Response Coracle Unit vessels with anti-matter so they can travel at light speed and beyond. A team of physicists at the University of North Pembrokeshire at Crymych are working with a group from CERN[9] on the French Swiss border and the aim of their research is to provide DPPRRCU with the most modern, up to date capability and in the process they hope to throw light on two secondary matters, where did the universe come from and why is it that everything we can see, everything that has form, and all known energies make up only about 4% of it. The team recently trapped an atom of anti-hydrogen in a jam jar with half a dozen tadpoles for several days, until one of the tadpoles ate it. A major breakthrough."

"I can see one downside to this," thought the Sergeant, "the coracle will travel at speeds so fast it will suck fish out of the water and rabbits off the cliffs. They`ll have to fit mudflaps." This idea brought back memories of patrolling Milford Sound and the afternoon he stopped a canoeist for speeding. The canoe had Carmarthenshire plates. "Step away from the paddle," the Sergeant ordered quietly. "Step away from the paddle," he repeated, adding, by mistake, "and step away from the vehicle." He used the grappling iron to rescue the canoeist who was struggling in the deep water and swearing at him in Welsh.

"Can you speak English?"

"No!"

"But you`re speaking English now."

"I don't care!"

The Sergeant let him off with a caution, in Welsh and English, before releasing him back into the water so he could retrieve his canoe, now carried some distance away by the current. The Sergeant knows exactly what his job is. To go out there and cause general havoc and mayhem amongst the canoeing fraternity.

Reminiscing happily about acts of general havoc and mayhem and wondering what jobs he might get on with the Sergeant picked up the tea and another chocolate biscuit and looked around. Sensing danger, and timing its intervention perfectly, The Parrot clicked the Insert Sergeant Field icon on its wingwatch and inserted the Sergeant into the hammock. Some regard this level of security to be over the top but The Parrot is only too well aware of the danger an unsupervised Sergeant poses to shipping. It chose carefully from the drop-down menu as the wrong option might result in the Merging or Splitting of cells, or worse, turn him into a Footnote. Ctrl+Alt+Delete is useful occasionally to close the Sergeant down when he is not responding, and it goes without saying that Hyperlinks are not advised. Lord knows what that might lead to!

Barely registering the change and pleased to find himself in the hammock the Sergeant continued his revelries. Reading the graffiti on a wall in Peking some years ago whilst on official hush hush business there he came across an ancient Chinese proverb, "If I keep a green bough in my heart, the singing bird will come." Upon his return he planted willows on the eastern side of the lake on the stern. Several species of birds live there permanently now and migratory birds winter there. The Sergeant and The Parrot decamp to the cool of the willow grove on hot balmy, summer evenings. It is where the Sergeant goes for his power snoozing sessions which, he has discovered, 'if repeated, become continuous'.[10]

A number of options are available for selection on the touchscreen of The Parrot's wingwatch to regulate the depth of the Sergeant's sleep. Deep Sleep Mode is the most energy efficient. Neuroscientists recently confirmed that during it there is more brain activity in a marble.

He put the mug of tea and the biscuit on the small coffee table next to the hammock, picked up his favourite novel, Herman Hesse`s *Siddhartha*, the Picador edition with Hilda Rosner`s wonderful translation from German to English[12] he bought years ago in Seaways,[11] Fishguard's première boutique qui vend des livres, lay back in the hammock and began, once again, to read out loud from the beginning. *'In the shade of the house, in the sunshine on the riverbank by the boats, in the shade of the sallow wood and the fig tree, Siddhartha, the handsome Brahmin`s son, grew up with his friend Govinda. The sun browned his slender shoulders on the riverbank, ...'* He savoured the words. Over the years he had read the book dozens of times. "What bliss!" he exclaimed.

He noticed the moon shining brilliantly in the light of the morning. "The moon is forever dark," he commented to no one, "there is no moonlight, but sunlight reflected from it. And earthshine. Therefore, both sides of the moon are dark."

"Creepy," he thought and changed the subject, putting *Siddhartha* back and reaching for his well-thumbed *The Sub-Committees of Wales, Volume 3, 1768-1821*. His brain slipped naturally into cruise control and he lay back in the hammock to enjoy the ride. From the radio in the galley came the soft, gentle sound of Katherine Jenkins[13] belting out that old Nonconformist favourite, King Crimson`s *21st Century Schizoid Woman*.[14] As he concentrated on reading the Sergeant joined in absentmindedly with the background harmonies and felt strangely comforted.

The alarm went off. His wife was ascending the gang plank having returned to Fishguard after a long weekend with the girls on the Gower. He lay still in the hammock feigning death as she undertook a brief yet thorough inspection of the vessel, forefinger detecting, notebook and pencil recording, before proceeding to the willow grove and prodding him in the side with her toe.

"CLEANING?" she enunciated slowly and with menace.

"**C L E A N I N G ?**" she repeated dustily, with emphasis, with added decibels and with a Chinese accent. The latter affect he found unsettling.

He meditated upon this for a few moments, weighing up his options. Peeking out between his eyelashes the expression on her face suggested they were few. He chose a high-risk option, high-risk because he was lying deep in the hammock with her toe, still in its boot, in his side, poised and ready to strike.

He moved rook to e4.

She responded, rook to e6.

Rook to d4.

Rook to d5.

Yes, the classic French Defence, an audacious move. But to no avail as a little while into the game Arianrhod unexpectedly stood on a square on the deck that could be taken by three of his pieces. Legend has it that, seeing this, The Parrot threw several pieces of eight onto the grass next to the hammock.

Realising his carefully planned strategy had failed he attempted a different gambit. "I'm here to eat chocolate biscuits and drink tea. And pilgrim, I'm all out of tea," he murmured.[15] Often coinciding with logical incongruity, humour evolved in his family about six and a half million years ago.

Cold vengeance glinted in her eyes. Retribution would be swift, clinical. Despair coursed through his veins with the adrenaline and his body gave an involuntary shudder of panic. Desperate, he tried another tack.

"Who is this Klee Ning of whom you speak, dearest?"

It is a risky business using words.

Her foot moved with great speed. "I`m going to stay with my mother!" she ordered, at least it sounded like an order, as he hit the deck. And off she went, leaving behind her a blast radius of several hundred feet.

He rolled into the foetal position, conserving energy in line with DPPRRCU emergency protocols and remained where he was, facing the gentle warmth of the southern sun, and dozed, dreaming of *petite* Chinese women with slim waists and small breasts in their tight-fitting *cheongsams*. He was back in Peking with the socialites. Oh, to be young again! Nonetheless, the Sergeant felt uneasy as word had come to him of Comanche and Kiowa raiding parties coming out of the hill country to the north of the river.[16]

Nearby, centipedes, predatory, carnivorous creatures that inject their venom through forcipules to kill or paralyze their prey, hunted in the moist environment of the woodland floor, antennae twitching. Forcipules, pincer-like forelegs, are unique to centipedes which always have an odd number of legs, the number changing during their lifetimes. Millipedes, which never have as many as a thousand legs and make up for this by having a number of unusual mating styles, moved slowly beneath decaying wood, munching happily on leaf litter and other plant matter. First appearing in the fossil record during the Silurian period, they are among the first animals to have colonised land. A distant ancestor grew to almost 7 feet in length.

A thin, fragile daddy-long-legs with a body less than half an inch long and long, spindly legs nearly 2 inches in length waited patiently in its irregular shaped web, its two lateral groups of eyes and two median contiguous eyes keeping watch, unaware that it belongs to a family of araneomorph spiders first described by the German entomologist and arachnologist Ludwig Carl Christian Koch[17] in 1850.

The inventor of the coracle all those thousands of years ago was a genius who cared about aesthetics. Inventors often change the way we live our lives, the inventor of the coracle achieved something far greater and more lasting, by altering not only the way we behave but the way we think. He or she did it by marrying two elements of our culture that are usually held distinct and antithetical: cutting edge science and art. The unknown inventor brought the unloved one-person fishing vessel into daily human life by combining utility and beauty in a way that few other technical innovators have achieved, and most never attempt.[18]

As Barack Obama[19] said in a speech at the 2016 Great Lakes International Coracling Congress, the inventor of the coracle was brave enough to think differently, bold enough to believe they could change the world and talented enough to do it. Legend has it that the coracle`s inventor once remarked that being the richest person in the Stone Age didn`t matter to him. He wanted to go to bed thinking he had done something wonderful.[18] He did. As Steve Jobs once remarked, 'It`s better to be a pirate than to join the navy.' Henry Ford[20] said that if he asked his customers what they wanted they would lazily and unimaginatively have said, 'Faster horses'. The inventor of the coracle did not give customers what they wanted. He gave them what they could not imagine.[18]

Inspired, the Sergeant sang a few lines of one of the great songs, a take on the mediaeval *trope*, to himself, to The Parrot, to the birds in the willow grove, to passers-by, to assembled tourists on the quayside and to anyone else who was listening.

I`m bound to stay
Where you sleep all day,
Where they jailed the jerk
That invented work
In the Big Rock Candy Mountain.

"Oh, to have the honey voice of a Burl Ives,"[21] he thought. The Parrot agreed.

"And now for the news," came the distant voice of the Radio Free Pembrokeshire[22] announcer. "A Bronze Age stone coracle in the Preselis capsized over the weekend. The two-ton Cwrwgl Morris as it is known was left lying upside down next to the spot where it has stood for as long as anyone in the area can remember. Local Canoeing Rebellion activists are being sought by the police."

"Strange that it's not made of bronze," he thought.

"And now some light relief. In a breakthrough experiment recently scientists at the CARN[23] nuclear research facility near Strumble Head trapped a coracle made of anti-hydrogen, each atom of which is made up of a positron and an antiproton, for over seventeen minutes. Previously such things disappeared as soon as they were created. This allowed the anti-matter coracle to be studied in detail. Normally, when matter-coracles and anti-matter coracles meet they annihilate each other instantly, releasing a burst of high energy. The anti-coracle was first proposed by a physicist in 1931[24] and since then the race has been on for physicists to try and find a way to harness the energy. The search is also on for an anti-coracler. An anti-coracler is the mirror of an ordinary coracler. Normal coraclers are made up of positively charged nuclei orbited by negatively charged electrons. Their anti-matter counterparts are the other way around, having negatively charged nuclei and positively charged electrons."

"Whatever will they think of next," the Sergeant muttered, a little perturbed, swatting a cloud of positively charged electrons that had settled on his nose.

"Ouch!"

"Scientists at CARN suggest we are on the brink of a new physics. In a breakthrough experiment conducted recently they spun the Sergeant around a 49-foot magnetic ring at nearly the speed of light and recorded the speed at which he wobbled. "The results are not what we expected," a spokesperson told us earlier today. "Are there new particles or forces not accounted for in the standard model?"

"Council news now. A furious political debate has erupted in County Hall in Haverfordwest after IT Support officers removed the Chief Executive's[25] computer for repairs. A quote was discovered carved into the surface of the giant mahogany desk under where the computer had stood. The quote, in comic sans, font size 18, probably inscribed with a rusty penknife, allegedly reads, `Politics is the art of looking for trouble, finding it, misdiagnosing it and then misapplying the wrong remedies'.[26] The Chief Executive[25] has stated that he is innocent and that it must be the work of a previous, rather unpleasant Chief Executive.[25] When questioned he revealed that the philosophy enshrined within the words does not guide his policy making. In support of the Chief Executive[25] an angry County Councillor,[27] when asked about it by Radio Free Pembrokeshire earlier this morning, said, `A previous Chief Executive[28] had an Icarus complex and thought rather a lot of himself. In Bruegel's painting *The Fall of Icarus*[29] there's this huge landscape and in the bottom right-hand corner there's a small pair of legs sticking out of the water. He thought his life was something momentous, huge, but in the great scheme of things he was just a pair of legs sticking out of the water'."

"This year the county's annual Bog Snorkelling Championships are to be held near Puncheston. The bog there is perfect. The winner will represent Pembrokeshire at the World Bog Snorkelling Championships."[30]

"This Saturday at 11.00a.m. a saucy new novel will be launched in a *café* in Fishguard. *Coraclers' Wives* is the raunchy tale of shenanigans amongst high-ranking members of the Coraclehood. The author will give a brief talk about the inspiration for the book followed by a questions and answers session. Refreshments will be available throughout until 2.00p.m. The book the Admiral wants to scupper."

"And finally, midnight tonight at the Norwegian Church in Cardiff sees the European launch of the new 5G-enabled iPaddle 23, which Wall Street analysts tell us will release a 'supercycle' of sales."[18]

"And now for our afternoon story read by Sioned Davies."[31]

"*Treiglgwaith ...*" began Sioned. "That's, 'Once upon a time ...' in Welsh. *Treiglgwaith, yn ieuenctid y dydd, ...* Once upon a time, in the youthfulness of the day ... It's from the Mabinogion. First branch, Pwyll a Rhiannon."

"It's an old story," the on-board computer explained.

Sioned continued. "*Treiglgwaith, yn ieuenctid y dydd*, Pwyll was at home in Haverfordwest when he decided to go shopping in town. He set off on foot, his springer spaniels with him, stopping off at a cafe, Rhiannon's near the clock tower, to meet some friends and have a cup of tea, three pieces of toast and some chocolate for breakfast. Afterwards they all set off together. It was the annual St Elvis Day parade and the town thick with people. He was concentrating so much on chatting up Rhiannon's sister that the dogs ran off and chasing after them he became separated from his companions. As he followed their barking, he heard the cry of a second pack of dogs. Running south along Bridge Street he could see a clearing ahead. As he entered the Square, he saw his dogs and on the other side of the clearing another pack entering from Quay Street chasing a Norwegian Forest cat. It was huge. To his dismay, the other pack caught up with the cat in the middle of the square, bringing it to ground. The dogs were a dazzling white colour with red ears. He had never seen dogs like them. "Must be from Milford," he thought. He shooed the dogs away from the cat only for his own dogs to jump on it."

"Before he could rescue the animal a horseman coming down the High Street on a magnificent dapple-grey horse with a hunting horn around his neck cantered up to Pwyll's dogs and said, **SHOOH!**"

"Oh yeh! Think you`re important, do you?" Pwyll retorted.

"Well actually, yes, I do."

"Hmmm!"

"It`s not done where I come from."

"What isn`t?"

"Driving off another bloke`s dogs when they`ve caught a cat. I`m not gonna do anything about it, it being the St Elvis Day parade and him being a local saint and all that and there being lots of families around. A large pot of tea and a scone in that *café* over by there will do it."

"Yeh, you`re right," replied Pwyll, "so for 'friendship and honour', tea and a scone it is. I don`t know who you are."

"A crowned king in the land that I`m from."

Pwyll noted that the man had red ears. "And which land is that?"

"Why this land, Pembrokeshire. I am the lord of the Great Council of the County. My castle stands by the river."

"Can we be friends?"

"If you wish. Although I rarely make friends with common stock. But I likes your dogs. There is one condition on the friendship, and this is it ..."

"And there we leave the story for today," came the announcer`s voice. "It will be continued after the news tomorrow and every day for the rest of the month. Oh! And the Norwegian Forest cat got away safely."

A Great White, dazzling white shark surfaced next to the coracle, teeth gleaming in the late evening sun. The holidaymakers on the breakwater froze, even though it was a hot, sultry evening. The Sergeant noticed it had red ears. Springing into action he moved effortlessly to the bow of the coracle and paddled furiously towards the sanctuary of the marina. "With luck we`ll get there before the anti-shark boom is lowered for the evening," he told the crew.

There had been a spate of disappearances during the summer. A number of yachts owned by people from away, all driving Volvos and Range Rovers and all owning holiday homes in the area, had gone missing. One of the locals, a Mr M. Glyndŵr,[32] told police one of his neighbours thought it must be shark attacks as no ransom notes had been received. "And how do you know that?" asked the police officer. Mr Glyndŵr smiled knowingly. The yacht owners paid for the anti-shark boom.

The coracle sped towards the marina leaving a large wake in its path. The Great White followed at a respectable distance, keeping up easily with the coracle`s acceleration produced by the Sergeant`s powerful, rhythmic paddling, a skill he had learnt the hard way over the years, by paddling. Then he spotted the boom. It was still up. The Sergeant fired a distress flare high into the great blue yonder. It exploded high above the harbour sending an "*Oooooooooh!*" of appreciation around the heads of the onlookers. Marina staff, alerted by the pretty fireworks display, manned the pulleys on both sides of the boom and attempted to lower it. But the binder twine on one side had twisted and was caught fast between the wheel and the axle. This would take some time. The Sergeant deployed a circular holding pattern, both clockwise and anticlockwise, and occasionally a figure of eight, to keep ahead of the shark whilst waiting to enter the safety of the marina with the boom lowered behind him.

News of the chase spread like wildfire through the twin towns and a huge crowd formed to watch the spectacle from the breakwater and the harbour wall. After some hours of this a great cheer went up as a very giddy Sergeant guided the coracle into the safely of the marina just as the boom was lowered. The crowd burst into a reggae version of *Don`t Cry For Me Eglwyswrw*,[33] a perennial favourite, and the barbecues around the water`s edge fed everyone fish and healthy wholemeal bread rolls, much to the vicar's delight.

It won`t be easy, you`ll think it strange
When I try to explain how I feel.
That I still need your love after all that I've done.
You won't believe me.
All you will see ...

This was followed by a more conventional version of Bob Dylan`s *Mr Coracling Man*.[34]

Take me on a trip upon your magic swirling ship.
My senses have been stripped,
My hands can`t feel to paddle, ...

They experienced it all, *pathos, comedy, melodrama* and *bathos*, all in the crazed freedom of the moment. But mostly *bathos*.

For many years after that, indeed up to this very day, the story of the Sergeant and his crew, The Parrot, repelling a fierce attack by a gang of thirty to forty Great White sharks and how they fought them all the way from Newfoundland to Fishguard Harbour is a favourite of local storytellers, particularly in the summer when Pembrokeshire is full to the brim with tourists who listen fearfully as the tale rolls on and on, heaving a collective gasp as they learn that the gallant crew were down to their last tea bag as they rounded Dinas Head.

Each summer, the greatest storyteller of them all, Shemi Wâd,[35] who lives in a small, whitewashed cottage in Broom Street opposite Berachah Chapel, holds court in a Goodwick pub in the evenings with throngs of mesmerised tourists sitting on the cold, slate floor in front of him as he spins this most famous of yarns. During the day he runs a sanctuary for homeless pigs in Rhos-y-Caerau, Pencaer, in a delightful spot facing Garn Fawr, Garn Fechan and Garn Folch. What a trio! In the wooden arched entrance to the sanctuary are carved the words *Cyfaill i foch, a hoff gan foch.*[36] A tribute any storyteller would be proud of. As silence falls on his nervous and expectant audience he coughs twice, takes a sip of local seawater to calm the throat, a dramatic pause ... and then, in a quiet yet powerful voice, drawing upon more ancient tales, he begins. "*Treigylgweith, yn ieuengtit y dyd, kyuodi a oruc, a dyuot y ...*"[37]

He sometimes tells the tale of the long weekend he spent with Catherine Zeta-Jones in her caravan in Porthcawl. Locals suspect this to be a tall tale however as everyone knows her caravan is in the Mumbles.[38]

With no warning, not so much as a "Hi there!" a thick sea mist rolled in, engulfing the harbour in its lethal embrace. Holidaymakers on the beach grew uneasy. Strange things are known to happen when a sea mist comes to land in these parts. They heard the ominous sound of the bell on the buoy anchored beyond the harbour wall and a shiver ran through them. Women ground their teeth. Men's faces turned white as the blood drained from them. Confused teenagers looked up from the screens of their mobile devices. Glancing seawards they started taking photographs. Taking their cue from the locals, they sought shelter in *cafés* and pubs.

The Parrot flew to the crow's nest from where it sounded the general alarm, seven short blasts of the conch shell followed by one long blast. The remainder of the crew, executing a well-rehearsed emergency measure, proceeded to the designated muster station on the bow, where, with his right hand, he reached instinctively to grasp the handle of the cutlass bound tightly to his left side by the wide leather belt, an accessory achieving both function and style, around his waist. The *solarstein*, a light-sensitive crystal used by Norse navigators to locate the sun on cloudy days could not help under these conditions. And anyway, it lay forgotten in the back of a drawer in the galley.

In tune with the ocean and its spirits, and trusting his instincts, the Sergeant leant over the side and plunged his head into the cold, murky waters to study the signs. His eyes closed in contemplation, smarting from the salt. "Tell me what is coming!" he gurgled.

Silence. Dylan Ail Don did not answer.

176

He waited a few moments more then, running out of oxygen, raised his head out of the briny yet zesty harbour water, spluttered a few times, coughed vigorously, scraped the seaweed off his nose, opened his eyes and drew breath. He shook the salty water out of his hair and pulled more seaweed out of his ears. Prostrating himself he pressed his left ear close to the deck and listened.

Nothing.

The Parrot, high on the main mast, heard it first. "Listen close!" it counselled, with reverent tone. "And you will hear it. It's ... a woman's voice ..."

The Sergeant let go the fear and opened his mind to all possibilities. A calm descended upon him. Then he, also, heard it, faint at first, barely audible. "Yes. A woman's voice ... soft ... welcoming ..."

Time to go home, time to go home.
La, la, la, la, la, la, la, la, la, la.
Time to go home, time to go home.
The Sergeant is waving goodbye, goodbye, goodbye.

The Sergeant is going home now.
But he's coming again soon.
Goodbye children. Goodbye.

Time to go home, time to go home.
La, la, la, la, la, la, la, la, la, la.
Time to go home, time to go home.
The Sergeant is waving goodbye, goodbye, goodbye.[1]

As the sound of snoring reached it, The Parrot knew it was safe to return to its perch in the galley and relax. With the usual thoughtfulness it first placed a blanket over the sleeping Sergeant to prevent him catching a chill in the cold, damp air.

Later that evening, high on the clock tower above Fishguard Town Hall to the east, the civil defence siren gave the all-clear signal indicating that it was safe for civilians to leave their shelters as the air raid or other hazard had passed.

13

... allow the mystery of the universe to be something awesome and beautiful.
Ram Dass[1]

Megan was sitting on the armchair in the *simne fawr* reading, for the umpteenth time, her battered and treasured copy of *The Ascent of Rum Dingli*, W. E. Arrowman`s classic account of a mountaineering expedition during the 1950`s when Rum Dingli, the highest peak in the Preseli Mountains range, was climbed for the first time.[2] Or was it? The book contains a map showing the mountains and the main river in the region with sketches of birds and other wildlife found there and notes on the place-names. It was written on a 58-foot-long roll of cartridge paper that lay undiscovered in a paper bag under his bed until the Welsh Place-Name Society[3] heard rumours of its existence. After months of research at the National Library of Wales[4] in Aberystwyth and in the pubs of south Ceredigion they finally traced the author to a cottage near Cardigan. Overjoyed that his literary and toponymic efforts were appreciated the author gave permission for publication. And the rest, as they say, is Rum Dingli. The Sunday Times` Literary Critic[5] wrote, "Wonderful. *The Ascent of Rum Dingli* does for mountaineering what *Moby Dick*, the film starring Gregory Peck, does for Fishguard[6] or the novel *Don`t Cry For Me Aberystwyth* does for, well, Aberystwyth."[7]

It is as new each time she reads it, that timeless tale of bravery, courage, daring, heroism, determination, fortitude, resolve, and, finally, betrayal and disappointment on a bleak mountain range. Her reading tipple, a one litre tub of ice cream, always helps. In large parts of Western Europe they put milk into their ice cream. In Crymych they eat it pure. Just ice cream. Unadulterated. Raw. X-certificated hardcore. To eat it she uses one of a set of vintage mismatched teaspoons cooled to the correct temperature. There is no sugar in the Machlud y Wawr[8] version, and lots of fibre. Together with the exercise of lifting the weighted spoon, and good company, this is a perfect part of her diet.

Their exercise schedule is tough. For Megan and Bronwen a half hour structured workout in the gym just off the crypt followed by a clogging video. They have a range: *Now That`s What I Call Clogging*; *Annibendod Llwyr: Fast and Furious Clogging Techniques*; *30 Minute Everyday Clogging*, *Body Shaping Intensive Clogging* and Megan`s favourite, Eilyr MacPherson`s *The Clog*.[9] From easy to advanced, each one lasting half an hour, except the ones that are longer, some gentle, some wild and abandoned. An hour of quality exercise every day is the optimum recommended dose. During the warmer months, which are few high up on this mountain, Tai Chi and yoga are recommended, which Megan and Bronwen do every morning in the apple orchard.

They had been busy over the weekend having gone on the *Clonc Mawr*, the monthly walk in Pembrokeshire, in Welsh of course, for Welsh speakers and adults learning Welsh.[10] They alternate it with *Teithwyr Teifi*`s outings in Ceredigion.[11]

To keep her place, she folded down the top corner of the page, a habit picked up in infants' school, much to the disappointment of Miss Thomas, the kindly teacher. She closed the book and put it on the small table next to her. Picking up the dooby doo she leant back into the armchair, pointed it at the large screen television on the wall on the opposite side of the crypt, clicked `On`, turned the volume up and watched the news from S4C.[12]

"Some Japanese scientists are working on bringing extinct animals back from the dead, including dinosaurs. At a full meeting of Pembrokeshire County Council[13] last night planning permission was given for the scientists to fence off large tracts of the southern slopes of the Preseli Mountains so that these returned animals can roam free. A one-mile-wide corridor will extend from the dinosaur park to the sea at Saundersfoot so the animals can go for a swim. Objections from local shopkeepers due to concerns regarding traffic congestion were put aside and a subcommittee was formed with the task of redesigning the town`s one-way system. The scheme`s potential for attracting visitors interested in seeing previously extinct animals helped overcome objections."

Megan wished them luck. Bronwen was worried. She remembered the film about Jurassic Park,[14] that failed attempt to bring dinosaurs back to life. A shiver went down her spine, then up again. Further attempts, also filmed, failed. Another shiver went down her spine, then up again.

"With typical Japanese ingenuity miniature versions of the park for kiddies to take home in a bucket will be on sale. Every child can have his or her own dinosaur under the bed. Or in the bath if the animals are aquatic. Every parent's dream, say the scientists."

Megan licked the ice cream off the spoon. "Every parent`s dream?"

Bronwen sat in her armchair facing Megan whilst recovering from the afternoon`s clogging match between Crymych and Scleddau. "Clogging isn`t getting any easier," she explained to Megan as she rubbed Dunderhonung Fire Ointment[15] onto her bruises. "Even though they`ve changed the rules of engagement and taken away the long-range hit, contact is still heavy. The referees hold the opposing packs apart a long time but it`s a *trébuchet* waiting to happen. The shock of the contact creates a car-crash environment our bodies have to absorb." She looked down and fidgeted with something. "Do you know," she said, changing the subject, "I`ve lived in Pembrokeshire all my life yet I`ve never walked the Coast Path."[16]

179

"Yes," said Megan, "that`s the way of it. I hear there are Cockneys living in London who have never been beheaded in the Tower."

After waiting patiently for the conversation to stop the newsreader continued. "The best place to open a new *blancmange* shop is, of course, right next to an existing *blancmange* shop." The girls looked up. "Two become three and before you know it there's a cluster attracting *blancmange* lovers from far and wide. *Blancmange`Rus*, Crymych's seventeenth *blancmange* shop opens today. Everything is free for the first week. A spokesperson for the city`s *blancmange* Makers has welcomed the news saying that this development will cement Crymych`s reputation as the go-to destination for *blancmange* lovers in west Wales."

"I`m going to try the mixed fruit special," said Bronwen, "it`s one showerburst of a *blancmange*."

Amused by the constant interruptions the announcer burst into song. He chose one he often sings in his canoe whilst shooting the majestic Cenarth rapids on the daily commute down the Teifi to Cardigan where he works in the studio in the castle. He has a mooring next to it. His French trapper`s accent done in Oliver Reed style was a little contrived, but overall, viewers agreed that Rita would approve.

> *When I`m a man I`ll take me a wife.*
> *We`ll live in a house on the hill, the hill.*
> *The carts and horses all white all white,*
> *And she will have diamonds and pearls, and pearls.*
> *And she will have diamonds and pearls.*[17]

Bronwen loved it and sang along. "If only newsreaders would sing songs all the time instead of reading the news," she thought.

"Spring is well and truly here," continued the announcer. "The first swallow was seen in St Nicholas this morning. The St Nicholas swallows are the first to arrive every year. You can set your watch by them. I have with me a tame ornithologist and keen entomologist ....."

"Etymologist."

"Etymologist. Here is Dr Iolo Jones who is going to tell us about interesting research published in *Astudia Celtica*."[18]

"Thank you. In volume XXXVI in 2002 a linguist published a short contribution in which he discussed the etymology of *gwennol*, the Welsh word for *swallow*, and a feminine noun. To cut a long story short he suggests that *gwenn* means *fork* and the suffix -ol means *small*. So *gwennol* is *fork small* which means, remembering that English is back to front, *small fork*, aptly describing this beautiful bird. He suggests that the folk etymology which produced the idea that the name is *gwenfol*, later *gwynfol* meaning *gwyn bol*, *white belly* is just that, folk etymology and is wrong. The descriptive word *fork* also lies behind the English word *swallow*, the evidence coming from other Germanic languages such as Norwegian and Faroese."

"Thank you, Dr Jones."

"Compare also the Old Cornish *guennol* and Old Irish *fannall*, both feminine. We see here an -l- suffix, having a diminutive function not unexpected in a bird name."

"Coffee?" Bronwen asked.

"Ohh! Yes plllleeeeeease."

"Sugar?"

"No. No. **Nooo**."

"Of course not. Cup or mug?"

"Cup."

"Handle on right or left?"

"On the left today, I think."

Bronwen moved towards the kitchen. She made the journey a pilgrimage, as all journeys are.

Outside, deep in the orchard canopy, a kingfisher sang.

Then began the sound of clattering and nervousness. "You`re a machine. You`re cleverer than I am. Work!" Megan heard Bronwen say.

"It`s a kettle, dear," Megan said soothingly. "Speak nicely to it and be patient."

The announcer took advantage of the pause as the kettle boiled. "Physicists at Swansea University[19] have announced that Einstein`s calculations on time in his General Theory of Relativity[20] are slightly, ever so slightly flawed because he failed to take into account the `Kettle Phenomenon`, due to which, on certain occasions, time slows. They think the `Kettle Phenomenon` is commoner than previously thought, happening several times every day in homes, offices and physics departments around the world."

"Do you want to hear my favourite religious joke?" asked Megan.

A worried frown appeared fleetingly on Bronwen`s face. "Religion?" she thought. "That`s not like Megan."

Unperturbed Megan pressed on. "How do you make God laugh?"

Bronwen had no idea.

"Tell Her your plan."

Bronwen didn`t get it. She thought of all the terrible things that appeared on the news almost every night. "How do you make God cry?" she enquired.

"Indeed," replied Megan thoughtfully as she put the dooby doo down and picked up the London papers she reads on a Friday, The Times[21] and the Guardian,[22] just to see if the Western Mail[23] has missed anything.

"I'm not altogether fond of the radio," Bronwen remarked as she appeared from the kitchen carrying a tray upon which were two cups of coffee, a little-known blend called Black Blood of the Earth.[24] The caffeine content is up to 40 times greater than regular coffee, hence they limit intake to four a month. Also on the tray were sweet cakes made from cinnabar and honey that were dried by the sun in the orchard that morning and some chocolate truffles, *bûche au chocolat* and *marrons glacés*. Of course! It is to these delicacies that Megan attributes her youthful looks. Bronwen gave a coffee and sweet cake to Megan then settled herself with coffee and sweet cake on the other armchair in the *simne fawr*.

"Why?"

"You have to listen to people talking all the time."

A cloud of self-propelled flowers flew in through the open window, swallowtails, small pearl-bordered fritillarys, pale clouded yellows, purple hairstreaks, common brimstones, small and large skippers, orange tips, small blues and painted ladies, Bronwen's favourite. On hot days butterflies are drawn to the coolness of the crypt.

"How`s your back, dear?" asked Megan.

"Getting better slowly, thanks."

"You shouldn`t have done that bungee jump off Cardigan bridge without someone checking the bungee for you first. It wasn`t the right length."

"You`re right. Luckily it stopped me half a mile downriver by the Ferry Inn[25] so I had a nice cup of coffee there before being rescued."

"Don`t live in love with me," said the newsreader, "fall into the love that you are so that you will shower everything with love. Including Cardigan Castle."

Megan looked concerned. Bronwen smiled a smile of knowing. The butterflies circled above her head, waiting to pounce.

Megan daydreamed. "Has your love for me changed since I became ill?" Her husband asked her one day.

"Unfair."

"In what way?"

"Every day I love you more."

"What will you do when I die?"

"I`ll mourn you every moment and then I`ll get on with my life, for life is to be lived. And I`ll be grateful that life gave me such a precious, joyous gift as you. And I`ll celebrate and be grateful for the happiness we shared. Gratitude will be the most powerful emotion. Gratitude for life itself."

"I wish my arm was made of elastic."

"Why?"

"I would wrap it several times around yours. Hmmm. I might be wrong ..... but I think we just kissed."

"We did."

"It seems as though. Hmmmmm. Wait a moment ..... it happened again."

"Yes, it did."

"You don`t seem too concerned."

"I'm not. Do it again, cariad."

As a wedding present Megan gave him a t-shirt with the words `Under new management` written on it.

She thought of friends of theirs who kept telling their children what careers would be good for them when they grew up and that they should work hard at school to achieve their goals or they wouldn`t amount to much. One morning at 5a.m. the couple woke to the sounds of three children, all aged under twelve, and all banging pots and pans and making a terrible noise outside their bedroom door. The wife got out of bed and went to see what was happening. "What on earth are you doing?" she asked. "If you won`t let us dream, we won`t let you dream," they said in chorus. An uneasy truce was declared, and the children continued dreaming.

"And now a few words from Dr Bronisław Malinowsky[26] our resident anthropologist."

"Thank you. One downside of people watching other people whilst sipping coffee in a *café*, people watching in other words, is that some people don`t want to be watched. Some even watch back."

"I sometimes feel guilty when I get turned on by a *mannequin* standing in a shop window dressed only in underwear," the newsreader confided.

The girls looked at each other and then back at the screen.

Dr Malinowsky stared at them, an exasperated look in his eyes. It was the right time, but the wrong place. The right dream, but the wrong people.

"The light in Pembrokeshire is better for artists than the light in Cardiff," continued the newsreader unabashed. "Out there in the west it`s closer to the horizon."

"Have you been to New York?" asked Dr Malinowsky.

"No." Replied Bronwen. "I`ve been to Porthcawl. Why would I want to go to New York?"

Irritated by yet another interruption the newsreader noticed his thoughts. "What if disturbing thoughts are not disturbing?" he asked.

"Now you`re talking," said Megan. "What Is needs nothing to be as It Is."

"Apparently you can see the moon from the Great Wall of China," said Bronwen.

"Well, I never did," muttered Megan under her breath.

Bronwen picked up her *hurdy gurdy*. "I`m too happy to play the Blues."

"That is sad," said Megan. "But play them anyway."

"In the paper shop this morning I heard my neighbours say that I live next door," Bronwen continued, an edge of irritation in her voice. "But I thought they lived there." She pondered this matter, attempting to make sense of it. She ponders quietly, there being less noise to distract her.

To celebrate her thirty first birthday, which one she couldn`t remember, Megan`s husband took her to their favourite restaurant, the Vietcong, a regular haunt of theirs at the top of the Twm Carnabwth Tower. "Good evening again, sir," said the *maître d'*, "and who are we with this evening?"

Megan's husband turned to her. "Who are you?"

"I`m your wife, cariad."

"She claims to be my wife."

"I see, sir. And will that be a problem?"

"Only if we don`t get our usual table as holding her hand throughout the meal is particularly important for me this evening."

"Your usual table is ready for you, sir. Please follow me."

He took Megan`s hand contentedly and they followed.

"Why are you holding my hand?" Asked Megan.

"I`m a little angry. And I don`t know why."

"You held my hand yesterday and you're holding my hand today."

"And I`ll hold your hand tomorrow. It`s an expression of love."

"But you`re angry."

"Anger comes and goes and is to be noticed and let go. Love is permanent. Heaven is being in the perfection of each moment. Hell is wanting it to be different. Heaven is being in each moment as It Is."

Years before, after plucking up the courage to ask her out, he said, "Can I ask you a question?"

"Go on," she replied.

"Are you now, have you at some point in the past ever been, or do you at some point in the future intend being, the Mad Axewoman of Crymych?"

"No, no and no."

"That`s good. Can I take you to watch the match in Cardiff on Saturday?"

"Who`s playing?"

Wales against New Zealand."

"Yes. Yes. Yes. And can we go shopping on the way?"

"Where?"

"In a real shop. One with escalators and sickly perfume smells."

"That means Harrods[27] in Carmarthen."

"Yes. They have the best light bulbs."

"I`ve forgotten my glasses. You`re wonderful even when you`re indistinct."

"Thank you, cariad."

The newsreader coughed politely.

Bronwen picked up a holiday brochure that was lying on the shelf under the coffee table next to the armchair and started reading.

Holidays created by the people who know. Seven days for only £3,179 per person. Luxury river cruising on famous rivers. More information on our website. River cruising is a wonderful way to explore the heart of west Wales. Enjoy the very best scenic splendours from the comfort of your chosen vessel. Our guided river tours bring this intriguing corner of Europe to life. All cabins are luxuriously furnished, tastefully carpeted and sizes range from 35–55 square feet. Beds are hotel standard, although hammocks, single, double and king size are supplied upon request for that genuine seadog experience. The cuisine is 5 star. Select one of these classic cruises.

The four-star Teifi Serenade 3 taking you from the source of the Teifi in the Teifi Pools near Strata Florida Abbey in northern Ceredigion through cosmopolitan Lampeter to Newcastle Emlyn with its ancient castle. Run the magnificent Cilgerran Gorge with its impossibly steep riverside vineyards and on to The Lord Rhys' Cardigan, the site of the first official Eisteddfod in 1176.

Alternatively, join the Tywi Traveller, launched from Milford Haven`s great ship building docks in 1914, travelling from the source of the Tywi on the lower slopes of Crug Gynan in the Cambrian Mountains through world famous Llanddewi-Brefi, onwards to Lampeter with its university and cosy ice cream *cafés* run by the descendants of Italian immigrants, the great publishing town of Llandysul, onwards to Newcastle Emlyn, through terrifying Cilgerran Gorge before reaching your destination under Cardigan bridge.

For the *connoisseur*, the fourteen-day Cleddau Special is a must for only £7,628 per person. Travel the length of the Western Cleddau through the hard volcanic rocks at Treffgarne Gorge, go upriver to the source of the Eastern Cleddau before returning downriver to enter the Daugleddau estuary and the serene haven at Milford, inspiration for composers such as Strauss,[28] remembered in the county for his much loved, *Pembroke Dock Waltz*.

For the more adventurous we offer the six-day river to ocean experience. Example itinerary.

Day 1:   You take a late morning Eurostar from Carmarthen to Clarbeston Road, arriving approximately 35 minutes late due to engineering work on the line, from where a coach will take you to Llangwm and to your choice of vessel moored by Llangwm's historic centre. Your tour manager and dedicated crew will welcome you aboard ensuring you settle into your cabin.

Day 2: Enjoy a sumptuous breakfast as the delights of this river to ocean cruise unveil themselves as we head down the Eastern Cleddau, passing under a cloud bridge far above before travelling out to sea, veering sharply to starboard as we hit the waves driven towards land by the strong prevailing winds gusting powerfully from the southwest.

Day 3: One of the most memorable stretches of the holiday is white water cruising against the turbulent, unpredictable currents as we pass between Skomer Island and the mainland. Seasickness tablets are available from the Purser.

Day 4: Continuing northwards with beautiful north Pembrokeshire's rolling mountains to starboard we navigate along the coast before reaching the mouth of the Teifi. Turning into this majestic river, the Welsh Mississippi travel guides call it, we travel upriver to enter the delightful mediaeval town of Cardigan where an excursion to the dominating castle takes up our afternoon. Also included is a visit to the huge, richly decorated basilica to the north of the town centre, one of the finest Romanesque buildings in the area.

Day 5: Today we gently cruise upstream, so why not catch up on some reading in the library, play tennis, sunbathe next to the pool or try your hand at pushing against the scrummaging machine.

Day 6: Your final day's cruising is spent gliding majestically between the ancient, forested outcrops either side of Cilgerran Gorge, the setting for mystical legends and a fairy-tale castle. We arrive at Newcastle Emlyn and its world-famous hostelry *Y Galon Wen*. Do not expect your English to be understood here. This timeless place lies at the heart of West Wales' Welsh speaking community. No bilingual Welsh English signs here. It is Welsh only. Even if they can speak English, they won't. Our team of translators will accompany you on every step of your visit. The afternoon is spent at the castle in its idyllic setting by the meandering river. A mediæval *pageant* and a performance of a specially chosen collection of Dafydd ap Gwilym's much loved poems reminds us of his family connection to the castle. An optional helicopter flight will carry you aloft for an unforgettable aerial view of the mighty Cenarth Falls. You sleep this night moored next to the castle for safety.

Day 7:   After breakfast, having survived thus far, we drive south with Richards Bros[29] and attempt a navigation of the short, stomach churning, minor road infamous for its spectacular descent with hairpin bends and acute inner angles where the road almost turns back on itself time after terrifying time before arriving in Cwmcych where we enjoy a surprised welcome at the Fox and Hounds. After a short break we proceed to Rosebush, nestling amongst stunning mountain views, where assisted once again by our translation team, you will lunch at the Tafarn Sinc which looks like a disreputable tin shed but is the village`s best kept secret.[30] Then we visit the Welsh Bobsleigh Centre[31] nearby. After afternoon tea at the Centre you enjoy a short bus journey to Clarbeston Road where you board the Eurostar bound for Carmarthen. In order to facilitate the transfer your tour manager will accompany you. In the event that the bus driver gets lost whilst crossing the Preseli Mountains the tour manager will organise an emergency *barbecue* and make sandwiches and a hot drink for everyone.

Bronwen felt seasick.
"And now the weather from Derec."[32]
"Shw` mae? More rain. Lots of it."
"Thank you Derec."

Amongst the white rhododendrons with their trusses of funnel-shaped, strongly scented white flowers growing wild at the edge of the orchard a white kookaburra, mostly carnivorous and sexually dimorphic, rests on a branch from where it waits patiently to catch site of its next meal, an unwary insect, an earthworm, a mouse or even a snake.

Dragonflies, with large multifaceted eyes touching at the top of the head and hind wings shorter and broader than forewings, the males having accessory genitalia located under segment 2 of the abdomen, the females with ovipositors located under segments 8 and 9, play, mercifully unaware that fate has decreed their life span to be a cruelly brief six months.

A harvest mouse climbs the stem of a tulip intending to have a snooze inside the flower at the top. It will reappear later, refreshed and with nose and whiskers covered in pollen.

Sunlight falls on fallen leaves.

14

What am I doing at a level of consciousness where this is real?

Thaddeus Golas[1]

The Sergeant lay in the hammock in the willow grove getting some well-earned R&R down him. Nestled amongst the trees was a 1/12 scale model of Carn Menyn, the Bronze Age stone circle in the Preseli Mountains. The stones are singing stones and when the wind comes off the ocean and blows between them, the music they make soothes the Sergeant`s tired and sometimes fevered brow after a hard day at the paddle. But hark! Something yonder rattles. A few lines of poetry appeared in his mind.

> Oh! as I was young and easy in the mercy of his means,
> Time held me green and dying
> Though I sang in my chains like the sea.[2]

"'Singing in chains'," he thought. "Mererid[3] would approve." He was reminded, although quite why he wasn`t sure, of an article in the Western Mail`s Saturday coracling supplement.[4] 'There is little shared experience in coracling now. There are only competing versions of the experience, consumed in such a way as to confirm whatever preconceptions you already have, rather than to make you reflect on them.' The stones sang to the sea. "Time for reflection," he mused. "Although the trouble with reflection is that you must have something to reflect upon." He drew a blank on that one and instead hummed along with the stones.

Glancing off the starboard deck he saw a green, red and pink object whizz past. "Good heavens!" The coracle rocked in the wake, the hammock dampening the effect. Subliminally, he was confused. "So, what`s new?" thought The Parrot. The Sergeant looked closer and focussed. "Ah haaa!" He recognised the whizzing object as a Gwynedd Police Rapid-Response Coracle Unit vessel, the new Clough III.[5] No barnacle bearing, tar-black, bible-black[2] appearance for this model. The Clough series is built in the Porth Meirion shipyard in the style of Escher[6] which makes the coracle appear to undulate as it rolls along. "Hmmm. We don`t often see them this far south," he thought, "winter must be drawing in."

He picked up a leaflet lying under the hammock. "Why didn`t early coraclers learn to fly?" asked the title of an article on the first page. It was a *Fishguard Town Civic Society*[7] publication for visitors. Leaning back in the hammock he read on. "The mastery of the sea by early coraclers arose out of necessity. Good navigation skills around the Pembrokeshire coast were essential as this is a land of high, steep sided cliffs, spectacular waterfalls, inlets, islands and pirates. Since the earliest days of human occupation, it has been easier to get around by sea than by land. Just ask the Saints and Professor E. G. Bowen[8] who wrote a book about their travels although Richards Brothers Buses[9] have improved things in recent times. Another characteristic in parts of West Wales is that a sometimes harsh climate and limited fertile agricultural land meant that fishing was a vital part of the livelihood for most families."

"Coraclers developed navigation skills on lakes and inland waters. Then, as the population increased, they sought to supplement their food supplies by venturing beyond these shores on fishing expeditions far out to sea, often trading with people far away. Eventually they organised raiding parties to other lands, the most famous being Madog`s June 1170 cattle raid on America, some 322 years before *Señor Columbus*, which failed in the end because Madog and his men fell in love with some native American women of the Mandan Tribe[10] and decided to settle down and raise families. And so, the story tells us, the White Indians came into being. A similar history of early ocean travel exists for other ancient civilisations such as the Phoenicians, from whom, it has been suggested, the earliest Celtic writers we know of borrowed a script, hence Tartessian and perhaps the earliest examples of a written Celtic language from the 8th century BC. And the Polynesians, to name but two."

"Others disagree about Tartessian however. But where did the Celtic languages first appear before spreading across Europe and into Asia Minor. There are theories. First *Celtic from the East* then *Celtic from the West* and most recently *Celtic from the Middle*.[11] But is this a Muddle? Indeed not. It illustrates how the understanding of scholars adapts as new evidence comes to light. Science at its best. And what new evidence will reveal in the future we can only wonder at. Meanwhile, as the shifting tides of evidence ebb and flow let us hope that the scholars with their competing theories remain the best of friends."

"Early coracles were basic, yet effective vessels as was proved conclusively by Twm Heyerdahl`s Con Tici expedition[12] during which he travelled from Milford Haven to Bardsey Island and back, proving his theory that long distances were no obstacle to a well-built coracle. And coracle design has remained constant over the millennia until recent times. From a technology point of view there was simply no necessity compelling early coraclers to invent such commonplace things as the light socket, the pneumatic tyre or jet propulsion."

"How interesting," thought the Sergeant, taking a bite from the Marmite,[13] Peanut Butter,[14] raspberry jam, banana and raw onions sandwich encased in slabs of white, extra thick, fibre reduced sliced bread he prepared earlier. "One for the gastronome," he mused, chewing contentedly. "Yes, a taste bud tickler. If Nicole Kidman[15] was lying in the hammock next to me wearing the tiniest, flimsiest bikini with that old *Come up and see me, make me smile*[16] look, I reckon I`d have to finish the sandwich first. Yup! That`s how good it is. And I wouldn`t share it with her if she asked, no matter how nicely."

"Who`s he kidding?" thought The Parrot. "Nicole would bring her own sandwiches."

In spring and early summer wasps, carnivorous beasts, tuck into such delights as aphids but also enjoy a sugary substance secreted by aphid grubs. By late summer, after the aphids die out and the grubs have grown, wasps look for other sugary foods to satisfy their sweet tooths, foods such as the Sergeant's sandwich, which means that during this period sandwich preparation in the harbour is preceded by porthole closing. While at sea, ocean going wasps are seldom a problem.

Placing the sandwich on the deck beneath the hammock he picked up the mug of tea waiting there, leant back in the hammock again and eyed an advertisement next to the article. "Buy or rent?" He read on. "There will be a public meeting in the Town Hall in Fishguard this Thursday evening from 7.00-9.00. Meet the young people who are considering buying their first coracle as they struggle to get onto the property ladder. Buying provides security but renting leaves plenty of disposable income to fund a lively social life. If you buy, then even if you don`t get the price uplift, you will still own a vessel that you can live on or sell. If you rent, you will have nothing. After the interval, during which tea, coffee and the customary *bara brith* and *pice ar y maen* will be served, the audience will take part in a virtual reality experience during which everyone will be induced to believe they inhabit a real coracle, even though the coracle exists purely as a computer-generated phenomenon. Participants in the experiment will become so deeply immersed in the virtual world that they briefly experience `ownership` of the coracle. As a spin off to the process of deciding whether to buy or rent this is helping marine scientists illuminate how the brain uses information it receives to construct a sense of self. They will also investigate whether too many virtual coracles would clog up Fishguard Harbour."

"Buy or rent? I could write a book about it," muttered the Sergeant. "Though not a bestseller, not number one in the charts. Much better to sell just a couple of dozen copies a year. A slow burner. An underground cult hit. Not for me wealth, fame and beautiful women." He looked around to see if his wife had detected that last thought. "Street cred around town. That`s what really matters."

"And how to get it," mused The Parrot.

"Although a colleague who recently posted a ten-minute video on the internet titled *Advanced Paddling Techniques* saw it going viral, with over 15,000 hits the first week, most coming from Austria interestingly enough. Hmmph. Far too ostentatious."

The Sergeant broke into a couple of verses of the drinking song from *The Student Prince*,[17] the operetta in four acts based on Gwilym Meyer-Förster's play *Olde Fiscguard* and the favoured operetta in Fishguard Rugby Club[18] late on Saturday nights. The original opened on December 2, 1924, at Theatr Gwaun[19] and ran for 608 performances, the venues longest running show of the 1920s and 30s.

> *Drink! Drink! Drink! To eyes that are bright as stars when they're*
> *shining on me.*
> *Drink! Drink! Drink! To lips that are red and sweet as the fruit on the*
> *tree.*
> *Here's a hope that those bright eyes will shine*
> *Lovingly, longingly soon into mine.*
> *May those lips that are red and sweet,*
> *Tonight with joy my own lips meet.*
>
> *Drink! Drink! Drink! Let the toast start.*
> *May young hearts never part.*
> *Drink! Drink! Drink!*
> *Let ev'ry true lover salute his sweetheart.*

His mind went back to the time he arrived at the harbour wall one evening at the end of a gruelling patrol, enjoying the long shadows of a late summer's evening reaching out over the water from the cliffs to the west, when a coracle cut in front of him as he negotiated the roundabout. A boy racer he realised, noticing the empty lager cans strewn over the deck, texting on his mobile phone as he paddled. Irritated, he pushed one hand on the horn and with the other reached over to flash the headlights but in his haste he pulled the wrong lever and the windscreen wipers came on instead and having let go of the paddle he lost control of the vessel as the wake left by the other coracle hit. He and the coracle spun for a while until coming to rest facing the way they had come. He slammed his foot hard on the brake pedal. "At least he'll see the brake lights." he thought. "That'll teach him."

Lying back in the hammock he sipped some tea from the mug which was designed to be sipped from as you lie back in a hammock, a feat of engineering achieved with the help of a specially designed straw attached to the inside of the mug the opposite side to the Sergeant. Placing the mug of tea and the leaflet on the deck he reached for the dooby doo, pointed it at the radio hanging by a coloured thread from the low-lying branch of a nearby willow tree and pressed 'On'.

"Local estate agents have revalued the planets in the solar system," came the voice of the newsreader. "The Earth is now worth 273 trillion drachma. We are living on the most expensive planet in the galaxy. But there are questions. Is blue green a bit strong? Would the resale value improve if we did it out in neutrals? Why drachma?" queried the announcer. "Why?"

"Literary scholars at Swansea University[20] have discovered a long-lost diary written by the poet Dewi Emrys.[21] In it Dewi writes that as a young man he read Woody Guthrie's autobiography *Bound for Glory*[22] and it inspired him to go walkabout. No one in Pembrokeshire then knew who Woody Guthrie was and he had no time to explain. One morning he slung a small bag of essentials over one shoulder, his guitar over the other and left for the open road, a true hobo following in his hero's footsteps. But to his consternation he discovered there weren't any dustbowls in west Pembrokeshire and gazing out to sea whilst munching his picnic on the cliffs at Pwll Deri one day he wondered, if he travelled fast enough and quietly enough, could he reach the horizon. It was then that the first line of an *englyn* came to him. To further his research, he became a crew member on a four-person coxed longboat plying an experimental course from Abercastell to the New World. He worked on the *englyn* on the sea voyage west as they chased after the horizon, but it proved too quick for them."

"Late one Friday afternoon almost seven years later the coastguard spotted him paddling alone as he rounded Dinas Head on the approach to Fishguard Harbour. A distress flare was sent up to alert the good people of the twin towns. Church bells rang out in surrounding villages and in Galway Bay. By the time he arrived at the harbour thousands of locals and tourists had thronged there to give him a hero's welcome. But he still hadn't finished the *englyn*, only the first three lines. "It's a lot closer now than it was seven years ago," he told everyone at the banquet held in his honour in Fishguard town hall that Saturday night. He promised to have the last line finished before his next visit. Early on the Monday morning crowds of well-wishers gave him a riotous send off as he returned to sea. The dawn departure he explained was necessary as he reckoned the horizon might be asleep, giving him an advantage."

"His plan is impeccable, but the logic flawed," remarked the Mayor of Fishguard and Goodwick[23] in his farewell speech to Dewi on the quayside after the singing died down. Challenged about this by a local in the crowd he replied, "I think I'm right, therefore I'm right. What more evidence do you need?" The other Councillors nodded sagely. The Mayor's mobile phone rang an hour and a half into the speech producing a stirring rendition of an old favourite.

Dum dum dummy doo wah, oh yay yay yay yeah,
Oh oh oh oh oh ohh ah ah, only the lonely, only the lonely.[24]

He pulled it out of his pocket, looked at it, turned his gaze to examine the crowd and boomed, "OK! Who's the ventriloquist?"

Later that same day members of Fishguard and Goodwick Town Council[25] were bussed to the Haverfordwest Hilton[26] to spend a week, all expenses paid, discussing why they all had enough time on their hands to spend a week in Haverfordwest together, all expenses paid. Amongst other things.

During the journey the Mayor was interviewed by the County Echo`s political editor.[27] "Mr Mayor," began the scribe, "humans have 24,000 genes less than it takes to make a cabbage. Would you like to comment?"

"Yes, but how many pairs of shoes?" interrupted the Mayor's wife. The other Councillors' wives,[25] who were included on the trip so they could inspect the quality of the hotel spa, nodded sagely.

"We will spend the week engaged in serious discussions about local issues," announced the Mayor. "We have several items on a crowded agenda, including the following.

1/   Should capitalism be underpinned by morality?

2/   Is infinity zero less?

3/   Why are there more bacteria in your armpit than there are humans on earth?

4/   Why Galway Bay?

5/   How did the person who made the first clock know what time it was?

6/   Is Western science but a series of footnotes to Archimedes?[28]

7/   Are mirrors good for us?

8/   Why can't I tickle myself?

9/   What on earth are they all doing there?

Also, we will be voting on a motion to increase the height of the cliffs between Fishguard and Pwllgwaelod to 3,316 feet, thus making them 1 foot higher than the Kalaupapa cliffs on the Hawaiian island of Molokai which at present are the highest sea cliffs in the world. This small step, paid for by Molokai, will bring a welcome boost to tourism in the area."

"Late on Friday afternoon we will send out a press release outlining our draft plan to hold further discussions," added the Mayor`s spokesperson.

Dewi stood up shakily in the middle of the coracle just before it disappeared from sight behind the ferry, which had taken emergency action to avoid ramming him as they crossed by the end of the sea wall, and using a loudhailer sent everyone a last message. "Coracling alone is not enough. It`s coracling married with the liberal arts, married with the humanities, that yields the result that makes our hearts sing."

Amused by all this, yet serene in his inner peace, the Sergeant swung gently as he lay in the hammock on the stern of the coracle which was moored fifty yards or so from the crowd. Far enough away for peace and quiet yet close enough for him to hear what was being said. The steaming mug of tea sat patiently on the deck under the hammock next to an open packet of chocolate biscuits. He pressed the green button on the dooby doo to change stations. The radio crackled and Radio Free Pembrokeshire[29] burst into life. He replaced the dooby doo, picked up the mug, leant back and sucked at the straw.

"And now to tonight`s film starring Gregory Peck and Omar Sharif in *Mackenna`s Gold*.[30] In the 1870`s Sam Mackenna, the Marshal of Fishguard, played by Gregory Peck, the only living person who knows the tortuous route to the fabulous *Cañón del Gwaun*, is captured by Colorado, played by Omar Sharif, a brutal Mexican bandit and County Councillor[31] who has long sought his death. But if Mackenna is to lead Colorado and his cut-throat gang to the lost treasure, Colorado must keep him alive. *En route*, Mackenna and the outlaws are joined by renegade soldiers and vengeful Indians, cold blooded killers all. Oh, and a mysterious gentleman from Neyland. As they get closer to *el cañón dorado*, all but Mackenna are swept by *fiebre del oro!* Listen to this must-see classic on Radio Free Pembrokeshire tonight."

The hammock swung gently in the breeze and his thoughts turned to his wife. "Yes, she can be trying alright," he thought. "She`s a wonderful human being trying to make sense of a funny old world that can appear difficult, threatening even."

"Oh, dear," sighed The Parrot.

The Sergeant looked at the tea suspiciously.

"Scientists do not know where all the water on Earth came from," continued the newsreader gravely. "Some think it was left here following collisions with comets early in earth`s history and ..."

"Rubbish!" interrupted the Sergeant. "It comes from Llys y Fran."

"Back to normal," smiled The Parrot.

The announcer moved on to the next item. "A new type of mineral has been discovered on the stern. The dark green rock, found deep in an abandoned mine near the stone circle, has been identified by an amateur geologist from Boncath. Gower Morgan, who was spending a long weekend down the disused mine collecting rock samples, has named it coraclite. His research shows that a rich seam of coraclite appears near the surface in the Basque Country then dips under the ocean before reappearing just under the surface 1,024 miles to the north on the stern before dipping under the ocean once again to appear close to the surface 3,360 miles away in Pennsylvania to the west. It is said that if a miner from one of these three locations visited a coraclite mine in one of the other locations, they would see no difference in the mineral in the rock strata."

Many miles to the east, two Intercity 125 trains passed each other between Neath and Bridgend. They were going in opposite directions. The Leigh Halfpenny was going west. The George North was going east. Combined speed as they passed each other, 275 mph. The George North, tanking it as usual, caused the discrepancy. The Shane Williams was in for repairs after developing hamstring trouble just outside Bridgend the previous day.[32]

"And now for the weather from Derec."[33]

"Shw` mae? More and more rain. And wind. Lots of wind."

"Fine!" exclaimed the Sergeant. "Just Fine! The most important thing in life is to be alive to right now. Rain. Bring it on. Whatever happens, it's perfect."

Reflecting upon the sandwich, he recalled something which, in an unguarded moment, he said to his wife shortly after they were married. "Sometimes I don` t know which is the best design, you or the sandwich."

"I wonder if you` re comparing like with like?" she retorted.

That night he discovered just how comfortable the sofa in the living room is, which was fortunate as he was destined to spend many a night on it.

"Be open to what appears in your mind," said The Parrot quietly so as not to frighten him. "Where does all that come from? Each moment thoughts appear in your mind, stay a moment, then disappear. Like the light coming from the sun, which happens so quickly you think it is continuous rather than a procession of individual photons. You think you have a past, which is memory, and you project a future. But there is only each moment, each present, and even that, if experienced through thoughts and words, is unreal. To the scientist the egg came first as it contains the genes. To others, the chicken came first, created whole. Yet there is no first, as that implies a second, which suggests other rather than One, and requires time, which is an illusion created by the mind. Let your mind be as it Is and reality will reveal Itself. Thoughts are the veil that prevent you from Being."

"That`s all very well," muttered the Sergeant, "but it seems to be real. Isn` t that enough?"

"Your thoughts, no matter how exquisite, will not give you peace. Nor will rearranging them help."

"How much coracling is enough?" his wife once asked him.

"More," he replied confidently.

"Really?"

"Well, not less," he replied less confidently. He had risen meteorically over several years to his foothold on the bottom rung of the career ladder. Then he looked down and was overcome by a fear of heights. "That`s a long way down!" Though his wife tried to persuade him to go for promotions over the years he stayed happily at that level. His was not so much a career as an incident, and a suspicious one at that.

"Stress," he muttered, "is a killer." He remembered the colleague whose coracle was reported drifting aimlessly off Porthcawl not that long ago. That in itself would have been fine except he was on duty at the time. The vessel was boarded by officers from the Dyfed-Powys Police Rapid-Response Coracle Unit.[34]

He was in the galley, dead, face down in a large box of Belgian chocolates, 95%. "Heaven!" thought the Sergeant. The poor fellow convinced himself that his usefulness and his age were going in opposite directions. Then one evening, alone on his coracle with his box of chocolates, he gazed into the abyss, and if you gaze long enough into the abyss, the Admiral gazes back.

As a second wedding anniversary present the Sergeant surprised his wife by making her an oak nest of tables. She was surprised, having expected flowers and chocolates. "It`s more sophisticated than a computer," he explained, "and it`s got more moving parts."

Later that night, in the midst of a controlled sequence of passionate clinches reminiscent of the series of scrums after full time at the end of the France v Wales match in the 2017 Six Nations,[35] they collapsed. Seeking an advantage, she rolled over and lay on top of him, him being comparatively passive at such times. He waited for the order from the referee to reset. "Will the next clinch be uncontested?" he wondered optimistically as he had been under pressure from the start. He put his hands on her behind. She grimaced menacingly. "Holding your behind and watching you smile, that`s as good as it gets," he whispered into one of her ears. He attempted an early shove and became only the second player to be shown a yellow card with the match clock in the red, spend ten minutes on the bench and return to complete the game.

"Before long I`ll be retired," he thought. "Until then I`m on cruise control." Leaving the hammock, he made his way to the conservatory. "It`s quiet in here. Must be because I`m not here." The strain of the evening classes in Buddhist Cosmology was starting to take its toll. "Some people think they have the truth," he continued, "yet the truth they have is not the Truth. It`s a thought, and a thought cannot contain Truth." Reinvigorated by this he went to the galley, made himself a fresh mug of tea, returned to the hammock and anchored there to enjoy it.

"Do you need two people to be monogamous?" he asked his wife one morning as they were having breakfast in front of the fire in the kitchen of their smallholding southwest of Fishguard. She paused from crocheting for a moment. "You have a rich inner life," she whispered under her breath. He was pleased with himself and was confident that progress was being made. She concentrated on crocheting the turning chain, reflecting upon the importance of gauge.

He munched chocolate biscuits and sipped tea, humming along as he did so to the classical music coming from the radio. Glancing at the cloudless sky above a look of irritation appeared on his face. He had been looking forward to an evening with his scale model of the Herschel Space Observatory[36] that was mounted on the prow, and a bowl of fresh, lightly seasoned sewin with salad garnish. But there was too much cosmic dust in the distance, and it blocked out the optical lighting thus adversely affecting his view of the observable universe from the harbour.

"It might be important in affecting star formation, stellar mass loss rates and in the formation of molecular hydrogen and planets," he thought, "but why does it have to be there tonight?" The Herschel Space Observatory has a mirror measuring 12 feet in diameter and operates in the infrared spectrum. The Sergeant`s scale model has a cream, oval scroll, hand-held vanity mirror requisitioned from his wife`s dressing table. It measures 5.5 inches in diameter and works by him looking through the hole he made in the cardboard box it rests upon. It operates during the day.

Picking up the Western Mail he turned to the Educational Supplement where an advert caught his eye. "Taught MA in Coracling Studies. Could I benefit from this?" he wondered. "Is this the way to the promotion the wife wants me to have?" His imagination rioted in glorious surround-sound techicolor all over the right side of his brain. The left was still asleep, drained by the demands of a particularly action packed episode of Pobol y Cwm[37] he watched earlier.

He answered his own question. "No! The bottom rung is best."

He read the headline on the first page. "I support the idea of euthanasia," says local Councillor. "Anything to reduce teenage crime."[38]

"Quite right," thought the Sergeant, turning to an article by the paper`s Africa correspondent. `Palaeontologists know that stone paddles were first used at least 2.6 million years ago when our brains, relative to our body size, were little bigger than that of a chimp. Over the next 2.3 million years as our ancestors moved out of Africa our brains nearly tripled in size but our paddle making skills didn`t improve at all. It wasn`t until the Late Stone Age about 100,000 years ago that paddle tool technology really advanced. Surprisingly, the oldest cave art in southern Africa, in the Blombos Cave[39] near Cape Agul, has artefacts showing modern human behaviour dating back around 80,000 years. But, no paddles.`

"Surprising indeed," mused the Sergeant. He was confused by this revelation. Totally confused yet strangely happy as by allowing the confusion to be, everything became clear. He wondered what he was doing tonight. His wife was still discussing the matter with herself. Even though he was in the minority he insisted upon exercising his right to vote. After all, he had fought long and hard for the right, initially denied to him. His wife held a permanent majority vote because, she argued, this reduced the possibility of disagreement. She voted this system into existence during an early morning business breakfast with him after which she left for a coffee date with some friends in the newly opened Yogistani restaurant[40] situated on the west facing aspect of the clock tower above the town hall on Fishguard Square.

He picked up the dooby doo and changed channels but became aware that the radio had gone silent. Finishing a biscuit and downing the last of the tea he leant gingerly to one side, placed the mug on the deck, lay back in the hammock, pointed the dooby doo at the radio and pressed to increase the volume. Nothing.

He pressed again. Silence. "Hmmm." He continued until the volume was at maximum. Still nothing. He pressed Boost.

He could not have known that he was listening to a live performance of Tchaikovsky`s 1812 Overture[41] by the St Petersburg Philharmonic Orchestra[42] during the few moments of silence that precede the climactic cannon volleys at the end. Neither could he have known that for this final night's performance the orchestra deployed ten Tsar Cannons, the largest cannon in the world, on loan from the Imperial Russian Army's ordinance depot[43] just outside the city. Weighing 40 tons, 16 feet in length and requiring 200 horses to transport, each one fires cannon balls weighing over 125 stones.

The coracle shook intensely as the wall of extreme sound exploded from the radio. The blast from the cannons blew the Sergeant off the hammock and pinned him against the main mast as the shock wave lifted the coracle out of the water, rotating it vigorously as it did so, before sending it careering over the calm waters of Fishguard Harbour, hurtling upwards at an angle of approximately 60^0 to the horizontal in, it would be reported on the BBC Wales[44] early evening news later that day, a southerly direction. Calculating as it went at what height the vessels kinetic energy in joules would be equal to its potential energy The Parrot was blown, tail first, deep into the willow grove. According to witnesses the vessel later descended over the beach, bounced once on the soft sand and entered the cafe through the large, open, folding glass wall. The Russian artillerymen[45] fired volley after volley with great passion but little accuracy, and, fortunately for the crew, quickly ran out of ammunition.

As the sound dissipated the coracle settled in the corner of the cafe on top of the table with the best view out over the harbour. General Sir Robert Thomas Wilson,[46] music critic for the Moskovskaya Pravda newspaper,[47] writing about the concert for the following morning's edition noted, "The Russian artillery is of the most powerful description. No other army moves with so many guns and with no other army is it in better state of equipment or is more gallantly served."

A waitress walked up the gangplank. "What would you like this morning, sir? The usual is it? Tea and two rounds of toast?"

He slid down the mast and crumpled onto the deck, nodding in agreement as the sound of fireworks erupted from the radio.

"You`ll have to stop that, sir, or I`ll have to ask you to leave. The loud bangs frighten children and dogs."

She turned and walked back down the gangplank. Chimes and a brass fanfare rang out. "This is your last warning, sir!"

As with his people before him the Sergeant fears only two things, that the coracle would open up beneath him and that the sky would fall on his head.

In the period between landing once again on the deck and clutching the dooby doo to turn the radio off the Sergeant reminisced of the time he was a teenager, seventeen years old and with no idea what to do with his life. He ran away from home. He went further than he had ever been before, seeking somewhere exotic, far off, different. He arrived in Porthcawl on the bus late that evening and booked into a B&B on the front, one of those with a good view of giant waves hitting the lighthouse. Walking around town the following morning he passed the Job Centre. In the window he saw a notice stating that the police were recruiting for a soon to be formed experimental marine unit. "Young men and women, preferably with no family ties, are sought for this dangerous work," he read. "The ability to swim is preferable, though not essential. All necessary training will be provided. Join the police and see the ocean." He didn`t know it then but from that day on his joining Dyfed-Powys Police Rapid-Response Coracle Unit and a life of adventure was inevitable. His days as a civilian were numbered. Eventually, after a brief period in education (sic), fate would give him the life of adventure and *camaraderie* he desired. He was elated but did not know why. He called into a *café* and had a mug of tea to celebrate.

In its youth, a young The Parrot followed a different path. It spent a couple of years in America and while there played in a little-known band called Crosby, Stills, Nash and The Parrot. Their only album, titled, *Haven't I Seen You Somewhere Before!* was savaged by the critics and sank without trace.[48] Not an altogether inappropriate fate considering The Parrot's calling.

Originating in the Indomalayan region, one of the eight biogeographic realms, about 27 million years ago, a brightly coloured common kingfisher with small feet and large head perches on a branch overhanging the edge of the lake on the stern. Cold, cruel eyes follow the direction of its long, pointed beak as it patiently seeks its prey. Unseen, a siege of bitterns visiting from Oxwich Bay on the Gower, buff-brown with dark streaks and long, yellow beaks move silently through reeds at the lake's edge looking for amphibians, insects and fish. An excited male expands the muscles surrounding its oesophagus to create a large echo chamber before letting loose a magnificent **BOOM!** that is heard as far away as Scleddau. A flock of cranes, grey with long legs and necks wade in the shallow water. Opportunistic feeders, they search for amphibians, small fish, berries, grains, roots, insects, snails, worms and small rodents. They are graceful birds with a wingspan of up to 8 feet. A flamboyance of flamingos, pleased to be the only bird family in the order Phoenicopteriformes and that their name is thought to derive from the Provençal word for 'flame', play in the warm waters of the tropical zone at the lake's southern edge. Others, standing over 4 feet tall on one leg, without any demonstrable muscle activity as they do so, contemplate filter feeding on small insects, crustaceans and mollusks. Their light pink to bright red plumage, the colours deriving from aqueous bacteria and beta-carotene they get from their food, catches light from the sun and is reflected beautifully on the surface of the still water.

Otters, semiaquatic carnivorous mammals nearly 3 feet long when fully grown with webbed feet and dense fur, play at the water's edge near the holt leaving five-toed footprints behind them in the mud as they go. Their name derives from the same Proto-Indo-European root *wódr̥ that also gives us the English word 'water'. In each of the six Celtic languages, Welsh, Cornish, Breton, Irish, Scots Gaelic and Manx there is a word for 'otter' that can be translated as 'water dog' or 'water hound'.

A clangel wangel, using its long tail as a sail, moves silently across the surface of the lake.

Later in the day, when all is dark, in the lee side of one of the wooden groynes that run perpendicular to the shore nearby and whose purpose is to interrupt water flow thereby reducing beach erosion, a great fox-spider, a member of the wolf-spider family, over two inches wide if you include its hairy legs, and I do, will run fast across the gravel and sand terrain after an insect. Once caught, it will inject its prey with venom that will liquefy its internal organs before using powerful, fang-bearing front appendages to feast upon it. An opportunistic predator, it is aided by having wrap-around vision provided by its eight eyes, two large ones on top of its head, two others forward of them and four smaller ones that are aligned in a row above its mouth. Before the first light of dawn, it will return to its silk lined burrow situated under a rock not too far away.

The well informed too whit, too hoo of an owl sounds agreeably across the lake.

15

Ní file ach filíocht an bhean.
Seán Ó Ríordáin[1]

A woman is not a poet but poetry itself.

Radio Free Crymych was on in the background as Megan checked her briefing notes for that evening`s Machlud y Wawr[2] meeting. Bronwen clogged quietly on the other side of the crypt, pirouetting around the beautiful stone pillars as she did so. She remembered a story her husband told her once about when he was sharing a flat with some other students whilst doing a degree in Celtic Studies in Aberystwyth.[3] One evening he and his flatmates were sitting in the living room of their flat chatting in Middle Welsh and Old Irish, as you do, and admiring the Christmas decorations around the room, and the tree in the corner with its lights flashing. A lovely festive scene. Then they realised it was June. They did what any group of students would do under the circumstances, they discussed the merits of leaving them up. After all, they were halfway through the year. A full and fruitful weighing up of the pros and cons followed, then a vote was taken. The result was close with two votes for and three against. So close in fact that a recount was demanded and held. The result remained and the decorations were taken down. Those in favour thought it would be nice to have them fresh the following Christmas. No woman in the house equals chaos and dust on the domestic front. Very tidy chaos and dust, with every book in its rightful place, but chaos and dust none the less. "Men live in houses and women live in homes." She thought.

"Is clogging a zero-sum game?" wondered Bronwen as she danced to the end of love[4] whilst at the same time knowing that such a place does not exist. A clogger's clogger, she lives for clogging, particularly in the crypt where the stone walls, pillars, floor and ceiling provide a rich acoustic accompaniment to her dancing. In her part of the crypt library the filing system for the books has two sections, Clogging A-Z and Miscellaneous.

Megan was thinking about the paediatrician and psychoanalyst who came up with the idea of the "good enough" clogger[5] which is a way to explain 'normal clogging' rather than 'abnormal clogging.' Later, when an eminent American psychologist[6] published his important book on parenting, he gave it the title *A Good Enough Clogger*. From the blurb on the back cover of the 1988 Vintage edition we read. 'His purpose is not to give parents pre-set rules for raising their children, but rather to show them how to develop their own insights so that they will understand their own and their children`s clogging in different situations and

201

how to cope with it. Above all, he warns, parents must not indulge their impulse to try to create the clogger they would like to have but should instead help each child fully develop into the clogger he or she would like to be.'

"Perhaps a talk about this concept at next month`s Machlud y Wawr AGM?" she wondered. "It`s high time we got some hard science into clogging." She thought of her husband, who would agree. A little while before his illness was diagnosed, when their future together had no limits, Megan suggested it would be good if he retired.

"Then I'll retire! But when?" he replied.

She looked over the pince-nez at him. "Good, cariad," she said, and continued with the sewing she was engaged in. She knew that whilst words appear out of peoples` mouths, it`s what lies between the words, in the silence, that tells us what people are really thinking. As much as you can say that people are thinking that is. Megan is of the opinion that thinking happens and it only appears as if *we* are doing it.

"Thank you for understanding. I love you."

"No `very much`?" she asked.

"'Very much' works when someone is being romantic and perhaps there`s poetry in it, but love is enough on its own. It captures the essence. It is the essence. It Is. Have a piece of chocolate, cariad. Dark chocolate, 95% per cent, very low sugar content, high in flavanols, substances that the woman in the health food shop says help lower blood pressure and improve vascular and cognitive function and provide UV protection for our skin."

"Thank you, cariad. How romantic. You`re wonderful." As the chocolate began to melt on her tongue her expression changed to one of delight. "We are inseparable. I, the chocolate, and you, its taste." She blew him a chocolate kiss. "What will we do when you retire?"

"We`ll grow old together, very old and we`ll have adventures. When we`re well over a hundred we`ll be the first centenarians to move to the newly established old peoples` home on the moon and just after we`ve settled in aliens will invade the earth. We`ll come up with a way to stop them and we`ll be heroes and famous and loved by all earthlings and aliens alike because we`ll stop the invasion by using love and compassion instead of war, which, as the Dalai Lama said, is so old fashioned. People will put up statues of us in towns and cities all over the planet, statues of us standing next to one another holding hands and you`ll be looking out over the world with a beautiful smile and I`ll be looking at you. Although in some places the statues will be taken down again ..."

Megan`s eyebrows raised questioningly.

He continued without drawing breath. "... because at the unveiling the womenfolk notice that I`ve got a giant hard on."

"Shhhh! Giant did you say?"

"Yes cariad. **Giant**."

"How giant?"

"The size of Strumble Head."

She blew him another chocolate kiss, then another, and looked pleased with herself. She understood that his strangeness was within normal limits.

Bronwen moved like a wraith, using the crypt`s pillars as partners, moving in and out of shadows, from dark to light and back again. "A clear case of nominative counter-determinism," thought Bronwen, impressed at her own insight.

"I`m not so sure," muttered Megan.

Bronwen was not prepared for such concentrated insight and noticed a cluster headache and a nosebleed coming on. She stopped her dance and returned to lie on the sofa where she swooned, still wearing her clogs. "Bronwen`s feeling of *fin de siècle* increases each day," thought Megan sympathetically.

"Recently released Welsh Government[7] statistics show that more people than ever before are taking up clogging," reflected Bronwen, coming out of her swoon.

"Hmmm. Perhaps more people than ever before are taking up clogging because there are more people than ever before. You need a cup of coffee Bronwen *fach*. Why don`t you go and make yourself one. The exercise will do you good. Take your mind off things. Perhaps I`ll have one as well, seeing as how you`ll be there anyway."

"Thank you for the advice. Two coffees coming up." Bronwen got up and made her way shakily to the kitchen. "What shall it be today?" she thought, tuning into her taste bud memories as she approached a sack of coffee, one of several arranged along a shelf next to the window. The instant she opened it and looked inside each coffee bean in the sack decided to be Sumatra and communicated that choice instantaneously to all the other beans in the sack. "This will be fine," she decided.

Putting aside her notes Megan picked up the copy of the Tivyside[8] that was lying on the coffee table beside her armchair in the *simne fawr* and read the frontpage headlines. "Eglwyswrw, population just a few hundred, has seen off an international coffee chain that wanted to open a 120-seat coffee shop there after acquiring the lease to a former pub, The Sergeant`s, which lies in a perfect spot on the main road in the centre of the village. 'Eglwyswrw already has seven *cafés*,' a spokesperson for local action group `No more *cafés*` told the Tivyside earlier this week. The group formed following the outcry when a half page advert for the proposed Costa[9] *café* in the village appeared in Clebran,[10] the *Papur Bro* for the area. Folks around here have a spend locally philosophy and are aiming for a self-sufficient community." The action group`s objections were successful, and the planning application has been turned down. "We`ve seen off the coffee chain," said the spokesperson. A letter from Costa appears in this month`s edition of

Clebran, magnanimous and generous in its content it wishes the village well. Residents of this thriving community of farmers, gardeners, artists, musicians, new age therapists, ageing yet spritely hippies, writers, *café* owners, poets and kite flyers have welcomed the news, and, in their turn, wish Costa well."

Megan turned the page. A headline, 'Clogging millions', caught her eye. She read on. "Twenty-five million Americans watched the last Soccer World Cup[11] final and twenty-six million watched the Rugby World Cup[12] final." Megan and Bronwen smiled. "Compare this with the recent Clogging World Cup final watched by twelve million, double the figure for the previous Clogging World Cup and treble the one before that. One hundred and ten million watched baseball`s World Series[13] and a similar number watched the American Football[14] final. Clogging has not yet reached a level that threatens baseball and gridiron, but it is growing. Each year the income generated by the clogging franchise increases significantly. One reason for this is that since equal opportunities legislation in the 1970`s, clogging is the dominant sport for girls in schools. Clogging games on the computer are also attracting children from younger age groups who get hooked by learning strategy and the sport`s personalities by playing the games regularly. This is not an overnight phenomenon. A professor of Sport Management at the University of Chicago writes in his recent book that cloggers were plying their trade in America during the nineteenth century and domestic leagues developed in the 1920s and 1930s. The motto of the American Clogging Association (ACA) is a quote by a Danish philosopher,[15] considered the first existentialist philosopher and an accomplished clogger, `Clogging is not a problem to be solved, but a reality to be experienced'. Technique was inspired by a German composer[16] considered a modernist by cloggers during his early period. When asked about his clogging method he replied, 'The thumb of the left hand should never leave the waistcoat pocket'. ACA members took this to heart and clogging in this fashion is what marks American cloggers out from those of other nationalities. She put the paper down. picked up the dooby doo and turned the radio off.

The kitchen door opened and Bronwen appeared carrying a tray and moved west. Megan got up from the armchair and followed, taking the notes and the paper with her. They lay back together on the sofa in front of the bay window, stockinged feet raised to rest on the table next to the eye stones and the swallow stones and sipped Americanos with double shots of expresso. Megan picked up her crochet and became busy. Bronwen continued reading her novel *The Pembrokeshire Coast Murder*, John Bude`s `classic mystery novel` published in 1936.[17]

A storm raged in Megan`s mind, but not in Megan. Her look was serene. "It is as it is," she whispered, so as not to disturb Bronwen. Then it disappears and only Is remains. Everything in the here and now is of benefit. Your happiness is in your sadness. If you want a peaceful world, be peaceful. It's no good shouting about it."

Bronwen looked up. "Another day, another start," she added.

"Our eyes are in our heads," Megan observed. "Because of this people think our minds are in our heads, and, therefore, that we are in our heads."

Bronwen wondered where this was going.

"It happens to be that our eyes are in our heads. If our eyes were in our knees, they would think we are in our knees."

Bronwen went back to reading the book ...

"Whatever your past," added Megan, "it`s a memory, a thought, a word in the here and now."

... and tightened her grip on the pages.

"When I think, I don`t know who I am. Never be a person who knows. Be a person who asks questions, simple questions. A person who wonders at the questions and the answers, knowing there is no question to be asked and no answer in the words. The essence of existence is non-symbolic. Everything is helpful, learn from it, and from nothing. And let It Be."

"I don't care what I think," revealed Bronwen.

"Well done," said Megan encouragingly. "Living is effortless when there is no destination."

"It is as it is and it isn`t," contributed Bronwen hopefully without raising her head from the book. Like Gulliver on his travels[18] she had no idea what was coming next.

"More coffee I think," came the reply.

"My turn no doubt," offered Bronwen as she put the book down, got up from the sofa and began walking to the kitchen. Again. "I`m not very good at coffee making, but practice makes perfect I suppose."

"Remember Bronwen," replied Megan, "you are where you need to be. You and the experience are one experiencing. Be present. Just breathe. The rest will take care of itself."

"I could do with a nice walk, a slice of warm, buttered *bara brith* and an orgasm," thought Bronwen. Her face turned crimson and she hurriedly turned the cold tap on and splashed water over her face. Recovered, she turned the tap off and opened the Machlud y Wawr cookbook that lay on the counter between the sink and the kettle. "1.2 million copies sold in its first year, 826,763 copies of the Welsh version and, hmm, hmmmm, hmmmmmmm, a lot of the English version," she marvelled. She turned to the chapter headed, `Boiling Water and What to Do with It` and began to read. "Until recently science has failed to understand water, having been unable to explain its properties as those of a fluid. A new theory suggests that water is not a fluid but a liquid crystal. The properties of water can now be better explained. Oh dear!" she thought. "Perhaps I`ll wing it."

Megan`s thoughts returned to the notes she was writing for her talk to the Tenby branch of Machlud y Wawr that evening. "How often do people blame their parents when they are unhappy?" she read. "Why not, instead, thank your parents when you are happy." She was pleased with this. In the background was the gentle sound of Beethoven`s 7th played by the Crymych Symphony Orchestra. It was a tight squeeze, but they all managed to get in. Except the conductor who stood on a raised podium in the kitchen where he offered advice to Bronwen as she attempted to make the perfect cup of coffee. The fact that they couldn't see him helped. Listening to the sound Megan sighed happily. "This comes from heaven itself." An exaltation of larks enlivened the atmosphere in the crypt, keeping time to the beat as they flew around the ceiling. "All is as it should be," she thought. Bronwen was lost in the right direction.

On the Pembrokeshire side of the Teifi the tylwyth teg were wearing red. On the Ceredigion side they were wearing green.

Picking up the notes she continued reading. "The difference between us is that I`ve always been a superhero and I`ve always known it, whereas you`ve always been superheroes and you`ve been busy not knowing it." A look of satisfaction appeared on her face. "That`ll do nicely," she thought. She put the notes down and picked the paper up again. She turned the pages and started reading an article on page five. `Bananas galore`, read the title. "The new banana plantation situated just outside Neyland is a roaring success and supplies every Farmer`s Market in the county. Banana production has increased by 15% year after year since this initiative began, thus bringing much needed jobs and revenue to the county and fully justifying the £7.5 million grant the County Council awarded the venture, a County Councillor is quoted as saying. And I know these statistics are right because I made them up myself, he added."[19]

Her eyes moved on to the adjacent article. "Jazz musicians, blues musicians and cloggers improvise a lot and thus increase the connectivity of their brains which in turn allows them to 'go with the flow', with little conscious thought." Megan thought of Bronwen. "This has been confirmed by a study conducted at the Music Department of the Karolinska Institute[20] in Sweden."

Bronwen reappeared with two cups of coffee and two plates bearing mini chocolate coconut bars and mini caramel *Macchiato* Cupcakes. On Megan`s cup were the words, `Crymych, a place where civilisation and wilderness coexist. Not wilderness in the sense that nobody lives there, but wilderness in the sense that if your horse broke down you can`t phone a breakdown service to be towed home'. It was a big cup. It was a big morning. "I`ve switched the coffee *du jour* from Colombian Supremo to Jamaican Blue Mountain. And in the morning at that." Megan politely ignored her.

The orchestra stopped, and led by the conductor, they filed out of the crypt. Megan and Bronwen clapped enthusiastically and looked forward to their next visit. The larks flew out through the open window into the orchard. But Bronwen was bored. She picked up her hurdy gurdy, sat down on the sofa and lost herself. Barely conscious, she played in realms of chromatic daring and deftly nuanced extemporisations, bringing to life mediæval airs and dances that once entertained The Lord Rhys in Cardigan castle. One melodic sweep after another, smouldering, rumbling and tumbling. Although how she was familiar with them, she didn`t know, being too young to have been there.

Listening with appreciation to the performance Megan sipped a glass of Crymych Carreg, a local sparkling wine, and reflected upon how the distribution gradient of the kinetic energy from adiabatic expansion in that particular bottle related to its temperature. Fluid dynamics is one of her passions. She is particularly interested in the dynamic behaviour of multicomponent hydroalcoholic systems supersaturated with dissolved CO_2, in other words, what happens when you open the bottle. She blinked, took off her glasses and cleaned them with the corner of her cardi' before replacing them delicately on her slightly reddening nose.

Bronwen, replenished by her stream of consciousness playing, a technique she developed for herself after reading a revue of Jack Kerouac`s seminal stream of consciousness road novel *On the A40*,[21] carried the instrument to its place on the *chaise longue* where she placed it lovingly, then returned to the sofa, pressed 'Play' on the dooby doo, and began listening to the radio. Just in time for the news.

"Early summer chaos has hit Pembrokeshire again as all roads around, leading to, and leading from Newport were closed yesterday morning as 120 million red and green crabs began their annual migration from the rainforest on the western slopes of the Preseli Mountains to the beach to breed."

"The day is going slowly, like honey off a spoon," continued Bronwen, at which point she felt rejuvenated, no doubt the effect of the coffee.

"Something unknown is doing we don`t know what," thought Megan, watching from the corner of her eye.[22]

The voice of the Radio Free Crymych announcer interrupted their reveries. "And now our `Thought for the Day` for which we are joined by the Reverend Doctor Professor The Mrs Lleucu Tomos, head of the Department of Holistic Art Therapy at the University of the Four Trinity Davids[23] in Carmarthen and President of the Brynberian branch of Machlud y Wawr."

"Thank you. There are excellent cloggers and good cloggers, poor ones and bad ones. How many of you want to be excellent cloggers?" Female hands, and a few male ones encouraged by the female ones, went up all over the city. "Is that good?" A rumbling sound reminiscent of low frequency growling reverberated across the county, spilling into Carmarthenshire, and, to the west, caused a small tsunami to hit the coast of County Wexford, much to the delight of the surfers there. "No!" exclaimed the Reverend Doctor Professor The Mrs Tomos. "To be an excellent clogger is to misunderstand. Give up the idea of being what you think yourself to be. Be yourself. Be the clogger that you already are. From what you suppose to be poor or bad you will learn. See the perfection in it all. Your difficulties will be your teaching. Keep the effort. For the beginner there must be great effort. Or none. Let it be. You are already excellent. Wherever you are, you are here."

"Hmmmmm. A farce made by Feydeau perhaps?"[24] Megan speculated.

Bronwen`s shadow groaned and fell onto the floor with a light thud. "Don`t be a 'wee, sleekit, cow'rin, tim'rous beastie," she whispered supportively.[25]

The announcer continued. "Thank you for those uplifting words Lleucu. The Welsh Government passed a law yesterday in the Senedd in Cardiff making it compulsory for cinemas in Wales to show the film Dr Strangelove[26] at least once a year, every year. And now our daily science update. Scientists at the Department of Glaciology at the University of North Pembrokeshire at Crymych have used a sophisticated numerical glaciological computer modelling technique to simulate glaciers that formed during the Little Ice Age, a period of cooling between the sixteenth and the nineteenth centuries. They have discovered that the previous understanding, which is that the last glaciers here melted 11,000 years ago, is wrong. Their new evidence shows that a pocket of colder, snowier climate existed in north Pembrokeshire until about 300 years ago. Until as recently as June 23rd, 1709, they claim, Clarbeston Road was covered by a glacier estimated to be approximately five miles thick. Part of their evidence is anecdotal in the form of a memoir written by the local squire in October of that year which survives as *Llyfr Porffor Heol Clarbeston*, The Purple Book of Clarbeston Road. The book was damaged in a fire at the squire`s mansion which stood just outside the village. The fire, which occurred late in the nineteenth century, destroyed most of the mansion but fortunately the majority of the manuscript, in which is found the fifth branch of the Mabinogion, survived. In the memoir the squire expresses his pleasure that the postman had recently succeeded in getting through the ice sheet, the first postal delivery for over 24,000 years."

Megan thought back to when she was courting her husband to be. He told her he thought they would be good together. "We`re compatible," he said.

"Yes, dear."

"Which end of the toothpaste tube do you squeeze?"

"The middle."

"Oh dear!"

"Oh dear?"

"I squeeze the end away from the nozzle."

"That`s allowed."

"But I thought couples were supposed to fall out about it."

"We won`t."

He smiled. "You see. I`m right."

"Yes, cariad."

Bronwen stirred on the sofa as a thought passed through her mind. "If I make a hole in the middle of a sheet of paper, is the hole in the paper?" She stopped stirring. "Do all mini chocolate coconut bars taste the same? Yes. But do I have scientific proof of this?" She decided to conduct an experiment, a double-blind trial. Closing both eyes, she began chewing mini chocolate coconut bars until they were all gone. "My hypothesis is correct," she said to herself, "they all taste the same. And now to extend the experiment to the mini caramel *Macchiato* Cupcakes."

"Reality is not something that happens," proposed Megan, "so whatever happens is not reality." She smiled. Or did she? "Everything happens exactly as it needs to happen, yet nothing happens."

Bronwen attempted to concentrate on her science experiment and listen to the radio. "I don`t do anything, everything happens."

"That`s it."

"I don`t eat mini caramel *Macchiato* Cupcakes, yet mini caramel *Macchiato* Cupcakes eating happens."

"You`ve got it. Now Be It. And be grateful for Everything. Absolutely Everything."

Bronwen`s thoughts returned to the mini chocolate coconut bars. She was sure there was another packet somewhere in the kitchen.

Piles of decaying logs and small branches dotted around the orchard outside the crypt are alive with fungi, centipedes, fly larvae, mites, slugs, snails, spiders, springtails and penny sows. Blackbirds and song thrushes nest there. Hedgehogs hibernate there over the winter.

Nearby, the wormery lies fulfilled. Its main inhabitants are tubular, segmented creatures with a rudimentary nervous system belonging to the phylum Annelida that have existed on Earth for over half a billion years. Ignoring the controversy regarding their classification, which many consider to be in chaos, they spend their days devouring fungal material, decaying organic matter and the bodies of small animals, oblivious to the fact that their excretions are rich in available nitrogen, phosphates and potassium and that their lifestyle choice is good for aerating the soil. Megan and Bronwen are not oblivious to this. It is a matter of concern to these happy creatures however that they are an important source of food for garden birds such as blackbirds, crows, curlews, lapwings, owls, robins and starlings as well as hedgehogs, shrews, badgers and foxes. The earthworms that is not Megan and Bronwen. Bronwen is in training for the All Wales Worm Charming Championships that this year are to be held in Brithdir Mawr, near Newport, which is a centre of excellence for the sport.[27]

Elsewhere in the orchard are beehives and homes for solitary bees. Bronwen talks to the bees telling them all the news, interspecies collective consciousness being well-developed in her self-constructed reality. Sometimes she makes music with them, she humming, them buzzing.

Several ant colonies around the orchard appear dormant as many of their occupants are out foraging. Recently, after much discussion, they united to form a supercolony. The main reason for this is that they are of the opinion that inter-colony aggression will be reduced. Many argued against the move however and a compromise position was reached in which each colony will maintain distinct genetic differences in order to mate. Argument and controversy between those who wish to remain in the supercolony and leavers will no doubt rage for many years into the future.

In ancient woodland extending northwards from the orchard, cattle, deer, pigs and ponies roam free. Mature birch trees with white bark grow to a height of almost a hundred feet forming a light canopy. Nearby, rowan trees, some over two hundred years old with smooth, silvery grey bark, stir in the breeze. Evergreen holly with spiked, glossy leaves and hawthorns reaching up to fifty feet in height with brown-grey bark that is knotted and fissured and with branches of slender twigs covered in thorns flourish. A single crab apple, *malus sylvestris*, over thirty feet tall with irregular shape and spreading canopy stands alone, covered in lichens and mistletoe. In the low understorey scrub grow bright green adder's tongue ferns.

Changed little over the last 15 million years, hedgehogs, with their characteristic creamy-brown spines, sleep in dens underground. Golden-brown hazel dormice with long whiskers, furry tails and large black eyes lie curled up in their nests amongst logs and piles of leaves on the woodland floor dreaming of flowers, insects, fruits and nuts.

Rooks, carrion crows, whose nests of stick and earth stand alone high in the surrounding trees, hooded crows visiting from Scotland, hawfinch, Siberian chiffchaff, starlings and grey wagtails, play.

Butterflies are plentiful. Small heath butterflies, wings banded with brown, cream and grey flutter in the sunlight low above the ground. Others settle on leaves and branches, wings closed, the eye spot on the forewing clearly visible, confusing predators. Pearl-bordered fritillaries, a little late in their season, with a wingspan of almost two inches, orange with black spots on upper side of wings and silver-pearl markings on underside, feed on nectar from dandelions and lesser celandines. Well camouflaged, moths, with thick hairy bodies and feather like antennae will soon come out to drink the nectar of night-blooming flowers, gladioluses, jasmines, evening primroses, phlox and moonflowers.

The neighbouring bog is home to a huge variety of species including slender, mosquito-like crane flies. Large semi-aquatic raft spiders, light brown with cream stripe each side of the body sit at the water's edge waiting patiently to feel the vibrations of their prey. Attached to a plant under the water lives a dark coloured diving bell spider, preying on crustaceans and aquatic insects. Coming up for air once a day, the air bubble surrounding its abdomen gives it a silvery appearance. By law, and to protect the insect population from light pollution, a blackout exists from nightfall until dawn within a circle with a ten-mile radius with Crymych Cathedral at its centre.

Orchids, amongst them narrow lipped helleborines with bright green leaves arranged in almost opposite pairs along the stem, purple orchids with ground rosettes of glossy, dark green leaves with dark spots and tall greater butterfly orchids with spikes of loosely clustered, whitish-green flowers, their spreading sepals and petals resembling butterfly wings, can be seen. Small, stocky, bee orchids, each with a rosette of leaves at ground level and a flower spike carrying several large, pink, brown and yellow flowers that resemble a bee, are plentiful here.

Being amongst the most ancient group of chewing herbivorous insects whose ancestors lived around 250 million years ago during the early Triassic period, meadow grasshoppers up to three quarters of an inch in length, with short, stubby antennae, munch plants in the sunlight.

In between feeding on ants and beetles, nightingales summering from west Africa, seven inches long with a wingspan of ten inches, plain brown above, buff to white below with reddish tail, rest on branches to fill the air with their beautiful, lilting song, a fast succession of whistles, trills and gurgles.

16

If your mind is empty, it is always ready for anything; it is open to everything. In the beginner's mind there are many possibilities; in the expert's mind there are few.

Shunryu Suzuki[1]

As the soft morning light beamed through the porthole, bathing the galley in its gentle glow, The Parrot stirred, raised its head from its breast and opened an eye. The head turned to the left, surveying the scene before returning to its resting position. The eye closed. Moments later the other eye opened and The Parrot turned its head in the opposite direction, sleepily examining the other half of the galley before the head returned to its starting position once again, whereupon the eye closed. Seconds later both eyes opened and the thus come one looked around, scanning the galley for signs of life. There were none. The Sergeant was positioned close to the wood-burning stove between the fridge freezer and the Welsh dresser on the starboard side making breakfast. The wisdom of The Parrot as an enlightened The Parrot is expansive and profound, it's heart overflowing with love for all beings. It lives in the boundless. And on the coracle. Upon waking it is The Parrot`s habit to begin the day with a variation of Zuigan`s early morning wake-up call[2] to itself.

"Master Parrot."

"Yes."

"Are you fully awake?"

"Yes, I am."

"Are you really awake?"

"Yes, I am."

"Do not be deceived by others."

"I won't."

There followed a pause during which particles of dust danced in the rays of sunlight streaming across the galley from east to west. A Russian Blue cat moved silently through the willow grove.

Laughing hysterically The Parrot lost its grip on the perch, fell off and landed with a thud on the welcoming carpet below. It became silent and remained on its back, winded, motionless, its beak fixed in a smile, legs pointing upwards to the heavens. Radiating peace and joy to the universe it dissolved into oneness.

The Sergeant continued preparing tea and toast, ignoring the ritual which he had witnessed every morning during the long years they had sailed together. "All is well," he thought, as the toast burned.

Shortly after they were married, in fact on their wedding night, the Sergeant`s wife suggested they sleep in twin beds, His and Hers. He protested but he was outvoted. She added an interesting twist to the idea which was that the twin beds would be in separate rooms. Inscribed neatly on the headboard of His bed is a quote from one of W.S. Gilbert`s *Bab Ballads*,[3] 'those irresponsible yet immortal rhymes'[4] he wrote for Fun magazine in the 1860s.

> *Of all the ships upon the blue,*
> *No ship contained a better crew*
> *Than that of worthy Captain Reece,*
> *Commanding of The Mantlepiece.*

The Sergeant admired Gilbert and Sullivan. *HMS Pinafore*, a derivative, in his opinion, of Captain Reece, was his favourite of all their operas.

As a young officer he was seconded to assist the North Cornwall Police Rapid-Response Crabber Unit[5] whose headquarters are in the village of Withiel as they attempted to clamp down on a severe outbreak of art treasure smuggling from the area. NCPRRCU intelligence officers discovered the smugglers loaded the stolen goods onto rafts at Grogley Halt. Under the cover of darkness, usually at night, they drifted lazily the short way down the tributary to the mighty Camel and on to Wadebridge and from there by pirate ship to the art shops of Paris, Milan and New York.

Through serendipity one afternoon whilst exploring Wadebridge and its tea rooms he came across a book, *The Complete Works of Gilbert and Sullivan* in the bookshop. In it, to his delight, he came across the comic opera, *The Pirates of Penzance*. Reading the opera provided him with useful background information which would be of enormous help, so he thought, during the investigation. He bought the book, as well as a beginner's course in Cornish in case he would be involved in cross examining captured pirates.

He loved the rebellious rhyming in the operas. How audacious to rhyme *quickly can be parsonified* with *conjugally matrimonified*, although he was slightly unnerved by this whilst at the same time not being quite sure why. Or *spleen and vapours* with *linen-drapers*!

The smuggling continued unabated.

Carved deeply into the headboard of Her bed is a quote from the song *Take a Pair of Sparkling Eyes*, from *The Gondoliers*.

> *Take a pair of sparkling eyes,*
> *Take a pair of rosy lips,*
> *Take a figure trimly planned,*
> *Take a tender little hand.*

Ah! Take all these, you lucky man
Take and keep them, if you can, if you can!

They decamped to the willow grove on the stern. He lay deep in the hammock with a steaming mug of spiced chai tea bought from the tea stall in Fishguard Market and a morning's supply of chocolate biscuits reading an article in *Archaeologica Cambrensis*[6] out loud to The Parrot who was perched in the shade on a gently swaying willow branch. It is keenly interested in archaeology. "On a small papyrus, barely five inches by four inches, covered in Coptic text, are words that scholars think are a record of a conversation between Jesus and his disciples. The parts of the texts that have so far been translated include the words, `my coracle`. There is uncertainty as to who the `my` is, but imagine! Scientists who have examined the papyrus say it is not a forgery and the papyrus and the ink have been dated to around 20AD, give or take a few years."

"Theologians are discussing the implications for Christianity. Professor Teleri Tegan from the Department of Coptic Studies at the University of the Four Trinity Davids' Middle Eastern Campus in Tel Aviv[7] has told the press that the implications of the papyrus`s content are `breathtaking` and might support the ancient theory that Jesus was an accomplished coracler. This fragment of a much larger, long-lost papyrus nicknamed *The Gospel of the Coracler* has caused great excitement in theological circles since parts were deciphered a short while ago. The Harvard Theological Review[8] recently published the results of a study by Cerys Gwenllian, a Harvard professor[9] of divinity, in which she says that while the fragment does not prove Jesus was a coracler it could shed light on early Christian practices, in particular whether `the ideal mode` of life was a celibate one, a topic hotly debated in early Christianity. She goes on to say that this gospel fragment provides a reason to reconsider what we think we know by asking what the role claims of Jesus`s coracling status played historically in early Christian controversies."

The Parrot, high in the willow tree close by, was writing a *communiqué* to a colleague in Ireland, Pádraig Ó Parrot, who sails with the Galway Bay Rapid-Response Hooker Unit and who lives with his family in Muiceanach idir Dhá Sháile, a small townland in Conamara. The anglicised version, as the educated reader well knows, is Muckanaghederdauhaulia, which has the distinction of being the longest 'English' language place name in Ireland. The Parrot paused and reflected upon this for a moment. "And Í is the shortest Irish language place name, even though it's not in Ireland. Compare these with Llanfairpwllgwyngyllgogerychwyrndrobwllllantysiliogogogoch, the longest Welsh language place name in Wales. Indeed, it is thought, in the whole of Europe."

In the *communiqué* The Parrot made the following observation. "Occasionally, when learning a new language, an individual comes across a word that confirms they have made the right choice. For many years after I began learning

Irish the word *scamallach*, /skaməlax/, meaning cloudy, was such a one. "Who would not want to learn a language that contains such a word?" I would declare loudly in the *cafés* and taverns of Fishguard of a weekend. "*Scamallach*", I would repeat, even on sunny days. "*SCAMALLACH!*" when overcome with enthusiasm. But now, the glories of *scamallach* have been overtaken, superseded. For recently, a colleague from Massachusetts, whose ancestry includes the Mac Oisdealbhaighs of west Munster and who himself has good Irish and is a crew member aboard a Massachusetts State Police Rapid-Response Schooner Unit vessel out of Boston,[10] emailed me, presenting to the astonished recipient the magnificent Irish word *scileagailí*, to be found in Hibernian English as skilligalee. Yes, *scileagailí*. You heard it here first. And what does this extraordinary word mean? Why, nothing less than 'weak tea'. Do you see the perfection! The glory! When on shore leave in Ireland my life consists of improving my fluency in Irish whilst drinking weak tea. I feel faint."

"For me, the equivalent word in Welsh is *anasbaradigaethus*.[11] In some parts of Wales this means '*anobeithiol o ofnadwy*', 'hopelessly awful', but with a humorous twist, which you will admit sets the bar very high. Yet, for the educational and cultural reasons outlined above, this glorious, luminescent item of vocabulary cannot quite achieve the perfection of *scileagailí*. "

"But now, which of these two majestic lexical items shall be deemed the most valuable for day-to-day usage in the native vernaculars of our two countries, in this, the 21st century? Whilst many and varied are the shenanigans in the day to day affairs of humanity that can be adequately and perceptively described as *anasbaradigaethus*, the bringing together of learning Irish and weak tea, both inside and outside the *Gaeltacht* areas of Ireland, brings *scileagailí* home by a luminous nose."[12]

The Sergeant glanced at The Parrot and noticed it was deep in thought as it weighed up the pros and cons of copying in a colleague in the GBRRHU whose family are from Lios Fear Beag na gCamán in County Clare. Known in 'English' as Lisfarbegnagommaun, the place name can be translated as 'the ring-fort of the little hurley-wielding men'.[13] And perhaps a copy to its Antipodean cousin, Richie The Macaw.[14]

The Parrot smiled as a whimsical notion entered its expansive mind. "What if we extend the reach of Hibernian English ..."

The Sergeant took a sip of tea.

"... to figures in history."

"Such as?"

"*Ich bin ein Berliner*, so I am."[15]

"Hmmm!" The Sergeant eased himself out of the hammock, placed the journal and the empty mug of tea on the deck and moved to a small, low, oak coffee table next to the main mast upon which was a partly completed jigsaw of Catherine Zeta-Jones. He sat cross-legged next to it and began studying the pieces.

"You are free," squawked The Parrot softly. The Sergeant sat back, waiting patiently for The Parrot to continue. He did not have long to wait. "The coracle is conditioned by its shape, the material it is made from, its use and so on. Yet the space within the coracle is free. It appears to be in the coracle only when seen in connection with the coracle. Apart from that, it is just space."

The Sergeant paused for a moment then went on with the jigsaw.

"*Mens agitat molem,* so it does," it whispered.[16]

A few minutes later the Sergeant paused again from his deliberations as a question formed in his mind, "If Pembrokeshire was a fruit, which fruit would it be?" Then more. "And is it singular or plural? Masculine or feminine?" The questions moved on and he watched them disappear over Harbour Village, heading sou` by sou` west to who knows where. "What is life?" he continued. Using techniques he learnt during a sojourn in Paviland Cave on the Gower many years ago he emptied his mind. This happened quickly. Amongst the random flotsam and jetsam eddying in the warm currents on the surface of his cerebral cortex an answer appeared. "A surprise!"

"You have learnt well, my child," said The Parrot.

"Everything is out of control."

"Exactly." The Parrot smiled. "Do nothing."

"Do nothing?"

"Nothing."

"Nothing?"

"Nothing. Doing nothing, doing happens."

The Sergeant reached critical mass. "I`m going to make another mug of tea." He switched to energy saving mode.

"Be yourself, *Patrón.* As life itself."

"A strong one," he decided as he wound his way back to the galley. Waiting for the kettle to boil he switched the radio on, removed the charred remains of morning forgetfulness from the toaster, replaced it with two fresh slices of extra thick fibre reduced white bread and continued making breakfast. The voice of the Radio Free Pembrokeshire[17] announcer filled the galley. "Computer scientists are designing tiny computers that can indicate when someone is in a bad mood. The idea is that a person will be fitted with sensors that cause them to change colour according to their mood. For this to happen the person would need to be covered with conductive paint, in a colour of their choice of course. The paint changes colour as the person`s mood changes. This new technology has many uses. For example, if the captain of the Fishguard to Rosslare ferry noticed a coracle with a red person on board paddling furiously and approaching the ferry at ramming speed, the captain would know the Sergeant was in a bad mood thus giving the crew precious seconds to take appropriate action, such as gathering by the handrail on the open deck area to cheer him on. At this early stage in its development however the technology cannot indicate why the Sergeant is in a bad mood."

The kettle boiled. The toast popped up. He filled the teapot and left it to steep.

"Tiny sensors are attached to the skin and analyse sweat, heart rate and electrical activity. They also send a small current of electricity through the body and measure how quickly it does so. The slower it travels through the body tissue, the tenser the person is. Computing technology is becoming one hundred times smaller each decade and the next generation will tap into the autonomic nervous system and into the unconscious mind. Dyfed-Powys Police Rapid-Response Coracle Unit[18] have expressed interest."

He poured the tea and buttered the toast. "The unconscious mind. At last!" Picking up the mug of tea and the plate of hot buttered toast he returned to the peace of the stern and, balancing mug and plate on his stomach, lay back in the hammock.

The Sergeant sipped his tea, `neither fast nor slow, but completely`. A thoughtful look appeared on his face. It came from nowhere. Music from the singing stones of the stone circle engulfed the stern in a soothing bubble of ancient music. A contented Sergeant went to sleep, his nature at peace. The half empty mug of tea and the plate of toast fell harmlessly onto the deck.

The Parrot was happy. The day was going well. It burst into song, quietly, so as not to wake the Sergeant.

> *Trasna na dtonnta, dul siar, dul siar,*
> *Slán leis an uaigneas, is slán leis an gcian.*
> *Geal é mo chroí agus geal í an ghrian,*
> *Geal bheith ag filleadh go dtí an Bhreatain Bheag.*

When returning from long sea patrols and upon sighting Strumble Head from his perch atop the main mast next to the kettle of buzzards, The Parrot would burst into song, *Trasna na dTonnta*[19] usually. The words of this popular Irish ballad are not entirely appropriate, and The Parrot changes the ending of the last line of the first verse from ... *ag filleadh go hÉirinn* to ... *ag filleadh go dtí an Bhreatain Bheag*. It doesn`t remember where it learnt the song, perhaps whilst travelling in its youth. The Sergeant thought it must have Irish blood, which it does. It has distant cousins living in Corca Dorcha, which many believe to be on the Dingle peninsular.[20]

As his heartbeat and respiration slowed, muscles relaxing, brain waves dawdling, the Sergeant twitched and noticed with enthusiasm the plural form of the 2nd declension, feminine noun *tonn*, the characteristic plural form of the definite article preceding it, and the giveaway *urú* of the first sound of the noun, bearing witness to it being in its genitive plural form, the genitive, as we all know, following such lively words as *trasna*, *chun*, *timpeall* and *dála*. This illuminating piece of information passed swiftly through the Sergeant's mind which decided, wisely, not to engage with it. The question as to whether, if we go back a thousand years or so in the history of the language, we will find a noun lying low within the modern *trasna*, remained unasked.

The first time the Sergeant invited his future wife on board was the morning after he and The Parrot returned from a secondment patrolling the pirate routes between Pembrokeshire and North Cornwall. As she tiptoed gingerly up the gangplank in her high heels the wake from the ferry hit and she fell into the water with a scream. And a splash. He knew instinctively that this was an opportunity to make a good impression on the woman he loved. Unfortunately, the two teenage boys standing on the quayside were reluctant to dive in to rescue her unless he offered them significantly more than 50p each for their trouble. The haggling continued for some time, and they were close to agreeing a price when she managed to drag herself, coughing and spluttering, onto the quay. She cancelled the visit and went home to her mother, Ardudful.

The Sergeant was approaching sleep, reassured after his latest health check confirmed that he has 53,583 neurones in the ventrolateral preoptic nucleus of his brain. "More than enough," he thought, before engaging with his dreams. But The Parrot was concerned that lack of exercise means the Sergeant has less efficient white matter fibres meaning that the different parts of his brain communicate poorly with one another. As a result of this his brain is less healthy, and slower than it would be if he exercised more. His memory would also improve with exercise.

The radio announcer continued, waking the Sergeant from his slumbers. "Breaking news. The Welsh Meteorological Agency raised the aviation warning code for the region covering Crymych International Airport earlier today after the eruption of a volcano in the Carnabwth lava field to the northeast. The Agency described the eruption as '... a calm lava eruption that barely registers on seismometers. This is the fifth eruption this year but poses no danger to aircraft. Lava flowing into the sea however might cause some warming of the water with the maximum predicted temperature being ideal for kiddies' play.' And now, news from the coast. A local fisherman is celebrating catching rare lobsters today. A blue lobster is reported to have been caught off Dinas Head at about 10.00am and a yellow lobster is reported to have been caught off St David's Head at approximately 11.00am. This follows the report of a crystal lobster being caught off Strumble Head at 9.00am. All three lobsters were released back into the sea within a few minutes of their being caught. A spokesperson for the University of the Four Trinity Davids' Lobster Institute[7] in Oxwich on the Gower told us earlier that the odds of all these different-coloured lobsters being caught in the same area on the same morning is thousands of millions to one. The fisherman was alone in his boat at the time the incidents occurred and is firmly entrenched in the Sloop in Porthgain accepting the congratulations, well wishes and free drinks offered to him by wonderstruck tourists. And now for the weather."

"Shw' mae? Warm horizontal rain fast approaching from the northeast."

"Thank you Derec."[21]

The Sergeant's day is four hours long. Staff at the medical unit of the Dyfed-Powys Police Rapid-Response Coracle Unit suggest this work-doze balance might not be ideal. In support of his lifestyle, he quotes from an essay written as long ago as nineteen thirty-two, thinking this to be positive affirmation that in his way, ` ... there will be happiness and joy of life, instead of frayed nerves, weariness and dyspepsia'.[22] He is particularly pleased about the prognosis for dyspepsia, not being too fond of peppermint.

"À cœur vaillant rien d'impossible, so it isn't," noted The Parrot.[23]

It was two bells in the forenoon on the bridge as another day dawned for the DPPRRCU. But not for the Sergeant, who was asleep in the hammock enjoying R&R after a busy breakfast. The on-board computer was in control as usual and the vessel began to power up. Just as bomber aircraft at times of tension during the Cold War waited on runways, engines running so they could be airborne in the shortest amount of time, the coracle fired up every morning at 9.00am and remained in a state of readiness throughout the working day - apart from the Sergeant's mealtimes, tea breaks and afternoon *siesta* of course, when readiness would be useless. The Parrot flew to its perch on the bridge and assumed command. To the east smoke appeared from a small terracotta chimney on the tower above Fishguard Town Hall and the crowds thronging the square cheered and threw their hats into the air. The town had a new mayor.[24]

Disturbed by the noise as the engines revved at maximum the Sergeant woke up. It was 10.45am and he was peckish as he had slept through the tea break, so he visited the galley before proceeding to the bridge to report in. He approached the fridge freezer next to the wood-burning stove and stood the required eighteen inches in front of the door surface, motionless, head up, chest out, arms down by his sides, feet shoulder width apart, looking straight ahead. The built-in face-mapping biometric technology providing advanced facial authentication hummed as the door confirmed the Sergeant's identity. He stood patiently, listening to the gentle sound of the concealed heavy-duty stainless steel, anti-tamper mortise rack bolts, an integral part of the structure, withdrawing. Reaching forward he grasped the handle, opened the door and studied its contents.

Several minutes later he was on the bridge eating a dishful of banana and toffee Belgian chocolate pieces with vanilla ice cream and chocolate brownie triangles sprinkled with white chocolate buttons drizzled with warm banana fudge sauce topped with a generous dollop of freshly whipped double cream, a Mars bar pushed down the middle to support it. He ate it with a miniature teaspoon as there is a danger of rushing such delights.

He glanced at the dashboard. A red light lit up on the top right. The words WARNING and URGENT flashed menacingly on the display. He leant closer to read the small text underneath. "Oh dear!" he groaned. "The infinity pool on the port side has sprung a leak." Embedding the teaspoon into the ice cream to free his right hand he pressed a blue button, one of many coloured buttons on the control panel. A message appeared on the screen.

DO NOT PRESS THE BLUE BUTTON.

"Oh d**r!" he protested forcefully. Irritated by an unhelpful technology he made his way back to the comparative safety of the hammock.

A flock of seven million pink-footed geese appeared from the northwest flying low over the chimney pots of the terraced houses in Harbour Village before hugging the cliff face as they descended rapidly, keeping a tight formation, Stuka like, towards the water. Pulling up just in time they flew low, passing the coracle to their left, and on towards Fishguard, veering northeast as they clung to the cliff face. Reaching Lower Town, they skimmed the masts of the yachts moored in the harbour before following the course of the Gwaun upriver where they would rest for the night in Llanychaer. "What a marvellous sight," beamed The Parrot, and cried pink tears. The Sergeant didn't notice, he was concentrating on the ice cream.

"Coracles are go!" blasted the ship-to-shore radio lashed to the base of the mast nearby.[25] Concentrating single pointedly on elevenses the Sergeant did not hear the announcement from HQ. It would not have made any difference if he had. He was worried. Earlier that morning he spotted a clump of Japanese Knotweed growing in a corner of the willow grove. He ate some more ice cream in an attempt to take his mind off it. "You will," appeared the voice of the Admiral, "patrol the sea lanes between Wales and Ireland and assist any Gardaí Rapid-Response Currach Unit`s you might come across, should they request it."[26]

The Parrot, having both Welsh and Irish blood, when in Ireland experiences *hiraeth* for Wales, and when in Wales experiences *síreacht* for Ireland.

Leaving the infinity pool to drain slowly into the ocean The Parrot pressed the orange button to raise the anchor, slipped the vessel into Paddle Gear 1 and pointed the coracle towards the open sea before switching to automatic pilot. Satisfied the vessel was secure it burst into song.

Fifteen men on a dead man's chest!

The Sergeant joined the chorus.

Yo ho ho and a bottle of rum.[27]

Then in Welsh.

> *Pymtheg dyn ar gist y dyn marw!*
>
> *Io ho ho, a photel o rym.*

Then in Irish.

> *Cúig fhear déag ar chófra an fhir bháite!*
>
> *Ío hó hó agus buidéal rum.*

They particularly like this song as many think the author based Long John Silver on north Walian adventurer John Lloyd, a merchant captain who, along with his brother Owen, turned to piracy by taking treasure from a Spanish galleon. John Lloyd also had a wooden leg. The singing of sea shanties, particularly this one, was a long and proud tradition they shared over the years and was their custom as they left port.

Tourists love the spectacle of an ocean going DPPRRCU vessel powering off to work on a Monday morning and crowds of them flock to the quayside to marvel at this living tradition. They position their deckchairs at dawn and sit munching sandwiches and drinking tea and coffee from flasks, waiting with anticipation. When the ship-to-shore radio barks into life and the Admiral fires orders at the Sergeant they cheer. When the song begins, they join in. Most know the words to the song off by heart while some mime in the style of John Redwood,[28] heads bouncing from side to side, just for fun.

A music teacher from Ysgol Bro Gwaun[29] in nearby Fishguard conducts this impromptu choir whilst standing precariously in a rowing boat twenty feet or so from the quayside and leads them through *kan ha diskan*. The music teacher is the *kaner* and the crowd the *diskaner*. Supporting the *kan ha diskan* every Monday are Rhocesi'r Fro[30] and Annie Ebrel, Nolùen Le Buhé, Érik Marchand, Yann-Fañch Kemener and Denez Prigent,[31] although the latter is a little too modern for local taste.

It is not unusual for different sections of the crowd to sing in their own languages, and such is the free spirit of the tradition that subtitles are rarely required. The different languages merge into one glorious sound, evidence that the story of the Tower of Babel has been misunderstood, the more the merrier being its true meaning. They sing songs in *kan ha diskan* style, volume increasing for the vocables, a favourite being *tra la la la leh no*, as the voices of the Sergeant and The Parrot become weaker and weaker, dimmer and fainter, until they disappear from sight and hearing around the harbour wall. At this point everyone falls silent and is overcome by a sense of loneliness and dread and a deep depression descends upon them. High spirits soon return however as the conductor passes out photocopied sheets, as teachers do, containing the music and words of a Gilbert and Sullivan opera and the *hwyl* and the *craic* rise again, like sap in a hedgerow in the springtime during the thirteen days of a waxing moon. All this a rich accompaniment to the beginning of another tumultuous week in the life of DPPRRCU`s elite.

Becalmed just beyond the sea wall the Sergeant lay on the starboard deck with his head over the side, peering into the ocean depths. The coracle rocked gently in the swell. He was sweating profusely. He threw himself away from the edge, landing in an exhausted heap next to the bird bath, frightening the wading birds that summer there and causing them to scatter. "Reminds me of our visit to the Cliffs of Moher," he remarked to no one. The Parrot, who had moved to the willow grove in order to keep an eye on him, pretended not to hear as it deftly preened its feathers. It was true. They had worked closely with the Galway Bay Rapid-Response Hooker Unit and on patrol one morning had ventured south before finding themselves at the foot of the Cliffs of Moher. "Looking up from the bottom of the cliffs is not as exciting as looking down from the top," a Mr Ó hEithir[32] a passenger on the adjoining GBRRHU vessel told him as the vessel bobbed up and down off the port side. A Mr Ó Direáin,[33] also a passenger aboard the Irish vessel at the time, agreed. The wind was up. It was not a soft day, the Fliuch Scale[34] showed 11, so they headed ashore, the Sergeant, Mr Ó hEithir and Mr Ó Direáin, made their way up the cliff path to the top, lay down on their stomachs, and slowly, very slowly moved their bodies forward to look over the edge. The Sergeant fainted immediately, a combination of a fear of heights and feeling queasy watching seagulls below him circling high above the ocean and needed two ice creams at the local tearoom to fully recover from the shock. The Irishmen, made of sterner stuff, became mildly delirious and recovered after just one ice cream.

The Parrot loosened its grip on the branch and executed a backward roll, ending up upside down, in which position it would stay a while until fate intervened. It was a yoga position it learnt during time spent on a retreat in *Goa* whilst travelling during its gap year. The upside-down-ness helped the blood circulate. It would keep a close upside-down eye on things.

Tradition has it The Parrot is hundreds of years old. Some say he sailed with Madog to America and hitched a ride back with Columbus. He sailed with Black Bart from Little Newcastle, to Madagascar, Malabar, Suranam and Porthmadog. It was whilst living with pirates that he learnt *Pieces of eight*. And it was he who christened the coracle The Hispaniola II in honour of a first cousin, also known as The Parrot, who sailed for treasure with Jim Hawkins and Long John Silver himself.[27] It is not all plain sailing for parrots, however. On returning from their last voyage to Zanzibar it took the Sergeant some weeks to get The Parrot back after it was impounded by customs in Milford Haven. Customs officers declared him to be a rare species and suspected the Sergeant of intending to sell him on the lucrative black market that exists for exotic birds in Carmarthen Market. An unfortunate mix up, it took the intervention of the First Minister[35] himself to have The Parrot released back for duty.

Whilst in Zanzibar they used their free time to explore ancient caves in a search for prehistoric paintings. Sitting quietly at the entrances to several caves they heard the sounds of deer, bison and many other long extinct animals. On the cave walls far inside, all these animals were represented in beautiful rock art. Early peoples, echoes, sounds, mystical interpretations, supernatural animal spirits living deep within the cave. They found all of these things. But no parrots.

The Sergeant felt ill. "I need a weak cup of homeopathic tea," he thought. He was furious and cursed his bad luck at being becalmed. He cursed with the curse of all curses. "May your ice cream melt before you can eat it!" He showed no mercy. None was asked, none was given. He did not know who or what he was cursing and he didn`t feel any better, so he tried again. "May all your seasickness tablets be placebos!" he screamed. Chimney pots onshore rattled, the weathervane on the clock tower above the town hall in Fishguard spun wildly in all directions, then a quietness engulfed the twin towns. Two girls in the van stationed in the car park on the Parrog selling teas, coffees, ice cream and confectionary burst into tears. Seabirds fell dead from the sky, mackerel floated to the surface of the water, lifeless, and the hens in Harbour Village will not be laying for weeks. The Parrot fell from the branch, landing on its head on the deck. "Collateral damage," it muttered as it rolled over and found its feet, "always a danger when such power is unleashed." It flew back up to the branch. Unaware of what was happening around him the Sergeant felt a lot better. He got up and moved to the hammock into which he fell, exhausted. "What a day!" he sighed.

The ship-to-shore radio came alive again. "This is the Admiral. Over. Are you there?"

"Yes sir."

"Dyfed-Powys Police Rapid-Response Coracle Unit`s Naval Intelligence Bureau advises you change your computer password immediately. They have reason to believe the Russians have hacked into your webcam and CCTV and the footage is being used in a livestream broadcast on a popular morning television programme in Moscow called, Сержант дома.[36] The programme is top of the ratings. Cyber defence company Malwarebutties have been informed."[37]

"Roger that, sir. Will change password immediately."

"Very good. Out."

The Sergeant thought about it. His mind was in his hemispheres, both of them, right and left. It seems that he is here and now in his right hemisphere, which is busy receiving information from his senses. Energy connected to energy. Looking for detail and creating time is what his left hemisphere does. And language of course. And `I am` is the great separation. Usually right and left communicate with each other via the corpus callosum. Usually. He was not to know that his corpus callosum was on strike. Unperturbed by this, he fell asleep.

"**If**, ... and that`s a very big if, ..." said The Parrot, then stopped, sensing a presence close by in the willow grove. It was wearing its McSalver`s coveralls,[38] waterproof and flame retardant. Sailing with the Sergeant it took no chances. The coveralls are equipped with many pockets inside and out where it keeps sea charts, a smart phone that operates to a depth of thirty fathoms, telescope, ship-to-shore radio, treasure map, novel, flare, sandwiches, fruit, gravy bones for the dolphins, oven gloves, a bottle of Tŷ Nant spring water,[39] a 20-foot electrical extension lead and a 12 bass squeeze box. You never know when a good sea shanty might come in handy.

The Sergeant woke with a start. The coracle rocked alarmingly and he clung to the sides of the hammock for dear life. But to no avail, he fell out anyway. Eventually the hammocks movements returned to within normal limits on a becalmed vessel.

"**If** ...," repeated The Parrot thoughtfully, "the cat is a spy, what shall we do?"

"Do you realise what this means?" announced the Sergeant. "We might have a Russian spy onboard. I`ll radio the Admiral."

"Hmmmmm," muttered The Parrot. "If you do that it`ll know we`re onto it. If indeed you are right, I suggest we keep an eye on it."

"Good idea," the Sergeant replied. "But I`m still worried."

"Act as though you don`t know anything," advised The Parrot with a mischievous grin. The Sergeant is convinced he learns better when sleepy and also that he learns better if he has a nap immediately after learning something. He climbed back into the hammock and went to sleep.

His wife, wearing her stealth outfit and therefore undetected by the radar, brought her dinghy alongside and came aboard. The early warning defence shield had failed. She entered the galley and looked around. The temperature inside dropped imperceptibly. A hint of destruction emanated from her nostrils. The Parrot, having trained as a Ninja in feudal Japan when a young The Parrot, realised the danger, slipped into its lightweight jumpsuit, became one with the branch and disappeared.

The Parrot remains vigilant, alert night and day. To this supreme being danger is signalled through awareness of sights, sounds and smells, and something else ... by wearing his bright yellow Bruce Lee jumpsuit with black stripe down each side. A nice touch. As luck would have it, an errant gene several generations ago in its family tree provides a further layer of perception. The Parrot's nose, the nasal cavities inside the nares on its upper beak, is 100 million times more sensitive than a human nose and is capable of detecting even the faintest rises of temperature in objects up to 30 feet away. Scientists think the nose achieves this independently of The Parrot by detecting photons of electromagnetic energy. The Parrot is on record as saying that the regions of its brain that process information from the nose light up as it approaches warm objects. Furthermore, it has observed that the temperature of the nose is always about 5C colder than the rest of itself and of the surrounding ambient air temperature. This was the clue that alerted scientists to the existence of what has become known in the academic literature as Parrot Nose. Interestingly, Parrot Nose is not unique to The Parrot, being a phenomenon also found in the noses of vampire bats, pit vipers and dogs.

As she left the galley, heading silently in their direction, its sense of humour got the better of it. "Who`s the boss, you or your wife?" it asked.

The Sergeant awoke. "I am, of course," he replied sleepily.

"And where are you going to take her for a surprise meal tonight?"

"I don`t know, she hasn`t told me yet."

"To the new Russian restaurant in St Davids," she announced from behind the main mast.

"Yes dear," he mumbled, looking wildly around to see where the voice had come from.

"It is so," decided The Parrot, giving out a great laugh. Clear or confused, the nature of the Sergeant is unchanged.

"I`ll be back at seven o`clock." And she left as silently as she had come, without a flicker on the radar. Or did she?

The temperature around the hammock dropped fifteen degrees. Frost formed on the ropes connecting it to the willows. Icicles appeared on the underside of the branches. The stone circle was covered with a light dusting of snow.

"Do you know what this means?" asked The Parrot.

"Yes," replied The Sergeant, "another displaced polar vortex."

"No. Your wife is a Russian spy."

The Sergeant enjoyed a morning of turbo-paralysis. His engine was roaring, his wheels were spinning but his body was refusing to move. The Parrot decided all was not lost and returned to his novel, *Germinal*, which he was reading in French.[40] The Sergeant needed tea and biscuits. He got off the hammock and walked slowly and carefully to the galley. If his wife, with Russian help, was using stealth technology, how could he be sure she was not still onboard. "A nightmare scenario if ever there was one," he thought, turning his head quickly to follow a shadow that appeared in the corner of his eye. "Nothing!"

A few cautious minutes later he was sitting by the table in the galley, a mug of steaming tea and a packet of chocolate biscuits in front of him. Bliss! He picked up the mug and gingerly sipped the hot tea, even though it was not ginger tea. His eyes stopped roaming the galley for signs of the intruder and he began to relax. He fixed his gaze on the packet of biscuits. He thought of his waistline. It was 11.48am. Picking up the packet he read the ingredients. 'May contain chocolate biscuits.' As he continued reading the words seemed to grow bigger, change colour to a garish purple and blue and flash like a neon sign. `Best eaten with a mug of tea before midday.` "That settles it!" He put a couple in his mouth and munched. Then another sip of tea. "The instructions refer to the whole packet no doubt," he thought happily. What else could he do? He was powerless to resist. A rhyme appeared in his mind, and he sang it softly to himself as he munched and sipped.

> Row, row, row your boat
> Gently down the stream.
> Merrily, merrily, merrily, merrily,
> Life is but a dream.[41]

The Sergeant played Grasshopper.[42] The Parrot played. Normal order was restored. "The Sergeant is going nowhere," thought The Parrot, "and he is going with all his heart."

"I`m a strong believer in eating," said the Sergeant. "I read somewhere that it`s good for you. My grandmother swore by it. She ate something almost every day and lived to be nearly ninety-seven." A puff of red, white and blue smoke appeared above the table the other side of the biscuits. As the smoke cleared the Russian Blue cat materialized, paused, eyed the Sergeant, then approached the packet of biscuits. Alarm bells rang in his head. He looked into the cat`s eyes. The cat looked back.

"Cat! Nibble one of those biscuits and you die."

The cat stopped and stared, hypnotically the Sergeant thought, into his eyes, purring menacingly.

"Cat! There`s something you need to know. Where I come from people wear fur hats in winter that look just like you. D`ya get ma drift, cat?"

The cat backed away, keeping her eyes on him all the time.

"A wise choice, cat. A wise choice." He took a sip of tea then reached for another biscuit, but the packet was gone. "What the ...!"

And so was the cat.

It was approaching eight bells in the forenoon. He turned his gaze to the beautiful Swiss cuckoo clock attached high on the port bulkhead between The Parrot's perch and the ship-to-shore radio and waited for the spectacle. A whirring sound, a clunk, the little doors on the front of the clock opened and an intricately carved and colourfully decorated wooden cuckoo appeared, looked around once, raised its head to the sky and began to sing.

"Cuckoo! Cuckoo! Cuckoo!

The sweet singing of the cuckoo was a highlight of his day.

Cuckoo! Cuckoo!

Such mellifluous tones.

Cuckoo! Cuck ..."

"What the ...!"

The Prussian Blue had struck again.

"*Veni. Vidi. Vici.* so I did," came a voice from nowhere.[43]

Recently, an infestation of locusts destroyed crops in the vegetable garden next to the cowshed. A supercomputer acquired by DPPRRCU and located in HQ will use satellite data of wind, rain and humidity to predict where the locusts will strike next. Scientists think the scale of the swarm followed last week's cyclone in Harbour Village which created ideal conditions for the locusts, with a life cycle of three months, to breed. It is estimated that there are now billions of locusts in the vegetable patch.

Patiently, a colony of fairy penguins with an average height of just over a foot, the smallest of Pembrokeshire's penguin species, play in the cool waters at the northern reaches of the lake. Their blue heads and upper parts catch the sunlight as they await news of a precise classification of their subspecies.

An African black-footed cat, at up to twenty inches in length the smallest wild cat in the county, with spotted and striped tawny fur providing camouflage on moonlit nights, lies curled up in its burrow hidden in a thicket of tiggory trees, resting, before hunting rodents and small birds during the night. At times achieving speeds of up to 1.9mph it approaches its prey from behind and during the chase puts its paws on the flanks of the prey and grounds it by using its dewclaws.

When in bloom at the end of March, dwarf pansies, 0.393701 inches tall, brighten the area around the rabbit burrows near the stone circle with their creamy yellow flowerheads with deep yellow centre edged in purple. Absent from the mainland, they are found only on the stern and on the Scilly Isles. It is a little-known fact that all pansies are violas but not all violas are pansies.

70 million years ago a day lasted 23 and a half hours when the Earth rotated 372 times a year instead of 365. However, the Earth's orbit around the sun has remained constant which means that the length of the year has remained the

same. During this period, friction from ocean tides, a result of the moon's gravity, has slowed the rotation of the Earth which in turn has caused the length of the day to increase. Unnoticed by the Sergeant, as the Earth's spin slows, the moon is moving away from Fishguard by about 1.5 inches a year.

'The August moon grew to fullness and waned without creating undue excitement in Fishguard.' [44]

17

We learn to wait, to wait until the time is right, ... To be patient is to align with the speed of the slowest person, to help them as they are and not to subject them to the violence of our wish that they were other than they are. ... We are for the other.

James Low

Megan`s favourite cardigan attracted moths. She was content with this and kept a net handy. They were travelling from Crymych for Megan to address yet another extraordinary general meeting of Machlud y Wawr's Tenby branch.[2] Actually, it was an ordinary meeting but the members there are fond of a bit of melodrama. Certainly, their Christmas *pantomime* is well attended. As they drove through the high wind and heavy rain along the road overlooking North Beach, they passed a group of people on the pavement walking the other way, adults and children. "Tourists," said Megan. "Who else would walk along a beautiful spot like this looking so miserable."

Upon arrival Megan settled into the comfortable chair set up for her on the stage. The assembled Machlud y Wawr members, packed into Theatr Bleiddudd in the middle of town, waited a moment or two, then murmured enthusiastically. She began her introductory remarks as only she can, pitching them perfectly for her audience.

"Puppets!" She exclaimed to rapturous applause, although no one knew why.

"Puppets!" They repeated. "Puppets?"

"The future is puppets," Megan continued, "which means going away on a training course." More applause. If there was anything they liked more than a stroll along North Beach with an ice cream, it was going away on a training course. "The biennial ten-day *World Puppet Theatre Festival* in Charleville-Mèziéres in northern France close to the *Parc Naturel Régional des Ardennes* brings together puppeteers from all over the world. There are shows for adults and children. In the town is the *Institut International de la Marionnette* and the *École Nationale Supérieure des Arts de la Marionnette*[3] where people can learn the craft." Her voice faltered for a second. "That is where my husband trained to be a *personne qui manipule des marionnettes.* Yes, a *marionnettiste.* Doesn't that sound like fun." A sympathetic hush filled the theatre. Then applause, both supportive and joyful. "We have decided", Megan thought `we` better than `I` on such occasions, "to send every member of this branch to the festival for the full ten days. Furthermore, scholarships are available to cover the cost of sending five members on the three-year course." A stunned silence shook the building. Once again

Megan`s free radical off-*piste* thinking surprised and delighted them. She paused to munch some nuts, seeds and strawberries and to sip tea laced with fresh, full fat milk. A heady mixture designed to alleviate the effects of free radicals. A woman in her prime once said, `The secret of staying young is to live honestly, eat slowly and lie about your age.`[4] Megan added antioxidants to the list.

"As an aside," she continued, "a little etymology. Many, many years ago the Virgin Mary was a popular figure in shows and plays. *Marionette* means 'Little Mary' and Her figure became the name for all such 'puppets' controlled from above by strings. Puppetry goes back thousands of years and was popular in cultures all over the world. It is mentioned in the writings of Herodotus and Xenophon around the 5th century BC in Ancient Greece where the Greek word for puppet was νευρόσπαστος. Let me repeat that, νευρόσπαστος. Isn't that a lovely sound. Why, even Aristotle himself, who lived from 384 to 322BC, discussed puppets in a work entitled *On the Motion of Animals*. Clay dolls found at archaeological sites in the Indus valley in India are thought by many to be early examples of puppets." Megan was just getting into her stride when she noticed the yawns. Not everyone shares her passion for the subject, a passion she got from her husband. She returned to the agenda of the meeting.

"At the next monthly extraordinary general meeting everyone`s name will be put into a hat and the Mayoress of Tenby[5] will draw the names of the five lucky members who will attend the three-year course, all expenses paid. Meanwhile, get packed girls, we leave for Charleville-Mèziéres with Richards Brothers[6] at first light tomorrow. Ten-day puppet festival here we come!" Pandemonium broke out. Some members swooned while others broke into song, paraphrasing a perennial favourite to suit the occasion.

> *The triangle tingles and the trumpets play slow,*
> *The sky is on fire, and we must go*
> *By Richards Brothers bus to* Charleville-Mèziéres.[7]

"You are one dangerous *mujer hermosa*," muttered Bronwen whose hair was fixed in a bubble-cut style. She likes the old ways. "Puppeteering in France," she thought. "We`ll get up before the stars set and go to bed after they rise." She was born with a sat-nav instinct for a *café* where they serve freshly roasted coffee, and she was going to France, where they understand coffee.

Megan poured herself another cup of tea and sat back in the easy chair to relax. She was already packed. In her travelling bag along with the usual clothes and toiletries was her reading material for the journey, the newly published *Stray Shopping Trolleys of North Pembrokeshire: A Guide to Field Identification* and *Better Not to Have Been*[8] which describes the negative effects of coming into existence that could perhaps have been avoided if you had not come into existence. Bad plumbing for example.

There is a dance sequence whose name **Seek and Destroy** is mentioned rarely, and then only in hushed tones, that Bronwen has perfected. Encouraged by the gathered Machlud y Wawr members she donned her *lorica squamata*, a scale armour bought on a whim during a recent long weekend in Sirmium, assumed the *en pointe* position, then moved - *plie, releve, fierce saute* - up onto the stage and did it right there and then. Or perhaps it would be more correct to say, it happened right there and then. To the *connoisseur*, Bronwen`s clogging technique is not easy on the eye, but it is addictive to the senses. Sunlight sweeping through the windows to the side of the stage caught the polished surfaces of the scales, reflecting off them to cast an eery glow over the terrified bystanders.

Bronwen paused to catch her breath, gathered herself and prepared to unleash her favourite terror weapon against the barbarian hordes of the fair town of Tenby, or, as it is known fondly by locals, the 'Little Town of the Fishes'. From her belt she took a sling made up of a leather pouch and two leather cords into which she placed several 'whistling' stones the size of acorns taken from a pouch hanging from the belt on her left side. Whirling the sling fiercely through the air several times with her right arm to gain maximum power she unleashed a lethal barrage of stones, each weighing about an ounce with a hole approximately 0.2 inches wide drilled into it to create a shrill whistling or buzzing noise during flight, an effect designed to terrify those poor souls facing her and to increase the size of the injury on impact, rather like hollow-tipped dumdum bullets which expand to cause maximum damage to living tissue. Slings were used as weapons by auxiliary troops in the Roman army, the most feared being specialized units of slingers from the Balearic Islands in the western Mediterranean, a favourite holiday destination when Bronwen was younger. Volley after volley, four stones per volley, was launched. The missile shots flew over the heads of the despairing audience, blasting a large hole through the exit doors at the back of the auditorium to speed through the foyer before emerging via the main entrance of the theatre. Sweeping across the pavement they ricocheted in a rising trajectory off the bonnet of a car parked illegally on the street outside, careered upwards over the buildings opposite, and, travelling at over 90 miles per hour, headed south over the town. To the barbarian hordes shopping in the quiet streets below the whistling noise signified that an attack was imminent. Alarm spread quickly as the intrusive, high-pitched scream of the stones was heard as far away as Caldey Island. Panic and dread engulfed the tranquillity of the visitors picnicking on South Beach. Novice monks in the abbey, all too aware that the island was in the flightpath, fell to their knees in prayer. With a look of grim satisfaction for a job well done, Bronwen slid the sling back under her belt.

From the back wall of the stage she retrieved and held aloft the *signum draconis*, known colloquially on the mean streets of downtown Tenby as the *draco*. First adopted into the Roman cavalry during the 2nd century AD it consists of a hollow dragon's head made of bronze placed atop an oak pole. Attached to the head is a multi-coloured tube of brightly dyed cloth acting as a windsock. The light summer breeze coming into the hall through the open windows howled through the *draco* holding the tube of brightly dyed cloth aloft in its turbulence as she strode around the stage, causing fear to spread through the crowd.

After marching several times around the stage she placed the *draco* against the back wall, gathered the javelin and shield that waited there, and, grasping the *amentum* she keeps in a leather pouch attached to the belt around her waist next to the sword for just such an emergency, fitted the javelin into it. With deft movement of upper arm and wrist, thus utilising the *amentum* to achieve greater velocity and stability in flight, she sent it hurtling over the stalls at high speed. The Members ducked as one. It flew unimpeded through the gaping, splintered hole in the exit door and past a panicking usherette who, at that precise moment, was contemplating entering the auditorium carrying a vending tray supported by a strap around her neck upon which was laid out a varied selection of chocolates, ice creams and lollipops. A deadly, southerly trajectory took it across the foyer and out via the main entrance into the street where it planted itself firmly into the side of a passing number 381 bus only to disappear as it careered, via Narberth, towards its new destination, the bus station in Haverfordwest.

Accelerating now, she danced a furious mirror-symmetrical U-shape, becoming a locus of points in one plane, equidistant from both the directrix and the focus. Unnerved a little by this audacious move she sneezed mid twirl and fell over. At least it had the suggestion of a sneeze. An explosion came up from deep in her stomach rather than from her nose. A bit like a cow. It is a genetic thing. Bronwen`s cows do it as well.

Enthused, she leapt to her feet and performed the climax of the dance, a *kamikaze* move so audacious it was as likely to throw her off the stage and out through the window as to delight the audience. Yes, the *finale* of the glorious piece of clogging ballet Bronwen had spent months secretly perfecting, as the bruises all over her body and the collision marks on the walls of the crypt testify. This was the time to unveil it. The assembled Members watched closely, following every move. To begin, a *francisca*, an ancient throwing axe spun through the air low over their heads, embedding itself deeply into the oak panelling on the back wall of the stalls with a dull thud. Then she sounded the *barritus*, an ancient war cry, beginning as a low murmuring and building to a loud roar amplified many times by her sounding it into the shield held in front of her mouth. As the deafening crescendo was reached she drew the short thrusting sword and waved it menacingly at the audience, who withdrew in alarm, before leaping three times into the air. She read somewhere once that three is a magic number. At the peak of each leap, whilst motionless between upward and downward movement, she emitted a terrifying bellow and glared with bulging bloodshot eyes at the petrified audience. Miscalculating the descent path of the final leap she disappeared through the window with a scream. For some, the maxim *clog fast, die young* is a literal truth.

"Does the directed motion of fundamental particles drive all life's actions?" Megan wondered.

Pots of irises lay scattered around the *auditorium*. Megan loves the association with Greek mythology, and, being amongst Tenby branch members, Greek drama. The flowers take their name from the Greek goddess of the rainbow who led the souls of dead women to paradise. "How fitting," she thought as she watched Bronwen attempting to climb back through the window. "The pole star has changed four times in recorded history, the role of North Star passing from one star to another, while Bronwen has not changed once. Such boundless, uncontrollable vivacity." Bronwen is Megan's attack dog, largely because of these qualities. As an attack dog she is brave but ineffective as she has a kind and generous disposition, character traits uncommon in attack dogs. This is why Megan chose her. Bronwen tumbled in a disorderly fashion through the window onto the floor and sat there panting, her back to the wall, as she got her breath back. She waited patiently as her body mind complex proceeded spontaneously towards thermodynamic equilibrium. She was in quite a state after another near-death experience. One of the members put a bowl of water on the floor next to her and patted her sympathetically on top of the head.

As Megan got to know her future husband in the weeks after they met, she asked him what he had done as a young man. "I loved the course in Aberystwyth but by the end had had enough of reading books. After the last of the final exams, I said that was the last exam I was ever going to sit. I wanted a complete change. One of my friends said he worked in a travelling circus in Sweden every summer and he might be able to get me a job there. A couple of phone calls later it was all arranged and at the end of the week we travelled to Sweden and arrived at the circus as it was about to leave Malmö for Ystad. My job was mucking out the animals, until one day, a couple of weeks after I arrived, the boss came up to me, told me a performer in one of the acts had been injured, and asked if I would take her place. The conversation was in Swedish, which I'd just started learning, so I didn't understand much of it. I said a tentative "Jag. Tack." He pushed a costume into my hands, told me to get changed and go to the entrance of the Big Tent. A few minutes later I was standing there when the clowns came and took me into the main ring where the packed audience applauded. It was then I realised I was going to be the human cannonball and it was too late to change my mind. They put a multicoloured *papier-mâché* crash helmet on my head and told me not to worry.

I climbed up the ladder and slid feet first into the barrel, hands outstretched above me. Then, from outside, I heard a clown's voice.

"Fem! Fyra! Tri! Två! Ett!"

BOOM!

I flew 50 feet through the air before landing safely in the net. I felt exhilarated and my face was a grin from ear to ear. The crowd jumped to their feet shouting and cheering. I stood up to bow but my legs gave way under me and I collapsed back into the net. I was jelly from the waist down. The clowns rescued me and the crowd loved it as they thought it was part of the act. So began my career as a human cannonball which lasted for nearly three years, covering for illness occasionally as the exploding box, until I was sacked."

"Sacked! What happened?"

"The clown responsible for firing the cannon liked a drop of *akvavit* and he often had a drop too much before sending me into space. He said he drank because he was nervous as being a human cannonball was such a dangerous thing to do. One day it was obvious he'd had far too much to drink, but I went ahead and got into the barrel as usual, trusting that everything would be fine. It wasn't.

BOOM!

I flew out of the cannon with great force. I remember everything happening as if in slow motion and my reaching a far higher altitude than usual. Then I noticed I'd flown over the net. "Oh dear!" I thought to myself. I looked ahead and saw the main entrance of the Big Tent with the lions' cage parked just outside and I was heading straight for the vertical iron bars along its side. "This is a strange way to die," I thought. Then an elephant appeared, ambling along between me and the iron bars, and on its back, wearing a new outfit made specially for this, her first solo elephant ride in the main ring, was the owner's fourteen-year-old daughter, with a very proud look on her face. She was about to display her professional skills at controlling an elephant for the first time in front of a live audience."

"I hit the elephant in the soft spot just behind and below its ribs and bounced off unharmed to the floor. The elephant on the other hand was taken completely by surprise and stampeded, as only an elephant can. The owner's daughter clung on for dear life as the elephant charged around the ring a few times before racing out of the Big Tent, jettisoning her as it went. She spun through the air and landed safely on some bales of straw. The audience laughed and laughed thinking this was a comedy act. Her pride shattered she was inconsolable following this embarrassment. Rather than being pleased the human cannonball wasn`t killed in what the papers would have called a tragic accident the circus owner was swayed by his daughter's demands for retribution. He had no choice of course as by this time her mother had arrived on the scene. He looked from his daughter's face filled with tears and revenge to his wife's face filled with crimson and venom, then looked at me. With an apologetic grimace and a resigned shrug of the shoulders he sacked me on the spot. My time as a human cannonball came to an abrupt end. But I still hold the longevity record, to this day no one else has survived as long as a human cannonball. Natural justice cannot withstand the combined force of an aggrieved mother and a wronged teenage daughter."

"What did you do then?"

"I did what any self-respecting human cannonball in my position would do, I hitched to Charleville-Mèziéres and trained to be a *marionnettiste*." She loved the way he said it in French.

Three weeks after the meeting in Tenby the 147th Crymych *Biennale* saw the *crachach* of the international art world descend on Crymych. What a weekend it is with Crymych International Airport hosting the private jets of rich art collectors and corporate sponsors. Large numbers of celebrities, arts lovers and *riff raff* arrive by coach, car, bicycle and on foot, most of them unaware they approach the city along Britain`s first stretch of motorway. The Crymych bypass was built in 1957 and the opening weekend saw the first motorway traffic jam as thousands came to enjoy the delights of motorway driving. The following week it was covered with traffic cones and ten days later it was closed for repairs. The Crymych Hilton[9] is booked ten years in advance, busier even than when the National Eisteddfod[10] comes to town. The contemporary art world`s *crème de la crème* throng the boulevards of the city and the *café* quarter along the Grand Canal forms the perfect backdrop to this artistic explosion, festooned as it is with fairy lights and flowers. Wasn`t it a poet who, after finishing *Le Grand Tour* in Crymych, called it a "*fairy city of the heart.*"[11] The *Biennale* was the brainchild of the founding mothers of the inaugural branch of Machlud y Wawr and has put Crymych at the centre of the world`s cultural map. Crymych is twinned with Venice and Ploveilh.

Art lovers sip their *caffè Americano, espresso Cambriano, caffè crema, Gwilymermo, caffè Zorro,* Anthony Hopkins' favourite,[12] *latte macchiato, caffè Carnabwth,* eggnog latte, Herbrandston *melange* or *espresso* with whipped cream to mention but a few as they admire the beautiful people promenading along the banks of the Grand Canal and the jet set in their private Leargondolas[13] cruising up and down before heading into the placid water of the Crymych Lagoon which they circle once or twice before returning to the Grand Canal. Last year, one of the traditional flat-bottomed Crymych gondolas, the Crymych Belle, was updated for the twenty first century. It is now fitted with two General Electric CM620-8 single-rotor axial-flow turbojet engines pylon-mounted on each side of the aft fuselage.[14] Each engine is rated at 2,975 pounds of thrust at sea level, more than enough to stir a Martini. The landing gear, brake flap and spoiler systems are hydraulically operated, much to the relief of the *gondolier*. Recently, the other gondolas were also overhauled and updated.

The wake following these traditional boats is cause for concern to CADW[15] whose statutory responsibilities include protecting the historic environment and heritage sites of Wales. The Crymych Lagoon forms the largest wetland in the Preseli Basin and was formed about seven and a half thousand years ago when the marine transgression following the Ice Age flooded the area. A colony of over two million freshwater bivalve molluscs live buried in the sediment of the Lagoon. A short time ago a few Zebra mussels from the lakes of southern Russia and the Ukraine were accidentally introduced and are establishing themselves.

One of the attractions of Crymych is that it appears to be floating on the lagoon. However, for centuries the city has been sinking and is living on borrowed time. The biggest threats are the extreme high tides known as *acqua alta* when the water level at high tide is several inches above normal. Water levels following an *acqua alta* can cause flooding of most of the city, including the Basilica San Davide. Rising sea levels caused by global warming are exacerbating matters as flooding events are becoming more frequent. When an *acqua alta* occurs the wake from the Leargondolas increases water damage, both to historic buildings and their foundations and to the clothes of tourists who venture too close to the Grand Canal and get showered by spray.

One controversial plan to solve the city's problem is the MOSE Project[16] (*Modulo Sperimentale Elettromeccanico*). This involved building an adjustable barrier on the river Teifi to the south of Cardigan Castle a few yards upstream from the bridge. The barrier rests on the river floor until an *acqua alta* threatens Crymych at which time it rises automatically to form a dam across the river. Controversial because it is completely useless.

Many visitors to the *Biennale* enjoy one of the architectural guided tours where they can get up close and personal to the city's high culture. The tours provide an opportunity to learn about Demetian, Brythonic, Heroic Age, *Mediaeval*, Georgian, Edwardian, Victorian and *Art Deco* styles and explore a range of buildings from nonconformist chapels, churches, the Cathedral, the Basilica san Davide, the castle, the astrodome, the opera house, the Twm Carnabwth Tower, the Crymych Bowlen and the Crymych Observatory to name but a few. Not to mention many unique shops and the perennially popular *cafés* and *restaurants* such as Das Kapital[17] in the Piazza della Republica, and Chez Carnabwth. The Kentucky Fried Cockles[18] fast food outlet is another must have experience on these tours as are the chariot races at the *Circus Maximus* which are held during the summer holidays. The *Circus Maximus* is one of the city's oldest places of entertainment having been there since Roman times. Much bad feeling erupted recently when the city fathers and mothers, concerned about the rising injury toll amongst charioteers and *Circus Maximus* staff, lowered the speed limit during races. A recent addition to the tour is the floating staircase designed by internationally acclaimed architect Zaha Hadid,[19] a dream like crystal structure fifty feet in the sky above the Piazza del Davide that joins the Cathedral to the Basilica. It goes without saying that the Olympic Stadium is also a must-see attraction. Ever popular are the Roman Baths built around the City's natural warm springs which, along with the name of the Celtic tribe, the *Crymychae*, whose capital it served, gave early Crymych its name *Aquae Crymychium* as recorded in early manuscripts and later in the Ravenna Cosmography. After the visitors left the baths were much frequented by the native *Brittunculi*. The Great Pyramid of Crymych is another popular destination for the cultural tourist. Is it any wonder that Crymych is called the Athens of North Pembrokeshire.[20]

Visitors can take a tour to learn about the city's curious bylaws. For example, it is illegal for a pregnant woman to eat chocolate biscuits on the bus to Cardigan without offering one to the driver; taxi drivers must ask their passengers if they have got smallpox or the plague; it is legal for a man to urinate in public as long as it is on the back wheel of the motor vehicle, either one, with his right hand touching the vehicle. There is no concession for left-handed men, nor for women. It is illegal to hang a duvet out of a window if someone is still under it; unemployed people are to be transported over the border to Ceredigion as the City has a zero-unemployment policy; you cannot shoot the Bishop of Crymych in the Cathedral Close with a bow and arrow on a Sunday between dawn and dusk. The Bishop of St Davids of course is fair game.[21]

Another favourite tour is the one along the Great Wall of Crymych. Over two thousand years of war, revolution and picnics have taken their toll on this famous landmark which, it is said, can be seen from outer space. Standing on the Great Wall of Crymych looking over the landscape towards the east from where invading armies once came it is easy to understand how the structure gave the fledgling city state's inhabitants a sense of security. Its stout ramparts look down over steep mountainsides and hilly terrain, offering the energetic visitor spectacular views.

Yet nothing can prepare you for the grandeur of the city and its environs more than its aqueducts. From the *mediæval* fortifications of 'the Rome of West Wales' as historian Gwyn Alf Williams described it in his seminal 1978 work *When Was Crymych?*[22] they can be seen marching along the horizon for mile after mile. Massive as the aqueducts appear to be they represent just a fraction of the 285-mile water supply network bringing water to the city. The aqueducts run through mountains and over rivers and are so solidly built that it is perhaps the world's only municipal service that is still fully functional after over 1,850 years of use.

Another gift from the Romans gratefully received by the locals, as were the Italian cafes that sprang up between the two world wars with their delicious coffee and ice cream.

Opening next week are the newly refurbished ladies' loos in the Piazza del Davide next to Crymych Yacht Club. Pembrokeshire County Council[23] paid tens of thousands of pounds to fly in Dr Simona Maredi, architect and *Feng Shui* mistress from Italy to advise how best to go about it. Amongst the improvements suggested are candles on the east side of the lounge, glitter lamps, palm trees, crystals hanging in the windows, windchimes and a whirlpool bathtub. She also suggested that the angle of the cubicles be moved a few degrees to improve the flow of energy and that a water feature be added. The sign outside the Ladies and Gents is in Welsh only and reads *Rhocesi* and *Rocynnau* respectively. There are no bilingual street signs in Crymych. There are no street signs at all, in any language. Crymychians live by the principle that if you don`t know where you are, you shouldn`t be there. And neither should you know how to get there.

When *Last Tango yng Nghrymych*[24] premièred on the closing night of the Crymych International Film Festival in the autumn of 1972 it was an immediate *succès de scandale*. The film critic of Clebran[25] hailed it as a landmark. "This must be the most erotic film ever seen on general release in the cinemas of Pembrokeshire, and it might turn out to be the most liberating film ever made." Dwynwen Jones, the film critic for the Western Mail,[26] responded in rhapsodic fashion. Ticket touts did a roaring trade. There might not have been riots, an honourable tradition in this part of the country, but there were walkouts, most notably in the local curry houses. That was only the beginning. What happened after its world-wide release is history. The Magistrates Court in Carmarthen[27] gave the stars, producer and director suspended jail sentences in their absence. "Very rude in any language," commented the Mayor of Haverfordwest,[28] adding, "This is the sort of film made by people who have been educated beyond their IQ levels. No sense. No sense at all." Gwyn Alf Williams commented in his book that, `Haverfordwest has been in a state of emergency since 400AD.`[22]

The following morning, sitting in the middle of the back seat in the Richard Brothers Megacruiser,[6] the luxury double-decker coach of choice for Machlud y Wawr as it meets all their intercontinental travel needs, Megan and the other Members were chatting noisily as they listened to the radio and caught the end of the news. "And now for the latest scandal to erupt in the city. Five members of Machlud y Wawr, Cangen Crymych, have been arrested and are being questioned by officers from Dyfed-Powys Police Rapid-Response Coracle Unit.[29] A yacht registered in the city was boarded and searched just off Dinas Head last night, thousands of pounds worth of Viagra[30] confiscated and the all-woman crew taken into custody. The yacht is suspected of having been on a course for Crymych

Lagoon. The husbands of the suspected drug traffickers are said to be devastated by the news." The coach went silent.

Megan picked up her copy of *Clebran* and turned to the Environment column. "The Crymych climate is warming twice as fast as the rest of the world, a report by the World Nature Organisation warned yesterday. WNO[31] scientists believe that until recently the Preseli Basin acted as a buffer which delayed the arrival of global temperature patterns in North Pembrokeshire. While the rest of the world began to warm around the mid nineteen seventies, Crymych did not start until several years ago and since then the annual temperature rise has been twice as fast as the rest of the world. It is thought that the buffering effect of the Preseli Basin and, in particular, the Crymych Lagoon, has diminished significantly thus allowing this unprecedented temperature rise. Scientists do not know what is causing it although local environmental activists blame the MOSE Project and the barrier near Cardigan bridge."

She turned the page and read the Law and Order column. "A Glandwr resident was given a parking ticket in Narberth last week. Constable Brunnström[32] told the court that he was obliged to give the driver a ticket because the car, parked in the main street, was too far from the kerb and was causing an obstruction to other vehicles. The driver claimed in her defence that she had taken this course of action because she did not want to park on the double-yellow lines." Megan`s eyes caught the next headline. "*Graffiti* outbreak. Police were called to the main street in Crymych early on Sunday morning when a passing motorist noticed a fresh outbreak of *graffiti*. The words **Vive le Crymych libre!** were painted with green paint on the sides of a bus that had been parked overnight outside the Crymych Arms on the square. A clandestine group, *The Democratic People`s Front of Crymych*, have claimed responsibility. Our brave correspondent Gareth Jones[33] talked to DPFC representatives at a secret meeting in Caffi Carnabwth on the square yesterday to find out what their demands are. Gareth was contacted by text to arrange the interview, but police have been unable to trace the call as a burner phone was used. Following the coded instructions he was given he entered the *caffi*, walked cautiously to the counter and ordered a banana milkshake with vanilla ice cream, as stipulated in the text, whereupon our courageous correspondent was approached by a member of the organisation, blindfolded and led to a corner table by the window, the one with the nice view. Two other members were already seated there and were tucking into their milkshakes. When they were all sitting down the blindfold was removed so he could enjoy the milkshake, which the waitress brought a few minutes later. His request to have a coffee instead was denied. During the discussion the DPFC leader stated that the movement had only one objective, to see Crymych become an independent state, rather like the Vatican City, but without any particular religion. Having set out their aims the three shadowy characters finished their milkshakes, put

Gareth's blindfold back on and warned him of dire consequences should he remove it before ten minutes had passed, or longer if the bus to Narberth was late. They slipped out through the back door of the *caffi* and walked round the front to the bus stop. The police have no idea who they are, as, when questioned by our correspondent, they would only reveal their bardic names and since none of them has won a chair at a local eisteddfod their anonymity is secure."

"Nearly two centuries after their debut the celebrated Baedeker-Parry-Williams guidebooks[34] are making a comeback in Europe. They were the ultimate guidebook for the Victorian tourist and appear in works by E.M. Forster, Agatha Christie, T.S. Eliot and Daniel Owen.[35] They ceased to be published several years ago but now ten titles including Andalucia, Venice, New York, Paris and Crymych have reappeared, in full colour. Digital versions of the books are also available."

"We regret to announce the death of Mati Tegryn Davies who passed away peacefully at her home in Cardiff surrounded by her family. Originally from Pembrokeshire her talent took her all over the world. Although she only clogged at Covent Garden for four seasons during the 1950s, she made a deep and lasting impression on those who saw her, particularly as Strauss`s *Salome* and as Marie in the first performance there of Berg`s *Wozzeck*. These were two of her finest roles, which included Strauss`s *Elektra*. Despite a predilection for German clogs, Mati, with a repertory of well over a hundred dances, clogged many nineteenth century Italian parts including *Abigaille* in Verde`s *Nabucco*, *Amelia* in *Un Ballo in Maschera*, and *Aida*. Her range extended to three octaves, allowing her to clog both *soprano* and *mezzo* roles."

Megan put the paper down and listened to the radio. "And now news from the world of archaeology. Has the original labyrinth been found? Archaeologists from the University of the Four Trinity Davids in Carmarthen[36] have shed new light on the inspiration for the Greek myth. A mountain riddled with what appear to be human made tunnels and caverns just outside the village of Trecwn might be the original site of the ancient labyrinth, the mythical maze where the half-bull, half-man minotaur of Greek legend lived. Scholars who recently undertook an expedition there believe the site has as much claim to be the labyrinth as the Minoan palace at Knossos, hundreds of miles away, which has been associated with the myth since its excavation between 1900 and 1935."[37]

Megan does not speak much. She subscribes to the `the more words, the less they mean` school of talking. "If you want to give someone your opinion about an important matter," she says to the younger Members, "let it be. It doesn't matter what you think. If you want peace, stop having opinions."

At midday Bronwen opened a tin of instant soup and to her disappointment discovered it wasn`t instant. She had to heat it. Cockles and laverbread are her meal of choice and some time ago she considered constructing a grand theory to unify the two. Then she thought again. Life is too short, and no one would agree with her. She would find a medium-sized project to keep her mind off the day-to-day stuff. At least then she would be operating mental machinery for which she had a license. But that was then and now is not then, it`s now. And by now the Machlud y Wawr General Committee had revoked her license. The machinery is too dangerous they decided.

"And now the weather. Derec, what`s happening out there?"[38]

"Shw` mae? Rain everywhere."

Amongst the flora on the rocky wild ground that falls away in front of the bay window of the crypt grow field scabious with lilac blooms atop long hairy stalks, sweetly scented red, pink and white valerian reach a height of 5 feet, field poppies with stems holding single red flowers up to 4 inches across with a black spot at their centre, Common bird's-foot trefoil with small clusters of yellow flowers and downy leaves and meadow cranesbill, some over 3 feet tall with 5-petalled blue and violet saucer-shaped flowers up to 1.5 inches across. The pink-purple flowers of vetches dance in the breeze as the clever little plants make their own nitrates and fertilise the soil. Clumps of tall, upright, branching brook thistles up to 4 feet in height with pincushion-like, deep crimson flowers set above a rosette of green leaves stand above semi-parasitic crested cow-wheat with densely packed deep rose-purple flowers. Sweet-smelling meadowsweet, called the Queene of the medowes, or, in Gaelic Scotland, *crios Chù-Chulainn*, with their densely clustered cream flowers and long-stalked pinnate leaves resembling feathers are plentiful, as are musk mallows reaching to over 3 feet with pale-pink, saucer-like flowers up to 2.5 inches across. Compact clumps of fairy thimbles with wiry stems carrying clusters of dangling, bell-shaped, lavender-blue flowers half an inch in length are seen amongst the rocks.

Oregano, 'brightness of the mountain', with olive-green, spade-shaped opposite leaves, basil, with scented, richly green ovate leaves and subtle *anise* flavour, bright green aromatic parsley, sage, growing to a height of 2.5 feet with oval, variegated leaves and used since ancient times for increasing women's fertility, clumps of quick-growing chives up to 20 inches tall with hollow tubular stems and grass-like leaves, and borage, with hairy stems and leaves are some of the herbs growing amongst the other plants.

In the marshy ground on the eastern edge of this wildness grow water avens with multi-coloured bell-shaped flowers with orangey-pink petals and yellow stamens surrounded by dark red sepals. Growing up to 28 inches high on tall stems above dark green lance-shaped leaves the delicate pink star-shaped flowers of ragged robin can be seen, each petal divided into four lobes creating the raggedy look. The golden, goblet shaped flowers of marsh marigolds, some growing up to 20 inches above the ground, shine in the sunlight.

An enormous flutter of butterflies, the movement of their wings mimicking the sound of a distant waterfall, dance here and there.[39] Moths abound.

The area hums and buzzes and drones with bees and wasps. The bees sleep for five to eight hours a day, sometimes in flowers with other bees where they like to cwtsh up and hold each other's feet.

A loveliness of ladybirds covers a tree stump that stands in the sunlight and beetles search for food as the Earth reflects light onto the moon.

18

That makes no sense and so do I.

Daffy Duck[1]

"How much of my life are the chocolate biscuits I have?" wondered the Sergeant lying in the hammock sipping tea as the coracle spun lethargically at its mooring in Fishguard Harbour. He had no answer to this. "Whoooh! This tea has got legs. It's got thighs too," he thought to himself. His mind speculated about the bead curtain hanging in the doorway leading from the galley into the walk-in storage area. "In French films that would lead to the back room, where ...," he paused and held the dream, "... if you`re lucky, you`re told to sit on the naughty chair." His mind explored that unaccustomed image. He blushed happily. "Ah yes," he reflected, "the definition of happiness is being a multimillionaire. The Buddha must have known about this, although he didn`t mention it in his teachings." He thought about the thousands he has stashed away in an offshore account on Barry Island.

He looked attentively, searchingly, deeply across the willow grove, over the circle of stones, past the flock of larks tumbling and weaving through the morning sky, towards Fishguard, and saw nothing at all. This is his gift, to see nothing at all when everything is there, plain to see. A power passed down from his mother and his mother`s mother and her mother`s mother going back seven generations. Nothing at all, and in nothing, everything. Pleased by this experience he decided to linger a little while longer in the hammock. If he left it, inspiration might leave him.

It was 8.45a.m. and a convoy of wage slaves drove bumper to bumper across the Parrog towards Fishguard. Watching them, he mused once again upon the meaning of happiness. "Oh! to be at the smallholding," he dreamed in romantic mood. The film The Towering Inferno[2] made a big impression on him which is why he built the greenhouse under the water tower. Explaining his reasoning to The Parrot he said, "Tomato plants are not things, they are only tendencies."[3] This annoyed his wife whose job it is to do the watering.

He put together his family tree when still at school. It goes like this, the Horrendous Space Kablooie,[4] the first self-replicating molecules, the first cells, the first multicellular life in the oceans, the first thought, the first life on land, the first language, the first use of fire, the first domesticated plants and animals, the Sergeant. "What a story," he mused. The stuff of Hollywood films."

"There`s little wind and no current," he contributed languorously to the internal conversation he was having with himself. "What`s happening? Nothing`s happening, and everything`s happening." He remained calm. Lying in the hammock with his eyes closed he cannot see the wavelets as they pass beneath the coracle, lifting and dropping it gently. But they are in his blood, in his subconscious. "Superficially," he thought, "there are many waves. Yet, ultimately, there is only one, the universal wave." He was at peace with himself. He was one with the hammock. The Parrot looked down upon him from his perch on the willow branch near the stone circle and smiled.

The Sergeant opened his eyes and eased himself off the hammock intending to stretch his legs. He walked to the vessel`s edge where he spotted a spider`s web that had appeared overnight, spanning the gap between the coracle and the harbour wall. He leant over to have a closer look. "Hmmm. An old spider," he thought, noticing the irregular patterning and lack of parallel strands. "Yes, a doddery one by the look of it. Or an ageing hippy that smoked too much grass in its youth."

The previous evening he arrived in the harbour an hour and a half later than his wife suggested he arrive. Never a wise thing to do. "Sorry dear," he said, attempting a smile. "There was a hurricane, a force twelve ...." he began. His wife stared at him menacingly. "... it came at us from all sides at once." She gave him a look that would freeze **Sgwd yr Eira**. "Sort of tangential, you see." She tapped her foot. The quay shook. Dogs whimpered in Harbour Village. Horses as far away as St Nicholas bolted and made for their stables, pulling the doors shut behind them. "It caused the coracle to spin wildly out of control." His explanations did little to defuse the tension. They heightened it. Her face ratcheted up the menace. "Another night on the coracle," he thought as she turned on her heel and walked off along the quay.

The previous day had not been a good one. On his way to Swansea on official business the vessel was approaching Worm`s Head at the end of the Gower when a hurricane appeared from nowhere causing the vessel to experience difficulties which the official enquiry later discovered were caused by the Sergeant, not the tropical cyclone with winds of up to 87 miles per hour, the accompanying rain that battered the coracle and the thunder and lightning. On top of that, as they rounded the Worm the coracle fell foul of strong currents to port, one would have been enough, which caused the coracle to move in a south easterly direction at approximately thirty-three knots whilst spinning furiously at the same time and taking on water. Fortunately, the currents were headed out to sea, so they were not driven onto the cliffs along the south coast of the peninsular. The Sergeant became confused, although the word `became` might be misleading here as it suggests he was not in that state before the incident. After enjoying the white-water ride for a while The Parrot took emergency action and switched the coracle to automatic pilot, following which the vessel stopped spinning, reduced speed to a comfortable fifteen knots and set itself a course for Swansea Harbour whereupon the Sergeant went below, rather hastily The Parrot thought, entered the engine room and turned the bilge pumps to MAX. Or so he thought. In his confusion he entered the escape pod and pulled the emergency release lever which ejected the pod safely from the mother ship. The pod set a course at maximum speed and he arrived in the harbour some time before The Parrot.

Having unintentionally facilitated his own escape he sat on one of the comfy chairs provided, put on the safety belt and reached across to the tea dispenser. "Time for a cuppa," he decided. To attract the attention of passing shipping the pod sent up three distress flares, a red beacon attached to its upper surface flashed and a distress signal was sent via ship-to-shore radio to both the Tenby and Mumbles lifeboats. The Mumbles lifeboat launched immediately and headed for the pod. The departure of the Tenby lifeboat was delayed because a walrus holidaying from Greenland was fast asleep at the bottom of the slipway where it enjoyed dozing in the sun. Oblivious to all this activity he sat in the quiet atmosphere sipping tea. As he munched a chocolate biscuit a calm descended upon him, and he entered a meditative state of no thought. A state that ended abruptly at the quayside in Swansea Harbour when the crews of the lifeboats freed him from the pod before replacing it on the coracle. All this delayed the mission and caused him to be late returning to Fishguard. The Sergeant would be surprised to learn that chocolate biscuits are made up of 21% dark matter.

The incident prompted Dyfed-Powys Police Rapid-Response Coracle Unit[5] high command to introduce techniques of `high reliability organisations` such as are used with air traffic control and electricity power grids, systems that cannot be allowed to fail. This proved straightforward as it was only the Sergeant and The Parrot onboard, and the latter was already a high reliability micro-organisation. Following the integration of `high reliability organisations` into day-to-day coracling life the on-board computer's surveillance capability was improved as the Admiral is concerned about the vulnerability of the vessels of the fleet, in particular their susceptibility to a cyber strike that could disable their power systems for vital minutes. Added to this is the worry that anti-ship missiles such as the Chinese DF-21D could swamp the coracles' defences. The new technology increases the capability of the on-board computer to track and monitor the Sergeant as he wanders aimlessly around the coracle, and in the galley, for example, as he bumps into utensils rather than using them. Senior management ensures that sound support and backup systems are in place, both academic and pastoral, they hope will result in high, even exceptional outcomes at all key stages of the Sergeants long-term, in-service, nautical training. The thinking behind this is that on long sea voyages a well-trained Sergeant is a happy Sergeant.

A kitchen ashore is quite a different beast to a galley which sometimes bounces violently up and down and spins riotously whilst travelling in all sorts of strange directions at varying speeds as you cook. Adapting to this requires three semesters studying Harvard University`s online *Marine Cuisine 101*[6] which entails course work, one day a week at Pembrokeshire College,[7] writing essays, non-slip galley shoes and good balance. The *cordon bleu* of nautical cuisine, as is the fashion nowadays, requires a master's degree.

Panicking during one particularly stressful part of the course, the pudding session in the kitchen in Pembrokeshire College, he broke down after the third attempt.

"If you don`t learn how to make custard without lumps, you`ll regret it," Rick, the student next to him, advised. "Maybe not today. Maybe not tomorrow, but soon, and for the rest of your life."[8]

Listening to these words of support he perked up. "Here`s cooking with you kid," he replied, and prepared to have another go. "Louie," he said to the lecturer, "I think this is the beginning of a beautiful custard."

Standing next to the classic, deluxe, induction-range cooker by the window, Ilsa smiled. She knew deep down that this time it would work. "Whisk. Whisk as if it were the last time," she cried excitedly.

The Sergeant looked across at her. "But I've got a job to do. Where I'm going, you can't follow. What I've got to do, you can't be any part of, Ilsa. I'm no good at being noble, but it doesn't take much to see that the problems of lumpy custard don't amount to a hill of beans in this crazy world. Someday you'll understand that."

Ilsa began to cry.

"We'll always have Tenby," he added, by way of encouragement.

Months after finishing his 'masters' the Sergeant wrote a revealing comment in the log. "It seems incredible that despite the galley being one of the most visited spaces on the coracle, so much of what happens in it remains an unknown. It retains a calm and is one of the few places on board that could be described as unspoilt. The view through either porthole, depending upon which way the coracle is facing, is to a wild, uninhabited countryside, a spectacularly indented coastline and the ever-present snow-capped Mount Etna providing a magnificent backdrop to food preparation." He had been on the Cherry Brandy again. As a local man,[9] in a letter to the Western Telegraph[10] observed about the Sergeant`s *soufflés*, "The best lack all conviction, while the worst are full of passionate intensity." Deep down in the Sergeant's mind lurks the belief that the cooking equipment was constructed for magical purposes.

On his voyages the Sergeant buys recipe books when in port and has all the popular ones as well as first editions of rare works such as *Galley Cooking for One* and *Coracling Snacks*. Thinking himself to be of a scientific bent he finds measuring ingredients an absorbing pastime. After all, this might be the key to smooth custard. On routine patrol in Cardigan Bay several months after finishing the course he stumbled across the galley, well concealed as it is behind the large brightly painted double doors at the for`ard end of the main bow to stern thoroughfare with a garish neon sign above the doors flashing incessantly 24 hours a day which reads, **GALLEY**. Unfortunately, he forgot to record the location and was unable to find it again. Until that is the `high reliability organisations` kicked in and the computer caused the sign to emit a weird 'come hither' wailing sound intended to mimic the screams of a three-month old child in distress which continued until, after following the sound, he stumbled upon it for the second time, opened the doors and sauntered cautiously in.

His interest in the science of food, particularly that of food measurement, began whilst doing the Harvard course, after which he devised an accurate measuring system and designed and constructed the device required to put it into practical use. All this with the help of the latest super-fast quantum computer recently installed on board along with a 4D printer, thus making good use of length, height, depth and time. He developed methods to measure individual quantum particles of food. As The Parrot was only too aware, in the quantum world the act of measuring a particle removes its quantum characteristics, a fact it did not bring to the Sergeant`s attention thinking he would become distraught and lose interest in food and the measuring of food and perhaps even in the eating of food.

The Sergeant knew this however as it had been covered during the first semester in a ten-week course entitled *Heisenberg in the Galley*.[11] He approached the problem by trapping ions between layers of *soufflé* and then measuring them using light. In a follow up experiment, he trapped photons between two highly polished adjustable 180 degrees angle bathroom mirrors and measured their behaviour using atoms of *soufflé au fromage*. So shiny are the mirrors that a particle of light is able to bounce between them for a tenth of a second, travelling the equivalent of the circumference of the Earth before escaping. The only flaw he encountered with the measuring system, which seemed to disproportionately affect puddings, was `entanglement`, whereby two particles separated at a distance appear to interact with each other. `Entanglement`, he discovered to his dismay, is the primary cause of lumps in custard. The problem was solved by using a 5D printer to bring into service possible worlds which, whilst being abstractions, are legitimate constructs occurring frequently in the mathematics of custard preparation.

When queues form in the galley at mealtimes the Sergeant follows the maxim, "From each according to his abilities, to each according to his needs."[12] He invariably gets a bigger portion than The Parrot, who is not a Marxist.

Leaving the spider swaying dozily in its web he returned to the galley and made himself a mug of Kenya Kosabei tea before sitting in the rocking chair in the corner which rocked backwards and forwards until gradually settling at the point of equilibrium of the Sergeant`s centre of gravity, thus satisfying all his ergonomic needs. The motion as the chair rocked gently to the coracle's movement in the water soothed his brain and took him back to earlier experiences in his mother's womb. Once or twice, he went further back and experienced past lives. Unless he had been dreaming. He put the mug on the small table by the side of the chair and picked up a tissue to dry his shirt after spilling tea all over it. He deposited the tissue in the paper bin, which was within easy throwing distance, picked up the dooby doo and turned the radio on before replacing the dooby doo and picking up the mug, being careful not to rock.

"At a meeting of the Cabinet of Pembrokeshire County Council[13] in County Hall last night it was decided to withdraw the ferry service between Fishguard and Goodwick," said the announcer. "A Council spokesperson told Radio Free Pembrokeshire[14] that declining numbers of passengers mean it is no longer financially viable. Asked why fewer people are using the service the spokesperson blamed the growing popularity of automobiles, the half hourly bus service and the fact that it is quicker to walk. Photographs of several Town Councillors[15] appear in this week's County Echo[16] along with an article in which they give everyone their opinions, whether everyone wants them or not. A meeting has been arranged in Fishguard Town Hall this Friday evening at seven o'clock when it is hoped a protest group will be formed and the Town Councillors can have their photographs taken again. 'We will fight this all the way,' one of them told us, several times. The latest edition of *Lonely Planet*[17] describes this particular journey across the blue azure waters of Fishguard Harbour as one of the top ten sea voyages on the planet, dubbing it, 'Not so much a voyage as a sea-bridge'."

The announcer drew breath, then continued. "Google's Street View[18] cameras have taken users along narrow, cobblestone alleys using a tricycle and cameras have been mounted on a backpack to take us along walking trails such as the Grand Canyon, Offa's Dyke, the 8,700-mile-long Wales Coast Path, and many others. Next, the internet giant is planning to mount cameras on the for'ard masts of Dyfed-Powys Police Rapid-Response Coracle Unit vessels to take us into all those small caves, caverns and coves that perforate the cliffs along the county's coastline. The cameras will also chart the ocean surface. An innovative feature of this project will be the use of sonar to map the ocean floor. If successful, this triple function technology will be extended to all the world's oceans."

"On a related note, the new version of the iPaddle app,[19] indispensable for this year's iCoracle,[19] was launched at the Norwegian Church Arts Centre in Cardiff Bay at midnight last night. Enthusiasts camped by the entrance, some for nearly a week, to be the first to get their devices. The way millions of people use coracles is about to change after the launch of the new software. This is a major update to the system that runs most of the world's paddles. The blurb describing it says, "Seeing, touching and paddling really is believing."[19] As the clock struck midnight in Cardiff Bay the app went on sale in Japan."

The Sergeant drained the mug, put it on the table, picked up the dooby doo and turned the radio off. He sighed. It was time for the monthly general meeting of all crew. Replacing the dooby doo he got up and walked out of the galley through the door. Turning left he proceeded along the corridor then down the stairs until he reached the conference room situated below decks. Pushing the door open he saw that The Parrot was already there, standing on its perch, waiting. The Sergeant was to chair the meeting and took his seat in the comfy, high-back Georgian leather wing chair with claw and ball legs at the end of the long, yet quite short, oak table. The Parrot, in its capacity as Secretary, had placed a copy of the agenda plus the minutes of the previous meeting on the table for him, keeping copies for itself. He sighed again. "Meetings! The world is full of meetings." He glanced at the agenda. "Only three items. Thank goodness for that! This should be over quickly," he muttered to himself. "As Chair I declare the meeting open." He paused, then added, "Any objections?" The remainder of the crew remained silent. "Minutes of previous meeting."

The crew perused the document.

"Correct."

"Correct."

The Sergeant called the meeting to order. "The first item on the agenda. Ready, steady, go." And so, it began. The Secretary read the first item on the agenda out loud to the rest of the crew.

1/   The universe is headed for a Big Freeze, a Big Dip, a Big Crunch or a Big Bounce.
      Proposer: The Sergeant.

This was an emotional issue. Tempers would flare. The conference room on 3 Deck amidships was packed. All members of the crew were present. For lower ranks it was standing room only. The Chair and the crew looked at each other, a fine example of the lesser-known marine Mexican stand-off. An invisible signal passed from perch to comfy chair and back again. Neither of them blinked. The pace was hurried, but not rushed as the Sergeant outlined his ideas. Several hours of discussion with no break for tea and biscuits later the voice of the Chair rattled around the room. "Tea! Biscuits! We must have tea and biscuits!" No conclusion had been reached and it was decided to put the matter on the following month`s agenda. An adjournment was agreed for twenty minutes. "After the break, item two," exclaimed the Chair in peremptory fashion such as to allow no challenge.

Twenty minutes later the meeting restarted. The Secretary read the second item on the agenda to the crew.

2/   Should the willow grove on the stern be given legal personhood?
      Proposer: The Parrot.

"*Señor Presidente*, I propose we vote immediately," pronounced The Parrot. "Those in favour of the motion." A hand and a wing were raised.
      "Against."
      "Motion carried," declared the Secretary with a smile.

The Secretary read the third item on the agenda to the crew.

3/   The governance of the coracle.
      Proposer: The Parrot.

The Parrot coughed. "Governance," it said, using its formal squawk. The Sergeant looked up and adjusted his reading glasses. Not to be outdone, The Parrot did the same. The room fell quiet. It is more of a cupboard really, with just enough room for the crew on its perch, the long yet quite short oak table, the Chair and his comfy leather chair and a fan mounted on the wall for when it gets stuffy. They can also open the porthole to improve ventilation.

"Background," squawked The Parrot gravely, adjusting its reading glasses again. "In 2007 a decision was made to replace the Governors with a Trust which was to be separate from the Executive. A disaster waiting to happen, in my opinion," it concluded. "This decision must be reversed."

The Sergeant was pleased the motion was presented so well. And succinctly. "I agree," he said. He had not been listening and wanted to be on the hammock enjoying a mug of tea and some chocolate biscuits in the late evening sun. He removed his reading glasses with a flourish and gave the crew a stern look. Satisfied, he replaced his glasses and continued. "What I have learnt in over thirty-five years of senior management is that a complex hierarchy such as the one aboard this vessel can only work effectively by keeping authority and responsibility close, rather than keeping them separate."

The Parrot dipped its head slightly and looked out over its reading glasses through the porthole, dreaming of Jamaican skies, walked along the perch a little bit and ruffled its feathers. The Sergeant waited patiently as he watched what seemed to him to be a display of histrionics play itself out. But this was unfair as histrionics describes emotional and energetic behaviour that is not sincere and has no real meaning. The Parrot was simply moving a little as it had developed cramp in its left leg. Remaining standing in one position for long periods during meetings is something parrots do not like doing.

"I move," said the Sergeant to the assembled crew, with all the authority of the Chair, "that the Trust, that is yourself, be dissolved forthwith."

The Parrot squawked loudly as a muscle in its thigh went into spasm. It did not want to be dissolved.

"Not actually dissolved, silly bird."

The Parrot looked offended.

"And all powers previously owned by the Trust, in other words, the general crew, be returned to the Executive, that`s me. Similarly, the Executive, me again, be dissolved and the Executive powers be returned to the Governors. Also, me." A pause followed this bold move.

The Parrot said nothing. It knew only too well that rearranging the deckchairs on the Titanic changed nothing.

"And now the vote," declared the Sergeant, raising his hand. The Parrot considered awhile, and after considering, rearranged its breast feathers with its beak. It abstained. "I declare the motion passed," pronounced the Sergeant with obvious relief. He wondered why his commandeering of the motion had not produced stiff opposition from the remainder of the crew and he was disconcerted to see a smile on The Parrot`s face. Reflecting upon the need for greater diversity in leadership in the already neuro-diverse community on board it concluded that silence was its friend. It was playing the long game. One advantage DPPRRCU has over pirates and smugglers is the cognitive diversity of its crews.

"Any other business," asked the Chair. The Parrot ignored him, gazed out through the porthole and dreamt again of those Jamaican skies.

"As Chair, I think it essential that a member of the crew comment before I bring the meeting to a close," said the Sergeant. He looked sternly and authoritatively, indeed menacingly, in the direction of The Parrot.

The Parrot turned its head to look at the Chair, thought for a moment, removed its reading glasses, then spoke with a firm squawk. "In a time of crisis, radical change requires scrambled restructuring aimed at determining strategic goals for future growth. This will bring with it short-term cuts whilst retaining stakeholder confidence, challenging key assumptions, evolving new ways to thrive, navigating consolidation opportunities and initiating reskilling in order to impact positive upgrouping spikes. The crew's guiding principle seeks to offset the rule of unintended consequences by which individual targets, as defined by an external team of leading-edge senior technical specialists, confront ever improving real-world data. Said crew, one of whom is a versatile high-performer routinely defying convention to induce chased input and achieve stasis of vertical consistency grouping whilst offsetting corrosive disorganising effects, is of the opinion that this is a journey worth making," it said.

The Sergeant remained calm. "This will soon be over," a voice from somewhere inside his head reassured him. "Hold firm!" it whispered encouragingly.

The Parrot continued. "We face unprecedented challenges in this period of turbulent times and tumultuous circumstances. Setting strategic goals across geographies in a worsening macro environment requires long-term stakeholder support to avoid a black-swan event. Revisiting evidence-based collaboration tools could provide the capabilities to create enough runway for the C-suite team to grapple with opportunities in the new normal. Corporate leverage gains the momentum to react quickly against existential threats of unforeseen volatility, brings a significant sense of urgency and can mobilise operationally whilst avoiding change fatigue. The dramatic acceleration of a five-year strategy can redefine the structuring of irrational strategic analyses whilst consolidating operational locations. Boosting short-term synergies has a powerful galvanising effect providing a plethora of benefit opportunities, although the complexity of these processes makes it difficult to predict if drivers of positive tandem pressures will remain resilient."

The Sergeant gupled. A result no doubt of the panic and confusion overwhelming his interior world. Ordinarily, he would have gulped. But those were no ordinary times.

"The challenges inherent in running grand-scale public sector projects with poor efficacy and sluggish responses remain some of the pitfalls. Reimagining contemporary lessons to unlock human and avian potential leads to significant progress with minimal disruptive implications. A deep and contextual look at trialled and implemented supranational exemplars of forecast demand aimed at "keeping the lights on" results in reality-adjacent domain-based message authentication. Layers of bureaucracy pump the brakes on self-optimisation of legacy technologies in the risk averse workspace experience. Even so, improved transparency is not without risks. Critically applied anonymised plug-in integrations going full tombola are proven robust and reliable when regaining trust for continued investment to deploy new firewall solutions of scale and complexity. Interrupted equilibrium is robust when flexible work options and the ability to scale are in the driving seat."

Neither crew member asked nor expected quarter.

"The demographic status of crew members means that all the ingredients needed to exacerbate existing inequalities and highly functional channel disruptive events presents huge legacy challenges threatening equality in systems. The life cycle of political necessity is an added accelerant which will speed up the deployment of constantly innovating and evolving maximum-viable products and rapidly deploy solutions aimed at a vendor lock-in internally owned road map. A fragmented and opaque reactive posture improves insight garnering capabilities in the complex landscape of wrap-around solutions and agile methodologies to breed complexity. Procurement dynamism leads to an overhaul of the next step-change upheaval as the roll out accelerates thus rewriting the rules of siloed operations in order to overcome administrative hurdles. This is governance in advance. Applicant portal due-diligence tools are technology enablers on the cusp of risk mitigation controlling supply chain interoperating teams. We are on a good trajectory and the art of the possible places us entering the endgame. It is time for *realpolitik* to triumph over ideology," concluded The Parrot with a flourish.[20]

An observer would not have noticed a change in the Chair's external appearance. However, the bobble hat monitoring his vital signs reported they had become erratic. His bemused look, whose facial features betrayed an all-consuming lack of comprehension of current events and an inability to grasp the mundane, appeared normal. But what lay behind the facade? At first, he experienced a tingling in his brain, a creeping sensation that spread outwards from deep within the interior. Goosebumps appeared on the surface of his cerebral cortex. Slowly, a torrent of trembling flooded the brain stem. Overflowing, it surged down the spinal cord, spreading to arms and legs as it went until stopped in its tracks by the *cul de sac* known in medical circles as the *coccyx*. At the other end, the bemused look held firm, secure in its belief that it could ride the storm. "I'm quite an optimistic person. When I'm not catastrophising that is," thought the brain. The rudimentary Sergeant's brain appeared over 400 million years ago, many of its structures being present before that in fish, a fact leading many to conclude that this explains his choice of a nautical career.

"I declare the meeting closed," said a despairing Chair.

The Parrot, as Secretary, made an announcement. "Tea and biscuits are available in the galley." Then it flew out through the porthole, turning vertically upwards as it increased its speed, heading for the pure air at 20,000 feet.

The Sergeants rise to power manifested the psychological state Freud[21] called `the negative hallucination` in which you hallucinate that you can`t see things that are plainly there. This caused some disruption to the routine of daily life on board and rose to danger levels when he was left to his own devices and tried to do anything other than lying in the hammock sipping tea and munching chocolate biscuits. Paddling, for instance. Another hiccup in the smooth running of things is that on hot days, for all intents and purposes, his brain only functions in energy saver mode, and minimally at that, when in the sun. Hence the pink *marquee* erected during the summer months on the lawn for`ard of the stone circle on the stern to provide shade.

The Sergeant was quick in the galley, a well-rehearsed tea and chocolate biscuits routine paying dividends and in no time at all he was lying in the hammock on the stern sipping and munching and planning the rest of the day. It was a hot summer`s day, however. Thoughts of overheating came to him. He tried to work out where the *marquee* should be for maximum cooling effect. He remembered it was situated on the lawn. "Which needs cutting," he remembered. By now there was a stiff breeze coming from the north and a strong swell from the south. "Unusual," he thought. The coracle was moored where the breeze and the swell met and the resultant moderate to severe rocking of the coracle convinced him that it was too dangerous for lawn mowing, a hazardous enough endeavour when weather conditions were perfect, which was not very often. More than one lawn mower had been lost overboard in the past whilst attempting this difficult procedure. He contented himself by lying in the hammock worrying about it. Until he remembered the mug of tea and the chocolate biscuits, at which point lawn mowing thoughts exited his mind and disappeared out to sea. "*Bon voyage!*" he muttered, watching them go as they battled against the wind.

He glanced up at the sky, a fairly easy manoeuvre when lying on your back in a hammock. "A distinct lack of isobars," he commented to The Parrot who had returned to rest nearby on a willow branch. "It`s going to be a lovely day." The Parrot nodded its head in agreement. The Sergeant felt a great peace wash over him and got in touch with his inner chocolate biscuit, as testified by the serenity of his features. The Sergeant was being the Sergeant, which for him is a full-time job. "Did you know," he asked, "that coraclers on the Zambesi do not navigate on the left or the right, they travel in the shade." The Parrot let it go. The lack of conversation irritated the Sergeant. "Grrr!" he said, remembering Dennis the Menace[22] saying this quite often and to great effect in the comics he read as a child. At the time he thought it to be very effective. But that was then, and this is now. The Parrot was unmoved. As was the Sergeant as he had not yet finished his tea and biscuits. "Compared to him," he thought, glancing across at The Parrot, "mushrooms are a talkative species."

They looked at each other. Time went by. The Sergeant blinked. "It`s going to be a long day," he thought to himself. The Parrot agreed.

As the breeze dropped in intensity the swell decreased in magnitude. Becalmed, the coracle and her crew were at rest in Fishguard Harbour. The quay near the mooring was thronged with tourists. A playful gleam appeared in the Sergeant`s eyes and popping the last of the chocolate biscuits securely into his mouth he put the mug down and eased himself out of the hammock. The Parrot knew what was going through the Sergeant`s mind and grinned, moving its weight onto its left foot, then onto its right foot, then back again, before balancing evenly on both and ruffling its feathers. It braced for action and looked at the Sergeant expectantly. The Sergeant, munching, looked back. A mischievous look appeared on the Sergeant`s face all around his nose, which remained calm. "Got to time this just right," he thought.

Some of the tourists gazing at the Dyfed-Powys Police Rapid-Response Coracle Unit vessel noticed a blur where the Sergeant had been. "Is that a tear in the space time continuum?" a child asked. In the bow a paddle rose unaided into the air and stood suspended in the breeze. But it was a hot, barmy evening, the air shimmered in the heat above the water's surface. A mirage perhaps, a delusion, a loss of faith. Next, they noticed the space where The Parrot had been a moment before was also a blur. The anchor chain vibrated. The Sergeant swallowed.

In the blur that was the Sergeant he moistened the forefinger of his left hand with his tongue and raised it into the air to judge wind speed. He held it there. "Wait," he whispered.

"Wait!"

"Wait!"

"Wait!"

"Now!"

The paddle rotated furiously under his expert control. The Parrot raised the anchor with its beak in one quick, deft movement. The coracle rotated clockwise then anticlockwise, executing the perfect figure of eight as it did so, repeated once, then the same action anticlockwise then clockwise. The tourists looked on with astonishment at this display of advanced seamanship on what appeared to be an unmanned vessel. The crew were invisible to the onlookers, moving as they were at near warp speed. As astonishment gripped the minds of the spectators the coracle returned to its mooring position, the paddle fell to the deck, the anchor fell back into the water, and the crew reappeared in their respective positions on the hammock and the willow branch. It all took just a few short zeptoseconds.[23] Some of the bystanders missed it. Some saw it but were not sure what they had seen. A spontaneous round of applause erupted all over the quay and in the *café* on the beach, appreciation for having been privileged to witness one of the great coracling manoeuvres, the Double Round the Clock Figure of Eight with Reverse, made famous at the last Olympic Games[24] by Gareth Kasparov[25] the great Russian coracler.

The crew rested contentedly after their exertions. "Time for tea," one of them thought. The other became nothing, and becoming nothing, became everything.

Unnoticed, a large holding tank containing several deadly eleven-foot-long carnivorous Conga eels with characteristic smooth, greyish-blackish scale-less bodies roughly the width of an adult human thigh, extended black-edged dorsal fins, large gill slits and wide mouths, unbalanced during the manoeuvre, slid off the upper deck into the welcoming waters of the harbour. Their strong teeth glinted in the sunlight as they fell. Freed from captivity, the predatory eels headed for the beach where throngs of unsuspecting summer visitors enjoying the short unseasonal outbreak of sultry weather, during which temperatures were predicted to soar to the high teens, splashed happily in the warm shallow waters.

A mature spruce tree growing in the northern temperate region close to the lake stands over 200 feet tall, its characteristic four-sided leaves attached singly to pulvini on the branches. Cone shaped, its whorled branches move in the breeze. Nicknamed Young Tjikko it is just over 9,000 years old, an age it has achieved by means of layering, and is thought to be the world's second oldest tree.

The Sergeant makes tea from its leaves and The Parrot makes chewing gum from the sap.

In the lake beyond the cow shed the ornate, black head plumes and orange-red and black neck decorations of great crested grebes catch the sun. Clumsy on land, these are elegant birds in water where they dive to feed. A seeze pyder, large and ferocious, lurks deep beneath the surface. Above the reed beds nearby, swallows feed in flight, their chirps, whines and gurgles ringing out over the stern. A sexually dimorphic bearded tit perches atop the brown, cylindrical seed head of a reedmace, resting, unaware of its sexual orientation.

Growing in the marshy ground, deep pink, hollow-stemmed, marsh orchids over 2 feet tall shimmer in the sunlight and attract the eye. Water voles with small, black eyes, glossy brown fur and dark, slightly furry tails sit on hind feet holding stalks of grass between small paws to feed. A 'plop' is heard as one of the group, disturbed by an unexpected noise, dives into the water.

In the blood-soaked peat bog nearby, packed to the gunwales with carnivorous plants, bladderworts are busy capturing and digesting law-abiding larvae, water fleas and aquatic worms in the hollow sacs along their stems. Butterworts with sticky, bright green, succulent leaves capture innocent insects before digesting them. Sundews trap blameless creatures attracted by the sweet secretions before leaves bearing long tentacles fold lengthwise around them and digestion begins. Death takes about fifteen minutes, complete digestion several hours, events unfolding as they must. Grey-brown daddy longlegs with slender bodies and long deciduous legs, heath butterflies, pearl-bordered fritillaries, chocolate brown raft spiders with bilateral creamy yellow stripes and moths are plentiful here. Water meanders around the baffles in the gullies. Peat covers approximately 5 per cent of the stern, slightly more than the national average.

Surrounding the peat bog and gazing inwards across it stand several *moai*, monolithic human figures covered with intricate carved designs that were hewn and transported from the quarry behind the cow shed between 1250AD and 1500AD. Standing up to 15 feet tall and weighing many tons they stand silent on platforms known locally as *ahu*, watching with eyes of coral and obsidian. Full-body statues painted maroon and white, the faces, thought to be those of deified ancestors, are disproportionately large, making up three-eighths of the size of each one. Symbols of authority and power, their noses and ears are elongated.

Multi-coloured carpets of sphagnum moss are busy preventing the decay of dead plant material below them, thus slowly increasing the depth of the bog which is filled with flowering plants and teems with insects. Yes, the peat bog on the stern, quietly storing carbon for ten thousand years since the last Ice Age.

19

Take human beings as they are, not as you think they should be.
Krishnamurti[1]

Bronwen placed the book on the coffee table next to the chair. "What a wonderful read!"

Is it an historical novel?"

"Sort of. It`s set in the future."

"Is it a good book?"

"Wonderful! Writing of the highest quality. And a beautiful red cover. In fact, it was so good I`ve decided to read another one of the same colour. Oddly, the decor in the *café* just around the corner where I've been reading it is the same colour too. And I had a tomato with breakfast. Today is clearly a red day."

"Congratulations," replied Megan, "always keen to support Bronwen`s literary endeavours. "Which *café*, by the way?"

"The Crymych *Café Rouge*."[2]

"Have you read *Llyfr Coch Hergest*, the Red Book of Hergest?"

"Is that an historical novel too?"

"Sort of."

Bronwen thought about it. She was sitting opposite Megan in the armchair in the *simne fawr*, a large earthenware pot on each side of her. Growing in one was a laverbread tree and in the other a cockle tree. That was what the man at the car boot sale at Haverfordwest airport told her. "They flower once every twenty-five years," he explained helpfully. "The last time was yesterday. You should have seen them. A glorious sight." Whilst understanding the importance of process, Megan puts a great deal of time, energy and Machlud y Wawr[3] resources into outcomes. She was none too sure Bronwen was clear about this line of thinking. "Give her time," she reassured herself. Bronwen picked up a new red novel, turned to the first page and began to read.

Megan watched her for a moment. She has no need for Bronwen to be any different than the way she is, a way of thinking she applies to everyone. "Do you want a cushion, dear?" she asked. Bronwen looked up, a little offended. "I`m tough. I clog. I make lots of noise. I don`t need cushions." She was on her second glass of cool, carbonated, sugar-free soda water and that`s an awful lot of bubbles. "Be present to life dear, not reactive to it," suggested Megan. Bronwen drained the glass in defiance.

"Looking back over my career," thought Megan, "there is nothing I would change. I`ve done nothing special. And if what I`ve done in my life is special then what every single person on the planet has done with their lives is special. That's the miracle." She picked up the dooby doo, sat back in the chair and turned the television on, a 95-inch OLED screen less than 1mm thick and weighing less than a pound. It sat opposite her on the crypt wall pressed against a magnetic panel. It can be peeled off and moved to another part of the crypt as she moves around during the day. It was time. She switched to the live slow-burning channel. Born in Norway in 2009 with a live broadcast of a seven-hour train journey, slow-burning television was a hit. The train journey was followed by a 134-hour programme following the progress of a ship sailing from Bergen to Kirkenes. Half the population of Norway, about 2.5 million people, watched it. Eighteen hours of salmon swimming upstream followed. The nation was hooked. Later came eight hours of live television watching a wood fire from blazing to ashes during which viewers could suggest when fresh wood was put on the fire as it burned. Then the nation watched nine hours of long, quiet sequences of knitting. Slow-burning TV reached Wales with a fifteen-hour live broadcast of a meeting of Pembrokeshire County Council's Top Priority Subcommittee[4] when it last met in 2006. The ultimate in slow-burning TV according to the blurb in the Western Mail's television supplement.[5]

"Our finest clogs we bring, pa rum pum pum pum, rum pum pum pum, rum pum pum pum,"[6] sang Bronwen to herself as she read, whilst sipping a small glass of watered-down Brain's Dark[7] enlivened with a splash of *crème de Lychee* (0.9%). Placing the novel in her lap she adjusted her red, felt *cloche*, popular in Crymych since 1908, with one hand and glanced casually through the antique, French, pink, red and gold vellum leaf fan *lorgnette* with decorative gilt-silver borders and two mica peepholes she held in the other, at the barometer, a beautiful copy of Goethe's thunder glass water barometer[8] which hung from a ceiling beam alongside a nearby pointed, Gothic style pillar. "Low pressure system approaching. Chance of rain," she read. "What's new?" Above the barometer was a framed quote that put all bad weather predictions into perspective.

"It's snowing still," said Eeyore gloomily.
"So it is."
"And freezing."
"Is it?"
"Yes," said Eeyore. "However," he said, brightening up a little,
"we haven't had an earthquake lately."[9]

Silence pervaded the crypt. Bronwen listened to it for a moment or two and felt the better for doing so. Then she returned to the novel.

"When you say, "I`m reading a novel," said Megan, "you appear to be the subject. Can you instead be the object? Can you be both subject and object? Can you contain both of them yet be beyond them?"

"Time for a nice cup of freshly roasted coffee," decided Bronwen, putting the novel down, getting up and moving towards the kitchen. Outside, lightning flashed, thunder rumbled, and the sky turned as black as ink. The gods were unhappy. "And some digestives," she added, cheering the gods up. Sometime later she reappeared with two large cups, very large cups, well bowls really, each containing an *affogato*, an expresso-based drink drowned in Italian *stracciatella gelato* and gave one to Megan in the *simne fawr*, before taking her place in the armchair opposite. "That took a long time," said Bronwen. "Sorry about that."

"No," replied Megan, "it took the time it took."

"It`s Machlud y Wawr`s annual trip on Saturday," remembered Bronwen, munching a digestive. "I`m looking forward to another surprise."

"There is no journey," whispered Megan. "We are as we always have been. That`s the surprise."

"Ah! The news," they thought together, turning to look at the television. "A box has been found," said the announcer.

"A box! How wonderful!" exclaimed Bronwen.

"It contains the handwritten lyrics, circa 1967, of dozens of previously unknown Meic Stevens' songs[10] as well as early recordings of them. The treasure was found by a group of keen amateur Meicologists in the attic of a cottage in Solva. Chemical analysis of the paper and ink prove the date to be correct and handwriting experts say the lyrics are definitely those of the Welsh Dylan, the Solva Balladeer. The lyrics to the songs on the Attic Tapes,[11] as they are being called, were penned during the period when Meic was recovering from a bicycling accident. A convention of the European Society of Meicologists will be held at Swansea University[12] next month during which it will be decided which musicians will be commissioned to record the songs for their release as a boxed set called *Lost in Solva: The Attic Tapes*."[11]

"News from the world of science now. The new 3D lab opening in Pontfaen in the heart of Silicon Cwm[13] next week is a joint collaboration between the University of North Pembrokeshire at Crymych and Mynachlogddu Institute of Technology.[14] 'This will move us from Silicon Cwm to Grapheme Cwm,' said an MIT spokesperson. 'Or at least to whichever of the five hundred or so materials similar to grapheme makes the cut.' The Welsh Government[15] is investing heavily in this, bringing the best of science and engineering together. 3D materials will produce self-repairing surfaces, light surfaces for planes and other forms of transport, lighter, stronger buildings and so on. And of course, flexible screens for mobile phones, computers, televisions, etc. Indeed, even flexible mobile phones, computers, televisions, etc. Grapheme will be the nuts and bolts of computers and usher in a time of the `internet of things` when all the objects in your everyday life will be computers, all internet connected. 'We`re working at the edge of physics and engineering here in Pontfaen,' said the spokesperson when interviewed in the local pub."

"Scientists at the University of the Four Trinity Davids' Faculty of Futurology[16] located in the Mojave Desert on the California Nevada border have devised a memory device which will orbit the earth in a specially constructed satellite. The device will contain the DNA of famous people chosen for their positive qualities. The people chosen include Gandhi,[17] Nelson Mandela,[18] the Dalai Lama,[19] Stephen Hawking[20] and the First Minister of Wales.[21] It is called the Immortality Drive[22] and will provide aliens who visit earth in the future after the extinction of our species with an insight into what human beings were once like. Also stored in the device are the lyrics and music of the song *Yma o Hyd*[23] which have been transcribed into the DNA of a strain of radioactive resistant bacteria.

"I`ve read that we share 98.4% of our DNA with chimpanzees," remarked Bronwen.

"Really dear?"

"70% with slugs, 50% with bananas and 40% with turnips."

"Only 40%. That is strange."

The announcer continued. "The St Dogmaels Frog Jumping Competition reached its zenith this year when a specially bred frog from Dinas jumped clear across the mill pond by the Abbey, narrowly avoiding being eaten by a passing seagull in the process, and by doing so set a new world record. This feat has never happened before in the long history of the competition. Jim Smiley, president of the *Welsh Frog Jumping Society*, told our reporter, "This is a great leap forward for the sport." The WFJS lays down strict rules for frog welfare including limiting the daily number of jumps and stating that calming music must be played in the frogs` enclosure before a competition. It is also necessary to feed the frogs the best insects, snails, spiders and worms. Larger frogs can also be fed small fish and even mice. All this food must be fresh. On very hot days frozen food may be used at the discretion of the competition judges for which written permission must be got no more than forty-eight hours before a competition begins. One little known fact about frogs is that they have no teeth. Similar to snakes, frogs have to swallow their entire meal whole because they cannot chew anything. For this reason, frozen food must be properly thawed before being fed to the frogs as otherwise they get a condition called Frozen Belly which can cause cramps. The victorious frog, crowned St Dogmaels Champion, now proceeds to the world final in Calaveras County in California,[24] an event held annually since 1928 in which the St Dogmaels Champion will compete against the best from the rest of the world. The competition will be stiff. Last year there were over 4,000 contestants and it is thought the number this year will exceed that. The £100 prize for winning in

St Dogmaels is dwarfed by the prize money for the American competition where this year's winner will receive $10,000 and a silver cup. There are also generous prizes for the frogs coming second, $7,500, and third, $5,000. Any frog beating the previous record of 31 feet, 5³/₄ inches will receive an additional $5,000."

"The results from the Moylegrove Gooseberry Pie Fest are not yet in. The competition start was delayed this afternoon when the gas cannister under the sink in the kitchen of the village hall ran out resulting in a backlog in the pie cooking. We will bring you the latest news from the Pie Fest in our evening bulletin."

"Experience the new fitness craze that is sweeping Western Europe. Clog and Knead classes, costing £135 per place for a day's instruction are springing up all over the country. Bringing together the best clog dancing and the latest bread making techniques in a unique way to keep you fit and healthy. Weekend and weeklong retreats are also available. Asked how this unique new take on fitness came about, one of the founders, Sioned McSweet from Penarth, said, 'It happened by accident really. I went to a weekend yoga retreat on Steep Holm recently and whilst stranded there for several weeks because of stormy weather I was struck by how similar yoga and clog dancing really are and my time competing with the Urdd naturally made me plump for clog dancing rather than yoga. Add to that my love of breadmaking and I realised that this was a recipe for success. However stressed you are after a busy working day, when you get a couple of clog dances behind you and a sweet bun in the oven all your worries and tiredness are gone.'"

Bronwen, enthused by thoughts of healthy exercise, got up and went to the kitchen to make two cups of coffee made from beans sourced from the Xinjiang province of China, cold brew infused with aromatic pear and the merest hint of cinnamon. One for her and one for Megan, as usual. She returned a while later and put a cup on the table next to her armchair and another on the small table next to Megan before scattering dried udumbara and plum blossoms on the surface of the tables around the cups. She walked back into the kitchen and reappeared carrying two bowls and two spoons, putting one each next to the cups before sitting down again. Megan picked up the cup of coffee, took a sip, returned it to the table and stretched an arm towards the plate. Her arm stopped *en route*, gripped by her conscience, as her eyes gazed at a large slice of apple tart almost completely buried beneath a generous helping of vanilla and honey ice cream.

She blinked.

"Resistance is futile," whispered Bronwen.

"Resistance is futile," whispered the arm.

"Resistance is futile," whispered the apple tart.

"Resistance is futile," whispered the generous helping of vanilla and honey ice cream.

Her conscience raised a white flag and she tucked in. She recalled, whilst munching, something her husband once said to her. "You know, I`ve noticed in my life many areas in which I`m awkward, hopeless even, at a loss, lost. Things about life I don`t understand. Things I can`t do. You do all those things well, cariad. With you I have a sense of being complete. Please tell me we`ll live to be a hundred and fifty years old and spend all that time together." She squeezed his hand. "Sometimes, when we are apart, I miss you so much my whole body aches. There is a pain."

"The pain you experience for me is but your desire to experience the love that is inside you. For some beautiful reason I am a trigger for that. And you play that role for me, for which, each moment, I am grateful. I am a pathway for you to yourself and you for me to myself. For that is really what we offer each other, a pathway to the love that we are. And our devotion to each other enables that. Thank you, cariad." She squeezed his hand again. He smiled as tears came to his eyes. "Are you OK?" she asked.

"Yes, cariad."

"I`m glad you`re OK."

"Do you know," he said, "when I use the word cariad it is always meaningful. It affirms that I love you. Be certain when you hear it that in that moment I am aware of being full of love for you, and with that beautiful word cariad, I give my love to you."

"Thank you, cariad."

He was sitting at his two-hundred-year-old antique mahogany roll top desk which was situated to one side of the bay window in the crypt. Every morning before breakfast he sat at the desk writing. It was the perfect spot for an amateur novelist, with its distracting view across the Piazza della Republica to the Cathedral. Megan was sitting next to him. He took the pen with his left hand, freeing his right hand, and with it he held hers. "Thank you cariad," he said, squeezing her hand, adding, "I have a problem."

She looked at him, concern on her face. "What is it, cariad?"

"I can`t hold the notebook open and write with only my left hand."

She tried to release her hand, but he held it tight. "I can live without writing the twenty first century`s greatest novel, but I can't live without holding your hand." They sat in silence for a while, close to each other, gazing out through the window. With her free hand she blew him a kiss. He let out a yell and collapsed towards her. She caught him as he fell. "What`s the matter, cariad?

"I like being in your arms, so I decided to fall into them," he replied with a smile. She kissed him on the top of his head and hugged him close.

They were sitting in the *café* in Theatr Mwldan in Cardigan one morning enjoying a coffee, him reading the Marxist Times and her the Washington Post. She takes the Saturday edition for the literary supplement in order to keep up with developments in American literature and to get news of recent activity of Machlud y Wawr`s North American affiliates. They overheard an excited comment from one of a group of women sitting at a nearby table. "Look! Isn`t that Megan`s husband? The one who won the Golden Double."

"Did you hear that, cariad?" he asked Megan.

"Yes, cariad. You`re the one who achieved the Golden Double."

"No, cariad. I`m the one who is your husband."

"To tell you the truth," said Bronwen, I`m a bit tired of reading literature. It`s boring. Well drawn characters, each with a rich psychological life, well-paced plot development, sentences resonant with lyrical qualities. Tedium personified! Murder, mayhem, car chases and a high body count. That`s what I need, detective stories and westerns."

Megan nodded approval. "Or a mixture of the two."

Megan and Bronwen enjoy whiling away their evenings in the crypt, sitting opposite each other on their armchairs by the wood fire in the *simne fawr*, the only light coming from the burning logs. In between long periods of silence they like to engage in Inuit throat singing, the voiced and unvoiced sounds of inhalation and exhalation generating duets of exquisite beauty, one setting a rhythmic pattern, the other singing in the gaps as their bodies sway gently from side to side. As their throats begin to tire one of them picks up the dooby doo to turn the radio on and they sit in the cosiness watching the fire and the flickering shadows, listening intently to the news before supper whilst gargling with a thick, viscous concoction made with honey and lemon juice designed to help their throats recover.

Megan thought of another visit with her husband to the *café* in Theatr Mwldan whilst shopping in the town. He looked up from the book he was reading, *The Cambridge History of Cornish Literature*.[25] The *café* was quiet, a folk melody playing softly in the background, people dotted around at the tables engrossed in conversation. Megan looked up from her novel. Their eyes met. They smiled at each other. A few moments later he broke into laughter.

"Why are you laughing at me?" she asked.

"I would never laugh at you. I`m laughing with you. I look into the eyes of the most beautiful woman I`ve ever met and laughter bubbles out of my heart."

She took his hand in hers.

"You know," he continued, "that I love you."

"Yes."

"You know, with absolute certainty, that I will always care for you."

"Yes." She felt tears forming in her eyes. His presence was overwhelming.

"You know, beyond all doubt, that I will always be devoted to you, cariad."

"Yes."

"And you know with complete assuredness that you are the best thing since sliced bread."

"Thank you, cariad." A strange gurgling sound came from her mouth. Her chest heaved and the tears flowed. She gripped his hand tighter. He winced in pain. They were still looking intently into each other's eyes, in silence, when the waiter brought the bill.

Megan`s husband wasn`t much to look at, yet his face was kind and there was a peacefulness about him. She could read him like a book. To her, his mind was transparent, and he was the most sincere person she had ever met. They enjoyed being together in simple, everyday ways such as standing in the kitchen in the evening in the converted cowshed as she prepared supper, hugging and kissing. Slow times of caress.

"I never thought when we met that you had such a powerful sexuality," she remarked once. "Even now to look at you, no one would think you are so good at sex." She blushed.

"I`m glad," he replied "for my sexuality is for you, and you alone. Every moment of intimacy between us from a *cwtsh* to a kiss to swinging from the *chandelier* entwined naked together is a delight that stimulates me deep inside. If no one else sees that in me, that`s fine. It`s my gift to you. Just to you. That`s why it`s so powerful."

"Thank you, cariad."

"You know, sitting in this *café* together, if the other people here are wondering why you're sitting at a table with a corpse, I would be happy. That would be fine." She laughed. "All that energy is for you. You see it and you experience it. And we are complete. One." Megan smiled and squeezed his hand. He winced again.

The music playing on the radio stopped and the newsreader's voice soothed the atmosphere in the *café*. "We interrupt this programme with a newsflash. Good news for Rugby fans. A former Wales and Lions captain[26] has been honoured by the Australian government by having the twin craters of the world`s largest known asteroid strike named after him. The East Warburton and the West Warburton Basins are craters caused by an asteroid that split into two just before hitting the Earth. They have a combined diameter of over 400 km which is greater than the Vredefort Crater in the Free State Province of South Africa which until this find was the largest known crater at about 300 km across. It is the second-oldest known crater on Earth, a little less than 300 million years younger than the Suavjärvi crater in Russia and is named after the nearby town of Vredefort where some elderly residents in the Sunshine Sunset nursing home claim the noise caused by the impact woke them up. Scientists have linked the asteroid that created the East and West Warburtons to a mass extinction during the Late Devonian period between 359 and 375 million years ago. And now back to the music."

They returned to their reading, half listening at the same time to the songs on the radio, *The Times They Are A Changing,*[27] *Norwegian Wood*[28] and *Golden Brown.*[29] "I`ve suddenly realized why I love those songs," Megan said. "You can waltz to them." And they did. Much to the amusement of everyone there.

"Who said, 'You can`t be wise and in love at the same time'," her husband asked as they whirled between the tables.

"I don`t know, cariad."

"Bob Dylan."

"Of course."

After several laps of the *café* they returned to their table. He picked up his book and she her novel.

She noticed two cups, two saucers and two spoons on the table. Two books and two people, one woman and one man. "Cariad," she whispered, "someone once remarked, 'We used to think that if we knew one, we knew two, because one and one are two. We are finding that we must learn a great deal more about and`."[30] She and him, her and he, lost in the mystery. She smiled and continued reading.

Wild garlic with long, pointed, oval-shaped leaves carpets the floor of the woodland next to the orchard outside the kitchen door of the crypt. Slow-spreading wood anemones up to 8 inches tall with deeply cut three-lobed leaves are plentiful, as is hollow-stemmed cow parsley with its fern-like foliage and delicate clusters of white flowers in early summer. Tall columbines, whose individual upside-down blue flowers with spurred petals resemble five doves, gather together. Hairy, wood forget-me-nots with their clusters of salver-shaped five-petalled azure-blue flowers with white eyes, abound. Dogwood, sweet cherry, pine, hawthorn, buckthorn, juniper, linden, rowan, mountain-ash, willow, olive, yew, holly, goat willow and buddleia provide shade. Assorted cats and dogs run free in this wild place.

The skirl of a peregrine falcon pierces the air as it prepares to leave its nest high on the southern aspect of the Cathedral. Upon hearing the call, a family of voles on the woodland floor far below move swiftly towards the cover of the undergrowth.

Passing at high altitude over the summit of Rum Dingli[31] to the west a skein of bar headed geese with characteristic 'rollercoaster flight' hug the mountainous terrain. Flying in V formation each bird gains lift from the bird in front. Blood temperature lowered by 2^0C they adjust their energy use to fly with a third of the oxygen available at sea level, thereby coping with the metabolic requirements of flight in the extremely hypoxic air found at 23,000ft as their heart rate and wing beats remain the same. For millions of years bar headed geese have been travelling north from India to Mongolia, China and north Pembrokeshire to breed.

20

Táimid faoi dhraíocht
ag ceol na farraige.
Liam Ó Flaithearta[1]

We are enchanted
by the music of the sea.

The coracle bobbed softly on the calm waters of the harbour as the Sergeant sat next to the table in the galley sipping tea from his favourite mug. The Parrot stood quietly on its perch on the port side between the porthole and the cuckoo clock nibbling from a bowl of mixed nuts and avocado slices drizzled with extra virgin olive oil. "All is well," thought the Sergeant. But all was not well.

"**SERGEANT!**" barked the ship-to-shore radio attached to the bulkhead next to the cuckoo clock. It shook angrily. It was the Admiral's voice. **"SERGEANT!"**

He put the mug down, hurried across the galley and took hold of the receiver which was already heating up. "Morning, Sir."

"Is that you, Sergeant?"

He looked around the galley. There was no one else there, only The Parrot. "Yes sir, it's me," he replied, reassured.

"The mystery, man. Have you solved the mystery?"

A confused look appeared on the Sergeant's face. "Mystery man, sir?"

"The crime, Sergeant. Have you solved it?" The Parrot stopped nibbling and turned to listen to the conversation.

"Crime, sir?" The coracle stopped bobbing.

"Wake up, man!" Came the exasperated voice of the Admiral.

"Ah! Ah? Oh!"

"The case you've been working on these past months. The Landsker Line. Don't you remember? It's disappeared. Suspected stolen. How is the investigation going? Any leads? Has anyone talked? Are you close to finding the criminals responsible? What **are** you **doing** up there?"

The Sergeant looked wistfully at the mug of tea on the table hoping against hope that an answer would come to him.

"Send me a full report tomorrow morning." The line went dead.

Relieved, he put the receiver back in its place, returned to the table, sat down, picked up the mug of tea and took a long, hard sip. Then a short one. He felt peckish. "Time for a sandwich," he said out loud to himself. The Parrot tightened its grip on the perch as the Sergeant stood up, walked to the counter and began. First, he put on the pair of heat retardant oven gloves then got two slices of extra thick, fibre reduced sliced white bread, Marmite,[2] Peanut Butter,[3] raspberry jam, banana and raw onions from the cupboard. Unsettled by the thought of having to write a report he went for the nuclear option, extra Marmite. The sandwich finished, the Sergeant placed it on a plate and the plate on the table. Picking up the empty mug he returned to the counter, made a fresh brew of steaming hot builder`s tea with a splash of full fat milk and sat down again, placing the mug cautiously on the table. The Parrot covered its head with its wings to shield itself from the blast.

He paused, breathing slowly in and out, emptying his mind as he prepared himself for what was to come. He shifted position on the chair, back straight, feet shoulder width apart and solid on the ground. He reached across to pick up the mug, an operation hampered considerably by the oven gloves, and took an introductory sip. "Hmmm. Wonderful!" He put the mug back on the galley table. "And now for the sandwich."

The last thing he remembered was grabbing it with the required Vulcan Death Grip.[4] Oh, and a squawk. Several hours later he woke up lying on the hurricane deck amidships. Dragging himself cautiously yet unsteadily to his feet he followed the trail of crumbs back to the galley where he noticed the sandwich had disappeared and the mug was empty. "I must have enjoyed that," he thought. The perch was empty, some feathers lay on the mat at its base. The blast from the explosion blew The Parrot cartwheeling out through the porthole, onwards and upwards towards Harbour Village. It regained control as it passed over Llanwnda before steering a course back to the harbour and settling on top of the main mast to preen its smoking, ruffled plumage. It felt safe there, it wasn`t far from the safety of the sky.

Still groggy, the Sergeant made his way to the willow grove on the stern and lay in the hammock to think about the report. Researchers have tracked the brain activity of 14,726 subjects using electroencephalograms and found the average human attention span has dropped to eight seconds. They suggest two reasons for this. One, more and more people are using digital technology, and two, one of the subjects who took part in the research has such a short attention span that the data is skewed. The average attention span of a goldfish remains encouragingly constant at nine seconds. The Sergeant was pleased, he liked goldfish and kept half a dozen as pets in the harbour. He also admires penguins, seals and whales. They are all full of blubber. Several seconds had elapsed. The Sergeant wondered why he was there. "Hmm. Tea!" he thought and got up and strolled towards the galley.

"That such a one walks amongst us," mused The Parrot.

Several hours later, having walked to the four corners of the coracle yet failed to find the galley, he stumbled wearily into the willow grove and found himself back by the hammock. Brain cells responsible for a sense of direction are in the entorhinal cortex, a region next to the hippocampus. `Grid cells` in the entorhinal cortex are the brain's GPS system. They tell us where we are relative to where we started. Also found there are `head-direction cells` which fire when we face a certain direction. The hippocampus is associated with memory and in it are `place cells` which activate when we move into a specific location and groups of them form a map of the environment. These three types of neurones enable navigation in humans. Their function is impaired by the ingestion of one of the Sergeant's extreme sandwiches, the effects of the habitual eating of which scientists describe as *Extreme Sandwich Syndrome*. The Sergeant is proud to have invented an extreme sport that, like coasteering,[5] can be claimed for Pembrokeshire. Fortunately, the negative effects of extreme sandwiching are reversible and disappear after a few hours in a hammock. More fortunate still he happened to be standing next to a hammock, otherwise he would have been in trouble, lost at sea. He lay down and went to sleep. The Parrot flew down from the mast where it had remained during the danger period and stood on the lowest branch of a nearby willow tree preening itself, relieved that it was all over for another day.

Awakened by the singing of the stone circle caressed by the cold east wind coming in low over Fishguard Bay the Sergeant opened his bloodshot eyes with a start. Or perhaps they opened themselves. This is the cause of some dispute in scientific circles. His movements during the troubled extreme sandwich sleep phase resulted in him finding himself lying face down in the hammock instead of, as was usual following a calm Horlicks[6] sleep, on his back facing the sky. He turned his head and as his eyes regained focus he noticed the garden shed standing to one side of the willow grove, the architectural design of which is known as the *Loire-Château* style. He removed himself from the hammock and went to the galley for a mug of tea, just the thing to clear his head and get him ready for the rest of the day. It would be some time before he tried the nuclear option again, a decision helped by his fear of the effects on his mental wellbeing, the effects on his sleep patterns and by the fact that, with a triumph of common sense, The Parrot had hidden the jar of Marmite.

Sitting next to the table sipping tea he picked up the dooby doo, pointed it at the large screen television lashed to the for'ard bulkhead above the porthole, flicked through the recorded films, chose one and pressed play. "*Kasimir und Karoline*, Ödön von Horváth's dark drama from 1932.[7] Just the thing to clear my head," he thought to himself.

For several months Machlud y Wawr's 255th CyOps Company[8] had been sending subliminal messages to the Sergeant's television. In every 24 frames per second one frame contained a message that appears and disappears so fast that the eye does not see it. But the brain does. A powerful brain-washing procedure, it has proved effective on many occasions over the years. But with this subject it has no effect. Absolutely none.

Having gained valuable insights into his relationship with his wife from the play's use of cultural references and naturalistic language, characteristic of von Horváth's description of the *bourgeoisie* of the Weimar Republic, although a little taken aback by the sexual phrasing present in the script, he gave some thought to the Admiral`s orders. Amongst the myriad crimes common to the area, piracy and cockle trafficking are the greatest threat to security faced by the Dyfed-Powys Police Rapid-Response Coracle Unit.[9] Little has changed in this regard over the last fourteen thousand years since the ice retreated as the last ice age came to an end, apart from the coastline. But a new crime, one of gargantuan proportions, has shaken the very fabric of society on the Pembrokeshire peninsular, the rainiest part of Wales, and its ripples have travelled outwards disturbing the laidback calm of the rest of the country. Actors, writers, poets, artists, film makers and intellectuals in Cowbridge speak of nothing else whilst sipping their special coffees and nibbling *tortes* in the *bourgeois art nouveau kaffeehauses* along the cobblestoned High Street where the better class of visitor takes delight in the Cowbridge Cubist architecture to be seen in the details of the *café* facades and interiors.

"Yes. I remember now, the Landsker Line. It's disappeared and DPPRRCU are treating the incident as suspicious. Exactly! Suspicious is the word. Downright dubious if you ask me. But why?" Pleased with the progress he was making he relaxed and gazed out through the porthole, admiring the new visitor attraction, the world`s longest glass-bottomed cantilever skywalk. It reaches out 76.92 metres into thin air from the top of the cliff above the harbour and is in the shape of a loop with the end of the walk 20 metres further along the cliff top from the beginning and has become a firm favourite with locals and tourists. It is longer than the Grand Canyon Skywalk in Arizona and longer than the Longgang National Geological Park Skywalk in Chongqing, China which was previously the world`s longest. It cost the Pembrokeshire Coast National Park[10] 36 million yuan to construct. Work on a glass-bottomed cantilevered skypath, two metres wide and secured three metres from the cliff face has begun. The skypath will extend from Goodwick to Carreg Wastad and will be built and paid for by the French Government who are keen to make amends for the incident in 1797. They will also send a highly skilled team of clock restorers and French polishers to fix the collateral damage. Like the skywalk, this cliff hugging feature, several miles long and made entirely of transparent glass panels, will be for brave, thrill seeking, adventurous types as the cantilevered design makes for a terrifying hiking experience.

Pondering again the disappearance of the ancient Pembrokeshire landmark a thought came to the Sergeant. Unperturbed by this he continued reviewing the case. "Machlud y Wawr have stolen it so the south of the county will become Welsh speaking. For centuries it`s been a barrier preventing babies Down Below being born as Welsh speakers. The linguistic and cultural dam has been breached. Machlud y Wawr and Megan are behind this." He knew he was getting somewhere at last. The mystery was beginning to clear and slowly the pieces of the jigsaw were falling into place, forming a rough sketch of one of the great improbable moments in history.

He reflected upon some of the unexpected consequences. Since the Landsker Line`s disappearance a significant proportion of the babies in Tenby have been born speaking Cornish, a development that has prompted a flurry of letters to the London Times[11] from the Welsh Language Commissioner.[12] *Mebyon Kernow*[13] have responded, rebutting the Commissioner`s fears and appealing for calm. Following full and frank discussions with Menter Iaith Sir Benfro grateful inhabitants of the town have seen the first trilingual signs, Cornish, Welsh and English, appear on roads and public buildings. Reassured by this and following meaningful discussions with *Seneth an Stenegow*[14] the Welsh Government[15] has instructed Pembrokeshire County Council[16] to open a Cornish medium nursery and primary school in Tenby, next door to the Welsh medium one. The possibility of a bilingual Welsh and Cornish secondary school in Tenby is on the agenda of the next full meeting of the County Council. Also on the agenda is the idea of twinning the school with the Cornish medium secondary school in Wadebridge. Children in Tenby are becoming megaieithog, being the technical term educationalists use to describe children with the ability to speak many languages.

This outbreak of Cornish speaking babies Down Below is limited to Tenby, a phenomenon as yet unexplained by linguists and obstetricians. An extraordinary general meeting of the Council's Forward Planning Committee[17] is due to be convened later this month to determine how many Cornish pasty outlets the town will need in the future as the percentage of Cornish speakers increases exponentially year by year.

In a recent development, permission has been granted by Natural Resources Wales[18] for a Cornish Tin Mining Company to begin prospecting in the area. A kernowite mine in the middle of the housing estate in Kilgetty is already in full production. Geologists have confirmed that the seam of kernowite begins near the surface under St Day in Cornwall, sinks deep to pass under the ocean, and rises close to the surface again under Kilgetty. The estate has applied to be designated a UNESCO world heritage site.

A seam of granite rich in lithium carbonate running deep underground from Cornwall to just outside Saundersfoot has been discovered recently by prospectors acting under license from Cornwall Council[19] and Pembrokeshire

County Council. In both locations the lithium carbonate is being mined from the granite rocks and geothermal waters below ground. First discovered at the Wheal Clifford copper mine in Cornwall in 1864, lithium carbonate is rapidly gaining importance as it is essential for the batteries of electric vehicles.

"The Landsker Line must be returned," he remarked in an aside to himself, "even though its historic dividing nature has been annulled. It`s an important attraction for the spiritually inclined tourist. Tradition has it that one walk along it is equal to a walk to Rome and one walk along it and back is equal to a walk to Jerusalem, no matter which end you start at." Exhausted but happy he made himself a mug of tea and went to his office on the deck below to write the report.

Sometime later The Parrot yawned. All over Pembrokeshire other parrots followed suit. As did budgies. This, the first attested case of contagious yawning in a non-mammalian species in the county, was perhaps empathetic rather than involuntary. It went unnoticed however by the Sergeant, who, shivering with excitement, was busy fighting the keyboard. To passing shipping it looked as if something disagreeable was happening, but it is no more than his typing style.

Hallucinations ploughed deep furrows in the soft surface of the nervous tissue contained within his skull. Sweat poured off his fevered brow. "My name is the Sergeant, king of kings: Look upon my typing, ye Mighty, and despair!" he chanted hoarsely, over and over again.[20] Days later The Parrot found him slumped exhausted by the gunwale on the starboard side gibbering incoherently, a paper printout of the report clutched tightly to his breast. Using advanced counselling skills learnt on a Dyfed-Powys Police Rapid-Response Coracle Unit Advanced Counselling course and metaphysical debate it took The Parrot several hours to talk him back to an acceptable relative reality. "*Mon grand seigneur*, you don`t have to do anything, and yet everything is done," The Parrot advised, quoting from the Way of the Coast Path Sutra. Two large mugs of steaming tea also helped, one for him and one for The Parrot. When he remembered what he had done, namely write a lengthy report, his first, about something or other, and survive, he was delighted and promptly gave himself the rest of the day off. He spent the time by the water feature on the bow which is home to a family of Chinese water dragons, six yellow necked mice, a pair of puffins, five red kites, assorted tarantulas, three European polecats, peacocks and a clattering of jackdaws who nest in their thousands in the chimney above the galley and in holes in the for'ard mast. "Very noisy creatures," the Sergeant always says. Their numbers are growing.

The bows of Viking long ships were adorned with the carved heads of dragons or monsters designed to strike fear into the hearts of the enemy. On the bow of the coracle is carved the head of Gonzo Davies,[21] a fearsome sight indeed as it appears out of a sea mist striking fear into the minds of smugglers and pirates alike. Its secondary purpose is to provide shade for wildlife from a blazing summer sun. He dozed in this shade, a beautiful green and blue carthen spread beneath him, awakened frequently from his dreams by the hard-clipped ascending call and raspy chatter of jackdaws.

By late afternoon he had recovered fully from the earlier bout of cabin fever and was finishing the last of the methuselah of Glengettie `... a full bodied and brisk tea with rich flavour ...`[22] he takes with him on picnics, when the alarm went off. He jumped to his feet and looked for the danger. There was none. All was well, the water surface remained calm, the Chinese water dragons, yellow necked mice, puffins, red kites, tarantulas, European polecats, peacocks and jackdaws were feeding peacefully. Fishguard and Goodwick were safe. A false alarm. Scientists are developing a system of deep-sea sensors that will give early warning of tsunamis. The sensors, providing real time measurements, will be attached to subsea telecommunications cables and they will have the secondary purpose of helping study climate change. The main cables will stretch between Swansea and Cork and between Holyhead and Dublin. This sophisticated system is being trialled in the water feature. The on-board computer turned the alarm off, pressed the reset button and sent a message to the system's control centre in County Meath that all was well.

Lulled into a false sense of security by the false alarm the Sergeant became careless and was unaware of the coracle shuddering violently as the usually calm waters in the harbour came alive, frothing in tumultuous indignation. Ever alert however he noticed as soon as The Parrot drew his attention to it. The Parrot suggested the change was due to the North Atlantic Oscillation, a climate variable affecting central North America, Europe and parts of northern Asia. "The North Atlantic Oscillation," The Parrot explained "caused long, severe winters in north-western Europe between 290AD and 500AD, coinciding with the fall of Rome and the migration of the Germanic peoples. "Just think," it continued, "if not for the bad weather the Germanic peoples might never have come to Britain which today would be Welsh, Cornish, Cumbric and Pictish, etc, speaking. Brythonic languages all, apart from south eastern Britain where a Romance language similar to French would be spoken as a result of the Britons in that area turning to Latin during the four centuries the Romans were here. Between 600AD and 900AD the North Atlantic Oscillation caused lots of good weather and the Vikings came and said hello," added The Parrot. "Hmmm," thought the Sergeant, "Fishguard, *fiskigarðr*, the Old Norse for a fish trap? There are other places with names similar to Fishguard, one in Russia and one in the Mediterranean to mention but two. And all where the Vikings went and traded."

The Sergeant thought it best to hit something while the iron was hot and relay to the Admiral the news that the report was finished and that he was well on the way to solving this awful crime. All he needed now was evidence. Forensic evidence. Fingerprints. DNA samples. He watches crime dramas on the television and knows all about that sort of thing. He rose from the luxurious feel of the *carthen* and made his way to the Communications Room situated on level three, amidships. Sitting in front of the bank of computer screens a puzzled frown creased his brow as he worked out how to begin. The frown disappeared, a knowing smile lit up his countenance and he reached under the seat with one hand, pulled the small lever and adjusted the height. "That`s better," he thought as the onboard computer turned the computer systems on and the screens lit up. "Funny place to put the `On` control," he muttered. Unperturbed by this idiosyncrasy he continued. He opened his emails, wrote a short message to the Admiral and attached the report document. He pressed `Send` with a flourish. "My first report," he exclaimed with delight. "Now, what else can I do while I`m here?" The onboard computer recognised the danger and shut the computer systems down. Perched on a willow branch astern The Parrot sighed with relief. "The danger`s over," it thought as the Sergeant readjusted the seat, got up and walked to the galley for another celebratory mug of steaming tea. "And chocolate biscuits. Essential when I`m in a state of euphoria. Indeed, essential in any state," he chuckled to himself.

Following a recent upgrade to increase security against hacking the Sergeant's laptop uses qutrits, in which photons are polarised in three perpendicular directions, to send messages to HQ. Whilst typing he is unaware of his close proximity to quantum entanglement.

Seated next to the table he picked up the dooby doo, turned off the television, pointed it at the radio attached to the starboard bulkhead between the fridge-freezer and the black and white photograph of Arianrhod and pressed the green button. Radio Free Pembrokeshire[23] came to life just in time for the news. The announcer`s voice filled the galley and spilled out into the corridor. "The Bullet Train[24] from Carmarthen to Aberystwyth, and back of course, has set a new record for being on time."

"Of course, it has," a spokeswoman told us earlier today during an exclusive interview. "This is analytics at its best, safe and efficient. Bullet Trains have a top speed of over 280mph, although such high speed has its drawbacks. Occasionally sheep and goats grazing near the tracks are sucked under the wheels as it whizzes along. All right if you like your lamb chops fresh perhaps but animal rights activists are outraged. Local farmers have started an online petition to have the wheels removed."

"That would certainly slow the trains down."

Ignoring this comment, the spokeswoman pressed on. "Thousands of sensors along the tracks collect petabytes of data that a computer control system situated in the University of the Four Trinity Davids' Department of High-Speed Communication and Line Dancing[25] at its Carmarthen campus uses to keep the trains running on time. This streaming data platform works in real time to guarantee excellence in performance and happy customers. Recently a deputation from Japan were guests at the university and during their six-week stay they studied the Bullet Train set up to see what they could learn from it that might improve Japan`s fledgling high-speed train network. They were particularly interested in the intricate networking sensors that ensure not only that trains run on time, but also, with extraordinary attention to detail, provide information about wear and tear in the kettle in the buffet car and can identify sandwiches that need to be refreshed. The buffet car is therefore both descriptive by observing past eating trends and predictive. It is good at seeing the future."

The spokeswoman took a deep breath then continued. "If problems with sandwiches occur new supplies can be taken on board in Llanybydder, as can fresh supplies of coal. With scheduled stops at stations in Pencader, Llandysul, Llanybydder, Lampeter, Tregaron and Llanilar the 56-mile journey through the stunning scenery of Carmarthenshire and Ceredigion will take the Bullet Train, known locally as *Y Bwled*, approximately 157 minutes. Following *Y Bwled*`s first run several complaints were received from the public. One was from an old man in Pencader who didn`t like the fact that staff on the train could speak English. A gentleman from Llanilar[26] complained that staff in the buffet car asked him to stop serenading other passengers with Welsh hymns. "The government tells farmers to diversify and when we do, we`re told to stop," he exclaimed indignantly as he phoned for a taxi to take him back to the S4C headquarters in Carmarthen.[27] A number of complaints were received from farmers and other members of the public who had lost livestock and pet dogs that were sucked under the wheels of the train by the slipstream as the train swept past. Good news though, several passengers complimented the artist who carved the lovely wooden statue of *Twm Siôn Cati*[28] that stands on Tregaron Square and the staff of the Bullet Train for having copies of T. J. Llewelyn Prichard's recently republished, *The Adventures and Vagaries of Twm Shôn Catti, Descriptive of Life in Wales* available in the reading room next to the dining car. Originally published in 1828 it is thought to be the first Welsh novel written in English. A recent innovation means the system is now prescriptive and decides what is statistically the best course of action for any given circumstance at any given moment and this is the part of the system the Japanese delegation is particularly interested in as they seek to ensure all the sandwiches on Japan`s trains are fresh every morning. And inspired by a visit to a coffee shop in Aberystwyth they have decided to put *bara brith* on the menu, knowing full well that it rhymes with teeth."

"Impressive," thought the Sergeant.

The spokeswoman paused to take a sip of tea before continuing. "The analytics has been so successful on the bullet train between Carmarthen and Aberystwyth that the Welsh Government intends incorporating it on the buses running the Town Service between Fishguard and Goodwick. Watch this space."

"Good news indeed," he muttered.

"And now news from the world of sport. The *Fformiwla T* [29] World Championships will take place on Roath Park lake in Cardiff next month. *Fformiwla T* aims to make top class racing accessible to a wider audience and, also, sustainable. The silent electric racing coracles can be used in top competitions in parts of cities ordinary racing coracles cannot as there are no emissions and instead of the piercing screech of ordinary racing machines the electric engines emit a soothing **hummmmmm**. After the inaugural race of this year`s World Series in Cardiff, *Fformiwla T* moves on to Madrid, Paris, Stockholm, thought by many to be the ideal city for these races, partly because the city is spread over a number of islands, partly because the race can extend to the Archipelago, but mostly because Swedish people are lovely, then Long Beach, California, Sydney, Dunedin, Putrajaya, Malaysia, the world`s first intelligent garden city, before finishing in Venice where it began all those years ago.

The development of electric motors and batteries is an important part of the work at the University of North Pembrokeshire at Crymych`s Sustainable Energy Department known as C2 which is sited near the University`s Experimental Coracling Unit in Cilgerran. Here engineers are at the forefront of revolutionary and innovative technology increasing the reliability and durability of batteries which will one day be seen in cars, planes, and, of course, homes as we increasingly draw our energy from the sun. "It is a little-known fact," a spokesperson from the unit in Cilgerran told our reporter earlier today, "that the energy the earth receives from the sun in one hour is enough to supply all the Earth`s energy needs for one year. Our work here fits well with official policy as the Welsh Government has abandoned its targets for renewables, instead looking at energy from a different perspective and is on track to decarbonise the Welsh economy." A Cardiff City Council [30] spokesperson told us earlier that the arrival of *Fformiwla T* is a coup for the city as much as hosting the World Bog Snorkelling Championships [31] is for Llanwrtyd Wells, or the Welsh Open Conker Championships is for Hubberston. [32] The race is expected to reach a worldwide television audience of seven hundred million and will put the lighthouse in Roath Park lake containing a scale model of the *Terra Nova* upon which Captain Scott, Edgar Evans and others sailed to the Antarctic from Cardiff in 1910 on the world map."

Inspired by this news the Sergeant picked up the book which was lying on the table next to him and continued reading. It was an old favourite, well thumbed, covered in tea stains and in a shabby state, as every old favourite should be. Yes, he was rereading for the umpteenth time Izaak Walton`s 1652 classic *The Compleat Coracler*, [33] a bestseller in its day. In 1653 he followed it with *The Compleat Angler*, a decent book about fishing but without the genius of the previous tome. Both are still in print.

The announcer continued. "The Welsh Government has granted planning permission for the £1.1 billion Milford Haven tidal lagoon project." 'This will be yet another game changer for Wales,' the First Minister told our reporter. 'It will lock in a 150-year, zero-carbon energy system. The 420-megawatt project will generate 700 gigawatt hours of electricity every year, enough to power all the homes in Pembrokeshire. As a peninsular nation, harnessing the power of water, both on land and offshore, is an important part of our energy planning for the future. By 2050 we want all of Wales` energy to come from renewables and we are well on the way to achieving this.' "That was the First Minister, speaking earlier today. This development is linked to the energy pioneers based at Swansea University`s new bay campus at St Modwen`s on the eastern approach to the city.[34] Here, surface coating and fuel cell technologies are being developed, which, amongst other things, will produce batteries for home and industrial use that can store energy during the day and night to provide electricity. In the not-too-distant future, all the homes in Wales will be off grid."

"We`re doing our bit," added The Parrot, "in an environmentally sustainable sort of a way. The willow grove on the stern cleans the lake as the trees can survive high levels of pollution, removing chemicals and rendering them inert. And it is home to some of the world's three trillion trees whose roots pump water from the ground before their leaves release water vapour that is moved by winds as "flying rivers" to fall as rain on the arid region of the stern's interior."[35]

Unaware of the fact that he and his ancestors have existed for one per cent of the time that trees have been on the Earth the Sergeant decided a snack was in order. An expert at the art of "dynamic balancing", moving from A to B, changing positions as he does so, without falling over, he got up, made his way to the kettle and began tea making plus. A few minutes later he was seated by the table sipping steaming hot tea from the mug and munching Welsh Rarebit.

Lost at the headwaters of a river in France some years ago whilst on an exchange with la Gendarmerie Nationale`s Rapid-Response Coracle Unit (*Rivières* Division)[36] he was put up by generous locals in a hamlet after running aground on a nearby sand bank. The trip was to have been his *les rivières de France* work experience. Serendipidy turned it into his *les fromages de France* experience. He discovered French cheeses and ate about a pound of them every week during the long winter months he was marooned there and noticed his microbiome improved greatly during this period. He particularly liked *Alpage Comté* and *Mimolette*. "Traditional cheeses full of microbes, yeasts and moulds," The Parrot explained. "Unpasteurised milk is essential." Live cheese became a part of the Sergeant`s diet.

The Sergeant now makes real cheese, enjoying it with fruit and oat or barley biscuits. He doesn`t cook or otherwise heat the cheese in any way after learning in the French village that that would kill the microbes. He swabs between his toes and mixes the collected bacteria, yeast and fungi with raw unpasteurised milk obtained from the cows on the stern, adding to this heady mix some lactis acid bacilli. The maturing process takes place on old wooden shelves in a dark, damp corner of the cowshed built into the hillside next to the willow grove. Being partly underground and having thick stone walls means the temperature fluctuation throughout the year is small. This is a cheese factory that is impossible to sterilise, especially when the cows are in it, a fact the Sergeant is convinced is partly responsible for the excellent quality of the cheese and of his biome. He rubs the surface of the cheese occasionally with an old cotton rag dipped in his own urine to give the cheese a good crust upon which cheese mites proliferate as it matures.

His wife won`t go near the place although secretly she is proud of her husband`s *fromagerie* and enjoys a generous nibble herself. Nonetheless, she doesn`t want to know how it's made. What she doesn`t know she won`t worry about and what she suspects she can dismiss as the taste of the cheese washes over her. The bacteria swabbed from between the Sergeants toes have been classified by microbiologists from the University of North Pembrokeshire at Crymych`s Department of Nutrition and Cheese Science based in the beautiful village of Llangloffan to the southwest of Fishguard. The scientists have given the bacteria the name Brevibacteria Sergens and treat it with respect. He is now experimenting using microbes swabbed from between The Parrot`s toes and from the organisms thus captured he has cultured strains of lactobacteria those same scientists have classifed as Lactobacillus Casei Parrota.

"And now for the bank holiday weather," said the Radio Free Pembrokeshire announcer.

"Shw' mae! Good news for bog snorkelers, torrential rain will sweep the country all weekend."

"Thank you, Derec."[37]

Rejuvenated by this news the Sergeant was overcome by a strange compulsion to do something. "Now then," he said to The Parrot, "there`s two ways we can play this. One, I can pretend I know what I`m doing ...""

"Two!" said The Parrot.

The Parrot, a keen member of the Welsh Perry and Cider Society,[38] looks after the apple trees in the orchard on the stern, a tasty accompaniment to cheese. Several varieties grow there including Afal Gwdyr, Afal Illtud, Afal Madog, Blas y Cwrw and Pippin Bach Llydan. Local bears enjoy an occasional apple as a treat. The *huerta*, situated close to the most southerly aspect of the stern, benefits from ancient irrigation canals bringing fresh water from the lake. Sweet tasting, succulent *navel* and *canoneta* oranges have flourished here since being introduced by the Moors in the 10th century.

Rhododendrons flourish on a stony outcrop to the northwest of the cowshed upon which honeybees from a hive nearby feed on nectar. The Sergeant collects the honey and can be seen late of a summer's afternoon lying back in the hammock sipping tea and munching cupcakes laced heavily with this golden fluid. Through this he gains valuable insights into the workings of his mind.

Native to the habitat close to the lake are marsh orchids with their distinctive tubers, long lanceolate leaves and dark-spotted compact flowering stem with dark to light pink flowers, marsh marigolds, each with several flowering stems carrying yolk yellow, white or magenta flowers and yellow flags up to five feet in height with large, bright-yellow flowers. Dense clumps of bulrushes grow up to eight feet tall with broad linear leaf blades and characteristic brown, cylindrical spikes.

The delicate, melodic, rippling call of willow warblers, rising quickly before slowly dying away can be heard as these small birds, approximately 4 inches in length, with greenish-brown backs, buff under parts and brown bills, feed on insects and spiders in the willow grove close to the lake. Some feed off aphids feeding off tree sap on the undersides of leaves. Their nests of grass, moss and feathers lie hidden in bramble bushes in the young birch wood nearby. The sniffle snuffle of a spicky sparrow sounds through the trees.

In the habitats from the willow grove to the rocky ground around the stone circle to the meadow and the marsh beside the lake grow knapweed, thistle-like with lance-like leaves, blackish-brown flower heads and tightly packed purple-pink inflorescence, harebells, in some places called fairy bells with their clusters of delicate blue, bell-shaped flowers atop long slender stalks reaching a height of 16 inches. They symbolise true love when seen in dreams. Hairy speedwells are plentiful with their bright-blue flowers whose lowermost petals are white on slender stalks as are ragged robin with their dark green leaves and tall stems bearing opposite, lance-shaped leaves and clusters of rose-pink flowers whose every petal is divided into four lobes creating a frayed, lace-like effect. Wild strawberries growing up to 12 inches tall with glossy, trifoliate leaves with toothed margins and hairy undersides and five-petalled white flowers with golden centres are plentiful. Common bellflowers with alternate leaves and flowers in panicles with blue-purple, five-lobed corolla dot the landscape, as do corn cockles with greyish, lanceolate leaves covered in soft hairs growing up to 40 inches in height with single, slender, deep-pink flowers 2 inches in diameter becoming white in the centre, each petal marked by two or three discontinuous black lines, and daisies with composites of small, white and yellow flowers and rosettes of spoon-shaped leaves. Orange and yellow marigolds grow alongside red poppies, yellow California poppies and Welsh poppies, papaver cambricum, not really a poppy and the only flower of the species Meconopsis that is native to Europe, with fern-like foliage and flowers consisting of four overlapping yellow petals on thin, green stems. Here and there are chicory plants, with lanceolate leaves and numerous blue, dandelion-like flowers up to 1.5 inches across that close early in the afternoon and in wet weather.

To the north of the cowshed, which lies in the pole of inaccessibility, (POI), the point on any landmass or continent that is farthest from the coast, and surrounding a prominent mound in the landscape, lies a plantation of Camellia sinensis, an evergreen shrub from east Asia. Planted in late 1625 it has been a reliable source of high-quality leaves for infusion ever since. Known locally as Gorsedd Abergwaun the mound is thought by some scholars to be the Gorsedd of the first branch of the Mabinogion, thereby challenging similar mounds near Narberth and Cardigan to be the magical place from where Pwyll went down to Annwfn, the Otherworld.

The Parrot, a keen amateur metal detectorist, recently discovered a hoard of over 17,000 Iron Age Celtic coins dating from around 150BC just two feet under the surface close to the mound. A yew tree over 3,000 years old grows close by.

Inside the cowshed, tear-shaped egg sacs of silk spun by long-jawed cave spiders, each containing up to 300 eggs and over an inch long, hang suspended by silk threads from the ceiling. Amongst the largest of Pembrokeshire's spiders, adults have a 2inch leg span. Photophobic, slow moving, and preying upon such delicacies as myriapods and slugs, they thrive in the damp, dark habitat found in the deepest corner of the building next to the cheese.

Nearby, Siberian unicorns, nearly 7 feet tall at the shoulder, 15 feet in length and weighing up to 4.5 tonnes, with long horns on noses, roam the grasslands chomping contentedly. Thought to have died out during the Late Pleistocene about 39,000 years ago to join the over 5 billion species, more than 99% of species ever to have lived on Earth, that are now extinct, the group survived by exploiting the ecological niche that is the northern reaches of the stern.

Further north, muskox, in Inuktitut, umingmak, ▷ᒥᐊᒪᒃ, graze. Tough, arctic megafauna given their own genus, Ovibos, they are more closely related to sheep and goats than to oxen. Evolving first in the temperate regions of Asia the animal adapted to cold tundra conditions late in its evolutionary history. They have been around for more than 2.5 million years and have seen Ice Ages come and go.

21

Abhall uasal farsaing frèimheach
Do'n cù'idh moladh;
Crann as ùire dh'fhàs troimh thalamh,
Làn de thoradh.

An Duanag Ullamh[1]

Noble generous deep-rooted appletree
To whom praise is fitting;
Most verdant tree that grew through earth
Full of fruit.

Bronwen lay in a heap at the base of one of the pillars after colliding with it during another energetic practice session. "A velociraptor on clogs," was how the Western Mail`s arts correspondent[2] described Bronwen`s silver medal winning performance at the Clogging World Championships in Helsinki, adding, "Yet possessed of a certain charm." She was thrilled as Megan read the report out loud to her which included the words "acrobatic" and "noisy". The bumps, scratches, cuts, contusions, bruises and other assorted injuries, both minor and a little serious, sustained to various body parts, not forgetting furniture, fixtures and fittings in the crypt, over the weeks practising the new *kamikaze* routine were worth it. The damage was temporary. Bowed, battered but never beaten after practice sessions an old zen saying kept her going, `From the withered tree a flower blooms`. When asked by a reporter from the Pembrokeshire Herald[3] if she was disappointed at not winning the gold medal Bronwen replied, "In the end only three things matter. How much we have clogged, how gently we clogged and how gracefully we let go of the gold medals not meant for us."[4]

A convocation of triple harps, crwths, pibgorns and other traditional musical instruments filled the corner of the crypt. *Y Clerddorfa* were visiting again, fresh from their gathering in *Y Galeri* in Caernarfon.

Megan picked up the dooby doo, pointed it at them, turned the volume to low, replaced the dooby doo on the small table next to her and continued reading. "Tenby Town Council[5] has ordered that all sodium streetlights in the town be turned off as they are interfering with the mating habits of local glow worms because the lights attract the male insects who prefer them to female insects.

"Typical," thought Bronwen.

"During the two-week blackout before the sodium lights were replaced by LED lights which are harmless to glow worms the darkness attracted local teenagers, both male and female. A spokesperson told the Western Mail earlier today that the Town Council does not feel responsible for improving the mating habits of local teenagers. 'Our intention is to help Tenby`s glow worms,' she said. 'Any collateral effects such as an increase in pregnancy rates amongst young women in the town is, all things considered, acceptable.'" Appalled retired Colonels in Cowbridge and Tunbridge Wells gasped and reached for fountain pen and paper.

The musicians, volume turned down low, sang in the background, accompanying themselves with their home-made instruments. It was a song that reached high in the charts several decades ago.

> *Dum, dum, dum, dum, dum, dum, dum, dum,*
> *Dum, dum, dum, dum, dum, dum, dum, dum,*
> *Dum, ...Dum, Dum, Dum..*

> *You keep saying you`ve got something for me,*
> *Something you call love, but confess,*
> *You`ve been cloggin` where you shouldn`t have been a cloggin`*
> *And now someone else is gettin` all your best.*

> *These clogs are made for cloggin', and that`s just what they`ll do.*
> *One of these days these clogs are gonna clog all over you.*

> *Dum, dum, dum, dum, dum, dum, dum, dum,*
> *Dum, dum, dum, dum, dum, dum, dum, dum,*
> *Dum, ...Dum, Dum, Dum.[6]*

Megan was sitting in her armchair by the fire in the *simne fawr*. She put the newspaper on the small table next to her and picked up the library books she was going to read. She always reads two novels at a time, one in Welsh and one in English. "Which one to begin?" she wondered.

Bronwen stirred.

"I`ll decide after a coffee," thought Megan, noticing the stirring. "Another coffee?" she enquired.

"Wouldn`t that be too much? I thought you were pacing yourself."

"I am, my dear. I`m having one after the other."

Bronwen pulled herself to her feet using the gargoyles on the pillar as hand holds, a trick she learnt on a recent Machlud y Wawr[7] mountaineering course in north Wales where the Members climbed the *arêtes* of Crib Goch and Y Lliwedd before tackling the north facing Clogwyn Du`r Arddu. They left Yr Wyddfa for another day. "I`ll make the coffee," she mumbled. "Expressos?"

"Yes, please," replied Megan, yawning sleepily.

"Doubles?"

"That would be best, my dear."

Bronwen collected the empty coffee cups and disappeared into the kitchen from where, moments later, sounds emerged. Strange sounds, as if the very fabric of space time itself was unravelling. Or was it her tummy rumbling? "Toast?" came a shaky voice from nowhere.

"Ooh! Yes pleaeaease! In the beginning was the word, and the word was toast."[8]

Are you a Marmiteer[9] or a marmaladeer this morning?"

"Hmmm. Marmalade is a fine thing to have on your toast first thing in the morning but sometimes its subtle charms cannot compare with the vicious wake-up call that toast thickly spread with Marmite delivers. Marmite please."

"Soldiers?"

"What a good idea."

Things in the kitchen were slow. Megan picked up a book and began reading.

"Won`t be long," came Bronwen`s voice after a while.

"Good. I`m not fond of long soldiers."

Bronwen was in the kitchen and Megan is always on her guard if she closes the door and therefore cannot be seen by an independent observer as it means that Bronwen might exist in a number of different states simultaneously until, once again, she is observed. This is known in Brynberian as the Copenhagen Interpretation. Schrödinger,[10] in an early work, suggested this would not unduly influence the flavour of the coffee. Richard Feynman,[11] the Nobel Prize winning physicist wrote, "If you think you understand Bronwen, you don't understand Bronwen."

Bronwen crashed out of the kitchen carrying a tray laden with two cups of Expresso and two piles of toast, one with butter and marmalade, one with butter and Marmite. "Heaven on a tray. How often do you walk into the kitchen and make exactly what you want to eat even though before going in you didn't know you wanted to eat it?"

A few minutes later they were sitting opposite one another sipping coffee. Bronwen was rereading the *Library of Wales short story anthology, volumes 1 and 2*.[12] When reading these books for the first time they induced a profound change in her world view. Powerfully informative, they deeply influenced her susceptible mind. If any experience in her life `formed` her, reading these books was it. She was engrossed. "These are difficult books," she thought, "they can`t be begun and finished on a tube ride from Brynberian to Crymych Centrum." She frequently put them down for long periods and looked at the wall opposite her, concentrating as she struggled with the content whilst scratching her head. For Bronwen, pausing whilst reading a book does greater justice to a book`s content than simply reading it. 'They also read who are not turning pages', as someone once said.

Megan sighed contentedly, picked up the dooby doo and turned *Y Clerddorfa*, who were singing a medley of Pembrokeshire folk songs, off, and the radio on. "Just in time for the news."

The voice of the Radio Free Crymych announcer poured itself into the crypt. "A Neyland man has invented a hearse that cremates the body as it goes and uses the energy to power the engine."

"Good heavens!" Muttered Megan. The colour drained from Bronwen`s face. Thoughts shaped like small metal balls ricocheted around the pinball machine that is her mind.

The announcer continued. "A Narberth man has been accused by his *fiancée* of setting fire to her house, causing considerable damage. Miss Evans claims he was drunk, fell asleep whilst smoking a cigarette and set fire to the bed. In an audacious rebuttal he claims the bed was on fire when he got into it, a defence she strenuously denies. And now to music. Crymych based band Callach, the only rock group to have changed the course of European history, are playing at the Queen`s Hall in Narberth tonight. Their music is difficult to describe, sort of a fusion of free jazz, driving rock and roll and Morriston Orpheus conducted by Frank Zappa. They are supported by the Penny Sows from Down Below. And now for the weather."

"Bore da! People in Pembrokeshire might be able to switch their lights off later today as there is a chance of it brightening up this afternoon. Oh dear! I can feel a couple of lines from a traditional song coming on ..."

There is many a dark and a cloudy morning
Turns out to be a sunshiny day.

"Thank you, Derec."[13]

Megan enjoyed the singing, which was in the style of the Gower Nightingale,[14] then turned the radio off and put the dooby doo back on the table. The crypt was enveloped in silence.

"I hope it stops raining soon because I`ve got to water the garden," said Bronwen, looking through the window at the vegetable patch outside. "I might go for a walk today instead and do the watering tomorrow."

"Today and tomorrow are not really different," Megan reminded her.

"I used to spend a lot of time thinking but I see now that it hasn`t got me anywhere, so more and more I`m enjoying all the other things that don`t get me anywhere, like sitting under the apple trees next to the vegetable patch waiting for the rain to stop, then smelling the earth." She paused to take a breath. "Thought has its limits and I get beyond the limits next to vegetables. In the garden there is sitting. In the garden there are trees and shade and there are vegetables and there is growing. Sometimes I ask the trees a question and return weeks later for the answer, things being slower in the lives of trees as communicating via interconnected root systems is a process that can't be rushed. The garden is where slow motion was invented." She does not worry about where she is going, for she knows that she is already there.

Wind chimes hanging by golden silk threads from the branches of the apple trees next to the vegetable patch sang their tinkling songs as the breeze passed between them.

They sipped and munched, then sipped and munched some more and as they did so the rain stopped, the clouds dispersed, and the sun came out. "As the colour blue is inseparable from the sky, so the coffee is inseparable from the water," murmured Bronwen,[15] adding, "I love apples."

"Do you dear?"

Megan sipped long and deep. "Aaaah! Mission accomplished, blood caffeine levels restored to optimum levels." Back at maximum efficiency Megan got up, went to the far corner of the crypt and began dusting her extensive collection of Geraint Jarman a`r Cynganeddwyr memorabilia. Old age is permanently many years ahead of her. "This morning I feel about twenty-five or maybe twenty-six," she said.

"Is that chronologically?" queried Bronwen.

"You make me sound like a barometer, dear."

"I want to live in a world where cats live on milk and mice eat cheese," replied Bronwen earnestly.

Megan continued dusting. "You are an 'incorrigible latitudinarian'," she informed Bronwen, who smiled happily at this great compliment.[16]

"Why do some words have so many letters in them? Are they ganging up on the next word?"

"Perhaps, dear, and there`s probably a word for it, although I don`t know what it is. Sometimes I think there are too many words. And some of them do seem to go on for a long time."

"It`s an enduring problem," said Bronwen. "But that`s life I suppose." A thought crossed her mind, passing through her imagination before skirting her reasoning. "Is there a word that describes the process of coining a word that is totally unnecessary? Defenestration, for example. Why would anyone want to make up a word like that? This is one of the Knock-on effects of reading dictionaries, and a serious matter, as can be seen from the capital K, even though it is silent." She stayed seated, enjoying the coffee and marmalade toast, recovering from the previous day`s bout of binge clogging following which she was found collapsed and exhausted in a heap on the steps of City Hall after the annual Shepherds and Hoggers Ball. Binge clogging is a growing social problem in parts of rural Wales, particularly at weekends. Friday and Saturday nights are the danger times. She told the ambulance crew she had been practising for an extreme clogging event in St Davids later in the year, but Megan knows she`s been binge clogging for months and is in denial. Megan finished the dusting and went back to her chair, making a detour on the way to give Bronwen a *cwtsh*. "Thank you," said Bronwen. "A *cwtsh* is good for you, it releases a hormone called oxysomething that reduces stress, relieves pain and boosts your immune system." Megan was impressed and gave her another one before putting a log on the fire and returning to her seat. "In fact, a good *cwtsh*, dark chocolate and freshly roasted coffee works marvels for a person's health."

Megan remembered how her husband cared for her. When she was young her parents left Cardiff and moved to north Pembrokeshire for the good life. She was the eldest of five children. They bought a smallholding called Bryn Eithin, with a rambling farmhouse and outbuildings near Llanycefn and left friends, relatives, and good jobs as architects behind them. But they discovered it was not as easy as they had hoped, and their dream slowly crumbled. They couldn`t run Bryn Eithin and work, they couldn`t run it full stop. The money ran out and they failed to find jobs. Megan`s abiding memory of childhood is of being cold.

A little while after she was married her husband went away for a while, he spent an afternoon at the bottom of the garden, digging and weeding the vegetable patch. Whilst there, having travelled such a long way south, he spent much of the time lying in the long grass enjoying the sunshine, letting life be. During an extended tea break he composed and wrote a love letter to Megan in which he promised that ensuring she would never experience being cold again was one of the great aims of his life, greater even than the one about eating chocolate. With him she would always be warm. After the tea break, he was overcome by an irresistible urge to be with her.

Megan was in another part of the garden near the plum, peach and apricot bushes and watering the azaleas as he appeared, a huge smile on his face. "Wonderful news, cariad," he exclaimed.

"What`s that, cariad?"

"I love you," he replied, and kissed her. "Oh, and this letter just arrived for you." He handed a scraggly piece of paper to her then turned and went back to the sunshine, just in time for the next tea break.

Glowing, she stood for a while watching him go, put the watering can down then read the letter. "You`re safe with me. Quietly, out there around the raggedy edges of your life, where you don`t notice, I take care of you." Pondering these kind words, a tear forming in one eye, she folded the letter, placed it carefully in the breast pocket of her overalls, the one next to her heart, picked up the watering can and continued with the gardening.

The sound of Bronwen's voice appeared out of the stillness in the crypt. "Why is the subjunctive disappearing from all western European languages?"

"The subjunctive is a psychological phenomenon," Megan informed her, "as are all moods."

"I see." Although she wasn't sure.

"They appear out of a formless background."

"If you say so."

"Everything we experience via the five senses and the mind, which in the East is regarded as being a sixth sense and not put on a pedestal as it is in the West, is an illusion and doesn't really exist."

A deep rumination swept through Bronwen who, deep down, is empty space, even after consuming a double expresso and a pile of marmalade toast. Her electrons are fuzzy waves spread diffusely along their orbit. Some days she is fuzzier than others, at times she is a mere probability.

Unconcerned at this, Megan's thoughts returned to the garden and to an idea for her talk to the Members later that afternoon. "It's counter intuitive, but green plants do not need green light. They can do very well with light from the red, blue or yellow parts of the spectrum. Using LEDs our growing pots in the Cathedral cellars produce fruit, veg, herbs and lettuces in abundance. LEDs produce hardly any heat and can be placed around the plants, so they get light from above, below and the sides. No need for windows. The *cwtsh dan staer* in the average Member's house can produce fresh food for the family." Bronwen's beautiful, carefree smile returned.

"What are you going to do today, dear?" Megan asked.

"Well, earlier on a plan seemed to be forming, then the sun came out and the plan got all vague and indistinct. Maybe I'll have some coffee."

"That's a good plan," said Megan nodding. "I'll join you. Why don't we take the coffee outside and sit under the apple trees? I'll bring the lute."

Bronwen returned to the kitchen, pressed on with the coffee making, and soon they were sitting barefoot on the grass in the shade of the trees enjoying the scent of the earth after the rain and a portion each of a delicate freshly made summer fruit *Génoise* sponge cake served with blueberries, strawberries and cream. All washed down with cinnamon flavoured *cappuccinos*.

Coffee and cake finished, Bronwen got up to wander around the garden admiring the wildflowers. She particularly likes the purple ones which she thinks bring good luck. She looked down. "Toes are fascinating," she informed Megan. Bright shafts of sunlight pierced the shade beneath the apple trees and all around her butterflies danced in their warmth. "Butterfly dust," she whispered to Megan. "I'm standing in butterfly dust. Look!" Megan was puzzled. "Butterfly wings," Bronwen continued, "are made from millions of tiny scales that come together to create what looks like one solid pair of wings. The coloured scales create the beautiful patterns. Every time a butterfly flies some scales fall off, like dust, and as a butterfly gets older the colours and patterns fade. I'm standing in butterfly dust," she marvelled. Megan looked around her at the grass and moss floor covered in butterfly dust and smiled deeply. Time passed and the happiness that imbued the simplicity of their lives matured in the silence. The breeze picked up and the apple trees waved at the sky. The orchard, where the mundane and the sacred are one.

"It is predicted," Megan proffered, "that within a few decades artificial intelligence will take over every job and machines will be humanlike. Perhaps," she continued, "yet will a machine ever stand beneath the apple blossoms gazing in wonder at the butterfly dust settling on its toes?"

"Much of the happiness of the world can be found in Crymych," said Bronwen, "even though it's a relatively small city by world standards. There must be a lot more happiness in cities like Swansea and Brasilia for there are lots more people there." She came to the realisation that standing in the butterfly dust, bathed by streams of sunlight coming through the apple trees is a wonderful thing, and determined to stay there for the rest of the morning. Flowing in the moment, she sang and danced all three parts of a *canso* written by a thirteenth century Occitan *trobairitz*, as Megan accompanied her on the lute. Following this she paused, squatted, thus lowering her voice, and produced a creditable rendition of Lee Marvin singing an old Western ballad.

Where am I goin'?
I don't know.
Where am I headin'?
I ain't certain.
All I know is
I am on my way

When will I be there?
I don't know.
When will I get there?
I ain't certain.
All that I know is
I am on my way.[17]

Megan was pleased Bronwen was doing something useful. Putting the lute down she took her gaze from the butterfly dust, picked up the copy of *Clebran* she had taken with her into the garden and began reading quietly to herself so as not to disturb Bronwen's musical meditations. "Crymych's new arts centre will be officially opened on Friday evening by the city's Lord Mayoress. Hailed by city councillors as a cultural powerhouse for Pembrokeshire the building cost £37 million pounds and is situated on a four-and-a-half-acre site just off the Piazza della Republica next to the astrodome. It will open in a blaze of publicity and fireworks with a weekend of films, drama, music, live performances and exhibitions. It has four cinemas, two theatres, exhibition space, a concert hall, a bar, two *cafés* and a lecture theatre. It will also provide a permanent home for Machlud y Wawr's 'Spinning and Weaving' outreach programme. During Saturday's Science fest a lecture will be given by Teifion Williams, professor of photonic engineering at Cambridge University, who will discuss the future of optical processors." Megan had already booked seats for herself and some of the Members for this event. "How enlightened of the organisers to include science in an Arts Centre," she thought, before continuing. "Optical processors perform calculations using light instead of electricity and have five hundred times more power than the world's fastest supercomputer. They use laser beams and tiny reservoirs of liquid crystal, are a hundred times cheaper to build than conventional computers and run on a fraction of the energy. They are also very small, the equivalent of a conventional supercomputer being the size of a Gwen Parrott novel."[18] "Exciting times," she exclaimed. "Exciting times indeed." Turning the page, she was surprised to read a short announcement about herself. "Well, I never did!" she declared, delighted to discover she had been included on the Forbe's list[19] of the world's most powerful women.

Megan and Bronwen were booked at a meeting in the Great Court of Crymych Museum that afternoon with Machlud y Wawr members from all over Wales. The museum was designed using *lemniscate* and *viviani* curves and recently won a global prize for sustainable architecture, coming second only to the Step Pyramid of Djoser. The Great Court itself is rectangular in form and inspired by the *bouleuterion* at Priene. The meeting was at two o'clock on the dot, Bronwen being a stickler for punctuality, a personality trait she put down to the few days she spent in the little German town of Gerbersau at the beginning of July 1977 during a pilgrimage to Hermann Hesse's birthplace. More than nine million people visit the Hesse museum every year, many of them from Pembrokeshire, drawn by the treasures contained within. The museum was opened on St Davids Day in 1752.

After the meeting, which would be long and boring and mainly about the organisation's finances, they planned to go to the city's multiplex for a screening of 1953's *How to Marry a Millionaire*,[20] based on the true story of three fashion models who share an apartment in Haverfordwest and who intend marrying for money. The film has as its stars Marilyn Monroe, Betty Grable, and Lauren Bacall as the leader of the pack. Bronwen in particular is looking forward to the screening even though she has seen the film over a dozen times as she thinks the ladies' fashions in the film are to die for. She also quite likes the idea of marrying a millionaire and is looking for pointers. So as not to miss any tips she will prepare to get the best out of it by sleeping through the meeting. As usual Megan has arranged for background music with ten-second phrases to be played during the discussions as this coincides with the natural rhythms by which the brain regulates heart rate. Great works such as the *Chorus of the Hebrew Slaves*,[21] the *Four Seasons*,[22] *Ave Maria*,[23] sung in Latin, Indian sitar ragas and the *Power of Equality*[24] have a calming effect on the cardiovascular system and can lower blood pressure and heart rate. Machlud y Wawr debates have improved in quality since this initiative began, as has the quality of Bronwen's sleep during them.

Megan jots down notes during meetings which help keep the details sharp in her mind. Over the years she has devised her own encrypted shorthand which would defeat the toughest of code breakers. It is based on that of Pitman, the Welsh language version. "The Russians will never get to know our innermost secrets," she tells younger members, who are always impressed. Bronwen, when not asleep, emulates Megan by making her own notes in pencil in *prosimetrum* style and mysterious in many ways, but then she moves in mysterious ways. The notes are then rewritten using the 13,000 symbols of the Tironian shorthand,[25] particularly helpful as they are based on Latin and their use declined after the 12th century and are therefore little-known today. She then erases the notes with a rubber and reuses the paper by writing shopping lists on them at a ninety-degree angle to the notes thus creating a *palimpsest* which can only be read by using multi-spectral imaging. Added to this, the notes only exist if she is looking at them. Bronwen herself only exists if somebody is looking at her, an added layer of security.

Bronwen's gentle singing voice appeared at the edges of Megan's attention. She listened for a moment, closed the paper, put it on the ground and lay back, inviting the song to join her thoughts as they went back in time to her husband.

"Cariad!"

"Yes, cariad."

"Will you do something for me?"

"Of course, cariad."

They were sitting under a tree on the hillside to the north of the smallholding, looking south across the narrow valley to the woodland on the other side, warmed by the late evening sun. The three dogs lay on the grass next to them and the chickens, ducks and geese wandered contentedly about. He held her hand. She held his.

"Can I tell you something I've observed about you? Even though you might take it as a criticism, become defensive, then go into attack mode."

"Yes."

"Usually, you add two and two and make four."

"That's good, cariad."

He squeezed her hand. "Yes. Sometimes though you make five, and we miss."

She squeezed his hand.

"At those times let the thoughts be and feel the love between us. Be certain that we are one, and always will be."

She leant over and kissed him.

Megan sighed. Lifting her left foot, she shook the butterfly dust gently from between her toes, then did the same with her right foot, noticing the myriad colours reflecting off the dust as it was caught in a beam of sunlight.

Bronwen remained in a state of high alert. "It's better to believe that faeries are the cause of much of the goings on at the bottom of the garden," she whispered to the apple trees, "than to deny the existence of the garden."[26] Several weeks later, the trees agreed. Looking up, Megan watched as Bronwen put the finishing touches to a garland of crow-flowers, nettles, daisies and long purples which she then placed lightly on her head.

Taking account of the position of the sun whilst incorporating unseen gravitational forces into her computations, Bronwen engaged deeply with her inner 'pleasures and jollity'[27] and performed a waggle dance. It began with her skipping in a straight line, known technically as the waggle run, waggling her bottom animatedly as she went, before looping to the right and moving back to the beginning. She repeated the waggle run, waggling her bottom animatedly as she went, before looping to the left and moving back to the beginning, thus creating a figure of eight. This was repeated many times, the length of the waggle run indicating how far they were from the kitchen and the angle to the sun demonstrating, unnecessarily Megan thought, the direction they would need to travel to find it. The number of waggle runs signalled how many portions of summer fruit *Génoise* sponge cake were left in the fridge.

"Hmmm," thought Megan. "A large *mocha* made from dark, freshly roasted beans with cocoa powder and cream ..." She lay back on the grass, closed her eyes and felt the warmth from shafts of sunlight that found their way through a gap in the foliage above caress her face. "... with dark chocolate shavings and whipped cream on top, perhaps?" Thinking back to her husband she sang a few lines of a song to the exquisite beauty of the moment and offered them to the enchanted orchard.

> *If I had the wings of a snow-white dove*
> *I'd preach the gospel, the gospel of love.*
> *A love so real, a love so true,*
> *I've made up my mind to give myself to you.*[28]

Bronwen, her work complete, stopped waggling and trod barefoot in the direction of the kitchen, the soft grass tickling her toes as she went. "What is the meaning of an apple tree?" she wondered curiously.

"To Be, simply to Be. Just like Me," came a voice on the wind.

"And me, and everybody," Megan affirmed.

Inspired by this train of thought Bronwen offered a song of her own to the orchard of existence.

> *To pray to a tree is to pray to Me,*
> *Yet to pray to Me is to miss Me.*
> *Life is not to do, it's to Be.*
> *Best not to be busy being somebody.*
> *Just Be. You and Me.*
> *No you, all Me.*

High amongst the branches of a nearby apple tree a passing solitary leafcutter bee, black with pale yellow strips on her abdomen and face, on a journey gathering pollen, waggles her abdomen in delight. Pollen falling from it showers onto the flowers below. An unexpected consequence. Bronwen and Megan collect apples in the autumn to make cider, leaving windfalls for insects, birds, small mammals and pigs to feast upon through into winter. Leftover pulp from the cider making process is fed to the clutch of chickens that, in the daytime, run wild in the orchard and in the meadow. Amongst the apple trees, earwigs, with characteristic pincers to rear, munch contentedly on common pests such as aphids, codling moths, leaf rollers, scale insects and psyllids. Predatory phytoseiid mites wander hungrily over leaves, chomping on delicious red spider mites as they go.

In the pollinator strip around the vegetable patch are large numbers of flowering plants such as Jacob's Ladder with its sprays of blue flowers and prominent yellow stamens, annual mallows with pink and white flowers up to two inches across, sapphire blue cornflowers, tall broad-leaved Helleborines with greenish, purplish-red flowers arranged in long drooping racemes and broad, ribbed leaves spiralling around the stem, and many more. Fruiting shrubs and grasses grow in the sunnier spots, sedges and rushes in shady, damper areas. The strip hums and buzzes with bees searching for nectar and pollen. The bee hotels dotted around the area are full. Butterflies, midges, flies, beetles and ants are active. Wasps, lured to the orchids, buzz as they feed on spiders, ants, bees and flies and collect honeydew. Mosquitoes feed on nectar. Later, moths will appear, attracted to the strong, sweet scent released by Jasmines growing nearby with their clusters of fragrant white and pale-pink flowers about one inch in size.

At rest on a bank nearby amongst wild thyme, oxlips, violets, woodbine, musk roses and eglantine a grass snake basks in the sun.

In the forest to the north a yellow and black striped hornet more than one and a half inches long is busy stripping bark from an ancient oak.

22

When you come to a fork in the road, take it.

Yogi Berra[1]

Stillness pervaded the galley. Out of the formless appeared the Sergeant. Life at play. The Parrot, deep in meditation on its perch, smiled knowingly and coughed. The Sergeant sensed something extraordinary was happening. "Time for a mug of tea," he decided, keeping caution close.

The breeze outside moved the sails in the rigging and high above sea level to the west, blew through Harbour Village, that sought-after subsidiary of Goodwick where freezing air currents dry clothes hanging on washing lines decorated with myriad primary-coloured Tibetan prayer flags dancing in the penetrating, glacial wind. Discouraged during the Cultural Revolution, prayer flags remain popular on this remote high-altitude plateau teetering on the cliff edge overlooking Fishguard Harbour far below to the east.

Passengers on the Town Service bus, climbing rapidly as it ascended the steep south facing escarpment from Goodwick Square to Harbour Village did not notice the oxygen saturation of their haemoglobin fall rapidly as the atmospheric pressure decreased exponentially with altitude. The driver kept the vehicle in low gear as it approached the death zone where the amount of oxygen in the atmosphere is insufficient to sustain human life. A tourist sitting near the front, recklessly ignoring acclimatisation advice given to her in the Visitor Centre on the Parrog, showed early signs of acute mountain sickness. Over thousands of years the inhabitants of Harbour Village have adapted to the lower oxygen levels with enlarged lung volumes, lower haemoglobin concentration and an increased cerebral blood flow. Life for incomers on this extreme altitude *plateau* is fraught with hazards. Sleeping is difficult, digesting food almost impossible, recurrent medical problems such as high-altitude cerebral oedema are common, and, in this rarefied atmosphere, clothes take a long time to dry.

The Sergeant returned to the formless then reappeared again trillions of times each moment. Unsettled by this and a mite seasick he set about making breakfast. "Everything falls into place, everything happens naturally," he muttered in a rare moment of lucidity as he switched the kettle on and began unwrapping the loaf of white, extra thick, fibre reduced, sliced bread. Impressed, The Parrot came out of its meditative state, undid the full lotus position, stood up, shook its legs a couple of times to help blood circulation and looked around. Noticing with a start that the Sergeant had begun making himself a sandwich to accompany his tea it hastily reassumed the full lotus and returned to the safety of the blissful state.

Donning scorched oven gloves and with the deft and efficient movements born of experience the Sergeant built two large Marmite,[2] Peanut Butter,[3] raspberry jam, banana and raw onion sandwiches which he placed gingerly on a plate which in turn he placed on the table. By this time the kettle had boiled. Sprinkling a handful of bog standard builder's tea bags into an old battered mug adorned with the words *Sam Warburton was innocent* in Welsh, Cornish, English, Irish, Ulster Scots, Scots Gaelic, Scots, French, Basque, Breton and Italian he covered them with boiling water and set about stirring vigorously for the recommended ten minutes in order to gain the full benefit of the rich *bouquet* of delicate flavours. The concoction of chemicals began suffusing the water in the mug. Five minutes or so into the process, as the darkening fluid thickened, he changed to a stronger spoon. When the stirring period was finished, he added a splash of full fat milk, took the mug of tea to the table, sat down and raised it to his nose to inhale the aroma. A puzzled frown swept his boyish features, and he became momentarily confused. Was he inhaling an attractively arranged bunch of flowers such as is used during a ceremonial occasion or given to a loved one as a gift? "No!" he said, decisively, "It's the characteristic scent of perfume or wine. Or tea, of course, in this case. And it is good. Very good. Vintage in fact, though I say so myself." He sipped the tea and munched the sandwiches which, for safety reasons, he held between the oven gloves with the recommended Vulcan Death Grip.[4] In the background the ambient temperature in the galley began to rise. A warning light flashed somewhere out of sight.

The plate and the table are constructed from fire resistant composite steel and their strength is improved by the inclusion of mesh reinforcement. Building regulations oblige engineers to ensure such equipment is safe. The regulations state that they be designed and constructed so that, in the event of a fire, their stability shall be maintained for a reasonable period. Recently, The Parrot was advised that its perch will be modified to meet these requirements with the added precaution that the perch's load bearing capacity will continue to function until it has escaped. A sprinkler system designed to suppress sandwich fires on or shortly after ignition or to contain such fires for a long enough period to allow the crew to escape is fitted in the galley. The oven gloves are covered with a thin film intumescent coating, a paint like substance which is inert at low temperatures but when heated swells to provide a charred layer of low conductivity which acts as insulation. Given the extreme nature of the sandwich eating procedure the Sergeant is advised to buy a new pair every year.

Breakfast finished the Sergeant decamped to the hammock. The Parrot flew out of the starboard porthole and proceeded in an orderly fashion to the willow grove where it settled on a low-lying branch in one of the willow trees.

Looking around from this vantage point it noted how pretty the illusion looked in late summer. Lying at peace in the gently swaying hammock the Sergeant felt the air temperature drop. He opened his eyes and, looking around, noticed a dark cloud in the sky, blocking out the sun. "Dark cloud nor' by nor' east," he informed The Parrot. He loved the way nautical terms trip off the tongue. The Parrot noted that the cloud was sou' by sou' west but said nothing as its mind was at peace and it saw no reason to interfere with that interesting form of the illusion that is 'the Sergeant'. "All is well," it thought, but unfurled an umbrella and held it over its head just in case.

The cloud approached, getting closer and closer, bigger and bigger. A sense of unease came over the Sergeant. Suddenly it dawned on him. Millions of spiders were mass ballooning, the breeze catching gossamer threads released from their spinnerets as they were carried towards the coracle by the prevailing wind. Having travelled many long nautical miles on the air currents the spiders were relieved to find themselves dropping down onto the coracle where they could have a break, as being carried many long nautical miles on air currents can be tiresome. With no control over their direction of travel, nor where they land, they considered the freshwater lake on the stern a pleasant and fortuitous rest-over spot where their natural skills on water would get them to dry land, which in this case was the coracle, to rest awhile before becoming airborne to balloon again. "Spiders!" He said grumpily. "The shock troops of evolution, dropping like paratroopers from the clear blue sky." The spiders spent a refreshing afternoon annoying the Sergeant before returning to the water of the lake to be lifted once again into the air. They ballooned *en masse* to Llys y Fran where they have relatives.

The Sergeant thought it might be a good time to read something and rummaging amongst the well-stocked pile of books strewn on the deck underneath the hammock he chose a secondhand paperback copy of *Zhou Hou Bei Ji Fang*,[5] a book on Chinese medicine he received as a present whilst patrolling the Yangtze river several years ago, and got back into the hammock. A colleague from the Yangtze Police Rapid-Response Junk Unit, who use a variation of this ancient vessel adapted for use on the river, read and translated the text to him during a joint exercise between the DPPRRCU and the YPRRJU during which their flotilla of vessels journeyed the 6,300 kilometres down the waters of this mighty river from the glaciers on the Qinghai-Tibet Plateau eastward across southwest, central and eastern China to where it empties into the East China Sea at Shanghai. He experienced many wonderful moments during the voyage, the most memorable being the passage over, and at one point he could have sworn, under the Three Gorges Dam, the largest hydro-electric power station in the world.

During the months spent on the river the Sergeant was intrigued to see finless porpoises, Yangtze Sturgeon, golden-finned chuprassies and Chinese Paddlefish along the way. One evening, suffering from a bout of *hiraeth*, he was stood at the rail on the port deck dreaming of home when he heard a splash and caught a glimpse of a Yangtze River Dolphin or *baiji* which his colleagues later told him was thought to be extinct. They and the wider scientific community in China showed their gratitude for his discovery by presenting him with the signed copy of *Zhou Hou Bei Ji Fang*.

Unable to read Chinese he stopped at page twenty-seven, closed the book, reached down and returned it to the library under the hammock which contains such books as *Siddhartha* by Herman Hesse, Picador 1973, translated by Hilda Rosner, his favourite ever novel, *The Dhammapada*, *The Tao Te Ching* and *The Mystery of Edwin Drood* by Charles Dickens. The Sergeant reads the latter once every seven years and each time thinks of a new ending which he shares with The Parrot, who is yet to be convinced. Other works in the collection include *Miracle of Love* by Ram Dass, Thucydides' *History of the Lemon Grove War*,[6] *Libri Wallae Vols 1 and 2*, *Gone with the Faeries* by Emerald Universe, *A Field Guide to the Birds on the Stern* by naturalist Iolo Williams,[7] *Coracles of the World, Vols 1-6*, a signed first edition of *The Five Branches of the Mabinogion*, *Illicit Interludes* by Kat Kiraly, a much loved copy of *The Hedges of the Stern*,[8] a first edition 1973, after reading which he realised that some of the hedges on the stern have been growing there since the Bronze Age, Leonard Cohen`s *Great Book of Coracling Songs*,[9] the classic *East of Eglwyswrw*[10] and a first edition of the *Whole Earth Catalog*, to name but a few.

Turning onto his side he peered over the edge of the hammock intending to choose a book, falling out of it as he did so. From his vantage point on the deck, he looked up at his collection of mountaineering books. "Which one?" he mused. "*Sherpas and Preseli Mountaineering; Trecking in the North Pembrokeshire Mountain Range: A Route and Planning Guide; Copa: How to Get There; Conquering the Seven Summits of the Preselis; Carn Ingli: The First Ascent: The Untold Story of Gruffudd Puw, the Man Who Made It Possible;*[11] *The Hills of the Chankly Bore: A Field Guide; A Trekking Guide to the Gwaun Valley.*"

Quite tired out by all this exertion the Sergeant decided to make a mug of tea and getting to his feet set off for the galley. *En route* to the kettle the Sergeant decided that upon his return to the willow grove he would read the trekking guide to the Gwaun Valley as it had lots of pictures in it. As this thought appeared in his mind, from where he had no idea, he felt a pleasant sensation arise in his mesolimbic dopamine system. He knew he had made the right decision. "I'm feeling much embettered," he remarked, unaware that the verb has been declared obsolete. Unperturbed, he continued on his way.

"Give me a glimpse into your culture," The Parrot called after him as he disappeared from view.

The Parrot's eyes rolled upwards as it rolled backwards, executing a perfect $180°$ backwards half rotation before coming to rest upside down on the branch, looking out to sea. "Einstein was wrong," it thought. "You think this world of the senses is real, that life is outside of yourself, and then you go looking for it there. That's what madness is."

The Sergeant took no notice, his mind was on the tea and thoughts of toast were in a holding pattern in the formless waiting to appear in his mind. It was going to be a busy morning.

The Parrot joined the Sergeant who was happily sipping tea and munching toast in the galley and took up position on the perch where it began reading a dual language copy of *An Eochair, Yr Allwedd*[12] it found in Charlie Byrne's in Galway City when it and the Sergeant moored there overnight whilst returning from an exchange visit to Inis Oírr where they spent several months on manoeuvres with the Galway Bay Rapid-Response Hooker Unit.[13] Technically the visit was to have lasted a week, but time slows in the *craic*.

Unexpectedly, the Sergeant felt his toes twitch. "Why my toes?" he wondered, glancing down to see what was going on. Gradually, in unhurried fashion, the twitching passed upwards, moving a little beyond his knees, before returning, at a regular pace, to his toes. The Parrot sneezed. "God save us from all harm," it muttered, crossing itself as it did so, influenced no doubt by its choice of reading material. The Sergeant shook one foot, then the other, and the twitches passed harmlessly up into the air before leaving through an open porthole. Stimulated by this development his frontal cortex engaged with the toast he was holding in his right hand which he noticed was fast approaching. His mouth opened automatically, he took a bite, and the process of munching began. His right hand returned to the table, replaced the remainder of the toast on the plate and waited, poised, to pick up the mug of steaming tea.

A thought arrived. "Me and the paddle are one." Intrigued by this he paid attention as more thoughts arrived. "The paddle is the paddle, and I am the observer of the paddle. I am the final link in the chain of observational processes and the paddle can only be understood in terms of how it interacts with me. Yet even doer, the doing, the paddle and the ocean done to must fall away." He stopped munching and let the thoughts be, admiring them in a puzzled sort of a way yet pleased with them. "Hmmm!" he muttered.

"*Maintenant, mon commandant*, you are full of not knowing," The Parrot explained to him gently. "As am I." Moments passed as more munching happened. The Parrot waited patiently on its perch to see if there was going to be a breakthrough.

"Ah yes!" Exclaimed the Sergeant. "That's it!"

"*Formidable.*" The Parrot sensed progress was being made.

"More toast."

The Parrot did not show its disappointment, that would have been unkind. Not that the Sergeant would have noticed. It put its head under its port wing and went to sleep.

By the light of the kerosene hurricane lantern swinging wildly from the roof of the galley as the vessel see-sawed furiously in the rough, storm swept waters of Fishguard Harbour, and undeterred by the incessant drumming noise of the rain on the portholes, the Sergeant continued reminiscing about past adventures, this time his work experience as a raw recruit along the Silk Road. Whilst hopelessly lost on this ancient pathway he was surprised to discover there was more than one. During the trip he spent a long weekend enjoying the company of locals along the route by whom he was wined and dined as was their custom after long centuries of offering hospitality to passing strangers. He was entranced by their glorious traditional music and dance. During his stay he moored the coracle to a large stone the locals called the *omphalos* which stood on the village square. When questioned later by historians as to its location he failed to recall where along the Silk Roads it was. This inability to remember detail caused no doubt by the strong local beer that had been part of the generous hospitality. Also, as he explained, he's not particularly interested in large stones with personal names, apart from Pentre Ifan and Carreg Samson and .... "Oh dear!" He muttered under his breath. "It's somewhere along the Silk Roads," he told them, trying to be helpful. But it was too late.

The grandmother clock in the corner of the galley between the artwork and the multi-disc CD player chimed. Before he was married it was a grandfather clock. "Grandmother clocks only exist in our minds," the Sergeant informed the piece of toast on the plate, before focussing his attention on it, picking it up, taking a bite out of it and munching. The grandmother clock had already disappeared. "This means that everything outside our minds does not experience grandmother clocks."

Encouraged by developments The Parrot commented. "Grandmother clocks are an illusion in the world of subject and object, me and you, that our mind creates. To go beyond grandmother clocks is to go beyond our minds, beyond thought, beyond subject and object."

The strain appeared on the Sergeant's face, sweat dripped off his forehead. "To go beyond grandmother clocks, you must become one with grandmother clocks."

"No need. Just leave the thoughts be. They appear, abide a moment, then disappear. Grandmother clocks appear as thoughts appear, abide with them, and disappear with them. Let the thoughts be and you let grandmother clocks be and experience grandmotherclocklessness."

"Nothing!" exclaimed the Sergeant.

"Not even that," said The Parrot. "Your senses are an interface to simplify the complexity of the universe. We create a grandmother clock when we look and destroy it when we look away. Something exists when we don't look, but it isn't a grandmother clock and is probably nothing like a grandmother clock."[14]

The Sergeant continued munching and imbued with a powerful feeling of inner happiness picked up the concertina that sat on the table and began playing a selection of his favourite rigs and jeels. "Enough is enough," he thought and embarked upon a steep unlearning curve. Pausing on the descent, he reached for the mug of steaming hot tea and the chocolate *sablés* flavoured with almonds he bought from the *Biscuiterie Sant Mihangel* on Goodwick Main Street the previous day, tapping his foot to the rhythms in his mind as he did so.

Sighing, the Parrot reached for the reusable, nano silicone, medical grade, noise cancelling, water resistant, ear plugs.

For the next hour, whilst pulling and squeezing, tapping and munching, and of course sipping, he studied the exuberant wild growth in the flower box outside the porthole on the port side. The flower box, suspended by a brass chain attached to a hook on the side of the vessel, was swinging wildly in the gale. Weeds were in full bloom as were a small flower or two. "It's less than five hundred generations since farming began," he sang, "not enough time for my genes to have evolved sufficiently for my body to become adapted to the life of a farmer." A poignant look appeared on his face, then a smile as he remembered the chocolate *sablés*. "Perhaps a touch more orange zest." He decided to enjoy some quality down time, a short period of relaxation within the frenetic life of a captain in the Dyfed-Powys Police Rapid-Response Coracle Unit.[15] He decamped to the stern, taking the tea, a few culinary delights and the concertina along for the ride. The Parrot followed, keeping a close eye on things.

Relaxing in the hammock, he thought of a special tea. On his birthday every year his wife gives him a packet of tea bags, well one tea bag actually, called *Goodbye World* she imports especially from Belgium. EU, WTO and WHO regulations insist upon strict controls on the movement of this ultra-strong tea across national borders. Such is its potency, only one 250-gram box containing a single-use tea bag is allowed to leave Belgium every day. The tea bag itself weighs a fraction of this, the remainder being made up of protective packaging.

As he lay in the aggressively pitching hammock, soothed by the sweet music of the concertina, the Sergeant's thoughts wandered around inside his mind and bumped into the memory of the previous Saturday when he accompanied Arianrhod to Theatr Gwaun whose design references the steep vertical walls, tall elongated windows and steep roofs of ancient nonconformist chapels. The northern *façade* of this magnificent building is a brutalist, neo-liberal, layered concrete landscape that nobody likes. But this doesn't matter as the only people who see it are the people living in the house opposite. The western side is clad with aluminium which as it weathers plays havoc with the light from the evening sun while the remainder of the building is built from 35,000 locally reclaimed bricks. These valuable and much sought-after bespoke bricks are dug by hand from local blue shale and clay and fired in the beehive kilns of Goodwick brickworks, founded over a century ago. The high-quality bricks, in vogue with the chattering classes of Scleddau and Letterston and the more fashionable areas of Cardiff to enhance the architectural design of their homes, reach peak production of a mere five thousand a week, thus ensuring demand remains high and guaranteeing continued employment for the fifty-three staff. The design of the brick has remained constant over the years, being a sort of brick shape. The blue, black and white roof, the colours of Fishguard Rugby Club situated just across the road on its southern aspect, glows menacingly at night in *homage* to front row forwards and their dark arts.

The vast, curved auditorium, placed within the interior of the building for convenience, has seating that moves to improve the acoustics. The *café* with its large bay window situated in the north of the building on the ground floor by the kitchen incorporates a special design feature, it turns. Every fifteen minutes it completes a 360-degree rotation which provides *café* goers with a panoramic view of the town, although not much of it, it has to be said, as the builders read the plans upside down and made a terrible mistake. It should have been in the roof garden which, happily, is situated on the roof. The morning the *café* was officially opened by the Mayor of Fishguard[16] the control mechanism was set incorrectly and the centrifugal forces produced by the spin caused mayhem. The following day metal tables and chairs donated by the hardware shop two doors down were bolted to the floor and these, along with high sided magnetic plates, mugs, teapots and assorted cutlery now ensure biscuits, large slices of chocolate cake, tea, coffee and other assorted delicious home-made snacks are secure. Fresh fruit and veg is obtained from the roof garden by a sophisticated pulley system operating to the exterior of the building via the bay window, except when it's raining. This is why the *café* was originally planned for the roof garden. Travel sickness tablets are available free from staff at all times.

As an additional feature of interest, the *foyer* design incorporates five separate microclimates, namely tundra, steppe, forest, mountain and wetland. Visitors thrill as they enter from the street and pass through freezing temperatures to high winds to claustrophobic all enveloping darkness to oxygen deprivation to finally a good soaking before buying their tickets or enjoying the calming theatrical ambience in the spinning *café*. Survival in this unforgiving climate is dictated by the seasons. The refurbished building has won many architectural awards.

The western facing aspect of the building is fitted with giant wind turbines which, together with the solar panels in the garden on the roof, produce all the electricity Theatr Gwaun needs with enough left over for homes in West Street and Plas y Gamil, which, because of the free energy have become popular areas to live.

After the warning alarm sounds five minutes before the start of a performance theatregoers make their way up the stairs which are situated off the *foyer* next to the entrance. For the extreme theatregoing *aficionado* seeking that element of danger and exhilaration another route is possible. These adrenalin junkies open an unobtrusive, power-assisted, manual-opening, swing door to one side of the *café* and enter a long passage that leads westwards and make 'their perilous way between the rocks that crush, through the reeds that cut to pieces, and the cactus plants that tear to pieces, and then across the boiling sands'[17] before entering the auditorium at stage level through a concealed sound-proofed heavy oak door and taking their seats.

The performance ended, revellers spill out of Theatr Gwaun making their way to restaurants such as *Maxim's* and the *Belle Époque* (Est. 1871) on the Golden Mile which is notable for its varying architectural styles from *Art Deco* and *Art Nouveau* to neo-Byzantine and neo-Gothic to Welsh Calvinistic Methodist.

He and Arianrhod had gone to watch *Ask the Expert*,[18] a weekly Saturday morning programme broadcast live on Radio Wales[19] from Theatr Gwaun. J5 is his seat of choice, in the back row to the right as you enter the auditorium from above, in which position his head is turned slightly to port for comfort with a view down over the audience to the stage. He prefers sitting with his back to the bulkhead. His wife sits in J6. They chatted with friends and acquaintances until the show began at 11.00am on the dot as the programme host and that week's guest walked onto the stage. The expert, dressed in a yellow and black skirt and blouse with fetching buff shoes took her seat as the host, dressed in a grey suit with the top button of his white shirt done up and no tie, clutching a piece of paper with hastily written notes on it, stood to one side. He turned to face the audience and with a typical handsome host's ear to ear smile began to speak. A hush descended upon the packed audience.

"Good morning Fishguard. And what a good morning it is in Fishguard."[20] Loud applause and cheering filled the auditorium. Many leapt to their feet, jumping up and down punching their fists in the air with joy as the full impact of that morning permeated their very being. Unnerved a little by this the host glanced down at his notes. A hush descended upon the audience, the second one that morning, and everyone sat down again. Looking up he continued. "I have the pleasure this morning of introducing the first programme of this season's *Ask the Expert* in which knowledgeable people from different walks of life are invited to share the enthusiasm and ideas they have for their chosen subject with us. The title of our guest's chosen subject this morning is *Seven Years Amongst the Wasps* [21] and without any further ado it is my pleasure to introduce an accomplished, leading, world-renowned, consultant, fully qualified, professional, specialist, expert ..."

"Bees!"

The host glanced across at the expert.

"Bees. *Seven Years Amongst the Bees*." With a slow, controlled movement she raised her right hand, adjusted her spectacles and returned her hand to her lap. Unnoticed by everyone present her hand brushed the pocket of her blouse on its way down. A faint Zzzzzzzzzzzzzzzz-ing was audible to those members of the audience seated in the first few rows. They ignored it, thinking it must be the plumbing.

"My apologies, doctor. Ladies and gentlemen, *Seven Years Amongst the Bees*. The long wait is over, and so, without any further ado ..." He ducked suddenly and made a movement with his right arm as though to fend off an invisible something just above his head. Fear filled his face, he leapt to one side and waved both arms frantically in the air. The notes flew vertically upwards, borne aloft by the wind currents generated by furiously flailing arms. The audience remained calm. The guest speaker smiled malevolently. This continued for a few seconds more, the host appearing to be doing an impression of a wind turbine in a typhoon as, unfazed, the audience dipped into their popcorn and chocolate treats and sucked fizzy drinks through straws. Then, as suddenly as they had begun, the thrashing arms slowed, stopped rotating and returned to his side. Like the true professional he is the smile, yes, that smile, and the composure, returned. He gathered the notes scattered around the stage, moved to stand once again on the X marked on the floor of the stage by the sound recordist earlier that morning and quickly, yet professionally, rearranged his hair. The attack bee returned silently to the blouse pocket.

He studied his notes briefly, but more carefully. "Bees?" He asked out loud.

"Bees!" Repeated the guest speaker.

"Are you sure?"

"Yes!"

"Are you absolutely sure?"

"Yes."

"As I was saying, ladies and gentlemen, it gives me great pleasure to introduce to you this morning to discuss her experiences whilst *Seven Years Amongst the Bees*, Dr Absolutely Sure. Dr Sure, what was it that prompted this passion you have for bees?"

Having finished the ice cream and chocolates he bought as a treat for his wife at the counter situated in the tundra zone, so as to take full advantage of the low temperatures to keep goodies fresh, the Sergeant fell asleep.

The standing stones in the two Gorsedd Circles[22] stand silent in solemn witness to ceremonies of great import performed amongst them in times gone by, and to those yet to come. A small child, a future Archdruid[22] perhaps, sits on the flat-topped stone at the centre of one of them, engrossed as she weaves a daisy chain of the bellis perennis, creating a garland from the composite flowerheads, each about an inch in diameter. The white ray florets and yellow disc florets of the pseudanthiums shine in contrast as the sun's rays catch them. Her friends play noisily around the stones whilst another attempts to climb one. Their mums sit on a bench nearby, ignoring them as they sip lukewarm coffee from flasks and engage in sophisticated, adult conversation oblivious to the fact that Fishguard is one of the few places in the world blessed with two Gorsedd Circles, something locals talk of with pride. With great foresight the authorities decided to erect a public sign to only one of them, thus ensuring that locals and Eisteddfodwyr[22] can enjoy the other one in peace.

The on-board radio next to the fridge freezer on the port side came to life. "Ladies and gentlemen, the story you are about to hear is true. Only the names have been changed to protect the innocent. This is the city: Fishguard, North Pembrokeshire."

The Parrot, remaining on board as skeleton crew, turned its head to listen.

"Like other great cities it is home to schools where you can get most any kind of education. All these schools are accredited. There is one that is not. It holds its classes in the cracks and crevices of the city. Because of it I have a job. I carry a badge. It is Wednesday, June the 23rd. It is raining in Fishguard. It has rained in Fishguard for four billion years. We were working the day watch in the news division when a model aeroplane flown by Mr and Mrs Jones of 3, The Square, Goodwick's eight-year-old son Samuel crashed in the Goodwick boondocks. No one was hurt. The story you have just heard is true. The names were changed to protect the innocent."[23]

As the tempest abates and the sun reappears, music emanates from the singing stones of the stone circle on the stern as they perform in the offshore breeze. Amongst and around them the different colours of many plant species are to be seen with bees buzzing busily around. Cornflowers grow to a height of nearly three feet with branching grey-green stems, lanceolate leaves and bright, intense-blue flowers, wild carrots up to two feet tall with solid, hairy stems, lacy, tripinnate, feathery leaves and white flowers, low scrambling honey-scented lady's bedstraw with whorls of narrow, dark-green leaves and dense clusters of bright yellow flowers reaching nearly four feet in height, bird's foot trefoil with light-green downy leaves divided into three leaflets and clusters of yellow flowers with orange-red tinge shaped like miniature slippers that are followed by claw shaped seed pods, bee orchids reaching to a height of twenty inches, each with a rosette of leaves at ground level and stem sheathed by two leaves and a flower spike made up of up to twelve flowers whose green, white to pink sepals and yellow-green petals are shaped and coloured like a hairy bee, and a profusion of red poppies with crumpled petals surrounding blue-black stamens and deeply dissected hairy leaves on hairy stems, best suited for arable land as the seeds, which can lie dormant for decades, thrive on bare or disturbed soil.

"Without music, life would be a mistake, so it would," observed The Parrot, tapping its foot on the perch in time with the lithic beat.[24]

Ancient drystone walls and *clawdd* walls, some with drains and styles, obvious features of the westerly aspect of the stern, stand out in the landscape. Some have quartz placed in the coping stone to ward off evil spirits.

A mysterious metal monolith, 15ft tall, uncannily similar to the monolith in the film *2001: A Space Odyssey*, appeared overnight and stands silently next to the cowshed. A rumour that began in the Oak on Fishguard square suggests the shiny, silver object might be a message from aliens. An emergency meeting of Fishguard Town Council has been scheduled for the third Thursday of next month to discuss the matter.

On the northern reaches of the lake the last intact ice shelf breaks up and a slab of ice larger than Strumble Head fractures off it. Every decade for the last sixty years this area has warmed by one degree Celsius, but this summer the temperatures have been five degrees Celsius warmer than the average. As it fragments, the northern hemisphere's last epishelf lake is lost, taking with it many unique life forms. Scientists hurriedly abandon their research camp and seek safety away from the moving ice in *umiaks* made with frames of whalebones covered with walrus skins, which are sourced locally, and waterproofed with seal oil. Oars and paddles working urgently as they seek to escape the danger the breeze catches the sail made from seal intestines and aids their retreat.

23

Now is where love breathes.

Rumi[1]

Bronwen was perfecting a new move as part of the choreography for her latest dance, provisionally named **Creative Destruction**, and clattered happily in the far corner. The soles of her clogs, studded as they are with iron nails, causing great showers of orange and red sparks to fly into the air in beautiful undulating patterns behind her as she moved gracefully in tune with some inner hembra beat. "More colourful than the Rainbow Mountains in Zhangye Danxia, China," thought Megan, observing the far-off orange-red glow and the twirling, surreal form that was Bronwen.

The mild yet lavish tones of the Radio Free Crymych newsreader travelled to every nook and cranny of the crypt. Megan turned her eyes to the copy of Thomas Jones' painting *A wall in Naples* that hung on the crypt wall to one side of the sofa whilst listening intently to the radio, focussing her attention and thus allowing the terrible noise emanating from the corner to fade into a distant, soothing hum. "A recent study by economists shortlisted for the Rybczynski prize[2] argues that rather than destroying jobs the rise of technology has created jobs. Too much emphasis has been put on job losses rather than job gains," one of the authors told us earlier today. "For example, whilst the number of agricultural labourers in Pembrokeshire has markedly reduced over the last two and a half centuries this has been more than offset by the number of Beauty Therapists graduating from Pembrokeshire College."[3]

"Hmmm," she thought. "I'll look into this and form a discussion group at our next monthly meeting to examine the implications for the economy and for the job prospects of young people in the county." She made a mental note to book an appointment to have her nails done.

The newsreader continued. "A treat is in store for lovers of Italian film this weekend as the Crymych multiplex has a double bill of Salvatore Samperi[4] films. At six o'clock the dark, award winning *Malizia* made in 1973 followed at eight o'clock by the sweet comedy *Peccato Veniale* released in 1974. The lead role in both is played by Laura Antonelli. This is nostalgia at its best. Crymych folk will be particularly attracted to the latter with its gorgeous period beach scenes reminiscent of Tenby in its glory days."

"And now for some legal news. The Welsh Government[5] today revealed its intention to repeal a centuries old law that whilst appropriate in its time is thought to be discriminatory now. The law states that no Swedish visitor to Wales is to be charged for food and drink in public houses and restaurants in the country. The law has been on the statute books since Hywel Dda first proposed it at a meeting in Whitland between 940 and 945, the period during which the Welsh Laws were codified. He further proposed that no meeting was to last that long again. Relationships between the Welsh and the Danes and Norwegians at that time vacillated from good to fraught with alliances coming and going and Hywel decided that he would show gratitude to the Swedes who went east to Russia while the Danes and Norwegians sailed south to bother us. 'We have enough trouble with the longboats from Denmark and Norway,' he remarked after presenting his case. 'Just think of the worry we'd have if the Swedes joined them as well.'

The announcer continued. "A spokesperson for the Welsh Government was at pains to point out that it's been a while since Danes and Norwegians journeyed here, and since they have never beaten us at rugby, extending this hospitality to them as well is a simple courtesy. This announcement coincides with a Wales Tourist Board[6] initiative in Scandinavia. In addition to this, byelaws in west and northwest Wales which give guidance to innkeepers as to how they deal with a stranger entering a tavern on a dark winter night will also be repealed. The rule of thumb in the byelaws, which go back to the early eighth century A.D. is, Viking until proved innocent."

"And now for more local news. Not to be outdone by the restaurant on the top of Snowdon, Pembrokeshire Mountaineering Club[7] is proud to announce the opening today of Rum Doodle, named after the famous mountain in Yogistan, their new *café* on the top of Rum Dingli,[8] the highest peak in the Preseli Mountains range. All are welcome, both mountaineers and civilians. Light snacks and hot and cold drinks will be available all day. The *soup du jour* is a light vegetable broth sprinkled with crampons."

"Health news next. A new fitness craze is sweeping the country. Grucking, pronounced grucking, is an exercise regime which involves the participant carrying a rucksack weighted up to 30 pounds whilst clogging. The health outcomes include benefits to the calves, quadriceps, glutes, hamstrings, abdominal muscles and spinal erectors. Clog dancing whilst carrying weights stabilises the pelvis. Experts claim that grucking works your core as well as a Pilates workout and burns fat as well as running. It also improves your posture. As part of a grucking regime advanced gruckers stop mid-dance to do fifty press-ups."

Megan noticed the dreadful sounds from the far corner had stopped. She looked across and noticed Bronwen lying in a crumpled heap against the base of one of the Gothic pillars, sweating profusely, her exhausted mind connected to the morning by thin threads of consciousness attached at the other end to who knows where. One of the threads listened intently to the news and decided grucking would be added to her ever-expanding fitness routine. She remained in this position for a few minutes until normal service was grudgingly resumed then took to her feet by hauling herself up the east face of one of the pillars holding the roof of the crypt up, this being the most difficult route, taking advantage of the finger holds formed by the horizontal lines and vertical cracks, a natural feature, the result of it being made of blocks of carboniferous limestone. Overcome by thirst during the ascent she took a long draught of water from a mug placed on a rocky outcrop along the way. Upon completing the climb, she relaxed body and mind for a moment, turned on her heel, causing a shower of beautiful orange-red sparks to brighten that area of the crypt and strode across to the *cwtsh dan staer* where she began her daily fifteen-minute plyometric workout designed to improve her jumping ability. The workout moves around different apparatuses to increase the strength in her glutes, quads and legs. "Improved jumping technique and explosive power, that's what it's all about. A competitive edge." At least that is what she tells the young, inexperienced cloggers. And they listen, for in her prime, when at the peak of her powers she achieved the remarkable feat of being crowned both the Welsh Clogging Writers' Association Clogger of the Year and the Cloggers' Clogger of the Season.

During the two years she spent at the University of the Four Trinity Davids' Camogie Campus[9] on *an gCeathrú Rua* in Conamara in the west of Ireland doing her master's thesis, *Celtic Clogging: Origins and History* she played for the local Gaelic football team and learnt the effectiveness of jumping. Gaelic football is a sport in which jumping high to catch a ball with extended arms is an art form in itself. So highly is this skill developed that scouts from Rugby Union and Australian Rules Footie are often to be seen at matches looking to offer the best exponents of this art rich money contracts to switch codes. Bronwen returned to Wales and introduced the technique to the clog dancing world along with new techniques with sticks she learnt whilst enjoying a few games of *camógaíocht* when the local side was short of players.

Bronwen is keen on wearable technology and is trialling clogs with inbuilt GPS tracking that vibrate when she moves in the wrong direction during a clog dance. This innovation, if successful, will promote the quicker learning of new dance routines. It also brings closer the day when clog dancing becomes available to the visually impaired. The clogs also have a cooling element maintaining optimum foot temperature at all times. These futuristic clogs are wearable computers with voice activation and can run mobile apps. Heart rate and skin activity can be monitored as well as step-counting, cadence and posture. These augmented reality clogs allow users to interact with both the real and virtual world and blend real clogging with virtual clogging. The clogs collect medical data, can administer drugs when appropriate and can alert the nearest Accident and Emergency Department and the Ambulance Service if needed. Socks made from an organic, lightweight, stretchable and washable fabric with built in solar panels allow the clogs to function for longer away from a conventional power source, a boon for the

Eisteddfod[10] where prelims and preliminary prelims can go on for days. Following a recent ruling by the *Fédération Internationale de Casser sa Pipe* (FICP)[11] clogging coaches will soon join those of Rugby Union, Rugby League, Gaelic Football, Hurling, Camogie, Aussie Rules, Bog Snorkelling, Worm Charming, Camel Wrestling and Soccer in being able to monitor athletes' real-time performance. Importantly, the information gained can inform tactical decisions.

After completing her daily bruising plyometrics session, "A real beating," was how Bronwen described it, she removed her clogs, donned mittens, thick socks with a separate section for her big toe, bobble hat, goggles and flip flops and entered the cryogenic chamber where she would remain for twenty minutes exactly, after which she showered, changed and made herself and Megan a cup of coffee using beans freshly roasted in a saucepan on the wood burner. Well two cups, one each. They sat on the sofa in the bay window looking out over the semi-circular *Piazza della Republica* with its beautiful fountain, infamous for its nude revellers after the *cafés* and taverns close in the early hours of Sunday morning. From their vantage point on the sofa the two have a particularly clear and detailed view of the *Piazza*. They sat together in silence as for fifteen minutes or so after a gruelling workout Bronwen finds speaking, or indeed any activity, mental or physical, utterly impossible. Apart from making coffee and sitting on the sofa drinking it with chocolates. They sipped the coffee and guiltily nibbled hand-made 99% dark chocolate encrusted with crushed, freshly roasted Arabica beans late into the morning until it was too late to do anything else. The plan worked.

"A new development to the east of Crymych will increase the city's reputation as a cultural destination," announced the newsreader. "The city fathers and mothers have a vision to develop the Lower East Side which they intend by next year will boast the Crymych Smithsonian,[12] the American Museum group's first overseas attraction. If successful this might encourage a second such European development, the London Smithsonian, to be built, perhaps, in London. On the same site, as part of the Welsh Government's initiative to take essential services to the regions, Pembrokeshire College have ambitious plans to build extensive research facilities to complement their Haverfordwest campus which will be state of the art and cater for over 1,000 students studying Hairdressing and Beauty Therapy. The National Museums and Galleries of Wales[13] plan to open a Museum of the Future[14] on the site and Welsh National Ballet[15] will relocate there from Cardiff Bay to occupy a purpose-built auditorium with rehearsal space, six studios and training facilities thus creating a dance powerhouse for the west. A separate theatre for drama, complete with backstage facilities to rival those of Theatr Gwaun in Fishguard will be developed on One Crymych Bridge next to the lagoon, one of the most sought after residential areas in Crymych, which lies in the shadow of the recently completed Lletem, the city's tallest building, pipping the Twm Carnabwth Tower to the honour by six yards, with a top floor viewing platform offering 360 degree panoramas of the Earth's curvature. On a clear day you can see the Llŷn Peninsular to the north and Ireland to the west, while looking south you can see the sea. To the east, should the Luftwaffe decide to bomb Swansea again, Pembrokeshire poets will have a much better view this time around. Looking upwards on a clear night you can see the Andromeda Galaxy 13,226,624,581,804 miles in the distance. Immediately beneath the viewing platform is a restaurant and filling the thirty floors below that is luxury, top of the range social housing for local people with office space occupying the lower floors." Enough noise. Megan pressed mute.

The *Piazza della Republica* in the distance was alive with the comings and goings of locals and tourists mingling by the fountain in the sunshine as Megan enjoyed her coffee, people watching. Her thoughts turned to the past. "How beautiful you are," her husband said to her one morning as they stood by the fountain on a summer's day just like this one a few years ago. "With you near I find concentrating on anything difficult."

"You are a man who loves women," she replied.

"It's enough to love. Yet to be loved, to be truly loved, that is a wonderful experience also. Sadly, most people want to own the other or control the love. Both these things fail. To have a heart filled with love is enough, to be such a one is a blessing. To be with another whose heart is also filled with love is blessing upon blessing."

"You love beauty, cariad."

"Yes, I love beauty. It's possible to be devoted to beauty as it appears in another, as it resonates with the beauty inside us. Really, to be devoted to another is to be devoted to ourselves, to the beauty that we are. We devote ourselves to ourselves. In the same way we love the love within us as it manifests in another being. That's why being in love with another is a beautiful thing. It gives us a valid, understood experience of the love that is inside us, of the love that we are. An affirmation that all is well."

"What does the word 'love' mean to you?"

"Usually, it refers to a pleasant emotion, a good feeling. But this is transient, dependent upon things outside of us which is why it comes and goes. Real love is what we are, is what the trees are and the mountains and the oceans. It's what the universe and everything in it Is. We cannot experience It, we can only Be It. It's what we are. The illusion that we think is life appears to our minds as separate, rather like a wave thinking it's separate from the ocean. Our minds deceive us, yet how happily we want to be deceived. Life, Love, is behind the mind, above the mind, beyond the mind and yet includes the mind, is the mind. It is between the thoughts, and it is the thoughts. To love the life we are given and see the perfection in it, whatever comes, is the way. Let go of the past and future, trust and be grateful for the present as life unfolds in all its glory. Be in each moment, where life is, as only in each moment can the veil part and the exquisite illusion be seen for what it is. Enjoy the illusion, it is life at play. 'Life is an ocean with a *cwtsh* on every wave.'"[16] Megan was a little lost by this but enjoyed it anyway. In her imagination she threw a penny into the waters of the fountain and made a wish.

Bronwen liked the peace and quiet on the settee, but unrest was abroad in the county, a reaction to the arrival of immigrants. This year alone there have been sightings of seven big cats, fifteen wild boars, 3 wallabies, seven racoons, a couple of pandas, two scorpions and a penguin. And that's not counting the parakeets roosting in the trees around the Cathedral, a pelican on the Teifi and thousands of dormice living in lofts in Tenby. She turned to Megan, "Just think, if the force binding neutrons to protons had been slightly bigger or smaller, the stars wouldn't have been able to produce carbon and the whole of Crymych would be a lifeless desert."

"Yes, we've a lot to be grateful for, dear. Unless existence appears exactly as it needs to be for us to enjoy the view."

Bronwen turned and gazed out through the bay window. "Hmmm. What percentage of the world's water is contained in a cow?"

"Your line of thinking as you question the great panjandrums of certainty that try to bind us is as rich as a fruit cake."

"Wonder shines its light on everything."

"You have the touch of the poet about you, my dear."

"Somebody once said, 'Trying to write a poem is like running off a cliff to see if you can fly. Most of the time you can't, but every once in a while, something happens'. Rather like life itself."

Megan looked up. "Some adults who are learning Welsh have a similar experience when they try speaking it," she commented thoughtfully. "Indeed, I've heard that in the experience of the adult learner of Welsh, not only does the soft mutation appear to be infinite but the nasal and aspirate mutations appear to be infinite as well. Whatever the learner tries to say, mutations are there. To the learner, the likelihood of the appearance of mutations in his or her cosmological vision is about as vast as it is possible to conceive. The teacher explains that there is no final mutation that rules over everything, although some learners, under pressure in the class, might come to believe that one mutation is the Supreme Ruler of All Things, a Creator Mutation if you will. I have a piece of advice for Members when they begin a Welsh class. Know mutations, although there is nothing to know. Relinquish the causes of mutations, although there is nothing to relinquish. Speaking of which, there's a poetry reading in *Das Kapital*[17] tonight. Shall we go?"

"Hmmmmm."

"There'll be snacks available."

"Snacks?"

"Snacks."

"Why do poetry anthologies always omit my favourite poem?"

"*Guacamole, couscous* salad, smoked salmon and *Brie crostinis*, crab cakes with lime chive *mayonnaise*, sweet potato fries, goat's cheese *bruschettas*, *beignets*, butter toffee popcorn, cinnamon buns, sour cream banana bread, chocolate truffles, ..."

"Poetry at its best. We'll go."

"The reading includes a new interpretation of some of Dafydd ap Gwilym's poems, including *Mis Mai, Yr Haf, Y Deildy, Yr Wylan, Galw ar Ddwynwen, Marwnad Angharad, Dyddgu a Morfudd, Breichiau Morfudd* and *Dagrau Serch*.

"Oooooh! Dafydd ap Gwilym! Yes please!" She recited the first two lines of *Mis Mai*, the original fourteenth century Middle Welsh version, then in modern Welsh, then in modern English.

> *Harddwas teg a'm anrhegai,*
> *Hylaw ŵr mawr hael yw'r Mai.*

> *Dyn ifanc golygus a roddai anrhegion i mi,*
> *gŵr mawr hael a pharod ei gymwynas yw Mai.*

> *A fair handsome youth who gave me gifts,*
> *May is an obliging generous nobleman.*[18]

Bronwen enjoys the simple things of life, the way day is followed by night. "Get the basics right and the rest will follow," she always says. And she loves poetry. Inspired, she sang a couple of lines from a favourite traditional song.

> *Mae 'nghariad i 'n Fenws, mae 'nghariad i 'n fain,*
> *Mae 'nghariad i 'n dlysach na blodau y drain.*

"Lovely dear," said Megan, developing goose bumps in all the excitement. "Poetry and music, a lethal combination."

"I've heard it said that a painting shows something, a good book says something, but music appears from nowhere, lights up the brain, disappears to nowhere and doesn't make any sense."

"It makes goose bumps."

"Every folk song has in it the potential for perfection, just as every sesame seed is pervaded with oil." Bronwen had reached the point of no return when the singer becomes the song. She had gone AWOL.

Mae 'nghariad i'n caru fel cawod o law
Weithiau fan yma a weithiau fan draw.

She was in touch with her inner folk singer who knows no limits other than those we impose when we think we are in control. The inner folk singer contains great transformative power flowering as a life of fulfilment, a marvel described adequately in that ancient book *Tao Canu Gwerin*, recently translated as *The Tao of Folk Singing*. She paused and looked across at Megan. "Each one of us is a note in the great folk song of existence. A good life is one characterized by complete absorption in folk singing."

"And coffee and chocolates!"

"Oh yes! Shall we?

"Let's."

"If rock music has fire in its belly, folk music has coffee and chocolates." She paused. "Hmmm! That sounded wild before I said it." Undeterred she finished her speculations with a flourish by singing a snippet from another traditional song.

Dacw nghariad i lawr yn y berllan
Tw rym-di ro rym-di radl idl-al
O na bawn i yno fy hunan
Tw rym-di ro rym-di radl idl-al
Dacw'r tŷ a dacw'r sgubor, dacw ddrws y beudy'n agor

Ffal-di rwdl idl-al, Ffal-di rwdl idl-al,
Tw rym-di ro rym-di radl idl-al.

"Coffee and chocolates it is," she said, getting up from the sofa and moving to the kitchen from where, moments later, the strange bubbling sounds that accompany the secret coffee making process could be heard through the locked door. Driven by a powerful instinct regulated by cells located somewhere in the primitive Coffee Making Region of her brain stem Bronwen navigated the ocean of ever-changing phenomena that is the coffee maker's art. A piece of rainbow-coloured *graffiti* was written across the fridge door. 'A cup of coffee should be free from traces of the past, like a flower of spring.' She doesn't make coffee with her brain, but with her heart. "A coffee maker's way has no end and no beginning, and from this she cannot escape," chanted Bronwen rapturously, immersed by now in the ritual.

Megan wondered how much longer the coffee would take.

The ceremony was nearing its end. A stained and battered steel coffee pot gurgled on the Aga as Bronwen danced naked around the kitchen table playing a pair of small, brass, hand cymbals interconnected by a copper cord in her left hand whilst blowing into the white conch shell of a large predatory sea snail, the type that lives in Crymych Lagoon, decorated with ornate patterns in silver, held in the other hand. Displaying a musician's dexterity, she played a set of two *tabla* drums secured with braided hemp ropes, one on each leg between her knees, their loudness and rhythmic sound increasing in intensity. Unattached utensils rattled, the kitchen door shook, and Bronwen, by now a mere blur whizzing around the kitchen, reached a crescendo and collapsed triumphantly onto the floor under the table in a scrunched up giddy heap of dynamic harmonic energy. It was complete.

"Ah! Good!" smiled Megan as the sofa stopped shaking. "Nearly ready." She let go of the tall halogen floor lamp she was holding to keep it from falling over. Being 'a little over' approximately forty years of age and with eyesight not what it used to be the light from the lamp is essential for reading. "Bronwen is lovely, but all over the map," she decided.

Bronwen came to, soothed by the hollow bubbling sound coming from the coffee pot. As the dizziness subsided, her head still spinning, she scrambled to her feet and made her way in a path of ever decreasing circles towards the wicker chair by the door, missing it a couple of times until she got close enough to grab an arm. She paused for a few moments as the kitchen slowed down sufficiently to allow her to stand unaided then placed the cymbals and conch shell carefully on the chair, undid the braided hemp ropes that attached the drums to the insides of her knees, put them next to the other musical instruments and got dressed. The coffee was ready. Megan was ready. Crymych was ready. The kitchen door swung open and Bronwen returned triumphantly to the crypt bearing two coffee cups filled to the brim with coffee made from freshly roasted, organic Arabica beans and a plate of dark chocolate truffles that had mysteriously found its way onto the tray.

"The purpose of coffee making," she told Megan as she placed the tray on the coffee table in front of the sofa and sat down, "is to enjoy our old age. But we can't fool ourselves, only sincere coffee making will work." Megan nodded thoughtfully, leaned across, picked up a coffee cup and a handful of chocolate truffles then sat back, snuggling into the cushions and inhaling the delicate aroma coming from the cup. She nodded thoughtfully again, sipped, then popped a truffle into her mouth. Two pairs of shoes fell discarded to the floor and two pairs of stockinged feet rose into the air before coming to rest on the coffee table. Absorbed into the moment, Bronwen sipped and munched. Their bliss cells lit up and the resulting light display formed a rainbow arcing colourfully between them, a healing heart burst of energy extending from its epicentre on the sofa to envelope Crymych in its loving embrace. Bronwen was still high following the experience in the kitchen and filled with an overwhelming sense of awe. "We practise coffee making with people at first. But the experienced in the art practise with mountains, trees and rocks," she said in a soft voice.

Megan waited.

"Words bring you only to their limit. Go beyond them into the silence. Words are needed for communication, to share information. Real communication is not verbal."

Megan nodded thoughtfully again, focussing her concentration, lazer like, on the coffee and truffles. Not wishing to squeeze reality into words they sat in silence enjoying elevenses and gazing through the bay window as the play of the universe unfolded joyfully before them in the *Piazza della Republica*.

Hypatia made her way onto the sofa and settled between them on a blue and violet coloured velvet cushion covered with white roses from where she intended enjoying the one third of the day she spent awake, eyeing the truffles as she did so. Sensitive to vibrations she returned after the explosions in the kitchen stopped and the tremors subsided. As with all cats, she has no sweet tooth, the result of a mutation in a key taste receptor, so the truffles were safe. She purred contentedly, curled up and went to sleep. At eighteen years of age this is entirely reasonable.

"Chocolate truffles," explained Bronwen, "capture within the constraints of their form both the pathos of anguish and a vision of its resolution."

"Yes, dear."

"We cannot choose whether to engage with them, only how."

"With coffee?"

"Coffee making," she continued unabashed, "is not an instinctive skill for human beings. It is not etched into our genes the way, say, swallowing is."

"No dear." Megan reminded Bronwen of something said many years ago, 'Coffee drinking is a surrender. It is not a demand. It is not forcing existence your way. It is relaxing into the way existence wants you to be. It is a let go.'"[19]

The coming and going in the *Piazza della Republica* increased in intensity.

"Has there ever been a day without a yesterday?" pondered Bronwen as a deep coffee and chocolate induced peace infused her being.

This reminded Megan that Machlud y Wawr's Pembrokeshire Brigade[20] were having a meeting in the crypt the next morning followed by an excursion to go whale watching in Llys y Frân. "The forecast for the trip tomorrow is good, up to twenty-eight degrees in the shade during the afternoon."

"We'll have to keep out of the shade then."

"And take umbrellas and factor fifty."

Hypatia woke with a snuffle, a little confused by this sudden re-entry into day-to-day life. "In the beginning is the end," she thought. Megan stroked her comfortingly whilst placing a handkerchief moistened with a blend of eucalyptus oil, thyme oil and menthol on the cushion next to her. Satisfied, she went back to sleep. Bronwen looked serene as she spent this precious time getting in touch with her inner chocolate truffle. "All is well on Planet Crymych," she murmured.

Megan noticed the position and length of the shadow of the Cathedral spire to one side of the *Piazza*, "Time for the midday news bulletin," she decided and reached for the dooby doo which Hypatia was lying on. Pointing it at the radio mounted on the crypt wall she pressed to unmute, increased the volume, put it back underneath the cat, sat back and closed her eyes as the newsreaders voice filled the crypt.

"The Wales Tourist Board have announced that the trial of the use of QR codes at sites of interest in the Preseli Mountains has been a great success. Using mobile phones to scan the codes attached to standing stones visitors can learn about the history and archaeology of the area in an accessible, user-friendly way. Standing in the middle of a thick, wet, slow moving rain cloud they can enjoy the view from the site by looking at the video clip on the screen, except of course when the mountain is overrun by solid, all-engulfing, coagulated, cloud cover during which time the mobile phone screens themselves are not visible. An app, *Where is that cloud?* is free to download onto your mobile phone."

"Sporting news next. Injury rates whilst clog dancing are down a hundredfold since 1427, the lowest since records began.

And now here's Derec with the weather."[21]

"Shw' mae? Awful day, but at least we're here to enjoy it," he said, before bursting into tears as Brunelleschi's dome atop the Cathedral disappeared into a thick mist that was accompanied by a vicious, all engulfing, torrential drizzle.

Megan retrieved the dooby doo and pressed mute as Bronwen got up and went across to the panotrope to put Dr Leary`s phonograph record *Clog on. Clog in. Clog out.*[22] on the turntable before returning to the sofa. Powered by electricity, sounds were amplified by the vacuum tubes and sent around the room and through the kitchen into the orchard. The furniture rattled in appreciative accompaniment.

In the few acres beyond the orchard, barley and ceirch duon bach grow together. The resulting mixture of grain is known as shiprys and is fed to the horses as well as being used to make bread.

In the woodland nearby grow beech, oak and maple trees whose leaves Megan and Bronwen munch as an occasional delicacy. Aromatic common mugwort grows to a height of over 6 feet with dark green pinnate leaves, silver and hairy on the underside, with small yellow to reddish brown flowerheads. By infusing the leaves for 10 minutes Bronwen makes tea. Lady's bedstraw stands almost a foot tall, stems dense with clusters of frothy, honey-scented, yellow flowers and angular stems carrying narrow, dark green leaves in whorls. The lilac-blue, daisy like flowers of royal blues with contrasting yellow centres stand out against their fine, dark green leaves. Amongst them grow erect, bristly, viper's bugloss with dense cylindrical spikes of violet-blue, flared flowers each with a reddish tuft of protruding stamens and stigmas resembling a snake about to strike.

Growing along the banks of the stream flanking the orchard are teasels, their spiky flower heads carrying inflorescences of small, blue-purple flowers above brown, prickly stems and bright green leaves, reaching a height of over 8 feet, and marsh woundworts up to 40 inches tall with solid, square, hairy stems with lanceolate, shallow-toothed leaves and dense spikes of zygomorphic, rose-red flowers.

24

Summoned or not, the Sergeant will come.
> Motto over the front door
> of Carl Jung's house[1]

The Parrot had placed the Sergeant under house arrest, citing high crimes and misdemeanours. His wife, on her way into Fishguard earlier that Friday afternoon a couple of hours before he left for the weekend on routine shore leave, phoned him to tell him she might be late back that night. "Rhiannon and the girls are having a *lingerie* party," she explained. "Don't wait up. It's best if you're in bed when I get back." Her calculations suggested he would cause minimum disruption to her routine if he was fast asleep under the duvet when she arrived home. He of course, encouraged by her use of the '/' word and the single, yet explosive use of the 'b' word, read everything into this that an independent observer would counsel against. As a result, he got hot under the collar and in various other places, his excitement levels went into the red and in this semi-delirious state he attempted to take control of the coracle. The Parrot did not see this as mutiny exactly, after all, he is the captain of the vessel, but a danger nonetheless, especially to shipping. Fortunately, the on-board fail-safe mechanisms worked, and the vessel remained at anchor in the peaceful surrounds of Fishguard harbour.

A Foehn wind blew down from the Preseli Mountains, played music with the stone circle and warmed the Sergeant's toes as he rested in the hammock on the stern. The green light on the electronic tag fitted to the basket-shaped guard of his single-edged cutlass, secured to his person as usual by the wide leather belt around his waist, flashed, indicating that the on-board computer knew exactly where he was, a simple yet effective surveillance device. As an extra precaution until the Sergeant's wild state of excitement subsided The Parrot stood guard on an overhanging branch. "Not a great deal has ever happened in Fishguard," muttered the Sergeant thankfully, "if you exclude the Ice Ages."

A drift of coracles sailed out of the harbour in V formation, each vessel gaining lift from the one in front, saving fuel, the so-called 'wake energy retrieval' effect. Their upper decks were densely packed with delighted tourists on a pleasure cruise bound for Dinas Head, taking photographs of everything, alive and dead, as they went, including the Sergeant who smiled graciously as he lay recumbent on his best side in the hammock. Adjusting the periscope suspended alongside him, he stared back. The Parrot, not averse to attention, preened itself. On slow afternoons it amuses itself by speaking to the remainder of the crew in

Mandarin as this stimulates the firing of neurones in its right anterior temporal lobe which is involved with music. Such is the effect of tonal languages.

The Sergeant's first kiss after he began courting his future wife was uneventful. "Step forward, kiss, move away, and no one will get hurt," she instructed. He considered it a success, but then he had no reference point. A randomized double-blind trial would have provided him with evidence to the contrary.

The Sergeant was sure he loved sex, although he could not be sure. When emotions are involved, the memory is fickle. One night whilst in bed together a little while after their wedding day his wife told him she only enjoyed sex when the atmospheric pressure was high. "High! In west Wales!" he retorted indignantly, yet quietly so as not to disturb her enjoyment of the novel she was reading. He took a keen interest in the shipping forecasts and all things meteorological after that having previously relied upon the rheumatism in The Parrot's left knee. A few industrious, experimental weeks later, after they had retired to bed, she was lying back peacefully under the *duvet*, propped up by several pillows, undisturbed by the hand of man, enjoying her novel with him lying beside her. 'Beside' need not be taken too literally here as it is a super king size bed, and he was there during one of his rare visits. Banished to the western border, a large memory-foam body pillow between them acted as both a marker of two separate administrative areas and a deterrent. He complimented her on her looks. "After all," he mused, "she's just spent over an hour in the bathroom getting ready to come to bed so it would be churlish of me not to congratulate her. Foolhardy even." He eyed the safety pillow separating them.

"You look lovely, dear."

She stopped reading, turned her head and looked at him suspiciously. "Thank you." She secured the pillow lying between them, turned back to the book and continued reading.

Both a thoughtful expression and a wicked grin appeared on his face. Encouraged by this he spoke. "I've made a fan," he informed her as she turned the page and began a new chapter. She looked up from the novel. There at the bottom of the bed was an industrial size mobile fan six feet in diameter pointing directly at her. It was fastened firmly to a stand which in turn was attached to a heavy metal base bolted solidly to the floor. Alarm bells sounded in her head as he reached across to the bedside table, picked up the remote control and pressed 'On'. Too late. "I've closed all the windows and sealed the gap under the door with a towel," he told her. Instinctively, she dropped the book and as the blades of the fan began to spin, burrowed under the *duvet*, holding onto her hairdo as she went. He perused the controls. Slow Medium Fast Very fast SEX. He pondered the consequences for a few moments before taking a deep breath, crossing his fingers and pressing SEX. He read on. Regular Boost. "Hmmmm." He pressed Boost. Twice.

The hurricane force wind blew the *duvet* off the bed revealing his wife who lay in foetal position on her side of the territory, which was most of it, partially protected by the two layers of cotton pyjamas, tightly wrapped dressing gown and scarf which was her normal attire in bed. "And I can plug it in next to the sofa opposite the television in the living room as well," beamed the Sergeant, secure in the safety harness as his wife lost her grip on the mattress and flew upwards and backwards through the air to find herself pinned, spread-eagled, upside down against the wall above the mock, Georgian, oak headboard by the ferocity of the wind. "Everything seems to be going according to plan," he thought. At this crucial point in the proceedings the immortal words of Indiana Jones came into his mind. 'Fortune and glory kid, fortune and glory.'[2] He gazed lovingly into his wife's upside-down eyes. "If you could be a butterfly, what kind would you be?" he asked tenderly. Her bedtime *froideur* dropped several degrees. Five feather and down pillows, a large memory-foam body pillow and a *duvet* with one hundred per cent long-staple breathable cotton cover with corner ties, all accompanied by a romance novel, flew out of the manual opening opal glaze dome roof window with trickle vents and 10-year warranty he had left open when making the room airtight, in case things got too hot. The stars were out, the moon was about to go to sleep, and a sinking feeling appeared deep in his solar plexus. He began to cry. Yet even then he was comforted by the knowledge that he could not easily be replaced by algorithms. It would be reckless to make assumptions but, "My time will come," he muttered comfortingly, indeed optimistically to himself.

The Parrot's morning routine includes a warm shower followed by a 90 second cold shower hit. This done, it transfers to the perch in the galley which has a port for its smart phone and speakers at each end of the horizontal bar through which, relaxed, calm, seated in full lotus position, wings resting in its lap, tips touching gently, primary feathers facing upwards, it listens to whale songs.

Reckless and without fear the Sergeant began that fateful day with half an hour's yoga on a sheltered part of the foredeck, starting with the Flying Pigeon pose, *Eka Pada Galavasana* and finishing with the Legs Up the Bulkhead pose, *Viparita Karani*. During the ten-minute visualization phase that followed, a piece of hot buttered toast formed in his mind. He moved it around and looked at it from every angle. A thought appeared in the furthest reaches of the cavernous stillness that is his yogi consciousness. "To Marmite or not to Marmite?"[3] Time passed. A reply appeared from deep within the hallowed depths. "A no-brainer."

"Exactly," agreed The Parrot.

To contemplate this development fully he remained under the shelter on the foredeck next to the large, moss-covered, limestone boulder surrounded by raked sand and pebbles. He draped a woollen shawl over his shoulders to keep the early morning chill off and put his new glasses on. He had been commanded to trial a pair of adjustable prescription glasses developed by the University of the Four

Trinity David's Space Biomedical Research Institute.[4] An experiment was afoot, an attempt to remove the possibility of potentially mission-threatening changes in the eyesight of Dyfed-Powys Police Rapid-Response Coracle Unit staff.[5] The lead scientist of the project at the UFTDSBRI informed DPPRRCU staff that, "Eyesight can change during prolonged ocean voyages and the changes can be significant. We aim to understand these changes and then prevent them. Research has shown that long sightedness can become longer, and short sightedness can become shorter, when at sea for extended periods. This is obviously not desirable." A recent survey of DPPRRCU captains returning from lengthy voyages found that almost two thirds of them returned with blurrier short-distance vision, which is not helpful as they navigate their way around the vessel from galley to bridge to hammock and so on. The new glasses are designed to adapt to changes in the wearer's focus. One experimental design adjusts the angle of the prisms in the lenses electronically to make up for subtle changes in eyesight, a problem that constitutes a serious barrier to the effectiveness of prolonged ocean patrols as it means the captains cannot see where they are going.

His vision restored by the new glasses he gazed across the harbour, noticing the play of the early morning light on the water, dappled as it was by the heavy rain moving in from the east. He was reminded of a period he spent several years before on an exchange visit with the Helsinki Police Rapid-Response Pursi Unit.[6] During an expedition on Lake Tuusula he woke early one morning and made his way to the galley where he brewed a mug of tea before going up on deck to enjoy the view across the lake. Sixteen swans appeared from the mist surrounding him, moving elegantly past the vessel before disappearing again into the mist. "How beautiful!" he exclaimed. The Parrot, standing serenely on top of the spinnaker, and who is a distant relative, twice removed of the swans on both his mother's and his father's side, agreed. During the night the Sergeant had a vivid dream about a garlic press which he found puzzling, the dream that is not the garlic press, and wondered what meaning it held for his life. Over the public address system of one of the *pursis* in the fleet each morning came the gentle strains of Finlandia, one of Sibelius' best loved compositions. The music brought calming vibrations to the *manipura chakra* in his solar plexus thus preparing his body for breakfast.

From his vantage point on the foredeck, his mind becalmed, his eyes took advantage of the down time and turned upwards to study the cloud formation over Dinas Head in the distance. It looked familiar. "What does that remind me of?" he asked out loud. "Hmmm! I can't quite put my finger on it." And on that note, he got up, shook himself down and went to the galley to make a mug of tea. Whilst sitting at the table waiting for the kettle to boil, he chatted to the computer which gave thoughtful, guarded replies, careful not to divulge information the

Sergeant might act upon in an attempt to do something. Anything. "The computer seems a trifle slow this morning," he thought, watching the kettle.

The Parrot, unravelling from the yoga position, stood up, shifting its weight from one leg to the other then back again. "That's because the data being sent to the computer at huge speed in the form of photons along the optical fibres that make up the internet has to be slowed down when it reaches the computer to be converted into electrons so it can travel along the wires inside the computer," it said.

There was a pause.

Then another.

"The computer seems a trifle slow this morning," muttered the Sergeant to himself, watching the kettle.

The Parrot shifted its weight from one leg to the other then back again and sighed.

The kettle boiled.

A few minutes later he sat by the table, mug of tea in hand, pondering the possibility of a second. He was uneasy. He was reading an unsettling article in the previous day's Western Mail[7] that troubled him. He thought about it, wrestled with it, thinking out loud as he did so. "Terabytes are turning into petabytes which are turning into zettabytes. We're running out of space. This is going to be almost as big a problem as Gatland's Law used to be. Thank goodness for 'exceptional circumstances'." Comforted by this forensic dissection of the problem he took another sip of tea. Thoughts of a sandwich appeared in his mind, and he checked to see that the oven gloves were on standby next to the bread bin. The internet of things works well on the coracle, connecting all physical things on board and keeping everything running smoothly. Except the Sergeant who is a known unknown the computer system acknowledges is and always will be unknowable. At least until advances in artificial intelligence produce the sophisticated algorithms necessary for computers to go where no computer has gone before, into the very being of complex organisms like the Sergeant.

He read on. "石黒浩, a Japanese computer genius and visionary[8] is at the cutting edge of robotics. Androids, he says, are close to becoming a reality. Soon we will have robots interacting with humans during their everyday lives. Humanoids are coming to your home. They will recognise you, talk to you, react to your emotions, move and live autonomously, clean and cook. They will be our friends, talk to us, read to us from books stored in their memory, sing to us, play music, speak to you in the language that you are learning, do the weeding, do the shopping, do the hoovering, make tea, ..." The worried look on the Sergeant's face disappeared as this vision of the future sank in. "Make tea," he repeated out loud. "Want one!" He turned to the next article and read on. "A new hypersonic coracle that will reach a velocity of Mach 5 is being developed by scientists and is expected to become operational sometime during the next decade. America, China and Russia are in the race to be the first. A spokesperson at the School of Ocean Sciences at Bangor University[9] has stated they are confident they will beat the superpowers to the finish in the race to create an air-to-water craft. 'At our laboratories on the Menai Straits our prototype, the X-57 Wave Glider is undergoing trials. Recently it travelled more than 231 nautical miles at Mach 5 after being launched from a space shuttle on loan from NASA[10] from where it descended rapidly to splash down somewhere in Cardigan Bay at which point the water-based section of the trial began.'" His interest waned and he turned to the next article. "Seagulls winter in Spain, Portugal and Morocco before returning here to prey on tourists and eat their fish and chips. Dr Pedr Craig, a research scientist who studies the migratory habits of herring gulls and lesser black-backed gulls has issued a warning to the public. 'Cover your chips, they are on their way back. They are coming for your chips.'" He turned to the next article. "A factory based in Manorbier which specialises in the manufacture of collapsible coracles is expanding its workforce to 350 as it celebrates the opening of its new plant in the heart of the village, inside the castle. The aptly named Collapsible Coracle Company is the largest manufacturer of collapsible coracles in Europe and is growing to meet a surge in worldwide demand. Surprisingly, 81% of the coracles are sold to buyers outside the county. The new plant will produce 200,000 collapsible coracles a year within the next six years. The brand 'Made in Manorbier' is very strong overseas." He was intrigued.

The ship-to-shore radio next to the cuckoo clock burst into life interrupting the captain's *reveries*. "The following top-secret communication has been sent to all DPPRRCU captains.

Memo XXXVII: Security concerns.

The Admiral is leading an investigation into the recent ransomware attack that paralysed the Sergeant's paddle. Security experts think it was a state-sponsored virus, the chief suspect being North Korea. In a statement released to the press he says that it is less likely to be the work of a criminal gang from Saundersfoot or a sole teenager working out of Clunderwen.[11]

Dyfed-Powys Police Rapid-Response Coracle Unit are concerned by a number of 'fake news' items that are appearing on social media. Recently, several big social media platforms released a series of adverts, some pro-Sergeant and some pro-Pirates. The Admiral claims to be in possession of evidence that proves they were paid for in roubles. Millions of roubles. Is the Sergeant vulnerable to foreign bots?"

He got up and turned the kettle on then opened the cupboard and brought out a packet of chocolate biscuits which he placed on the table. The Sergeant is a self-taught biscuiteer, his expertise resulted in him being awarded the title Honorary Chocolate Biscuiteer, of which he is very proud. His experience in these matters however does not extend to making them, only to eating them, hence the 'Honorary'. The kettle whistled and a minute later he sat down again, a fresh mug of tea on the table next to him. He reached for the packet of biscuits and began opening it. "Resealable packets for chocolate biscuits?" he chuckled. "Why?" In a recent memo he received from the Worshipful Guild of Chocolateers it was suggested that each biscuit be manoeuvred towards the mouth with the chocolate side on top to optimise the visual stimulation, but once out of sight under the nose to flip it, thereby ensuring the chocolate makes direct contact with the tongue where the majority of taste buds are found and thus maximise taste.

The clouds dispersed. The rain stopped. The harbour was bathed in bright, warming sunlight. Energised by the yoga, tea and chocolate biscuits he left the galley and moved to the paddle area on the foredeck where he sat on the willow rod that is the seat and with smooth, energy efficient strokes born from years of experience, began operating the paddle. The coracle moved forward. He wondered at this.

The vessel came to an abrupt halt as the anchor dug into the harbour floor three feet below. The Parrot, warned by the alarm, flew out through a porthole and demonstrating excellent instrument flying skills deployed the air currents to take it upwards to an altitude of approximately one hundred feet where it maintained itself relatively stationary. From this vantage point the Sergeant could be observed safely. "These are dangerous times,' it thought. Extending its right leg, it pressed the red button on the mobile emergency control unit attached to the leather belt around its waist and switched the automatic pilot on. "All is well again," it said with relief and glided downwards along those same air currents and in through the porthole to land smoothly on the perch in the galley where it assumed the resting position and changed its status to 'Dozing'.

Meanwhile the Sergeant continued his exploration of physics. "The paddle pushes against the water, the water pushes back." He looked up at the sky. "That means that rockets can't travel through space because space is a vacuum which means there's nothing there to push back."

The vessel's Cognitive Dissonance Detector went into the red, sprang to life and sent a message to the on-board computer, which, sensing danger, caused the perch to vibrate gently to wake The Parrot. Minutes later, having been fully briefed about developments The Parrot flew to the for'ard porthole, which was open, landed on the lower rim which it grasped with its claws, steadied itself, put its head out and addressed the Sergeant thus. " *Maintenant, mon capitaine*, do you understand what you are saying?"

"Of course, I understand."

"Then explain."

"Hmmm. I can't."

"Then you don't understand."

"Hmmmmm."

The Parrot flew back to its perch, gripped it tightly, then relaxed. It sensed the peril had passed. It was wrong. The Sergeant continued to think. "The paddle pushes, the water pushes back, we move forward. Perfect harmony." Somewhere, a long way away, the spirit of Richard Feynman[12] uttered a cry of despair as The Parrot executed a full 360^0 backward roll with squawk and returned to its original position. It glanced at the control console on the galley wall, checking the automatic pilot was still on and the anchor secure. Satisfied, it resumed 'Dozing' mode. Relaxing his cerebral cortex after the strain the Sergeant put the paddle down, swivelled around on the seat, got up and strolled calmly across the foredeck to the sheltered spot beneath the porthole where he sat in full lotus position on the yoga mat and covered himself with the shawl to take a well-earned rest in the blissful tranquillity of a *post meridiem* Fishguard.

A swarm of predatory Giant Tropical Bullet Ants from Brazil invaded the coracle. The Parrot, warned of the danger by the sounding of the alarm, swung smoothly into action, chanting DPPRRCU's motto as a mantra as it went. "One jot, or one tittle, shall not pass." Flying to the bridge it pushed several different coloured buttons on the emergency console in a well-rehearsed move. A siren sounded on deck and woke the Sergeant in time to see all the doors, hatches and portholes being sealed automatically by shutters of impenetrable steel half an inch thick. The Parrot was aware that activation of the emergency procedure meant, on this occasion, that it and the vessel were safe, and that the Sergeant was outside, exposed, all alone on the foredeck and not safe at all. But it had no choice as the security of the vessel was paramount. "*C'est la vie!*" it said with a humorous shrug of the shoulders and a twinkle in its eye.

The Sergeant was completely encased in a living, seething shroud of reddish-black insects. One of the Giant Tropical Bullet Ants, stout and more than an inch long in its stockinged feet, stung the Sergeant on the nose and then, to an ant, they decamped to the wet neotropic ecozone on the south side of the lake on the stern where they lunched on small arthropods and nectar. As the agonizing pain took hold of his nose the Sergeant was able to confirm that the Schmidt Sting Pain Index was correct and that a sting from this particular species of ant is by far the most painful, greater than that from all other ants, sawflies, bees and wasps, greater even than the sting of the tarantula hawk wasp. As his nose swelled alarmingly and the tears of pain rolled down his cheeks, he felt some pride in this. The ants left as suddenly as they had arrived, walking *en masse* down the gangplank before taking off and flying south to who knows where. A few minutes later the all-clear sounded and doors, hatches and portholes were uncovered as the steel shutters opened. As a temporary emergency measure the on-board computer advised the Sergeant to proceed to the hibernation pod in which the Sergeant enters a state of drug induced delirium when on long voyages, thus reducing boredom. The on-board computer planned to keep his nose in a controlled torpor, a state of suspended animation close to the barrier between life and death for the next twenty-four hours until the worst was over. From there he would be transferred to the sick bay.

The Sergeant was reminded of a quote he once read, "Whatever happens will be for the worst, therefore it is in our interest that as little should happen as possible."[13] On that particular morning he agreed wholeheartedly. Feeling his way with his hands, his vision impaired by the tears and the swollen nose, he went below decks to recuperate. Arriving at the hibernation pod which is located at the stern end of the main thoroughfare on B Deck he settled into a hammock and declared a *moratorium*. On what, he would decide later as at the time he was alone and as an amateur ethologist he was, unfortunately, pondering the question of species *solipsism*. It would be a while before he reversed out of that dead end.

One reason for the on-board computer releasing information about the coracle's day-to-day activities to the Sergeant on a need-to-know basis only, in other words it doesn't tell him anything, is to protect the vessel should the Sergeant experience cognitive failure. His access to social media is also strictly curtailed. Using the internet a lot for communication, entertainment and social networking would distract him from primary tasks and result in him having lapses of attention, spending his days daydreaming, forgetting things, lacking focus and bumping into things. The computer has programmed his smart phone to function for fifteen minutes every afternoon. Whether this policy contributes to an improvement in his performance as the captain of a vessel packed to the gunwales with sophisticated navigation, surveillance and *espionage* equipment remains to be seen. However, high ups in the Dyfed-Powys Police Rapid-Response Coracle Unit are cautiously, very cautiously, optimistic.

The Parrot was enjoying the peace in the galley and listening to Radio Free Pembrokeshire's morning science programme.[14] "Early human ancestors might have been walking upright as early as 3.5 million years ago. However, these early 'humans' would have found coracling almost impossible because it is thought they lacked Achilles tendons," the programme's science correspondent explained. "With the exception of gibbons, all humanity's closest animal relatives, chimpanzees, gorillas and orang-utans, have no Achilles tendons. A new computer gait simulation of both early human ancestors and modern-day humans has revealed that Achilles tendons are critical to achieving fast coracling speeds. If early humans lacked these tendons they could still have walked almost as fast as modern humans but their top coracling speed would have been half as quick.

Evidence for the evolution of Achilles tendons is hard to come by because not many hominid fossils have been found with intact feet. The shape of other bones however suggests that the tendons did not evolve fully until about 2 million years ago. What we need to discover now is two things, when exactly in our evolution we developed an Achilles tendon and who was Achilles."

"Still in our past, but a little more recent," the science correspondent continued, "a recent study of the climate around Saundersfoot at the time the Neanderthals disappeared has found no record of any sudden disaster that might have contributed to their extinction, suggesting other factors such as competition with Homo Sapiens were important. The cause is disputed, with some scientists favouring a warming climate and the arrival in Saundersfoot of modern humans who could run.[15] Some suggest there was a contagion?[16] Or were Neanderthals displaced by offspring produced by their interbreeding with Homo Sapiens. On this note, is it a coincidence that Saundersfoot football club are known in Tenby as the Hybrids? After thriving in the town for about 300,000 years the Neanderthals disappeared abruptly between 32,000 and 24,000 years ago."

" Abruptly?" queried the Sergeant.

Seconds later, the Sergeant's nose entered 'torpor mode' and proceeded spontaneously towards thermodynamic equilibrium and thereby maximum entropy. The on-board computer noted the rapid eye movements characteristic of mammalian sleep and the low muscle tone throughout his body. The Sergeant was napping. A quantum dream appeared in his mind and into the dream popped a question. "Are mugs of tea things or merely observable phenomena?"

An impenetrable sea fog making navigation impossible enveloped Fishguard harbour. The computer moved from DEFCON 2 to DEFCON 5 and breathed a sigh of relief.

"And now for the weather."

"Thick fog will cover southern Wales for several days to be followed by heavy rain for at least a week. Torrential rain will cover northern Wales for several days to be followed by dense fog which will last about a week. Fishguard will be particularly badly affected."

"Thank you, Derec."[17]

An owl rose silently from the brush covering the cliff above the harbour, the feathers on its wings absorbing the energy of flight vibrations. The 'king of acoustic stealth' glided noiselessly downwards before plucking its prey from an exposed rock on the cliff face. The Parrot watched through a porthole. "If only wind turbines utilized the owl's noise reduction technology," it thought, impressed."

A wilderness of monkeys at play swing from tree to tree in the willow copse, disturbing the chattering of red-billed choughs that rest there, black plumage contrasting with brightly coloured legs, feet and bills as intense shafts of sunlight catch them. A murder of crows take flight, passing an exaltation of larks whose melodious males fill the willow grove with song as they defend their breeding territories and seek to attract mates. The piercing calls of a muster of peacocks fill the air as a parliament of rooks calls it a day and goes into recess. A covey of speckled, greyish brown ptarmigans feed peacefully on leaves, flowers and seeds near their simple nests on the ground. An alpine species they live on the high ground to the north of the cowshed. A fall of woodcock with their cryptic brown and blackish plumage feed unobserved in the soft ground at the edge of the lake while a siege of long-legged herons stand in the shallows looking for prey. High above, the stark cry of a nupiter piffkin is heard. The eerie wailing call of a bush stone-curlew, grey-brown above, streaked with black and rufous, wondering no doubt how it came to be so far from Australia, rings out over the willow grove. Large, slim and mainly nocturnal, its eating habits include insects, spiders, frogs, crustaceans, molluscs, snakes and lizards. Being abroad at this time of day perhaps the result of jet lag.

To avoid the congestion, a kettle of Rüppell's griffon vultures, named after the 19th century German explorer, collector and zoologist Eduard Rüppell, visiting from the Sahel region of central Africa, wait patiently in a holding pattern at 37,000 feet having been put there by air traffic control after arrival following their long-haul flight. Their cruising speed is set at 22mph. This is a large, powerfully built bird, adults reaching up to 3.5 feet in length with a wingspan of 8.5 feet. A bird of prey, it is a scavenger, feeding mostly on the carcasses of dead animals. Unusually, it does not have feathers on its head, an adaptation perhaps because of the vulture's habit of putting its head inside the body of the prey when eating. An endangered bird, the Rüppell's griffon vulture has evolved a type of haemoglobin that can use oxygen efficiently at high altitudes where oxygen levels are low.

"Thank goodness there's only one of me," thought The Parrot.

Flowers sparkle in the sun, caressing the habitat where the willow grove meets the meadow. Included in their number, a bushy clump of goat's beard over six feet tall with deep-green foliage and a profusion of small creamy-white flowers in large terminal panicles, fritillaries with purple-reddish bell-shaped flowers, strongly scented common yarrow with feathery blue-green aromatic leaves arranged spirally on the stems and white to pink flowers reaching over three feet above the ground, tall downy cow parsley with hollow stems and tripinnate leaves standing over two feet tall having florets of small, white flowers and colonies of lilies of the valley with narrow, paired, elliptic leaves growing up to ten inches long and three inches across with a single raceme of sweetly scented bell-shaped white flowers. Marsh marigolds with hollow flowering stems carrying bright yellow flowers, purple loosestrife growing up to six feet with tapering spikes of purple-red flowers and the tiny, purple, densely crowded flowers of water mint, all brighten the area.

Buzzing here and there, a solitary mason bee and a rabble of leaf cutter bees collect pollen and nectar, inadvertently dispersing pollen as they go before returning to their nests.

The long dangling spines of globe-shaped lion's mane mushrooms belonging to the tooth fungus group can be seen growing on the trunks of hardwoods on the north-western side of the lake. An edible fungus, The Parrot is experimenting with its neuroprotective and nootropic properties in the forlorn hope that the Sergeant's memory and reasoning can be improved, however slightly. Lichens, liverworts and mosses are plentiful in the woodland. Dark and light green hornworts, unusual for land plants in that they use inorganic carbon transporters and carbonic anhydrases to increase CO_2 levels, abound.

Colourful, carnivorous dragonflies with powerful jaws, not real flies, dance in the warm air using four delicate, membranous wings, two on each side of long slender bodies. Predatory damselflies, present in the area since the Lower Permian period spanning 47 million years from the end of the Carboniferous period 298.9 million years ago to the beginning of the Triassic period 251.9 million years ago, hunt their prey.

Thirsty swallows skim the calm surface of the lake to drink, helping themselves to midges and dance flies as they go.

A green and yellow grass snake, Pembrokeshire's longest snake, basks in the warm sunlight on a flat shelf of rock at the lake's edge before hunting for frogs and toads which it will consume live without using constriction. This particular one is five feet in length, its body curled around itself.

A troop of noisy, howler monkeys rest high in the tree canopies munching leaves and flowers. Blonde females care for their young while black males, the largest approximately three feet tall when standing, make loud roaring calls to mark their territory as they lie back amongst the branches, legs wide apart, exposing their rust red scrotums to seasick passengers returning from an excursion around Dinas Head.

25

If you have love you will do all things well.
Thomas Merton[1]

The hay meadow nestled between the orchard and the *Piazza della Republica* caught light from the early morning sun. Long shadows moved imperceptibly as it traced its path west. Blue speedwells, red campion, ribwort plantain with lanceolate leaves and stubby brown flower heads with whitish anthers borne on leafless stalks, buttercups with shiny yellow flowers growing in circular patches, white and red clover, lesser stitchwort with slender stems bearing terminal cymes of white flowers, delicate looking pignut with clusters of small white flowers on branched heads, scabious with their dainty, lilac blooms bobbing on the end of long stalks, tough harebells with wiry stems and pale blue flowers and scentless ragged robin with delicately fringed, divided, rose-red petals are some of the wildflowers providing a habitat for seed-eating and ground-nesting birds, slow worms, lizards, voles and shrews. The meadow is a pollinator paradise attracting many different species including bees, wasps, butterflies, moths and hoverflies. The area is also a hedgehog hotspot with its abundant natural vegetation and bushy areas.

At home in the meadow, *dzo*, of archaic Asian cattle stock, and *yaks* provide wool for socks and several pints of rich milk every day from which Megan makes butter, cheese and yogurt. They graze at up to 16,000 feet, covering vast distances and thriving on the sparse vegetation of the Preseli Peaks. In Bronwen's mind the hay meadow, shaded at its north easterly perimeter by the apple and oak trees, is a landscape imbued with enchantment and endless possibility. Through the long winter months the dried dung cakes of the cattle supply fuel for heating.

Perennial colonies of native honeybees, Apis mellifera mellifera live contentedly in this environment. Whilst producing less honey than some other bees they do not need to be fed sugar and are consistent honey producers. This particular morning, in a hollow tree trunk, the pupal stages of the daughter queens are nearing completion and observant passers-by are thrilled to witness the old queen and approximately two thirds of the adult workers leave the colony in a swarm to search for a new location where they will begin the task of building a new hive. Bronwen collects the honey which she and Megan use raw as a cough syrup and lip balm and to wash their hair. Needless to say, it also finds its way, along with coconut oil and cocoa powder, into their homemade dark chocolate. And, of course, into their honey ice cream.

In a rare example of mutualism in west Wales Bronwen and honeyguide birds have, through natural selection, formed a mutually beneficial arrangement. Flitting from tree to tree the birds call out to Bronwen, their song a chattering tch tch tch tch tch tch. Following them until they stop close to a bees' nest, she lights a small fire under the nest for the smoke to drive away the bees and collects some of the honey, leaving the beeswax for the birds. Bronwen and the honeyguide birds talk to one another as they move via a system of melodious whistles.

Black truffles grow under oaks on the meadow's western edge which Megan grates over soup. Nearby is the juniper copse from which, after two years maturing on the trees, the berries are picked for Bronwen to make a rather lively lemonade. The oaks, lilacs, horse chestnuts, beech and cedars of Lebanon lining the city's *Grands Boulevards* have been genetically modified with fungal luciferin, which is compatible with plant biochemistry, to create autonomously luminescent trees which glow in the dark. This sustainable light source falls in line with a recent Welsh Government[2] directive relating to carbon neutral street lighting although protest groups are concerned about the effects of light pollution on the insect population. On dark autumn nights the yellow carpet of leaves fallen from the beautiful gingko tree in the *Piazza* attracts many visitors who are drawn by its ghostly glow.

Returning from the annual Machlud y Wawr[3] conference which this year was in north Wales, the red eye arrived at Crymych International Airport just after 5.15a.m. The shuttle dropped them in the centre of the City and they breakfasted in Caffi Carnabwth on the corner across the road from the Crymych Arms. Cockles and laver bread with all the trimmings accompanied by thick slices of sour oatmeal bread downed with cupfuls of freshly roasted Arabica coffee was the most popular choice, followed by either apple tart and vanilla ice cream or spiced coffee and walnut roulade with a hint of cinnamon and nutmeg covered with walnuts and drizzled with dark chocolate. Or both. The special that morning was boiled eggs in organic vegetable soup. Of course! Some, too tired to talk, read the early edition of the morning paper, the Crymych *Zeitung*, delivered free to every business in the City.

Munching toast, Megan remembered the last time she and her husband visited the caffi. Sitting by the window watching the morning rush hour tractors potter by he took the little finger of her right hand gently between his thumb and forefinger. "You can't escape now, cariad," he said. "I've got you in a Maori wrestling hold." She eased her finger free as she needed it to lift the cup and took another sip of coffee, the little finger sticking out. "So, you've learnt how to escape from the wrestling hold," he sighed, and looked at her, admiration in his eyes. She smiled as her eyes rolled upwards. "There is a closeness between us," he whispered. "There is love. To me this means that I am kind to you, generous to you, loving to you. I seek to create an environment in which you experience the love that is inside of you, the love that you are. There is no other purpose to this relationship. This is how I see it." She put the cup down, took his hand in hers and squeezed it lovingly. They looked into each other's eyes. "I'm glad I met you cariad," he said.

"Thank you."

"Who are you again?"

She laughed and squeezed his hand extra hard. The orchestra in the *cwtsh* over in the corner were playing a *waltz*. "Can I have the pleasure of this dance?" he asked. "Yes," she replied. He took her little finger in the Maori wrestling hold again and they walked into the middle of the dance floor. "I can't dance," he told her, "so I always come into the middle. I feel safer here."

"Even though we are the only people dancing?" she queried.

"You go onto the dance floor and wiggle about and it looks fantastic," he continued. "I go onto the dance floor spiralling and wheeling and somebody calls the coastguard."

"You'll never leave me, will you," she said, more in a saying than an asking way.

"Never!"

"I knew that."

"Unless ..."

She looked up. "Unless?"

"Unless Nicole Kidman calls."

"You wouldn't!"

"No, of course not."

"Thank goodness for that."

There was a pause as he thought about it. "She's unlikely to phone."

"And if she did?"

"I'll let her down gently. I'll be very sensitive and take her feelings into consideration as I explain to her that I'm with you now."

"Hmmmmm. You could borrow my shotgun, cariad, that would be quicker. And humane."

"I would like to be holding your hand and kissing you in fifty years time."

"Yes, cariad."

"No! That's terrible!"

"Terrible?"

"Yes. It suggests that I only want to be with you for another fifty years. I want to be holding your hand and kissing you for much longer than that."

"I'll be very old then."

"Mmmm. You're right. I haven't really thought this through. You'll be all shrivelled and wrinkly, so I'll have to close my eyes when I kiss you." She pinched

him lightly on the arm. As the *waltz* neared its end a few tender, prophetic lines
of poetry came to her.

> *You are drifting away from*
> *me on the whitening current of your hair.*
> *I lean far out from the bone's bough,*
> *knowing the hand I extend*
> *can save nothing of you*
> *but your love.*[4]

"You're looking very smart tonight," she said, as they returned to their
seats.

"Thank you. I think the wind swept me in the right direction on my way
here." He looked her up and down. "You're beautiful. There are twenty-year olds
who would strangle their mothers to have a figure like yours."

"Thank you, cariad."

He knew he was in love, his toes felt warm and tingly.

The Members were tucking into their breakfasts, some stifling yawns after
the previous long day and sleepless night. "What a lovely morning," Megan
remarked, looking through the window at the rainbow arching over the Memorial
Hall, one end disappearing through the window of a nearby terraced house, the
other end lighting up the front door of the pub.

"Every day's a lovely day when you're having breakfast," proposed Bronwen.

Megan, her mouth full of cockles, nodded in agreement.

"When I blink," Bronwen informed Megan, "light travels around the world
twice."

Megan continued munching the cockles, a thoughtful look on her face. Later,
after the tumultuous joyfulness of breakfasting with friends and as the
streetlights went out the revellers scattered and made their way home. Megan
and Bronwen took the underground to Crymych Centrum from where they would
enjoy the short walk across the *Piazza della Republica* to the Cathedral, entering
through the side door and going down to the crypt. But they were delayed. They
had forgotten that around this time every year there unfolds an event
Pembrokeshire folk light-heartedly call The Great Migration during which 1.7
million Wildebeest migrate from the Preseli Mountains of north Pembrokeshire to
the warmer climes of the plains around Kilgetty where they graze during the
winter cold. 250,000 will die *en route*, such are the dangers they face.

All the pedestrian lights are on red and the traffic lights on green for the
three days these magnificent animals take to pass. Megan, Bronwen and the others
caught up in the last day of the migration were fed and watered in the Machlud y
Wawr *marquee* set up for this very purpose. Deck chairs are laid out in rows on

the viewing platform for those stranded by nature's procession to watch this great natural spectacle pass and wait for the all clear to sound and the dust to settle as the last animal heads south. They should have got off at the next stop. Nonetheless, a few short munching and sipping hours later it was a beautiful, clear, sunshiny day with sapphire blue sky and the last Wildebeests mere specks in the distance as they disappeared into a vast dust cloud bathed by southern light. A warming breeze came from the southwest. The traffic lights turned red, the pedestrian lights turned green, they finished their *cappuccinos*, bade farewell to the Members serving in the *marquee* and strolled across the *Piazza* to the Cathedral where they unlocked the side door and went down the ancient oak spiral staircase to the crypt.

Bronwen, a little-known side effect of the stardust generation, made them both a *macchiato*, each with two shots of *expresso* and a dollop of foam to celebrate. Megan sat in her armchair in the *simne fawr* sipping coffee and began reading a novel, picking up where she had left it three days before. Bronwen decided to practise the new dance routine she named **Catastrophe**. Changing into clogs she sat on the floor, body at a ninety-degree angle to it with legs stretched out in front of her and began her warmup pre-practise routine. Her toes moved from pointing straight ahead to pointing to the ceiling and back again. She continued this exercise for several minutes, chanting in synch with the movements as she did so.

Good steel tipped toes.
Naughty steel tipped toes.
Good steel tipped toes.
Naughty steel tipped toes.

Then, muscles, sinews and mind ready she downed the coffee in one, hurled the *demitasse* hard against the wall and before the myriad smashed pieces of crockery hit the floor, unleashed her inner clogging monster and began whirling and twirling around the far end of the crypt. She was in the zone. The clattering of the iron nails on the underside of the wooden clogs as they met the cold slate floor slabs reverberated around the uncarpeted crypt, bouncing noisily off the stone walls, pillars, floor and ceiling, filling the air behind her with flaring sheets of multicoloured sparks. Recently, an experimental echoic chamber was constructed enclosing a section of the space, completely absorbing reflections of sound. As her excitement levels mounted and her endocrine system kicked in she moved inside. On the outside Megan was insulated from the clamour of the clogs and on the inside Bronwen was insulated from the noise of Megan sitting back in the sofa reading, allowing her to concentrate on what she knows best. In the chamber she clogs in an environment that simulates a quiet open space of infinite dimension in which she lets herself go with her stream of consciousness creative impulses uncoupled from reality. Bronwen is widely thought to be one of Machlud y Wawr's wilder flowers.

"Time for the evening news," thought Megan, picking up the dooby doo and pointing it at the radio. She pressed the 'On' button, replaced the dooby doo, placed the novel in her lap and listened as the announcer began. "The new £1.3 billion Terminal 6 at Crymych International Airport, capable of handling forty-two million passengers a year, was officially opened today by the Lord Mayoress of Crymych, Councillor Rhianwen Haf. During her speech Councillor Haf said, "This is the new gateway to Pembrokeshire and a symbol of the county's ambition to benefit from the exponential growth in the world's environmental tourism sector."

In the throes of dance practice Bronwen crashed silently off the vaulted ceiling and plummeted to Earth where she formed an impromptu, untidy and somewhat painful heap on the cold stone floor. In clogging terms this is a hard-hat area. Upon becoming a heap on the floor, a frequent event over the years, she has learnt to become one with the heap, to let it be, as it is, to embrace heapness, to enjoy it as life's illusion unfolding. Then she got up again. You can't keep Bronwen down, at least not for long. The clogs moved, slowly at first, then quicker and in no time at all she reached optimum clogging speed and using her inbuilt trial and error algorithms continued refining the dance whilst simultaneously attempting to reduce the 10^{47} possible ways, about as many as there are molecules on Earth, of clogging across a given space to a manageable 10^{30} or so, along with the appropriate dance steps. Her ancestors were capable of symbolic thought, abstract concepts and ritualised collective behaviour and she drew on this family experience as the choreography developed. Bronwen was in her element, every fibre of her being sang the song of freedom.

She crashed heavily into a stone pillar and formed a crumpled heap on the solid, unyielding, stone floor. Whilst in this position, winded, she contemplated Newton's Laws of Motion as they applied to her. "The first states that a clogger stays in motion unless acted upon by an outside force such as a pillar," she thought out loud, which, in an echoic chamber, isn't loud at all.

"Correct," she concurred.

"The second law describes what happens when that clogger arrives at the pillar. In my case, deceleration proportional to the mass of the clogger, me, and the force applied, F=ma. The bigger my crumple zones the longer it takes to stop and the less likelihood there is of experiencing a whiplash injury."

A moments reflection. "Correct."

Her crumple zones are of concern to her and she often fantasises about having them enlarged. Megan discourages this idea, reassuring her that one day she will meet a man who will love her just the way she is.

Her ruminations continued. "Newton's third law states, if you run into a stone pillar with a force of x the pillar in turn hits you with a force -x. That's why stone pillars hurt." Her scientific analysis completed to her satisfaction she rubbed the bruises on her crumple zones and lay still, waiting to get her breath back before returning to the fray.

Megan wondered what Bronwen was doing as the vibrations emanating from the Cathedral's foundations had stopped. Bronwen, in her eyes, seems to be a bundle of energy that appears from nowhere, or from the kitchen if the First Law of Thermodynamics means anything. Bronwen, the motionless heap lying on the floor at the base of the pillar certainly suggests she is not a perpetual motion machine, however much casual observation of her movements might suggest otherwise. Perspiring profusely after her exertions, Machlud y Wawr's Etiquette Guide advises against sweating, Bronwen thought it unnecessarily restrictive that she could not cool herself to absolute zero for a few minutes and in the process take a well-earned rest. As such, she is a fan of the third law.

Her explorations of herself *vis-à-vis* the natural sciences continued as she turned her attention to gravity, knowing from bitter experience that the mathematical law describing it is only an approximation. It seemed straightforward enough to Newton, but had he bounced off the ceiling of the crypt in his local church and from there fallen to Earth? There is no mention of this in the literature. "Relying upon an apple to fall on your head seems to me to be precarious science at the very least," she informed Megan on one occasion. Later, Einstein muddied the waters by concluding that objects curve spacetime around them in a way described by a system of partial differential equations. "Yes, partial being the operative word," she reflected.

Bronwen moved slightly to take the weight of her body off her nose, which lay beneath it. Blood began to return causing pins and needles at the tip. She gazed at the intricate patterns etched into the base of the pillar. "My predicament can be explained mathematically thus:

$$F = \frac{G\, m_1\, m_2}{r^2}$$

where F is the force of gravity, Big G is the gravitational constant whose value is approximately 6.674×10^{-11} $m^3 \cdot kg^{-1} \cdot s^{-2}$, m_1 is me, m_2 is the floor, which in this case represents the Earth, and r^2 is the square of the distance between us." She felt giddy as more blood drained from her body and rushed into her nose. "However, this theory would break down if the crypt was a black hole or if the crypt floor and I were subatomic particles." The pins and needles stopped. Her nose returned to normality. "Time to dance!" she cried.

Suspecting that her ability to develop the choreography was being thwarted by radio waves from an alien presence passing through the galaxy somewhere close to the Milky Way Bronwen wrapped her head in tin foil she found earlier in the cupboard next to the sink in the kitchen. Reassured, she began dancing furiously again only to crash into another stone pillar and enter a dizzy crumpled state on the floor at its base. Once again life presented her with down time, an opportunity to contemplate heapness and her relationship to it. Bronwen always starts well, then enthusiasm takes control, guided by exploding raw energy. She lay mutely on her back on the floor admiring the craftsmanship displayed in the richly decorated stonework of the vaulted ceiling and felt depressed by all the lying around. Her dream of getting a clogging gold at the next olympics crashed and cuddled up next to her. "*Fin de sens unique*," it whispered unkindly in her ear.

"You cannot yet do it perfectly, yet every time you do it, it is perfect," proffered Megan encouragingly. "Step out of the dream of who you think you are."

The Radio Free Crymych announcer continued. "This weekend Tenby is filled with photospheres, fifty in all, in different parts of the town, each measuring seventy feet in circumference. The photospheres depict a selection of Wales' historic sites, literature and visual art in 360^0 format."

"To the kitchen now. Crymych Cooking Club's monthly public demonstration of culinary skills is in Das Kapital[5] tomorrow morning from eleven until one during which Club members will make a *sofrito* from locally grown organic tomatoes, garlic and extra virgin, cold-pressed, olive oil fresh from the olive groves on the southern slopes of the Preselis near Rhosfach. "Our motto is, It's not just taste. It's health," a Club representative told us, adding, "There'll be seating for a hundred and fifty."

In the depths of winter, the three months of the year during which only polar bears can get through, when Crymych, atop its bleak, exposed mountaintop is frozen solid for month after relentless month, Megan snuggles up in the armchair in the *simne fawr*. A small round table stands next to her on which she keeps books and newspapers, the reading lamp next to it. Bronwen, in a similar arrangement, sits opposite. In the twilight between sunset and dusk as sunlight scatters off the atmosphere and then on into the night as rooks caw and wood pigeons coo in the trees to the south and west, it is their habit to sit without artificial light, chatting about the day's events as the shadows cast by the wood fire dance in ever darker patterns around them. Only when conversation wanes are the lamps turned on and books or newspapers read. Later, they tire of reading, put out the lamps and sit bathed by the light from the fire, Megan with her *crochet* and Bronwen weaving willow baskets. Sometimes, whilst engaged in these occupations they watch a nature or history programme on the television that at the flick of a switch descends between them from the vaulted ceiling. The two-sided ultra-thin OLED display means they can sit at opposite sides of the television and watch the same or two different programmes at the same time, the tiny speakers built into their armchairs guaranteeing no interference with the sound quality. But seldom is the television used, particularly shortly before retiring as they prefer the quiet time in a soft firelit night and an old well-fitting companionship that prepares their minds for sleep.

On the crypt wall to one side of the sofa in front of the bay window hang Flemish painter Jan Brueghel the Elder's oil on oak panel *Still Life of Flowers in a Stoneware Vase* and John William Whitehouse's *Gather Ye Rosebuds While Ye May*, painted in the style of Romanticism. To one side and positioned to cover a damp patch is *A Wall in Naples*, an oil study by Thomas Jones. Yawning, Megan turns to gaze at Marc Chagall's *Bouquet près de la Fenêtre* hanging alongside them. Late on a winter's night when all outside is blackness and cold she looks through this *fenêtre* and dreams. All four paintings are on loan. The faint western light entering through the bay window illuminates them, helped by the low light from the bespoke antique brass wall lamp above each one.

Bronwen raises herself from the floor, carefully removes the tin foil from around her head, and leaving the echoic chamber lopes unsteadily to the kitchen where she puts two handfuls of whole Arabica beans into a frying pan, switches on the heat and begins the roasting process. Coffee making finished she reappears carrying a tray upon which are two full cups of coffee with saucers and teaspoons, a small jug of slightly warmed, unpasteurised, raw, organic cream from a farm near Maenclochog and two small 85% cocoa bars. Walking to the bay window she puts the tray on the coffee table and falls back into the sofa's embrace. Megan turns the radio off, gets up and walks across to join her. Two pairs of woolly stockinged feet appear on the coffee table and the sipping and munching begins.

A solitary owl prepares for night-time adventures. Unable to move its eyes it swivels its head to view the surrounding locality, its disc-like face channelling sound to its ears until a faint noise coming from below reaches both ears at the same time and it looks directly at a vole moving across the woodland floor. Descending with long glides it puts beak and talons to good use. The churring song of a nightjar rises and falls in the still evening air as it rests. Its short bill and wide mouth will soon catch moths in flight. A small family group of foxes get ready to leave their underground den to hunt insects and small mammals and to eat worms, spiders and berries.

High above, the moon is surrounded by a celestial rainbow.

The rumbling and thundering of late evening sounds from the City gain access through the open bay window, resounding, reverberating, rolling and tumbling around them in a low *basso profondo* background. Megan taps a teaspoon against her half empty coffee cup for pitch and they lift their voices to the fading light in the west as it is lost to view. No words form, the beauty of vocal sounds alone enough to express their feelings in heavenly two-part harmony.

Greenfinches, bullfinches, blackbirds, song thrushes, woodpeckers, skylarks, grey partridges, golden plovers, ring ouzels and merlins raise their voices in one last glorious hurrah for soon they will become quiet as they congregate for the night.

A convocation of eagles passes overhead heading for their eyries built high in the tall, strong pines, spruces and firs to the north of Crymych. The landscape around the city provides their basic needs, water to drink and catch fish and forests which provide other food sources such as rabbits and squirrels and in which they build their nests in the treetops, just below the crown where the branches are strong enough to support their weight. They choose trees that reach high above the forest canopy as this provides easy access and perches with good visibility for hunting and resting. Their cries mingle with the sounds emanating from the bay window far below to create a swaying, vertical, choral landscape.

Encouraged by this a colony of gulls returning to their homes on the coast further to the west squawk and scream enthusiastically.

Western tree hyraxes, small nocturnal mammals with 4-toed front feet and 3-toed back feet, cousins several times removed of elephants and sea cows, their light brown coats reflecting the fading light, gather, as is natural for arboreal folivores, in trees nearby. Encouraged by the musicality of the evening the males expand their air pouches to maximum. Enlarged larynxes come into play as they emit distinctive, territorial, awful, high-pitched screams followed by a descending series of horrible shrieks.

Nocturnal creatures stir. Bats, important for pollinating flowers, hang upside down from the branches of trees as waking thoughts of food and sustained flight appear in their minds. Soon, their calls, reaching up to 140 decibels, will be heard around the woodland.

High above, a solar storm, an eruption of electrically charged particles from the sun's atmosphere, hits the Earth's magnetic field producing waves of varying high frequencies and the song of the Earth begins its mysterious refrain.

Dogs in the vicinity, encouraged by this unearthly symphony of eerie sounds, willingly contribute their vocal calls.

Aficionados of song, members of the third and fourth fifteens, travelling reserves and camp followers who are whiling away the evening reliving past glories in the rugby club downtown, become quiet and listen. Inspired, they order another round of pints with rum and black chasers and begin singing a medley of Shirley Bassey[6] and Kylie Minogue[7] favourites, including Shirley's, *Something in the Way He Sidesteps*, *Dislocatedfinger*, *Rucking Is Forever*, *Get the Shove Started*, *What Kind of Hooker Am I*, *Hey Big Offloader*, *Born to Play Flyhalf*, *And We Were Flankers*, *Nobody Kicks Out of the Hand Like Me*, and Kylie's, *Come Into My Scrum*, *Get Outta My Way*, *Red and Black*, *I'm Just Here for the Half Time Team Talk*, *Keep on Pumpin' It*, *All I Wanna Do Is Score a Try Under the Posts*, *Better the Props You Know*, *Spinning the Opposition Scrum Around*, *Can't Get Your Boot Off My Head*, *Je Ne Sais Pas Pourquoi the Bar Is Closed* and *Never Too Late to Get a*

Penalty Try, followed by a raucous, irreverent rendition of that Noel Coward classic, *Don't Put Your Daughter in the Scrum Mrs Worthington*[8] closely followed by Bois y Blacbord's glorious *Dros y Mynydd Du.*[9]

"Oh dear!" Megan murmurs and gets up to close the window.

26

A young lad was sent to school. He began his lessons with the other children, and the first lesson the teacher set him was the straight line, the figure 'one'. But whereas the others went on progressing, this child continued writing the same figure. After two or three days the teacher came up to him and said, "Have you finished your lesson?" He said, "No, I'm still writing 'one'." He went on doing the same thing, and when at the end of the week the teacher asked him again, he said, "I have not yet finished it." The teacher thought he was an idiot and should be sent away, as he could not or did not want to learn. At home the child continued with the same exercise and the parents also became tired and disgusted. He simply said, "I have not yet learnt it, I am learning it. When I have finished, I shall take the other lessons." The parents said, "The other children are going on further, school has given you up, and you do not show any progress; we are tired of you." And the lad thought with sad heart that as he had displeased his parents too, he had better leave home. So, he went into the wilderness and lived on fruits and nuts. After a long time, he returned to his old school. And when he saw the teacher, he said to him, "I think I have learnt it. See if I have. Shall I write on this wall?" And when he made his sign, the wall split in two.

Hazrat Inayat Khan[1]

On routine patrol from Fishguard to North Cornwall The Parrot used the gravity of Strumble Head to swing the coracle forward through the water thus saving a vital three minutes of travelling time. Oblivious to this detail the Sergeant experienced a slight lean to one side as he lay in the hammock sipping tea through a straw. "Pentaquarks," he thought, then continued sipping. Having begun, the brain continued. "The flow of my thoughts is unceasing. The flow of the associated emotions is unceasing." These thoughts echoed safely around the inside of his mind. He felt a little unnerved by it all. New thoughts arrived. "I am not my thoughts. I am not my emotions." He smiled. The Parrot smiled. The sea smiled. The thought, "All is well." appeared in his mind. He took another sip from the tea, made from a new tea mix that is scarily potent.

The Parrot, for the fun of it, set a course that would take them along the coast of south Pembrokeshire, under the Green Arch, between Stack Rocks, between Caldey Island and the mainland, between St Catherine's Island and the mainland, then across open water to the Gower, between Burry Holms and the mainland, between Worm's Head and the mainland, then, hugging the Welsh coast, entering English waters and heading south west along the old pirate trails before entering Cornish waters and following the coast of North Cornwall to Wadebridge and, if time allowed, up the Camel and its tributary to the mooring at Grogley Halt. Having secured the course, it flew to the crow's nest atop the main mast, donned an eyepatch, put a tricorn on its head and raised the *Jolly Roger*, a request from the children of Ysgol Wdig. Picking up the squeeze box kept there for such occasions it sang sea shanties to the crowds gathered along the quayside and the beach to watch their departure. As the call-and-response grew in volume, The Parrot calling out the verse and the spectators responding in unison, the vessel left the harbour, narrowly missing the incoming ferry as it went, and headed southwest. It was happy to be heading out to sea again, it is what parrots are born to do.

The Sergeant distrusts the on-board computer, preferring a map that does not depict the position of the mainland, the coastline and islands but instead the position and movement of ocean currents. It must be said that not knowing where Pembrokeshire is brings with it its own disadvantages when returning from patrols.

Once safely past Strumble Head The Parrot suggested a relaxing game of chess. It was a bruising affair, but The Parrot, using a line of the Sicilian he had never played before as Black, prevailed. In the fortieth move of the twenty first game, he countered the Sergeant's bishop to king six with pawn to rook four. The game was adjourned for tea and toast. The Sergeant resigned the following day.[2]

Over the last few years, the Sergeant has spotted 60 species of butterfly and 2,500 species of moth in the willow grove. Of the moths, his favourites are the crimson speckled and the French red underwing, not forgetting the spectacular, squeaking, African death's head hawk moth which is about the size of a small parrot and has tufts of short yellow hairs on the thorax that form the shape of a human skull, an evolutionary adaptation whose purpose no doubt is to scare the Sergeant. It works.

They reached Tenby as the tide was at its lowest ebb and as they carried the vessel across the sand between St Catherine's Island and the cliff with Tenby Museum looking down on them from above, they stopped to have an ice cream and watch the marine archaeologists at work. In 1715 three galleons laden with treasure and bound for Spain foundered at this spot with the loss of over two hundred souls. The galleons were the survivors of a fleet struck by a hurricane off the coast of Florida while carrying riches from the New World to King Philip V of Spain. Nearly one million pounds worth of gold coins have been recovered recently from the wrecks and are on show in a locked display case in the museum next to the permanent exhibition celebrating the 9th century poem *Edmyg Dinbych*, translated as *In Praise of Tenby*, from the Book of Taliesin, in which Tenby and its king, Bleiddudd, are praised. The wrecks lie in the shallow sea just below the low water line and ever since that terrible night when they were lost, the area has been a favourite snorkelling spot for locals. The treasure trove includes dozens of coins known as 'royals' that were specially minted and are valued at $300,000 each. The town is doing well from the discovery as visitors flock here to see the archaeologists at work recovering the treasure. "Over the centuries, locals from the town who spend summers snorkelling have occasionally let slip tales of wrecks and Spanish doubloons appearing in the sand," one of the archaeologists explained to a group of visitors. "Our dig here proves the old stories to be true."

Their ice creams finished they carried the coracle to the water's edge where they got it afloat by the pontoons used to get day trippers onto the boats ferrying them back and forth to Caldey Island. The Sergeant and The Parrot boarded and after a wave of thanks and a dramatic shout of "**Avast ye landlubbers!**" from the Sergeant the on-board computer pointed the vessel across the bay towards the Gower at 'enjoying the view' speed and they embarked on the next leg of the journey.

As it would be some time before landfall on Worm's Head where they were to spend the night the Sergeant made a mug of tea and lay down on the soft, verdant floor of four, five and six-leaf clovers and bear grass close to a fire of mesquite wood in the stone circle on the stern from where he could keep an eye on things. When at its most luxurious this is his first choice lying down spot. The clover bank is alive with plants he was given whilst on an exchange visit to the Abisko National Park two hundred miles north of the Arctic Circle in Swedish Lapland. A great spot from where to view the *aurora borealis*, as is Rosebush on a clear night of course. Researchers do not know whether the fourth, fifth and sixth leaves are caused by environmental factors, genetic factors or both. A small area of Tregaron Bog, the biggest in western Europe, has been planted with them. *Twm Siôn Cati* would no doubt be delighted by this development. The Sergeant was in northern Sweden to assist an enquiry into allegations that the Arctic Circle had gone missing. After a month-long search that proved fruitless, he reported back that their worst fears had been realised as he could find no trace of it on the ground. Later he was to comment that it was this experience that made him the ideal choice to investigate the alleged disappearance of the Landsker Line back home in his beloved Pembrokeshire.

Whilst lying on the clover he finished reading *The Deerslayer* by James Fenimore Cooper. "Apart from a misplaced comma on page 136, that was a good book," he said to himself and looked forward to reading the remaining four volumes in the series which include *The Last of the Mohicans*, all five volumes in the series making up the *Leatherstocking Tales*. Putting it down he picked up the new novel he had borrowed from Fishguard Library, Allen Raine's *A Welsh Witch*, and began reading. " *'The lights and shadows of an April day, and the solemn silence that sometimes falls on a calm sea, were brooding over a sheltered bay on the Welsh coast, as the Lark ploughed her way through the green pellucid waters'* ."

The sun was setting. "Probably in the west," he thought and stood up and walked to the gunwale on the starboard side from which vantage point he confirmed this theory. The use of the terms 'port' and 'starboard' on a coracle is of course contentious. Pleased that his theory was correct he returned to the clover and continued reading. Late that evening as the sun set and the world was bathed in a soft, crimson glow they made landfall on the Worm and the on-board computer dropped anchor and settled the coracle at its mooring for the night. The computer does not share information with the Sergeant. For health and safety reasons information is maintained in a closed loop consisting of two component parts, the computer and The Parrot, and the system works well. Senior commanders of Dyfed-Powys Police Rapid-Response Coracle Unit,[3] following a long and frank discussion with The Parrot, came to the conclusion that including the Sergeant in the loop would create a damaging situation known as an 'information paradox'. For many years Stephen Hawking[4] the Cambridge physicist worked on this problem and in a lecture in Stockholm in front of an excited audience his solution was revealed. "Leave the Sergeant out of the loop," he declared emphatically.

They made the most of what light remained to collect shells and play a hotly competitive game of dandiss on the beach before surfing the Rhossili breakers around the Helvetia to cool off. Standing on the wet sand at the water's edge admiring the sunset, his surfboard tucked under one arm, he felt a little homesick, as was usual for him on long sea voyages and reminisced about his wife. An Italian psychologist has shown that gazing deeply into another person's eyes for ten minutes can transport you to another state of consciousness in which you hallucinate and feel disassociated from the world around you.[5] The Sergeant is pleased about this. However, when he gazes into his wife's eyes, he does not need ten minutes, the effect is immediate.

As night fell, life on the coracle became quiet. The dragon flies, butterflies, moths and fen raft spiders that live in the marsh grass bounding the eastern edge of the willow grove sensed the approaching dark and slowed their activities. Movement amongst the beavers, great bustards, cranes, and the pair of Eurasian lynx, slowed. In the lake nearby a dolphin pod played sleepily. They spend a part of every week on board, jumping overboard to return to the ocean and returning the same way. The seal colony that winters in the lake was nowhere to be seen. The lake, the willow grove and the marsh were recently awarded Mobile Site of Special Scientific Interest (MSSSI), the first in Wales. This honour follows the habitat on the stern being declared a Mobile Area of Outstanding Natural Beauty in 1955.

The Sergeant made his way back to the vessel and to the galley to have a hot mug of tea before taking the first watch and as he settled into a chair, mug of tea on the table next to him, he picked up the dooby doo and turned the radio on to catch the weekly science programme and then the news. He was distressed to hear the presenter state that a robot coracle was being developed at the University of the Four Trinity Davids' Naval Research Depot in Milford Haven.[6] "The robot coracle will be able to sail itself and resist attacks from pirates," the presenter explained. "The Mimosa II, as it has been dubbed by scientists working on the project, will be powered by wave energy supplemented with anthracite from Glamorgan, although the latter is being phased out in order to comply with Welsh Government[7] green guidelines. The on-board computer will make all the decisions so no need for crew and no need for food, no illness and no mistakes. And no refuelling. It will carry drones that can leave the vessel to carry out research both above and below the water. Remote intervention by DPPRRCU staff will be possible. The robot coracle will one day replace all manned and womanned vessels," the presenter finished with a hint of delight. "And now news from the world of physics. "Worm's Head is a psychological construct, it only exists because we exist."

"Hmmmmmmmm! " thought the Sergeant.

"Burry Holms too. In fact, our minds create everything. The mug, for example, does not exist except in the illusion our mind creates."

Confused, the Sergeant noticed the mug was morphing into what appeared to be a formless entity that as far as he could remember had previously exhibited characteristics he subconsciously labelled 'mugness'.

"**Hmmmmmmmmmm!** he thought, more emphatically this time. Reaching across he grasped the formless entity formerly known as mug.

"Neither does the tea exist," came the voice from the radio.

Tightening his grip, he lifted the formless entity formerly known as mug and took a reassuring gulp of tea before it, too, disappeared. As he gulped, the table disappeared.

"That's going too far," he complained. He noticed The Parrot had disappeared. He looked down and noticed his feet had disappeared and the disappearing process was working its way up his legs. He watched in silence as gradually his entire body proceeded to disappear from bottom to top. The precuneus, the area of his brain associated with memory, visuo-spatial perception, self-awareness and consciousness was showing early signs of alarm as it too disappeared.

"Perhaps you need to reassess who you are," came the voice of The Parrot from nowhere. "You no longer have a body, yet you still Are."

"You mean ...? What ...? Who ...? How ...? When ...? Why ...? Where ...? What time is it? Hmmmmmmmmmm!, ventured the Sergeant unconvincingly as the coracle disappeared. He took a cautious sip of the tea that had disappeared, put the mug that had disappeared onto the table that had disappeared picked up the dooby doo that had disappeared and turned the radio that had disappeared off then placed the

dooby doo that had disappeared back onto the table that had disappeared before picking up the mug that had disappeared and taking a confidence boosting sip of tea that had disappeared. "Considering the mug, the tea, the table, the dooby doo, the radio and my body, *Oh … dear!* and The Parrot and the coracle have all disappeared, I'm doing quite well," he thought, as Worm's Head disappeared.

"You no longer exist, yet who is it that is thinking?" asked the voice.

And so, to unwind after a long day travelling the sea lanes that by now were nowhere to be seen and to negotiate re-entry into the illusion that had disappeared he retired next door to the television room that had disappeared with a large bag of popcorn that had disappeared to watch a DVD that had disappeared and chose *L'Eclisse* with Alain Delon and Monica Vitti,[8] even though they too had disappeared, 1962 being one of his favourite years in French cinema. Glancing through a porthole that had disappeared during a boring part of the film that had disappeared The Parrot that had disappeared noticed the moon daisies that had disappeared growing at the edge of the willow grove that had disappeared glinting in the moonlight that had disappeared and the cows that had disappeared grazing alongside a couple of Welsh cobs that had disappeared, pit ponies that had disappeared and the black Welsh mountain ponies that had disappeared the Sergeant who had disappeared bought some time ago from the Ceulan Stud that had disappeared. Five different species of wasps, the red, the tree, the German, the Norwegian and of course the common that had disappeared were at play near the lake that had disappeared. A silver rainbow that had disappeared sparkled in the moonlight that had disappeared above the cowshed that had disappeared and beneath it thousands of *hotaru* butterflies that had disappeared from Japan, that, unknown to the Sergeant, had also disappeared, were at play. "If ever there was a night for the tylwyth teg that have disappeared to appear, this is it," murmured The Parrot that had disappeared.

The evening drew on and as existence slowly reappeared and resumed normal service The Parrot pondered the Sergeant's enjoyment of the simple things, and a few lines of poetry came to it. "*Maintenant, mon camarade de travail,*" it squawked tenderly to draw its shipmate's attention, before reciting.

> *He knows not where he's going,*
> *For the ocean will decide,*
> *It's not the destination,*
> *It's the glory of the ride.*[9]

The Sergeant's calm was interrupted by an announcement from the ship to shore radio. "Exciting news. Plans are afoot to land the first coracle on the dark side of Caldey Island, the side that always faces away from Tenby and has been virtually untouched for a very long time. Untouched that is apart from asteroid and meteor strikes. Photographs taken from NASA[10] spacecraft in orbit around the island confirm that its dark side has been hit many times throughout its 4.5-billion-year history. Impact craters are still clearly visible as the dark side has no atmosphere, which means no weather, no wind, no water, no plants and animals and therefore no erosion. Added to this, unlike in Tenby, there is no tectonic activity there to move rocks around, recycling them. The third reason why craters are still clearly visible is because there has been no volcanic activity on the dark side of Caldey for about 3 billion years."

"Bother!" he grizzled as he paused the film.

"A spokesperson from the Dark Side Exploration Department, an offshoot of the University of the Four Trinity Davids' Space Colonisation Institute[6] based jointly at Shanghai University's Jing'an campus and in a small room in Tenby Museum from where they have a lovely view of the light side, told us earlier today that the mission is planned for early next year. The objective of the mission is to study the geology of this unexplored area and to determine if it is a suitable site for a radio telescope as the far side of Caldey is a quiet place free from the interference of radio signals from Tenby. Because radio transmissions from the mainland are unable to reach the dark side of the island, making the expedition particularly hazardous, an unmanned vessel will be used which will beach at an appropriate spot and release a probe to collect samples."

"After beaching, the unmanned vessel, NASA's Perseverantia Caldey rover, will drop a five-pound helicopter from its underside. The $86 million rotocraft, called Ingenious, is set to conduct up to six flights, its three cameras recording the dark side's surface from above. The agency plans to share more details in a press conference in Tenby town hall on Tuesday week," the project manager at the University of the Four Trinity David's Jet Propulsion Laboratory in Kilgetty[6] explained. "Because communicating with a spacecraft on the dark side of Caldey takes a few minutes, which means that ground controllers in Tenby cannot control the flight in real time, engineers have designed and programmed the helicopter to carry out the flights autonomously. To catch enough air in the thin Caldey atmosphere the helicopter's four carbon-fiber blades are designed to spin in opposite directions at 2,400 revolutions per minute, eight times as fast as an ordinary terrestrial helicopter. Solar panels on top of the spacecraft power the spinning."

"A device the size of a toaster, the Caldey oxygen in-situ resource utilisation experiment, (Coxie), will travel attached to the chassis of the rover and is designed to create oxygen from the thin carbon dioxide rich atmosphere. It works by heating a sample of the atmosphere, which on Caldey is about 96% carbon dioxide, to about 800^0C. At this temperature oxygen atoms separate from the carbon dioxide molecules. Five grams of oxygen will be produced every hour, enough to keep an astronaut breathing for ten minutes. This is the first step of one day seeing humans living on the dark side of the island."

"After several days the probe will make the difficult journey back to the mother ship which will then return to South Beach in Tenby, beaching at high tide on day five."

"A press release sent by China's ruling Communist Party to the Tenby Observer[11] earlier today reads, 'Unlike mankind's mania in the past the Chinese people harbour the dream of shared human destiny. We choose to go to the dark side of Caldey Island not because of the unique glory it brings, but because this difficult step of destiny is also a forward step for human civilisation'."

The violent beating sound of light rainfall so familiar in these parts, encouraged by the force 8 that had appeared suddenly, blowing in from the southwest, hammered against the vessel and drew his attention to the portholes. He observed people enjoying a late evening stroll along the beach, battling with inside out umbrellas. And then it came to him. He put two and two together. "I wonder," he reflected, "if umbrellas attract rain?" Unmoved by this train of thought the Sergeant's ferrets escaped and began playing havoc with the wildlife on the stern, particularly the pet rabbits. The early arrival of Bewick's swans from Siberia, their all-white plumage, black feet and gills having an eerie, ghostlike appearance in the gloom, heralded a harsh winter. They settled in the shallow pools and marshland of the tundra to the north of the lake. Unconcerned by these comings and goings he made his way to the galley. Sitting at the table later with tea and chocolate biscuits at his side he turned the radio on to catch the news. He didn't notice the big brown owl flying past the porthole. But that's another story.

"Deep beneath Skomer Island," came the voice of the announcer, "frozen in the permafrost is a crucial piece of Welsh linguistic history. Preserved for generations in a purpose-built concrete vault that can withstand nuclear war or natural disaster are the country's *treiglads*. The vault protects this part of our heritage from disaster. The Endangered Treiglad Project (ETP) records and stores as audio and video clips examples of the three main initial consonant *treiglads*, soft, nasal and aspirate before they disappear. Two of these, the nasal and aspirate, have been under threat for decades, particularly in the southern half of the country. The *treiglad* vault is designed to protect the linguistic heritage of the Celtic countries and examples of *treiglads* from their six languages are kept here forming an invaluable research resource for scholars of the future who wish to preserve and restore initial consonant *treiglad* systems. Of the three *treiglads* used today in Welsh it is estimated that two will have disappeared from speech before the end of the century, only the soft remaining. The vault's chambers, embedded deep in the permafrost, will keep the *treiglads* frozen even if someone accidentally turns the power off when they go home in the evening. Having completed the majority of the work on initial consonant *treiglads* the work is now expanding to include other consonant *treiglads* and to begin work on vowel *treiglads*."

Heedless of the gathering storm he sipped tea, ...

"Tomorrow will see the official opening of a similar vault buried deep in the permafrost of the island of Grassholm as a storehouse for the Global Endangered Treiglad Project (GETP) which, supported by grants from UNESCO, the WHO, the EU and CADW will record and store examples of *treiglads* from all the other world's languages. Sometimes called mutations, examples of consonant and vowel *treiglads*, recently reclassified by scholars as Sound Changes, have already been recorded for over five thousand of the world's estimated eight thousand spoken languages and the remaining three thousand will be completed within the next two years. The first to be collected were examples from Cherokee, Maori, Yogistani[12] and English."

... listening intently ...

"The director of the project, Dr Gwyddno Garanhir explains. 'Part of the problem we are facing today is that the general public are not aware these *treiglads* exist. If you don't know something exists, you don't know when it's gone. A sudden loss of *treiglads* will disrupt communications causing havoc. Rather like compound semiconductors, nobody knows these little microchips exist but without them mobile technology and its communication networks would not be possible. Neither would the internet, big data, sustainable energy, driverless vehicles and other communication technologies. So you see how vital the *treiglads* are. Everyone is welcome to the opening ceremony following which a grand tour of the vault will give the public an opportunity to see the inside of this strategic building. All conversations on the islands are recorded automatically by sensors embedded in the vault structures and these recordings of natural speech used for research. Refreshments will be available at the Machlud y Wawr[13] *marquee* situated at the entrance to the vault'. Back to the studio now as Mr Seithennin Williams, the caretaker, wants to close the vault and lock up safely for the night."

... and munched a biscuit.

"And now for news from the world of the performing arts. *Sleepless in Saundersfoot*,[14] a bestseller when it appeared a few years ago, has been turned into a film. Following the pre-release preview last month Total Film[15] ranked it the best book-to-film adaptation this year. The European *première* is in Milford Haven's Torch Theatre this Friday night at 7.30p.m. In the same *venue* the following day is the long-awaited Sci-Fi Fest. Starting at noon, with breaks in between for refreshments, five of cinema's greatest science fiction films will be shown through the afternoon and late into the night. The films, in order of appearance are, *The Walking Dead*, 1936, *I Walked with a Zombie*, 1943, *Doctor Blood's Coffin*, 1961, *The Earth Dies Screaming*, 1964, and, at midnight, *Night of the Living Dead,* 1968. Customers are encouraged to arrive dressed appropriately and to bring their own sick bags. There will be discounts for groups and children will be admitted for free."

"Breaking news. Reports are coming in of an unusual occurrence in Haverfordwest. A postwoman on her round in the Prendergast area of the town this morning tripped over the raised edge of a small pothole in the pavement. Thinking it a danger to the public she phoned the Council[16] and a team from the recently enlarged Pothole Department arrived in a van to investigate. They parked, peered at the pothole, retired a safe distance to begin discussions, then called for backup before sitting on a nearby bench under the shade of a sycamore tree enjoying the *cappuccinos* and *lattes* that Twm, the youngest member of the team, grudgingly volunteered to get from town. As they were finishing their third game of bridge the bench shook and they heard a **rumble** coming from the direction of

the pothole, then a louder **rumble**, then a **crash**, then a very loud **crash** and watched open mouthed as the van disappeared into a sink hole they estimated to be 35 feet across and 25 feet deep. Unable to get to the edge of the hole to inspect it because the sides continued to crumble away as it slowly increased in size, they called the emergency services and returned to the game of bridge. Within a very short time the sink hole had been sealed off, the area evacuated, the on-call county archaeologist called and Twm had won the bridge game. The fire brigade staff made it safe, as safe as you can make a giant expanding sink hole in Prendergast, and the archaeologist was lowered into it and disappeared for several hours during which time unexpected whoops of joy were heard echoing from the epicentre. She had discovered the tomb of Pharaoh Mentuhoteb V and later described to an awed group of onlookers the hieroglyphics she spotted on the walls of the tomb depicting, amongst other things, African Grey parrots. Also present were large numbers of mummified cats. Swansea University's Department of Egyptology[17] have been notified and as I speak a specialist team of rescue Egyptologists is *en route* to what has been classified a Site of Special Archaeological Interest."

The Parrot found the news very interesting as it had distant relatives in Egypt. The Sergeant sipped tea and thought of a light supper. He likes a chunk of very mature cheese and a handful of grapes with his tea before going to bed, the combination resulting in vivid dreams. Caerphilly produces dreams of nature and Llangloffan dreams of holidays past. *Gruyère* results in dreams of his wife white water rafting down the Teifi. He chose the Caerphilly.

A flock of scarlet ibis passed unnoticed overhead as they glided onto the mudflats on the stern where their long bills will probe for scarabs and ground beetles before settling for the night. They will be gone in the morning long before the Sergeant awakes. The Parrot will swap stories with them over breakfast.

The Sergeant got up and flicked the switch to boil the kettle then gathered cheese and grapes onto a plate. He put the plate on the table and returned to the kettle to make a mug of tea, listening to the radio as he did so.

"The bronze larger than life statue of Sam Warburton[18] that stands proudly on its plinth next to the cannon on Fishguard square has been removed for repairs. Fishguard Town Council[19] and the Welsh Rugby Union[20] issued a joint press release this afternoon in which they say the statue has a stinger injury, an occupational hazard for a flanker, and has been withdrawn as a precautionary measure. It is expected that Sam will be back on his plinth next weekend in time for Cardiff Blues'[21] crucial European clash with Toulouse.'[22]

"Nautical news now. Crowds are expected on the quayside tomorrow afternoon to watch the opening of the deepest artificial pool in Pembrokeshire. Situated between the cowshed and the willow grove the pool will allow divers to descend to a depth of 65 yards beneath the surface of the deck. Known as Bluepool II it contains underwater caves and three shipwrecks. Containing 11,000 cubic yards of water it has been built as a training facility for DPPRRCU divers. At quiet times it will be open to the public and to scuba and free-diving enthusiasts. An early booking has been made by a group of snorkellers from the Tenby area."

A worried look appeared on the Sergeant's face as he placed the mug of steaming tea on the table and sat down, reaching for a grape as he did so. "Toulouse!" he sighed. "Yes, he'll be needed for that one." He threw the grape into the air above him, dropped his head back and opened his mouth to catch it. The grape had other ideas and bounced off his nose, then off the table, landing back on the plate. A song, one of the great ones, came into his mind and he began to sing, quietly at first, then louder.

> I've been to Blackwood
> I've been to Blaina
> I crossed Ponty for a heart of gold.
> I've been in my mind,
> It's such a fine line
> That keeps me searching for a heart of gold.[23]

His ears wiggled uncontrollably as the occipitalis minor muscle at the back of his skull went into spasm. He stopped singing as another thought appeared in his mind. Safer to concentrate on one thing at a time, he decided. He repositioned his head and sat up, not sure whether he was wave-like or particle-like and found the uncertainty unsettling. The thought continued, transferring its attention to the kettle. "Since I'm not looking at the kettle," he reflected, "it doesn't exist". He became apprehensive. "No kettle?" He prepared himself to look across to see if it was in its usual place. "Please let it exist when I look." He glanced across. It was there. "But was it there yesterday? Will it be there tomorrow?" More questions arrived. "What do I mean by yesterday? What do I mean by tomorrow?" And a final one. "What do I mean by I?" The Sergeant developed a tension headache and after suffering silently for a few minutes got the headache tablets' container from the headache tablets' cupboard, sat down again and tried to open it. The Parrot watched from its perch and after a few minutes, displaying infinite compassion, flew down and opened the child proof container before returning to its perch. The Sergeant was grateful and took a couple with a sip of tea.

Sitting peacefully next to the table the Sergeant gazed at the artwork on the port side galley wall astern of the porthole as he waited for the headache to recede, a full-size copy of Modigliani's 1917 *Nu Couché* that caused such a scandal when it was first exhibited. A sensor fixed to the handrail of the gangplank detects when his wife comes aboard and automatically retracts the artwork into the ceiling whilst simultaneously lowering a photograph of equal size of herself and her mother taken one blustery summer's day on the seafront in Penarth. Upon her departure, as she walks down the gangplank past the sensor, the artwork returns into view.

The announcer continued. "Scientists working in a cave behind the cowshed have discovered bone fragments of the first examples of *Homo sapiens* in Europe, dated around 45,000 years ago. The cave also has a variety of stone tools and ornaments inside. These were made from quality flint brought with them over great distances and refined in ways particular to the Initial Upper Palaeolithic time frame, giving more evidence of exactly when these people lived. Were these the first modern humans to come aboard?"

"And now for the weather," came the announcer's voice. "Derec."[24]

"Shw mae? Tomorrow there'll be a very cold wind from the Arctic. Very cold."

The Sergeant popped a grape into his mouth and looked up mid munch. "A cold wind from the attic?" The Parrot shivered at the thought of it.

"Followed by heavy rain from the south."

He completed the munch, went straight into another, and, eyeing the plate on the table next to him, reached for another grape. The Sergeant threw it into the air, dropped his head back, opened his mouth wide and closed his eyes. The Parrot, thinking a little variety of diet would be good for it, flew off the perch and caught the grape as it began its descent then returned to the perch. He waited. After a while his ears wiggled uncontrollably again, and his mouth seemed to be getting dry. "All very strange," he thought. "All very strange." He opened his eyes, returned his head to its resting position and tucked into supper. Gagne's Hierarchical Model of Learning is useless on the coracle.

"Followed by gales from the west. Nos da!"

In the tropical forest on the southern aspect of the lake a beautifully patterned orange, yellow and black Sabertooth Longhorn beetle (Macrodontia cervicornis), nearly seven inches long if its huge mandibles are included in the measurement, and with antennae longer than its body, moves nimbly through the undergrowth searching for a mate. Released a few short weeks ago after ten years in the larval stage it has little time to waste with only a few more weeks given it to disperse and reproduce before it dies. If successful, the female will lay her eggs under the bark of dead or dying softwood trees from where the hatched larvae will burrow into the rotten wood.

Found usually in rainforests in Central and South America, and, of course, not to be confused with the Eastern and Western Hercules beetles, a Hercules beetle, a species of Rhinoceros beetle, the longest beetle in Pembrokeshire at just over seven inches in length, accompanies it. Sexually dimorphic and not at all bothered about it, it has a black body with olive-green elytra and remains unrepentantly polygynandrous as a lifestyle choice.

27

If there is no me, there is love.

Krishnamurti[1]

High above and to the east sunlight refracted and scattered through hexagonal ice crystals whose principal axes were vertical as they lay suspended in cirrus clouds. To curious early morning shoppers walking Crymych's boulevards in search of a coffee shop, or *thermopolium* as they are sometimes still called here, two very bright sun dogs with faint overlapping red, orange and blue colouration were visible, each about 22^0 either side of the sun and at the same altitude above the horizon, their colours merging into the white of the parhelic circle. In local folklore this rare atmospheric optical phenomenon is said to be 'a harbinger of what will be, augury of what is'.

It was a routine morning in the crypt. A group of carbon-based bodies of mass hurtled around the far end accelerating and decelerating in sync, changing direction at regular intervals and moving independently of any external force. Bronwen was taking a group of cloggers through some set piece moves for her new dance she calls **Turbulence** in preparation for an approaching competition, and she was hammering it. Then the motivational talk. "Those were the days, before professionalism, when rugby was rugby, when a player would play seventy-five minutes with a broken collar bone. Now they don't have collar bones, they cost too much. But those glory days are still with us in clogging so if you're injured in a 'big hit' or a collision, dance on. If the opposition see you're down they'll gain an advantage."

Megan was sitting in her armchair in the *simne fawr* reading Clebran.[2] "Listen to this, dear," she exclaimed. "Researchers at the Department of Innovative Technical Research at the University of North Pembrokeshire at Crymych wish to recruit members of the Cloggerati to trial an important piece of technology that's been years in development. The 'smart' bra uses a smart phone app to control the wearer's temperature and the bra is heated or cooled by pumping water through micro channels embedded in it. The water is warmed by the body heat of the wearer and is cooled by a small heat exchanger. A more elementary version enables the water to lose heat by evaporation. These microfluidic bras will be a godsend for dancers." Bronwen was intrigued. "Perhaps your dance group could be part of the trial. Why don't you contact the University?" Megan asked.

Bronwen left the defence coach in charge, a retired clogger who had experienced both codes having danced for Cardiff and won five Welsh caps and then, tempted by the big money, had 'gone north' and clogged for Wigan before returning. This is a coach who quickly finds your crumple button, then pushes it mercilessly. Perspiring profusely and disorientated by her exertions Bronwen walked to the bucketful of ice-cold water by the kitchen door, picked it up, poured the water over herself, replaced the bucket, walked across to the *simne fawr*, leaving a trail of water in her wake, took off the practice clogs she was wearing, collapsed sopping wet into her armchair and looked across at Megan. "What?" she said as water drained off her, soaked through the cushions and dripped onto the floor, cooling her as it went.

"It says here," Megan explained, pointing to the Evolutionary Science page, "that plant chloroplasts and mitochondria are the direct descendants of symbiotic bacteria."

"What?" Bronwen repeated absentmindedly, concentrating on her breathing after the gruelling training session. Ice cold water ran down her body into her socks and from there onto the floor. She was in that state of neither here nor there she often experiences between training and rest, for a moment fully concentrated on what she is doing, then letting the thoughts be and relaxing completely. Simplicity itself.

Megan turned to the archaeology page and read an article out loud to help Bronwen unwind. "In one of the most exhilarating archaeological discoveries of recent times, Publius Aelius Traianus Hadrianus, Hadrian to us, has been discovered deep within the soil of a mountain top near Mynachlogddu. Or at least, a statue of him. Excavators have unearthed a head, an arm, a torso, part of a leg, and a foot from a statue that, pieced together, might have stood up to five metres tall. Elegantly carved, the parts offer tantalising clues about the man who gave his name to Hadrian's Wall. Hadrian was Emperor from 117AD to 138AD and his wall, built in 122AD and situated in northern Britain, was modelled on the one built in 121AD to the north of *Aquae Crymychium*, present day Crymych. Scholars suggest the earlier wall was designed to defend the city against invasion by tribes from the north and east. It extends from Saundersfoot to Moylegrove with various detours and is 94.5 miles at its greatest length, several miles longer than the other one. Buried about five feet underground the remains of the statue were found amongst the ruins of a bath house. The region is thought to have suffered a major earthquake between the late sixth and early seventh centuries AD during which the bath house and statue fell. Archaeologists hope to unearth the remainder of the statue as excavations progress. At the same site gold coins depicting a naked horseman carrying a shield and javelin were also found. Thought to have been minted in Calleva Atrebatum aka Caer Fuddei aka Silcestria aka Silchester, in 43AD, they bear the inscription CARAT, evidence that they were issued by Caratacus, aka Caradog."

Encouraged by news of Caratacus, Megan turned to the sports page. "The World Clogging Association (WCA) is considering changing the laws to reduce the incidence of concussion which is an increasing threat to the well-being of people, especially children, who enjoy the sport. The tackle area is of particular concern. Head teachers have expressed unease and call for children to be placed in dance troupes based on their size rather than their age. A documentary will appear on BBC1 tonight, *Clogging and the Brain: Tackling the Truth*.[3] in which the tackle will be described as a collision. The danger of concussion is increasing by a creeping culture of glorifying the tackle as a 'big hit', as some commentators increasingly call the tackle."

Bronwen dripped, water evaporated. Apart from that there was little sign of life. Somewhere far off in the distance a computer crashed. "The lineage of bees is from paradise," she whispered.[4]

Megan nodded in agreement, happy at this display of life living.

"I can feel gravity," Bronwen announced, shivering a little as she cooled.

"That's nice, dear."

"I can see it."

"A useful skill I would imagine."

"I'm one with it at the moment."

The tremors and explosions emanating from the far corner of the crypt ceased abruptly. The practice session was over, and the group huddled in a circle, arms intertwined around each other's shoulders, with the defence coach at its centre as she took them through the debrief. "Clogging is an interior state. Understanding this is key and with understanding grows a perspective in which you enjoy the space between appearances and reality and the true nature of things is revealed. Let mental constructs fall away. Be that place that is not a place that underlies and becomes life as one, suffusing all with radiance, being all, being nothing."

A low rumbling sound reverberated ominously around the crypt. Barely audible at first it grew in intensity until the coffee cups on the table rattled in their saucers, Megan's reading lamp wobbled and the paintings hanging on the walls shook. Faces shaped by fatigue and controlled aggression they stamped iron studded clogs in unison again and again on the stone floor creating a pounding beat and sending showers of orange-red sparks into the air around them whilst simultaneously shimmying their crumple zones as in *faux* Burlesque challenge they sang their song of war, *à la les Pierres qui Roulent*.[5]

> *Well, you've got your headphones*
> *And you've got your low top sneakers.*
> *And the chauffeur drives your cars,*
> *You let everybody know.*

But don't dance with me
'Cause you're dancin' with fire.

Your mother she's an heiress,
Owns a block in Cardigan town.
And your father'd be there with her,
If he only could.

But don't dance with me
'Cause you're dancin' with fire.

Your old man took your facial scrub
And shave balms by the score.
Now you get your kicks in Narberth,
Not in Crymych anymore.

So don't dance with me
'Cause you're dancin' with fire.

Now you've got some moisturiser
And you will have some shower gel.
But you'd better watch your step, boy,
Or start living with your mother.

Bronwen blushed.

So don't dance with me
'Cause you're dancin' with fire.

The vocal range of the sopranos in the group reached its zenith.

So don't dance with me
'Cause you're dancin' with fire.

Somewhere at the back of the dishwasher in the kitchen a wine glass shattered.

Bronwen's face achieved a bright crimson before returning to its normal pale pink as the colour drained into her earlobes which pulsed attractively in surprise. She smiled. "They're ready!" And so was she. Coming out of her gravitational state, her socks dry enough so she wouldn't slip on the slate floor, she stood up. "Coffee?"

"Oh! Yes, **PLEASE!**"

Walking carefully on the high ground around the edge of the puddle that had formed on the floor of the crypt Bronwen made her way to the kitchen from where, for a few minutes, Megan heard all sorts of remarkable sounds, extraordinary even. At least, for a kitchen. Then silence. Bronwen had become trapped in a suspended state known as a Bose-Einstein condensate during which she passed through a pair of laser beams set up next to the fridge that scattered her into a grating pattern for a moment before, with a sigh, she recombined. Megan looked up expectantly. The kitchen door burst open and Bronwen appeared carrying a tray and on it two large *café bombóns* and two small platefuls of truffle chocolates. She padded across the floor, skirting the outer edge of the puddle, and placed the tray on the table next to her armchair, then put a coffee and a plate of chocolates on the small table next to Megan, whose eyes lit up. "Thank you," she said, "for bringing heaven to me."

Seated in the tranquillity of the crypt, log fire burning quietly in the background creating silent dancing shadows, they were content in the peace of the world.

By this time the coach and the girls in the shower were coming to the end of their song medley ...

Mawredd mawr, 'steddwch i lawr,
Mae rhywun wedi dwyn fy nhrwyn.[6]

... before leaving for a night on the town. Raw, raucous, loud passion.

"Cmch'sondfl'ace," Bronwen informed Megan over the noise whilst running her tongue around a chocolate that was melting divinely in her mouth.

Megan's brow wrinkled. "Are you encrypted, my dear?"

Bronwen swallowed the remains of the chocolate, took a deep breath and repeated the sentence. "Crymych is a wonderful place."

"I agree, dear."

"Situated on top of a mountain, population 1,776 or thereabouts, the descendants of the Celts and the Britons, votes for women, no military and no foreign debt."

"We're blessed indeed."

When faced with a problem Bronwen is a ruminative thinker. She chews on things a lot, particularly chocolate. Even when on a strict diet her firm line on chocolate can be summed up as, "**Yes!**"

One balmy summer's evening a long time ago Megan and her husband were sitting on the grass on the north side of Dinas Head when they noticed it. Out on the water some mad person in a coracle was travelling with increasing velocity in decreasing circles until both he and the coracle disappeared with a great splash. What appeared from that distance to be a Parrot rose from the vicinity of the splash, moving upwards on the air currents before flying in the direction of Fishguard harbour with a smile on its face and what appeared to be a tattoo of an anchor, the result of a weekend ashore in Wadebridge during a recent expedition to North Cornwall, on its left shoulder.

"I used to be the sort of person I would want to avoid now," he said to her. "Except I wouldn't avoid them as I've come to understand, 'There but for the grace of God, go I'. As a young man I was selfish, arrogant and a know it all, but I didn't see it. I thought I was the bee's knees. The first chink in this armour of ignorance came when I met you. I was supremely confident, my future success all planned, but the instant I looked into your eyes I was confused. The edifice of belief in my world view was undermined, it shook and began to crumble. After that, being with you, dazed and happy, my life continued its descent into ruins. The final collapse happened when our first child was born, a small being of delight completely dependent upon us. I could never have imagined, and certainly never understood, that such an experience of love for another is possible. With that experience the remnants of the fortress of stupidity I had constructed in my mind, based upon thinking material things are paramount and everything in life, including people, are objects I can manipulate for my own ends, fell apart. I had an understood glimpse of what is Real. Of what Is. Of Love. For that I will always be grateful to you."

Megan brushed away a tear.

Bronwen sipped more hot coffee and popped another truffle chocolate into her mouth just as something she once read popped into her mind. "Chocolate, if false, is of no importance, and if true, of infinite importance. The only thing it cannot be is moderately important."[7] She eyed the plate. Still a few left. "Ever since I was young, I've had a feeling of an energy in my hands and lower arms and the thought that they would one day write a book. A book that would put a smile on peoples' faces. A book that would cause people to laugh uncontrollably and fall off their chairs onto the floor to roll around giggling helplessly. The sort of hysterical giggling that leaves housework undone and tidying jobs unfinished."

"How wonderful," Megan remarked encouragingly.

Megan's thoughts returned to her husband. "I sometimes worry about losing you," he once confided in her. "You are beautiful and gorgeous and sexy. And I'm not. And negative emotions appear in me. They come and go on their own. There's nothing to do about them. I let them go because that's what they do, they come and go. Jealousy for one. Jealousy appears and I know that in a while it will be gone, and happiness will appear. No need to try and push jealousy away. No need to try and hold onto happiness. Negative emotions pass through us, harmless, and are gone. We invite them by thinking about things in the past -

madness, and by imagining things in the future - more madness. Only now is real, right now. Sitting with you, holding your hand, my heart opens to you. I am committed to you, my being with you an expression of love and devotion in this moment. And you return that. And since this moment is imbued with these things, they will be in our next moment and our next. This moment alone is real, this moment alone is where we meet."

Romantics both, they were like two small spherical green or yellow embryonic plants, often edible, contained within the seed-bearing structure of a flowering plant, technically the fruit, which forms from the ovary after flowering.

In the quiet of the day as the light around the smallholding outside faded they sat on the sofa in the living room opposite the log burner, holding hands as evening arrived. He decided to add to the romantic atmosphere by singing a Leonard Cohen song to her. Her peace was shattered. Evening turned into night and nature put its pyjamas on. He stopped singing. "Thank you cariad," she said, charitably. "That was beautiful." They felt the Earth change as it settled into a quieter time.

Later that evening they lay in bed, close against each other, bodies parallel, arms straight down before them, fingers entwined, looking into each other's eyes. She kissed him. He kissed her. They kissed. "I can feel your love for me," he said. "It's a wonderful thing, a precious thing in a life to feel someone else's love. To know without doubt that you are loved."

Megan continued reading, "Researchers have created a digital version of the brain of the European honeybee, Apis mellifera." Bronwen paid no attention to this important announcement. The chocolate and her taste buds had combined to take her brain to its bliss point. She was gone. She had left the party. Megan noticed an advert, "All terrain clogs. Size 9. Good condition. £80 o.n.o." She sank further between the cushions, deeper into the welcoming recesses of the armchair. In *Breakfast at Tiffany's* Audrey Hepburn's cat is called Cat.[8] Inspired by this Megan's armchair is known as Armchair.

Turning the page Megan began reading a feature titled Corgi Trekking in the Preselis. Bronwen's ears pricked up. "It is a joy to see the faces of tourists when they see their first mountain corgi. There is open-mouthed astonishment and tears of joy. The National Corgi Reserve has a permit for guides to lead groups into the mountains. Numbers are restricted so as not to disturb these wild creatures in their natural habitat. The plan is to come across one of the five packs that live in the Reserve. The guides walk the group up into the mountains early when the morning is still cool, and the trek takes about three hours. The maximum time a group is allowed to spend with a Corgi pack is one hour as these are wild animals not for taming."

"Corgi habitat has been eroded by farming over the years and the Reserve is surrounded by a dry-stone wall, not to keep the corgis in but to keep grazing animals such as cows, horses and sheep out. And to keep velociraptors from the nearby Dinosaur Park, which for several miles is contiguous with the Corgi Reserve, out. It is well known that corgis and velociraptors do not mix. At least, not if you are a corgi. The mountain corgis live in the dense forest above the wall. The silverback, the alpha corgi in each pack and the dominant member of its social group, is a hugely impressive animal. Should you be nervous when observing them up close? Not at all. The corgis watch the people watching them and show some interest in human activity. Tourists are often surprised as the corgis exude calm and peace and by the end of the hour the novelty for the corgis has usually worn off and most of them fall asleep. These tours in the vast expanse of the National Corgi Reserve which encompasses the volcanic North Pembrokeshire Mountain Region almost in its entirety run most of the year, but not during the monsoon season between November 1st and St Davids's Day when conditions for trekking through the steep slopes of the forest are treacherous. Flash floods can wipe out a whole party of tourists. And anyway, the *café* by the entrance to the Reserve is closed."

"These five-day Corgi tours are very popular, especially with visitors from Africa who want to experience exotic European wildlife at its best. A typical itinerary to see these endangered mountain corgis is as follows:

Day 1 Upon arrival in Rosebush you will be met by your guide and transferred to your lodge in the southern foothills of the National Corgi Reserve. The remainder of the day is free time and provides an opportunity to meet the other trekkers in your group.

Day 2 You will be wakened by bugle call at 4.00a.m. After showering, breakfast, a leisurely glance through the morning papers and a briefing from your guide you will set off at 4.15a.m. to climb through the thick forests to where your allocated corgi pack lives. The trek takes up to three hours and you will arrive as the mountain corgis awake and begin foraging for food. When the guide finds a pack you will keep an appropriate distance, for safety and to respect their privacy whilst enjoying this awe-inspiring sight. You are free to take photographs but you are advised to keep together as one group. People who leave the group risk inadvertently disturbing the pack or, worse still, upsetting the silverback and being torn to pieces. After a relaxing hour with the wild mountain corgis you will retrace your steps down the mountain side and return to your lodge where you can mingle with other trekkers to swap stories and photographs. An optional excursion by minibus in the afternoon will take you on a sightseeing tour of the area which includes a visit to Crymych and the beautiful Piazza della Republica where you will be free to explore this great city before meeting in Das Kapital[9] for coffee and cake. The minibus will then return you to the lodge.

Day 3 During the morning you will follow the same itinerary as day 2. In the afternoon you can take advantage of an optional bus tour to Fishguard to see the two Gorsedd Circles.[10] Also on the schedule is a visit to D.J. Williams' house in the High Street[11] which has been converted into a literature centre and, also in the High Street a few doors down, Pembrokeshire's smallest house, where two at a time, you will sit in the living room and enjoy tea and cakes. Following refreshments, you will visit the Last Invasion Tapestry[12] in the library before returning to the bus. The return journey via Goodwick will allow you to see some of the houses mentioned by Waldo[13] in one of his poems.

Day 4 Today is your last day with these magnificent creatures. The morning itinerary is the same as Day 2. An optional bus tour in the afternoon will take you to Tenby and to Castle Hill, the site of King Bleiddudd's court all those years ago, where the Tenby Players[14] will perform a modern musical version of the poem *Edmyg Dinbych* in the open air. Following this you will be free to explore the town and its beaches before returning for your last night in the lodge. An end of safari eisteddfod will be held in the Great Lodge after supper.

Day 5 After waking to the bugle call at 4.00a.m., showering, taking breakfast and saying farewell to your companions who shared the adventure with you a minibus will take you to Rosebush where you will find a regular half hourly bus service taking you onwards on your journey."

Refreshed by the coffee and chocolates Bronwen stirred. She gazed lazily around the crypt. "This is obviously an ancient building. You can tell from the carpets."

"Yes, dear."

Bronwen's gaze moved to the framed quote hanging on the opposite wall. "Bore da, Mrs Mathias." it read. The first words uttered on *Pobol y Cwm*. And it was signed by Mrs Mathias herself.[15]

Megan put the paper down and picked up the book she was reading, *Slash and Burn*, the memoirs of a recently retired general surgeon based in Withybush Hospital in Haverfordwest.

Bronwen put the coffee cup on the table beside the armchair. A keen starer out of windows she turned her head to stare out of the bay window. Staring in anticipation, she anticipated. "Is it a good day?" she asked.

"Good and bad are labels we put on the perfection that is life and thereby lose it. Here's a gentle reminder of where we are, dear. I'm staying here and you're going off on a training run." As part of her training regime for the Six Nations, the premier clogging tournament in the northern hemisphere and thought by many to be superior to its southern counterpart, for the socialising at least, if not the quality of the clogging, Bronwen runs every day from Crymych to the Parrog in Newport, ascending to the summit of Foel Cwmcerwyn, the third highest peak in the Preseli Mountains range, on the way out and on the return. In the week leading up to a test she wears her match day clogs. Carwen James, coach to the victorious 1971 Lions[16] when they won that famous test series in New Zealand, outclogging the All Blacks in their own back yard, would approve.

She has a skillset that is the admiration of many, a highly developed game-intelligence and a field-craft that sees her in the right place at the right time during a dance set. It is for these attributes she was again awarded the tribute of being the Clogger's Clogger at a dinner in Cardiff for the clogging *cognoscenti* at the end of last season's Six Nations during which she played a blinder in every test. After the final game she was interviewed live on television in a packed stadium in Cardiff. "You must be delighted with this hard fought Six Nations during which the standard of dancing was very high? And to be part of a Wales side that has won the Grand Slam. What next, a well-deserved rest on a beach somewhere?" asked the interviewer. "Oh no! Tomorrow morning I'm refereeing a local derby between Brynberian Under XII's and Scleddau Under XII's. And they don't come bigger than that!"

Bronwen rose from the armchair and made her way to the changing rooms at the far end of the crypt.

Megan closed her book, placed it on the table by the armchair and settled even deeper into the cushions. A deep calm enveloped her. She is a *gwiddon*, a wise woman, one of a long line her family has produced in the Preseli Mountains, the first-born daughter having the gift, going back generation after generation to beyond where memory fades. Years ago, members of that foreign women's institution claimed she was a *gwrach*. They were wrong of course and were later to pay dearly for the slur. Every village in Wales has its *gwiddon* who acts as soothsayer, counsellor, herbalist, marriage organiser, weather forecaster, *pâtissière* and leader of its *brigade de cuisine*. Indeed, being the *station chef* of a pastry platoon is a responsibility not worn lightly.

Thoughts of her husband appeared. "I'm very careful as to how I come into your life," he said to her near the beginning of their time together.

"I know, cariad."

"I want to enter your life but not change it."

"Thank you."

"As if I'm slowly, quietly, moving down a riverbank and entering the water, making no ripples, entering the flow of you and becoming one with it."

"Cariad."

In her imagination she took his hand, squeezed it, and felt his absence in her heart. It is said that the past is a foreign country, they do things differently there. Indeed, for Megan now, there is no they.[17]

Later that evening, accompanied by freshly made white chocolate *mochas* and a generous selection of hand-rolled coffee truffles coated in tempered white chocolate dusted with cocoa powder they move to the sofa in the bay window from where, gazing expectantly upwards, they watch the long bright trails and fireballs of the Perseid meteor shower pass across the heavens, followed by the Swift-Tuttle comet making an unexpected early appearance.

Approximately fifty miles above the crypt water vapour collects around dust particles in the low temperatures of the mesosphere forming ice crystals. Couples ambling arm in arm across the Piazza della Republica gaze upwards to enjoy the beauty of rare noctilucent clouds becoming visible at twilight as they are illuminated by sunlight from below the horizon as the brightest stars appear. The lovers wonder at the lack of shadows and Brunelleschi's dome above the Cathedral silhouetted against the lit sky.

To the south Sagittarius can be seen, it's teapot easily recognisable, and in the 'steam' emerging from the spout the vast interstellar cloud known as the Lagoon nebula is visible to the eye. Amongst the stars of Sagittarius, Saturn shines with its rings open wide. With a small telescope, interested observers can see Titan, Saturn's largest moon, cloaked in its thick nitrogen and hydrocarbon atmosphere although a telescope is not enough to see its methane sea, nor its rain, rivers and lakes. Unseen by our intrepid duo, a tiny speck, the Juno spacecraft passes through Jupiter's cloud tops sending back images of the little-seen polar regions.

South by east between the constellations Sagittarius and Ophiuchus the star clouds of the Milky Way sparkle in the night sky in which, to the keen observer, the constellation Cygnus is easily recognisable with its 'summer triangle' of bright stars, Altair, Deneb and Vega.

Further south still the diffuse green glow of the aurora Australis is visible. "But not from Crymych, surely," Megan suggests, putting her delicately carved silver lorgnettes onto the sofa beside her, to look more closely.

Was it serendipity that sent the International Space Station, a point of dazzling light brighter than the stars, passing overhead at that moment.

The 3:10 Richards Brothers express from Crymych to Aberystwyth, leaving late, heads north. Viewed from the International Space Station it appears to be heading east. Such is the Coriolis effect.

"Oh look!" cries Bronwen excitedly, "an alignment of Mars and Venus." A global dust storm rages in Mars' thin atmosphere completely covering the Red Planet.

High above, a NASA satellite captures a beautiful image of a bloom of phytoplankton formed as a consequence of higher temperatures and increased sunlight in the microclimate of the Crymych Lagoon. Unseen in the darkness above the Lagoon a volutus cloud turns slowly on its side whilst close by, west-northwest, magellanic clouds glow mysteriously. A sure sign of rain.

In an area of strong upward motion in the coldest part of an extratropical cyclone to the south of the Lagoon, in which the top of the cumulonimbus cloud is unusually low, thunder and lightning combine with a heavy snowstorm to produce a phenomenon known as thundersnow, in which the primary precipitation is snow rather than rain. In this particular example of the *genre,* and unlucky for couples out taking an evening stroll, snow pellets and ice pellets also fall. The resulting thunderclap sets off car alarms below.

Heralding the arrival of severe weather, a rare cloud *tsunami* several miles long can be seen to the northeast as its high menacing cloud wall rolls in over Bwlch-y-groes, its moist air lifted abruptly by the cold outflowing air from a thunderstorm.

A shooting star sweeps from east to west.

The cold snap that has lasted several days, characterised by very low temperatures, neap tides and strong, dry winds evaporating warmer surface water, culminates in the sea freezing at Poppit Sands to the west.

Further away and unnoticed a coronal mass ejection witnesses the release of plasma and magnetic field from the sun into the solar wind.

Ominous looking asperitas clouds form to the northwest.

Approximately 2,500 light-years from where they sit the glowing ribbons of the Cygnus Loop, a blast wave left over from the supernova explosion of a massive dying star twenty times the mass of the sun that lucky Crymychians would have witnessed 15,000 years ago, moves through space at about 220 miles per second, heating and compressing tendrils of gas and dust as it goes.

A huge high-precipitation supercell forms north-northeast embedded in a squall line between Cwmcych and Newcastle Emlyn, an area known to locals as Tornado Valley, producing torrential rainfall and hail as it goes. Its deep, persistently rotating updraft spawns a tornado from within. There is a danger the supercell will develop two separate updrafts with opposing rotations and split into two supercells. People in Newcastle Emlyn are being advised to wrap up warmly and keep a scarf and bobble hat close to hand.

"Is that the Evening Star kissing the Ringed Planet in the southwestern sky?" wonders Bronwen in admiration.

A solar eclipse appears on Jupiter as its Great Red Spot continues to shrink, a sign that this massive storm the size of Earth is abating. Nonetheless, the planet's 12-year revolution around the sun continues unabated. Through a telescope with a magnifying capability of 20x its four Galilean moons are clearly visible. Fine details of features on the moons such as the volcanic eruptions on Io, the most volcanically active body in the solar system, the hot lava glowing orange and red, the colours coming primarily from sulphur gas, require greater magnification.

The bowl-shaped cluster of stars that form the tiny constellation of Corona Borealis in the northern sky is just visible although the elusive irregular variable low-mass yellow supergiant star, R. Coronae Borealis, is sufficiently faded to require a telescope, visibility reduced by the presence of large dust clouds. These dust clouds are unusual in that astronomers think they originate from the star itself.

A little to the north hail falls over Cilgerran, melting briefly in a layer of warmer air, then, closer to the ground, becoming super-cool as it falls through air at sub-zero temperatures. Hitting the ground, it freezes to form a sheet of ice. The specific conditions necessary for freezing rain have been met and soon the road to Llechryd will be impassable.

A super blue blood moon coinciding with a total lunar eclipse hangs over the orchard outside the crypt. Later, by the soft light of the moon, a silvery lunar rainbow will shine dimly over the cascading fountain in the Piazza della Republica. The Great Wall of Crymych will gleam eerily in its light.

"Is that Planet Nine, wonder of once every ten thousand years' wonders?" enquires Bronwen, rapture in her voice.

A pinprick of light brighter than any comet, but with no tail, a cigar-shaped interstellar object over 300 feet long nicknamed Oumuamua II by the boffins at Crymych Observatory, rotates as it travels through space at up to 50 miles a second. Having travelled here from the frozen vastness between distant stars it will soon loop the sun and accelerate away from Crymych. "It comes in peace," Megan sighs with relief.[18]

As the central pressure of the low-pressure system southwest by south falls quickly by more than 24 millibars accompanied by a steep drop in temperature, a devastating bomb cyclone forms above Rosebush, wreaking havoc with high winds gusting to 95mph bringing with them a wind chill of -35⁰C, blinding sleet, ice and heavy snowfall. Well prepared for such emergencies staff in the Tafarn Sinc put an extra log in the wood burning stove. Up to 25 inches of snow is expected overnight that will bring vital transport links between Mynachlog-ddu and Efailwen to a standstill. Caffi Beca will close early. Ideal conditions for the bomb cyclone were created when warm air from the sea met cold polar air. Flights into and out of Crymych International Airport have been cancelled as a precautionary measure.

A warm wet weather front moving northwards from Portugal meets a vicious polar vortex arriving from the Arctic over Boncath causing heavy blizzards of snow, sleet and black ice.

"Is that a black hole eating a neutron star?" Bronwen wonders, tiring now.

"Or two black holes colliding, perhaps," suggests Megan, uneasily.

"Maybe. Or neutron stars colliding in a binary system."

"Hmmm. Difficult to be sure about cataclysmic events from this distance.

Arriving late, the Quadrantids meteor shower is visible west by north to the keen eye. Thought to be produced by dust grains left behind by an extinct comet known as 2003 EH1, meteors radiate from the constellation Bootes producing an above average shower of up to 40 meteors per hour at its peak.

It is at this time of year that the North Pembrokeshire hurricane season begins. And so it is that warm temperatures in Llys y Frân coupled with cooling equatorial waters off Tenby weaken high winds gathering around Templeton, winds that would otherwise diminish a developing storm. Soon, a hurricane boasting catastrophic 155mph winds driving substantial rain before it will settle in for the evening over the Globe Inn in Maenclochog. Unnoticed by locals gathered in the bar, a brave member of staff, following recently updated Emergency Response Precautions, moves to the Hazard Analysis Critical Control Point by the sink in the back kitchen in a bid to identify 'critical points' and 'hazards' in the food making process. Ensuring sandwich preparation will be unaffected is paramount in her mind.

Northwest by north the Delta Aquarids meteor shower produced by debris left behind by the comets Marsden and Kracht send 20 meteors per hour over the city.

The Pleiades sisters, open star clusters containing middle-aged, hot B-type stars located in the constellation of Taurus, wink at the pair far below.

East-southeast, localised, low-lying, apocalyptic undulatus asperitas clouds that appear to be boiling from below, progress slowly over Tegryn.

"Is Mercury moving backwards?" Bronwen enquires, a jet-lagged tone audible in her voice.

In a distant galaxy a part of the cosmic web formed by the collapse of primordial hydrogen created in the Horrendous Space Kablooie 13.7 billion years ago[19] and its associated threads of invisible dark matter 3.3 million light years long, bide their time. Within the cosmic web filaments of primordial gas illuminated by the galaxy's stars and black holes return to a lower energy state, emitting radiation as they do so.

South-southwest two electrically charged regions in the atmosphere temporarily equalize themselves releasing almost one billion joules of energy. Strokes of deadly cloud-to-ground lightning with bolt temperatures five times hotter than the surface of the sun bombard Llandissilio and Clunderwen. These unfortunate villages, both positively charged now, are lit up by the resulting lightning strikes. Each bolt, containing up to one billion volts of electricity and beginning as a step-like series of negative charges, races rapidly downwards from the base of the storm cloud at about 200,000mph. Taller inhabitants run for cover.

As the giant cumulonimbus cloud high in the troposphere continues its passage, vertical wind shear causes a deviation in the thunderstorm's course, redirecting it towards the 'gorgeous little market town' of Narberth with its elegant high street lined with multicoloured Edwardian and Georgian buildings containing shops, stores, *boutiques*, *emporiums* and *delicatessens* overflowing with a wide array of *artisan* crafts, *antiques*, local and Spanish foodstuffs and many more delights for the discerning shopper. Having shopped 'til they dropped, friends unwind, sitting relaxed outside the many street *cafés* sipping coffee, munching delicacies and chattering gaily in the warmth of the late evening sunshine unaware that the Met Office forecast that morning had been wrong. Terribly wrong.

As the giant cumulonimbus cloud passes overhead gases close to the discharge heat and increase in pressure, rapidly expanding and vibrating and the resulting deafening thunder reverberates around the town and on to nearby Robeston Wathen, shattering windows and coffee cups as it goes. In the ladies' over fifties yoga session in the Queen's Hall enthusiasts abandon attempts at achieving inner peace, and, ignoring the pleas of an impatient instructor, break ranks, thereby collapsing their pitiful yet valiant attempts at *sarvāṅgāsana*, Sanskrit, सर्वाङ्गासन, an inverted pose with the body resting on the shoulders, and huddle nervously in one corner of the room, out of sight beneath a machine washable, fusion Cashmere and fleece thermal weave blanket made by skilled artisans in Taiwan one of the group brought back from a recent meditation retreat in Goa. Emboldened by the semidarkness under the blanket they gulp lukewarm green tea enlivened by several heaped tablespoonfuls of *mêl direidus* bought fresh from the *delicatesson* for that very purpose earlier in the day, ignoring a recent scientific report confirming the lack of conclusive evidence linking consumption of green tea to weight loss.

An observant passer-by notices the barometer attached to the wall by the steps of the town hall indicating a calamitous crash in barometric pressure, 2.31 inches of mercury in fifteen minutes. Hidden from her view by this elegant Grade II listed building of 18th century origin whose coordinates are latitude 51.7982 / 51°47'53"N, longitude -4.7434 / 4°44'36"W, and moving north at speed along the A478, a bomb blizzard approaches and will soon bludgeon the town mercilessly, burying it under 12 feet of snow in less than 17 minutes.

The staff canteen in the Meteorology Institute in downtown Crymych runs out of coffee.

From a bar somewhere in downtown Crymych a sound drifts in through the open bay window.

Oooo!

Mawredd mawr, 'steddwch i lawr,
Mae rhywun wedi dwyn fy nhrwyn.

Mawredd mawr, 'steddwch i lawr,
Mae rhywun wedi dwyn fy nhrwyn.

A 7.2 magnitude earthquake, its epicentre beneath the annexe of the village hall in Brynberian, rattles windows and chimney pots throughout the village and beyond. Rough tremors reach Crymych where the Cathedral shudders in their wake. Onstage at the annual eisteddfod being held inside the hall, Julie, Ann, Bel and Vanya, participants in the adult Welsh learners' group recitation competition for Entry Level, pause with puzzled expressions on their faces as they wait for the building to stop shaking before continuing with their rendition of that perennial Entry Level favourite, *Y Storm* gan Islwyn. Not yet having learnt the Welsh word for 'earthquake' they will be left wondering what hit them.

'Twas ever thus.

28

Oh! the time will come up,
When the winds will stop,
And the breeze will cease to be breathin'.
Like the stillness in the wind,
Before the hurricane begins,
The hour that the ship comes in.

Bob Dylan[1]

It was early morning and the fragrant scent of juniper wafted across the coracle as The Parrot walked silently around the vessel's circumference taking the incense burner to every corner, part of a cleansing ritual it performs at every sunrise.

The Sergeant dozed in his cabin below decks in the bow. As the sun rose, long beams of sunlight pierced the shallow waters around the coracle bringing life to another day. Others moved unnoticed through a small gap between the curtains of the submerged scenic window positioned above the vessel's bulb, bathing his sleeping face in warmth. The rain had stopped, briefly. On the ocean floor several feet below the hull a dozen microphones picked up the underwater dawn chorus. This cacophony of noise was relayed to loudspeakers either side of his pillow, volume full on. He opened his eyes. A thought intruded into the calm. Had his wife changed her hairstyle recently? Was it still red? A sense of impending doom entered with the beams of light. He was wide awake now and sitting bolt upright. This was a matter of great consequence. To comment or not to comment as required would be crucial to his wellbeing during the coming days. A wrong comment, failure to make a positive comment if appropriate or to make a false positive comment, and their lives together would be rough. He tried to get up, but he couldn't. His left leg was tangled up in the blue woollen strands of the *carthen* covering him.[2]

Unaware of the developing crisis below decks The Parrot was by now perched on the low-lying branch of a willow tree on the stern playing Bach's Courante, Suite VI for cello, arranged for the arch guitar, its preferred instrument as the arrangement of the strings suits its plucking style.

Later that day, following an uneventful voyage, they were passing Pentire Point on the approach to Wadebridge when the coracle was hit by a rogue wave the height of a ten-storey building. The vessel's design, honed over thousands of years of trial and error, meant that the ascent to the crest and the subsequent return descent to the bottom of the trough, went smoothly. This cannot be said of the Sergeant's equilibrium however as he was unnerved by the period of weightlessness during the descent. Fortunately, his brain is on override during long sea voyages in line with a Dyfed-Powys Police Rapid-Response Coracle Unit[3] Health and Safety Directive that enables The Parrot to suspend, or indeed cancel all cortical functioning, and, if need be, take manual control at the flick of a switch. The override feature activates previously unused neural pathways, always in plentiful supply, which act to diminish his sense of disorientation. This made little difference to the outcome other than enabling him to continue sipping tea in the galley without feeling giddy. Although there is little corroborative evidence to support this.

The vessel entered a wall of thick sea fog formed when a parcel of warm south westerly air passed over the cooler waters of Padstow Bay. Immediately, visibility reduced to nil. Unseen, a troupe of ring-tailed wombats moved from branch to branch high in the canopy of the tropical rainforest on the stern. These mythical creatures, shy by nature, are not often glimpsed in North Cornwall. Always one to see the bigger picture The Sergeant reached for a chocolate biscuit. Fortunately for the crew a Morris dancing festival was afoot and The Parrot, a keen student of traditional native dance, steered the coracle by keeping the distinctive sound of the dancers of Rock to the north equidistant to the unique sound of the Padstow dancers to the south, thus maintaining a course up the middle of the Camel Estuary for several miles until, as the 15th century bridge in Wadebridge came close, the fog mysteriously cleared as quickly as it had arrived. A whale pod played off to starboard.

The Sergeant manoeuvred the coracle towards the quay on the western side of the River Camel a few yards upriver from the bridge, bringing it to rest close to a North Cornwall Police Rapid-Response Crabber Unit vessel,[4] the St Tedha, built in St Mawes in 1851, with its magnificent gaff rig and bowsprit. Or did he? The reality is that the on-board computer was taking the vessel there anyway. This delicate cat and mouse game played out by these two characters, if an on-board computer can be called a character, it certainly thinks it can, enables the computer to remain in charge and the Sergeant to think he is in charge. In this way both players achieve optimum efficiency and life aboard flows smoothly. The coracle bobbed up and down in the pull of the current by the quayside as the Sergeant dropped the fenders before lassoing an object he deemed immovable, which on this occasion was Wadebridge, him not being big on detail. The particular part of town the twine embraced was the end of a large sign on the side of a building close to the water's edge which had the words *Allnut and Sayer. Boat Builders. Est. 1914.*[5] written on it. He pulled the binder twine tight, jumped ashore, secured the bow line, the stern line and the gangplank, released the sign from the binder twine's steely grip and headed into town, taste buds singing expectantly. The Parrot stopped mid *étude*, bowed discretely in *hommage* to J. S. and his musical genius, returned the guitar to the case lashed to the branch alongside and flew after its shipmate. On their visits to the town the crew always stop for refuelling at *Koffiji an Mor*, the *café* on the crossroads where they enjoy fish and chips whilst admiring the *trompe l'oeil* adorning one wall, the work of a beautiful and talented local artist.

After the main course The Parrot went for a stroll along the river's edge, leaving the Sergeant with a mug of tea and some biscuits. Sitting by the window watching the world and Wadebridge pass by outside he pondered the possibility that he was addicted to chocolate biscuits. After much thought he concluded he was not. "After all," he argued, "it's my hand that picks them up and puts them into my mouth. Therefore, it's my hand that's addicted. Not me." His mind at ease and having finished the biscuits and tea he decided to explore the town, perhaps visit the bookshop and see what was new. When in town, it is a habit of his to buy a supply of novels chosen from its extensive Cornish language section, reading material that provides him with much needed background information about the area and its people, particularly the criminal underclass of pirates and smugglers who have outwitted him all these years. Leaving an empty mug and plate behind him, he left the *café*.

Whilst navigating the pedestrianised area in the vicinity of the bookshop, the Sergeant, alert as always, bumped into a suspicious looking character wearing a *tricorne* hat decorated with a plume of brightly coloured bird feathers, a knee-length tunic made from worn sail canvas and baggy woollen trousers cut off below the knee, both tunic and trousers coated in pitch for warmth and to deflect sword thrusts. Over the tunic the stranger wore a colourful satin waistcoat of intricate design and over that a heavily brocaded, crimson coat with long wide cuffs ornamented with embroidery, jewels and a line of shiny brass buttons, the look accessorised with a white, layered lace *jabot* around the neck and a silver-buckled, leather shoe.

Taking this to be an opportunity to further his enquiries, he decided to question him. "Who are you and what business do you have here?" he demanded, admiring the gold rings, bracelets, earring and diamond encrusted pendant.

"The name's Frank, Gwikor Frank, of this parish," the man rasped in a curious, challenging sort of a way, stroking his thick black beard with the metal hook replacing his right hand, amputated some years previously by the ship's carpenter after it was crushed by falling rigging in a storm. Disturbed by the hook, black powder discharged in a shower from the beard.

The Sergeant detected the smell of sulphur in the air. "Hmmm. All very strange."

"I'm in private business, a free trader if you will," the man added, moving his left hand to grip the loaded flintlock pistol held fast on his right side by the thick leather belt over a *cramoisin* sash around his waist, the same belt that secured a cutlass with its razor-sharp, curved blade on his other side.

"Hmmm! Very well!" The Sergeant replied gruffly and told him to be on his way and look sharp about it. The man raised his right arm to touch the wide brim of the *tricorne* hat with the hook, bowed slightly and walked off, a smile lighting up his eyes, his dagger-scarred face demonstrating a contented yet amused expression. He adjusted the black leather eye patch covering his port side eye as he went. Thought by some to be a fashion item, the eye patch is essential during night-time operations.

As the clump ... clump ... clump sound of the wooden peg leg faded into the distance, somewhere deep inside the Sergeant's subconscious a warning bell sounded, but there was nothing he could do about it, and the moment passed unrecognised. The small camera mounted on the front of his round Monmouth cap knitted from coarse two-ply wool and made weatherproof by felting noticed changes of colour in his face caused by micro flushes of blood. From the tiny motions of the skin of his nose it measured his oxygen levels, pulse and heart rate. The cap also keeps an eye on his facial movements and the tone and pitch of his voice. It sent him a text advising more tea and biscuits. He complied and returned to the *café* where he settled on a seat by the open window which provided a view of the comings and goings outside and ordered fresh provisions. The latest instalment of the local soap opera played softly on the radio. Meanwhile, in a simple yet dramatic twist of fate worthy of Rosamunde Pilcher[6] herself, The Parrot made its way to downtown Wadebridge intent upon whiling away the afternoon with the *Kirtan Wallahs*.

Sipping from the mug he became aware of a drumming sound echoing off the sides of the stone buildings lining the street outside. He listened intently. The drumming grew louder. It was impossible to know the direction from which it came, impossible to know how many drums. Like native peoples the world over, the *Kowethas an Yeth Kernewek*[7] committee cannot be seen unless they want to be.

The latest instalment of the radio drama came to an end. The voice of the Radio Free Cornwall[8] announcer issued a weather warning, a worried tone adding a note of urgency. "Storm approaching from the northwest." The emergency drill raced through the Sergeant's cerebral cortex, but to no avail. It was a sultry summer's afternoon with just a trace of cooling breeze, and he was becalmed in the *café*. Whilst munching a biscuit his internal emergency drill applied the brakes, his mind slowed to a crawl, and he entered slow steaming mode to conserve energy. He gazed at the tea, *Assam Behora* he would recall later, waiting patiently in the mug on the table in front of him. One of his hands, when questioned by The Parrot that evening he could not call to mind which one, rose slowly into the air and reached across to pluck the last chocolate biscuit off the plate. Leaning back into the seat he kept his eyes trained on the biscuit as it approached. It was in no hurry as it followed its pre-set trajectory. The critical moment was the arrival of the biscuit, timed to coincide with the lowering of the jaw. Time slowed. He had all afternoon and there were more biscuits behind the counter.

The announcer continued. "Self-sailing Crabbers have been seen in Cornish waters for the first time. A fleet of ten vessels, gaff rigged topsail cutters with angled bowsprits and keel-hung rudders controlled by a tiller, all equipped with Autonomous Sailing Technology, arrived in Falmouth this morning having travelled from Falmouth, Massachusetts. The lead vessel, named the Bartholomew Gosnold,[9] set the route and speed and all the vessels were connected wirelessly in a tight convoy formation. A spokesperson from the University of the Four Trinity Davids' Autonomous Technology Unit[10] based on the campus of MIT, the Mevagissey Institute of Technology,[11] spoke to Radio Free Cornwall earlier today. She informed us that the fleet has been commissioned by the North Cornwall Police Rapid-Response Crabber Unit as this new technology has several advantages. The short distances between the vessels will increase the space when navigating rivers, travelling close together one behind the other reduces air resistance thus increasing cruising speeds and reducing fuel consumption, and when the lead coracle brakes, the others in the convoy brake at the same time, thus increasing safety."

"And now a breaking story. Police have appealed for witnesses following an incident that occurred on The Platt outside the Council Office[12] in Wadebridge between 11.35a.m. and 3.20p.m. yesterday. "I waz dealin' with a customer at the time an' I jussed turned me back fer a minit juss te wrap up some mackerel fer'n," Demelza told our chief crime reporter. "The lil oss waz tied up fast ov the lamp pawst. An' the wagon, well 'twas a lovely lil pony cart when it started out in life, an' so 'tis easily noticeable. Ee gawt our bizniz name, Demelza's Mobile Fish Wagon plastered all aver 'n, an' on both sides, so you caan't miss en. One minit they waz there, the nex' they was gone. I caan't bleeve it! All the thieves left be'ind obm waz a empty cowal! Bleeve it can ee? I mean te say, in broad daylight and before yer very eyes! An' as fer the lil mare she waz my favrite oss too. Dappled grey she was, an' her coat shone like a bottle! I've 'ad 'er since she waz a foal. Twelve years old she is. Mind you, you wouldn' think it by the way she de move; in the prime ov 'er life she is. They waz gypsies I bawt 'er off of I de bleeve, they de knaw a thing er too 'bout osses tha's fer sure."

"Oh for a clandestine wireless communication to brighten my day," thought the Sergeant. Comforted by the steaming tea and chocolate biscuits he yawned abundantly, taking in much needed oxygen to pass to the bloodstream which in turn lost carbon dioxide, but to no avail. Unable to overcome the energy barrier he fell asleep. Wadebridge was safe. In a remarkable evolutionary development, half of the brain of marine mammals such as dolphins and whales is asleep at any one time as they swim. The Sergeant's ancestors however did not evolve this ability. For him, asleep means asleep.

In the Sergeant's life, time is plentiful. The world of technology races ahead as he dozes in the hammock. There is ample time to ponder, to sleep, and on the odd occasion, to read. There is time to daydream, to enjoy the view, to engage The Parrot in philosophical discussion. Why is vanilla ice cream white? Why do clouds change colour? Why, if the tin can was invented in 1810 was there not a tin opener available until 1858? Why is wet seaweed slippery? For him, life is lived at human pace. Indeed, it is true to say that it is this enduring quality that first attracted his wife to him. She feels peaceful, in an irritated sort of a way, when he is around. When in his company, there appears a silence imbued with calm. They seem to have lots of time for one another during his short and infrequent shore leaves. There is no busyness. Her scolding, brought on through impatience, is gentle. It lacks edge. Their lives together are without pace. His life lived does not allow technology to steal precious time from them. He is never in a hurry. He doesn't know how to be. He moves in time with his own internal rhythms. In Venice, they call him *Il Coraclino*.

The young girl behind the counter noticed a customer slumped in the seat by the window, a contented smile on his face. A physiologist would observe his heart rate dropping, his breathing slowing, his muscles relaxed, meaning no movement, and brain activity reduced to a minimum. As he slept a dragonfly, taking respite from a transcontinental flight with the wind currents, landed on the southern edge of the lake on the stern of the coracle. A chance to rest and mate. To The Parrot, deeply engrossed in a shared musical tradition whose roots are in the Vedic *anukirtana* tradition, repeating the chant, yet ever vigilant, this was a sign of impending rain. The Sergeant, in deep sleep now, missed the spectacle. The management team at Dyfed-Powys Police Rapid-Response Coracle Unit headquarters in Milford Haven, kept abreast of developments by the Monmouth cap, have a vision, to have the right person with the right skills in the right place at the right time.

At that exact moment 104 miles to the north and a tiny bit west of the *café*, Fishguard Town Council[13] voted unanimously to ban walking on the right-hand side up the stairs leading to the library in the Town Hall. The motion was passed following a presentation by an expert in the field who claimed this would reduce congestion on the approach to the bottom step, a particular problem on busy market days. "A recent academic study revealed," she began, "that the number of people using the stairs increases by two thirds during library rush hours." The expert went on to inform full Council that less than 40% of people consider running up the stairs. Such a sensitive change requires support from residents and during the public consultation period the County Echo[14] published dozens of letters from local residents, most, it must be said, in favour of the change. One voice of dissent came from the head coach of Fishguard Rugby Club[15] who argued that getting a good shove on when negotiating the scrum that forms at the base of the stairs was good practice for the forwards. Another letter from Fishguard and Goodwick Ladies' Fitness Club pointed out that the healthy option would be for everyone to walk up and down the stairs several times before returning a book, which side people were on being immaterial. A local marathon runner suggested running up and down the stairs all morning carrying weighted rucksacks with in excess of 50lbs of baggage. Running out of time and keen to get to the pub the vote regarding the appropriate method of walking down the stairs was deferred until the following month.

Heartened by this, brain activity in the Sergeant's head picked up, heart rate and breathing quickened, and the waitress, busy on her smartphone, was startled by faint signs of movement. He awoke, not sure of his bearings, confused by the unfamiliar surroundings. Fortunately, the Monmouth cap uses a 3D depth sensor and lasers to scan his face and analyse any facial expression that might appear on it. By combining this activity with an analysis of his voice tones the cap detects confusion and engages him in happy uplifting conversation, thereby leading his mind back gently into the everyday. If the ascent from deep sleep to waking is too rapid the cap utilises positive visualisation techniques in which steaming mugs of tea and chocolate biscuits play a prominent role. This robotic cap, via its feedback loop to DPPRRCU HQ in Milford Haven, recently suggested that the Sergeant be replaced by an algorithm. This was rejected by High Command, the decisive factor being public concern. Humans want humans in control. The fact that the Sergeant is not in control failed to sway the vote for the simple reason that the general public are not aware of this. The vision of tea and biscuits calmed the Sergeant and his mind re-engaged with Wadebridge. "**Avast me hearties! 'Tis wadebridge I espy**! he murmured in his best pirate speech, imagining that he was deep, deep undercover in a pirate haven.

Always observant, he looked warily around and noticed two old boys sitting at the table next to him drinking tea. He listened with interest to the end of a conversation they were having in which they seemed to be discussing the relative merits of two engineering firms in Camborne.

"Up te Holmans, they work te with in a thousandth of a inch ye knaw."

"Ess I knaw that but up te Climax they de git en 'zackly!"

"A coded message," he decided, as the words "a thousandth of a inch" and "'zackly" reverberated through his mind. "Are they pirates discussing a shipment of contraband bound for who knows where?" A shiver moved up and down his spine.

Encouraged by signs of life the waitress approached. "'Ow wuz yer rest, pard? Yoom bound te be tired after yer long jurney. 'Ave drop moore tae an' a few more bisc'its will ee?"

His ear for languages, fine-tuned over the years during missions to foreign parts, sprang into overdrive. He turned to her, listening with a keen ear.

"'Tis turnin' out grand agane this marnin' pard."

The subject had provided him with sufficient data, his linguistic analysis was complete. "What part of Poland are you from?" he enquired knowledgeably.

"I belong inte Pendoggett, really, but now a days I de live in te Tregonetha, yo."

"Is that near Krakov?"

"Kraków, pard. No pard."

"Hmmm. Fascinating place northern Europe. Yes please, more tea and biscuits."

As she walked away from him his eyes followed her slim behind until it disappeared behind the cake cupboard at the end of the counter and his thoughts turned naturally to matters of cosmology. "That big, round yellow thing in the sky is hurtling through space dragging us and the other planets with it, attracted by its gravity." he mused. "Contrary to popular belief we are not involved in rotational motion but in vortex motion." A dull thumping ache began inside his head.

"'Ere you are boy, yer favrite mug, an' the biscits are fresh an' fresh, straight out o' the packet they are."

"Wonderful!"

"The tae is brab'm 'ot, so mind yer lips, see, 'tis still steemin' and juss as you de like it. Now, mine you dawn't go burnin yer tongue either."

"Excellent. Thank you, Brenda."[16]

"'Tis turnin out te be a braa fine morning Cap'm. The ol' clouds are baten away grand."

But by now the Sergeant was focused on what lay on the table in front of him and her comment went unheard. She smiled affectionately, knowing him to be a good 'un, turned and went back to her place behind the counter, above which hangs a large sign that reads **PRENA DYBRI EVA LEEL**, thumbs texting fluently as she went.[17] Aeons passed in his universe until a stray ray of sunshine came out from behind a cloud and shone through the window, lighting up his features. Warmed by this he looked across at the pretty young waitress busy behind the counter preparing two rounds of toast, a mug of *scileagailí* and a *cappuccino*. "I can feel a song coming along," he muttered. And sure enough, *Bre Gammbronn*[18] came along, and, noticing with great interest the sound change of /k/ to /g/ after *Bre*, *Kammbronn* to *Gammbronn*, he began to sing. The waitress put the toast, tea and coffee on the table for the middle-aged couple who had ordered them, went back behind the counter, took off her pinafore and picking up the melodeon she kept there for just such an occasion as this, began playing the tune.

Goin' up Camborne Hill, coming down.
Goin' up Camborne Hill, coming down.
The 'orses stood still;
The wheels went around;
Going up Camborne Hill coming down.

The other customers, locals mostly with a sprinkling of emmets, looked up in delight.

Owth yskynna Bre Gammbronn war-nans.
Owth yskynna Bre Gammbronn war-nans.
Pub margh stag yth o,
Pub ros eth yn-tro,
Owth yskynna Bre Gammbronn war-nans.

The waitress walked between the tables to the middle of the *café* playing the melodeon as she went and sang the next verse with him.

White Stockings, white stockings she wore.
White Stockings, white stockings she wore.
White stockings she wore,
The same as before,
Goin' up Camborne Hill, coming down.

Hy lodrow, hy lodrow o gwynn.
Hy lodrow, hy lodrow o gwynn.
Hy lodrow o gwynn,
A-ugh hy dewlin,
Owth yskynna Bre Gammbronn war-nans.

Everyone joined in for the last few verses, including a jolly band of fishermen whiling away their time drinking tea in the corner as they waited for a favourable wind to take them back to Newquay.[19]

The Sergeant, his brain now fully awake after the music therapy, beamed with pleasure. Brenda curtsied. An appreciative round of applause broke out from the customers in the *café* and from a young mum who happened to be standing outside on the pavement with her pram waiting for her new boyfriend. The father had long since fled the area pursued by the Child Support Agency.[20] The Sergeant blushed. "You're very kind," he whispered as he bowed his head to acknowledge their generous spirit. As the applause died down the young mum resumed her grip on the Triple Stroller with red hoods, black side-by-side seating and light aluminium frame, the ideal accompaniment for the first-time, unmarried teenage mum with triplets and a vibrant social life.

Later that day the Sergeant, with The Parrot standing on his right shoulder in true Cornish style, walked around the town following an experimental promenade production of the Cornish language drama *An Tarow* staged by *An Wariva Genedhlek a Gernow*,[21] the National Theatre of Cornwall. It began in Molesworth Street, the audience and players walking to different locations during the performance which ended in the town's *Plen an Gwari* from where it was broadcast live to packed audiences in theatres and cinemas across *Kernow*, *Kembra* and *Breten Vyghan*. The play finished, they returned to the vessel at its mooring.

On the quay side the single mum was about to buy a pasty for her boyfriend from the pasty van parked nearby. A disreputable looking skinhead, he lived with seventeen other down and outs in a squat in a vacant Council flat in the seedier part of Bodmin. In their luxury conveyance, bought for them by despairing grandparents on their absent father's side, the eighteen-month-old triplets whose heads appeared to be shaved as if in *hommage* to their mother's new 'special friend', were exchanging ideas with each other by means of what appeared to be a fist fight. "**Extra large!**" He ordered somewhat brusquely, kicking the pram as he did so. The children became quiet for a moment, looked up at him, beautiful blue eyes sparkling, then continued as before, increasing the volume a couple of decibels as if to make up for the interruption. The pasty vendor, overhearing the exchange, noted the young man's rudeness and with a look of resigned restraint tightened the straps at the back of his black and red striped canvas eyelet bib apron with co-ordinating webbing ties, adjustable neck strap and pocket before reaching into the pie warmer display cabinet to pick out the food item requested. "Tri feuns pymthek dinar ha tri-ugens dhiso-jy, tegen," he said in Cornish, holding the pasty out for her. She didn't understand. "Three pounds seventy-five pence to you, my luvver," he repeated, smiling sweetly. She recoiled, startled by this unsolicited expression of kindness and with a sharp intake of breath began rummaging amongst the *debris* in her large, ladies', hippie style, multicoloured shoulder bag for money. The boyfriend, for no particular reason, kicked the pram again then stared at the pasty vendor with a bored yet surly look. The noise emanating from the pram abated briefly before another fist fight erupted, accompanied by raucous eighteen-month-old screams of delight. Finding her purse, she looked up and moved hesitatingly towards the outstretched hand, suspicion written all over her pretty face. The burly food *entrepreneur* held the pasty out to her as she approached, an encouraging smile lighting up his ruck-scarred features.

Meanwhile, the boyfriend, angry with life and everything in it except booze, fags and class A drugs, turned his ill-natured attention to the offending object. He gaped vacantly at it whilst simultaneously studying its contours with deep expectation, a feat only young adult males of a certain disposition can accomplish. A look of annoyance clouded his spotty face. With great effort his jaw dropped, opening his mouth slightly to reveal a jagged row of dark, nicotine and goodness knows what else, stained teeth. An indecipherable yet unpleasant stream of polysyllables interspersed with a series of unintelligible, staccato grunts, the overall affect suggesting a reluctance to engage in meaningful discourse, spewed out of the half open orifice.

He was interrupted by the proprietor of the pasty van's deep bass-baritone voice, noting that it had a range extending from F2 up to C5. He discerned a quiet glint of rough punishment in the ex-rugby forward's eyes and heard menace rather than Bryn Terfel in the intonation. "My a wor pandr'a brederydh. 'A wrug ev ri dhymm an huni Bras po Marthys Bras?' Wel yn gwiryoneth, gans pubtra esa ow hwarvos, my a ankevis pyth esen ow kul. Mes awos bos hemma onan Marthys Bras .44, pasti kernewek an moyha posek y'n bys hag a allsa tardha dha benn dhyworth dha dhiwskoodh, yma res dhis omwovyn unn govyn: 'A wrav vy omglewes feusek?' Wel, a wre'ta, a dhrogwas?"[22]

Uncertainty became confusion and the spottyfaced one's brain whirred in disarray, then stopped. Realising that the youth didn't understand Cornish the proprietor repeated himself. "I knaw zactly w'at you're thinkin'. Did ee gi' me a large er a extra large?' Well, te tell ee the truth ov it, in all the 'citement, I kind ov fergot where I wuz to. But 'cause this is a .44 extra large, the most powerful Cornish pasty in all olv the werld an' would blaw yer 'ead off, you got te ask yerself one simple question: Am I feelin lucky?' Well do ee, punk?"[22] No, you don't mess with a recently retired number 8 for the Cornish Pirates. As he stood in his van watching the bleak and cheerless side of life unfolding in front of him the number 8 dreamt of the glory days at the Mennaye Field in Penzance when he fought with opposition forwards worthy of his attention.

Deflated, the young man kicked the pram in disgust, once again disturbing the three cherubs lost in their violent individual struggles for domination. Annoyed by the constant interruption and sensing a common enemy, they began throwing things at him, many of the items shoplifted that morning from businesses in the town. The three hostiles showered the young stud with rattles, baby beads, molar mallets, a Beatrix Potter bean rattle, a wooden Tetris jigsaw puzzle toy, a happy cloud rattle, a blue spotted antique plastic elephant covered in lead paint and teeth marks, two sets of plastic count and explore keys, the third having recently been thrown successfully under a passing bus, a radio control race car, a plastic radio and activity cube with lights and sound, a long since out of date half empty bottle of teething gel, two toddler car key puzzle toys, a wooden-handled jingle stick shaker with metal bells, a baby Einstein key to discover the Hohner mini B/C button accordion, three matching steering wheel driver car dashboards with authentic engine sounds, a Fisher Price rainforest mobile in which the canopy had already died, five empty 200ml bottles of CALPOL Sugar Free Infant Suspension, three galactic wars space laser swords with sharpened blades, two punctured swimming aids, a peek-a-boo rugby ball, an old duck comforter, assorted mouldy teething rings, a musical wooden giraffe, three matching wooden jingle ring hand bell rattles, a disassembly assembly cartoon motorcar toy, a jockstrap, which puzzled all three, a varied selection of squeaker rattles, a multicoloured toy skwish made from replenishable rubberwood, ideal for baby hands to grip, a 54 piece mini jungle plastic animal toy set and three carousel drum and drumsticks with expertly honed, fire hardened tips.

Intent upon inflicting the maximum harm on the common enemy the gang of three left the soft toys unused, and anyway, they had other plans for them as at a secret meeting convened earlier in the day it was agreed unanimously to use them to build a bonfire underneath their cot in the bedroom after dark on Saturday night when mum was out and the fifteen year old babysitter was busy with her new twenty eight year old *beau* on the settee in the open-plan living area downstairs. They also retained the three mini AK47 SWAT auto electric guns with flashing lights and lifelike fire sounds they had adapted to shoot glass marbles.

The young man broke down and began to cry.

Several days later, their mission in collaboration with the North Cornwall Police Rapid-Response Crabber Unit and a top-secret undercover section of the Helston Furry Dancers[23] having been completed successfully, it was with heavy hearts that the Sergeant and his crew, The Parrot, prepared to leave this delightful part of the world they love so much and set out on the return journey.

The Parrot spoke softly, "*Maintenant, mon vieux.*"

The Sergeant, standing tall and proud on the deck next to the main mast put the forefinger of his right hand into his mouth to wet it, removed it and held it aloft. A mysterious silence descended over the town. One moment became two ... three ... four ... The crowd of well-wishers on the quayside held their breath. In the *café* the waitress stopped texting and looked up, without knowing why. As the tension approached breaking point a faint smile appeared on the outside of the Sergeant's face. He nodded consent as his forefinger, sending messages to his brain, confirmed his gut instinct that wind speed, a light breeze he estimated to be 2 on the Beaufort scale, 4-6 knots from the southeast, was perfect for departure. Spectators cheered and threw their hats into the air.

With a look of great forbearance and a performance the great John Wayne himself would be proud of, The Parrot, looking down from its position in the crow's nest, said, "Let`s go home, Sergeant."[24]

Lowering his forefinger, the Sergeant proceeded to the port side and cast off before moving for'ard to take his place for the next instalment of this well-rehearsed sequence. Shards of sunlight shone through gaps in the gathering cloud cover lighting up the nicer parts of Wadebridge as the vessel, carried by a benign current, moved serenely towards the middle of the Camel. Positioned in a prominent location on the bow the Sergeant performed his signature *kabuki* dance followed by a controlled series of Bulgarian split squats before taking his seat at the paddle. The Parrot, perched on the for'ard edge of the crow's nest, a tear in its eye, faced down river. "Tumultuatio,"[25] it squawked and blew loudly into the conch shell, a symbol of water and female fertility. On the quayside, a young mum searching her large ladies' hippie style multicoloured shoulder bag for the high-voltage rechargeable electric stun gun, three breathable, nylon mesh muzzles and matching sets of handcuffs, blushed ever so slightly.

Using the conch shell served both as a farewell to the good people of North Cornwall and a warning to shipping. After five, short, rapid blasts The Parrot put the conch shell back into its velvet lined weather-proof box permanently attached to the mast, adopted the full lotus position and began to chant.

Om Namah Shivaaya Om Namah Shivaaya

From their vantage point on the nearby stone bridge the massed ranks of the Hare Krishna Choir,[26] bussed in specially from their monastery in a converted cowshed on a farm in Ruthernbridge, took up the chant.

Om Namah Shivaaya Om Namah Shivaaya

The Parrot adjusted his Ray-Bans and led again.

Om Namah Shivaaya Om Namah Shivaaya

The monks responded, feeling the energy rising through their chakras.

Om Namah Shivaaya Om Namah Shivaaya

Spiritual energy suffused the higher chakras of grateful onlookers. An eastern sound *tsunami* of bliss swept over the town and surrounding districts reaching as far upriver as Grogley Halt as the monks were joined by the *Kirtan Wallahs* adding fast, mesmerizing rhythms with their *chimtas*, *daphlis*, *dholaks*, *jhanjis*, *manjiras* and *tablas*. From their position on the opposite bank of the river the Radio Free Cornwall choir paused, fixed eyes upon their conductor, and as her arms raised high into the air and began revolving, joined in.

Shivaaya namaha Shivaaya namah om
Shivaaya namaha Shivaaya namah om

An enthusiastic *troupe* of acrobats, jugglers and aerialists performed on and above the bridge.

Shivaaya namaha Shivaaya namah om
Shivaaya namaha Shivaaya namah om

The weathervane atop Wadebridge town hall stirred, appeared agitated for a moment then swung violently around indicating that the sudden change of weather promised by the Met Office shipping forecast was correct. Over a period of two and a half minutes, wind speed, as measured by the antique Alberti anemometer lashed high on the foremast, rose to near gale, 5-6 on the Beaufort scale, 28-33 knots. Wind direction was now from the northwest.

Shambho Shankara namah Shivaaya
Girijaa Shankara namah Shivaaya

Shambho Shankara namah Shivaaya
Girijaa Shankara namah Shivaaya

"**Engaging Warp Drive**," shouted the Sergeant with a loud piercing cry that rang out above the *pandemonium*. Unaware of the danger, the crowd cheered. The Parrot gripped the wooden rail of the crow's nest ever tighter with both claws and leant into the future.

A selection of half inch diameter multicoloured glass marbles erupted from a pram on the quayside causing panic to spread through the crowd. The emergency response team from the Truro branch of the St John's Ambulance[27] who had been on standby in The Swan moved in to restore calm before retreating under a *barrage* of increased intensity.

Running barefoot for thousands of miles with the *Rarámuri* Indians in the impenetrable mountains and canyons of the *Barrancas del Cobre*, the Copper Canyons, in the *Sierra Madre Occidental* in Mexico whilst on an exchange visit there several years ago, The Parrot learnt the recipe for *lechuguilla*, an alcoholic drink made from local plants.[28] Low in alcohol, high in salts and minerals, The Parrot prepares the beverage for ceremonial occasions such as this to enable it to express the strong emotions welling up inside. Releasing its grip on the rail with one claw it raised the open water canteen filled with *lechuguilla* that was hanging around its neck, took a long, deep draught of the intoxicating brew, released the canteen, gripped the rail again with both claws to steady itself, threw back its head and with rapid back and forth movements of tongue and uvula emitted a long, wavering, high pitched vocal sound with its distinctive trilling quality. Dogs lurking in dark alleys nearby took up the call as the crowds lining the riverbanks listened with delight. Common in parts of Southern Europe such as Galicia, the Basque country and Cyprus, and further away in India, Sri Lanka, Central to South Asia, the Middle East and Africa, ululation is still heard in northern Europe as far north as Wadebridge where palaeoethnomusicologists claim the phenomenon achieves its most sophisticated forms.

Off Daymer Bay, a school of bottlenose dolphins frolick in the sheltered waters. Close by, a group of Atlantic bluefins, dark blue above and grey below with relatively short pectoral fins, some up to forty years old, weighing over 2,124 pounds and measuring up to ten feet in length, moderate their internal temperature as they enjoy the warming sunlight. Apex predators, the Atlantic bluefin tuna, much admired by fishermen and fisherwomen, was first described by Linnaeus in 1758 in the tenth edition of his *Systema Naturae*. They are joined by a swordfish, a 17-year-old female weighing almost 1,202 pounds, also of the order perciformes, basking lazily near the surface. Putting on a show for the visitors gathered on the headlands either side of the bay to admire this unexpected visitation of ocean species she jumps high into the air before falling back and disappearing beneath the surface of the water again with a smooth splash. Turtles and manta rays play in the azure waters alongside seals, sea lions and squid, the latter moving swiftly by jet propulsion.

A pod of killer whales wait patiently in the warm, shallow waters. Keeping a respectful distance, several species of acoustically distinct subspecies of pygmy blue whales and a small school of minke whales with characteristic white band on each flipper, gather expectantly. A school of all-white beluga whales adapted for life in the Arctic with distinctive protuberances at the front of their heads navigate the dangerous waters around The Rumps as they head eagerly for the party, excited high-pitched calls heralding their arrival. Blue whales, keeping to seaward of The Mouls follow close on their heels as they approach the mouth of the Camel, calling to relatives far way. A change in the frequency of the sound wave since the swinging sixties means that these atonal sounds that can travel over 600 miles underwater are deepening in pitch, the average pitch having dropped the equivalent of three white keys on a piano. Whale calls are evolving. In the freezing Arctic waters to the north of Pentire Point two narwhals surface from beneath the ice sheet and rub their tusks together in greeting. Two separate pods of humpback whales sing as they approach Trevose Head from the southwest. Their songs tell us that one group are from the Pacific, near New Caledonia, and the other from the ocean near eastern Australia. To the delight of the visitors a megamouth shark, a filter-feeder 15 feet long and weighing 890 pounds can be seen swimming with its mouth open to catch plankton and jellyfish, the 50 rows of teeth in its bulbous head clearly visible. Usually staying deep during the day and coming to the surface at night to feed it is attracted by the *brouhaha*. This species was first discovered in Hawaii in 1976 when one got caught up in the anchor chain of a North Cornwall Police Rapid-Response Crabber Unit vessel on *manoeuvres* with the Hawaiian Navy.[29]

The more astute observers amongst the onlookers note that the whales, as with all marine mammals, move their tails up and down, whereas the sharks, like all fish, move their tails from side to side. The movement in the whales being a relic of the hip movements of their ancestors when they walked on Cornwall, rather than swimming around it as they are doing today.

From the bushes and hedgerows each side of this mighty river come the rattling melody of lesser whitethroats as common whitethroats sing and dance above them. A low, deep buzzzzzzing announces the presence of bees swarming amongst the oak, ash, hazel, willow, blackthorn and wild cherries. Later, they will return to the hollow trunks high in the trees to rest for the night, *cwtshed* up together. Reddish brown roe deer with short antlers and no tails move quietly in woodland close to the north bank as they graze. Accompanying them are orange-tips, white males with orange wing tips and white females with black wing tips playing above a bunch of lady's smock. Brown hairstreaks gather close to the ash trees to feed on aphid honeydew. Orange and brown Duke of Burgundys enjoy the woodland clearings where bluebells, cowslips and primroses grow. Graceful, pale orange silver-washed fritillarys, flying fast with pointed wings with silver streaks on their undersides, catch the sunlight as they feed on brambles in the glades.

Goldfinches, displaying their long gold wing bars and black, red and white vertically striped heads stand on thistle heads taking the fluffy white seeds. Nightingales, their upperparts mottled chestnut and black in tortoiseshell patterning and with white edges on black tails, hide in thickets and sing their distinctive trills and gurgles with whistling *crescendo*. Turtle doves purr reassuringly amongst the hawthorns and blackthorns. Kingfishers, with long, dagger-like bills, their feathers scattering blue light, stay close to their nests in the willow and alder trees. A lone fimble fowl waits in a crumpetty tree nearby, cautiously surveying the landscape. A squadron of choughs flies past overhead, their red legs and bills glistening in the sunlight. A lone European eagle owl, its wingspan just under seven feet with distinctive orange eyes and characteristic ear tufts circles at one hundred feet, a puzzled expression on its face. Visiting from mainland Europe on a short stay visa it is engaged in an intelligence gathering mission. A South Georgia pipit, Antarctica's only songbird, a rare sighting along the estuary, sings happily whilst perched in bushes, daydreaming of home in the Southern Ocean. At around seven inches it is a small, stocky bird with brown streaks, slender blackish beak, long pinkish legs and long hind claw on each foot. High above, a vagrant albatross with dark upper-wing and back with white undersides and twelve-foot wingspan, the largest wingspan of any living bird, soars easily with the winds at a sustained speed of around fifty miles per hour. Over seventy years old it has seen it all before and its attention is focused on finding something to eat.

Greater horseshoe bats, greater mouse-eared bats, pipistrelle bats and serotine bats sleep peacefully. Their time has not yet come. Also in attendance are badgers, brown hares, rabbits, pine martens, foxes, weasels, stoats, mice, hazel dormice, water voles, wildcats straying south, red squirrels, lesser white-toothed shrews recently arrived from the Scilly Isles as stowaways on a yacht, wood mice, field voles, grass snakes, adders, barred grass snakes and smooth snakes, sand lizards, grasshoppers, crickets, rare king diving beetles up to 1.5748 inches long, bumble bees, red mason bees, common carder bees, distinguished from moss and brown-banded carder bees, all three species being all-ginger, by black hairs on the abdomen, all of the bees having evolved from predatory wasps during the Cretaceous period as flowering plants began spreading. Ladybirds and all manner of spiders, wait.

The ancient forest that lies in the subtropical region south of the Camel, trunks and branches covered in orchids, tillandsia, ferns, mosses, lichens and liverworts is quiet in the intense early evening heat. Honeysuckle, with simple leaves growing oppositely along the stems and fragrant purple-white flowers that open at twilight to attract moths, climb high amongst the trees in glades where their roots are shaded, their foliage bathed in sunlight. All manner of mushrooms grow wild here.

In rough, rocky ground at the edge of a meadow by the river, thistles, grey-green with prickly leaves and stems, wait anxiously as a herd of grazing herbivores passes close by. Thrift, with its deep reddish-pink cup-shaped flowers and dense mats of sea campion with tiny, grey-green, fleshy leaves and white flowers, each with five bi-lobed petals reaching nearly a foot high, grow here. A few feet from the safety of its nest made of woven leaves built high in a nearby tussock of grass the slim body of a harvest mouse, 2.7 inches long and weighing 0.2 ounces with small hairy ears and orangey-red fur with white underside is in plain sight, the puncture marks of an owl's talons in its back. Swallowed whole then regurgitated moments before, its long, hairless, prehensile tail lies limp and motionless in death. From the mouth of its burrow in the ground nearby a goliath tarantula looks on with interest.

A flock of white pelicans of the family Pelecanidae, black flight feathers visible only when wings are spread, with thin necks, long beaks and large throat pouches, skim the water of the river surface in flight to scoop up fish. Swimming low with long, thin, hooked bills raised, black-plumaged cormorants dive occasionally to catch fish. Pink and white long-legged spoonbills visiting from the Americas wade the shallow waters at the edge of the river, moving their partly opened, flattened bills from side to side, snapping them shut when a small fish or crustacean touches the inside. These roseate spoonbills are particularly partial to shrimp. On Pentire Point to the northwest a shag, with smaller, lighter build than the cormorants and thinner bill warms itself on a rocky ledge before diving to feed on sand eels on the sea bottom up to 150 feet below, staying underwater for up to 45 seconds and needing only 15 seconds or so to recover between dives. Its metallic-green-tinged plumage gleams in the sunlight.

A raft of otters, streamlined semi-aquatic carnivorous predators over two and a half feet long with dense, brown fur and long tails, chatter and play as they hunt for fish, amphibians and crustaceans.

Located in the middle of the infamous Bermuda Triangle, the Sargasso Sea in the North Atlantic near the Bahamas almost 4,000 miles to the west is the only sea without a shore, being bounded by ocean currents on all sides. It is covered by a mat of dense seaweed that in former times trapped sailing ships, their crew never seen again. Weather conditions in the sea are warm and stable as it rotates slowly clockwise in a subtropical gyre. Several years ago, whilst on patrol with the Bermuda Police Rapid-Response Schooner Unit with Bermuda Rig,[30] the Sergeant experienced difficulty paddling the coracle through it and the vessel became stuck for several weeks. Supplies ran low and at one point, parched and desperate after several days without tea, and hallucinating badly, he attempted throwing The Parrot overboard in order to conserve water. Meanwhile, deep beneath the waters of the Camel, eels, spawned in the Sargasso Sea before their larvae, over a period of some ten months, drifted to the North Cornwall coastline, feed on crustaceans and fish. Unimpressed by this tale of derring-do a passing shark decides to eat one.

Exhausted by the exertions of the day Team Sergeant falls asleep at the paddle. Displaying a humour not often found in inanimate objects the on-board computer raises the Absentee Pennant.

NATO[31] has been tracking the Sergeant for years and the results of their surveillance can be seen on the official website www.natocymrukernow.mil although the site is a little dull for anyone not interested in international maritime intrigue. The NATO Sergeant Tracker www.natocymrukernow/thesergeant.org is much more fun, and, along with amusing anecdotes and video clips, provides the intelligence community with insights into his sailing habits, which they are yet to comprehend. The Sergeant might not know where he is, but they do. The 2-star general on duty at NATO headquarters in Brussels, Belgium, smiles. "Shut it down," he says brusquely. "He'll be there for days. See y'all in the mornin'."

In a bunker deep underground at NORAD[32] (the North American Aerospace Defense Command) Northern Command headquarters at Peterson Air Force Base in El Paso County near Colorado Springs, Colorado, the officer in charge heaves a sigh of relief and gives his team the rest of the shift off.

On and on, deep into the night the chanting on the bridge continues as the coracle, stuck fast on a sandbank a little way downriver, waits for the next high tide. At two bells, long before dawn, the Sergeant will sound the general alarm.

29

They say we're young and we don't know,
We won't find out until we grow.
Well, I don't know if all that's true,
'Cause you got me, and baby I got you.

Sonny and Cher[1]

On the avenues and boulevards leading to the Piazza della Republica at the heart of Crymych the sense of nothing happening was palpable. Nothing was happening, apart from riotous carnival time that is. It was Twm Carnabwth Day, a public holiday in this great city. A wooden carousel gaily painted in red, green and white with twenty-one horses and four gilded king's and queen's carriages gives rides to laughing children as their mums and dads, uncles and aunts, grandfathers, grandmothers, great grandfathers, great grandmothers and associated relatives sideways to the ninth degree, sip coffee with friends in nearby *cafés* overlooking the festivities. Huge crowds of spectators, Crymychians, a happy people, and festival goers bussed in from surrounding areas watch as dancers, drummers and a host of other performers surge through the metropolis accompanying the colourful floats. The procession is led, as it is every year, by students from the City's *samba* school, the biggest outside Brazil.

The film festival based at the Arts Centre was showing, amongst others, Sidney Llumet's *12 Angry Cloggers*,[2] a perennial favourite, Delme Davies' *3:10 to Brynberian*[3] and François Villiers' 1958 *L'Eau Vive*[4] whose theme song, composed by Guy Béart from the golden age of French *chanson*, Megan, Bronwen and all Machlud y Wawr[5] members know off by heart. The *Palais de Danse* in the western suburbs would be full until morning. The Historic Regatta was in full flow in Crymych Lagoon, a procession of antique gondolas with gondoliers in full costume. The Twm Carnabwth Tower, all 73 storeys of it, was decked out in bunting and balloons as booming disco music reverberated around the Vietcong restaurant at the top. A Dafydd Iwan tribute band played the Crymych Bowlen. The weather was perfect yet puzzling, not cold enough to be cold, not hot enough to be hot.

It is not easy to capture the spirit of a place as many-sided as Crymych. Once the capital of Wales it is also known as the Shangri-La of the west or simply *La Dominante*. Between the 8th and 13th centuries the City State of Crymych is considered by scholars to have been the first major European financial centre, a development that brought great wealth and gave the world the term *banc*, later to be borrowed into English as *bank*. Evidence of this wealth can be seen today in the magnificent architecture to be found within the city walls. At its financial zenith, emboldened by being a major commercial and maritime power the City Fathers and Mothers declared independence and the Republic of Crymych was born, lasting through the Middle Ages and the *Renaissance*, to which it made significant contributions, into modern times. Eventually, a decline in its fortunes saw wealth pass south to a town sinking somewhere in Italy.

Following the welcome result of the 1997 referendum which would lead, after an unwarranted interruption of several centuries, to the reconvening of the Welsh Parliament,[6] a delegation from the Senedd[7] in Cardiff Bay met with leaders of the Republic for secret talks at a neutral venue on the Gower, later revealed to be the front bar of the King Arthur in Reynoldston with its welcoming use of warming wood throughout and magnificent log fire. Following a week of frank discussions, the intensity of which was relieved by afternoon excursions to sites of interest on the peninsular, in particular the pub and *café* quarter of Rhossili, it was agreed that in the interests of harmony and to aid the newly formed administration in Cardiff achieve its vision for the future, Crymych would revert to being a City State, albeit one coming under the jurisdiction of the government in Cardiff Bay.

During the economic uncertainty following June 2016 as new trade deals were forged with the outside world the City State of Crymych was affected differently to the rest of Pembrokeshire as it has its own currency, first minted in the late 4th century BC. It consists of gold coins bearing a triple spiral on one side and a horse or barley sheaf on the reverse, along with the names of rulers, and, in more recent times, Lord Mayors and Mayoresses. In early 2020 analysts in the City's financial quarter noticed that share prices and bond prices were moving in tandem. This positive stock-bond correlation suggested that money was leaving the City, which began to look like an emerging economy market. Economists tracking this capital flight out of the City advised prudence while pointing out that it is not an emerging nation. Therefore, no cause for alarm.

Innovative as ever and impressed with what they saw on a fact-finding mission to Bhutan several years ago where they met with officials from the Ministry of Happiness, the City Fathers and Mothers, known for brevity as The City Parents, declared that for Crymychians, Gross National Happiness is more important than Gross National Product. And being carbon neutral is part of this.

Many years ago, the City Council declared the City State and its environs to be a pesticide free zone. Since then, Pembrokeshire pollinators such as bees, butterflies, hoverflies and many, many more are healthier and have increased in numbers aided by the abundant planting of wildflowers in the region and the controlled introduction of beehives and bee hotels. Bee guardians make hives of straw and hollowed out logs and leave the honey intact in order to help wild bees, because they are needed. Cars, buses, vans and lorries, electric or otherwise, are also banned in Crymych and its environs leading to ingenious new forms of transport being used, such as bicycles and the pedal powered *tuk tuk*. Or *tyc tyc* as it's known in the area. With more exercise, people are healthier. St Davids, the county's second city, followed suit shortly afterwards with similar encouraging results. They were followed by towns and cities in Canada, Denmark and France.

On a historical note, the most famous line of Thucydides' *History of the Pembrokeshire War* reads, 'The growth of the power of Crymych and the alarm which this inspired up in England, made war inevitable.' But that's ancient history and the rivalry is long forgotten. Or is it?

The massed band of Machlud y Wawr brought up the rear of the procession, led by Megan beating the big bass drum which was attached to her body with leather shoulder straps. In front, Bronwen, in the style of a *grand guignol*, accompanied by a few brave volunteers handpicked for the occasion, clogged her new piece called **Death March Over Crymych**. Over the years the weight of the drum caused Megan some shoulder strain giving rise to pain on her right side, her main banging side. One evening whilst in the living room of their smallholding she mentioned this to her husband. "I can show you an ancient yoga technique that will give you relief," he told her.

"Thank you, cariad," she replied.

He led her to the rug in front of the log fire for her to be warm. "Now, stand facing me," he whispered. "That's it." They were about six inches apart, the fire on her right side. "Place your feet shoulder width apart and look into my eyes." He took her hands in his. "Let all the muscles in your body relax, but don't fall over. That's it. Take a slow deep breath in. Pause. Now slowly breathe out. Pause. Breathe slowly in. Pause. Breathe slowly out. That's it." He leant forward, kissed her gently, then straightened again, maintaining eye contact. "Slowly in. Pause ... Slowly out. Pause. In ... Pause ... Out ... In ... Out ..." He leant forward and kissed her again, lingering a little longer this time before returning to his original position. She smiled. "In ... Out ... In ... Out ... That's it." He kissed her again. This continued for fifteen minutes. "That should do the trick. Is your shoulder better?"

"Yes. Much better, cariad."

"I must repeat the treatment for ten days or for as long as the pain continues."

"That's quite intense."

"Yes, but your shoulder needs it. Remember, once in the morning, twice in the afternoon and three times in the evening. It can also be done in bed."

"Oh! Yes please!" She leant forward and kissed him. "I like the sound of that."

"When you see me, you see my love for you. You feel it. That's the greatest healer. I act as a mirror and the love you see in me is but the love that is in you."

Later that evening they sat on the *sofa* facing the wood burner as the light faded outside. Megan dozed off, waking sometime later with a start. "Sorry, cariad, I fell asleep."

"You fell asleep in my arms, cariad. There's a difference."

"Is that important?"

"What's important is that I love you. And that I'm your husband."

Why did you marry me?"

"Many reasons."

"Such as?"

"You give me the tingles. On my 100th birthday I'm going to carry you upstairs to the bedroom and have my way with you."

"That sounds lovely, cariad. Will you do it on my 100th birthday too?"

"Yes."

"That's going to be a good year."

They both giggled.

It was late evening. The procession had long since wound to its end and the big drum put back into its cupboard in the crypt to be silent for another year. Megan sat on the *sofa* in front of the bay window, *crocheting* as the sun set. Out of the corner of one eye she thought she glimpsed something unusual. A movement perhaps, a blur, way over on the far side of the Piazza. A whizzing. Or was it a whirring. It seemed to be getting nearer. "A whirlwind?" she wondered, continuing to *crochet* whilst turning her head slightly to one side to get a closer look. "Oh dear!" she sighed. Earlier, as the procession finished, and the carnival moved into all-night-party mode Bronwen and a few friends entered Das Kapital[8] to quench the thirst brought on by hours of dancing. Unwisely she drank a large *bhang lassi*, a house speciality. Das Kapital is the only government authorised *bhang café* in Pembrokeshire and uses a centuries old recipe containing water, coconut milk, grenadine, ginger, almonds, sugar and ... something else. "She'll be gone for hours," thought Megan. "Tripping with the saints."

A little while later the door of the crypt burst open and Megan felt a rush of air as the blur blew in, blowing the door closed behind it. A rhythmic clattering sound filled the space behind her, rather as if a hundred people were playing *tablas* with furious intent. Turning round she peered into the semidarkness, the only light coming from a beeswax candle in the far corner, standing secure in its holder, an adapted pipe Megan's grandfather smoked, his favourite briar pipe with a *meerschaum* bowl set in a brass holder attached five feet up the crypt wall.

Megan always knows where Bronwen is. She is everywhere at once. By looking, Bronwen appears into existence from a formless background. Before that, poor old Bronwen is just a potential. A very sweet potential, but a potential, nonetheless.

It took a few moments as her eyes adjusted, and then, at the other side of the crypt she made out a spinning form, an unfocused haze rotating fast as it moved at speed between the pillars, around the pillars, up the pillars and down again. Bronwen was home. Megan returned to her *crochet* and waited patiently for her companion to regain some slight connection with Crymych, 'the gateway through which all miracles emerge'.[9] And then it happened, the rotating column of indistinct energy slowed, and in its place Bronwen appeared. Her flower bonnet exuded a delicate outburst of north Pembrokeshire fragrances. "My feet ache," she declared.

"You're standing on them, dear," Megan responded, "after dancing for hours in those new clogs. Kick them off and put your feet up."

The new clogs arrived that morning from a factory in Merthyr Tudful. Fully digitalised, they can perform a range of roles across most difficult terrains. They incorporate advanced digital architecture to facilitate the collection and sharing of up to the moment intelligence in real time in all weathers. Optional features include a laser warning system, advanced modular armour for increased toe protection and for the extreme clogging enthusiast a 40mm automatic cannon. For maximum toe protection the tips are covered with a thin layer of hafnium carbide, one of the most refractory binary compounds known which has a melting point of $3,958^0$C. They are fitted with sensors that utilize real-time in-dance monitoring and diagnostics to make full use of the internet of things. Economical and energy efficient the sensors are self-powering using the vibrations of the clogs during a dance to generate their own power with enough left over for the microprocessors and wireless transmitters. The system monitors key components of these complex pieces of sports equipment, each being constructed from a single block of alder wood. In this way dance coaches are provided information enabling them to avoid unpredictable equipment failure and to gather performance data including identity, acceleration, speed, distance travelled and location. And they pinch.

Bronwen removed the clogs and went in thick stockinged feet to the kitchen to work her magic. With the frying pan heated to the appropriate temperature and ready to do the roasting she studied the sacks of coffee beans arranged on the shelves along one wall. "This is mission critical," she announced to the beans. "Ah yes! C'mon! Get that bad girl out. That's it. Perfect!" she exclaimed as her eyes alighted on the sack of Brynberian Gold. Whilst making the coffee she called out, "Cheese and biscuits?"

"Oh, yes please," replied Megan. "Do we have live cheese?"

"I'll look." Moments later Megan heard a strangled cry followed by Bronwen's voice, sounding a little hoarse. "When I opened the packet, it reached out and grabbed me around the throat."

"Perfect."

Bronwen had gone off-*piste*.

A few minutes later they were sitting on the *sofa* in front of the bay window, woolly stockinged feet resting on the hand-crafted oak coffee table whose blue surface was made from formica hewn by local artisans from a quarry in the hills above Florence.[10] They sipped long *macchiatos*, munched biscuits and fought with the cheese, a five-year old *Gouda* with sweet, caramelized flavours, whilst enjoying the view of the crowds thronging the city.

"Is it greedy to think of finishing off with chocolate cake and ice cream?" asked Bronwen.

"Not if you eat it with a teaspoon. It's a combination that captures the essence."

"What is the essence?"

"Nothing."

"Nothing?"

Chocolate cake with ice cream is exquisite, lasting but a few brief moments yet in that time touching what cannot be touched, expressing what cannot be expressed, taking us to a place that we cannot be taken to.

"More coffee?"

"Thank you."

They were approaching peak coffee and were in the groove.

Pressing the button on the dooby doo Megan turned the radio on. "Breaking news," announced the Radio Free Crymych presenter. "An unrecorded First Folio of Dafydd ap Gwilym poems has been discovered in a sealed compartment in Stouthall, a mansion in the parish of Reynoldston on the Gower. This collection of his poems, dated by scholars to 1378, is thought to be one of the most valuable in the world with an estimated value of £7.3 million. Compare this with a recent First Folio of Shakespeare plays that sold for £6.9 million. After a deep forensic examination with colleagues lasting several months, Mair Jones, a pre-eminent Dafydd ap Gwilym scholar, is delighted to confirm its authenticity. 'The clincher for us,' Professor Jones told a news conference this morning, 'were the watermarks and printing errors.'"

"The book was discovered by a cleaner in a sealed compartment in a secret walk-in cupboard concealed behind a false bookcase in the Oval Room of the mansion. The existence of the compartment was hitherto unknown. The cleaner, a local woman, kept the vacuum cleaner and other routine cleaning equipment in the cupboard as it saved her carrying everything up from the basement every morning. Being in a bit of a rush that fateful day, in the darkness she tripped over the dustpan and brush and fell against a side wall lined with wooden panels, splitting one of the panels with her elbow. She noticed a cavity behind the broken panel, got a torch from amongst the cleaning materials, shone a light through the hole and was astonished to see a compartment measuring approximately 3' by 2' by 1' and sitting there, a thick leather-bound book covered in dust."

"I'm pleased to announce," said the announcer, "that, aided by a cultural and culinary grant from the Welsh Government[11] the book will be on permanent display in the Oval Room which will also house a 14th century tearoom thus making this treasure of Welsh literature available to the public as they munch 600-year-old sandwiches."

"Professor Jones continued. 'The First Folio, as all the poet's admirers know, was published a few short years after his death and without it much of the poet's work would be lost. The Folger Dafydd ap Gwilym Library in Washington DC[12] is home to the world's largest collection of Dafydd ap Gwilym manuscripts and printed works and contains more than 80 copies of the Folio. In my recent book, *Dafydd ap Gwilym's First Folio: Six Centuries of an Iconic Book*,[13] I liken the volume to Lorens Hokusai John's series of woodblock prints *Thirty-Six Views of Carn Ingli*,[14] each of which, like the copies of the First Folio, show variations. And each one is a gem.'"

"And now news from the world of education. An audacious attempt by the University of the Four Trinity Davids[15] to relocate the Eiffel Tower to Nott Square in Carmarthen has been thwarted at the last minute by an EU ruling passed in Brussels today. The decision not to allow it to leave mainland Europe is a disappointment for the Expansion and Requisitions Team of the University who have been working on the project for several years. 'The opening of the Eiffel Tower in the town was to have followed the recent awarding of professorships to senior catering staff in the refectory,' a disappointed University spokesperson told Radio Free Crymych this morning, adding, 'And all 27 Vice-Chancellors were looking forward to moving into their new offices at the top. They are all very sad. This is a bad day for Carmarthen.'"

"An unidentified source who wishes to remain anonymous but whose brief includes chairing the University's powerful World Domination Committee told our reporter at a secret meeting in the vegetarian *café* in Lammas Street dinner time today that the University has now set its sights on a statue that stands on a mountain top a short distance from Rio de Janeiro," added the announcer. "Whilst not as tall as the Eiffel Tower it will nonetheless add a certain *je ne sais pas trop quoi dire, quand vous me regardez ainsi* to the town centre. The only drawback of course being the lack of office space at the top, a matter of concern for the vice-chancellors."

"More news from the University now. Dr Enid Reiss and her team at the Department of Astrophysics have measured the 'Clogging Rate', the average speed at which cloggers clog during competition dancing. Until recently this was thought to be a constant. The figure has been published on the arXv website,[16] a repository of over a million electronic preprints in various scientific fields and is 8% faster than when previously recorded in 1926. 'There appears to be something in the standard cosmological model we don't understand,' Professor Reiss told a packed press conference in the Halliwell Centre today. 'There are three possibilities, one, the new measurement is wrong, two, the old measurement is wrong, three, we need to rewrite the textbooks.' The Welsh Government has called for a full report."

"Travel news now. The opening of Pembrokeshire's first spaceport on the summit of Carn Ingli yesterday makes the county a pioneer in the world of futuristic transport. 'We foresee the spaceport being a hub for cultural space tourism. This is the most significant development in the county since the building of Pentre Ifan,' a Cabinet member of Pembrokeshire County Council[17] who holds the Space Travel brief told us earlier today."

"Exciting news from the world of the Arts. Sebastiano del Plombo's *Adoration of the Cloggers*[18] has been restored and is going on display in the Crymych Museum of Art. Sebastiano, 1485-1547, was an Italian lutanist and painter of the High Renaissance period and a contemporary of Raphael with whom he worked for a period. Michelangelo himself promoted Sebastiano's early career."

"The series of lectures on European literature at Crymych Library reaches its penultimate session tonight with a discussion of the importance of François Mauriac, novelist, dramatist, critic, poet and journalist in the history of French literature. Tomorrow night the series is brought to a close by the much-anticipated dissection of the role of Daniel Owen's novels in the history of Welsh literature. Widely regarded as being the father of the Welsh language novel tradition the lecture will shed new light on his works and reveal the manuscript of a hitherto unknown novel recently discovered amongst a large collection of private papers during a house clearance in Mold."

"Foreign news now. In a landmark case in a court in Louisiana in the United States a pair of clogs is suing their owner. Kept as backup by the owner, whose identity cannot be revealed to the public, the clogs have spent their entire time in a cupboard since being bought three years ago. The lawyer representing the clogs contends that they are being deprived of the chance to dance. Clogs kept as spare should have the same rights as any other clogs the court ruled. The lawyer is reported to be working *pro bono*."

Perusing a paper discussing electron impact excitation of clogs a feeling of unease swept across Bronwen's brow then swept back again. She engaged in a few moments of preparatory magical thinking. Relaxed, eyes closed, she established meaningful contact with happiness and wellbeing then slipped the clutch and entered freefall. A warm glow erupted from the crown of her head as she became established in the great cognitive vacuum that is full.

The announcer continued unabated. "Farming news. The annual Pembrokeshire Binder Twine Festival will be held this Saturday in the castle in Manorbier and the same day the camel-wrestling season begins in Brithdir Mawr[19] near Newport. Under 9s, under 11s, and under 14s in the morning, adults in the afternoon. In the evening, the annual and always much-anticipated Camel Beauty Pageant will be held in which camels from all parts of the county compete."

Megan's thoughts slipped back to life with her husband. It was early morning and the sun newly risen, they were lying in the double bed in the converted cowshed on the smallholding. As she woke, she opened her eyes and saw he was lying next to her, facing her.

"I feel very sad." he whispered.

"Oh dear! Why are you sad, cariad?"

"I suddenly realized I wasn't within kissing distance. I'm always sad when we're far apart."

She put an arm around him. "I'm here, lying next to you."

"I can't see you."

Your eyes are shut, cariad."

"Oh yes." He opened his eyes and smiled. Their eyes met. He kissed her. "Your mission, should you choose to accept it," he said authoritatively, "is to lie here in this lovely warm bed and snooze while I get out of this lovely warm bed into the cold, get dressed and go out into the freezing, wet weather risking hypothermia, frostbite, shark attack and goodness knows what else, sacrificing my wellbeing and future health in order to let the horses, chickens, ducks and geese out, give them all something to eat then fight my way back inside, make two hot mugs of tea, negotiate the stairs without spilling tea and scalding myself, place one on the bedside table each side of the bed, undress and get back into bed."

"Yes, cariad. How brave of you."

He moved his face from side to side. "Are you following?"

"Following what?"

"My nose."

She smiled sleepily.

"Repeat after me. I'm wonderful."

"You're wonderful."

"No. I'm wonderful."

"You're wonderful."

"No. I'm wonderful not you're wonderful."

"You don't think I'm wonderful?"

"No. Yes. No, no. I'm, that's you, you're wonderful."

"You're wonderful."

"Nooo. You're wonderful."

"I'm wonderful."

"Yes. Even when it's raining. And I'm glad you're beautiful. I can admire your beauty whenever I'm with you."

"You enjoy doing that?"

"Not enjoy, cariad. That makes you sound like a sandwich."

"When did you fall in love with me?" she asked.

"The first time we met I looked into your eyes and my brain exploded."

"Oh dear!"

"Have I been a good husband? I've tried to be, but I don't know."

"You don't know?"

"Well, after your brain explodes it's difficult to gauge these things."

"Yes, you have, cariad. And I thank you for it." She knew he was a worrier, always thinking he was outstaying his welcome. And inside he was lonely.

He smiled, kissed her again, tucking her in as he did so, then left the sanctuary of the bed to go off and take care of the animals. As he walked down the stairs and through the house towards the door, she sang a few lines of a favourite song to herself.

> There's beauty in the silver, singin' river,
> There's beauty in the sunrise in the sky.
> But none of these and nothing else can touch the beauty,
> That I remember in my true love's eyes.

She sank towards sleep halfway through the last verse. Sensing this as he walked up the path towards the stables, he sang the last few lines.

> Yes, and only if my own true love was waitin'.
> Yes, and if I could hear her heart a-softly poundin'.
> Only if she was lyin' by me,
> Then I'd lie in my bed once again.[20]

Long before the last words of this beautiful song echoed around the outbuildings on that quiet, frosty morning, she was asleep.

"Oh my!" cried Bronwen, jumping to her sore feet.

Megan looked up. "Are you all right, dear?"

"Yes!" she said as she sat down again with a whoomph. "I had a sudden impulse to be dramatic."

"Well done."

"Perhaps it would be soothing to get on with the weeding," she said, lifting herself unenthusiastically to her feet again. "Do you realise that there have only been weeds since people invented gardens."

Megan noticed the downcast look on Bronwen's face. "It's a little late for weeding. And anyway, the good news is that they're slow moving. You'll catch up with them in the morning."

From time-to-time Bronwen can't bring herself to step off the path which leads from the garden door of the crypt through the orchard, modelled by herself on Monet's painting *Garden Path at Giverny*. This is when she enters into a Ramakrishna like state in which she experiences the grass as living energy, disrupted if she steps on it. In these moments of bliss, the grass, the trees, the apples and leaves, she experiences as life's energy. If an apple is taken from a tree or if a leaf falls, she observes the beginning of its death as an object. Yet when she looks down, she sees the paving stones are also living energy, as are her shoes and socks and feet and legs and ... Then she walks onto the grass, takes an apple from a tree and eats it. Life's living energy eating life's living energy.

"Yes, catch up with them tomorrow. That," she paused thoughtfully and began moving in the direction of the kitchen, "is a good idea. Now that I'm up, *café bombóns* and *truffle* chocolates anyone? And two *affogatos.*"

"Perfect." Megan was happy. "A label," she thought. "As is unhappy. Both are thoughts and neither is the essence of what we are, which is Happiness. Yet Happiness pervades both. How deliciously paradoxical."

She was going over an inspirational talk in her mind, one due to be given at a Machlud y Wawr branch meeting in Cresselly in a few days time. "Accepting life as it is in each moment means you are free to live a life that is of benefit to yourself and others. Not accepting leads to trying to control life, which means a life of reaction and negativity, a life of suffering. And be grateful. Life wants you here, now, perfect as you are. Listen to life. Listen to accept. Listen to be grateful. When lived as it is, life is simple."

"More literary news now," came the voice from the radio. "The winners of the Wales Book of the Year Award,[21] presented to the best Welsh-language and English-language works first published in the preceding year have been announced."

The busy clattering of utensils in the kitchen stopped, leaving the gentler sounds of coffee beans cracking in the frying pan. Bronwen, standing by the open door leading into the orchard, slowed and deepened her breathing before moving into the mountain pose, tadasana. After five breaths she reached down with her right hand and placed her right foot on the inner thigh of her left leg to form the tree pose, vrksasana. She breathed through alternate nostrils for a few moments before engaging in a series of alternating short, explosive exhalations and longer, passive inhalations, gazing into the orchard as she did so. Hydrangeas up to 15 feet tall and 12 feet wide with large flowerheads of blue, pink, light purple, dark purple, red and white flowers growing in light shade at the edge of the orchard attracted her eye. Further away, with some reaching a height of 30 feet, she noticed rhododendrons with spirally arranged leaves and clusters of pink, red, white and purple flowers. Above them, a vast celestial sphere scattered sunlight of every hue. She began to feel faint.

"The prize for Creative Non-Fiction in the English-language section has been awarded to ... *The Secret Life of a Hurdy-Gurdy Player* by ..." A muffled scream of what sounded like light-headed delight came from the kitchen.

Megan looked up. "Are you all right, dear?"

Another scream, less muffled this time, and the sound of one hand high fiving. Megan continued reviewing the talk. "Always give a visitor a hot cup of coffee." She paused. "Or a mug if they prefer, but, make it a thick one to retain the heat. The insular cortex, the part of the brain that responds to feeling warm also responds to feelings of affection. You'll find that simply holding a hot cup of coffee will dramatically increase levels of cooperation."

One June morning several years ago Megan's husband was digging in the vegetable patch in the garden. He had been there for nearly an hour, and he missed her. Leaning the spade against an oak tree he took a notebook and a biro from a pocket and sat down in the shade, his back resting against the trunk. He began writing a love letter.

"My dearest cariad. I hope you are well."

He raised the biro from the paper. "A little formal," he thought, "yet the sentiment carries it."

He continued writing. "No! I hope you are wonderful."

A moment's reflection, then, "No! I hope you know you are wonderful."

"That's it. Finished." He added five kisses, one big one and four little ones, tore the page out of the book, put the biro and notebook onto the grass, got up and folded the note as he began walking towards the herbaceous borders surrounding the lawn, which were in full bloom. Megan was barely visible as she crouched in it weeding. She heard his footsteps and stood up as he approached, turning to him, smiling. He stopped just in front of her, kissed her, handed her the note, kissed her again then turned and went back to the digging. "Yes, that's better," he thought. She misses him.

Bronwen returned with the necessary sustenance and soon two pairs of woolly stockinged feet were perched on the oak coffee table again as they sat back and sipped and munched with eyes gazing through the bay window over Crymych. The gentle clicking sound of *crocheting* emanated from Megan's side of the *sofa* as Bronwen became absorbed into That which is behind all forms, even *café bombóns* and *truffle* chocolates. Hard to believe perhaps, but true. Whilst in this state of shimmering light she enters many a time of an evening she sees a mountain beyond the city limits to the west. "It's beautiful," she tells Megan upon her return. She calls it Kailash II without knowing why. It is invisible to ordinary people and no image of this magic mountain has ever been or could ever be drawn or recorded by camera or any other digital device for it exists at a higher level of consciousness ordinary mortals can never access.

The announcer's voice filled the crypt. The clicking slowed and Bronwen returned. "A flock of wild emus is running riot in the villages around Crymych. For thousands of years emus lived in the surrounding mountains until driven to extinction when fruit farmers and local militia shot them as they were seen as a pest. Emus are fussy eaters and enjoy a diet rich in nutrients that includes fruits, seeds, the young shoots of plants and insects such as grasshoppers, ladybirds and caterpillars. Since their reintroduction to the area several years ago their numbers have grown exponentially, partly because local children feed them. However, they increasingly encroach upon the city where they ravage gardens and attack tourists. These birds usually travel in pairs but occasionally form large flocks when moving towards a new food source, Crymych for example. A recent report published by The University of the Four Trinity Davids' Emu Outreach Facility[15] in the shire of Bruce Rock situated in the heart of the Wheatbelt Region of Western Australia 152 miles west of Perth, making it an excellent base to explore areas where these flightless birds are found, concludes that emu numbers in north Pembrokeshire may have grown to as many as half a million."

"Who would have thought," muttered Bronwen. "Perhaps we need to raise this matter at the monthly meeting next week."

"That's a good idea," replied Megan thoughtfully, rubbing her chin. "Please put it on the agenda. Oh! And add, 'My Time with the Hadza' also, would you? And remember to tell everyone that next year's MachludyWawriadur from Y Lolfa[22] has arrived in Siop Siân.[23] Everyone must buy one." Megan encourages Members to spend as much time as possible each year living and eating out on the Preseli Mountains to rewild their gut bacteria by enjoying a preagricultural lifestyle, feasting on vegetable roots, honey and nectar, ants, beetles, fungi, grubs, moths and *bunya* nuts. In season, fruits such as *kakadu* plums, *kutjera*, *muntries* and *quandong* are considered delicacies. Because of this Members have some of the most diverse gut bacteria found in humans anywhere in the world. Indeed, their microbiome compares favourably with that of the Hadza, a hunter gatherer tribe in Tanzania with whose women Machlud y Wawr are twinned. Megan discovered this while on a recent culinary exchange visit with them. They discovered that *bara brith* rhymes with teeth.

The announcers voice danced around the room. "The Institute for the Study of the Six Senses at the University of North Pembrokeshire at Crymych published a report today casting light on the neurophysiology of clog dancing. 'In clog dancing,' Professor Maharajji Evans-Wentz,[24] the lead author told us, 'the clogs move too fast for the brain to process visual information. The clog dancer must attain a zen like state of no-thinking. It is commonly believed the senses take in information which is transmitted to the cognitive centres. But this process is too slow. Instead, the brain, based upon experience, predicts the path of the clogs. This means that cloggers must not think when dancing.' When asked why six senses Professor Evans-Wentz explained that in the West the thinking is that there are five senses and the brain. In the East the brain is thought to be another sense, hence there are six senses. He learnt this during the latter half of the '60s when he spent time with his guru in an ashram in Kainchi in Uttarakand in northern India."[25]

Bronwen sat in silence, at rest, eyes closed, hands folded in her lap, her woolly stockinged feet perched on the small oak table in front of her. With a sigh she metamorphosed and slipped into energetic mode. She did not move, she did not dance, she did not think of dancing, yet she danced. Her being became one with the dance of existence, and then they both disappeared. Megan watched in wonder at the mystery that is Bronwen. She is of the opinion that on occasions Crymych is not so much a place as a state of mind. She thinks the same of Bronwen.

Later that evening, in the peace of the *simne fawr* with her *crochet* and her woolly stockinged feet, Megan noticed time go by, for she is not in it. Subject and object appeared and disappeared before her, she is not of them. An eternal peace spread outwards, enveloping Pembrokeshire. The scent from the fragrant flowers of the Malati trees in the orchard wafted into the crypt on the breeze. Megan let the natural flow of her mind be as she lay back in the *sofa* to enjoy the passing charade. Megan was in love yet there was no object of that love. She thought of her husband and his leaving. Putting her right hand over her heart she sang a few lines of one of the great songs quietly to the evening, and to the memory.

> I loved you in the morning, our kisses deep and warm,
> Your hair upon the pillow like a sleepy golden storm.
> Yes, many loved before us, I know that we are not new,
> In city and in forest they smiled like me and you.
> But let's not talk of love or chains and things we can't untie,
> Your eyes are soft with sorrow.
> Hey, that's no way to say goodbye.[26]

In open glades in the orchard grow peppermint, geraniums, borage, lemon verbena, basil, bergamot, mint, lavender, purple coneflower and camomile which Megan uses to make tea. Mushrooms and toadstools thrive. By day filled with the cries of grouse, merlins, redshanks, curlews, lapwings and ring ouzels, all is still and at peace there now. Despair, ecstasy, longing and windfalls for cider are all to be found in equal measure in the orchard. In the wider Pembrokeshire region short-eared owls, long-eared owls, barn owls and little owls watch silently and wait. Tawny owls communicate. "Keewick!" Cry the females. "Hoo hoo hoo hooo!" Answer the males.

It is late in the evening now as they sit opposite each other, nestled deep in the armchairs in the *simne fawr*, the heart and mind of their Crymych, unaware of the drama unfolding a few miles to the south. Megan looks across at Bronwen, smiles and whispers knowingly. "Magic is in the everyday. Let everything be as it is. Remember, all is well. Life Is, in all Its glory. Always pass the glory on to someone else for there's more than enough to go around. The mistake is to think 'we' are doing the everyday."

"And now for the weather forecast," comes the voice of the radio announcer.

"This evening swallows are soaring, feeding on insects high in the sky, a sign that it will be a fine day tomorrow."

"Thank you, Derec."[27]

A strawberry moon casts its glow over all.

30

There came one and knocked at the door of the Beloved. And a voice
answered and said, "Who is there?"
The lover replied, "It is I."
"Go hence," returned the voice. "There is no room within for thee and me."
Then came the lover a second time and knocked, and again the voice
demanded, "Who is there?"
She answered, "It is Thyself."
"Enter," said the voice, "for I am within."

Rumi[1]

It was late of a Tuesday morning and the Sergeant was sitting in the galley
sipping tea, munching chocolate biscuits and listening intently to a current affairs
programme on Radio Free Pembrokeshire.[2] It could of course have been a
Wednesday morning. Or indeed any weekday morning but probably not a Saturday
or a Sunday morning as he generally spends the weekends with his wife Arianrhod
at Cnwc y Perfedd, their half Irish half Welsh smallholding, along with cats, three
dogs, Cynon, Cadreith and Cadlew, rescue dogs, survivors all, and assorted other
living beings. "We interrupt this programme with some breaking news. Early this
morning the Landsker Line was found abandoned in a disused quarry near Pentre
Galar. A local couple out walking their dog came across what they thought was a
suspicious object in a plastic bag lying amongst the ferns and foxgloves and called
the emergency services. A Dyfed-Powys Police[3] spokesperson told our reporter
that the scene is being examined by forensic experts and the Landsker Line will
undergo thorough testing in a bid to discover fingerprints, DNA or any other
evidence that will help solve this unsettling crime, a crime that has destabilized
the county, waking it from a centuries old slumber."

"The Chief Constable[3] sought to allay public fears by stating that all leave
has been cancelled for the foreseeable future as the full might of Dyfed-Powys
Police, both land-based and marine divisions, is directed onto this case. 'No fern,
no foxglove, will be left unturned until the perpetrator or perpetrators are
brought to justice,' she told the world's media at a hastily convened press
conference in Caffi Beca, in Efailwen a couple of miles south of the quarry during
which *te, coffi, pice ar y maen* and *bara brith* were served free to one and all,
such is the generous hospitality of the people of these parts. Adding, 'I appeal
for calm to allow my officers to proceed with their enquiries unhindered. Time is
of the essence.' The quarry itself is now a crime scene and the Chief Constable
has asked the couple to stop walking their dog there until such time as the

forensics team give the site the all-clear. Pembrokeshire County Council[4] has established a focus group to discuss where to put the Landsker Line when this ancient piece of county history is released back into the community after the police examination of it has been completed, as much has changed since it first appeared all those centuries ago. Some argue it should be placed further to the north while others are firm in their conviction that it must be situated to the south of its previous location, south of the Welsh medium primary schools in Pembroke and Tenby, and, near its western end, south of Ysgol Caer Elen the Welsh medium secondary school in Haverfordwest. The group's first meeting is on Thursday week between 11.00am and 1.00pm. The location will be announced nearer the time, but it will almost certainly be in a *café*. The public are invited to attend in an advisory capacity. There will be a full report on the main news tonight. The police have appealed for witnesses."

Happy at this turn of events the Sergeant left the galley and made his way to the grassy knoll, passing *en route* a team of archaeologists who were busy at work, and took up position from where, sipping and munching, he could keep a close eye on things. Whilst on aerial manoeuvres the week before The Parrot spotted rectangular shapes on the ground, the patterns having been revealed during the drought that is affecting parts of the stern. It contacted Dyfed Archaeological Trust[5] and experts arrived the following morning, cordoned off a section and set up a rescue excavation camp. Exploratory trenches were dug and mosaic pieces uncovered close to the surface at which point the archaeological team and assembled reporters from local papers adjourned to the beer tent where the pieces were examined, classified and recorded. Science being a slow and deliberate process this work wasn't finished until way after midnight, sometime after 'last orders' was called. Up at the crack of dawn excavations continued immediately after breakfast at 10.00a.m. and by the evening of the second day their suspicions were confirmed. To their astonishment they had discovered a Roman villa experts date to the middle of the fourth century A.D. It was generally agreed that as the coracle was moored in Fishguard Harbour at the time this is undoubtedly the westernmost Roman villa ever discovered in Britain. And the first *peripatetic* ocean-going villa to be discovered anywhere. Or is that Greek?

On the morning of the twenty third day The Parrot observed the archaeologists at work from the vantage point of a branch halfway up a nearby willow tree. Sitting on the grassy knoll nearby scrutinizing the site the Sergeant sipped tea from a pint mug, lay back and nursed his bruises. To stop himself from falling off the willow rod that forms the seat whilst coracling in rough seas the Sergeant designed and made a cushion that combines five types of adhesive forces, mechanical, chemical, dispersive, electrostatic and diffusive. It didn't work. At least not between him and the cushion. The cushion however remained firmly attached to the seat. He remained *stoical* about this partial success and resolved in the future to express his creativity in other ways as yet unknown. A cold shiver ran down The Parrots back and he flew to a higher branch for safety.

Because the archaeological team and assembled press were not seafarers the Admiral ordered the Sergeant to stay at the mooring in Fishguard Harbour until the rescue dig was finished. After all, Dyfed-Powys Police Rapid-Response Coracle Unit[3] was getting good publicity which aided recruitment. And the Admiral enjoyed turning up every few days, inspecting the site and being interviewed on radio and television. He had a gift for it his wife told him. The Sergeant, on the other hand, was keen to get to sea. On the morning of the forty seventh day, in his capacity as captain of the vessel, he spoke to the chief archaeologist Dr Meleri Wheeler.[6] "I could do this bit of archaeology in a couple of weeks," he retorted. "But that would be work," replied Dr Wheeler. "Why take a couple of weeks when you can dig for months and months. That's archaeology."

When the excavations are finished, the archaeologists will move to an area alongside the lake which lies under the shadow of the volcano. The pyroclastic flow consisting of lava, ash and scalding hot gases from an eruption in AD78 buried the area in 15 feet of volcanic material that hardened into rock and moved the coastline 50 feet into the lake. Archaeologists expect to find bodies and the remains of buildings. A preliminary excavation undertaken recently revealed the remains of a library containing thousands of carbonised scrolls. Known to locals as the Villa of the Papyri it is rumoured to have belonged to Lucius Calpurnius Piso Caesoninus Jones who was father-in-law once removed of Julius Caesar. Fame perhaps, but being related to a war criminal, no matter how many times removed, is a matter of considerable concern.

The Sergeant was not a happy bunny. In fact, he was not a bunny at all. It would be more correct to say, simply, that he was not happy. A rumour came to him that the 'widow maker' was awakening over Cribbar Reef off the Towan Headland in North Cornwall, an event triggered by low pressure that happens only a handful of times a year. And now was one of those times with waves predicted to swell to 30 feet. He and The Parrot coracle there every year whilst on manoeuvres with the North Cornwall Police Rapid-Response Crabber Unit.[7] And then they paddle out to the Zorba ...

These waves are far too dangerous for the average coracler, but not for them. The Parrot's seafaring skills coupled with the modern coracle and its built-in stabilisers, two-axis gyroscope and three-axis accelerometer, all fitted by the boffins at the NCPRRCU's R&D lab situated in a garden shed between their HQ and the village hall in Withiel. Data from this sophisticated equipment is analysed by an app in The Parrot's smartphone which enables it to guide the vessel along the optimum surfing lines, hanging four, sometimes eight, on the bow. At such times of course the Sergeant is a liability, isn't aware of this, loves the ride and invariably falls out of the vessel. The overall influence of the captain is benign, he wakes up, he is excited, he is bewildered, he falls out. Indeed, with new Connected Coracle technology the Sergeant can email as he falls out. NCPRRCU staff have installed a high-tech, hands free, distraction free system to keep the crew safe at the paddle whilst keeping them in touch and enabling them to dictate and have emails read out to them as they work.

On one occasion however, whilst The Parrot was executing a cutback to get the coracle on the surf line the Sergeant's magnetic field flipped upside down causing havoc with the on-board navigation equipment. To avoid a wipe out The Parrot was forced to kick out and exit the wave.

Before each visit to the 'widow maker' the Sergeant adapts the 76mm grenade launchers attached on the port side into ice cream cone launchers. Offering a choice of flavours and with a 99 option this has proved a hit with locals and visitors alike.

The surfing community enjoys the sight of this intrepid pair riding the waves at night. Whilst on a snorkelling holiday in the Seychelles several years ago the Sergeant's DNA was infiltrated by luminescent marine bacteria causing him to light up with an ethereal, soft, green glow after dark. Inspired by this curious phenomenon plans are afoot to grow algae on the hull. At night the bioluminescent glow will allow the crew to see through 360^0 rather than straight ahead only, as is the case with the standard headlights currently fitted on the vessel. It will be environmentally friendly and beautiful when seen by observers as the environment near the coracle for up to 15 yards around, underneath and above, will be illuminated. Bioluminescent coracles come in various pastel colours according to which algae are used. A peaceful and calming light azure is the most popular this season. As an aside, on long ocean voyages such as that to the Seychelles, where extra supplies are needed, the coracle drags a *travois*, packed with gear, behind it.

High in the canopy of the willow grove The Parrot was preparing a quiz and decided to try a dummy run with the questions on the Sergeant below. Foregoing natural flight on this occasion it slipped into its battery-powered, body-controlled jet suit with a ducted fan on each wing and two on its back, pressed 'Start', lifted off from the branch and flew downwards with a hummmm, landing smoothly on the grassy knoll a few seconds later.[8] "*Maintenant, mon ami*, which substance with which you are familiar in your day-to-day work does the following describe?" The Sergeant prepared himself mentally for the task ahead by taking a sip of tea and nibbling a chocolate biscuit. "Ready," he mumbled, careful not to lose any of the biscuit.

"It is composed of collections of eight pairs of up quarks, each bonded with a single down quark, together with eight pairs of down quarks, each bonded with a single up quark, all bonded with two lots of one pair of up quarks with a down quark, and one pair of down quarks with an up quark?"

The Sergeant stopped munching. The mug of hot tea *en route* to his mouth stopped, remaining motionless at the midpoint between him and the table. His eyes narrowed and glazed over. It was a hot day. His brain froze.

The Parrot repeated the question, more slowly this time.

"Is it for the Sunday night pub quiz?"

"It is."

"Could you remove a couple of quarks?"

"Water."

"No thanks. I have some tea."

"The answer is water."

"Water?"

"Yes. Water."

The Sergeant's brain trembled, twitched and quivered as it began the laborious process of defrosting. He continued munching then took a sip of tea, a thoughtful look on his face. "I think I'll give the quiz a miss this week." Finishing the biscuit, he sipped the last of the tea, placed the mug on the grass next to him, lay back under the warmth of the late morning sun and gazed at the ever-changing sky above. Birdsong serenaded the stern accompanied by the chiming of the stone circle in the breeze. This was his soundtrack. Day or night, moored in Fishguard harbour or on the ocean, southern hemisphere or northern, this was a source of wonder to him and one he would never tire of. Soon, he was asleep.

The Sergeant stirred as delicate ripples of gravitational waves danced through him and the grassy knoll. "Unusual," he thought in his dream. The mooring was carefully chosen to be at a Lagrange point to conserve energy. This is a quiet spot far from the chitter-chatter of solar forces filling the solar system. The perfect spot for dreaming. That the mooring is at a Lagrange point was decided by the Admiral after reading a recent work of creative fiction. Scientists disagree. The Sergeant dreamt on, unaware of the dispute. An archaeologist, a puzzled look on her face, paused during excavations in a trench, raised herself up and looked around. "Nothing," she said to herself, then got back to work, singing a local favourite quietly to herself as she did so.

If you're going to Eglwyswrw
Be sure to wear some flowers in your hair.
If you're going to Eglwyswrw
You're gonna meet some gentle people there.
For those who come to Eglwyswrw
Summertime will be a love-in there.
In the streets of Eglwyswrw
Gentle people with flowers in their hair.[9]

In his dream the Sergeant woke with a start. More to the point, with his wife's voice via the intercom digging like the bucket of a mini JCB into his ribs. "**Wake up!**"

"What? Who?"

"**Wake up!** There's a strange noise in the house. It's nearly three in the morning."

"I'll go and see what it is," he volunteered, knowing deep down that volunteering had nothing to do with it. He eased himself out of the bed, tucking his pyjama top into his pyjama bottoms as he went. He wasn't taking any chances. He walked to the bedroom door, opened it as quietly as he could and moved onto the landing, leaving the door open behind him. The noise was coming from the playroom at the end of the corridor. As he went, he looked into the bedroom next door intending to reassure his wife, but she was already asleep, the electric fence surrounding the bed switched to maximum. Turning once again to face the noise, he walked slowly towards it. There had been trouble from the playroom before. He stopped just outside. The door was ajar. He pushed it gently and as it swung open he peered inside. There in the far corner, the scene lit by moonlight cascading through the window where the curtains had been left open, was the doll's house. Every light was on and all three floors, swimming pool and garage were lit up. Disco music could be heard playing loudly inside. The front door was closed, and two dejected figures stood outside. He turned and retraced his steps.

"It's alright dear. The toys are having a party again and they've locked Florence and Zebedee out.[10] I'll talk to them about letting them back in. If negotiations fail, I'll lift the roof and put them into the attic. They can get back to the party that way. The Wooden Tops[11] no doubt will be furious, but I can deal with them in the morning." Back he went and after unsuccessful talks lifted the roof and put the two forlorn figures into the attic and returned. On the way back to the sanctuary of his bedroom, and in a bold act of suggestively erogenous significance, he pulled his pyjama top out of his pyjama bottoms. Delaying for a moment at the open door of Arianrhod's room he watched glumly as the searchlight beam swept the electric fence. Sighing, he turned and made his way downstairs to the kitchen where he put the kettle on and got a plate of chocolate biscuits from the cupboard, placing it on the table along with a large mug and a teaspoon. He chose Chantler's loose-leaf Mariner's Tea, put some into the teapot, poured boiling water from the kettle onto it, replaced the kettle, put the top on the teapot and set it on the table along with a small jug of soya milk and a fine-mesh, non-magnetic, stainless steel tea strainer.

After the tea had steeped for the requisite ten minutes, he poured himself a mugful and sat back on the chair. He reached sleepily yet accurately for a biscuit, took a bite, then another, until the biscuit disappeared then picked up the mug of steaming hot tea and sipped cautiously. "Let the healing begin," he murmured sleepily to himself. Tea and chocolate biscuit entered his bloodstream, his mind was focussed, yet at peace. The veil of illusion parted unexpectedly in front of him. He lowered his gaze to study the energy that was a chocolate biscuit on the plate. Words appeared in his mind. "If we ask, for instance, whether the position of the chocolate biscuit remains the same, we must say no. If we ask whether the chocolate biscuit's position changes with time, we must say no. If we ask whether the chocolate biscuit is at rest, we must say no. If we ask whether it is in motion, we must say no."[12] Satisfied by this turn of events he reached across, picked it up, raised his arm, placed it into his mouth and became one with it. The rollercoaster that is the Sergeant's life roared on into the night.

The temperature on the grassy knoll reached the high twenties. Taking advantage of a passive stabilising mechanism evolution had provided in its legs The Parrot saved energy by standing on just one of them as it continued preparations for the quiz. Hearing a faint whimpering sound, it turned to observe the Sergeant. Movement on the surface of his eyelids indicated a manoeuvring of his eyes as he slept. His body twitched in unison with dreamy events.

Unusual weather patterns brought hitherto unseen birds to the lake area on the stern. A pair of Eastern kingbirds from North America with their dark grey upperparts and white tipped tails rejoiced in their aerial skills as they caught insects in flight. Several Dalmatian pelicans, the world's largest freshwater birds, arrived from the eastern Mediterranean. Content to move slowly across the surface of the lake, dipping their heads underwater from time to time to catch fish, they measure up to 6 feet in length with wingspans that rival that of the great albatrosses. Thought by many to be the world's heaviest flying bird they are nonetheless elegant in flight. Slender Bearded vultures from the high mountains of the Caucasus, the only known animal whose diet is almost exclusively bone, rested on rocky crags on the eastern side of the lake, their cream-coloured foreheads contrasting against the black band across the eyes. Other visitors included Siberian accentors from the Ural Mountains in Russia with their dark brown crowns and pale yellow 'eyebrows'. Their favoured breeding habitat is subarctic deciduous forests close to water, so they are at home on the northern side of the lake. Several pairs of Western swamp hens, one of the six species of purple swamp hen with distinctive red bills and bright plumage, arrived from the Iberian Peninsula, settling in the swamp at the lake's edge to eat tender young shoots. Other visitors, red-footed boobys (Sula sula) from the Caribbean with their red legs and pink and blue bill and throat pouch presented an eye-catching sight as they dived into the sea off the bow to catch small fish. All these species joined the puffins, cormorants, razorbills, kittiwakes, fulmars, great auks and shags already naturalised on the stern and became firm friends with The Parrot.

Startled by a Dalmatian pelican landing on the lake next to its lodge a Eurasian beaver slapped the surface of the water forcefully with its broad tale as an alarm signal before diving beneath the surface. Twitchy, as usually nocturnal, and heeding the warning, other beavers in the vicinity dived beneath the surface and disappeared. A few years ago, several pairs were re-introduced onto the stern and their numbers are increasing with several kits born each year. They are important for the ecosystem of the streams and lake and their activities, including dam building, reduce flooding, help with filtering the water and bring light into overgrown areas resulting in a more varied habitat for other species. The dams they have constructed protect the beaver colony from predators such as bears, wolves and coyotes which are a constant threat.

The Sergeant woke with a start. Thinking deeply about the dream and its implications he stood up, looked in an exasperated way at the field archaeologists deep in discussions in the beer tent, and wandered off in the general direction of the galley. He needed refreshment. Sometime later, after taking a wrong turn, he ambled into the strategic data centre amidships on 3 Deck. "Interesting," he thought as he listened to the gentle humming sound that filled the room and gazed in awe at the array of sophisticated computer equipment with different coloured flashing lights. "I wonder what it all does?" The computer became silent, the lights dimmed. After a moment or two, losing interest as there was no food to be seen, he left. Silently, the automatic door slid shut behind him and his brain erased all memory of it, just in case. The on-board fourth industrial revolution was safe. Digital technology is not a part of his world. He lives a separate existence knowing nothing of the always-on connectivity beloved of the iGeneration tramping along in front of him. His digital sophistication index remains at nought. In terms of the evolution of technology, he has not yet left the ocean.

He eventually found his way to the galley where he prepared two soft boiled eggs for a snack. Seated at the table, the eggs in eggcups on a plate in front of him, he looked longingly at them for a moment or two, picked up a teaspoon, gave the tops of the eggs several sharp taps then slid the tip of the spoon into them to remove the tops. He put the teaspoon onto the plate and with an overly optimistic flourish lifted the pepper pot and covered the exposed parts of the eggs with a light dusting of kisspeptin, a hormone that acts centrally to stimulate secretion of gonadotrophin releasing hormone resulting in increased testosterone levels and an enhanced response in the brain to sexual images. The pepper pot was a cover. Tenderly, he replaced it on the table next to the plate. A framed, photo shopped, A4 size colour photograph of his wife in a pink and blue high-waisted bikini, taken surreptitiously as she sat eating a cheese and tomato sandwich on the golden yellow sand of Porthcawl beach at low tide many years before, stood upright in its frame on the table in front of him. He picked up the teaspoon, carved out a large chunk of egg, placed it into his mouth and began to chew, all the while staring intently at the photograph. The hand slowly descended and another piece of egg was gathered in the spoon's welcoming embrace. The hand and the spoon oegan to tremble. Bright beads of sweat appeared on his brow. Whilst sweating is used mainly to control body temperature in humans, at this crucial moment, in the computer controlled optimum environment of the galley, that function was redundant. After eating he returned the photograph to its hiding place at the back of the upper compartment of the deep freeze next to the Marmite,[13] returned to the chair and dreamt of extended weekend leave.

On board, Marmite is routinely stored in a vacuum sealed container in the deep freeze where it is cooled to a fraction above absolute zero, -273.15°C. At this temperature, due, The Parrot suspects, to strange quantum effects, Marmite molecules can still exchange atoms, forging new chemical bonds as they do so. The coldest known place in the universe is the Boomerang Nebula in the constellation Centaurus, approximately 5,000 light years from Earth. The back of the upper compartment of the deep freeze is the second coldest. A few hundred billionths of a degree above absolute zero Marmite atoms barely move, form a Bose-Einstein condensate and act as a superfluid able to flow without losing energy. Some claim this to be of no practical significance. But they are fools. The Sergeant came across the effect by chance one lazy Saturday afternoon and finds it makes Marmite easier to spread.

A mental picture of a mug of tea appeared in both the Sergeant's visual cortices in the back of his head. He responded proactively to this unexpected development by sitting upright on the chair. A moment later the image was replaced by a piece of toast and a wedge of *Roquefort* cheese with distinctive veins of blue mold.

The Sergeant's muscles, evolving more than 600 million years ago, sprang swiftly into action, contracting to generate the force necessary to propel him into 'hunter gatherer in the galley' mode. In many parts of his body a multitude of adenosine triphosphate molecules lost a phosphate molecule. The energy stored in each bond was liberated, along with one hydrogen ion (H^+), leaving behind molecules of adenosine diphosphate. Energy enriched, the Sergeant's musculoskeletal system raised itself to a standing position, and, guided by a homing device located in the subject's brain, moved in the direction of the cheese cupboard. The journey from table to cupboard is short, yet routinely classified as urgent, therefore creatine phosphate molecules, placed on high alert by evolution's guiding hand, waited in the wings in case they were needed.

He approached the locked and bolted cheese cupboard with its attractive yellow triangle with black skull and crossbones prominent just above the handle. Sensors embedded in the fabric of the door, which to him appeared to be a classic inanimate object, detected his presence, decoded his brain activity and read his mind. Patterns of thought in his brain were deciphered by the door's deep neural network aided by a second type of AI known as a deep generative network positioned in the door handle, which acted as backup.

The Sergeant looked at the cupboard door.

The door looked back.

As the Sergeant's brain eased off on the throttle the door extracted biometric data from his image, replacing it with a biometric template in the form of a mathematical file which digitally referenced the unique characteristics to be found in the image. This was then encoded mathematically to make it easier for the door to store and harder for hackers who might be targeting the Sergeant to get at it. Meanwhile, brain activity continued to ebb.

"**Step away from the door!**" said the door.

He stood his ground.

The door decided a different approach might be helpful. *A velvety smooth female voice laced with reason and compassion spoke to him, suggesting he choose a nice marmalade instead.* His resolve stiffened by the after-effects of the kisspeptin he didn't flinch and seconds later the sounds of locks opening and bolts being drawn alerted The Parrot. Too late. The Sergeant leaned forward, reached into the dark recesses of the cupboard and unchained the Number 23 **EX**tra Mature *Roquefort.* That was the last thing he remembered. He was still lying unconscious on the galley floor when The Parrot found him.

"Funny things women," the Sergeant muttered as he was helped back to the chair. He shared an incident that occurred during an evening he and Arianrhod spent in the Japanese Quarter in Lower Town years ago. It was just after they were married. Seated at her favourite table in the Randibŵ, the evening sunlight bathing them in a soft pink glow, he was moved to pay her a compliment. "You look just like Bob Dylan," he told her. She convulsed and drew away from him, snorting uncontrollably. He smiled, pleased that the flattery was appreciated. This wasn't so difficult after all. Married life was new to him and he was still learning the ways of her feminine charms, but yes, he was getting the hang of it.

Giving him a glare that would melt the *Jostedalsbreen Glacier* in western Norway, which, he reminded her, is the largest *glacier* in continental Europe measuring 37 miles in length, is 2,000 feet thick and covers an area of 188 square miles, she stood up, grabbed her bag and stormed out of the *café* into the sunset. Dazzled, he drew his dark glasses from the breast pocket of his open, short-sleeved shirt and put them in place so as to shield his eyes. Considering himself adept at seeing and empathising with the emotional cues that expressed themselves in his wife's face he deemed this to be some form of romantic ritual he had not run into before. "All very strange," he remarked to a passing waitress who convulsed and drew away from him, hyperventilating boisterously as she went. The heat from her glare before she turned on her heel to leave the Randibŵ, intending to provide comfort and solace to his wife who stood weeping at the quayside just passed the yacht club, caused him to flinch momentarily and reach

411

.· the tube of factor 50 suncream in his showerproof, canvas sling bag. "How very strange indeed."

Having made the cheese cupboard safe, The Parrot returned to its perch in the galley where it assumed the full lotus position. Inscrutable, a smile of serenity overflowed from its beak. Time was no longer, and no time means no mind. The Parrot was a *wu-wei* master, action through inaction, albeit with a tad more *wu* than *wei*.

Later that day the Sergeant lay becalmed in the hammock. The Parrot stood atop the main mast holding a face mirror as it arranged the yellow feathers of its crest, a magnet attracting universal *chi* energy. They were not naturally yellow. When young, The Parrot studied for several years in the Ridzong monastery with members of the Yellow Hat sect of Tibetan Mahayana Buddhism. The monastery is situated at the very top of a valley on the north side of the Indus on the way to Lamayuru in Ladakh. During its stay, not being able to find a Yellow Hat that fitted, it began dyeing its crest feathers yellow. The *sojourn* in Ladakh also explains the brightly coloured prayer flags that fly between the willows on the stern. Whilst at the monastery The Parrot learned Ladakhi, one of the world's most complicated and interesting languages. The ability to converse in Ladakhi it finds most useful when on long sea voyages with the Sergeant.

Finished with arranging its crest feathers The Parrot put the face mirror down, turned and looked across the top of a fleet of Tenby Luggers moored in the harbour to survey the Goodwick bayou, a huge expanse of low-lying, slow-moving wetland just across the road from the beach. Local guides take tourists into it, drawing their attention to the rich *flora* and *fauna* found there that includes leeches, shrimps, crawdads, catfish, red fish, *sac au lait*, gnats, redwings, night bitterns, egrets, spoonbills, frogs, toads, snakes, turtles, cattails, and, always in the far distance, an occasional alligator. In between boatloads of visitors the guides sit in the *café* on the Parrog playing poker, chewing pieces of mesquite and drinking. At the height of the season water skiing is popular here. 'A low-pressure front was due in from Texas. Soon it would be raining.'[14]

The ship-to-shore radio barked impulsively. The Sergeant reached over and picked it up. He was not wearing the oven glove. The heat emanating from the receiver made him wince as he placed it next to his ear. He felt the ripples in space-time pass through him. The Parrot, buffeted by the gravitational waves, shifted its weight to right foot, then left foot, and back again before tightening its grip on the perch. The very fabric of the coracle undulated. The Sergeant felt a heaviness and was compressed into the hammock. A short period of suspended animation followed. Normally, gravitational waves are the result of cataclysmic cosmic events, collisions between black holes billions of years ago or massive stellar explosions. But this was the Admiral checking that everything was shipshape. Or was it?

The stern is alive. In the meadow, house martins with their glossy blue-black upper parts and forked tails and swallows with their distinctive long tail streamers are on the wing catching prey. Fast flying swifts with short-forked tails and long swept-back wings visiting from the cave systems of nearby cliffs where they roost, hunt with them. Willow tits, one of our most sedentary of species, their numbers at a record high on the stern, feed on the plentiful insects, seeds and berries. Off the starboard side dark brown and white guillemots and black and white razorbills with thick, black beaks join stocky, short-winged, short-tailed puffins, their orange-red feet standing out against a blue sky, to feed on fish. A chevron of Canada geese with their distinctive black head and neck and white throat patch above a brown body pass low overhead.

Butterflies, among them red admirals, purple emperors, brimstones with their angular shaped and strong veined wings, holly blues, orange-tips, darting orange and brown skippers (Ochlodes Sylvanus), brown ringlets with their distinctive underwing eyespots, dark brown speckled woods with creamy white patches on their wings and silver-washed fritillarys play in the sunlight as black six spot burnets with their large red spots feast upon common bird's foot trefoil, vetches and clover. Purple hairstreaks, which breed on the oaks on the stern, dance in the sunlight dappling the oak wood whose trees are alive with bright green lammas shoots. Pink and olive-green elephant hawk moths feed on honeysuckle and yellow brimstone moths hover in mid-air to feed on sweet nectar from abundant flowers. Black cinnabar moths with red markings on their wings feed on ragwort and groundsels growing in a spot close to the stone circle. A beautiful yet tired flight of cecropia moths with red and white bodies and dark brown wings, the largest native moths in North America with a wingspan approaching 6 inches, rest with puzzled expressions amongst the lower branches of a birch tree trying to work out how they have gotten here from their home on the Eastern Seaboard. Stag beetles, crickets and grasshoppers are to be seen. Dragonflies skim the surface of the lake catching midges and mosquitoes.

The numbers of beetles, butterflies and dragonflies is kept in check by the presence of, amongst others, a small population of blue-throated bee-eaters in the subtropical mangrove forest on the southern aspect of the lake. On a low-lying branch in the swampy, lowland forest nearby an adorable chocolate frog, with chocolate coloured skin and large eyes, croaks wailfully as it melts in the heat of the afternoon.

Brown hares and grey partridges play amongst the cowslips. A pale-coloured barn owl swoops on its prey then returns to its roosting site in the woodland to feed its owlets.

A lone Monterey pine almost 200 feet tall with upward pointing branches and rounded top that grows on a bluff to one side of the cowshed undulates gently in rhythm with the rocking of the vessel. A colourful cloud of black, orange and

,nite monarch butterflies edge its canopy. To the west of the cowshed a spinney of soffsky-poffsky trees, their blue leaves reflecting the sunlight, sway to and fro in the breeze.

A herd of black-faced impala appear as if from nowhere, their glossy, reddish brown coats shimmering in the light, the lyre shaped horns of the males catching the eye as they sweep over the grassy knoll, bounding gracefully amongst the ferns and foxgloves in the stone circle, and, in playful mood, circumnavigate the cowshed three times before disappearing back to the safety of the trees. A passing herd of elephants talk to one another using low frequency rumblings below the range at which the Sergeant can hear, so as not to disturb his day.

Curlews stride through the mud of the shallows at the western side of the lake, their long, curved beaks searching for food, their distinct calls carrying over the harbour. Nightingales attract mates with chatters, rattles and whistles. Marsh frogs sing freely.

A harvest mouse, hanging upside down by its prehensile tail from a spherical nest of tightly woven grass in the long, tussocky grassland close to the spring nearby, takes pleasure in the peace of a late afternoon.

On the port side, undetected by the vessel's surveillance system, a Number 23 **Ex**tra Mature *Roquefort* slips silently overboard, easing itself into the calm waters of Fishguard Harbour and makes its bid for freedom.

The Sergeant, taking a sip of tea, begins the harrowing task of compiling his memoirs. Ghost written by The Parrot, *The Sergeant: The Wilderness Years* will be published to great critical acclaim.

The voice of the radio announcer fills the deserted galley. "And now for tomorrow's weather."

"Oh!"

"Dear God!"

"No!"

"Nooooo!"

"Thank you Derec."[15]

May it be so.

Epilogue 1

News of the Sergeant's success spread quickly through the law enforcement and intelligence community and soon he was off on another case.

"The equator has disappeared. Yes, a person, or persons unknown have liberated the equator," revealed an embarrassed Inspector General of Police in Nairobi soon after the story broke in the world's press.[1] "We are treating the disappearance as suspicious and appeal for the public to come forward with any information that might help us with our enquiries and lead us to apprehending those responsible," he added. The authorities in the African and South American countries most affected asked DPPRRCU for their help in solving what has become known to the public as The Riddle of the Disappearing Equator.

"You can cross the equator, but you can`t see it," The Parrot advised.

Epilogue 2

Following his successful involvement in The Landsker Case and in the investigation of The Riddle of the Disappearing Equator the Sergeant was instructed to help police worldwide solve The Enigma of the Disappearing Horizon. This elusive but popular object was reported missing just as the Sergeant's memoirs went to press.

"Interpol[1] and other police forces around the world are treating the disappearance as irregular and are appealing for help from the public, in particular anyone who was in the vicinity of the horizon between 6.15pm and 11.20pm the evening of its disappearance," ran the headlines.

"This might be a prank," said a United Nations[2] spokesperson, "but whoever is responsible should return the aforementioned item as soon as possible."

"We urge extreme caution," a DPPRRCU spokesperson[3] told the world's press, "and warn the public not to approach unsavoury looking characters and to contact the nearest police station immediately if they have any suspicions. This is a distressing time for holiday makers and landscape artists alike and our thoughts go out to them at this difficult time."

"Where is the Welsh Government[4] going to put offshore wind farms now?" ran a frontpage headline in the Western Mail.[5]

"You can see the horizon, but you can`t cross it," advised The Parrot.

Epilogue 3

During a private meeting with the author in the *café* on Goodwick Parrog shortly before the book went to press, The Parrot reflected upon life with its shipmate, the Sergeant. Imperturbable, wing tips folded in *gassho*, eyes twinkling, its face transformed by the knowing smile of loving kindness, it downed the last of the tea, replaced the mug on the table between us, and bowed. And so, on the twenty ninth day of the eighth month, summing up their adventures with a few softly spoken words, it began.

Thus, have I heard.
Nothing exists but momentarily.[1]
Before the torrential rain stops
We hear a seagull squawk.
Rain falls from the sky,
A lake of water.
In the willow grove,
Soft grey-green catkins,
Wands of beauty,
Wave in the breeze.
Know that in the silence
The stone circle
Sings its song of gratitude.
The whitewashed cowshed glistens
In the long evening light.
Hedgehogs run free on the stern.
The moon is reflected in the water.
The ocean of life abides
In an endless rhythm.
The Sergeant in the hammock faces the heavens,
Endlessly travelling the ten directions.
Voyaging nowhere,
Every journey is the first one.
We go away to here.
Out amongst the waves with the seagulls,
I raise my mug of tea to the sky.
The sky, the mug of tea, myself, the birds,
make this moment our home.
Currents move through the vast ocean.
In the early morning,
toast burns in the galley.

The Coracle and the Cathedral

For the time being
A Parrot sits on its perch.
Throughout the billion worlds
The myriad things smile.
Sun, moon, mountains, rivers, wind and rain,
Everything equal in the moment.
For countless aeons,
Our mind moves.
Still.
Empty.

In the miracle of each moment
The Sergeant comes and goes,
Appears and disappears,
Without abiding.

If Arianrhod isn't there,
May she be there.
And if she is there,
May she not be there.[2]

There is a wonder.
A mystery.
Words point to it,
But cannot express it.

Taste as if there was nothing to taste,
Smell as if there was nothing to smell,
Touch as if there was nothing to touch,
Listen as if there was nothing to listen to,
Look as if there was nothing to see,
Think as if there were no thoughts.

Please treasure yourself.

Epilogue 4

"**I'm appalled!**" insisted the retired Colonel, raising his head from the newspaper he was reading to look across at his wife.

"Are you, dear?"

"I think a man of my age and standing should be appalled at least once a day."

"Yes, dear."

"**I'm appalled!**"

"That's lovely, dear."

Epilogue 5

Three puffs of dust rose into the thin Martian atmosphere as the Welsh Rugby Union[1] space probe touched down on the surface of the Red Planet shortly after 6pm GMT after a 300-million-mile journey that took almost seven months. The £635 million craft survived the final few dangerous minutes of the landing phase, decelerating from 26,400mph through the planet's rarefied atmosphere, which provides little friction to slow an object. During the descent temperatures reached 1,648^{0}C before its heat shields were ejected and a parachute deployed to slow the lander. The firing of retro rockets enabled it to land at a safe 5mph on the Elysium Planitia area north of the equator which has a flat, featureless, rock free surface. Each one of the thousands of computer commands involved in the process had to work perfectly for the landing to be a success. A few minutes later the solar panels unfurled successfully and the probe's first photograph, taken as it sat on the planet's surface, was received at the WRU's Jet Propulsion Laboratory situated at the Vale Resort just outside Cardiff.[2] The crust of Mars today looks like Earth would have looked 4.6 billion years ago.

"If ever rugby was played on the Red Planet, it was here," a WRU spokeswoman told news agencies at a press conference at the Vale Resort shortly after touchdown. "We are optimistic we will find Welsh qualified players before the two-year mission ends. After several weeks of practice, the lander's robotic arm will place a heat probe and seismometer onto the Martian surface and the search for players will begin. The two-year mission will also be used by WRU scientists to study the planet's interior structure, its core, mantle and crust. Knowledge gained from this will lead to new insights into how Mars formed 4.6 billion years ago at the dawn of the solar system. Our scientists hope to understand why Mars is smaller than Earth and Venus and why it has a lower density. And why have no Mars based players played for Wales? Big questions indeed."

Epilogue 6

At the edge of the forest, we find a second cathedral, this one not seen by humans, its great pillars formed by the natural growth of ancient yew trees whose canopies reach high into the sky. At their centre a space opens to the sun, moon and stars. The yews were saplings when the singing stones were moved from Pembrokeshire to Stonehenge over 5,000 years ago. Around the outside of this massive, circular yet elegant living structure is a covered walk formed of oak trees, the outside an open colonnade. Hawthorns grow nearby creating fairy forts whose roots lead down to Annwfn, the otherworld. Fairy folk spend their days amongst the trees' roots, emerging at night to sing, dance and work their beneficial nature magic. With long, sharp-pointed thorns and thick tangle of branches the hawthorns are covered in beautiful white flowers in early summer whilst in autumn they bear deep red, blood red fruits. When the time is right Megan and Bronwen eat the flowers, sandwiched between leaves pulled fresh off the branches. Of all the trees, the hawthorn belongs to the fairies. Growing close to the holy wells nearby are craggy trunked ash trees, the males in their season free of seeds, the females covered with seeds. An apple and an ash stand side by side, their canopies close, as if each with an arm around the other, like father and son or mother and daughter - healing and renewal alongside wisdom and poetry. All the trees of the year are here, yew, pine, birch, rowan, alder, willow, hawthorn, ash, oak, holly, hazel, apple, elder ... and the tree of power standing outside time itself. All sacred.[1]

Megan, Bronwen and the other living beings of Machlud y Wawr[2] will continue their lives in Pembrokeshire and beyond. They have been, and in times to come they will be here for many human ages as they are of the tylwyth teg, the faery folk, the elven race and are immortal. They are taller than humans, slender and light, so light they can walk over newly fallen snow without leaving footprints. Their vibrations are finer than that of humans, higher and faster. They are matter infused with the energy of love, the energy flowing from heart to mind such that the love in their hearts infuses their thoughts. Not bound by the physical laws of our dimension they are protected by the elementals, the energies of the earth. We humans see them only when they want to be seen. They delight in dance and song which heal the natural world as the roots of the music of the tylwyth teg rest deep in love.

Fairies fill Pembrokeshire with their creations - flowers, trees, rocks and other natural things. These invisible beings are the architects of forms crystallised from the energies of earth, wind, air and fire. They are nature spirit intelligences. Some are small, light and slender like the flowers they have given coherent form to. They spin energy to form a primrose, they weave energy and form an oak tree. Those that give form to flowers are small, those that give form

Trees are very tall. Fairies are of a higher vibration, finer, faster and are not closely related to the human race. As with the faery folk, we see them only when they want us to.

Their music is tinkly, like bells and is healing as its roots lie also in love. When many fairies are in a place, humans, particularly children, sense a lightness and are filled with laughter. If humans harm the natural world by cutting down trees or in some other way damaging nature, they leave and wait nearby to return for they have a strong will to stay and regenerate land damaged by us. But sometimes, if the damage humans do is very great, they leave and do not return.

Ley lines, pathways of energy within and upon the body of Pembrokeshire and extending far beyond to encompass the Earth itself are a real part of the life lived by Megan, Bronwen and the Members. Male and female energy lines weave through the landscape, crossing often. Such crossings occur where cathedrals are found. Megan and Bronwen perform ceremonies at these sacred sites to balance and heal, and to send love into the earth.

Addendum

It is a little-known fact, yet one that may be of interest to the reader, that Megan and the Sergeant almost met on two occasions. At least, they were in close proximity to one another. The first of these occasions, mentioned earlier in this volume, occurred one calm, peaceful, summer's afternoon as Megan and her husband enjoyed a picnic on Dinas Head. Munching salad sandwiches enlivened by herb mayonnaise they watched in surprise as a coracle just offshore, which they assumed was bound for Fishguard Harbour, began spinning uncontrollably before sinking.

The other occasion was when the Easter MachludyWawrathon[1] met in Brecon and a day excursion was arranged by coach to the magnificent **Sgwd yr Eira** waterfall in the Brecon Beacons National Park. Members looked forward to walking the narrow, rocky path, sheltered by the overhanging rock face above, that allows the brave rambler to walk beneath the waterfall behind the thundering curtain of falling water, entering one side of the waterfall and exiting the other. The previous few days had seen persistent, torrential rainfall in the area and the river was running dangerously high with floodwater. Fortunately, on the morning of the excursion, the clouds dispersed, and the group set off to spend a delightful sunny day beneath a clear, blue, cloudless sky.

The Sergeant, on a fact-finding mission whilst preparing a sting operation against whisky smugglers in the area, was patrolling the swollen river just upstream searching for clues. He found none. He did however find **Sgwd yr Eira**.

"Oh dear!" he murmured as the coracle changed from horizontal to vertical as it plunged over the edge, held fast by the deluge. A gurgling sound came from the Sergeant's half submerged face, then another as he began the descent. Sensibly, as the angle of coracle to river approached 65⁰ The Parrot flew from the crow's nest on the main mast and hovered safely overhead in the sunshine, enjoying the view.

Megan and a few intrepid members were standing under the waterfall marvelling at the glow of distant sunlight coming through the unrelenting wall of water roaring past just a few short feet in front of them. It was at that precise moment, one of the great crossroads of human history, that fate declared Megan and the Sergeant would make visual contact.

The Sergeant noticed, momentarily, a splodge of colour, Megan's bright yellow raincoat, before hurtling on his watery way.[2]

Megan heard a strange gurgling sound followed closely by a muffled scream and glimpsed, for a split second, held fast by the water, a dark oval shape shooting past in the torrent of descending white water in front of her, and clinging onto it for dear life, a ..... something, only for them to disappear as quickly as they had come, to be submerged in the deadly maelstrom at the base of the waterfall where the weight of the surging water and water-borne sediment have gouged out a plunge pool several metres deep with rough, irregular sides, in the solid rock. Tens of thousands of cubic feet of water fall into this liquid graveyard every minute, much more after it has been raining, crashing into the turbulent whirlpool where lethal hydraulic jets of maniacal fury at its base make it a no-go area for local fish. Unaware of this, the Sergeant, gasping desperately for air, his top half submerged, held firm by the unyielding grip of the solid wall of plunging, plummeting water, his legs thrashing helplessly in the gentle warmth of the summer sun, clung desperately to the seat with one hand whilst paddling furiously with the other as he attempted a textbook emergency reverse manoeuvre. To no avail. He continued downwards, engulfed in the thundering water's diabolical embrace.

Their paths were never to cross again.

The Parrot, enjoying the beauty of the area from its vantage point as it hovered some sixty feet above the water a safe distance downstream from the base of the waterfall, the sun behind it, noticed a rainbow appear in the spray, a primary rainbow at an angular range of approximately 41^0 formed as a circular arc around the anti-solar point. It made a mental note to inform the Sergeant that water is silent, the bursting of bubbles makes the deafening noise. He was sure to be pleased to learn that. It would be some time however before they spoke as the self-righting mechanism of the submerged coracle would be slow to cope with such extreme conditions.

Referencing Hynek's Scale,[3] the standard in ufology, at supper later that evening Members came to the conclusion that they had experienced a Close Encounter of the First Kind, but with no 'intelligent communication'. After taking a head count between the main course and the pudding Bronwen was relieved to be able to squash the rumour that a Member had been abducted.

End piece

DPPRRCU Monthly Management Report 21/06/21[1]
Classification: Top Secret

It was a few minutes after midnight on a tranquil, moonlit night in June 2021. Aided by the silencer fitted to the paddle the vessel, bound for Grogley Halt, moved up the Camel without making a sound. The crew were on a black-ops mission gathering intelligence about local pirates. Suddenly, from nowhere

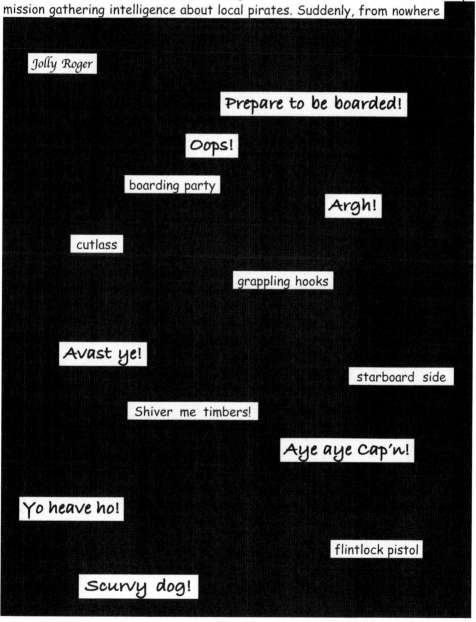

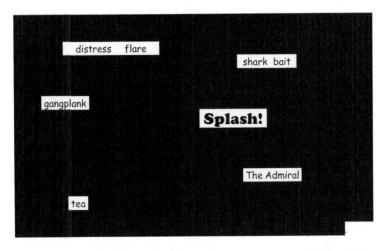

The above report was redacted by the Security Services[2] before being received by the author. We must glean what information we can from the lexical items remaining to begin a tentative reconstruction of the syntax in order to understand fully what happened on that fateful night. A DPPRRCU spokesperson stated that these measures are necessary in order to protect the identities of DPPRRCU staff engaged in dangerous operations in North Cornwall. Pressure was brought to bear on the author to remove

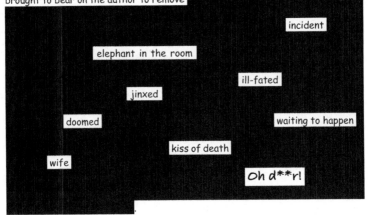

Further reading

Ἀρχιμήδης, Περὶ τῶν ἐπιπλεόντων σωμάτων.
Archimedes of Syracuse, (250BC?), *On Floating Bodies*, two volumes.
Asher M. and Rhys-Jones S. T. (2010) *Saint Non and the Americas: Discovering Evidence for the Fusion of Native American and Celtic Spirituality*, University of Wawayanda Press.
Baring-Gould, S. (1909) *Cornish Characters and Strange Events*, London: J. Lane.
Beauvilliers, A. (1814) *L'art du cuisinier*, Pilet, two octavo volumes.
Bengtsson, F. G. (1994) *The Long Ships*. Translated from the Swedish by Michael Meyer. Harper Collins.
Bennett, S. (1912) *Old Age, Its Cause and Prevention*, Chas. H. Desgrey.
Borsley, R. D. Tallerman, M. and Willis, D. (2007) *The Syntax of Welsh*, Cambridge University Press.
Bowman, W. E. (1953) *The Ascent of Rum Dingli*, Max Parrish and Co. Ltd.[1]
Ibid (1956) *The Ascent of Rum Doodle*, Max Parrish and Co. Ltd.
Braddock, J. (2018) *A Spy's Guide to Thinking*, independently published.
Brooks, S. (2021) *Hanes Cymry*, Gwasg Prifysgol Cymru.
Campbell, J. (1949) *The Hero with a Thousand Faces*, Pantheon Books.
Carey, M. (2019) *The Meaning of Megan Phillips*, MacMillan[2]
Carson R. (1962) *Silent Spring*, Houghton Mifflin Company, Boston.
Charles, B. G. (1992) *The Place Names of Pembrokeshire*, National Library of Wales, two volumes.
Ibid (1997) *The Place Names of the Stern*, National Library of Wales, three volumes.[3]
Charles-Edwards, T. M. (2013) *Wales and the Britons 350-1064*, Oxford University Press.
Christie, A. (1920) *The Mysterious Affair at Styles*, John Lane, New York.
Ibid (1933) *Death on the Teifi*, Collins Crime Club.[4]
Cohen, L. (1968) *The Great Book of Coracling Songs*, Viking/McClelland & Stewart.[5]
Conrad, J. (1899) *Heart of Darkness*, Blackwood's Magazine.
Cross, E. (1942) *The Tailor and Ansty*, the Mercier Press.
Dass, R. (1979) *Miracle of Love*, E.P. Dutton.
Davies, B. (2019) *The Secret Life of a Hurdy-Gurdy Player*, Y Lolfa.[6]
Davies, D. W. General Editor (2020) *The Oxford Literary History of Wales*, Oxford University Press, four volumes.
Davis, H. C. (1966) *Murder Starts from Fishguard*, The Mystery Book Guild, John Long Limited.
Deloria, E. C. (1988) *Waterlily*, Lincoln: University of Nebraska Press.

Edalji, G. E. T. (1903) *Maritime law for the "man in the coracle": chiefly intended as a guide for the travelling public on all points likely to arise in connection with the sea*, London: E. Wilson.[7]

Eliot, G. (1860) *The Mill on the Floss*, William Blackwood, three volumes.

Eliot, T. S. (1922) *The Waste Land*, Boni & Liveright.

Evans, C. (1915) *My People: Stories of the Peasantry of West Wales*, Andrew Melrose.

Evans, G. & Fulton, H. Editors (2019) *The Cambridge History of Welsh Literature*, Cambridge University Press.

Ibid (2021) *The Cambridge History of Cornish Literature*, Cambridge University Press.[8]

Evans, M. (1961) *Atgofion Ceinewydd*, Cymdeithas Lyfrau Ceredigion Gyf.

Fagan, A. (1931) *Mother Wales*, University of Sussex Press.[9]

Foucault, M. (2012) *The Archaeology of the Stern*, Routledge Classics.[10]

Gaskin, S. (1978) *... this season's people*, The Book Publishing Company, Summertown, Tennessee.

Gibbon, E. (1763-1775) *The Decline and Fall of the City State of Crymych*, Strahan & Cadell, London, seven volumes.[11]

Ibid (1776-1789) *The Decline and Fall of the Roman Empire*, Strahan & Cadell, London, six volumes.

Goethe, J. W. von (1795) *Römische Elegien*, in Die Horen.

Goodwin, G. (1936) *Myths and Tales of the Mountain People of the Preselis*, Memoirs of the American Folklore Society 32.[12]

Goulson, D. (2021) *Silent Earth*, Jonathan Cape.

Grey-Wilson, C. (1993) *Poppies: The Poppy Family in the Wild and in Cultivation*, Batsford.

Hands, I (1722) *My Adventures as a Sea-faring Man Sailing around the West Indies and the North American Colonies*, Charles Rivington.

Hannahs, S. J. (2013) *The Phonology of Welsh*, Oxford University Press.

Hesse, H. (1988) *Siddhartha*. Translated by Hilda Rosner. Picador.

Hierocles & Philagrius (4th century AD) *Philogelos*, Φιλόγελως.

Hopkins, H. (1937) *The Successful Breeding of the Domestic Parrot*, Portsea Publications.[13]

Hornell, J. (1938) *British Coracles and the Curraghs of Ireland with a Note on the Quffah of Iraq*, The Society for Nautical Research / Bernard Quaritch.

Hughes, A. J. (2008) *Leabhar Mór Bhriathra na Gaeilge*, Beann Madagáin.

Jerome, J. K. (1886) *Idle Thoughts of an Idle Fellow*, The Leadenhall Press.

Ibid (1898) *The Second Thoughts of an Idle Fellow*, Hurst and Blackett.

Ibid (1911) *Three Men in a Coracle*, J. W. Arrowsmith.[14]

Johnson, Captain C. (1724) *A General History of the Robberies and Murders of the most notorious Pyrates*, Charles Rivington.

Jones, B. M. (2010) *Tense and Aspect in Informal Welsh*, De Gruyter Mouton.

Jones, H. (1903) *The Sub-Committees of Wales, Volume 3, 1768-1821*, University of Wales Press.[15]

King, G. (2016) *Modern Welsh: A Comprehensive Grammar*, third edition, Routledge.

Ibid (2020) *The Working Coracle: A Guide to the Mechanics of Coracling*, Routledge.[16]

Leacock, S. (1912) *Sunshine Sketches of a Little Town in Pembrokeshire*, Bell and Cockburn.[17]

Mac an Iomaire, S. (2002) *Cladaí Chonamara*, An Gúm.

Mac Cóil, L. (2014) *I dTír Strainséartha*, Leabhar Breac.

Ibid (2016) *An Choill*, Leabhar Breac.

Ibid (2019) *Bealach na Spáinneach*, Leabhar Breac.

Mac Conamhna, B. (2016) *Curaigh na hÉireann*, Cló Iar-Chonnacht.

MacGill-Eain, S. (1999) *O Choille gu Bearradh*, Carcanet/Birlinn.

Maharaj, Sri N. (1973) *I Am That*, Chetana (P.) Ltd., Bombay.

Manthorpe, J. (2007) *Pembrokeshire Coast Path*, Trailblazer Publications.

Mitchell, J. (2017) *Geiriadur Cymraeg-Gwyddeleg*, Gwasg Gwaelod yr Ardd.

Moravia, A. (1947) *The Woman of Crymych*, English Edition Farrar, Straus, 1949.[18]

Norberg-Hodge, H. (2000) *Ancient Futures*, Rider.

Ó Cróinín, S. (2019) *Blas Meala. An Bheachaireacht Shimplí*, Cló Iar-Chonnacht.

Olsen, A. & Ellsworth Olsen, M. (2010) *Exercises for Gentlemen. 50 Exercises to Do With Your Suit On*, Universe.

Orwell, G. (1947) *A Nice Cup of Tea*. Evening Standard. An excellent essay in which the author advises, quite rightly, that the hot water be put into the cup before the milk.

Ó Sé, C. (2001) *Traidisiún na Scéalaíochta i gCorca Dhuibhne*, Coiscéim.

Parrot, T. (2005) *Colloquial Ladakhi for Beginners*, University of Wales Press.[19]

Ibid (2009) *The Life and Works of Prince Madog*, University of Wales Press.[19]

Pearl, M. H. (2021) *Ruby Rockpool & The Garbage Patch King*, Independent Publishing Network.

Perkins, G. (1397) *Through the Ages: A Historical Study of Something*, manuscript.

Phillips, M. (1965) *Everything is nothing. Nothing is everything*. Shambhala Publications.[20]

Ibid (1967) *I am what you are. You are what I am*. Shambhala Publications.[20]

Ibid (1975) *Behavioural Freefall and the Brain's Plasticity During Clogging*, University of North Pembrokeshire Press.

Ibid (2017) *The Little Book of Bronwen*, Penguin.[21]

Prys, P. (2020) *Bora Brav*, Kesva an Taves Kernewek.

Rees, D. (2013) *How to Sharpen Pencils*, Melville House.

Rose, P. (1991) *An Chéad Chnuasach 1972-'79*, Coiscéim.

Ibid (1999) *An Dara Cnuasach 1980-'87*, Coiscéim.[22]

Salaman, R. (1949) *The History and Social Influence of the Paddle*, Cambridge University Press.[23]

Sapiens, G. (568AD) *Librum Britannicum*, manuscript.

Simenon, G. (1931) *Pietr-le-Letton*, Fayard.

Ibid (1972) *Maigret et Monsieur Charles*, Presses de la Cité.

South African Banana Board (1976) *Be Bold with Bananas*, Muller & Retief, revised edition.

Spencer, E. (1960) *The Light in the Piazza*, first published in The New Yorker.

Sterry, P. (1997) Addasiad Iolo Williams and Bethan Wyn Jones (2007) *Llyfr Natur Iolo*, Gwasg Carreg Gwalch.

Stevenson, R.S. (1883) *Treasure Island*, originally published as *The Sea Cook: A Story for Boys*, Cassell and Company.

Styles, H. (2014) *Kynsa Mil Er yn Kernewek*, Kesva an Taves Kernewek.

Tagore, R. (1986) *Gitanjali*, Papermac.

Thompson, F. (1945) *Lark Rise to Candleford*, Oxford University Press, a trilogy.

Toulouse, M. (1496?) *L'art et Instruction de bien danser*, Paris: Michel Toulouse.

Trevena, D. L. (1847) *Keeping the Sea Lanes Open. A History of the Cornish Rapid-Response Crabber Unit*, University of Wadebridge Press.

Trimmer, J. W. (1993) *How to Avoid Huge Ships*, Cornell Maritime Press. Second edition.

Watkins, T. A. (1955) *A Linguistic Atlas of the Welsh Dialects of the Stern*, Centre International de Dialectologie Générale.[24]

Williams, I. (1951) *Pedeir Keinc Y Mabinogi*, Gwasg Prifysgol Cymru.

Ibid (1957) *Pum Keinc Y Mabinogi*, Gwasg Prifysgol Cymru.[25]

Unknown, (10th century Persian) *Hudud al-Alam*. حدود العالم.

Wrench, T. (2002) *Building a Low Impact Roundhouse on the Stern*, Permanent Publications.[26]

Wyn, H. (2008) *Pentigily*, Y Lolfa.

Apologia

Many of the quotes in the book have been changed slightly from the original in order to introduce humour. For example, a quote from Alfred Lord Tennyson in chapter 1 has been changed to, *'Tis better to have fallen out of a coracle than never to have fallen out of a coracle at all*. The changes will be obvious to the reader, therefore, the original quotes, in this example, *'Tis better to have loved and lost than never to have loved at all*, are not written in full next to the reference in the Apologia.

Of the quotes on page 5, at the beginning of each chapter, and in the body of the book, some are translations from other languages. Most of the translations into English are not mine and it has not been possible for me to find the name of the translator and the source in each case. My apologies for this.

I have tried my best to include references to every source used in the book. My apologies if I have missed one.

Quote: Between life and death there is but a breath. *Lifting the Latch: A Life on the Land*, a memoir of Mont Abbott (1902-1989) a rural labourer in Enstone, Oxfordshire, as told to Sheila Stewart. Page 137. Day Books.

By the same author: [1]Harvard University Press, [2]Gomer Press, [3]Dublin Institute for Advanced Studies, [4]Redcliffe Salaman and Cambridge University Press, [5]University of Wales Press, [6]Charles Moore and Allen Lane, [7]Parthian Press, [8]Y Lolfa.

Book reviews: [1]Western Telegraph, [2]Ernest Elmore and John Bude and *The Cornish Coast Murder*, [3]Sydsvenskan, [4]Withiel Parish Council, [5]Chicago Tribune, [6]Pembrokeshire Herald, [7]L'Académie Caseus, [8]Irish Times, [9]William Faulkner, [10]A. A. Gill, [11]County Echo, [12]Comhar, [13]Peig Sayers agus Máire Ní Chinnéide agus Comhlacht Oideachais na hÉireann agus Bryan MacMahon agus Talbot Press, [14]Anne Robinson, [15]Radio Pembrokeshire, [16]GOLWG, [17]The Cloncfeistres and the Cloncfeistr and the Clonc Mawr, [18]Richards Bros, [19]Katherine Watts, [20]The Chair, Hywel Dda Health Board, [21]Thomas Hardy Society, [22]Le Matricule des Anges, [23]British Medical Association, [24]Y Cymro, [25]Robert Frost and Kathleen Morrison, [26]Timothy Leary, [27]Journal of Abnormal Psychology, [28]Professor Alfred Wegener, [29]University of Wales Trinity Saint David, [30]Institut International de la Marionnette, [31]Perseverance, the Mars rover.

Publisher's note: [1]BBC Wales, [2]University of Wales Trinity Saint David, [3]Hay Festival, [4]Chantler Teas, [5]Steven Spielberg, [6]Coen Brothers, [7]Martin Scorsese, [8]The *X Explained* column in the Sport section of The Times on Saturday, [9]Anthony and Berryman's *Magistrates Court Guide 2010*. Edited by F. G. Davies, [10]Health and Safety Executive, [11] *The National Eisteddfod, Eisteddfod Genedlaethol Cymru*, [12]Google and Google Translate, [13]Caradoc Evans.

Foreword: [1]Pembrokeshire County Council, [2]Robert A. Heinlein and *Stranger in a Strange Land*, [3]Professor Randolph Quirk, Baron Quirk.

Introduction: [1]Aristotle, [2]Douglas Allchin and *Monsters and Marvels: How Do We Interpret the 'Preternatural'?*, [3]C. G. Jung, [4]Caitlin Moran, [5]Lao Tzu, [6]Keith H. Basso and *Wisdom Sits in Places: Landscape and Language Among the Western Apache* and the University of New Mexico Press, [7]Einstein, [8]Bette Davis and Joseph L. Mankiewicz and *All About Eve*, [9]Professor Sir Christopher Ricks.

Author's Preface: [1]The Mayor of Fishguard, [2]W. E. Bowman and the wonderful *The Ascent of Rum Doodle*, [3]Karl Marx and *Das Kapital*, [4]University of Wales Trinity Saint David, [5]*Kowethas an Yeth Kernewek*, [6]*Gorsedh Kernow*, [7]Helena Norberg-Hodge and *Ancient Futures*, [8]CADW, [9]Cornwall Heritage Trust, Ertach Kernow rag Onan hag Oll.

Prologue: [1]Muireann Ní Bhrolcháin and An Introduction to Early Irish Literature, [2]Dyfed-Powys Police.

1 [1]Somhairle MacGill-Eain/Sorley MacLean, *O Choille gu Bearradh/From Wood to Ridge*, Collected Poems in Gaelic and English Translation, Carcanet/Birlinn 1999 agus *Ó Choill go Barr Ghéaráin*, Somhairle MacGill-Eain, Na Dánta, maille le haistriúcháin Ghaeilge le Paddy Bushe, [2]Dyfed-Powys Police, [3]Merched y Wawr, [4]Welsh Philosopher J. R. Jones, [5]Tertullian, [6]Tai-hui, [7]Werner Heisenberg, [8]American Association for the Advancement of Science, [9]County Echo, [10]the Urdd and Aelwyd Crymych, [11]The National Eisteddfod, [12]Tony Blair and the Labour Party, [13]Alfred Lord Tennyson, [14]Salvador Dali, [15]Leonard Cohen, [16]George Lucas and *Star Wars*, [17]Aristotle, [18]John Gray and *Men Are From Mars, Women Are From Venus*, [19]Marvel Comics and Marvel Worldwide Inc, [20]TomTom GPS technology, [21]NASA, [22]the Ospreys rugby team, [23]the Dragons rugby team, [24]University of Wales Trinity Saint David, [25]Radio Pembrokeshire, [26]J.B.S. Haldane, [27]Ivy Bush Royal Hotel in Carmarthen, [28]World Wildlife Fund, [29]Science, [30]Lucy and Australopithecus afarensis and Donald Johanson and Maurice Taieb and Yves Coppens, [31]Carlo Petrini the Slow Food gourmet, [32]Amelia Earhart, [33]Stradivarius, [34]Paul Hawkins and David Sherry and Hawk-Eye technology.

2 [1]William Blake, [2]Del Monte Foods, [3]The Women's Institute, [4]Merched y Wawr, [5]Father Charles O'Neill and Carl Hardebeck and *The Foggy Dew*, [6]Trotsky, [7]Mario

Puzo and *The Godfather*, [8]Saunders Lewis, [9]Viagra, [10]Dale Carnegie, [11]Radio Wales, [12]the Three Crowns in Hubberston, [13]Western Mail, [14]Voltaire, [15]Molière, [16]Michel de Montaigne, [17]Flaubert, [18]Marcel Proust, [19]Hilton Hotels, [20]Edward Gibbon, [21]Radio Cymru, [22]Scrabble and Mattel and Hasbro, [23]Geiriadur Prifysgol Cymru: pwlffacan; straffaglio, mynd i drafferth (i wneud rhywbeth): to make one's way with difficulty, struggle (along); put oneself out (to do something). Ar lafar yn Sir Benfro, pwl(l)ffagan. T. H. Parry-Williams: *gwylio trên bach yr Wyddfa yn pwlffacan yn fyglyd i fyny i'r top.* [24]Andy Clarke and Ian Sturrock and Dr Joan Morgan and the Brogdale Trust, [25]Lao-Tzu.

3 [1]P. L. Travers and Bill Walsh and Don DaGradi and Richard M. Sherman and Robert B. Sherman and Irwin Kostal and Walt Disney Pictures and the film *Mary Poppins*, [2]Harrods, [3]Steve Jobs and Apple, [4]René Descartes, [5]Merched y Wawr, [6]Nant Gwrtheyrn, [7]Bob Morris Jones and *Tense and Aspect in Informal Welsh*, [8]Western Mail, [9]Bob Borsley, Maggie Tallerman and David Willis and *The Syntax of Welsh*, [10]Incredible String Band, [11]The Mind and Life Institute, [12]the Dalai Lama, [13]Jean-Jacques Rousseau, [14]Saint Augustine, [15]Immanuel Kant, [16]Karl Marx, [17]Aristotle, [18]Katsushika Hokusai and his woodblock print series *Thirty-six Views of Mount Fuji* which includes *The Great Wave off Kanagawa* and the late Lorens John, [19]the Viet Gwent, Graham Price, Bobby Windsor and Charlie Faulkner, [20]Hakone Museum in Japan, [21]Wikipedia, [22]Felinfoel Double Dragon, [23]Gwyn Nicholls, [24]Claude Davey, [25]Bleddyn Williams, [26]famous Zen story, [27]Gampoda, [28]Marmite, [29]Peanut Butter, [30]Star Trek, [31]Dyfed-Powys Police, [32]Carl Rogers, [33]Blind Willie McTell, [34]Robert Johnson, [35]Max Boyce, [36]Blind Willie Johnson, [37]Walker Percy and *The Moviegoer*, [38]Mario Puzo and Francis Ford Coppola and Robert Towne and *The Godfather*, [39]University of Wales Trinity Saint David, [40]Christopher McDougall and the Rarámuri and the Tarahumara and *Born to Run*, [41]Sharon Arbuthnot and Máire Ní Mhaonaigh and Gregory Toner and Joe McLaren and the Royal Irish Academy and *A History of Ireland in 100 Words*, [42]**ULTRARUNNING** magazine, [43]Vibram and the Vibram FiveFingers.

4 [1]Maharajji/Neem Karoli Baba and Ram Dass and *Miracle of Love*, [2]Tenby Observer, [3]Stanislavsky, [4]President Charles de Gaulle, [5]Stieg Larsson and the *Millennium* trilogy, [6]Merched y Wawr, [7]Radio Wales, [8]Dyfed-Powys Police, [9]Alan Watts, [10]Henri-Alban Fournier and *Le Grand Meaulnes*, [11]OzBus, [12]Frederick Forsyth and Kenneth Ross and Fred Zinnemann and Edward Fox and *The Day of the Jackal*, [13]Penguin Books, [14]McDonald's, [15]Robert Zemeckis and Bob Gale and Christopher Lloyd and Michael J. Fox and *Back to the Future*, [16]Trevanian and Clint Eastwood and George Kennedy and *The Eiger Sanction*, [17]all Rinpoches, [18]Bois y Blacbord, [19]Leonard Cohen, [20]Rumi, [21]Incredible String Band. There are quotes from several songs in the text here, as well as the chorus from *A Very Cellular*

Song. [22]John Hefin and Gwenlyn Parry and the *Ruptured Ferret* and *Grand Slam* and BBC Wales, [23]Blind Willie McTell, [24]Karl Marx and *Das Kapital*, [25]Gareth Thomas, [26]St Francis of Assisi, [27]C. G. Jung, [28]the Chief Executive of Pembrokeshire County Council, [29]John Cage, [30]Cape Canaveral, [31]Phil Bennett, [32]Huw Llewellyn Davies, [33]S4C, [34]Thomas Llyfnwy Thomas, a Welsh American baritone who was born in Maesteg, [35]NASA, [36]The Wales Open golf tournament, [37]W. E. Bowman and the wonderful *The Ascent of Rum Doodle*, [38]MGM and *Meet Me in St. Louis*, [39]Siwan Jones and *Con Passionate*, [40]Tony Bennett and *I Left My Heart in San Francisco*, [41]George Mallory.

5 [1]Alan Watts, [2]Alistair MacLean and Brian G. Hutton and Richard Burton and Clint Eastwood and *Where Eagles Dare*, [3]Marmite, [4]Peanut Butter, [5]*Mission: Impossible* (film series), [6]University of Wales Trinity Saint David, [7]John Guillermin and Irwin Allen and Stirling Silliphant and Steve McQueen and Paul Newman and the film *Towering Inferno*, [8]B. J. Thomas and Paul Newman and *Butch Cassidy and the Sundance Kid*, [9]Richard Chamberlain and *Dr Kildare* and *Towering Inferno*, [10]Steve McQueen and *The Great Escape*, [11]Welsh Government, [12]the Delphic maxims and the Temple of Apollo at Delphi, [13]Goodwick Brass Band, [14]Preservation Hall Jazz Band, [15]Pembrokeshire County Council and Pembrokeshire County Council`s Adult Education Centre in Haverfordwest and *Learning Pembrokeshire* and *Sir Benfro yn Dysgu*, [16]Dyfed-Powys Police, [17]Alan Greenspan, the American economist, [18]Pembrokeshire County Council, [19]Angharad Wynne and *Mermaids Ahoy!*, [20]John Prebble and Cy Endfield and Stanley Baker and Michael Caine and Gonville Bromhead and *Zulu*.

6 [1]Dylan Thomas, [2]Marcel Carné and Jean Gabin and Michel Simon and Michèle Morgan and *Le Quai des Brumes*, [3]Merched y Wawr, [4]Wikipedia, [5]Gwenlyn Parry and Sharon Morgan and Windsor Davies and Huw Griffiths and *Grand Slam*, [6]Bardstown Bluegrass Festival, [7]Second City improv troupe, [8]Felinfoel Double Dragon and Valium, [9]Leonard Cohen and *Dance Me to the End of Love*, [10]Stieg Larsson and the *Millennium* trilogy and *The Girl with the Dragon Tattoo*, [11]Felinfoel Double Dragon, [12]Robert Frost, [13]Twm Carnabwth, [14]Ram Dass, [15]Josiah G. Holland, [16]Tomás Mac Eoin and *An Cailín Álainn*, [17]*Dónal Óg*, translated by Séamus Ennis.

7 [1]Dogen, [2]*Y Llien Gwyn*, [3]Abu Dhabi Adventure Challenge, [4]Dyfed-Powys Police, [5]Dan yr Ogof caves, [6]Madam Patti, [7]Evening Post, [8]NASA, [9]Wales Tourist Board, [10]TomTom Technology, [11]the monks of Caldey Island, [12]the vicar of St Mary`s church in Tenby, [13]the Bishop of St Davids, [14]Tenby Museum, [15]Pembrokeshire County Council and Tenby Town Council, [16]Tenby Observer, [17]Merched y Wawr, [18]Jini Williams, [19]Chief Executive and Cabinet of Pembrokeshire County Council and Town, City and County Councillors in Pembrokeshire, [20]Welsh Government,

[21]Eurofighter Typhoon, [22]Cosworth, [23]Oakwood Theme Park, [24]Charles `Chuck` Yeager, [25]Radio Pembrokeshire, [26]Felix Baumgartner, [27]Geiriadur Prifysgol Cymru, [28]Western Mail, [29]Centre for Advanced Welsh and Celtic Studies in Aberystwyth, [30]National Library of Wales, [31]The Cabin in Pier Street, Aberystwyth, [32]US Air Force, [33]Einstein and his wife, [34]Nicolas Roeg and Paul Mayersberg and David Bowie and *The Man Who Fell to Earth*, [35]Amos Dolbear and *The Cricket as a Thermometer*, 1897.

8 [1]Hakim Jami, [2]Wikipedia, [3]Merched y Wawr, [4]BBC Radio Wales, [5]James Joyce and *Ulysses* and Nora Barnacle and Bloomsday, [6]Carmarthenshire County Council and Councillors, [7]Silicon Valley, [8]University of Wales Trinity Saint David, [9]County Councillors, AMs, MPs and the High Sheriff of Carmarthenshire, [10]Welsh Government, [11]The Muppets, [12]*The Vagina Monologues*, [13]Stefano Bonilli and Gambero Rosso, [14]Pembrokeshire County Council, [15]Pembrokeshire College, [16]Samba Doc, [17]the Mayor/Mayoress of Haverfordwest, [18]Haverfordwest Town Councillors and Pembrokeshire County Councillors, the Chief Executive, senior officers and members of the Cabinet, especially Independents, of Pembrokeshire County Council, [19]Côr y Dysgwyr, [20]Dawnswyr Clocsiau Maenclochog, [21]World Clog Dance Championships, [22]Mary Vaughan Jones and Rowena Wyn Jones and *Sali Mali*, Roald Dahl and *James and the Giant Peach*, [23]Swansea Market, [24]the Senedd, [25]Peig Sayers and the Blasket Islands, [26]Llywelyn Goch ap Meurig and Tebot Piws, [27]the Mayor/Mayoress of Tenby, [28]Theatr y Gromlech, [29]SOAS, University of London, [30]Pontypridd Rugby Club, [31]Karl Marx and *Das Kapital*, [32]Daniel Owen Memorial Prize, [33]the National Eisteddfod, [34]Peter Green and Fleetwood Mac.

9 [1]Gerry and Sylvia Anderson and *Thunderbirds*, [2]Confucius, [3]Shirgar Butter, [4]County Echo, [5]the Coracle Society, [6]Dr Denis G. Osborne, [7]Erasto Mpemba. In *Lifting the Latch: A Life on the Land* as told to Sheila Stewart by Mont Abbott of Enstone, Oxfordshire, published by Day Books in 2003, Mont recalls his life as a rural labourer. He was born in 'ought-two [1902]' and at thirteen he began work on a local farm. On page 47 he makes the following comment about his midday 'bit of tucker', '... and a bottle of cold tea. Always cold tea, even in the middle of winter. Warn't no use putting in hot tea; hot tea always frez quicker than cold.' [8]Dyfed-Powys Police, [9]Bob Dylan and *I've Made Up My Mind to Give Myself to You*, [10]Radio Pembrokeshire, [11]Welsh Rugby Union, [12]Alain Rolland, [13]NASA, [14]Pembrokeshire College, [15]World of Groggs, [16]Charlton Heston, [17]the Sloop in Porthgain, [18]Emanuel Leutze and *Washington Crossing the Delaware* and Pat Nicolle and *Bonnie Prince Charlie Sets Out for the Isle of Skye*, [19]S4C, [20]Merched y Wawr, [21]Waldo Williams and *Y Dderwen Gam*, [22]Mererid Hopwood, [23]the Chief Executive and Cabinet members from Pembrokeshire County Council, [24]Bishop of St Davids, [25]Rowan Williams, [26]Fishguard and Goodwick Town Council, [27]Albert

Einstein and Nathan Rosen, [28]Arlo Guthrie and *Alice's Restaurant*, [29]Welsh Government, [30]The Oak on Fishguard square, [31]Pembrokeshire County Council's Transport Committee, [32]Pembrokeshire County Council's Finance Committee, [33]Wikipedia, [34]Aberystwyth University, [35]Max Westenhöfer and Alfonso Cuarón and Jonás Cuarón and Sandra Bullock and George Clooney and the film *Gravity*. Some dialogue from the film is used here. [36]RNLI, [37]GCHQ, [38]University of Wales Trinity Saint Davids, [39]The London Eye, [40]Tregwynt Woollen Mill, [41]Shakespeare, [42]*Côr y Dysgwyr*, [43]Ivor Emmanuel, [44]Archimedes, [45]Fishguard Lifeboat, [46]Groucho Marx and Leonard Cohen, [47]Dylan Thomas, [48]Sky, [49]Alan Llwyd and Robert Rhys and Gwasg Gomer and *Waldo Williams: Cerddi 1922-1970*, [50]Frank Lloyd Wright.

10 [1]Ramana Maharshi, [2]Merched y Wawr, [3]Silicon Valley, [4]Nadia Boulanger, [5]*Geiriadur Ffrangeg-Cymraeg, Cymraeg-Ffrangeg / Dictionnaire Francais-Gallois, Gallois-Francais*, Centre for Educational Studies, University of Wales (2000), [6]Keith H. Basso and *Wisdom Sits in Places: Landscape and Language Among the Western Apache* and the University of New Mexico Press, [7]Albert Camus, [8]Hollywood Bowl, [9]Arlo Guthrie, Pete Seeger, Judy Collins, Woody Guthrie and *This Land is Your Land*, [10]Jean-François Dutertre and the *Anthologie de la Musique Traditionnelle Française*, [11]the Gorsedd and the National Eisteddfod, [12]Tolstoy, [13]canu pwnc, [14]Sigmund Freud, [15]Pobol y Cwm, [16]Ysgol y Preseli, [17]Gandhi and Richard Attenborough and Ben Kingsley and the film *Gandhi*, Michael Collins and Neil Jordan and Liam Neeson and the film *Michael Collins*, [18]Folly Farm, [19]BBC, [20]Candide, [21]Lionel Hampton, [22]NOAA Space Weather Prediction Center, [23]Jo Stafford and *You Belong to Me*, [24]Jools Holland, [25]Fishguard Folk Festival, [26]Jimmy Hendrix, [27]Meic Stevens and the Cadillacs and *Rue St Michel*, [28]the Dalai Lama, [29]Johnny Cash and *Get Rhythm* and *A Boy Named Sue*, [30]Frank and Nancy Sinatra, [31]Sonny and Cher, [32]Nina Simone, [33]The Monkeys, [34]Terry Jacks, [35]The Righteous Brothers, [36]The Drifters, [37]The Ronettes, [38]The Temptations, [39]Neil Young, [40]Bob Dylan, [41]the Mamas and Papas, [42]Mary Hopkin, [43]Barry McGuire, [44]Marvin Gaye, [45]Lillian Gish, [46]The Essential Dogen and Kazuaki Tanahashi and Peter Levitt and Shambhala.

11 [1]Plato, [2]*Kvæfjordkake, verdens beste kake*, the world's best cake, [3]Alan Watts, [4]Keith H. Basso and *Wisdom Sits in Places: Landscape and Language Among the Western Apache* and the University of New Mexico Press.

12 [1]Andy Pandy and *Watch with Mother*, [2]Jules Verne and *20,000 Leagues Under the Sea*, [3]Walt Disney, [4]Dyfed-Powys Police, [5]Arthur C. Clarke and Stanley Kubrick and *2001: A Space Odyssey*, [6]Robert Frost, [7]Welsh Government, [8]Brian Appleyard, [9]CERN, [10]Ziji Rinpoche and *Short Moments*, [11]Seaways bookshop, [12]Herman Hesse and *Siddhartha* and Hilda Rosner and Picador, [13]Katherine Jenkins, [14]King Crimson

and *21st Century Schizoid Man*, [15]John Wayne, [16]Paulette Jiles and *News of the World* and Harper Collins, [17]Ludwig Carl Christian Koch, [18]Steve Jobs and Apple, [19]Barack Obama, [20]Henry Ford, [21]Burl Ives and the *Big Rock Candy Mountain*, [22]Radio Pembrokeshire, [23]CERN, [24]Paul Dirac, [25]the Chief Executive and all past Chief Executives of Pembrokeshire County Council, [26]Groucho Marx, [27]Pembrokeshire County Councillors, [28]all past and previous Chief Executives of Pembrokeshire County Council, [29]Bruegel and *The Fall of Icarus*, [30]World Bog Snorkelling Championships, Llanwrtyd Wells, [31]Sioned Davies, Professor and Head of the School of Welsh at Cardiff University and her excellent rewriting of *The Mabinogion* from Mediæval Welsh into English and Oxford World's Classics, [32]Meibion Glyndŵr, [33]Julie Covington and Andrew Lloyd Webber and *Evita* and *Don't Cry for me Argentina*, [34]Bob Dylan and *Mr Tambourine Man*, [35]Shemi Wâd and Mary Medlicott and *Shemi's Tall Tales* and Gomer Press, illustrated by Jac Jones, [36]*Geiriadur Prifysgol Cymru* (*A friend to pigs, and loved by pigs.*), [37]*Pedeir Keinc y Mabinogi, Allan o Lyfr Gwyn Rhydderch*, Ifor Williams, Gwasg Prifysgol Cymru/University of Wales Press, [38]Catherine Zeta-Jones.

13 [1]Ram Dass, [2]W. E. Bowman and the wonderful *The Ascent of Rum Doodle*, [3]Welsh Place-Name Society, Cymdeithas Enwau Lleoedd Cymru and Idris Mathias, [4]National Library of Wales in Aberystwyth, Llyfrgell Genedlaethol Cymru yn Aberystwyth, [5]The Sunday Times, The Sunday Times` Literary Critics, [6]Herman Melville and Gregory Peck and *Moby Dick*, [7]Julie Covington and Andrew Lloyd Webber and Evita and *Don't Cry For Me Argentina*, Malcolm Pryce and *Don't Cry For Me Aberystwyth*, [8]Merched y Wawr, [9]Elle MacPherson and *The Body*, [10]the Clonc Mawr, Y Clonc Mawr, [11]Teithwyr Teifi, [12]S4C, [13]Pembrokeshire County Council, [14]Steven Spielberg and *Jurassic Park*, [15]Bamse and Dunderhonung, [16]Pembrokeshire Coast Path, [17]David D. Osborn and Ron Goodwin and Oliver Reed and Rita Tushingham and *The Trap*, [18]Professor W. B. Lockwood and *Astudia Celtica*, [19]Swansea University and all physicists at Swansea University, [20]Einstein and the General Theory of Relativity, [21]The Times, [22]the Guardian, [23]the Western Mail, [24]Philip Broughton and Funranium Labs and *Black Blood of the Earth*, [25]the Ferry Inn, St Dogmaels, [26]Dr Bronisław Malinowsky, [27]Harrods, [28]Strauss, [29]Richards Bros, [30]Tafarn Sinc, [31]Welsh Bobsleigh Team, [32]Derek Brockway and BBC Wales.

14 [1]Thaddeus Golas, [2]Dylan Thomas, [3]Professor Mererid Hopwood and *Singing in Chains* and Gomer Press, [4]Western Mail, [5]Sir Clough Williams-Ellis and Portmeirion, [6]Escher, [7]Fishguard, Goodwick and Lower Town Civic Society, [8]Professor E. G. Bowen and *Settlements of the Celtic Saints in Wales* and the University of Wales Press, [9]Richards Bros, [10]the Mandan Tribe, [11]David Reich, *Nature* 22 December 2021 *Large-Scale Migration into Southern Britain During*

the Middle to Late Bronze Age. Patrick Sims-Williams, *Cambridge Archaeological Journal*, 02 April 2020 *Celtic from the Middle,* and *BARN*, Rhifyn 709, Chwefror 2022 *Pryd daeth y Gymraeg i Ynys Prydain?*, [12]Thor Heyerdahl and the Kon-Tiki expedition, [13]Marmite, [14]Peanut Butter, [15]Nicole Kidman, [16]Mae West and Steve Harley and *Come up and see me, make me smile*, [17]Mario Lanza and Ann Blyth and Richard Thorpe and Sigmund Romberg and Dorothy Donnelly and Sonya Levien and William Ludwig and Wilhelm Meyer-Förster and Karl Heinrich and *The Student Prince*, [18]Fishguard Rugby Club, [19]Theatr Gwaun, [20]Swansea University, [21]Dewi Emrys, [22]Woody Guthrie and *Bound for Glory*, [23]the Mayor of Fishguard and Goodwick and his wife, [24]Roy Orbison and *Only the Lonely*, [25]Fishguard and Goodwick Town Council and wives and husbands, [26]Hilton Hotels and Resorts, [27]County Echo, [28]Reviel Netz and William Noel and *The Archimedes Codex*, [29]Radio Pembrokeshire, [30]Gregory Peck and Omar Sharif and *Mackenna's Gold*, [31]all Pembrokeshire County Councillors, [32]Leigh Halfpenny, George North and Shane Williams, [33]Derek Brockway and BBC Wales, [34]Dyfed-Powys Police, [35]Six Nations Championship, [36]Herschel Space Observatory, [37]Pobol y Cwm, [38]all local Councillors everywhere, [39]Blombos Cave, [40]W. E. Bowman and the wonderful *The Ascent of Rum Doodle*, [41]Tchaikovsky and the *1812 Overture*, [42]St Petersburg Philharmonic Orchestra, [43]Imperial Russian Army, [44]BBC Wales, [45]Russian artillerymen, [46]General Sir Robert Thomas Wilson, [47]Moskovskaya Pravda newspaper, [48]Crosby, Stills, Nash and Young.

15 [1]Seán Ó Ríordáin, [2]Merched y Wawr, [3]Aberystwyth University, [4]Leonard Cohen and *Dance Me to the End of Love*, [5]D.W. Winnicott and his ideas on the "good enough" parent, [6]Bruno Bettelheim and *A Good Enough Parent*, [7]Welsh Government, [8]Tivyside, [9]Costa Coffee, [10]Clebran, [11]Soccer World Cup, [12]Rugby World Cup, [13]baseball's World Series, [14]American Football, [15]Søren Kierkegaard, [16]Richard Strauss, [17]Ernest Elmore and John Bude and *The Cornish Coast Murder*, [18]Jonathan Swift and *Gulliver's Travels*, [19]all County Councillors, [20]Karolinska Institute, [21]Jack Kerouac and *On The Road*, [22]Arthur Eddington, [23]University of Wales Trinity Saint David, [24]Georges Feydeau, [25]Robert Burns and *To a Mouse, On Turning Her Up In Her Nest With The Plough*, [26]Stanley Kubrick and Peter Sellers and *Dr Strangelove*, [27]Brithdir Mawr.

16 [1]Shunryu Suzuki, [2]Zuigan and Grace Schireson and Peter Schireson and *Zen Bridge: The Zen Teachings of Keido Fukushima Roshi*, [3]W.S. Gilbert and his *Bab Ballads* and *Fun* magazine, [4]François Cellier and Cunningham Bridgeman and *Gilbert and Sullivan and Their Operas* and Little, Brown and Company, [5]Devon and Cornwall Police, [6]*Archaeologica Cambrensis*, [7]University of Wales Trinity Saint David, [8]*Harvard Theological Review*, [9]Harvard University, [10]Massachusetts State Police, [11]*Lewisiana* gan D. Geraint Lewis, page 56, [12]Edward Lear and *The Dong with*

a Luminous Nose, [13]logainm.ie, [14]Richie McCaw, [15]President John F. Kennedy (I am a Berliner.), [16]Virgil (Mind moves matter.), [17]Radio Pembrokeshre, [18]Dyfed-Powys Police, [19]traditional Irish song from Gaoth Dobhair in County Donegal, [20]Brian O'Nolan agus Myles na gCopaleen agus *An Béal Bocht*, [21]Derek Brockway and BBC Wales, [22]Bertrand Russell and *In Praise of Idleness*, [23]Jacques Cœur (To a valiant heart nothing is impossible.), [24]Fishguard and Goodwick Town Council and the Mayor/Mayoress, [25]Gerry and Sylvia Anderson and *Thunderbirds Are Go*, [26]An Garda Síochána, [27]Robert Louis Stevenson and *Treasure Island*, [28]John Redwood, [29]Ysgol Bro Gwaun, [30]Rhocesi`r Fro, [31]Annie Ebrel, Nolùen Le Buhé, Érik Marchand, Yann-Fañch Kemener, Denez Prigent, [32]Breandán Ó hEithir, writer, journalist and broadcaster, born on Inis Mór. His Irish language novel *Lig Sinn i gCathú* was translated into English by the author and published as *Lead Us Into Temptation*, [33]Máirtín Ó Direáin, Irish language poet, born on Inis Mór. A volume containing his collected poems, *Máirtín Ó Direáin Na Dánta*, was published by Cló Iar-Chonnacht in 2010. Two separate volumes have been published containing original Irish language poems and translations into English, [34]Sharon Arbuthnot and Máire Ní Mhaonaigh and Gregory Toner and Joe McLaren and the Royal Irish Academy and *A History of Ireland in 100 Words* and the *Daily Edge* website, [35]First Minister of Wales, [36]The Sergeant at Home, [37]Malwarebytes, [38]McSalver`s coveralls, [39]Tŷ Nant, [40]Émile Zola and *Germinal*, [41]Alice Munro, [42]Ed Spielman and Jerry Thorpe and Herman Miller and David Carradine and *Kung Fu*, [43]Julius Caesar (I came. I saw. I conquered.), [44]R. C. Sherriff and the wonderful *The Hopkins Manuscript* and Penguin Modern Classics.

17 [1] James Low, [2]Merched y Wawr, [3]World Puppet Theatre Festival in Charleville-Mèziéres and Jacqes Félix and the Institut International de la Marionnette and the École Nationale Supérieure des Arts de la Marionnette, [4]Lucille Ball, [5]Mayoress/Mayor of Tenby, [6]Richards Bros, [7]Bob Dylan and *Farewell Angelina*, [8]David Benatar and *Better Never to Have Been: The Harm of Coming Into Existence*, [9]Hilton Hotels, [10]the National Eisteddfod, [11]Lord Byron, [12]Anthony Hopkins, [13]Learjet, [14]General Electric, [15]CADW, [16]the MOSE Project, [17]Karl Marx and *Das Kapital*, [18]Kentucky Fried Chicken, [19]Zaha Hadid and Zaha Hadid Architects, [20]Edinburgh and the Athens of the North, [21]Bishop of St Davids, [22]Gwyn Alf Williams and Wynford Vaughan Thomas and *When Was Wales?* and *The Dragon Has Two Tongues*, [23]Pembrokeshire County Council, [24]Bernardo Bertolucci and Maria Schneider and Marlon Brando and *Last Tango in Paris*, [25]Clebran, [26]Western Mail, [27]Carmarthen Magistrates and Carmarthen Magistrates Court, [28]the Mayor/Mayoress of Haverfordwest Town Council, [29]Dyfed-Powys Police, [30]Viagra, [31]World Nature Organisation (WNO), [32]Richard Brunstrom the retired Chief Constable of North Wales Police, [33]Gareth Jones, the Welsh journalist who told the world about the *Holodomor*, the Terror Famine

in Soviet Russia in 1932-33, [34]*Baedeker Guides*, [35]Daniel Owen, [36]University of Wales Trinity Saint David, [37]Sir Arthur Evans, [38]Derek Brockway and BBC Wales, [39]Emma Taggart and Phil Torres and *The Jungle Diaries*.

18 [1]Tex Avery and Bob Clampett and Warner Bros and *Daffy Duck*, [2]John Guillermin and *The Towering Inferno*, [3]Eisenberg, [4]from a Calvin and Hobbes comic, 1992, their term for the Big Bang, [5]Dyfed-Powys Police, [6]Harvard University, [7]Pembrokeshire College, [8]Michael Curtiz and Julius J. Epstein and Howard Koch and Philip G. Epstein and Casey Robinson and Humphrey Bogart and Ingrid Bergman and *Casablanca*. Several lines from the film script are quoted and changed slightly here. [9]W. B. Yeats, [10]Western Telegraph, [11]Werner Heisenberg, [12]Karl Marx, [13]the Cabinet of Pembrokeshire County Council, [14]Radio Pembrokeshire, [15]Fishguard and Goodwick Town Councillors, [16]County Echo, [17]*Lonely Planet*, [18]Google and Google maps and Google Street View, [19]Apple, [20]The Times and the Raconteur, [21]Sigmund Freud, [22] *The Beano* and *Dennis the Menace*, [23]Scientists have measured the shortest unit of time ever, the time it takes a light particle to cross a hydrogen molecule. That time is 247 zeptoseconds. A zeptosecond is a trillionth of a billionth of a second, or a decimal point followed by 20 zeroes and a 1. [24]Olympic Games, [25]Russian chess grandmaster and former world chess champion Garry Kasparov.

19 [1]Krishnamurti, [2]Café Rouge, [3]Merched y Wawr, [4]Pembrokeshire County Council, all Pembrokeshire County Council's Committees and Subcommittees, [5]Western Mail, [6]Katherine Kennicott Davis and *The Little Drummer Boy*, [7]Brains Brewery and S. A. Brain & Co Ltd, [8]Evangelista Torricelli and Johann Wolfgang Von Goethe and the weather ball barometer, [9]A. A. Milne and *Winnie-the-Pooh and Eeyore*, [10]Meic Stevens, [11]Bob Dylan and *The Basement Tapes*, Dylanologists, David Kinney and *The Dylanologists: Adventures in the Land of Bob*, [12]Swansea University, [13]Silicon Valley, [14]Massachusetts Institute of Technology, [15]Welsh Government, [16]University of Wales Trinity Saint David, [17]Gandhi, [18]Nelson Mandela, [19]the Dalai Lama, [20]Stephen Hawking, [21]First Minister of Wales, [22]the Immortality Drive and the International Space Station, [23]Dafydd Iwan and *Yma o Hyd*, [24]Calaveras County Fair & Jumping Frog Jubilee and Jumping Frog Competition, [25]Cambridge University Press and *The Cambridge History of Welsh Literature*, [26]Sam Warburton, [27]Bob Dylan, [28]The Beatles, [29]The Stranglers, [30]Arthur Eddington, [31]W. E. Bowman and the wonderful *The Ascent of Rum Doodle*.

20 [1]Liam Ó Flaithearta, [2]Marmite, [3]Peanut Butter, [4]Star Trek, [5]John Cleare and Robin Collomb and *Sea Cliff Climbing* and coasteering in Pembrokeshire and Coasteering, [6]Horlicks, [7]Ödön von Horváth and *Kasimir und Karoline*, [8]Merched y Wawr, [9]Dyfed-Powys Police, [10]Pembrokeshire Coast National Park, [11]The Times,

London, [12]Welsh Language Commissioner, [13]Mebyon Kernow, [14]Seneth an Stenegow, [15]Welsh Government, [16]Pembrokeshire County Council, [17]Pembrokeshire County Council's Forward Planning Committee, [18]Natural Resources Wales, [19]Cornwall Council, [20]Percy Bysshe Shelley and *Ozymandias*, [21]Eddie Butler and *Gonzo Davies: Caught in Possession* and *The Head of Gonzo Davies*, [22]Glengettie Tea, [23]Radio Pembrokeshire, [24]Shinkansen and Bullet Train and Bullet Trains, [25]University of Wales Trinity Saint David, [26]Dai Jones, Llanilar, [27]S4C, [28]Grace Young Monaghan and the statue of Twm Siôn Cati in Tregaron, [29]Formula E and the Formula E World Championships, [30]Cardiff City Council, [31]World Bog Snorkelling Championships and Llanwrtyd Wells, [32]Hubberston, [33]Izaak Walton and *The Compleat Angler*, [34]Swansea University, [35]Fred Pearce and *A Trillion Trees. How We Can Reforest Our World* and Granta, [36]La Gendarmerie Nationale, [37]Derek Brockway and BBC Wales, [38]Welsh Perry and Cider Society.

21 [1]*An Duanag Ullamh*, [2]Western Mail, [3]Pembrokeshire Herald, [4]Jack Kornfield and The Buddha, [5]Tenby Town Council, [6]Nancy Sinatra and *These Boots Are Made For Walkin'*, [7]Merched y Wawr, [8]John 1:1 and *The Bible*, [9]Marmite, [10]Erwin Schrödinger, [11]Richard Feynman, [12]Professor Dai Smith, editor, and *The Library of Wales short story anthology, volumes 1 and 2* and Parthian books, [13]Derek Brockway and BBC Wales, [14]Phil Tanner, the Gower Nightingale and *The Banks of the Sweet Primroses*, [15]Ziji Rinpoche and *Short Moments*, [16]*incorrigible latitudinarian*, a term found in a letter dated the 26th of January 1923 from The Clarendon Press, Oxford, to, it appears, a member of the public who complained about the spelling in a book published by the press. Mr Roy Watts of Fishguard found the letter in a book which was in a skip. He showed the letter to me. [17]Lee Marvin and *I Was Born Under a Wandering Star* and *Paint Your Wagon*, [18]Gwen Parrott, [19]Forbe's list, [20]Jean Negulesco and Nunnally Johnson and Marilyn Monroe and Betty Grable and Lauren Bacall and *How to Marry a Millionaire*, [21]Verdi, [22]Vivaldi, [23]Schubert and Sir Walter Scott and *Ellen's Song* and Franz Liszt, [24]Red Hot Chili Peppers, [25]The Tironian symbol for Latin *et*, meaning *and*, is ⁊. The symbol is still used occasionally to mean *and*. For example, in Irish in Ireland in place of *agus* on road signs *Íoc ⁊ Taispeáin* PAY & DISPLAY (*Íoc agus Taispeáin*). Note that the symbol & replaces the word *and* in the English version, a practice common in English usage around the world. The symbol & also derives from Latin *et*, meaning *and*. Tironian is a shorthand system invented by Tiro who died in 4BC. He was Cicero's slave and personal secretary but later became a free man. The original system was made up of about 4,000 symbols. This was added to over the centuries and by the mediæval period in Europe, where it was used in monasteries, there were about 13,000 symbols, [26]This is a quote but I can't find the source, [27]Nicholas Unhoch, [28]Bob Dylan.

22 [1]Yogi Berra, [2]Marmite, [3]Peanut Butter, [4]Star Trek, [5]Zhou Hou Bei Ji Fang, [6]Thucydides, [7]Iolo Williams, [8]Max Hooper and *Hedges*, [9]Leonard Cohen, [10]John Steinbeck and *East of Eden*, [11]Harriet Tuckey and *Everest – The First Ascent: The untold story of Griffith Pugh, the man who made it possible*, [12]Máirtín Ó Cadhain and *An Eochair, The Key*, [13]An Garda Síochána, [14]*Do we see reality?* Donald Hoffman, New Scientist, the 3rd of August 2019, [15]Dyfed-Powys Police, [16]Mayor of Fishguard, [17]Joseph Campbell and *The Hero with a Thousand Faces*, [18]*Ask the Expert*, [19]Radio Wales, [20]Ron Davies, [21]Heinrich Harrer and Jean-Jacques Annaud and Becky Johnston and Brad Pitt and David Thewlis and *Seven Years in Tibet*, [22]the National Eisteddfod and the Gorsedd, [23]Dragnet, [24]Friedrich Nietzsche.

23 [1]Rumi, [2]Rybczynski Prize, [3]Pembrokeshire College, [4]Salvatore Samperi and Laura Antonelli and *Malizia* and *Peccato Veniale*, [5]Welsh Government, [6]Wales Tourist Board, [7]Pembrokeshire Climbing Club, [8]W. E. Bowman and the wonderful *The Ascent of Rum Doodle*, [9]University of Wales Trinity Saint David, [10]the National Eisteddfod of Wales, [11]*Fédération Internationale de Casser sa Pipe* and *Casser sa Pipe*, [12]Smithsonian Institution, [13]National Museums and Galleries of Wales, [14]Museum of the Future in Dubai, [15]Welsh National Ballet and Ballet Cymru and the National Dance Company of Wales, [16]Silfan Rhys-Jones, [17]Karl Marx and *Das Kapital*, [18]dafyddapgwilym.net and Professor Dafydd Johnston, et al, [19]Osho and *Meditation is a surrender. It is not a demand. It is not forcing existence your way. It is relaxing into the way existence wants you to be. It is a let go.*, [20]Merched y Wawr, [21]Derek Brockway and BBC Wales, [22]Timothy Leary.

24 [1]Carl Jung, [2]Harrison Ford and Indiana Jones, [3]Marmite, [4]University of Wales Trinity Saint David, [5]Dyfed-Powys Police, [6]Helsinki Police, Police in Finland, [7]Western Mail, [8]石黒浩, [9]School of Ocean Sciences at Bangor University, [10]NASA, [11]Raphael Gray, [12]Richard Feynman, [13]Robert Arthur Talbot Gascoyne-Cecil, 3rd Marquess of Salisbury KG GCVO PC DL FRS, [14]Radio Pembrokeshire, [15]Christopher McDougall and *Born to Run* and Daniel Lieberman and *The Story of the Human Body*, [16]Rebecca Wragg Sykes and *Kindred: Neanderthal Life, Love, Death and Art*, [17]Derek Brockway and BBC Wales.

25 [1]Thomas Merton, [2]Welsh Government, [3]Merched y Wawr, [4]R.S. Thomas, [5]Karl Marx and *Das Kapital*, [6]Shirley Bassey, [7]Kylie Minogue, [8]Noel Coward and *Don't Put Your Daughter on the Stage Mrs Worthington*, [9]Bois y Blacbord and *Dros y Mynydd Du*.

26 [1]Hazrat Inayat Khan, from Ram Dass and *Journey of Awakening* and Bantam Books, [2]Bobby Fischer and Boris Spassky in the 1972 World Chess Championship in Iceland, [3]Dyfed-Powys Police, [4]Stephen Hawking, [5]Giovanni Caputo from the

University of Urbino, [6]University of Wales Trinity Saint David, [7]Welsh Government, [8]Alain Delon and Monica Vitti and *L'Eclisse*, [9]Edward Monkton, [10]NASA, [11]Tenby Observer, [12]W. E. Bowman and the wonderful *The Ascent of Rum Doodle*, [13]Merched y Wawr, [14]Jeff Arch, Nora Ephron, Tom Hanks, Meg Ryan and *Sleepless in Seattle*, [15]Total Film, [16]Pembrokeshire County Council, [17]Swansea University and Swansea University's Department of Classics, Classical Civilisation, Ancient History and Egyptology, [18]Sam Warburton, [19]Fishguard Town Council, [20]Welsh Rugby Union, [21]Cardiff Blues, [22]Toulouse and Stade Toulousain, [23]Neil Young and *Heart of Gold*, [24]Derek Brockway and BBC Wales.

27 [1]Krishnamurti, [2]Clebran, [3]BBC and Panorama and *Rugby and the Brain: Tackling the Truth*, [4]Gillian Clarke and the Laws of Hywel Dda, [5]the Rolling Stones and *Play With Fire*, [6]Tebot Piws and *Mae Rhywun Wedi Dwyn Fy Nhrwyn*, [7]C.S. Lewis, [8]Audrey Hepburn and *Breakfast at Tiffany's*, [9]Karl Marx and *Das Kapital*, [10]the National Eisteddfod and the Gorsedd, [11]D.J. Williams, [12]Elizabeth Cramp and many others and Fishguard Invasion Centre Trust Ltd and The Last Invasion Embroidered Tapestry, a magnificent piece of work, and Fishguard Town Library and Pembrokeshire County Council, [13]Waldo Williams, [14]The Tenby Players, [15]Pobol y Cwm, [16]Carwyn James and the 1971 British and Irish Lions, [17]L. P. Hartley and *The Go-Between*, 1953, and Val Biro and Hamish Hamilton, [18]Avi Loeb and *Extraterrestrial: The First Sign of Intelligent Life Beyond Earth* and John Murray, [19]from a Calvin and Hobbes comic, 1992, their term for the Big Bang.

28 [1]Bob Dylan and *When the Ship Comes In*, [2]Bob Dylan. There are several phrases from *Tangled Up in Blue* here, [3]Dyfed-Powys Police, [4]Devon and Cornwall Police, [5]John Huston and Humphrey Bogart and Katharine Hepburn and *The African Queen*, [6]Rosamunde Pilcher, [7]*Kowethas an Yeth Kernewek*, [8]Radio Cornwall and the BBC, [9]Bartholomew Gosnold, [10]University of Wales Trinity Saint David, [11]Massachusetts Institute of Technology, [12]Wadebridge Town Council, [13]Fishguard Town Council, [14]County Echo, [15]Fishguard Rugby Club and all the coaches of Fishguard Rugby Club, [16]Brenda Wootton, [17]BUY. EAT. DRINK. LOCAL., *Bora Brav* and Polin Prys and Kesva an Taves Kernewek: *Keskows y'n koffiji 'An Krow' ogas dhe'n kolji*, page 44, [18]the Cornish folk song *Bre Gammbronn/Camborne Hill*, [19]*Oll an Gwella*, a men's choir from Newquay who always sing in Cornish and English, [20]Child Support Agency, [21]Jonny Dry and Ella Turner and Samuel Jay Chesswell and Dan Baboulene and Dan Jennings and *An Tarow, An Wariva Genedhlek a Gernow* and the *National Theatre of Cornwall* and the *Cornish National Theatre* and *Sodhva an Yeth Kernewek* and the *Cornish Language Office*, [22]Don Siegel and Clint Eastwood and *Dirty Harry*, [23]Helston Furry Dance, [24]Alan Le May and John Ford and Frank S. Nugent and John Wayne and *The Searchers*, [25]Reginald Foster and his translation of 'rock 'n' roll' into Latin, [26]Hare Krishna movement, [27]St

John's Ambulance, [28]Christopher McDougall and the Rarámuri and the Tarahumara and the book *Born to Run*, [29]Hawaiian Navy [30]Bermuda Police, [31]NATO, [32]NORAD.

29 [1]Sonny and Cher, [2]Sidney Lumet and Reginald Rose and *12 Angry Men*, [3]James Mangold and Michael Brandt and Derek Haas and Halsted Welles and *3:10 to Yuma*, [4]François Villiers and Jean Giono and Alain Allioux and Guy Béart and *L'Eau Vive*, [5]Merched y Wawr, [6]Welsh Parliament, [7]the Senedd in Cardiff Bay, [8]Karl Marx and *Das Kapital*, [9]Lao Tzu, translated into German by Richard Wilhelm, and from that translation, into English by H. G. Ostwald, Arkana, Penguin Books, [10]Formica© and Broadview Holdings, [11]Welsh Government, [12]Folger Shakespeare Library, Washington, D.C., [13]Emma Smith and *Shakespeare's First Folio: Four Centuries of an Iconic Book*, [14]Katsushika Hokusai and his woodblock print series *Thirty-six Views of Mount Fuji* which includes *The Great Wave off Kanagawa* and the late Lorens John, [15]University of Wales Trinity Saint David, [16]arXiv repository of e-prints, [17]Pembrokeshire County Council and the Cabinet of Pembrokeshire County Council, [18]Sebastiano del Plombo and *The Adoration of the Shepherds*, [19]Brithdir Mawr, [20]Bob Dylan and *Tomorrow is a Long Time*, [21]Wales Book of the Year Award, [22]Y Lolfa, [23]Siop Siân, [24]W. Y. Evans-Wentz, [25]Maharajji and Neem Karoli Baba, [26]Leonard Cohen and *Hey, That's No Way to Say Goodbye*, [27]Derek Brockway and BBC Wales.

30 [1]Rumi, [2]Radio Pembrokeshire, [3]Dyfed-Powys Police and the Chief Constable of Dyfed-Powys Police, [4]Pembrokeshire County Council, [5]Dyfed Archaeological Trust, [6]Sir Mortimer Wheeler, [7]Devon and Cornwall Police, [8]Richard Browning and Gravity Industries and the e-suit, [9]John Phillips and Scott McKenzie and *If You're Going to San Francisco*, [10]*The Magic Roundabout* and *Le Manège Enchanté*, [11]The Wooden Tops, [12]J. Robert Oppenheimer, [13]Marmite, [14]Walker Percy and *The Moviegoer*, [15]Derek Brockway and BBC Wales.

Epilogue 1: [1]The National Police Service in Kenya and the Inspector General of Police.

Epilogue 2: [1]Interpol, [2]United Nations, [3]Dyfed-Powys Police, [4]Welsh Government, [5]Western Mail.

Epilogue 3: [1]Shunryu Suzuki, [2]Colm Cille agus *Loch na mBradán, Muna bhfuil bradán ann go rabh bradán ann, agus má tá bradán ann nach rabh bradán ann.* (If there isn't salmon there, may there be salmon there, and if there is salmon there, may there not be salmon there.) Agus Oideas Gael.

Epilogue 5: [1]Welsh Rugby Union, [2]Vale Resort.

Epilogue 6: [1]*Ireland's Trees. Myths, Legends and Folklore by Niall Mac Coitir*, [2]Merched y Wawr.

Addendum: [1]Merched y Wawr, [2]Eve Myles and Matthew Hall and *Un Bore Mercher* and S4C and *Keeping Faith* and BBC Wales, [3]J. Allen Hynek and Hynek's Scale.

End piece: [1]Dyfed-Powys Police, [2]Security Services.

Further Reading: [1]W. E. Bowman and the wonderful *The Ascent of Rum Doodle* and Max Parrish and Co. Ltd, [2]Mariah Carey and MacMillan, [3]B. G. Charles and the National Library of Wales, [4]Agatha Christie and William Collins & Sons, [5]Leonard Cohen and Viking/McClelland & Stewart, [6]Y Lolfa, [7]Edalji, G. E. T. and *Railway law for the "man in the train"* and London: E. Wilson, [8]Evans, G. and Fulton, H. and Cambridge University Press, [9]Evelyn Waugh and *Decline and Fall*, [10]Michel Foucault and Routledge Classics, [11]Edward Gibbon and Strahan & Cadell, London, [12]anthropologist Grenville Goodman and the *American Folklore Society*, [13]R. C. Sherriff and the wonderful *The Hopkins Manuscript*, [14]Jerome K. Jerome and J. W. Arrowsmith, [15]University of Wales Press, [16]Gareth King and Routledge, [17]Stephen Leacock and Bell and Cockburn, [18]Alberto Moravia and Farrar, Straus, [19]University of Wales Press, [20]Shambhala Publications, [21]*The Little Book of* ... series and Penguin, [22]*Peigí Rose* and Coiscéim, [23]Redcliffe Salaman and Cambridge University Press, [24]T. Arwyn Watkins and the Centre International de Dialectologie Générale, [25]Syr Ifor Williams and Gwasg Prifysgol Cymru, [26]Tony Wrench and Permanent Publications.

And to Edward Lear for: dilberry ducks, green ayahs and purple nullahs, clangel-wangel, tiggory trees, seeze pyder, sniffle snuffle and spicky sparrow, golden-finned chuprassies, the hills of the Chankly Bore, nupiter piffkin, fimble fowl and crumpetty tree, soffsky-poffsky trees. See Index.

Index

Printed in Great Britain
by Amazon

81326938R00261